JACK WHYTE

VIKING
CANADA

VIKING CANADA
Penguin Group (Canada), a division of Pearson Penguin Canada Inc.,
    10 Alcorn Avenue, Toronto, Ontario M4V 3B2

Penguin Group (U.K.), 80 Strand, London WC2R 0RL, England
Penguin Group (U.S.), 375 Hudson Street, New York, New York 10014, U.S.A.
Penguin Group (Australia) Inc., 250 Camberwell Road, Camberwell, Victoria 3124, Australia
Penguin Group (Ireland), 25 St. Stephen's Green, Dublin 2, Ireland
Penguin Books India (P) Ltd, 11, Community Centre, Panchsheel Park,
    New Delhi – 110 017, India
Penguin Group (New Zealand), cnr Rosedale and Airborne Roads, Albany, Auckland 1310,
    New Zealand
Penguin Books (South Africa) (Pty) Ltd, 24 Sturdee Avenue, Rosebank 2196, South Africa

Penguin Group, Registered Offices: 80 Strand, London WC2R 0RL, England

First published 2003

(FR) 10 9 8 7 6 5 4 3 2 1

Manufactured in Canada.

NATIONAL LIBRARY OF CANADA CATALOGUING IN PUBLICATION

Whyte, Jack, 1940–
    Clothar the Frank / Jack Whyte.

ISBN 0-670-88783-8

I. Title.

PS8595.H947C56 2003   C813'.54   C2003-905835-2

Visit the Penguin Group (Canada) website at **www.penguin.ca**

To my wife, Beverley

AUTHOR'S NOTE

In approaching this story, I was forced to come to terms with a few historical realities that bore heavily upon my vision of how the legend of King Arthur came into existence. In my mind, the entire story revolves around the Arthur/Guinivere/Lancelot triangle, and everything that occurs in the legendary tale is attributable to the humanity—and the human weaknesses—of the King himself, the dysfunctional nature of his marriage to Guinivere and their joint attraction to the brilliant foreign warrior known as Lancelot.

But there's the rub: Lancelot of the Lake, Lancelot du lac, is a French name, and Lancelot himself, the legend tells us, was a French knight who crossed the sea to England expressly to serve as a Knight of the Round Table at King Arthur's Court. Well, even making allowances for legendary exaggeration, that simply could not have happened in the middle of the fifth century, because in those days England was still called Britannia and what we call France today was still Roman Gaul.

It would not be until at least a century later, when the Anglo-Saxon invasions of Britain finally came to an end with the tribes called the Angles emerging as the dominant force, that the country would begin to become known as the land of the Angles—Angle land, and eventually England. By the same token, Roman Gaul would not become known as France until much later, when the invading Franks finally established their dominance over their arch-rivals, the Burgundians. Over time, the Frankish territories became the land of the Franks—France—while the Burgundians remained in their own territories of Burgundy.

ix

Reputedly wonderful horsemen, the Franks are the people generally credited with bringing the stirruped saddle to western Europe, and from the time of their first appearance in the Roman Empire, along the Rhine River in the third century, they had a reputation for being blunt spoken and utterly tactless, probably because their original tongue contained few of the subtleties of Latin or Greek. Be that as it may, we still use the term "speaking frankly" to denote directness and an unwillingness to mince one's words. There were two main tribal branches of Franks: the Salian Franks lived in what is now northern France, Belgium and the Netherlands, and the Ripuarians lived in the southwest of France and in what is now Switzerland.

Clothar is my interpretation of Lancelot. Academic opinion indicates that the name Lancelot probably developed from the Latin word *lancearius,* a Roman military denomination that was probably similar to the European lancer regiments of the nineteenth century. In Clothar himself, I have posited a Frankish horse warrior who comes to Britain, befriends the High King and earns himself an undying reputation as an archetypal hero, the character who will be called Lancelot centuries later by French storytellers who have heard of his fame and his exploits but have lost awareness of his real name.

The Names

It was an anomaly of Roman society that the names given to children appear to us to be relatively unimportant, but it is true that many children were named simply according to the order of their birth. The first three or four sons of a family might be called Gaius, or Caius, Marcus or Paulus, but the fifth son was likely to be Quintus, which means fifth, and thereafter, in large families, would come Sextus and Septimus or Septimius (sixth and seventh). Octavius Caesar, who would name himself Caesar Augustus, was the eighth son of his parents.

Roman place-names give us problems today, too, because they are Latin names and the modern cities that have replaced the Roman originals all have different names. For the sake of authenticity in a story like this, however, it would be jarring and unnatural to use the modern place-names, and so I have supplied a list below of the most important place-names in this story, along with their modern equiv-alents. The most obvious and enlightening example of this usage is the Roman fort at Lutetia in Gaul. It was built during the Gallic Wars of Julius Caesar, and its sole purpose, situated as it was on a crucial river ford, was to keep a lid on the warlike activities of the local tribesmen, a clan called the Parisii. That fort, Lutetia, has since grown to become the city of Paris.

Roman Name	*Modern Name*
Autessiodurum	Auxerre
Carcasso	Carcassonne
Cenabum	Orleans
Dubris	Dover
Genava	Geneva
Gesoriacum	Le Havre
Glevum	Gloucester
Lugdunum	Lyons
Lutetia	Paris
Massilia	Marseille
Treves	Troyes
Verulamium	St. Alban's

Language

The major difficulty an author faces in writing historical fiction is that of language, because language is constantly evolving and we have no real knowledge of how people spoke and sounded, in any language, hundreds of years ago. I have chosen to write in standard English, but even that is a relatively new development, since the language was only "standardized" in the nineteenth century. Until that time, there was no orthographically correct way to spell anything.

Most of the characters in my stories would have spoken in the ancient Celtic, Germanic and Gallic tongues, while the better educated, Romanized characters, like Bishop Germanus and his associates, and even Clothar as a student at the Bishop's School, would most probably have conversed in Latin. When people of mixed tongues met and mingled, they would have spoken the lingua franca of their time, although the real lingua franca—literally the language of the Franks—had not yet come into common use. But throughout history, whenever people of diverse tongues and races have come together to trade, human ingenuity has quickly developed basic, fundamental languages to fit their needs. In Africa, in the eighteenth and nineteenth centuries, that language was Swahili. In Oriental Asia, it was Pidgin. We do not know the name of whatever trading language was dominant in fifth-century Europe, but I have chosen to call it the Coastal Tongue, because the coast was the interface point for most traders.

Many terms and expressions used in this story, however, have no modern equivalent, and others sound modern and up-to-date when in fact they are genuinely ancient. I have addressed a few of these in the notes that follow here. Modern readers are sometimes surprised, for example, to find the title Duke being used in the ancient world, but the word originally sprang from the Roman army, where a man who had distinguished himself by demonstrating spectacular heroism and leadership could earn himself the title of *dux,* which is the Latin word for a leader, a man who is foremost among his companions, and out of that title came the English title of Duke.

In much the same way, people in North America today tend to feel proprietorial about nouns like *corn* and *bannock,* not realizing that *corn* has always been the generic Old World term for any kind of grain and that bannock—the simplest form of unleavened bread—is common to every primitive society, no matter what they call it. The Celtic clans of Scotland and Ireland have always called it bannock, and it was their use of the name that the aboriginal peoples of America adopted. The plant Americans call corn, on the other hand, is known as maize in Europe, where it is a coarse, mealy grain fed to cattle. American sweet corn came to be known in Europe only during and after the Second World War.

Another problematic word for us is *mile*. A modern mile is 1,760 yards, or approximately 1,500 meters, whereas the Latin word *mille* meant a thousand, and a Roman mile was one thousand paces long. Bearing in mind that the average Old World Roman was less than five foot six inches tall, their marching pace would have been short, probably in the range of twenty-six to twenty-nine inches, making their mile shorter than a modern kilometer.

And then there are the *latifundiae*. Few people today have any concept of how highly organized, and even industrialized, the Roman Empire was sixteen and seventeen hundred years ago. The Romans had a thriving stock market and a highly refined and regulated real-estate industry, and the food production and distribution system they constructed to feed their citizenry, founded upon a system of enormous ranches and collective farms called latifundiae, was extremely sophisticated even by today's standards. These private enterprises, run by corporations and funded and owned by investors, produced grain, cattle, wines, fruits and vegetables and other commodities in vast amounts for shipment to markets throughout the Empire.

The Latin word *magister,* which gives us our modern words *magistrate* and *magisterial,* was in common use in the Roman army in the fifth century. It appears to have had two levels of meaning, and I have used it in both senses throughout this book. The first of these was the literal use, where a student or pupil would refer to his teacher or mentor as Magister (Master), with all appropriate deference. The second usage, however, resembled the way we today use the term *Boss,* denoting a superior whose title entails the accordance of a degree of respect but falls far short of the subservience suggested by the use of the word *Master.*

Similarly, the word *ecclesia* gives us our modern word *ecclesiastical,* but the original meaning of the word was a church, particularly a permanent church, built of stone.

Citrus wood is well documented as being the most precious wood in the Ancient World, but we have no idea what it was like. No trace of it survives. It is one of the earliest known instances of a precious commodity being exploited to extinction.

And finally, a word about horse troopers. Roman cavalry units were traditionally organized into *turmae* (squadrons) and *alae* (battalions). There were thirty to forty men in a *turma* (the singular form of turmae), and the strength of the alae ranged anywhere from sixteen to twenty-four turmae, which meant that a cavalry battalion could number between 480 and 960 men. The *contus,* a substantial, two-handed cavalry spear, was the weapon of many heavy cavalry turmae, and those troops were known, in turn, as contus cavalry.

Clothar the Frank

ROMAN GAUL &
SOUTH BRITAIN:
450–480 A.D.

Caledonia

Britannia

Verulamium
[St. Albans]

GERMANIA

Glastonbury
Camulod

Lutetia
[Paris]

Gesoriacum
[Le Havre]

Treves
[Troyes]

Auxerre

Roman Roads

Towns & Forts

Clothar's Journeys

Lake Genava

Benwick

Gallia

ITALIA

Lugdunum
[Lyon]

Massilia
[Marseille]

Carcasso

IBERIA

MARE
INTERNUM
(MEDITERRANEAN)

PROLOGUE

I saw the bird lying in a pool of sunlight as soon as I came into the room. It was in the far corner over by the fireplace I built when I first came here a score and more years ago. I recognized its still form and felt immediate regret as I realized why its familiar song had been missing from my bedchamber that morning. The brightness of the pool of light in which it lay told me what had happened: the bird had flown in through the window and then, blinded in the sudden darkness of the room, had dashed itself against a wall and died.

It was a blackbird, a tiny, glossy creature whose only other color was its brilliant orange beak. As I bent over it and peered at the forlorn way one of its wings lay spread on the stone floor, the thought came to me that nothing about this little being gave any hint of the miraculous power and volume of pure song contained within its fragile frame. When this bird sang, men could hear it from miles away on quiet summer evenings. Its voice, its song and its magical power transcended and confounded the physical smallness of the singer.

I crouched cautiously, aware of the brittleness of my aging knees, and picked the dead bird up, cradling it in my hand and folding its already stiffening wings, noting the way the tiny head lolled on its broken neck. So small it was, and yet such a great loss to me in my early-morning awakenings and to everyone else whom its song reached. A blackbird—a *merle,* to the local Franks—a voice of purity and immense beauty, silenced forever. And then, merely thinking of its Frankish name, another, heavier wave of grief swept over me without warning; connections and associations swarmed in my mind, and my eyes were all at once awash with tears. I drew myself erect and inhaled a great, deep breath to steady myself, reaching out to lean on the stone breast of the fireplace, and then I wiped my eyes with my sleeve and looked about me at this bare room that holds so many memories and uncompleted tasks.

We have no need of open indoor fires here in the warmth of southern Gaul, but when I first came to these parts many years ago, my mind was filled with memories of long, pleasant nights spent in another land far to the northwest, sprawled in comfortable chairs before a roaring fire set into a stone-built chimneyed hearth, and so I indulged myself and built such a hearth here, in my new home. Once I had built it, of course, reality asserted itself, and to my wife's gentle amusement the fire was seldom lit. But I would often sit for hours in front of the silent hearth in the long autumn evenings, gazing into the dried logs and dreaming of things gone, and as time passed the habit endured while the memory of warm firelight faded. Since my wife died, I have been the sole user of this room, and I have lit the fire four times, purely for the pleasure of gazing into the heart of flames and interpreting the pictures I imagined I saw there. Today would have been the fifth occasion, had I not found the bird.

Moments after I had picked the small corpse up, I found myself outside, scraping a shallow hole with my heel in the grass beneath the window, then kneeling to use my dagger to deepen the hole into a grave. I buried the blackbird there, refusing to ask myself why I should be doing such a thing, and then I returned directly here and dragged this heavy table to the window, after which I sat down to write for the first time in years. And here I am, writing about a dead songbird and the memories it brought back to me.

Ten years ago, a full year after the death of my beloved wife, and prompted by an urging I could not deny, I made the saddest journey of my life, although at the start of it I thought nothing could surpass the sadness I had known throughout my later years. I laid aside my rich clothing and dressed myself as an ordinary, undistinguished man, then made my way, in a strong, tight boat that belonged to an old and honored friend, across the narrow seas to Britain.

I did not go alone. That would have been extreme folly for a man of my age, even although I refuse to consider myself *old*. Besides, those who love and care for me had quickly decided, upon hearing what I had in mind, that I must be mad to think to risk my life upon the seas and journey to a land notorious for its savage people and their alien ways. They thought at first to prevent me somehow from going at all, but then, seeing I was determined to go despite them, they insisted that I travel with an escort. So I selected the youngest of my three sons, Clovis, and nine of his closest friends and companions to accompany me. These were all young warriors, still unwed and approaching their prime, and armed with the finest weapons our armorers could make—long-bladed swords and axes of the finest tempered iron—so that no one could have denied that they were the best protection I could have. And thus accompanied, I set out for Britain with the tolerance, if not the unstinted blessings, of my advisers.

My youthful escorts called themselves knights, claiming adherence to the order established decades ago in Britain when I was their age, and I had long since become tolerantly inured to the images their fancies conjured in me. I no longer made any attempt to dissuade them from their error, for they paid my protestations no attention when I did, considering me an old and querulous man, worthy of honor and respect, perhaps, but a relic nonetheless of a generation whose time had passed, and hence no longer quite aware of the potency and immediacy of modern events, customs and times. Despite my silence, however, and notwithstanding their own insistence upon believing otherwise, they were not knights. All their enthusiasm and all their dedication to the ideals they cherished was mere self-delusion, because they had never knelt before the King to undergo the Ceremony. And so I had come to tolerate both their delusions and their deference to me, aware that they sought no more than to honor me and my long-dead friends in their insistence upon cleaving to the form and rituals of what we had once called knightly conduct.

That said, however, I did not permit them to journey with me as knights. They traveled as I did, in plain, dull, homespun clothes that, while they did nothing to disguise the strength and bulk of the wearers, yet made them seem less visible than their normal, rich and brightly colored clothing would have. I made it plain to each and to all of them that we were traveling into danger in a land that I had once known well but which had since degenerated into chaos and anarchy, peopled by savage hordes of invaders, and that sumptuous clothes and rich armor and trappings would invite unwelcome attention. We would not be making a triumphal progress, I warned them time and again. This journey was mine alone and it was one of contemplation, a pilgrimage. They would escort me, at their own behest, purely to keep me safe from harm in a strange land. If they chose not to dress themselves in drab colors and walk afoot, they were at liberty to remain at home in Gaul.

They brought their weapons with them, of course, but the armor that they wore was plain and old—sturdy, well-worn leather instead of metal, yet serviceable and strong. Our intention, and again I went to great lengths to make this very clear before we left our home, was to appear strong enough to defend ourselves wherever we went but not wealthy enough to attract predators. They grumbled and complained as I expected, but they soon recovered their good humor in the prospect of a great adventure, and we set out in early summer, as soon as the spring gales had blown themselves out.

We gained our first sight of Britain near the island men call Wight, and turned west immediately to make our way along the coast, sailing towards the setting sun until we eventually cleared the hazardous, rock-strewn tip of the peninsula of Cornwall and swung back to head northeastward along its other coastline, seldom varying our distance of a quarter mile from the land. Cornwall was a bleak and inhospitable place, protected by high, precipitous cliffs and jagged, broken rocks over which the breaking waves spumed constantly. Although the sight of it brought back a flood of memories, I kept my mind directed farther north, to where the location of the single stone church the King had built would be visible from far out to sea. Glastonbury, men called the place, and its high tor reared up from the marshes that surrounded it, protecting Britain's first *ecclesia* in its lee. We sighted it the following afternoon, when the sun was halfway down the fall from its zenith, and overcome by sudden, deep misgivings, I decided immediately to turn our boat around and find a sheltered beach to the south, where we could disembark and spend the night before approaching Glastonbury early in the day.

There were people watching us from the slopes of the rising ground to the northeast as we approached the shore in the pre-sunrise light the next morning. They stood in groups of two and three, or stood alone, and I could detect no signs of hostility or fear in them as we drew closer. Nevertheless, I scanned them carefully as our oarsmen brought us in towards the land, and only when I could distinguish them individually did I allow myself to breathe peacefully again. All of them were men—no women in sight anywhere—and that single fact assured me that these were the latest of the line of anchorites that had subsisted here in this barren yet sacred place for hundreds of years.

I had never been able to discover why this lonely, inhospitable place, huddled among its surrounding salt marshes, should be held sacred. Its origins were shrouded in ancient mystery, but tradition held that the Druids in antiquity had inherited the hallowed place from the priests and worshippers among the ancient race who had ruled this land and called it Alba since the beginnings of time, long ages before the founding of the village in Italia that would one day grow to be known as Rome. The Druids themselves had never made a dwelling of the place, to the best of my knowledge, and yet the legend went that Glastonbury had always been a place of worship. The high tor that reared above it was said to be hollow, constructed by the gods themselves to shield a gateway to the Underworld, and wise men shunned it, afraid of being lost forever in the enchanted maze of twisting paths that girdled and encircled the tor's heights and slopes.

Two of my young companions leaped into the shallows before we grounded on the sand and offered to carry me ashore, but I waved them away and lowered myself carefully until I stood in knee-deep water, and then I waded ashore and waited, eyeing the people who stood there watching us. For a long time no one spoke, on either side, but eventually one frail and bent old man moved forward, leaning heavily on a long staff, and made his way to where I stood, and as he came I noted the plain wooden Cross he wore about his neck, suspended on a leather loop. I waited until he reached me and then bowed my head to him in greeting. He was older than me by far and I recognized him, although I could not recall his name. As his rheumy eyes gazed into mine, I watched for a similar spark of recognition. None came, and I gave my son Clovis the signal we had arranged.

Clovis stood slightly behind me, his arms filled with a thick roll of heavy woolen cloth, woven on our broad Gallic looms from the spun wool of the hardy sheep of southern Gaul. At my nod, he stepped forward and knelt to lay the roll of cloth at the feet of the old Master, whose eyes softened with pleasure as he looked at it. It was not a great gift, from our viewpoint, having cost us nothing but the time it took our weavers to make it, but it would clothe this entire community in fresh, new garments, perhaps for the first time in many years. The old man looked back at me then, and I addressed him in the language known as the Coastal Tongue, the trading language, an amalgam of a score of languages that had been used along the coasts of Britain and the mainland for hundreds of years, asking him if we could leave our boat in the shelter of his bay for several days. He nodded deeply, maintaining his silence, and I bowed again and turned back to my boat to make my final arrangements with our captain. He and his men would wait for us here, and I assured them we would be gone for mere days: five at the most, and probably less.

Within an hour of stepping ashore, my ten companions and I were on our way inland, striking first to the northeast around the base of the tor and then swinging south and east again, following the fringes of the extensive salt marshes on our right. I was the only one of our party who was mounted, riding the single shaggy garron owned by the community of Glastonbury, and it occurred to me now, looking down on them, that my youthful companions, used to riding everywhere, were unaccustomed to walking for any sustained length of time. They would be sore and weary when they laid themselves down that night and the nights that followed, for long miles stretched ahead of us, and every pace would be across rough country unworn by human passage. For the first time, the reality of that troubled me.

None of these men, I knew, had any idea of why we were there or why it was so important to me to make this long and seemingly pointless journey. But they had come, and they were ready for anything I might demand of them, simply because I had invited them to accompany me into this foreign land on a quest of some kind, a quest whose roots lay hidden in bygone times, in what was to them my unfathomable past. Looking at them now, I felt the difference between my age and theirs. They saw themselves embarking upon an adventure, whereas I was more than half convinced that this journey was folly, bound to generate nothing but grief and pain and disillusionment. Knowing nothing of this Britain, they were filled with excitement over what it might hold in store for them, whereas I had known the land too well in former times and knew it could now hold nothing for me that was good. All that was good and wholesome in my youth, Britain had sucked from me long since, condemning me to exile in the place across the seas that had once been my home and had since become my prison. There was nothing I could hope to find here except perhaps the remnants of a dream, the last, tattered shadows of a vision that had once, for a brief time, achieved blinding reality before being destroyed by the malice of ignorant, venal men.

Thinking of that, I called my company to a halt and sat facing them, moving my gaze from face to face as they stood looking up at me, awaiting instructions of some kind. I smiled at them, incapable of resisting the inclination.

"Well, my young friends," I began. "Here we are, in Britain. Look about you now and take note of what you see, because I doubt you may have really looked since we landed here." I watched with interest as their eyes began to register their surroundings, their initial, tolerant indifference gradually giving way to a range of emotions, none of which approached happiness or excitement. I broke in on their thoughts just as they began to show signs of starting to talk among themselves.

"Britain," I said loudly, bringing their eyes back towards me. "It may not seem the fairest land you have ever seen, but I had friends here once who swore that it was. There are no vineyards here, no hillsides rich with grapes, and the summer sun that shines later today might leave you cool and longing for your own warm breezes. It can be hot here, but in fact it seldom is. The winters are brutal, too, cold and long and wet . . . always damp and dank and chill. And yet this is a land where great ideas and noble ideals took root and flourished for a time, a time you have all heard about . . . and although it was a tragically short and strife-torn time, yet it was wondrous. It was a time without equal, and a time without precedent, and it was *my* time in the way that today is yours . . . the time of youth, of dreams and high ideals."

Their expressions were thoughtful, their eyes flickering back and forth from me to each other and sometimes to the drab landscape surrounding us. I nodded and spoke on.

"Such a time might never come to Gaul, lads, for in Gaul we love our comforts far too much. We have grown too somnolent for such things, too lazy, basking in the warm sun of our provinces. It takes a place like this island, Britain, where the sun is frequently a stranger and cold is more familiar than warmth, to keep men moving and to spur them on to pure ideals, great deeds and high activity. And on that point of high activity, you are about to discover what I mean. You will walk today as you have never walked before . . . fast and far and over rough country." I saw a few smiles break out. "You find that amusing, some of you. Well, that pleases me. But save your smiles and guard them close, and bring them to me fresh when we camp tonight. I warn you, there are no horses out there waiting to be taken and bridled, not today—or if there are, I shall be much surprised. By the time the sun goes down today, before we are halfway to where we are going, you will all be footsore and weary, with aches and pains in places you don't even know exist at this moment. And then, once we reach our destination tomorrow or the day after, depending upon what we find, we will turn around and retrace our path." I looked at each of them, one after the other, moving from left to right, and they stared back at me with ten different expressions, ranging from tolerant amusement to shining eagerness, and even to truculent suspicion. I reached down to fondle the ears of the beast beneath me.

"None of you is used to, or prepared for, what I will demand of you within these next few days—" I threw up my hand to cut short the mutterings of protest as they began. "And I know, too, that your military training has been long and thorough." That sounded better to them and they shrugged, appeased and slightly mollified, preening themselves and flexing their muscles gently. "But you are trained as horsemen. Mounted warriors. Knights, if you will. Not infantry. Not foot soldiers. And foot soldiers is what you are become, here and now, today and tomorrow, and you will find the effort overwhelming. And so I wish to make it clear immediately that if any one of you—anyone at all—finds the effort too much for him within the next few days, he must say so, and we will leave him safe, with a companion, to await our eventual return. There will be no disgrace attached to that. Some efforts are too much for men not trained in the discipline required, no matter their proficiency in other things. We all have limitations, and none of you has been faced with this hardship before. You may find, any one among you, that your limitations lie in this . . . and if so, you must make that clear to me. Do you understand me?"

There came a rumbled chorus of assent, and I nodded again. "Good, so be it. Now we must move quickly and quietly—not in silence, but it would be best to make no noise that might be heard from afar. We have no friends in this land. Bear that in mind until we are safe afloat again, and let's be on our way."

We moved on immediately, having established among ourselves that the march would be endured by all without complaint of any kind, no matter how grave the nuisance of blistered feet or the pain of cramped and aching muscles.

We camped that night in a quiet woodland glade between two low hills, having seen not a sign of human habitation since we left the settlement at Glastonbury, and sometime before dawn a gentle, steady rain began to fall. We rose up in the predawn darkness and broke our fast as we moved on, huddled against the weather and chewing on roasted grain and chopped dried fruit and nuts from our ration scrips. Some time after noon the rain dried up, although the clouds grew ever more threatening and sullen, and towards mid-afternoon I began to recognize landmarks: hill formations and a single grove of enormous trees, sheltered among the hills, that was achingly familiar. I stopped there, signaling a halt, and as my escorts spread themselves out to rest, vainly trying to find dry spots beneath the towering trees, I sat on my garron, gazing north-eastward towards the mist-shrouded brow of one particular hill that, had it not been there, would have permitted me to see beyond it one of the dearest sights of my young manhood. I was glad the hill was there, however, for I had no desire to see beyond it and I felt not the slightest temptation to approach closer to it.

From its crest, I knew, I would have been able to look out across a stretch of forested plain to another distant, solitary hill that stood like a sentinel among the rich lands surrounding it, its crest crowned by a strong-walled fortification that had once housed the first true High King of all Britain, Arthur Pendragon, with all his family and friends, his armed might and his great and lofty and ultimately impossible ideals. I had no doubt it would be inhabited still, but it was no longer Camulod, and I had no wish to know who ruled there now. I climbed down from my horse and ate and rested with my young men, and then I marshaled them again and struck onwards, south by east on the last leg of my journey, just as the clouds above us pressed even lower and the rain began to fall in earnest.

For three more hours we made our way through trackless, sodden countryside, our wax-smeared woolen foul-weather cloaks rendered almost useless by the hissing, incessant downpour and the sheer volume of water that cascaded upon us from every tree and bush and blade of grass we touched in passing. I rode following the contours of the land, half blinded by the downpour, remembering clearly that once there had been pathways here, but, little used now, they had disappeared in all but a few barren or sheltered places. I pressed on in silence, saying nothing because there was nothing I could have said to comfort my hapless companions, who must have been grieving, I had no doubt, for the open, sunny June skies of their homeland far to the south, beyond the seas.

And then we arrived at the point I had been seeking, a point invisible to everyone but me. I slid down from my mount's back, mindful of the steep and treacherously muddy slopes that lay ahead of me, and guided the garron carefully down the narrow, winding path that led beneath the crown of trees that obscured all evidence of the small, hidden valley below. Clovis and his friends followed me, muttering quietly among themselves and treading with great caution as they wondered where we were going and why I had brought them to this desolate and forsaken place. They fell silent, however, as I led them out of the dark tunnel of the descent into the open, grass-floored glade that lay beside the tiny lake at the bottom of the hill. A small building of gray stone at the far end of the glade betrayed no signs that anyone lived there, although its roof appeared to be intact and the door looked to be solid and tight-shut. I told my companions to wait where they were, handed the reins of my horse to Clovis and walked alone towards the small house.

I have no idea how long I stood in the semidarkness of the single small room within the four stone walls, but it was long enough for my son to grow concerned and come looking for me. The sound of his voice calling me brought me back to awareness, but even so I made no response until he pulled the door open and stood there, peering in at me.

"Father? Are you well?"

I sighed then, I remember, surprised by the effort it required, and turned to gaze at him, hovering there on the threshold, unsure whether he should enter. Looking out at him from the dimness of the interior, it seemed to me that he shone with a peculiar brilliance, his sodden cape glittering strangely in the pale light cast by the watery late-afternoon sun that had emerged from a break in the clouds. Two of his friends stood a few paces behind him, still closely wrapped in their foul-weather cloaks, watching tensely.

"I'm well enough," I answered and told him to come inside, alone, and close the door. As he obeyed, I said the first thing that had come into my mind, and my tone was chill, even to my own ears. "Pharus and Lars, behind you—they were still wrapped in their cloaks when you opened the door. And you, your hands are empty."

He stood blinking at me in the dimness, too surprised by my words even to look about him. I gave him no time to respond. "I thought I had trained you better than that. Why did you come to the door?"

His lips moved several times before he could frame his words. "I— You had been in here a long time. I thought—"

"No, Clovis, you did not think. You came because you were concerned for me. Concerned that something might have befallen me. And what if something had? What if I had surprised an enemy in here and had been killed? You opened that door with no blade in your hand. That could have been the death of you, too. And Pharus and Lars might have died before they could even throw back their cloaks, let alone draw their swords. That kind of carelessness invites death."

He stared at me for long moments, biting his lower lip gently, then nodded. "You're right, Father."

"I know I am. Now look about you, now that you are here. This is what we came to find."

His guileless face registered renewed surprise, and I watched his eyes scan the tiny room, noting how they passed across the dusty bed and then wavered before snapping back to what he thought he had seen. I heard the sibilant hiss as he sucked in a shocked, sharp breath that stuck in his throat.

The figure on the cot, beneath the rumpled, dust-coated bedding of animal skins, had been dead for a long time. There was no way to tell how long, but all signs of putrefaction had long since dried up and withered into dust, leaving only a skeleton partially covered with scraps of dried skin. The vault of the rib cage was barely discernible beneath the coverings, and the hair that had once adorned the skull had fallen free and now lay scattered in wispy clumps like silken, ash white cobwebs. Clovis swallowed hard and licked his lips, vainly trying to moisten them, then looked sideways at me.

"Did you expect . . . this?"

I answered him without removing my gaze from the bald dome of the partly covered skull. "I had hoped otherwise, but I feel no surprise. He was an old man even when I last saw him, and that was nigh on twenty-five years ago. Had he lived until now, he would have been more than eighty years old." I stepped towards the bed, avoiding the two large bundles that lay between it and me, and knelt on one knee, bending forward to remove the bear skin that covered the lower part of the skull, and as I lifted it to bare the smooth, almost toothless jaws, my mind supplied a memory of the face that had once covered these grinning bones. "Farewell, old friend," I whispered, and covered his head completely. "We will bury you decently now."

"Who was he, Father?"

I looked up at my youngest son, noting his hushed voice and seeing the curiosity and wonder in his wide eyes, and then I pushed myself to my feet and looked back again at the lumpy shapes of the bones beneath the bed skins.

"A friend, Clovis, and more than that, trusted above all others save one, yet trusted equally with that one. A dear and priceless friend, although his very name struck terror into other people's souls. The man who fleshed these bones was a hero in the truest sense, greater than any hero you have ever dreamed of. Larger than life itself and more marvelous than any tale could tell of him."

I stooped again and tucked the dusty coverings more securely around the ethereal form on the bed. "In addition to that, he was the sole man in Britain who had perhaps more integrity and honor than the King himself; a champion, born of the noblest blood of ancient Rome . . . as well as a teacher and a mentor greater than any I have ever known, including the blessed Germanus." Again I straightened up, my eyes still fixed on the body's outline. "Above all else, however, first and last, he was my friend, although he forced me to abandon all my friends and thereby saved my life. This is Merlyn, Clovis."

I heard a strangled, gurgling gasp. My son's face was now filled with fear and horror. "He was a leper!"

I fought to swallow my sudden, unreasonable anger. It was I myself who had told Clovis of the leprosy, but I had no control over the fear the very mention of the dread disease could generate. I willed myself to smile, disparaging his fear without demeaning him. "At least you didn't say he was a sorcerer. Most people did, and many thought he was both: leper and sorcerer, cursed by Heaven." The lad stood motionless, gazing at me wide eyed, and I stepped closer to him, placing one arm about his shoulders and sweeping the other towards the bed. "He has been dead for years, Clovis, you can see that, so any threat of leprosy that ever was is long since gone. And he was never a sorcerer, despite what silly people say. You have nothing to fear from Merlyn, nor would you have were he alive and sitting here today, so take that awestruck look off your face. We have work to do here."

My son swallowed and made an effort to empty his face of fear. "What kind of work, Father?"

"A burial, for one thing. And we have to make a litter to carry those." I gestured to the two large bundles lying between us and the bed. "If you look, I think you'll find they are for me."

He blinked, frowning, then bent over to peer at the bundles before stretching out one hand to tug a small oblong package free from the leather strips that bound the larger. He held it up to his eyes, squinting in the gloom of the tiny room as his lips formed the letters of the single word written on it.

"*Hastatus*? What does that mean?"

"It means I'm right. That was his name for me. It means spearman in the old Roman tongue."

"No, that's *lancearius*."

"Aye, it is now, but a lancearius is a spear *thrower* and he's a cavalryman, throwing from horseback. The old word was *hastatus,* and the hastatus was an infantryman. He held on to his spear. Had he thrown it, he would have left himself weaponless."

Clearly mystified, Clovis frowned and held the package out to me. I took it, hefting it in my hand and gauging the weight of it as being equal to four, perhaps six sheets of parchment.

"Spearman," he repeated, as though testing the sound of the word.

"Aye, Spearman. Sometimes he shortened it to Spear—*Hasta*."

"I thought the old word for a spear was *pilum*."

I glanced at him again, surprised to hear that he had even heard of the weapon. "It was, but the pilum was a different kind of spear from the hasta, heavy and cumbersome with a long, thin iron neck—a rod that made up half the length of the thing. It was too heavy to throw far, a defensive weapon, designed to be thrust into an enemy's shield. The pilum would bite deep and then the iron rod would bend and the weight of the thing would drag the man's shield down, making it useless. The hasta, on the other hand, was a fighting spear, designed to be held by its wielder. Nowadays the lancearius uses a light throwing spear, a javelin. I used to be very good at throwing them myself, and that's how I got the name. It's a long story and someday I'll tell you about it.

"In the meantime I want to read this, and I would like to be alone while I do it, so take those tools from the corner there, if you would, and set your friends to digging a grave as close to the lakeside as may be, yet far enough above the waterline to overlook the scene and remain dry. Select the site yourself. But tell no one who we will bury there." I raised a pointing finger to him and lowered my voice. "I mean that, Clovis. I need you to be discreet in this. No mention of Merlyn's name. Say only that we found a dead man here, long dead—no hint of who he is or might have been." He nodded, and I inclined my head, accepting his agreement. "Good. We'll lay him down above this little lake of his and pray for him, then let him rest in solitude and dignity. But if any one of our companions should even guess at who lies here, word will get out, inevitably, and my old friend's rest might be disturbed at some future time by idle fortune seekers . . . although God knows there's little in the way of fortune to be found in this place. Go now, and when you've found the best spot you can find, come back and tell me before you start them digging."

He looked at me for a moment longer and then collected an old, rusted mattock and a spade from where they had sat unused for years, festooned with cobwebs.

When I was alone again I looked about me one more time, scanning the small room's few contents and furnishings. Merlyn's life here had been spartan. Two ancient cloaks hung from pegs behind the door, and the only other item in the place, apart from bed, table and a single chair, was a battered wooden chest, a footlocker, at the end of the bed. I opened it and found it held nothing more than a few folded old garments. I lowered the lid gently and then sat on it while I slid my thumb along the flap that edged the letter that bore my name, hearing the dried wax of its seal crack and fall to the floor. There were five sheets inside, written in the wavering scrawl of an old man's hand. I held them up to catch the light from the small window and I began to read.

Hasta:

Greetings, dear friend. I hope you will read these words someday and think on me with kindness.

I have lost track of time. Strange now, for me even to think of that after so many years. When I was young, time was the most important and demanding element in life. But then things changed when the world and all I knew in it fell into Chaos. Since then I have been alone, and time has no significance to one in perpetual solitude. The days pass unremarked and become months, then years, and one thinks more of seasons than of days. New snow, or green buds, mark the passage of the years, and one year is much like another. Only now, when the need to think of time has returned to me with thoughts of you, do I realize that I have no knowledge of where or when I am, or of how long I have been in this same, empty place. When last I thought of it, I had been here, pursuing my task, for a decade and a half. But I lost track of such things soon after that, when I fell ill of a fevered wound dealt me by a visiting bear. I spent I know not how long a time after that in some nether world, from which I returned eventually, alive but weak and confused. Since then, I have not bothered to attempt to mark the passage of time.

You may be dead by now, even as I write these words. Or perhaps you are grown too old to journey here to find the things I leave for you. I do not know, so I can only write and hope it is not so. I know that I am very old—older than I had ever thought to be. The sight of my hand, writing, shrunk to a claw and covered with thin, shiny, blemished, sagging skin that shows the bones beneath, tells me that I am ancient. (My other hand is fingerless today, but without pain. It serves to keep the parchment steady as I write.) Yet it surprises me to think that I know not how old you are today. Young enough to remain alive, and strong enough to come and find my bones and these my words? I know not.

No matter. I must place my trust in God and in His wish to have my tale made known. He has sustained me for long enough to finish my task, so I must believe that He has His reasons for keeping me alive to complete it. The fruits of that labor lie before you now, if you are reading this. Two of three bundles, as well protected against time and weather as my one-handed efforts can achieve.

The largest of these three contains the written words of Caius Britannicus and Publius Varrus, as well as my own tale of my young life. The smaller bundle holds my thoughts on what happened here in Arthur's final days, and in the days before you and we met. I have not sought to write of the time when you were here with us, since you yourself can achieve that more fully than I.

The third, most precious bundle I have hidden where only you will know to seek it, in the spot you helped me to prepare on the summer afternoon when first you found my valley here among the hills. You will know what it contains as soon as you see the shape and feel the weight of it. Do what you will with it, for it now belongs to you. Its destiny achieved, it is become a mere tool, albeit the very finest of its kind that ever was. But with his death, whatever magic it contained was spent, vanished with his lustrous soul into another time and place.

And yet be wary. Call it not by name. It will attract attention of itself, even in Gaul. Name its name aloud, and you will be inviting grief and strife and misery from covetous creatures who would stop at nothing to possess the thing.

You will also find the two items that you helped me place in the spot of which I write. Destroy them for me now, if you will, for they are packed with evil tools—poisons and vehicles of death in many guises. I have used some of them myself, at times, and know their potency, but I spent years in learning how to know and use them, and with my death they now pose lethal danger to any finding them, including you yourself. Be highly cautious. Handle none of them. I would burn them myself, but I have waited and deferred too long and now I have too little strength to deal with them. Should you not arrive, they will molder and rot, eventually, unfound. But if you come, burn them and complete the task for me.

My blessings upon you and on your sons, if a sorcerous old leper may bestow such gifts. I trust your wife is well, and that she is the wife whose husband fell to set you both at liberty.

And now, at last, this is complete and I am free. I am so very tired. It is winter again, and a harsh one. The snow lies thick outside and my little lake is frozen hard, its backing wall thick with sheets and ropes of ice. It only remains for me now to bind this missive and lay it with the others. Should someone else than you find it, it may remain unread, since none here, save me, can read today. But should they pull apart the other bundles, they will find more to read—far more—and they might well destroy what lies here, burning or scattering it all. So be it. They will not find the third gift I leave for you.

Now I shall go outside, one last, cold time, and gather wood for my fire, and I shall eat the last of some good rabbit stew I made but yesterday, and after that I will lie down on my old cot and sleep the sleep I have long wished for.

Farewell, Hastatus! May your lance fly straight and true forever, and may God grant you the power to tell of what we both knew here in Britain. Your friend,

Caius Merlyn Britannicus—how long since I have used, or seen, that name!

Excalibur! No shred of doubt existed in my mind that this was what lay in the third treasure set aside for me. He had been careful not to name it in bald words, but Merlyn had known that there had been no need. I was the only one besides himself who knew about the hiding place, the cave that I had helped him excavate behind the hanging slab of rock at the back of the hut, at the lake's farthest end. He had found it by accident one day, more of a recess than a cave, in truth: a natural space left between the hillside and the enormous broken slab that was the farthest end of the long stone cliff face that formed the rear of the little lake. A steady sheet of water flowed silently down that rock face from a source hidden on the steep, densely overgrown hillside above, and gave the tiny vale much of its magical, almost supernatural beauty.

Naturally, being Merlyn, he had seen the little hollow, screened by hanging roots and a huge clump of bramble bushes, as an asset that might be useful someday, and had labored long and hard thereafter to widen and deepen it, digging out the soft shale hillside behind the slab until he had formed a dry, enclosed space in which two men could stand upright; a space that might someday be used to conceal anything valuable, including his own life, from unwelcome eyes. I had helped him, on my first visit to this valley, to carry two iron-bound wooden chests there. He had told me at the time that they were filled with the poisonous leavings of two Egyptian warlocks called Caspar and Memnon, who had once served the villainous Lot of Cornwall and had died in Camulod for the murder of Merlyn's own father, Picus Britannicus. But he had made no move to open them to show me what they held, and I had not asked him to. And there, too, he had concealed Excalibur, years later.

I had often wondered what had become of the sword after Arthur's death. Now I knew, and I felt no surprise. Indeed, I should have known that Merlyn would have found a way to keep it safe, aware that its legendary brightness might have been put to evil purposes in the wrong hands. And thinking thus, I wondered, too, if there could be any *right* hands to own it, once its true possessor was dead. But now it was mine, by Merlyn's decree, passed on in trust to me and mine, albeit with a warning not to reveal its name or its true provenance. In Gaul, far removed from Britain and its memories, that might be possible, providing I contained my knowledge safe inside myself.

"Father?" I had not heard the door opening behind me. "I have found the place, I think. Would you like to come and look before we start digging?"

I folded up the sheets in my hand and went outside, where Clovis led me to the grave site he had chosen. It was perfect, situated on a little knoll overlooking the placid surface of the tiny lake, and doubly appropriate because I knew it housed a double grave already. Merlyn would share his final resting place with his own beloved wife and unborn son, laid in this selfsame mound more than sixty summers earlier. The rest of our party stood about there, silently watching me, their faces showing curiosity. I nodded in approval of the site, then raised my hand.

"I knew this place, long years ago," I said, moving my eyes from face to face, "and it holds many happy memories for me. It also holds possessions I had never hoped to see again; things that I had thought and hoped were safe here, in its hidden isolation. Treasures," I added, seeing the sudden stirring of interest that the word evoked. I paused, watching them closely. "But treasures that have no worth to anyone but me. I'll show them to you, and ask you to carry them for me. I will even share them with you, should you so desire. How many here can read?"

All of their faces twisted into scowls and only one besides Clovis raised his hand. "Lars? I had no idea. Where did you learn?"

Lars, a heavyset warrior, immense across the chest and shoulders, shrugged and dipped his head as though suddenly shy. "In boyhood," he growled in his great, rumbling voice. "My father had a crippled scribe whose task it was to teach me. But that was long ago."

"And do you still read, today?"

He looked me in the eye, defiantly, as though I might challenge him to prove his next words. "I could . . . had I the time or the will."

"Then you might like to read the treasure we will take from here, for it is all in words, written on fine parchment. Piles and piles of it, covered in fine script over a period of several lifetimes by men long dead. Would you wish to read what it has to say?"

Lars laughed suddenly, a harsh, deep bark. "Nay, Lord, I would not. But if there be as much as you describe, it will make a heavy burden. I'll gladly help you carry it, but I would rather die beneath the lash than have to read it." The others joined in his laughter, and I waited, smiling still.

"You're right, it will be heavy, three large bundles. So I suggest you and another make a litter of poles, the easier to carry it between four men. Four more of you to dig this grave, working in pairs."

"Who was he, Lord? The man we are to bury?" The questioner was Origen, the youngest of our group but already famed among his peers for his coolheaded courage and a wisdom beyond his years.

I shook my head. "As easy for you to say as for me, Origen. A vagrant, perhaps, who stumbled on this place and remained here to die."

"Then why the labor of a burial, Lord? Why not simply leave him where he is?"

That stopped me short, because I recognized the danger hidden in the simple question. Why, indeed, go to the trouble of burying a long-dead pile of unknown bones? But my tongue had already gone ahead of me so that my answer was as glib as any long considered, and my smooth response evoked another burst of laughter from my listeners. "Because he's in my bed, my friend."

As the laughter died away I looked up at the rapidly darkening sky above our heads. "Laugh as you will, but I mean it. We will stay here tonight and return to the coast in the morning. This is as safe a place as we could find in all this land, for no one knows it exists. The rain seems to have passed, but should it return we can all sleep beneath the old roof, there, packed in like grapes on a stem, but warm and dry. But there is only one small bed, and I lay claim to it, as senior here. Our bony friend will not feel the dampness of cold earth atop his bones, but I would find his dusty presence irksome, sharing the bed with him." That drew another chuckle, and as it died I spoke into it.

"So, the three of you who are left idle for the moment will have a task as well: two of you to gather up the bones of our dead friend and wrap them carefully for burial in the blanket that covered him, while the other shakes out the remaining bedding and the sleeping furs. Clovis, I leave it to you to do the shaking out. Take pains to shake out all the dust here in the open, if you will, but do so with respect. We may not know who this man was, but we know he died here alone and friendless, probably unmourned. And looking about the place in which he died, we found no weapons . . . not a sword, an axe, a knife or even a club. No means of self-defense at all, which tells me that this dead man was a man of peace."

"Either that or a base-born, gutless fugitive." The whispered comment had not been meant for me to hear, but it reached my ears nonetheless. The speaker, Armis, known as Blusher to his companions, knew I had heard his comment, and a deep red flush swept up his face.

"Perhaps so, Armis. You may be right. But we will never know, will we? And thus, we'll look at it my way. Do you agree?"

Armis said nothing at all, the red tide in his cheeks growing even deeper, and I turned back to the others, none of whom had yet laughed as they normally would at Armis's discomfiture.

"We will tend him as though he were one of us, treat his remains with dignity, and see him to a decent burial at last. After all, but for the seas between this land and ours, he might have been grandsire to any of you, who can tell?"

This last produced no laughter from my suddenly sober-faced audience, and I nodded. "Let's be about it, then, before it starts to rain again or grows too dark to see. Clovis, come you with me for a moment. There is much of your father here in this small valley, and since you are my youngest son, I want to share it with you."

I felt no qualms about the subterfuge as I led him away, leaving the others to dispose of the tasks I had set them. As soon as we were out of their sight, however, I changed direction, circling around behind the hut until we reached the hanging screen of roots, briars and creepers that concealed the entrance to Merlyn's hiding place. It took me mere moments to work my way around the hanging mass and rip away the living curtain to expose the narrow entrance, and I used my body as a brace to hold back their weight as Clovis eased his way past me into the interior. It was dry inside, and dark, but there was light enough to show us what lay therein: two massive chests and a long, straight-edged package that obviously contained a box, tightly bound in some kind of uncured hide that had been

soaked, then stretched tightly around its contents before being
bound with narrow leather thongs and left to dry in place, forming
a hard, stiff casing. Clovis turned to me, his eyebrows raised in
query.

I pointed at the long, narrow package. "This one is mine, from
Merlyn. Bring it when we leave here and place it with the other two
bundles in the hut."

He pointed a thumb towards the chests. "What about those?"

"Those we destroy. They contain sorcery—*real* sorcery. Merlyn
took them from two warlocks, many years ago. I helped him bring
them here. He always intended to destroy them, but he was curious
about the things they held and could not bring himself to dispose of
them before he knew their secrets. I suspect he eventually forgot
that they were here and only found them when he brought—" I
stopped short, on the point of saying "Excalibur." "When he
brought this other box to leave safely for me. By that time, he was
too old and weak, too tired, to destroy them effectively. And so, in
the letter that he left, he asked me to complete the task for him.
We'll burn them when we leave, tomorrow. Right now, we have to
empty them and scatter their contents on the floor here. But he
warned me that they are more than simply dangerous: they all
contain death, in one form or another, and in some cases, he insists,
mere contact with the skin can bring about a painful end. So be
careful not to touch anything that lies inside either of them."

I opened the larger chest, then stood gazing in surprise at what
I saw. The interior seemed to be a narrow, shallow tray, filled with
leather thongs and surrounded on all four sides by wide, ribbed
borders. It took me several moments before I saw that the "ribs"
along each edge were the edges of a nested series of trays, each
deeper than the one above, and that the leather thongs were handles,
one pair attached to each of the trays in series. I folded back the
thongs, draping them over the edges of the chest, then found those
for the first tray, the shallowest, which had contained nothing other
than the layered thongs. I lifted it out and laid it aside, revealing the
tray below. It was twice as deep as the first one, its interior divided

into rectangular boxes, some of them empty but many filled to varying degrees with what I took to be seeds and dried berries of many colors. All of them would be poisonous, I told myself, lifting out the tray and resting it on one corner of the chest. I gripped it by the sides and turned it over carefully at arm's length, scattering the contents on the floor of the cave before setting the empty tray aside and reaching for the third set of handles. This tray was deeper and heavier, with fewer compartments, containing jars and vials. Those, too, I tipped out onto the floor, using my boots to free the lids and tip the containers so their contents ran or oozed out into the dirt. I looked up then and nodded to Clovis, bidding him open the other chest and follow my example. Three trays remained in my chest, the topmost filled with oblong boxes of green glazed clay filled with some kind of greenish paste. I dumped them out onto the floor, too, kicking their lids away and turning the boxes over with my booted toes, so that their contents lay face down on the dirt.

The next tray contained what I took to be hanks of dried grasses and small tied bundles of twigs and dried herbs. I didn't know what those were, but they would serve as kindling for the fire I would light the following day. I piled them in the center of the floor. The bottom of the chest, the deepest compartment, was empty, save for a fat, squat wooden box containing what looked like a handful of granular black powder, which I shook out onto the pile of grass. The array of trays on my left would burn well.

"Look at this, Father." Clovis was holding something out to me. "It looks like a man's hair and face, peeled off the bone."

"It's a mask. A mummer's trickery. Throw it with the rest."

In less time than it has taken me to describe, we had emptied both chests, and their contents lay piled on the floor, surrounded by the half score of trays and the empty chests themselves.

"Those are wondrous chests, Father, well made. It seems a pity to destroy such things."

"We need them to burn, to destroy what they contained. Merlyn was quite clear about that. But there's not enough fuel in here to do that properly, so tomorrow morning, as soon as it's light, I want you to start gathering wood and bringing it in here. Have your friends help you. There'll be little dry wood, but no matter. Find what you can and chop it up into pieces small enough to bring through the entrance. Pack this place to the ceiling, if you can. The hotter the fire we make, the more completely we'll destroy what's here. But if your friends pay any attention to what's scattered on the floor, discourage them. Don't let them touch anything on the floor with their bare hands. If they ask you what we've done here, or why we did it, tell them it is my wish—that these are useless things too heavy to take home to Gaul. Tell them I have decided I have no wish to see them again, because of memories they stir in me. They will believe you. This is a day for memories, they have seen that. But on no account will you allow any of them to touch anything, unless you want to see them shrivel up and die before your eyes. Is that clear?"

His eyes were wide and full of conviction. "Yes, Father. I'll watch them closely. They won't touch anything."

"Good. I'll trust you to see to it. Now pick up my box, if you will, and let's get out of here. It's almost too dark to see, so it must be near nightfall."

The rain held off that night and we slept well, and at dawn we were up and about. Clovis and his friends made short work of filling the cave with wood, and if any of them even noticed the spillage on the cave floor they made no mention of it. I spent that time alone, sitting on the cot and reading over Merlyn's letter several times, resisting the temptation to open any of the three parcels. When I smelled the tang of smoke from green wood, I went outside where I could see thick white smoke drifting from the trees fronting the vent that formed the entrance to the cave. My escort, their work over, were standing around, idly watching the increasing clouds of smoke. I called them together and brought them to order, and they stood grouped around the open grave as we lowered the tiny bundle containing the brittle bones of Merlyn Britannicus to rest.

I found myself unsure of what to say over his grave, not having known if he was Christian or Druid. I had never been curious about his creed before. He had simply been Merlyn, sufficient unto himself, unbeholden to anyone, god or man. Now, however, I felt a need to say something aloud, notwithstanding that I could not name his name, and as my companions stood with lowered heads, just beginning to stir and shuffle with impatience, I cleared my throat and spoke, trusting my instincts.

"We know not who you are, or were, nor do we know what God or gods you cherished. We know not how you lived, or how you died; how long you knew this place, or whence you came. We only know we found your bones awaiting us, reminding us that all men come to death. Rest you in peace here, now, surrounded by the beauty of this hidden place, and may none disturb your bed from this day forth. Fare well, wheresoever your spirit roams."

We arrived back at Glastonbury at noon the following day, having met or seen no living soul on our journey, and as we approached, the anchorites began to gather in silence to watch us. The same old man was there at their head, but this time as I drew near he watched me keenly, his eyes slitted, and I knew he knew me now.

I dismounted in front of him and held out the rope reins of his garron. "Safely returned," I said. "These old shanks are grateful for your generosity in sharing."

Another man stepped forward to take the reins, and the old leader nodded.

"You are the Frank," he said.

"I am. And you are Declan." The name had come to me as he spoke. "How do you know me now, but not before?"

"It was the horse. I saw you in the way you sat as you came in. Before, when you arrived, I had not thought to see you, so did not. I have something for you."

"Something for me? How could you have anything for me?"

"Come you." I followed him, waving to my men to stay where they were. The old man made no attempt to speak again and I went with him in silence until we reached one of the simple huts surrounding the stone ecclesia, where he stooped to enter the low doorway.

"The building looks well," I said, gazing up at the stone church and feeling the need to say something, hearing the banality of my words as they emerged. "Is God still worshipped here?"

Declan stopped on the threshold of his hut and looked back at me over his shoulder as though I had broken wind. "It is His house," he said. "Where else would men worship Him? Come."

Feeling foolish, I bent to follow him into the tiny room that was even barer than Merlyn's hut had been, and so low that I had to stand bent over. It was dark in there, and smelled of straw, and the old man moved directly to the rough-edged hole in the wall that served as a window, where he picked up a flat, square wooden box a handspan long and held it out to me.

"What is it?" I asked, taking it and holding it up to the light from the window. It was well made and had been richly polished once, but years of sitting in that window space, open to whatever weather prevailed, had deprived it of its luster, leaving only a fragmented pattern of flecks of ancient varnish, cracked and peeled.

"It is yours," Declan said. "See for yourself."

I replaced it on the window ledge and opened the hinged lid, which squeaked in protest. Inside, lying on a hard, textured bed of what might once have been brushed leather, was a pair of blackened, tarnished Roman spurs, their straps hardened to the consistency of wood, cracked and fissured by time. I lifted them out, one in each hand, and felt their solid, heavy weight. Blackened as they were by the years and lack of use, their delicate engravings were invisible, but I knew them well. I had been with Arthur when we found them among the rubble of a ruined house close to the ancient Roman fortress of Deva, far to the north and west of Camulod. The engravings explained that these were the ceremonial spurs of Petrus Trebonius Cinna, a senior officer of Equestrian rank, serving in the Twentieth Legion, the *Valeria Victrix,* that had served long and honorably here in Britain since the days of the early Caesars. They must have lain where we found them for hundreds of years, for the decorative arch of their ancient leather straps bore the insignia of Claudius Caesar, and three hundred years had passed since he ruled Rome.

I looked at the old man, deeply perplexed. "Who gave you these to hold for me? Merlyn?"

He shook his head. "The King." The old man's voice was barely audible but filled with awe and reverence. "Arthur, the Riothamus himself, may God's light shine on him forever. He stayed with us the night before he left for Camlann, where they killed him. 'Declan,' he said to me, 'the Frank will come back someday. When he does, give him these, from me, and bid him give them to his son.'" He cocked his head. "I never thought to see your face again, but he was right. You came. And now I have done as he wished." He glanced down at the spurs in my hands. "I have never touched those. His were the last hands to hold them. Do you have a son?"

My throat had closed as though gripped in an iron fist, and I had to swallow before I could respond. "Aye," I said, my voice rasping. "I have three."

"Your firstborn, then, he must have meant."

"He did. But my firstborn was a daughter."

"Well, then, let her hold them for her son."

"She has one. His name is Tristan."

He cleared his throat. "Aye, well, they are for him, then. Is he worthy of them?"

I pictured my grandson's open, shining face with its strangely brilliant, gold-flecked eyes. "Oh, aye," I breathed. "More than worthy, I think. He possesses many of the characteristics of the Tristan in whose honor he was named, even if he is of different blood. He will wear these spurs well, when he is grown."

"Good. Then may he wear them with honor. Now we had better go outside again, before your back is locked into that stoop forever."

The next afternoon, as the shores of Gaul came into our view again, I caught my son Clovis staring at me with a strange expression on his face. He quickly looked away when he caught me regarding him. I went to sit beside him on the rower's bench he occupied.

"Something is on your mind," I said, keeping my voice low. "Bothering you. What is it?"

He looked wide eyed at me. "What d'you mean, Father?"

"Just what I said. Three times now I have caught you gazing at me as though I were suddenly a stranger, so I want to know what you are wondering about."

"I'm not wondering about anything, Father. Not really."

I sighed. "Clovis, you know me well enough to know that I keep little from you and I seldom react with anger to a straightforward question. So humor me, if you will, and tell me what you're thinking. Or ask me the question plainly on your mind."

He sat staring off into the distance, watching the distant coast rise and fall with the swell of the waves, and then he muttered something indistinct.

"What? I didn't hear that. Speak up."

His face flushed. "I said I was wondering who you really are."

"What?" I laughed aloud. "I'm your father. What kind of a question is that?"

"Aye, sir, you are my father, and I thought I knew you, but now I am unsure."

He would not look at me, so I reached out and poked him in the ribs. "How so? What are you trying to say?"

He turned, finally, and looked me in the eye. "You have two names I never knew before, Father—two names I've never heard. Hastatus, and the Frank. And now I find myself wondering how many more you have, yet unrevealed. The old man yesterday recognized you and said, 'You are the Frank.' Not simply a Frank, any old Frank as we all are, but *the* Frank. The name held great significance for him."

I could see the hurt and bafflement in his eyes and had a sudden insight into his distress, seeing how important it must be to him that he should know me better than he did, to understand the impulses that drove me and to know why I had dragged him and his friends on this long journey for no more reward than some piles of parchment and a tight-wrapped box left waiting for me in an isolated, alien place where those who had once known me did so by names other than those my loved ones knew at home. And as I stared at him, the immensity of all he wished to know overwhelmed and confused me, striking me speechless with the similarity between his case and my own when I had been but half as old as he was now.

I, too, had ached to think I had never known my father, for the father I had known throughout my life had stood revealed, without warning, as but a substitute—loved and admired but nonetheless a stranger. My true father had died shortly after my birth, struck down and slain when I was barely starting out in life. Clovis's case was different from mine, for I was his true sire, but nonetheless I knew what he was feeling, and I knew that, to some extent, he was correct.

The truth was that I had told my children almost nothing of the details of my early life, the life I had lived before I came to Gaul and fathered them. They knew that I had ridden with the Riothamus, Arthur, High King of Britain, serving as one of his equestrian knights, and that I had been one of his true, close friends. But they had no suspicion of the role that I had played in his undoing. That part of my story, all of it, I had concealed from them, with the collusion of their mother. They had had no need to know such things, she and I had convinced ourselves, and besides, such knowledge would have been dangerous to them, and to my wife. And so I sat there in that boat on a summer afternoon ten years ago and thought about what I must now tell my son, beginning with who I was, and who I had once been.

BOOK ONE

Fathers

BAN

1

I cannot recall much about my early childhood, but I have always been grateful, nevertheless, that I survived it, and that the memories of it that remain with me are happy ones, steeped in the eternal sunlight of long, bygone summer days and unaffected by the truths I learned later. The Lady Vivienne of Ganis, who occupied the center of my life then, since I grew up regarding her as my mother, was in fact my mother's twin and therefore my aunt. Her husband, whom I also believed for years to be my father, was called Ban of Benwick, King of the Benwick Franks who settled the Ganis lands in southeastern Gaul before my birth.

I was seven years old when first I heard the story that my mother had abandoned me, and I remember the occasion well. I scoffed at first, pointing out to Frotto, the loudmouthed lout who was tormenting me, that my mother was Vivienne, whom people called the Lady of the Lake. Everyone knew that, I told him smugly, except him.

Not so, he yelled at me, in a jeering voice that contained an awful note of conviction. *His* mother had told him that the Lady Vivienne had taken me in as a homeless baby, after my true mother had abandoned both me and my father to run off with another man. Infuriated, and strangely frightened by his outrageous accusations, I charged at him. He sidestepped my rush easily, being two years older than me and almost twice my size, and kicked me hard on the shin. While I was hopping on one foot and clutching my injured leg,

35

he punched me twice with large, meaty fists, bloodying my nose with one and then knocking me down and blackening both my eyes with the other.

Of course, I went running home, half blinded by tears and bruises and bleeding from my nose like a gravely wounded man, and Lady Vivienne was horrified when I burst into her rooms, dribbling blood and mucus all over her clean floor. She rushed to me and held me, uncaring about damage to her clothing, then hugged and comforted me and listened to my distraught tale while she tended to my wounds, holding my head back gently but firmly until the bleeding from my nostrils had dried up, then cleansing and dressing my cut leg. As soon as my face was free of blood and snot, she laid me on her own enormous bed and bathed my swollen eyes with a cool cloth, holding me to her bosom and crooning over me until I was pacified, while her women made sure that none of my siblings made their way in to gawk at me in my distress.

The major part of my comfort that day sprang from Lady Vivienne's immediate denial of Frotto's tale. She told me I must pay no heed to him or to his wicked lies, and I believed her. How could I not? She was my mother, the most beautiful being in my world, and it was inconceivable to me that she could lie, even to save me from pain. And so three more full years passed by before I learned the truth.

Once again, it was Frotto who precipitated things. By then he and I were implacable enemies, although he had learned to curb his tongue and keep away from me, most of the time at least. He was still larger than I was, and fatter, but I had grown too, gaining height more quickly than he and thickening steadily towards the strength and bulk that would sustain me as a warrior thereafter. I was larger than any of the other boys I knew of my own age, and that in itself might have been enough to keep Frotto away from me; he liked his victims to be much smaller than himself. And his father was a wheelwright, whereas mine was the King, so while he spent his time roaming at large with his cronies—and I was often jealous of his freedom—I spent most of mine, from the age of eight, in training to be a warrior. Chulderic, my father's Master-at-Arms, was my official tutor in such things, and he kept me hard at work, learning to ride and fight with sword and spear, and I was an apt pupil.

On the day I was to learn the truth about my parentage, I ran into Frotto and two of his friends while leading my injured horse, Rollo, to a lush pasture, a clearing in the woods I had discovered days earlier. Rollo and I had taken a fall that morning, and while I had been no more than slightly scratched and winded by the event, Rollo had gashed his pastern on a splintered branch that lay hidden in the thicket we had tried to gallop through. Now, a few hours later, his injured leg cleaned and firmly bandaged, I had thought to make reparation to him for my carelessness by taking him where he could eat his fill of succulent grass. I was walking slowly, allowing him to pick his way carefully as he hobbled beside me, favoring his sore ankle, and I was daydreaming, fretting about the damage I had caused to my beloved horse through my own enthusiasm and lack of thought. We Franks have always been proud of our prowess with horses, and we regard ourselves as natural horsemen, born to ride. But it had never really dawned on me until that day that the invincibility and invulnerability I felt, once mounted on my horse's back, were foolish. My poor horse was anything but invulnerable. By sending him charging into that copse the way I had, into its hidden dangers, I might easily have killed him and myself.

Thinking that, I led him around a bush, and found myself face to face with Frotto.

He was as surprised to see me as I was to see him, and it was pleasant for neither one of us. His first reaction was to draw back guiltily, leaping away from what he had been doing and looking beyond me as his two friends scattered, too, to see who else might emerge from behind the bush. For my part, I immediately looked to see what he had been doing. A skinny eight-year-old child I recognized as the daughter of one of my father's house servants lay on her back in the long grass, naked, her legs spread wide to expose everything that made her female. Her eyes were wide with fear, although whether she was frightened by what they had been doing to her or afraid of being caught doing it I could not tell. The truth is, I did not know myself what they were doing. I simply reacted to the guilt on Frotto's face.

"What's going on here? What are you up to, Frotto?"

My question broke his momentary panic. He had seen that there was no one with me, and so he charged at me, catching me with a shoulder to my chest and sending me flying to rediscover aches and bruises that I had sustained earlier in my fall from Rollo's back. Winded for the second time that day, I sprawled in the grass, looking up at him towering above me, his fists clenched and his face contorted with anger.

"What's it matter to you, shit spawn, what I'm up to?" He drew back his foot and swung a kick at me, and I rolled towards him, catching his flying foot between my arm and my chest and twisting to pull him off balance. He landed on top of me, and the sour stink of his stale sweat flooded my nostrils as I pushed him away and rolled again to regain my feet. Before I could rise, one of his friends kicked me behind the knee and I went down again, this time on all fours, just in time to take a third kick, full in the ribs, from the third boy. My vision hazed with red and I fought to keep from vomiting from the pain, but I could see Frotto scrambling away from me and I thought he was going to run.

I was wrong. He scrabbled on hands and knees until he reached the place where they had abandoned their fighting sticks, and he picked one up and rose slowly to his feet, hefting the short, thick club in his hand while measuring me with his eyes and grinning the grin that I had learned to detest. Seeing what was coming, I tried again to stand up, but again his friends prevented me, one of them sweeping my legs from under me with a wide, looping kick. And as I huddled there, face down, half lying and half kneeling, Frotto struck me across the shoulders with his cudgel.

Pain flashed across my back, but he had not hit me as hard as he could have; I knew that even as the blow landed, and a part of me wondered why. Chulderic, my trainer, had long since taught me that, once committed to a fight, it was sheer folly to hold back and be anything less than ruthless in disabling your enemy. Now, despite my pain, I was wondering what was going on in Frotto's mind. Perhaps he was still afraid of my status as my father's son. I fell forward onto my elbows, my face brushing the grass, and then I gathered myself and lunged, pushing upwards and forward, forcing myself to my feet in a shuffling run that caught all three of them by surprise.

The largest of the three came close to catching me. As his fingers closed on my tunic, pulling me around, I seized his own tunic in both my hands, then head-butted him hard. His nose crunched and he fell away from me, howling and falling hard to the ground, his hands clamped over the blood spewing from his ravaged face. Before either of the others could recover from the shock of what had happened, I leaped over the distance remaining between me and the other two cudgels that still lay on the ground. I snatched them up, one in each hand, spun towards my tormentors and dropped into a fighting stance.

The fight should have been over at that point. I had cut their strength by one-third and now I held two clubs to their one. And they must have seen how angry I was, in the set of my face. They knew I had been training hard for more than two years with cudgels very like those I now held, except that my own were longer and even heavier. It was plain to me that neither of them wanted to be the one who would put my training to the test. But poor stupid Frotto couldn't simply back away and accept the situation for what it was. Perhaps if he had, and had kept his mouth shut, I might have allowed him to walk away, even then, but that was not Frotto's way. He had to try to convince his dullard friend that they had bested me and that I wasn't worthy of their time or attention, and so he went into his customary diatribe about my parentage, and how my "real" mother had been a faithless slut.

I had heard the tirade many times by then, and I had almost grown immune to it, accustomed to letting it flow around my ears without heed. This time, however, I decided I had had enough, and I knew that Frotto's additional height, weight and years were no longer significant to me. I raised my right hand high and lowered my left, advancing towards him slowly and daring him to swing at me. He did, and I parried his blow with the club in my left hand, then smashed him on the wrist with the other. He howled, his club went flying, and he spun away in agony, tucking his injured wrist beneath his armpit. I followed him, moving quickly, bringing one cudgel and then the other down as hard as I could on his bent back, driving him to his knees.

The lout with the broken nose had managed to struggle up, but there was no fight left in him. The third, uninjured one stood gaping at me, hovering between flight and fight. I lunged at him and he broke, running for his life. As he went I noticed that the little girl had vanished, probably having escaped as soon as our attention had been removed from her. Broken Nose rose to his feet, one blood-covered hand upraised palm outwards, mutely begging me not to hit him again. I jerked my head at him and he, too, ran off, leaving me with Frotto. My tormentor had regained his feet by that time and stood looking at me, still hugging his wrist under his arm, his face the color of bread dough.

My anger had all drained away, leaving me cold, but I was far from finished with Frotto. I jumped towards him and slashed the club in my right hand downwards, striking him brutally on the left knee, and his leg gave way, pitching him at my feet.

"Now listen to me, you fat pig," I hissed. "If I ever hear you say another word about my mother, or about anything to do with my family, I'll kill you. Do you hear me?"

He groveled, whining and blubbering, and the coldness I had been feeling suddenly welled up in me, blinding me to everything but the infuriating sight of him. I hit him again, this time on his upraised arm, wanting to break it, but as I raised my cudgel yet again I became aware of violent movement beside me. A powerful blow sent me spinning to fall flat on my face.

"Enough, I said!" The voice roaring above me snapped me back to my senses. "God's teeth, don't you know when a fight's over? Are you trying to kill him? Pick that sack of guts up and get him out of here. See to him, and hold him with the others."

I raised myself on one elbow and saw two of my father's men-at-arms pulling the blubbering Frotto up between them. Beside me, Chulderic, the Master-at-Arms, was livid with rage. I looked away from him, shaking my head to clear it, and saw four more men holding my other two assailants by the arms. Both of them looked terrified.

I had caught the rough edge of Chulderic's tongue and temper before, but I had never seen anything like the fury that drove him now. King's son or not, he hauled me up by the back of my tunic and sent me sprawling again with his boot in my backside before recapturing me and dragging me, kicking and struggling, to his own horse. He picked me up and threw me face down across his saddle, yelling at me to stay there and not move if I valued my hide.

2

We made an inglorious entry to the settlement surrounding our fortress and attracted much derisive attention, me hanging head down over Chulderic's saddle and my three former assailants limping and dragging between their pairs of stern-faced escorts. Chulderic strode in front of me, holding his horse's reins, and I could only suppose that another of the men-at-arms was leading my injured mount.

"Bring those idiots over here!" We had stopped just outside the main gates of the castle and, face down as I was, I had seen Chulderic's legs striding towards me. He grasped me by both shoulders and heaved me bodily towards him, jerking my torso up so that my legs hit the ground and folded just as he let me go. I fell forward on my arms and then pushed myself back up until I was kneeling, and then as the other three were brought towards me I struggled to my feet. We stood side by side facing our glowering captor, all four of us swaying unsteadily. Chulderic's face was filled with disgust as he looked from one to the other of us, his eyes moving up and down the length of our bodies.

"Warriors, are we?" he snarled. "Fighting men? Brawling animals, more like. Three against one, too. And him barely half the size of any one of you, and he bests all of you. Warriors. Hah!" His eyes came to me, the disgust in them no less than it had been for the others. "And you, kinglet. Training to be a murderer, are you? Set to dash out the brains of anyone who crosses you? A fine king you'll make, raving and foaming at the mouth like some mad Hun. Is that what I've managed to teach you in two years, to take no prisoners? To lose your mind and give yourself up to killing anyone you dislike, even though they're down and finished?"

I started to protest.

"Quiet!" he roared so that everyone watching could hear him, even from the top of the walls at his back. "I don't want to hear your puling tales of how it was. I saw for myself how it was. You won your fight, and then you set out to wade through blood that shouldn't have been spilt."

He barked a command to Stegus, the commander of the detachment. "Punishment. Stones." My heart sank, and I wanted to weep with shame and frustration.

The castle we lived in had dominated the shores of the great lake of Genava for hundreds of years, built originally as a standard Roman cohortal camp to garrison six hundred men. But it had been fortified and enlarged steadily over the course of half a millennium, until it could now house more than four times its original complement. And as the art of siege warfare had progressed and expanded, so had the defenses of the stronghold, so that the fortifications were forever incomplete, each new improvement giving way upon completion to another, newer development. The most recent addition, still under construction, was a matching pair of barbicans—high stone towers jutting far out from the regular line of the walls, flanking and protecting the main gates, from which heavy artillery and concentrated bow fire could be brought to bear on any attacking force below before it could approach close enough to engage the main defenses.

Such massive constructions required an endless supply of stones, and a constant flow of carts and heavy wagons brought stones and boulders from all around the countryside to a dumping ground outside the castle walls. That area was known as the stone fields, and stones were the only crop anyone had ever known to grow there, the inexhaustible piles of them rising and falling constantly, fed by the unending stream of wagons and depleted by the laboring prisoners. It was standard punishment duty, and had been from time immemorial, for criminals, miscreants and malcontents to carry these stones, one at a time, from the place where they had been dumped to the area where the masons and builders needed them on any given day. It was bleak, crippling labor, the most detested punishment in the entire region. I had never been assigned to it before—the very idea of it had been unthinkable—and neither, to the best of my knowledge, had Frotto or either of his friends. But I knew there was no recourse open to me, and that it was going to be a painful, miserable day until the sun set.

By mid-afternoon, my hands were sore and bleeding, my nails broken and splintered, and every muscle in my arms, back and legs felt as though it was being torn into shreds. But time passed with no respite other than a cup of water at the end of every trip to the walls, and eventually the sun began to sink towards the horizon. Twice I fell to my knees under the weight of individual stones, and both times was convinced that I could not rise up again. But the guard set over me was unyielding. He carried a supple length of willow, peeled and cut to leave only a grip for his hand, and he stood over me, counting aloud as I knelt in exhaustion, and with every fifth count he lashed me with the wand. He was not vicious, not malevolent, but merely dutiful; he took no pleasure out of whipping me, but neither had he any pity. His arm rose and fell mechanically, and its remorselessness inspired me to find wells of energy inside my aching body that I might not else have known existed. Both times I rose up and continued my punishment.

Long before the middle of the afternoon crawled around, however, I had sworn an oath to all the gods in the universe that I would never let myself be consigned here again; not as a boy, and not as a man. Nothing, I had decided, no fleeting self-indulgence, even the most sublime, could be worth this much agony and misery. And yet I knew that we four were escaping lightly. We were but boys and the stones we were made to carry were boy-sized, back-breaking though they were. The men who labored there fared far worse, and they were committed to weeks, months and sometimes years of punishment. The rocks they carried were enormous, and they were forced to make two trips before receiving water.

"Stop."

It took me several moments to realize that my guard was speaking to me. I stopped, hugging the stone to my chest, heaving and hitching it higher, trying to gain a better grip on it.

"Drop it," he said. "You're being summoned."

Too dazed and tired to feel any elation, I opened my arms and let the stone fall to my feet. It landed with a heavy thump and I stood for a moment looking down at it, aware again, as I had been at the end of every trip to the masons' area, that my hands and arms seemed unaware of being freed of their burden. The throbbing ache in them was too bone-deep to permit any instant relaxation at the mere dropping of a stone. I glanced up then to see Stegus, the guard commander, heading towards me, the speed of his walk lifting the material of his long cloak so that it seemed to float about him rather than hang from his shoulders. I tried to stand straighter as I waited for him, but my shoulders felt as though they might be permanently bowed.

Stegus came directly to me, and nodded to my guard. "I'll take him now. See to the release of the other three and then go back to what you should be doing today." The guard snapped him a salute, turned smartly on his heel and marched away.

I knew Stegus well, and liked him, for he often supervised my training at times when Chulderic had other tasks to perform, but there was no trace now of the easygoing officer with whom I was used to dealing. His face and eyes expressionless, he looked me over from head to foot, taking in the condition of my filthy, torn clothing, and his gaze lingered very briefly on my bloody,

dirt-crusted hands. He offered me no recognition, no acknowledgment that he even knew my name.

"King Ban wants you. Come."

As I trudged behind him, fighting to keep my back straight and
wanting only to fall down and cry like a baby, the misery of my day
deepened and grew more malevolent. Now I had to face my father,
something I had not anticipated. As angry as Chulderic had been, I
still had not thought he would tell my father about my disgrace.
Now it was obvious that he had, and considering the truth of that, I
realized that it had been inevitable from the start and cursed myself
for a fool for believing, for even one moment, that it might not be.
Chulderic, as my father's Master-at-Arms, had condemned me to
the stones for a day, and I was the King's son. Impossible for him
to conceal that, or his reasons for doing it, from the King.

I walked in a daze, scarcely aware of my surroundings as we
passed through the castle gates, crossed the main yard and entered
the central fortress. Only the flickering of torches and the echo of
Stegus's iron-shod boots on the flagged floor of the passageway to
my father's duty quarters brought me back to reality.

"Come," my father's voice boomed in response to Stegus's
knock on his door. Stegus leaned on the handle and swung one of
the heavy, iron-studded doors open until he could lean inside.

"Your son is here, Sir."

"Thank you, Stegus."

Stegus held the door open for me while I stepped across the
threshold, and then he closed it quietly behind me, leaving me alone
with my father, King Ban of Benwick.

3

As usual, the first thing I noticed was the chill. It was always cold
in my father's day quarters, even at the height of summer, because
they lay at the north end of the central stone-walled building of the

fort and had large, open windows with high arches, set with a heavy iron grille, that looked out onto a walled garden. The windows had shutters, both internal and external, with wooden slats that could be closed against foul weather, but I had never known them to be closed. On this occasion I did not even look at the windows. I had eyes only for my father's shape, outlined against the brightness beyond them.

He was standing behind the enormous wooden table he used as a desk, gazing down at a wide, unrolled parchment that was held open on one side by his sheathed dagger and on the other by a heavy, squat ink horn mounted on a carved ivory base. His bronze and iron helmet, crested with tightly packed short, prickly dark brown horsehair, sat by his right hand, and his plain brown cloak lay beside it, casually folded and thrown where he had dropped it. A row of high-backed Roman chairs of the type known as *stellae* faced the table, their backs to me. On the far side, where he stood, there was only his massive armed chair of black and ancient oak, carved over every point of its surface.

I stood motionless and waited for him to take notice of me. He was engrossed in whatever he was working on, however, and paid me no attention at all for a long time, and as I waited I felt my initial fear abating. I had no fear of him as my father, none at all, but I knew I had earned the punishment I had endured thus far that day and I expected more to come. Patience and tolerance my father had in abundance, but when discipline was called for he could be ferocious and unsparing. Looking at him now, when he was unaware of being watched, I saw that the light behind him made him appear different, in some subtle fashion, older than I had thought him. In fact I did not know how old my father was, but I knew he was much older than my mother, Vivienne of Ganis, for his firstborn son, Gunthar, had been born out of wedlock to a different mother, who had died birthing the boy years before Ban and Vivienne of Ganis ever met. My mother, who had given him four sons—Samson, Theuderic, Brach and me—was, in effect, his second wife. It was perhaps that difference that made it easy for the four of us who were

Vivienne's sons to believe that our half-brother, Gunthar, was both mad and dangerous, but then, we were all mere boys and Gunthar was a disapproving and unfriendly elder who also happened to be a sibling, so we felt justified in regarding him as both alien and inimical.

The light shining in on my father from the windows behind him outlined the deep, vertical scar on the left side of his face where a hard-swung sword had almost cloven his skull in some long-past fight but had glanced down the side of his head instead, trenching his face and separating the flesh of it from the underlying bone, so that even his skilled surgeons had been unable to repair the damage. His hair, iron gray, was cut short, close to his scalp, in what I had heard called the warrior's crop, and he was wearing his standard, daily armor, a sculpted cuirass of layered, hammered, highly polished bullhide embossed with broad bronze rosettes on his breast and a delicate tracery of bronze inlay outlining the abdominal muscles beneath. Heavy, armored epaulettes protected his shoulders, and from waist to ankles he wore breeches of soft, supple, carefully tanned leather. Over those, he was still wearing his armored leggings, which meant that he had not long since come in from riding, for the leggings were heavy and cumbersome things to wear when not on horseback.

My father was proud of his leggings, because they were an innovation that he had designed himself, years earlier and in cooperation with a few of his friends, after the *cataphractus,* the heavy, armored blanket developed by the Romans to protect their horses against weapons and projectiles. The cataphractus had worked so well as a protective device that riders had soon begun adapting its design to protect themselves in the saddle, reshaping and extending the blanket so that one flap of it could cover their legs. My father had taken the adaptation one step further, fashioning a kind of divided skirt that covered him from waist to ankle, separate from the cataphractus itself but serving the same purpose for the rider that the armored blanket served for the horse he rode. The resultant leggings were little more than hanging flaps of ring mail, leather panels held in place by a thick belt and encrusted with thousands upon thousands of tiny rings of bronze, sewn to overlap each other thickly enough to deflect a sword blade or a spear point, but they could be laced at knee and ankle to wrap around and cover the vulnerable parts of a rider's legs. It was obvious to me that before I entered his quarters that day he had already started to remove his leggings, for the laces at both knees and ankles hung free, and the belt tongue threaded through the heavy bronze buckle at his waist had been pulled through on one side, then left hanging. He had removed his scabbarded sword belt, too—it was worn over the belted leggings—and hooked it over the back of his chair.

As I watched him, thinking he had already lost awareness of my being there, he crossed one arm in front of his chest to support the other, drew back his upper lip in a rictus of frowning thought, and began to tap the back of one fingernail against his upper teeth. The sound of it carried clearly to me, and I listened as the tempo of his tapping increased, then stopped. He sniffed sharply, then sighed and looked up at me, sweeping me from head to toe with his eyes before turning away to gaze out of the window.

"You look like a casualty. Mud, blood and crusted dirt. Your mother's going to be very pleased with you."

I gazed at his back, unsure whether to speak and trying to gauge how angry he was with me. He hadn't sounded angry. But before I could respond he spoke again, still facing the garden.

"You're ten years old now, boy, more than halfway to manhood and big for your age. Do you think you'll ever make a decent man?" He didn't wait for a reply this time, but swung back to face me. "Chulderic thought you would, until today, but now he's not so sure. And from what he has told me, I have to wonder, too." He gazed at me for three long, pounding heartbeats, then closed his eyes, leaving his face expressionless. "Now tell me, do I need to wonder? What happened out there?"

My face was crimson, my chest crushed with shame.

"I got into a fight."

He opened his eyes wide and raised one eyebrow high. I did not know the word *sardonic* at the time, but I recognized the expression on his face.

"I know *that*. You against three others, bigger and older than you. You won. That's not what worries Chulderic. He's the one who taught you to fight, and he might have been proud of you. But he tells me that when everything was over, and you had thrashed all three of them, you went wild and tried to kill the biggest one. Frotto, is it?"

When I nodded, he frowned. "Aye. Well, Chulderic is my Master-at-Arms, and a fighter born and bred, not some terrified old woman. He says you stopped, stepped back, chased off the other two and then went after the big one again, even though there was no fight left in the fellow. Chulderic believes you were trying to kill him. He says he yelled at you and you ignored him. He says that if he hadn't torn you away and thrown you down you would have smashed the boy's head in. So you tell me, now, the truth. Is Chulderic lying?"

I shook my head, trying to swallow the lump in my throat and blinking my eyes fiercely to stem the tears that threatened to spill out of me. "No," I whispered, almost choking as I tried to speak. "But I wasn't trying to kill him . . . I only wanted to beat him badly, to teach him a lesson."

My father's eyes narrowed to slits. "Why? And what lesson?"

"To keep his big mouth shut and stop telling those lies about me."

"What lies?"

I was crying openly now, the hurt spewing out of me. "The same ones he always tells. Every time I meet him he tells all his friends that I'm not really who I am. He tells them you're not my real father, and that my real mother was a—was a faithless whore who left me and my father when I was a baby to run away with another man. He says his mother says that you and Mother took me in out of pity, and he says anyone can tell, just by looking at Gunthar and Samson and Theuderic and Brach, that I'm not their brother. I hate him and he's always lying and I wanted to make him stop, to make him afraid of me so that he would stop."

I squeezed my eyes shut, scrubbing at my face with my sleeves to dry my tears, and when I opened them I saw my father frowning at me in stupefaction.

"How long has this been going on?"

I knew then that my mother had never mentioned the first incident to him, and young as I was, something inside me shrank and withered. "For a long time. Since I was seven."

"Three *years*? Why haven't you told me this before?"

What could I say to that? I knew that if I spoke the truth my mother would have to answer for it, and in my confusion, wondering myself why she had said nothing to him, I could think of nothing else to say. He was glowering deeply now. "Answer me, boy. Why didn't you come to me?"

"I . . ." And suddenly the answer sprang to my lips, along with the knowledge that I could protect my mother. "You told me not to," I said, and saw his eyes widen. "When I told you about Ector stealing my knife you were angry at me. You told me that you had more to think about than silly boys' squabbles and said if I came running to you every time someone did something to me that I didn't like, I would never grow up."

He gazed at me for a long time, his lips moving together soundlessly as though he were nibbling something, and then he drew himself erect and breathed out through his nose.

"That's true, I did, didn't I. But that was a long time ago. You were, what, six at the time? And I had a fresh war on my hands. That very day you came crying to me over your stolen knife, as I recall, I had just received word that an entire unit of my men had been ambushed and wiped out by marauders, less than ten miles from here." His hands moved to the heavy buckle at his waist and he undid the belt of his leggings, folding them over one arm and dropping them heavily over the back of his chair, beside his sword belt. "But at six, I suppose you would have been too young to know anything about the seriousness of that. You saw your own problem that day as the most serious one in the world, and I barked at you like an angry dog and sent you off to resolve it by yourself. And you've never brought me another problem since, have you? Not until now."

He walked to the window again and stood staring out at the garden, clasping his hands behind his back. "I need to think about this, but I'll tell Chulderic he need have no fears about your savagery—that you did what you did for good reason—good enough to satisfy me, at least. Leave me now. Go to the bath house and clean yourself up. Tell Lorio I want him to look at your injuries. I'll have someone bring you fresh clothes. And we'll say nothing to your mother about your punishment today. When you're presentable again, come back here." He turned back to face me. "Show me your hands."

I went to him and did as he had asked. He took one of my hands in each of his own, turning them over to inspect my swollen fingers and mangled nails. When he was satisfied, he grunted and released me. "Well, they're not permanently damaged, but you'd better be sure to have Lorio bandage those two fingers on your left hand. I imagine that's all he'll be able to do for you, other than to rub in some liniment. The bruising will go away and the nails will grow back, but you're going to be sore for a few days. I think that, and the punishment you've already undergone, will be sufficient for the sins you've committed. What about Frotto?"

I blinked at him. "Frotto? What about him, Father?"

"What am I to do with him and his friends? Do you want me to have them whipped?"

"No!" I surprised myself with my vehemence and with the realization that I was no longer angry with Frotto. "No, if you please. Let them go."

"I already have, but I could bring them back and have them flogged. Are you sure you want to let this quarrel end that simply?"

"Yes, Father."

He shrugged, but I could tell he was pleased with me for some reason. "As you wish. We'll say no more about it. Do you think you frightened him enough to make him stop baiting you?"

I frowned. "Perhaps not, but I think Chulderic did."

My father's face broke into the wide-mouthed smile I loved. "Aye," he said, "I believe you might be right about that. Off with you now, and see Lorio, but waste no time. Come back here as soon as you're clean and dressed again."

4

How easy it is for us to delude ourselves in matters we simply do not want to confront. Thinking back on that afternoon—and it is a scene I have revisited countless times—I am constantly astounded by my own lack of perception. Of course, I was only ten years old, no matter how grown up and worldly I believed myself to be, and yet it has often seemed to me that the mindless relief with which I sought my freedom, scampering off to the bath house to be tended to and fussed over by Lorio, would have been unchanged had I been twice the age I was.

I threw myself into the task of washing away all signs of my misadventures that day, accepting the stinging pain of hot water on my bruises and injuries as an easily bearable penance. When I was clean and dried, Lorio massaged my aching hands, then smeared them with unguents and bound them carefully in clean, bright, white bandages of boiled linen. I was appalled by that clean brightness, for the sight of it filled my mind immediately with the impossibility of concealing the bandages from my mother. She would immediately want to know what I had done to myself. The fact that my father had told me we would say nothing to her about my escapades that day became meaningless. Neither of us, I knew, could lie to her, for my father's celebrated courage and heroism were all confined to what he did in battle. Even at ten, I knew they counted for naught in his own household whenever he clashed with his wife. My father would tell her the truth, and she would be angry.

Thinking such thoughts, I made my way slowly back to my father's day quarters in the gathering dusk. It did not cross my mind that my father had not denied Frotto's taunts, as my mother had; I had too many other thoughts to occupy my mind. Because of the shame and humiliation I had already brought upon myself that day, I was convinced that nothing could make matters worse than they already were that afternoon.

My father was still reading when I returned. The broad chart he had been studying earlier, whatever it might have been, was still spread on the table in front of him, but his attention was now focused elsewhere. He was sitting in his huge chair, deep in concentration and whispering to himself as he deciphered the script on a thick wad of paper sheets held stretched between his hands. As I entered the room he finished reading one page and moved it to the back of the pile, and the entire wad sprang back into the tubular shape in which it had been delivered, rolling itself up over his left thumb. He anchored the moved sheet carefully against the others in his left fist and then straightened the bundle again before he continued to read. I could tell from the speed of his whispering that he had already read the script at least once before, for first readings were always slow and hesitant as the eyes and the mind struggled with deciphering the written words and separating them from each other, trying to make sense out of the densely packed mass of characters that covered the paper.

I stood patiently until he reached a natural stopping point, when he released the right edges of the missive again and allowed it to snap back into shape before he rolled it tightly and slid it back into the leather tube in which it had come to him.

"That's better," he grunted in my direction. "You look more like your mother's son now. How do you feel? Are your hands sore?"

"A little," I admitted, and he placed the leather tube carefully on the table.

"Aye, well, they will be for the next few days, I suspect. Come."

He led me from the room and past his guards, along the stone-flagged passageway to the wide, curving staircase of hand-carved steps that led up to the King's Quarters, where our whole family lived in a sumptuously appointed privacy that was unique in the kingdom. These quarters, elaborate and grand, formed the official center of the fortified castle and had been built for a Roman procurator more than a hundred years earlier, when this region had been one of the most prosperous provincial centers in the Empire. The broad, shallow stairs swept grandly upwards to a deep and spacious oval landing facing three tall and imposing doorways, the central one slightly taller and wider than those on either side, its double doors of dark, polished wood more elaborately carved. The doorway on the right was the entrance to the King's bedchambers, and its double doors opened into a suite of four large rooms, two of which were bedchambers, while the others were a living room and a private bath house for the sole use of the King and his wife. The imposing central doors concealed our opulent official reception rooms, the third and farthest of which was a private dining room that could seat upwards of fifty people in comfort and was built directly above the main kitchens on the ground floor. The third set of doors, to the left, led to what had originally been sleeping quarters for important visitors and imperial guests and now served the rest of our family—a long row of sleeping cubicles for myself and my siblings, with an extra common room, all of which opened off the left of a long passageway that ran along the wall of the central reception hall.

"Wait here."

I remained obediently on the landing as my father entered his own rooms, closing the massive doors behind him and leaving me to wonder idly what was going on. I let my gaze fall to the familiar colors on the floor beneath my feet, illuminated by dim, late-afternoon light from a narrow, open skylight far above my head. I slid the toe of one shod foot over the tiny bright mosaic tiles that formed an enormous and intricately worked oval depiction of the Chi-Rho symbol of the Christian Church. My mother had commissioned this work years earlier, when I was still a crawling tot, engaging the services of a brilliantly gifted artisan named Polidorus who traveled all the way from Antioch in Asia Minor to design and install the floor over the course of three years. I could still recall the rapt awe with which, as I grew older, I had watched the old man work, meticulously selecting tiny square fragments of polished stone—he called them *tesserae*—from the piles of red, white and blue. He would place them effortlessly but with great precision so that, from day to day, the picture he was creating grew in size and complexity. It had been endlessly fascinating to me to wonder how the old man would be able to fill the shrinking work space to perfection, completing the design with squares of stone so that the irregular, shapeless and rapidly dwindling space would be filled without obvious flaws to indicate where he had left off working. For every stone he set in place diminished the open area remaining for his work, and I was incapable of seeing how he would reduce the ragged, asymmetrical work area that remained so that it would eventually accommodate and accept exactly, at the very last, one final, perfect square of stone. But flawless he had been to the last, so that nowadays, although I knew the approximate position of the final tessera he had set in place, I found myself unable to identify the spot.

Alone on the landing, gazing at the floor, I became aware of the silence surrounding me. There were no guards up here. Only when King Ban was receiving guests and envoys did he station guards at these doors, more for display than for security, and even then my mother disapproved. These were her quarters, too, and she saw no need for guards. In truth, there were many things for which my mother saw no need—frequently to the great frustration of my father, I knew—and one of those was concern over the opinions that other people held of her. She was a conscientious and committed Christian, and that alone set her apart from the majority of the people whom her husband ruled and governed, as Christianity was something of a novelty among the pagan folk who peopled our land.

It amused and delighted my mother that the people around us thought her both unnatural and magical. Her Christianity they could take in stride, although they might wonder at it among themselves, but they truly believed she was a faery creature: a water sprite, a supernatural being whose true element was water and who lived as easily beneath the surface of the lake, communing with the spirits there, as she did on land by day, where she mixed with normal folk. They called her the Lady of the Lake, and although others assumed that this name derived from our castle's position on the shores of the lake the Romans called Genava, they knew within themselves what the name really signified, and they smiled at the foolishness of others. They knew all about my mother and her strangeness, our local folk, for my mother's magic was that she could swim, and she did so as easily and naturally as did a fish, for the sheer pleasure it gave her.

But what our people saw as strange and unnatural was perfectly straightforward and unremarkable in lands not much farther to the south and west. My mother had learned to swim as a child, on a long-ago visit to the imperial island of Capri in the Middle Sea when she and her mother had been privileged to accompany her father on official business for the Emperor Honorius. For an entire summer there, in the warm, pellucid waters surrounding the beautiful island, she swam every day and developed a lifetime love of the pleasures of swimming underwater, marveling at the beauties that abounded there. The waters of our lake of Genava were far colder than those of the Middle Sea, but such was my mother's love of being underwater that she had grown inured to the discomforts of our more northerly climate and plunged into the lake every year as soon as the chill temperature grew bearable in summer. Once begun then, she swam every day, sometimes for hours on end, stopping with great reluctance only when autumn was far gone and the winds and frosts of each new approaching winter threatened to bring ice.

To our local people, such behavior was incomprehensible. They had a passing familiarity with hot-water bathing, thanks to their hundreds of years of association with the ruling Romans, but even that activity seemed alien to them. They themselves simply did not bathe, in the sense of immersing themselves in water, hot or otherwise. Bathing, voluntary self-immersion, was madness to them, since no one could breathe in water without drowning. By that logic, therefore, swimming in the open waters of a vast lake demonstrated complete insanity, or, alternatively, it endowed the swimmer, my unique and beautiful mother, with supernatural attributes. People chose to believe the latter, because they could see in their daily dealings with her that the Lady Vivienne was as sane as they were. Besides, the alternative explanation provided rich fodder for their imaginative murmurs and whispering over the long winter nights.

And so my mother was perceived and talked about as a water-sprite, which caused her great amusement and enabled her to go about her life as a conscientious Christian wife and mother without being concerned that her true beliefs might attract unwelcome attention. That reluctance to be noticed as a Christian was no empty fear, because outside the primary Roman spheres of influence—the towns and fortifications throughout the province—Christians were few, and because they had a reputation for meek submissiveness in turning the other cheek to aggressors, they made easy targets for predators. Tales of slaughtered, robbed and despoiled families of Christians were commonplace, although such depredations were usually carried out by strangers or wandering bandits, rather than by any of my father's people. On the whole, the ordinary people of our lands were pagan in their beliefs, but not savage; a large proportion of them were completely godless, but the remainder shared their worship, when they did worship, among an entire pantheon of gods imported over the ages from all parts of the far-flung Empire.

King Ban was Christian, too, of course, as were we all, his sons and daughters. But even at the age of ten I knew that Ban's was a nominal Christianity, held and observed more to please his wife than to save his soul. Left to himself and living his life as King Ban of Benwick, nominal vassal to whatever sub-emperor might be in power at any given time, my father was a responsible warrior king first, an administrative imperial official next, and a working Christian last and least.

As these thoughts of my father filled my mind, the door opened and he stepped out halfway, looking at me with one eyebrow raised.

"Come," he said, and stepped back inside, holding the door open for me. I entered the long lamp-lit hallway that I had not seen in more than two years and stood there, blinking, waiting for my eyes to adjust to the dimness. My father walked directly towards the brightness spilling from the room at the far end, and I trailed behind him, glancing at each of the doors on my right as I passed.

The first, I knew, concealed a deep, narrow storeroom lined with shelves, and the second led to the family's private bath house. I also knew that behind that door, at the end of a short, narrow passageway, hung double floor-to-ceiling curtains of heavily waxed cloth that contained the steam and moisture from the baths and prevented it from spilling out into the passageway. The next room was my parents' sleeping chamber, containing an enormous bed, framed in dark, richly polished wood and surrounded by curtains of the finest, most diaphanous cloth made by the nomads of Asia Minor. My mother would be in there, I assumed, but the thought had barely entered my head when I saw her instead peering anxiously towards me from the room my father had just entered, the family room at the end of the hallway.

This spacious room was the heart of their private quarters, and it was filled now with the evening light that shone through the hundreds of small, translucent rectangles of colorless glass in the high, arched windows in the outer wall. There were six hundred of these glass panels—I had counted them many times—all uniform in size and held in place by a mesh of lead strips, and they were the wonder of all our land. People marveled at them, I knew, because I had often heard them speaking of their beauty and speculating on the cost of them. They were unimpressive from the outside, looking up at them, but the light that poured through them during the day transformed the room's interior in a manner that seemed magical.

As I stepped into the room, I lost awareness of all else as my attention became focused instantly on my mother's distress. Her face looked gaunt and distraught, her eyes deep set and haunted, but she did not appear to be angry at me, and I felt an instant of selfish relief. She seemed afraid, more than anything else, and that frightened me in turn, for I could not imagine what kind of terror might have frightened her here, in her own castle, with her husband by her side and his warriors all around us.

"Mother?" I said, beginning to ask her what was wrong, but the moment I uttered the word she rushed to me and drew me into the kind of enveloping embrace she had not shared with me since I had entered training as a warrior. Her hand clasped behind my head and drew me to her bosom and her other arm wrapped about my back, pulling me close, so that I felt the womanly softness of her body as I had never been aware of it before, and as she held me I felt her shuddering with grief and heard her anguished sobs above my head. Mystified, I did not know what to do or how to respond and so I simply stood there, letting her crush me to her until I felt my father's hand gripping my shoulder, pulling me away. As I obeyed and stepped back, I saw that he was grasping both of us, one in each hand, prizing us apart.

"Enough, Vivienne," he said, and his voice was gentle. "The boy's unhurt. A few scrapes, no more than that. Nothing that will not heal and disappear within the week." I saw him wince, as though in pain himself, as he uttered the last words, and I understood immediately that he wished he had not said them. My mother groaned and swung away from his now gentle grasp, catching her breath in her throat and turning her back on both of us. My father looked from her to me and shook his head tightly in what I recognized, even at ten years of age, as frustration with the behavior of women.

"Sit down," he said to me, pointing to one of the room's large padded armchairs, and then he slipped his arm about my mother's waist and murmured something to her that I could not hear. She sniffed and fumbled for the kerchief in her sleeve and then, wiping her eyes, she permitted him to lead her to a couch, where she sat staring at me for long moments until fresh tears welled up into her eyes and spilled down her cheeks.

"Vivienne." There was a warning tone to my father's voice, and she looked up to where he stood beside her, watching her.

"Must we, Ban?" Her voice was plaintive, beseeching him.

"Yes, we must. Now."

Both of them turned their eyes on me then, and I spoke through the panic that had been building in my breast since this strange behavior began. "What is it, Father? Mother, what's the matter, what's wrong?"

"Nothing. Nothing is wrong, Clothar—not in the way you mean." My father perched on the arm of Mother's couch and leaned slightly to rest one hand lightly on her shoulder, his thumb moving soothingly against her neck. "I said something to you earlier today, when you first came to me, about your age. You were ten, I said, more than halfway along towards manhood. Do you remember?"

I nodded.

"And then I asked you if you thought you would ever make a decent man." He was looking intently at me now. "I had never doubted that you would, until I heard that report from Chulderic today, and your explanation satisfied any doubt I had then. You will be a fine man when you are grown, and you are growing quickly. You have the makings of a warrior and a king, both. Any father would be proud to have you as a son."

He glanced down to where his thumb still stroked his wife's neck, comforting her. My mother had stopped weeping and sat gazing at me, and I frowned in puzzlement at what my father had said—not about his pride but about having the makings of a king. I was the youngest of five sons, with little chance of ever becoming King of Benwick, and I had known and accepted that all my life. Mine would be a warrior's life, but not a king's.

"This fool, Frotto . . . Your mother told me earlier today, while you were at the baths with Lorio, that you came to her three years ago, when he first began taunting you. She told you then he was lying, but she said nothing to me at the time, thinking it was no more than a boys' spat and would pass." He glanced sideways at my mother, who showed no reaction but stared steadfastly at me. "I am not displeased over that. I might have said and done the same things, at that time, had I been faced with the dilemma you presented to her.

You were left to deal with Frotto's bullying for three years, but that's a normal thing that all boys have to undergo, in one form or another."

I felt myself frowning at him now. He saw my confusion and rose to his feet, sighing deeply and expelling the air noisily through pursed lips. "Damnation, boy, you understand nothing of what I'm saying, do you?" He did not expect an answer and moved away, pacing the length of the floor three times before he spoke again, and by the time he did, nameless terrors were clawing at my guts.

He approached and stood directly in front of my chair, holding out his right hand palm downwards in the ancient, imperious gesture that demanded fealty and obedience. I leaned forward and took his hand in both my own, feeling the calluses of his weapons-hardened palm.

"Time for truth, boy. Time to grow up, to leave childhood behind and face the world of men. Do you fear me?"

I shook my head, wide eyed. "No, Father."

"Do you doubt my love for you as a son?"

"No."

"Good, so we are as one on that. In all respects save one, you are my son, and I am proud of you."

"What?" My question emerged almost as a bleat, betraying all my sudden fears and consternation, and he turned his hand, grasping both of mine tightly but not painfully.

"Frotto is a fool, Clothar—a loudmouthed, mindless, empty-headed fool who gabbles about things he neither knows nor understands. But he is not completely wrong, and I will not lie to you. Most of his mouthings are mangled, foolish, ignorant noises, almost completely untrue in all respects, yet nonetheless, when all is said and done, even in his wrongness he is correct, and I should have his idiot tongue cut out." His fingers tightened on mine. "I am not your father, nor is your mother your true mother. Your real father and mother died many years ago, murdered when you were a tiny child, still suckling at your nurse's breast."

I know I must have cried out, because the Lady Vivienne sprang to her feet and rushed to kneel beside me, and as her arms closed around me, pulling me close again, King Ban released my hand and moved away. I was vaguely conscious of the stiff set of his back and shoulders as he went, but I have no other recollection of how I actually felt. All I can recall is a reeling numbness, a yawning emptiness and a deep-seated, aching coldness in my chest and belly.

"Vivienne! Leave him and sit down. This has to be finished quickly, the needless pain of it. There will be time to comfort him later, once he is ready for comfort. Right now he needs to hear the truth, to take away the strength of Frotto's lies. Step away, if you love him."

She did as she was bidden, slowly, leaving me to huddle in the depths of my large chair.

"Clothar? Clothar!"

I looked up again at the man who had been my father all my life and now was not. I saw the familiar size and strength of him and the unusual severity in his face, but all I could think was that he was not what he appeared to be. He was not my father. I was not his son.

"Listen carefully to what I say. Listen to me, and put all thoughts of what Frotto said out of your mind. What I will tell you now is the truth, the only truth. Do you understand me? Do you?" He watched for my nod, and then perched himself on one corner of the large table by the wall opposite my chair. This was a favorite position for him, in any room, braced on one long, rigid leg and sitting with his back straight and his head erect, his other leg crooked over the table's corner; it allowed him to look down upon anyone seated elsewhere, or to gaze eye to eye with standing men from a position of authoritative comfort.

"I know you feel betrayed by both of us. I can see it in your face. You think your life has been a lie and that we have gulled you. Well, that's not true, and the quicker you accept that, the sooner you'll reach manhood. The only thing we have concealed from you is the truth of your identity—of who you really are—and that was for your own protection."

His words were echoing in the hollow emptiness of my mind, but I could understand them, if not their full meaning. He spoke of protecting me, but from what, or from whom? The only threat I had known until then had stemmed from Frotto, and no one had protected me from him. I wanted to challenge the King on that, but I did not know where or how to begin, and he was already speaking again.

"You are high-born, boy, of bloodlines nobler and far older than mine. The truth of that is demonstrable, and the time has come for you to know about it. You were your father's firstborn son and the sole heir to his kingdom. You would have died for that alone, slain like your parents, had your father's murderer known where to find you. But he did not know where you were—nor was he even certain that you remained alive. And no one here, except my most trusted warriors, Clodio and Chulderic, knew where you came from. That kept you safe.

"But you are a king's son. Your birthright and standing are the same as those of Gunthar, my firstborn. So you will be a king someday, although not here in Benwick. When you are old enough and strong enough to claim your own and take your vengeance for your parents' blood, I, or your brother Gunthar if he is king by then, will assist you in claiming what is yours by right of blood and birth, and the man you must strike down will know who you are and why he is being destroyed." He had my full attention now; I could feel my own eyes wide upon his. He knew I wanted to speak, and he nodded. "What is it?"

I had to swallow before I could make any sounds. Even then, however, in my extreme youth and in the shock of having my entire world reshaped, there was a doubt in my mind. It was not a doubt about my father's truthfulness—even now I think of him as the father of my boyhood—but rather of his blindness concerning the nature of his firstborn son, for I knew with complete conviction that Gunthar, son of Ban and future king of Benwick, would be no source of help to me, ever. Gunthar was simply not an amiable or accommodating person. Even at ten years old I knew better than to trust him in anything, and I had grave misgivings, shared with my other brothers, about his sanity. We joked about it among ourselves, but none of us believed that he was normal in his mind. Gunthar's was a cold, calculating mind well matched to an emotionless, distrustful personality that considered his own welfare and his personal advantage first and foremost in all things. But there were times when he could also be terrifyingly irrational, and at those times you could practically smell the threat of rabid violence in him. None of us had ever voiced the thought aloud, but none of us doubted, either, that Gunthar would kill us without a thought if we provoked him far enough.

I thrust those thoughts aside, dismissing them as unimportant, and condensed all my newfound pain, my wonderings and curiosity and my sudden, soul-deep longings into one simple question.

"My father . . . my real father . . . Who was he?"

"His name was Childebertus. He was my closest friend for many years, though he was much younger than me. We served in the legions together, long ago, during the reign of Honorius, just after the death of Stilicho, and your father was no more than a lad when first we met—a bright, sparkling lad, only seven years older than you are now. I was his first commanding officer, but he was talented and won promotions quickly. He grew level with me quickly, then went on to outrank me. He was a brilliant soldier."

Chillbirtoos, I thought, repeating the name in my mind as he had pronounced it. *My father was Chillbirtoos, a brilliant soldier.* The skin on my arms rose up in gooseflesh, but the King was still talking.

"We became close, he and I, over the ten years that followed, brothers in arms, closer than blood brothers—him and me and one other friend who outranked both of us and commanded an entire army group. And then, one day about twelve years ago, your father and I met and married twin sisters—the Lady Vivienne, here, and your own mother, the Lady Elaine, both daughters of King Garth of Ganis." He stopped suddenly, then waved his hand towards his wife in an unmistakable order for her to hold her peace. He kept his eyes fixed on mine. "Stand up."

I rose to my feet obediently.

"Would you ever call my wife a whore?"

The question stunned me, and I felt my face blaze with a sudden rush of blood and shame at the awfulness of what he had asked me. I did not dare to look at the Lady Vivienne, nor had I words to answer him, so I merely shook my head, blushing harder than ever.

"What does that mean, that mum show? Answer my question."

"No! I never would. Never."

"I thought not. But yet you called her sister one—your own dead mother whom you never knew."

My humiliation was complete. I lowered my head in an attempt to hide the hot tears that blurred my sight.

I heard him moving, rising from his perch and coming towards me, and then I felt his rough hand grasp my chin, not ungently, and lift my head to where I could see him peering into my watery eyes. I blinked hard, trying to clear my vision and look back at him defiantly, but I knew nothing of defiance then, and he had no thought of seeing any.

"Frotto lied, boy, because he is a fool and knows no better. You are more man, at ten years old, than he will ever be. But a man must quickly learn to recognize the truth when he hears it, and to know the difference between truth and lies. Hear the truth now, from me, witnessed by my wife who is your mother's sister. What you have heard about your mother is a malicious lie, spread by this Frotto's mother, who is even more stupid than her witless son. She worked here once, when you were newly arrived, and we cast her out for lying and for clumsy thievery. Her tattling afterwards was the result of that—malicious gossip bred of sullen resentment, nothing more.

"Your mother was Elaine of Ganis and she loved you. She loved your father, Childebertus, who was my friend, even more. She and your father both died because of an evil man—she by her own hand—and you yourself survived only by good fortune and the bravery of the same man who set you to work on the stones today, Chulderic of Ganis. He brought you here to us, and here you have remained. Apart from Chulderic and ourselves and Clodio, who led

Chulderic to us when he first arrived, no one here knows who you really are, including Frotto's vindictive mother. You became our son because you were already dear to us as the child of those we had loved and lost. And you will remain our son for as long as you wish to do so. Do you understand what I have told you?"

I nodded, half blinded by, but now uncaring of, the tears that streamed down my face. He nodded back at me and sucked in a great, deep breath. "Aye, well, that's good. So be it. And so be it that you never think another thought of your mother having abandoned you. She bought your life with her own and died in your defense. Don't ever forget that."

"I won't." I looked again to where the Lady Vivienne sat watching me. "But what will I call you now?"

"Hmm?" The King's deep-chested grunt betrayed his surprise, but he answered me immediately. "You'll call us what you always have—Father and Mother. Why should you not? Nothing has changed. We will still call you Clothar and you will continue to be as much a son to us as you have always been. We will continue to be your parents, in the eyes of everyone who knows no better. It's safer to keep it that way."

"But why, Father? Why is it safer, I mean?"

His swift frown of impatience with my slowness died as quickly as it had sprung into being. "Because you are yet at risk. Your father's murderer is still alive and well, and he is powerful, damnation to his black, worthless soul. Better that we do nothing that could betray you to him, for if he even suspected that you live he would send men to kill you, and he would not stop until you were dead, because fatherless boys grow up to be men capable of seeking vengeance for their fathers' murders."

I thought for a moment, then asked, "Who is this man, Father?"

"His name is Clodas. Clodas of Ganis. At least, that's what he calls himself now and will for a few more years, unless God smites him dead in the meantime. But he was no more than plain Clodas, a minor chief among your father's clans, before he set eyes upon your mother and began his scheming. In the end, he slew both your

parents and your grandfather and usurped your grandfather's holdings, stealing his very name."

"But why didn't you fight him, kill him, take revenge on him?"
In my ten-year-old eyes, Ban of Benwick was omnipotent and
invincible in war. I found it incredible that he should not have
exacted vengeance long ago on the slayer of his friends and family.

His mouth twisted wryly before he glanced from me to his wife
and back. "A fair question, I suppose. And one that I have often
asked myself, even knowing all the answers. I couldn't, Clothar.
That's the only answer I can give you. I could not, for many reasons,
none of which might make any sense to you today."

"Why not? Because I'm just a boy?"

He shrugged and almost smiled, but then he sobered. "Aye.
That's right."

"But you've just told me I'm to be a man, from this day on. It's
time to grow up, you said, and face the truth . . . to leave childhood
behind and face the world of men. Isn't that what you said? Tell me,
then, as a man."

He inhaled deeply, straightening his back, then blew the air
from between pursed lips. "Very well, as a man, then. I had my
hands full here when all this happened, and the news came but
slowly to us. We heard nothing about it for months—more than half
a year. It was only when Chulderic arrived the following summer,
bringing you and your nurse, that we found out what had occurred."

"Ludda came with me? She is from Ganis, too?"

"No, not Ludda. Your first nurse died. She was sick with a fever
from the journey when she arrived and she died within a few days.
Ludda came to us after that, because she had lost her own child at
birth and had milk, so she could feed you."

"How old was I?"

"Young—not yet a year."

I thought about that, then dismissed it. "You said you couldn't
fight this man Clodas because your hands were full. Full of what?"

He half grinned at my unconscious humor. "Many things," he
said with a shrug, "and most of them like sand, threatening to run

through my fingers and be scattered on the winds no matter what I did. I had a war to fight, first and foremost. The Alamanni were threatening to wipe us out, and my father was newly dead, killed fighting them. I had to take his place or see our home and our people go down into ruin and destruction."

I nodded gravely, trying to impress him with my understanding, for I knew the truth of what he said from my own lessons. The man whom I had always thought of as my grandfather until that day, King Ban the Bald, had been the first true king of Benwick, awarded the title by the Emperor Theodosius in recognition of thirty years of loyal service to the Empire. He had ruled Benwick well for twenty-five years after that and had fallen in battle against the Alamanni, at seventy years of age, the year before I was born.

Before becoming a kingdom, Benwick had merely been a territory settled by our people. Frankish tribes had swept into Gaul years earlier from the north and east, overcoming all opposition to become the predominant people in most of the ancient Gaulish lands that lay west of the Alps, with the exception of the central and south-western territories held by the Burgundians. The rulers of Benwick were from a far-wandered clan of the tribes of Franks known as the Ripuarians, who had drifted southward in large numbers from the Germanic regions of the Rhine River over the course of more than a hundred years. Ban the Bald had been hereditary chief of the clan, but from the moment he returned to them at the head of a small army of Roman-trained warriors, they had prospered under his new kingship and had established a new society, complete with laws and defenses, within a very short time.

Even so, they had not enjoyed sole possession of their new lands for long, for the route their forefathers had followed down and across Gaul attracted other wanderers, most notably the German tribes the Romans called the Alamanni, who were also looking for a place to settle. When the first of these new arrivals saw the beauty of our rich lands around the Lake of Genava, they decided they had wandered far enough, and so they spread out among and around our settlements and began to set down roots of their own.

For some time after that, we coexisted peacefully with them. But the Alamanni kept on coming south, in ever-increasing numbers, and soon there was no more room for newcomers. Tensions sprang up between the incoming land-hungry migrants and our own people and soon grew into hostilities that quickly escalated into full-scale war. That war had lasted longer than my lifetime and had ended only two years before, when our forces, better trained and more disciplined than the masses of Alamanni migrants, finally won a decisive and bloody victory over an army more than twice their numbers.

After that battle the enemy, shattered by their enormous battle losses, had sought terms to end the conflict, and it had been agreed by the leaders of both sides that the Alamanni would withdraw their southern border northward by fifty miles, leaving us to live unrestricted in our own small region on the southern shores of Genava. It was a great triumph for Ban of Benwick. But still, I thought, the war had been over now for two years and our whole country was at peace and growing prosperous again, yet Ban had done nothing about seeking vengeance against this Clodas. Even as the thought formed in my mind, however, the King anticipated it.

"Even although we are now at peace, I can make no move against Clodas yet. He is too far removed."

"Where is he?"

"Far to the north and west, in the Salian regions on the borders of Germania. Five hundred miles from here, at least."

"Five hundred *miles*?"

"Aye. What did you think? I told you it took Chulderic more than half a year to reach us after the murders. He could have been here sooner, had he been mounted and had an escort, but he was alone and on foot, traveling through hostile territory all the time, and he had a woman and a baby with him."

"Five *hundred miles* . . ."

"A long way, Clothar. Not a journey to be undertaken lightly, even with an army at your back. It would take years of preparation for us to wage a campaign that far away from home, even if it did not mean having to fight our way every single step from here to there. And even were I ready now, I couldn't take my army away for that length of time. The Alamanni would break the treaty as soon as we set out, and there would be nothing left for us to come home to when our campaign was over."

This was information I did not want to hear, and yet it puzzled me. "Why would you have to fight every step of the way, Father?"

"Because we would be traveling through other people's territories. No one wants a foreign army marching through their lands, even if it doesn't threaten them with war. Armies have to eat, and they eat off the land, and that land already belongs to people who need the food themselves, so they will fight fiercely to protect it. We would have to fight our way northward and westward for five hundred miles. That would be madness. And we are not a seagoing people, so we could not make the journey by water."

"Then we can never take revenge for my father and mother."

"No, that is not what I said." He paused, gazing directly into my eyes until he was sure I was listening intently. "What I *said* was that when *you* are ready—strong enough and grown into your own manhood—Benwick will give you soldiers enough to claim your kingship."

"Germanus," my mother said, and both of us looked at her, me thinking that she had meant Germania, the land King Ban had mentioned moments earlier. But then she said it again. "Tell him about Germanus."

The King frowned. "I intend to, Vivienne, as soon as I may."

I looked from one to the other of them. "Who is Germanus?"

"A friend." The King looked at me again, his eyes narrowed. "You'll remember what I said about your father and I being brothers in arms. I said there were three of us, one of them a man who outranked both of us by far. That was Germanus, Legate Commander of the Imperial Armies of Gaul, appointed by the Emperor Honorius himself."

"An Imperial Legate Commander? He was my father's friend?"

"Friend and brother, as he was to me. The three of us were as peas in a pod for years. But whereas your father and I were warriors and minor kings, Germanus had great power at his command, with almost a hundred thousand troops at his disposal before he left the legions. He left the same year your father and I left, but where we returned to our former lives, Germanus joined the Church. He is a bishop now, still wielding great power, though of a different kind, and people are saying he has become a worker of miracles, a very holy man."

He thought about that for a moment, and then smiled. "Your father would find that amusing. I do, too, God knows, because the Germanus we knew as young men loved to laugh at other people's folly and he was no one's idea of a very holy man. He was a fine man, completely admirable, among the best of the best by anyone's standards: strong, courageous, afraid of nothing and absolutely trustworthy." He smiled again, a savage kind of grin. "And now that I think of it, he worked miracles even then, years ago . . . but those were miracles of soldiering—achieving the impossible, it sometimes seemed, with very few resources." His smile faded but remained in place, as though at something only he could see. "He was always a noble man, Germanus, when we three rode together . . . honest and straightforward as the day is long . . . But we would never have thought of him as *holy*."

"What does holy mean?" I asked.

"Mean? I'm not sure what it really means. Devout, pious, unworldly and possessing sanctity, I suppose. A man of God. It means all of those things yet more than all of them, for a devout and pious man—an ordinary bishop, for example—cannot expect to cast out devils easily or bring dead people back to life. A man needs true holiness to do such things. Yet I have heard tales of my friend Germanus doing them, and often. And they are tales from people I know and trust."

"Where is he now?"

"He's here, in Gaul. He is the Bishop of Auxerre, about two hundred miles northwest of where we sit now."

"Oh-zerr?" I had never heard of such a place. "What kind of name is that?"

"It's what the local people there call their town. What more explanation do you need? Its old Roman name was Autessiodurum, back in the days of the Caesars when that part of Gaul was officially called Gallia Comata. But I suppose Autessiodurum was too much of a jawbreaker for the local folk, much the same as Gallia Comata turned out to be. It's been hundreds of years since anyone has called that region Gallia Comata."

"Comata? That means long-haired. How could that be the name of a country?"

The King grinned at me, his fine white teeth flashing. "Because all the people who lived up there were long-haired back then, when Julius Caesar first came strutting, thinking to conquer us. That was the explanation I was given, anyway, when I asked my tutor the same question at about your age."

"What were we called, then?"

"We?" He laughed. "*Your* people were Salian Franks. They lived up there, below the Rhine River. This part of Gaul down here was called Gallia Cisalpina, Cisalpine Gaul, because the Alps lie between us and the northern borders of Italia. My people called themselves Ripuarian Franks—but do *not* ask me what that means because I have no idea. The Romans, however, called us all Gauls."

"So why did people in Auxerre stop calling it Autessiodurum? I like that name."

Another smile and a shake of his head. "Why do people do anything? I can't tell you anything about that, lad . . . other than that they were Gauls and they wanted nothing to do with any Roman place called Autessiodurum. They'd had their own name for the place, long before the Romans came.

"Anyway, it's Germanus's home country. His family have been there for hundreds of years and own most of the land for many miles around. Or they used to own it. It has new owners nowadays, apparently. I've heard tell, again from people who know, that when he swore allegiance to the Church, as a bishop, Germanus turned over all of his possessions to his superiors, keeping nothing for himself, since he has no heirs."

"He gave away *everything*?"

"Aye, to the Church."

"Why?"

"You will have to ask him that for yourself. He will be here within the month. The letter I was reading when you came to me today was from him. We have not seen each other since our legion days, and he will be passing close to here on one of his missions, so he will stay with us for a few days."

"Will you be spending lots of time with him while he is here?"

"All of it. Why would you ask that?"

"Will you tell me more about my father before he comes?"

He looked slightly surprised. "Aye, I will."

"When?"

He turned his eyes away from mine to look at his wife, and I looked at her too, wondering what was passing between them. The Lady Vivienne simply smiled at him, her lips curving faintly upward, but her face was very pale. He nodded, tensely, I thought, and then looked back to me.

"Tonight, if you would like that. It's almost dinnertime now, and I have guests to look after. You eat, then go to bed at your appointed time, and I will wake you when I am done with my tasks. You and I can talk then and no one will interrupt us."

As though she had received some signal that I missed, my mother—and that word seemed suddenly strange to me—rose and crossed to where I sat, then stooped to kiss my cheek and told me gently to go and take my place with my brothers in the dining hall. As I left the room, I could feel both of them watching me.

5

I was so excited that evening that I did not believe I could possibly sleep when bedtime came. I ate without awareness of eating, my eyes fastened on King Ban and his guests at the head table as I

willed the King to look towards me and nod some kind of acknowledgment of his promise. But he paid me no attention, his entire
being focused upon the entertainment of his guests at the high table,
and shortly after they had finished their meal and left the hall,
Ludda came looking for me to gather me up and supervise my
bedding down for the night. Ten years old and more than halfway to
manhood I might be, but my nurse's word still ruled my behavior.

On this occasion, however, I made no demur about going to bed.
I was looking forward to lying awake in the warm darkness, thinking about my real father and mother and imagining the tales King
Ban would have to tell me. And of course, once in bed and warm, I
fell straight to sleep.

I awoke to the sound of my name, to find the King standing
above me, holding a flickering lamp.

"Up, boy. Or would you rather stay there and go back to sleep?"

Almost before he had finished speaking, I was rolling out of
bed, wide-awake, my heart already hammering. In anticipation
of being summoned, I had gone to bed still wearing my tunic and
leggings, and as I groped for my felt shoes the King threw me a
heavy, fur-lined robe that had been folded over his arm.

"Here, put this on. It's cold tonight."

I followed him quickly, clutching the warm, heavy robe around
me as he led me down the great curved staircase and back towards
his day quarters. I had no idea what time of night it was, but I knew
it must be very late because it was so cold, and because the hallways
were utterly deserted and several of the bracketed torches lining the
walls had burned themselves out. King Ban did not look back at me
but strode directly to his private quarters, where he threw open one
half of the heavy doors and swept through. I closed the door quietly
behind me, looking around me in surprise. The room was awash
with the leaping light of flames from a huge number of fine candles
and a roaring log fire in the brazier in the hearth. The windows were
firmly shuttered and secured against the night, and it was warm in
there for the first time ever, to my knowledge.

"Sit, over there."

I sat in the comfortably padded chair the King had indicated, on the left side of the hearth, and he crossed to its twin on the other side, but he did not sit down immediately. He stood with one hand on the back of the chair and stared back towards the door. I looked to see what he was staring at, but there was nothing.

"Where *is* the man?" As he spoke the words, the door swung open again, and Guntram, Ban's veteran personal servitor, entered carefully, holding the door ajar with his buttocks as he stooped to gather up two steaming jugs.

"Worthy lad," the King addressed him, "I was beginning to think you might have died in the kitchens."

Guntram, who was many decades beyond being a lad of any description, paid no attention to his lord and master. Carrying one large jug in each hand, he crossed the room quickly and placed them gently beside an array of mugs that sat on a long, narrow table flanking the King's big work table. He stood quietly for a few moments, gazing down at the table as though taking stock of everything it held, then turned to the King.

"Will you need anything else, Lord? Shall I pour for you?"

Ban finally smiled. "No, and I have kept you from your sleep for far too long. Get you to bed now, and sleep well. I may just have another task for you tomorrow."

Again the old man ignored the raillery. "Aye, sir." His eyes moved from the King to me and he nodded slightly. "Late night, for a young lad. Tomorrow, then."

I watched King Ban watch Guntram leave the room, and as soon as the door closed with a thud, he swung away towards the table with its steaming jugs. He filled a mug for himself, then poured mine from the first, larger jug, and topped it up from the second before bringing it over to me.

"Spiced wine and honeyed water. For me, spiced wine alone. I dislike the taste of water, honeyed or otherwise."

I could scarcely believe the privileges I was enjoying: first a uniquely private audience with the King, deep in the night, in quarters I could never have imagined being so intimately comfortable, and now this. I held the mug up to my nostrils, inhaling the fragrant steam that rose from it.

"I've never had this before," I said.

"I know," the King said, bending to thrust the long iron poker deep into the heart of the fire. He left it lodged there and sat back again. "But tonight is for talk of manhood and the preparations for it. Spiced wine is part of that. Try it. You might find the taste even better than the smell of it."

I sipped, cautiously on two counts, alert to the high heat of the brew and to the unimaginable taste. Both were acceptable, the flavor of the sweet, diluted, spicy wine indescribably delicious. The King watched me suck in my cheeks and smile my pleasure before he raised his own cup to his lips, nodding gently.

"Sets the mouth a-jangling, doesn't it?" He sipped a mouthful and savored it, rolling it around his tongue before swallowing, and seeing his pleasure I raised my own mug again.

"Be careful. Drink it very slowly, a little at a time. We have much to talk about tonight and you are not used to wine. I warn you, even watered down, it will go straight to your head. Especially when it is hot."

I sipped sparingly at the delicious potion, wondering what he meant by saying it would go to my head.

"Well," he said then, lounging back into his chair and stretching out his long legs to the fire. "Take off that robe now, if you're warm enough." I placed my mug on the floor and stood up, shrugged out of the warm fur-lined garment and folded it carefully over my chair back, and when I was seated again he sipped again at his own drink. "I'm glad you slept. It was a long, wearisome night and I was feared you might have lain awake, waiting for me."

"I meant to," I said, suddenly more shy than I had ever been in his company. "But I fell asleep anyway."

"Hmm. I wish I could have. Instead I spent useless hours listening to the mutterings of drunken fools. So, you have had time to think about the things I told you earlier, which means you must have questions. Fire away, then. What do you want to ask me about?"

"My mother, if it please you, Sire."

"Your mother. Of course that is what you would want to know . . . and it is what I am least qualified to tell you about, for I did not know her well. Your mother was my wife's sister and my best friend's wife, but I only ever met her twice and so knew little of the lady herself, apart from what others told me of her. But I can try to answer you. What would you like to know?"

"I . . ." I stopped, thinking hard about what I wanted to ask him. "You said Clodas did not begin his scheming until he set eyes on her. What does it mean?"

He sighed, and sat staring into his cup, his lower lip protruding in a pout. "What does it mean? I don't know, Clothar . . . In plain truth, I do not know . . . That is a deep question, and there is much more to it than meets the eye, so let me think about it before I answer. What *does* it mean?" He drew one leg up, away from the fire's heat, and looked into the flames. "It means, I suppose, that something was transformed in Clodas the moment he first saw your mother, the Lady Elaine of Ganis. Something happened inside him, at the sight of her; something dark in there, and shapeless, changed and grew hard and took a form it had not had before. It means all of that." He threw me a fierce glance. "But your mother was no more guilty of willfully affecting or attracting Clodas than the winter frost is guilty of turning the waters of a pond to ice. The frost freezes the water but is no more than the breath of winter. The sight of your mother's beauty undid Clodas, but her presence could have been no more than a beam of light shining into the blackness of his soul, showing it what might have been. And what was within that blackness we can never know.

"Would Clodas have been a better man had he never seen your mother? No, he would not, because the thing that changed inside him was already there." He paused, looking at me curiously. "Can you guess what it was?"

I shook my head, and he nodded, unsurprised.

"What was inside him, boy, was plainly a sickness, unseen before then and unsuspected by anyone else, and it was born of a mixture of poisons: malice, gross ambition, discontent, and envy of anyone he thought of as being better off than he."

"Was my mother that beautiful?"

"Aye, she was. But you must ask my wife that question. I am only a man, and men see women differently from women. Vivienne will tell you the truth. But be sure not to ask her when she is surrounded by the lovesick young admirers who swarm among my followers. I doubt she would thank you for that. Famed for her beauty as she is in these parts—and I know there is none more beautiful, within as well as without—my lady will tell you that she always felt plain around her sister. They were twins, born but an hour apart, but they were not identical. Elaine was the beauty of the pair, tall and upright, with raven hair and bright blue eyes, where Vivienne's height was normal, her hair golden and her eyes were that sparkling green they are today. Elaine's—your mother's beauty, seen unexpectedly, could make a man's breath catch in his throat."

"Was— was the Lady Vivienne jealous of her?"

"Jealous, of Elaine?" He laughed. "God, no, boy! They almost breathed as one, the two of them, so close were they. They may have had their disagreements from time to time, as all siblings will, and each might have felt some envy of the other from time to time, but there was never any lack of love between them, and certainly no jealousy. Jealousy is a bleak and bitter thing, Clothar. Those two loved each other too much as friends and sisters to be jealous, and each was happy when the other found a man to marry—two men as close to each other as the sisters were to themselves."

I digested that in silence, then continued with my catechism. "Clodas." I hesitated. "What was it that made him want to kill my mother?"

"He had no desire to kill your mother. It was your father he set out to kill. Your mother took her own life, in the end, but his murder of her husband—and of you, she thought—was the direct cause of her death. He destroyed her family and loved ones, yet expected her to consent to being his wife. That is insanity. You understand that word, insanity? Well, Clodas was insane." He paused, considering that, and then went on. "Clodas *is* insane. I suppose it might be possible to find some depraved woman, somewhere, who could accept that kind of thing, but Elaine of Ganis could never be such a one. Clodas was a monster whose existence she could not accept, and at the thought of having him control her life, she chose to kill herself."

Another long silence while the King stared into the fire, then: "I do not often trouble myself to think about whatever it is that makes men do the things they do. If they do something I find it necessary to condemn, I will condemn them, discipline them—slap them down or cut them down, depending on the gravity of what they've done.

"I am not a talker. I'm a soldier—a fighter. But I am also a king, and that often complicates things for me because a king must speak out forcefully from time to time . . . I am forever surrounded by people waiting for me to tell them what to do and what to think. Most of the time, when something angers me or when someone has offended me by breaking a law, or when I'm displeased and have a strong opinion to make plain, I attend to it with a sword in my hand. But this is a time for thought, and for clear words, so let me think, and then listen to what I have to tell you."

I waited, and he soon began again. "Clodas is a monster. But monsters come in many guises, Clothar, and not all of them are frightening to look at. Some are born monstrously deformed, and they grow ever less pleasing to the eyes as they age. But that is no more than misfortune, pure and simple. Ill formed as they are, they are not often ill natured. Many of them are meek and gentle souls. We call them monsters because they frighten us, but that reflects our failings, not theirs."

He thought for a while. "And then there are some men who grow to be monsters. They *learn* to be that way. You'll see more than you want to see of that as you grow older and become accustomed to war and killing, and as a Christian you will deplore it while the warrior within you learns to recognize it and to use it. That kind of monster you will learn to recognize on sight, and even to employ at times, for many of them you will number among your own men. Their disfigurement—" He paused, shaking his head impatiently and clearly searching for another word. "Their *affliction* is a wanton disregard for human life, born of too much hatred and bloodshed. Those men become rigid with hate, incapable of kindness or compassion. They see all but their own—and sometimes even their own—as enemies deserving death, and they are masters of spilling blood and spreading havoc. They are cold and pitiless, devoid of love, or mercy, or even hope, and that is their crippling misfortune. Life holds no value for them, not even their own, and nothing seems to them worth living for." His voice faded, but just as I was beginning to think he had finished, he began to speak again, his tone low and troubled, almost as though he were speaking to himself.

"But yet another kind of monster walks among us, sharing our daily lives and giving us no sign, until it is too late, that they are deeply different from us." He turned his head to look at me. "Clodas is one of those, and they are almost impossible to guard against."

"Why, Father?"

The word *father* sounded alien in my mind as I spoke it, but I used it because at that moment I could think of no other name to call him. *Uncle* would have seemed ridiculous.

"Because they are so different from the ruck of ordinary, honest men. They take the trust on which we live and turn it into poison."

"I don't understand."

"That does not surprise me. Trust is not . . . it's not something we *think* about very often, but we depend on it for everything worthwhile. We all deal in trust, Clothar—people's lives are *founded* on trust. D'you understand that?"

"I think so."

"It's true. We form our own opinions of the folk we live among, the friends and neighbors and companions and soldiers with whom we share our lives, and we trust them to behave in certain ways—as they do us—with honesty and dignity and respect for themselves and for their neighbors. And based upon that trust, that mutuality of

trust and common interests, we make laws and rules to govern how
we all live with one another. But these monsters I speak of now,
monsters like Clodas, are governed by no laws, no rules. They are
predators, wild beasts who prey upon honest, ordinary men as
victims—perceiving them and treating them as weaklings and helpless fools created solely to fulfill *their* needs. They have—they
know—no honesty, these creatures. Worse, they have no understanding of what honesty is, and that, alone, makes them dangerous to all
who cross their paths. They see no worth in trust, because they
themselves have no belief in it. It is alien to their nature, and therefore they exploit the trust of other people as a fatal flaw.

"By far the worst part of such beings, however, is that they
quickly learn to keep their true natures hidden from the eyes and
knowledge of others. They learn to ape the manners and behavior of
others unlike themselves, behaving outwardly as they believe others
think they ought to behave, and concealing their own monstrous-
ness. Their entire existence is a lie. They deal in a kind of treachery
that ordinary men cannot imagine, and that treachery grants them a
power against which no one else can be prepared."

His words chilled me, because as he spoke them I found myself,
without warning, seeing my brother Gunthar in my mind instead of
the faceless Clodas who was no more than a name to me, albeit a
name I had already begun to hate. The King's voice had grown
quieter as he spilled all of this out, and when he had finished he sat
frowning into the flames, his eyes fixed on some far-distant recollection. I remember wondering whether he was thinking about the
treachery of Clodas or whether he, like me, might be aware of
another, similar monster, closer to home and even more troublesome to his peace. I waited again for him to continue, but this time
he showed no signs of having anything to add and so eventually I
prompted him, clearing my throat three times before he noticed.

"What? There's a question in your eyes."

"You said they have a power no one else is prepared for. What
kind of power is that?"

"The power to deceive. And to betray."

I blinked at him. "But anyone can deceive anyone else."

"True," he conceded without hesitation. He looked away briefly and inhaled sharply before turning quickly back. "You can deceive someone without betraying him, Clothar. Deceit is usually self-serving, but it need not be harmful to others. Betrayal, on the other hand, is *always* harmful. And when someone who has gained a high position of trust betrays that trust as Clodas did, its effect has the power of a hard-swung axe, smashing through everything it encounters because there are no barriers, no armor or defenses, to stop it. Clodas was your father's blood kin, his first cousin. His mother and your grandfather were brother and sister. He destroyed your family and part of mine because he had placed himself in a position from which no one expected treachery, and until he struck no one had ever suspected that he might. His betrayal was monstrous, a crime no normal person could have imagined . . . your father least of all."

He emptied his mug at one gulp and I sipped at my own, surprised to find that I had drunk most of it and what was left was almost cold. The King rose to his feet and pulled the iron poker from the fire. It was bright yellow, whitening towards the tip. He tapped it against the side of the iron fire basket, then held it out to one side and crossed to the table where the pitchers sat. He plunged it into first one and then the other, sending clouds of fragrant steam billowing across the room.

"Bring the mugs."

I did as I was bidden, then returned to the hearth to add more fuel to the fire, thinking about all the King had said. He rejoined me moments later, bringing my drink with him, and when we were seated again I asked him the question foremost in my mind.

"Do you really think Clodas would send men to kill me, Father?"

His eyes narrowed. "Without a doubt, if he suspected you were still alive. Not because you are a harmless boy, but because you will soon be a man. So we can take no risks in that matter. None at all. Bear that in mind above all else and say nothing of this to anyone. Not to *anyone*. We have no control over the way tales spread. One word leads to another and the information spreads like ripples on a pond."

"But you said he is five hundred miles away."

"Aye, he is, but that changes nothing about the risk. You have five more years to go before you reach full manhood, and much could happen before then. I can protect you against an invading army, but no one could defend you against a hired, faceless murderer acting alone. So by keeping your mouth shut, you might save your own life."

I fell silent again, then remembered something else. "You said no one—and least of all my father—could have imagined Clodas's crime before it was committed. What did you mean by that . . . that he was least of all?"

The King shrugged, dipping his head. He drank again, then clasped both hands around his cup. "I have never known anyone like your father, Clothar. He was my best and dearest friend, closer to me than anyone else has ever been or could ever be today, and yet the two of us were totally unlike each other. We saw things differently, thought differently, and responded differently—often very differently—to the same things. In this case, I would never have trusted Clodas the way your father did. I had met the man, although only once. But with some people, once is enough. I disliked and distrusted him on sight, without reason. He set my teeth on edge and made me feel suspicious, even although I had no reason to suspect him of anything at the time."

"Did you tell my father that?"

"Aye, and he laughed at me and called me an old woman, reading omens and portents where there were none to be read. Clodas was his cousin, he said, a loyal chieftain and a fine warrior. His deeds spoke for him, your father said, and they were many and worthy. He would put no credence in my doubts. I wasn't surprised, but nor was I offended. He and I had differed on such things in the past—probably more times than we agreed, if truth be told—and so I shut my mouth and said no more. But when Chulderic brought me word of what had happened, it only confirmed that I had been right from the beginning, and by then it was far too late and useless to seek any comfort in thinking that."

"What was he like, my father?"

"What was he *like*?" He twisted in his seat and looked at me more closely than he had before, scanning my face. "He was much like you, to look at—or you will be much like him, when you are grown. Same eyes, same hair, same mouth, I suspect, once your face fills out. You'll certainly have his nose when you reach manhood, although yours will be straighter. I do not normally pay attention to such things, but even I can see you resemble him far more than you do your mother. Her hair was glossy black, like crow feathers, and in bright light it sometimes looked almost blue, like the sky at night. Yours is not quite black—it's more like your father's, dark, deep brown, and your skin is dark, like his. Your mother's skin was very fair."

"That's how Frotto's mother knew I am not really your son. I'm too dark skinned."

"Nonsense. She knew because Vivienne had not been with child—you can't hide that—and you were suddenly here. It's true our boys are all tow-headed like me, but that counts for naught."

I bowed my head, afraid that what I had to say next might anger him. "If it please you, Sire, I asked you what my father was like, and you told me how he looked, but what I really meant was, what manner of man was he?"

"Hmm." His mouth quirked upward, but not in a smile. I could see him nibbling at the inside of his cheek. "I know not how I can answer that . . . He was the kind of man who turned heads everywhere he went. He had . . . he had a certain way about him that told everyone, without a word being spoken, that here was someone to note and admire—not because he was comely to look upon, although he was that, too, but because he filled a room with his presence and he . . . he seemed to *glow* with authority and *promise*."

"Tell me about him, if it please you."

"I suppose if I ask you what you would like to know, you'll say *everything*." He was smiling again and I nodded. "Aye, well, let's see what comes to mind." A log collapsed in the brazier and sent up an explosion of sparks, some of which swirled outwards, one of them landing on the King's leggings. He flicked the tiny ember to the floor, then rose to his feet again. He picked up another length of fresh wood and used it to poke the fire down before he thrust it deep into the heart of the flames. "He wasn't a Frank, you know, not really, although his mother was. That's how he got his Frankish name, Childebertus."

"Chillbirtoos," I repeated, savoring the sound of it.

"Aye. You're three-quarters Frank yourself, through your grandmother and your mother, but the other fourth is all your father's blood."

That stunned me, for I had never thought of myself as being anything other than a Frank. "What was he, then?"

"He was a Gael, from Britain. Remember, I met him in the army, when I was with the legions. He came to us from Rome, as a recruit, and had been living there for most of his life, but he was born in Britain. By the time we left the legions, his father, Jacobus, had died, and so he had no reason to return to Rome. He came here to Gaul with me instead and met your mother shortly after that, when I began to pay court to her sister."

"A Gael . . ." There was something wondrous in the sound of that.

"Aye, but there was more to him than that, according to his father's account. I never met your grandsire Jacobus, and Childebertus never spoke about him much, but Germanus told me more about your family, years later. He had come to know your grandfather in Rome, where they were both lawyers, and it was Jacobus who later introduced Germanus to the woman who would become his wife. She was a kinswoman of the Emperor Honorius, so that in marrying her, Germanus himself formed some kind of kinship with the Emperor. They became friends, too. It was Honorius himself who convinced Germanus, after the death of his wife, that he should give up the law and become a soldier. But that's Germanus's story, not your father's.

"What Germanus told me was that your father's family could trace their paternity, the bloodline of their fathers, directly back through twenty generations to the province of Judea, to the time of the Christ himself and beyond that. That seemed unbelievable to me when I heard about it, but Germanus said it was a solemn matter of great family pride and he had no doubt of the truth of it."

I had no interest in that story, for my mind had fastened on the place-name he had mentioned. "Judea?" The name was strange to me. "Is it in Britain?"

"No, nowhere near it."

"But I thought the Gaels all came from Britain."

"No, that's not so, either. Many are from northern Gaul . . . Gaul, Gael, it's the same basic word. But Judea is the land where Jesus, the Christus, was born."

"That was Galilee."

"No, Galilee was the *region* he lived in, just as this place we live in now, Genava, is a region of Gaul. The Scriptures tell us Jesus was born in a place called Bethlehem, but he lived in the town of Nazareth. All three—Galilee, Nazareth and Bethlehem—are in Judea. The people who live there call themselves Jews."

I had heard of the Jews, but I had thought they all lived in a place called Jerusalem. I knew nothing more about them, or what being a Jew entailed, except that I had been told long before, by my earliest tutor, that the Jews had used the Roman law to crucify the Christ and were therefore *guilty of the Blood of the Lamb*. The words still rang in my mind, and although I had never understood their meaning, the condemnation they contained had sounded grim and unforgivable. This sudden revelation that my father might have shared that guilt appalled me. "My father was a *Jew*?"

"No, he was a Christian. Well, by his ancestral blood and descent he was Jewish, I suppose, but by belief he was a Christian. One of the most sincere Christians I ever met. It can be confusing, all this talk of Jewish creed and Jewish blood, but I've seen enough spilt blood to know that it's all red—doesn't matter who it comes from. It's impossible to distinguish the shed blood of a black

Nubian from that of a blond Northerner or a flat-faced, brown-skinned Hun. I don't even know who my own grandfather's grand-sire *was,* let alone where he came from, and I don't care. I know where I belong, and that's enough for me. But according to your own family historians—and they took great care of their clan's history—your father's ancestors have been Christians for four hundred years, and numbered among the very first followers of the Creed."

"Are they small people, the Jews?"

The King smiled, perhaps at me, perhaps at a memory. "You mean in size? No, not if they resemble your father. He was taller than me, by the width of his fist, and broader across the shoulders. He was a big lad, Childebertus. But he was half Frank, half Gael, remember. Most of his Judean traits, if ever there were any, might have been bred out of his clan long since. He was dark of skin, as you are, but no darker than many a Roman I've met born and bred in Italia, so I can't judge by that.

"But Judea is a desert land with a fierce sun, from what I've heard, so the people there must be dark skinned, and they probably dress differently because of the heat in their homeland. Here in our land, however, wearing the same clothes we wear, who would know how to tell them apart from others? You'll meet some folk who'll tell you that the Jews are accursed, because they crucified the Savior. That might be true, might not. I prefer to make no judgments on it. And I know, that when it comes to God and godly matters, there will always be people who claim to have exclusive access to God's ear and wishes. Well, let them all make their judgments without involving me. They will, anyway. What I know is that my dearest friend, the finest man I ever knew, took pride in his Jewish descent and was taught to revere the memory of his Judean forefathers. So why should I believe what others mutter when I have my own memories to prove that they are wrong?"

I sat rapt, absorbing his every word and believing, and a sudden question came to me. "Why did you say my nose will be straighter than my father's?"

Suddenly his grin was wolfish. "Because his was bent, broken in a brawl."

"Were you *there*?"

King Ban of Benwick laughed. "In the thick of it. I saw the blow that did the damage, a flying fist. I was flat on my back between your father's feet and he was defending me when someone—I didn't see who it was—smacked him from the side. A wide, fast, looping swing from a clenched fist—almost ripped his head off. I saw the punch land and the blood fly and poor Childebertus went sideways, head over heels. I tried to go to him, but I couldn't stand up. So I stayed on my hands and knees until my head stopped spinning, and by that time things had begun to settle down. Tavern brawls seldom last long. They're undisciplined, and they tire people out quickly because everyone is drunk. Anyway, by the time I got to him, still on all fours, your father was sitting up, trying to stanch the bleeding. He bled like a throat-cut pig—I can still remember it—and his nose was twisted right across his face, from left to right. We tried to straighten it—myself and a few others—but we didn't get it quite right, and it set crooked. That was the real start of our friendship."

"You were drunk? *You*?" I was awestruck, barely able to believe what I was hearing, but the King had no thought in his mind now of his dignity, enjoying the recollection of his tale too much.

"We were all drunk that night. We had just come back that afternoon from a long ten-day patrol in which we'd lost two men during a freak storm, when we were near to drowning in torrential rain. It happened four days into our patrol and to this day I have never seen anything to equal it. We were blinded by it, deep among the trees. The light simply vanished—went from day to night before we could adjust to it—and our horses were terrified by the lightning and the noise. We were, too, for that matter.

"Anyway, we could see nothing and lightning was striking all around us, huge trees splitting and exploding into flames. It was absolute chaos, but we couldn't stop, not there. We had to keep moving, hoping to find a clearing where we could dismount and calm the horses.

"Instead, we found a big raiding party that had crossed from the northern Outlands on the other side of the Rhine. We rode right into the middle of them without seeing them, and I doubt if they saw us, either, until we were among them. They were sheltering, too, hundreds of them, among the trees and bushes. We had to fight our way out of there, outnumbered by at least five to one, but they were afoot and we were mounted. We were lucky, nonetheless. Things might easily have gone much worse for us. We were in heavy forest and the underbrush was thick. Our horses couldn't make headway, let alone maneuver, and they were fetlock-deep in mud. If the raiders had been able to surround us completely we would all have died there. Fortunately they were as surprised as we were, and equally hampered by the storm and the darkness. But two of our men went down before we could ride clear of them."

"Did you leave them behind?"

He glanced at me sharply. "Our men? No, we did not. We don't do that. We rode clear of the area and waited until the storm broke and the raiders moved on, the following day. Then we went back and buried our two men, and after that we followed the raiding party at a distance until they emerged from the forest. As soon as they were out in the open where we could fight to our own advantage as cavalry, we attacked and destroyed them."

"But you said they outnumbered you five to one."

"Aye, but one cavalryman is more than equal to five men on foot, unless they're Roman infantry."

"How many of them were there?"

He wrinkled his nose. "Close to two hundred, perhaps a score or so more."

"And you were forty? Two squadrons?"

"No, only one squadron, a full *turma*. There was myself, the squadron commander and his two decurions, and forty troopers, one of whom was your father—minus the two killed in the first encounter. That's why we were drinking the night your father had his nose broken. We were bidding farewell to our dead comrades."

"Then why were you fighting one another? Would your two dead comrades have enjoyed that?"

The King's eyes went wide with surprise and then he smiled, shaking his head. "Aye, they would, could they have seen it. But we weren't fighting among *ourselves,* Clothar. There were other soldiers there that night, from an infantry detachment. They thought we were being too noisy and we thought they were being insulting. One word led to another, and eventually someone swung a fist or threw a drink, and it was all of us against all of them. Someone hit me with something—probably a pitcher or a table bowl—and I went down and your father jumped across to protect me, straddling me and fighting off all comers until I could regain my senses. Unfortunately, I was not quick enough and someone got him, too."

"Why didn't you straighten his nose properly?"

"We couldn't. We could barely see it, let alone straighten it. By the time we started, his face had swollen up like a cow's udder. His eyes were puffed into slits and turning black already and his cheeks looked as though he had apples stuffed in them. Even without all the blood, he was a disastrous sight. It took him more than two weeks to look normal again. Besides, his nose looked better afterwards, bent as it was. It simply added character to his face. He'd been almost too pretty before that, a boy wearing soldier's clothing. The broken nose made him look more like a man and . . . dangerous. That was how your mother described him to her sister when she first met him. She said he looked dangerous. Evidently not sufficiently dangerous, however, to frighten her."

"Had you and he not been friends before then?"

"No. I barely knew him before that night. He had been with us for less than a year—a recruit, and an outsider, at that. Most of the men in my command at that time were my own—my father's men, I mean, from here in Genava—and we had been together from the start. We were part of a cavalry division based on the Rhine River, which is too heavily forested to be good cavalry country at the best of times. It was a mobile force, never less than four hundred strong, never more than five hundred, and it was constantly being split and reformed, elements distributed as needed at any time among the serving legions in the region. I was one of five senior commanders, all of us under the overall command of the legate Suetonius Marcellus, who we used to say must have been born astride a horse. He was a fine man—killed in a silly little skirmish a few years after that, shot out of his saddle by an arrow that deflected up off his cuirass, went between the guard flaps of his helmet and caught him under the chin. Germanus gave me the division after that, but while Suetonius was alive he and I worked well together, which means he trusted me well enough not to interfere in the way I ran my own command. I had three squadrons of forty, and a full hundred of those were Genavans from Benwick. I was not yet their King at the time, but I was my father's firstborn son and therefore his heir, and that meant that my men were *mine* ahead of Rome's, so be it that we did as Rome required of us. Suetonius respected that and never tried to split us up.

"Your father was the youngest of our officer trainees. And he was also the best looking, which might have been unfortunate. In soldiering, a comely face can be a disadvantage. Some of my veterans thought that anyone who looked so young and pretty could not possibly be taken seriously. Fortunately for him, however, he was a fine horseman, a natural rider even among our Franks, who consider themselves the Empire's best. That saved him much grief, because it won him the respect his physical appearance might otherwise have cost him, and over the months since he had joined us a few of my younger officers had grown to like him and befriended him.

"By the time the fight was over that night, he was one of us. Things began to change between him and me. I had been impressed by the way he had fought above me, straddling me while I was down—it's difficult not to like someone who will fight and fall for you—and so I began paying more attention to him.

"He was six years younger than I was, seventeen to my twenty-three, a man in years and yet not fully grown, but big and strong, with every sign of becoming formidable. And as I watched him, I recognized him as a natural leader. The men assigned to him behaved well for him, always, and he was never at a loss in the training exercises we set for him. According to all the reports I had heard, read and evaluated, Childebertus was resourceful, intelligent, adaptable and above all flexible in his thinking. Without exception, all his supervisors had the same thing to say about him, although their words may have varied: "The more difficult the problem we set him, whether in logistics, tactics or strategy, the more easily he seems to solve it."

Somewhere beyond the heavy shutters a cock crowed and the sound startled both of us, bringing the King's head up sharply. He crossed quickly to the window, where he opened both sets of shutters and peered out and upwards, into the darkness, waiting for the sound to be repeated. Some time later, when he was satisfied that it would not be, he secured the shutters again and came back to the fire.

"Sky's clear. Clear enough to confuse that stupid bird into thinking it was dawn. For a moment there I thought we had lost the entire night and we still have much to talk about. Are you tired?"

"No! No, Father, not at all. I'm wide-awake."

He squinted sideways at me, pursing his lips, and then evidently decided I was being truthful. "Good. You can sleep late tomorrow. I'll tell Chulderic." He busied himself replenishing the fire, then set the poker among the embers to heat again. I could tell from the way he kept his eyes on his task that he was thinking deeply about what he would say next, but I dared to interrupt him anyway.

"Father?"

"What?"

"Will you tell me about how my father died?"

He was bent over the brazier, keeping his eyes on the fire, and he twisted the iron poker in its bed before straightening up. "No, because Chulderic can do that much better than I could, so you should hear that tale from him. He was there at the time, and he had been your father's loyal man for years. I'll tell him you need to know what happened, and he'll tell it to you as he saw it." He read the expression on my face accurately. "Don't fret yourself, I'll make sure he wastes no time before telling you. But in the meantime, you and I have something else to talk about."

I gazed at him, wondering what he meant.

"Germanus," he said, as though that should have been obvious to me. "We need to talk about Germanus, you and I. He will be here within the month. I told you that. What I did not tell you is why that is important, for you." He cleared his throat loudly and spat into the brazier, then wiped his lips with the sleeve of his tunic before he continued. "He is to be your teacher."

I heard the words, but they went winging over my head like passing geese, observed but insignificant, their meaning lacking any import to me. And then I heard them again, this time in my mind. *He is to be your teacher.* I was aware of the King's watching me closely, and I shifted nervously in my chair, wriggling in discomfort as though I could avoid the awareness that was growing in me. *He is to be your teacher.*

"Wha— What do you mean, Father?"

"Simply what I said. Germanus will be your teacher from now on. When he returns to his home in Auxerre, you will go with him."

"But . . . but this is where I live."

"Aye, for now, and perhaps sometime again in the future, but for the next few years you will be living and studying with Germanus. The years between ten and sixteen are the most important of your life, and Germanus is the finest teacher you could have in living them."

"But he's a bishop . . . a *holy man* . . ."

"Aye, he is, but he is also a famed and powerful lawyer and a victorious and unconquered battle commander—a soldier's soldier. He has always been a teacher, too, no matter what his calling was at any time, and that has not changed. In fact it is more true than ever. Since he became a bishop, Germanus has established a school for boys in Auxerre, and he tells me he plans to create many others. You will be one of the first students in that school, and it will be the making of you."

"I don't want to go."

My stepfather shrugged his broad shoulders. "That is unfortunate, Clothar, but you will change your mind once you are there and settled, for you are going, whether you wish it or not. This is not a passing whim of mine. It has always been intended, decided upon many years ago, soon after the death of your parents, when Germanus and I met to talk about your future. We decided then that since I was married and Germanus had no wife to care for you, you would spend your childhood here under my protection, living a normal boy's life among children your own age. Later, when you were grown enough to be aware of who and what you are, your education would pass into the care of Germanus, who would be responsible for teaching you all the things you would need to know—the things I could never teach you, since they are unknown to me: logic and debate; Latin and other languages; history, both civil and military; theology and the study of religion and a whole host of other things I could not even begin to guess at. But you'll also continue your existing studies there, your riding and military training, weapons craft and warfare, strategy and tactics. Bear in mind, Germanus was a legate; you could have no finer teacher in such things.

"When you came here to my quarters yesterday, in the afternoon, I was reading a letter. Do you remember that?" I nodded. "Well, that letter was from Germanus and it concerned this very matter. That is the real reason for his visit."

I knew, listening to the finality in his tone, that there was no hope of a reprieve from this decree, and my initial reaction was one of sadness at the thought of leaving this place that had been my home for most of my life—for all of it that I could remember. But I found, to my surprise, that I was not nearly as dejected as I might have expected to be as recently as the previous day, because I had learned this night from King Ban that I was the son of a heroic warrior called Childebertus, who had been befriended by a king and by an imperial legate, and that the same legate would now become my teacher, merely because I was the orphan son of his friend. There was a promise of adventure there, and of fulfillment. Besides,

I had always known that at some point I would have to leave home to continue my military training, earning my manhood in the service of some other leader. All of my older brothers had already done so and were now scattered among the territories of King Ban's allies. Gunthar had only recently returned home, a fully grown man and warrior, after four years spent in the service of Merovech, another Frankish king far to the northwest.

I suddenly became aware that King Ban was staring at me, obviously waiting for me to say something, and I realized that he must have asked me a question that I had not heard. I felt my face grow red.

"Forgive me, Sire, I didn't hear what you asked me. I was dreaming."

"I asked you if there was anything else you wanted to ask me, about all of this."

I thought about that for a few moments, then shook my head. "No, Sire. I can't think of anything."

"Excellent!" He rose to his feet, stretching up onto tiptoe and raising his arms high above his head. "Perhaps now we can get some sleep before the dawn breaks. Come, bed for both of us, for an hour at least."

CHULDERIC

1

Even though I had gone to sleep filled with excitement and wonder mere hours earlier and had slept right through until mid-morning, I awoke feeling angry, confused and resentful, my mind reeling with half-remembered statements and hazy, maddeningly elusive images of some of the things King Ban had described to me. My old nurse, Ludda, had been waiting for me to wake up—the Lady Vivienne had told her of my late night and of the King's decision that I should be allowed to sleep late—and as soon as she heard me moving about she brought me a breakfast of ground oats, savory seeds and crushed nuts, all roasted dry and bound together with honey from the King's beehives.

I was in no mood to eat, however—nor, for that matter, to be courteous or civil—and so I finished dressing and stormed out without acknowledging either her or the food she had prepared for me. I had a momentary twinge of guilt over my ill manners as I ran down the stairs from my quarters, but I thrust it aside easily, consoling myself with the thought that I had every right to be self-concerned today, since no one else appeared to have been truly concerned for me prior to the day before. Had anyone really cared about my welfare, I told myself, they would have told me the truth about myself much earlier and not left me to go blithely on my way, filled with foolish thoughts of belonging here.

By the time I reached the outer yard, having scowled my displeasure at everyone I met between my sleeping chamber and there, I had worked myself into a truly unpleasant frame of mind filled with self-pity, bafflement, hurt feelings and shapeless, threatening fears—all of them completely without justification. I reached the gates to the outer bastion, but then I broke into a run and swung directly to my left to head towards the stables, although I had no idea what I might do there, and as I reached the dark entryway, I almost ran full tilt into a figure emerging from the darkness.

It was Clodio, the strange but loyal man who had been Ban's lifelong friend and had consistently refused all advancement except his current and permanent post as Commander of the Castle Guard. He reached out and grasped me by the right shoulder, digging his fingers in hard and bringing me up short almost in mid-step.

"Ah, there you are! I've been looking for you. Where are you running to, so fast? Is someone chasing you?"

He sounded quite pleasant and not at all put out by our near collision, but I was in no frame of mind to tolerate pleasantness, especially from one of the group who had conspired to keep me in ignorance of my real identity. I pulled myself loose from his grasp and thrust his arm away from me.

"Leave me alone. And stand out of my way."

Clodio's head jerked in shock and his eyebrows rose high on his forehead. "Stand out of your way?" His face quirked in what almost became a smile. "Since when did you start ordering your father's officers around?"

"Since I found out he's not my father and he has been deceiving me—and you're no better than he is, because you knew, too. My father was a *real* king, and you know it, and I'm his son. So stand aside and let me pass."

I knew that what I had said went beyond insolence and far beyond ingratitude to King Ban, but even as I spoke the words I took a malicious satisfaction in mouthing such things. Clodio, however, merely stood looking at me, his eyes narrowed in concentration, and then, after what seemed like a long time to me, he nodded, once, abruptly.

"I heard you. But are you really sure you want me to step aside?"

"Yes, I—" But he had already held up a warning palm.

"Before you answer, consider this, my young kingling. *If* I step aside, at your command, it will only be to give myself purchase to swing my boot properly at your kingly little arse as you pass by me, and I'll kick it so far up towards your shoulders that you'll be a hunchback for the rest of your life . . . Now, I'll ask you again. Are you sure you want me to step aside?"

There was not a trace of humor in his eyes or in his voice, and so I knew I had to draw his fangs. I pulled myself up to my full height and put all the disdain I could muster into my tone.

"You will stand aside, and you will not dare to lay hands on me. I am the son—the *firstborn* son—of a king."

Clodio turned his back on me, his hands on his hips, and slowly completed a full turn, his head tilted back to look at the sky and his feet taking high but tiny steps, almost marching in place but turning very slowly and incrementally until he faced me again, and as he did so I heard him blow air loudly and rhythmically from his lips, in time with his footsteps. As he came back face to face with me, however, he grasped my tunic in both hands, on either side of my chest, and hoisted me effortlessly into the air, to where he could look directly at me, eye to eye, from a distance of less than a handspan, and when he spoke next, even though he spoke very quietly, I felt the flutter of his breath against my face.

"You are the *orphaned* son of a *dead* and *landless* king who was once a fine man and much loved by everyone who knew him. But he is gone now, long since dead, and the lands he ruled are hundreds of miles from here, governed now by the man who killed him and usurped his title and his holdings. You are still a boy—a mere child, ten years old—and you have nothing . . . no prospects, no wealth, no hopes at all, other than those for which you are beholden to King Ban. Do you hear what I am saying, boy? I knew your father, and I was proud to know him. I knew your mother, too, although no more than by sight, but she was the most beautiful lady I ever saw, more beautiful even than her sister, the Lady Vivienne." He shook me gently, tilting me from side to side and never taking his eyes off me. "I thought to have known you now, for years, but what I'm hearing spilling from your lips today is unlike anything I would ever have believed you capable of saying."

He brought me even closer to his face, so that I could see the individual hairs on his cheeks and the scar at the end of his nose where he had once been bitten in a fight. "Do you know how far your feet are off the ground as I hold you here, Clothar son of Childebertus? I could throw you like a pebble, and leave you lying where you fell. But here is a promise I will make to you freely. If I ever, *ever* hear you speaking of your uncle Ban like that again, I'll strip off your breeches and flog you with my belt until you bleed. Is that clear?" He shook me again, a single, violent jerk. "*Is* it?"

I nodded my head, suddenly overcome with shame and struggling to hold back hot tears. Clodio continued to hold me. "Good," he said. "Let's hope I never have to do that. Now, it's obvious that you've only recently found out about what happened to you as a babe in arms, and I suppose that could be seen as grounds for being angry. Before I put you down, however, I have one more thing to tell you. Are you listening?"

I was, but I was also beginning to grow astonished at the ease with which this man was holding me aloft. He showed no sign of strain at all. His breathing was easy and his voice relaxed. "Yes," I said through the lump in my throat, and nodding for emphasis. "I'm listening."

"Then listen well. I want to tell you something about your father. His soldiers and his people worshipped him. Do you know why? I do. I know why. Some people might give you a hundred other reasons, and they would all be true, to some extent . . . He was tall and strong and good to look upon. He had a pleasant nature and laughed easily. He had a beautiful wife and generous, loving friends. But none of these things explain why he was so much loved. But this one reason that I know, this one thing alone, explains it, and the explanation is very simple, yet very profound: your father treated all people with dignity and truthfulness.

"That may not sound like much to you, at the age of ten, but it is an awe-inspiring thing, almost impossible for ordinary men to achieve. And yet your father lived his entire life behaving that way. He never lied; he never looked down on anyone as being lesser than himself; he never treated anyone badly, unless that person had behaved badly and merited punishment. Your father never had an unkind word or an insult for, or about, anyone who had not earned them. Childebertus of Ganis would never have spoken to me, or to anyone else, the way you did here today. Bear that in mind. If you are going to announce yourself to be your father's son, then be true to his memory and to his honor. Be *worthy* of his name.

"Now, I am growing tired, so I am going to put you down, but when I do, you will stand there and wait until I have finished what I have to say to you. Are we agreed?"

I nodded, wordlessly this time, and he lowered me to the ground.

"So be it." He stood glaring down at me now, plucking at his lower lip, his right elbow resting on his left fist. "Do you have any of that poison left in you? If you do, this is the place to spit it out, because I've heard it now and I won't be too disgusted to hear more of the same . . . disappointed, perhaps, but not disgusted. Have you more to say?"

"No, sir." The words emerged as a husky rasp.

"Good. Then we will treat this little episode as a bad dream, and neither one of us will mention it again, to anyone. Agreed?"

I cleared my throat. "Agreed."

"*Bene*. I have been looking for you. That's why I was in the stables. Chulderic asked me to keep an eye open for you and to send you to the old oak tree on the riverbank when I found you. That was about an hour ago, perhaps half an hour more than that, so he might be there now, waiting for you, or he might not. If he is not, then you are to wait for him. Why are you not in school today?"

I told him about my all-night session with King Ban, and he listened closely, nodding his head from time to time.

"Well," he said when I had finished, "I can see now why you were so upset. Understandable, I suppose, that you would react badly to having your whole life exposed suddenly and unexpectedly as being different from what you had believed. But there's no reason to flog yourself over it. You see that now, don't you? Good. Now you'd better go and find Chulderic. You know he doesn't like to be kept waiting, by anyone. And if you value your life, don't use that tone of voice you used with me and *don't* tell him you're a king's firstborn son and that he must now show you respect. He'll puke all over you and then beat you senseless. Respect, you will soon learn, is something that has no price. You can't buy it and it's a thing you'll never get by demanding it. You have to earn respect, boy, from one man at a time, and you can't cheat in any way while you're about it. You'll see, someday, because you'll earn it yourself and you'll pay it willingly to others. Now go on, get out of here and find Chulderic."

I had much to think about, although from an entirely different perspective now, as I made my way from the stables to the huge old oak that spread out over the placid, muddy waters of the deep stream that wound through the valley and formed part of the defenses in front of our castle. I set out still smarting from the shame that had swept over me as I caught the rough edge of Clodio's tongue, but as I walked, my understanding of what had happened began to settle into a new appreciation, one that had been there all along but had been overwhelmed by my delayed reaction to all that I had learned the previous day and night, so that by the time I reached the riverside I felt far better than I had felt since wakening that morning.

Chulderic was not there when I arrived and so I made myself comfortable on the lowest bough of the great tree, my back braced firmly against its bole, then set myself again to reviewing the events and disclosures of the previous night.

"I saw your father sitting like that once." I jumped, startled to hear Chulderic's voice so close to me. I had been so deeply involved in my thoughts that I had not seen him approach. "But he was higher up, hidden among the leaves, waiting to jump down on a party of raiders as they rode underneath. He was sitting the same way, though, hands clasping his left knee, just like you now, and his right leg stretched out along the branch."

I swung to face him, flushing guiltily as I prepared to scramble down from my perch, shamed to have been caught slacking when I should have been at my lessons.

"No, stay where you are."

I froze, caught awkwardly in the act of turning my back to him, my belly against the tree limb as I spread my hands against the rough bark, ready to push myself out and away. Carefully, I eased my body around to where I could see him again, and he made a flapping motion with his upturned palm.

"Stay up there for now. Stay as you were, otherwise I'll have to look down at you."

Moving awkwardly and in danger of falling, I cautiously hoisted myself up to where I could regain my secure perch against the bole of the tree, and only after I was firmly seated did I dare to look over again to where he sat astride a tall, black horse, looking back at me. He had not sounded angry, and now it seemed to me he did not even look angry, and a sense of wonder began to stir in me. He had always been a stern, unsmiling and demanding taskmaster, this dour old soldier, and I would never have suspected that he could be as soft-spoken as anyone else. And yet here he was, addressing me courteously without either scowling frown or rough-edged tongue.

"The King has told me that you knew my father, Magister." The sense of the words was strange to my ears, and stranger still was my boldness in speaking to him directly without invitation. Magister was the term all of us boys used in addressing Chulderic, and it was a term of respect, as well as an accurate description of his rank. He was Master-at-Arms to King Ban and as such, in times of peace, his duties included acting as our instructor—we being the young men and boys who would eventually, God willing, become the commanders of the armies of Benwick. Chulderic was our tutor and our trainer in the crafts of war that we studied constantly. He knew everything concerning weapons and warfare and honor and the ways of officers and warriors, and we depended upon him entirely for enlightenment and guidance.

There were twelve of us in the boys' corps at that time, ranging in age from eight through sixteen, and there was no implication, in our calling him Magister, that we might all be slaves to his mastery . . . except that, of course, we were, utterly and abjectly. Chulderic was not a man to defy, to deny or to challenge. His discipline was renowned, and none of us would ever have dared to question it or to rebel against it. He was merciless, demanding and implacable in his expectations and pitilessly critical of all our efforts to do well and to win his praise. And yet sometimes he would relent, and would bark or grunt an unintelligible sound that was his only indication that one of us might have—*might have*—achieved a barely acceptable standard in something we had attempted. But now here he was, speaking to me in a quiet voice like a normal man.

He had swung his horse to face me as I addressed him and for a moment I quailed, expecting him to rebuke me for impertinence, but he merely looked at me with a peculiar expression, then nodded, almost imperceptibly.

"We could not tell you, before now. You were too young to know such things. They were too dangerous for you to know because, being a child, you would have asked a thousand questions and prattled to anyone who would listen, and sooner or later word would have reached the wrong ears." He scratched at his beard with his fingertips, then tucked in his chin and peered down along his nose, stretching a single long white hair out to where he could see the end of it. "Hmm," he grunted, and then twisted the offending hair around his finger and jerked it out by its roots. "More and more of those in there, nowadays."

I had no way of knowing if he had meant me to hear that, but I was stricken with awe to see this unexpected aspect of a man who had terrified me for years, and yet all I could think to do then and there was look more closely at his beard. It was black and long, neatly trimmed at the ends and very straight, with little curl to it.

But I could see white strands among the black, now that he had drawn my attention to them.

"I knew him longer than I've known you," he continued. "And I've known you all your life, since the day you were born. He was my friend, your father, as well as being my employer."

"Your employer?" I was no longer afraid, my apprehension swept away completely by his suddenly revealed humanity. "You mean you *worked* for him?"

"Aye, I did. Does that surprise you? I worked for him gladly. I was his Master-at-Arms long before I came here to join King Ban."

"But the King said he was in the army with you, and that you first met my father there, too, when he joined you fresh from Rome."

Chulderic nodded, deeply and slowly. "That is true, we all met in the army, and we grew close over the next ten years. Mind you, I was no more than a common soldier in those days, only newly appointed to command a single squadron, whereas the three of them—Ban, your father and latterly Germanus—were all field officers. But they chose to trust me and my judgment, for reasons of their own, and I somehow became their confidant, their messenger whenever they had need of one. But the day came, as such days always must, when we left the armies, all four of us at the same time, because we had fulfilled all our obligations. Our campaign was finished and our work was done and we were finally freed to go home. *They* were free to go home, I should say. I had no home to go back to. Your father knew that, and so he invited me to ride with him and be his man, in return for my board and keep and a parcel of land to call my own, an undisputed place to lay my head at day's end. Sounded to me as though I wouldn't find a better offer, and I never did."

"Did you know my father when he lived in Rome?"

He shook his head. "No, I did not. He had done his stint in Rome before he joined us, and I know he was glad to get away from it."

"What did he say about it?"

"I can barely remember, it has been so long, but it will come back to me if I take time to think." His chin tilted upward as he gazed at me with narrowed eyes. "Jump down now and run to the stables. Pick yourself a horse and come back here as quickly as you can. King Ban would have me tell you what I know about your father and mother, all of it in one day, and so I will, but I will be able to do it more easily if we ride. I never was a man for sitting indoors and talking. I need fresh, blowing air to keep my head clear when I am thinking. Go you now."

I ran like the wind all the way to the stables, where I quickly found the senior groom and told him why I needed a horse. I picked out my favorite, a black gelding almost as tall as the one Chulderic rode, and saddled it quickly, tightening the girth securely before I swung myself up onto the big animal's back. Then, mounted, I sat for a few moments inhaling the odors of the stable before I nodded to the groom to open the door, and I listened, as I rode out, to the sounds my horse's hooves made on the floor of packed earth and straw. I remember quite clearly the sensations of stretched tension and thrilling excitement that filled my chest that day as I rode back to where the Master-at-Arms was waiting. He watched me approach and kicked his horse into motion as I drew near him. For a while we rode in silence, side by side, as we walked our mounts among and between the buildings outside the walls of King Ban's castle.

As soon as we had passed the last of the houses, Chulderic kicked his horse to a canter, then to a lope, and finally into a gallop, and I kept close to him, barely half a length behind him and to his left, exulting in the surging power of the big animal between my knees and the way the wind ruffled my hair. We did not gallop far, however, before he pulled back on his reins and slowed to a canter, saying there was no point in overtaxing the animals.

The path he had chosen stretched upwards, rising gently and consistently over the course of two miles to the crest of a ridge that ended in a high cliff and offered a breathtaking view of the lake hundreds of feet below. As we approached the summit and the steepest part of the climb, we dismounted and led our horses, but they were both panting as hard as we were when we reached the top and stopped, overlooking the vista before us.

"Now that is a sight worth beholding," Chulderic said. "Large enough to be a sea, yet still a lake of fresh water."

He looked about him, then dropped his horse's reins on the ground and went to sit on an old log that some previous visitor had dragged close to the edge of the cliff.

"Come. Sit."

I did as he bade me, and for a while we sat staring at the view and waiting for our breathing to return to normal.

"Your father joined the army on his sixteenth birthday, did you know that?" I shook my head. "Aye, well, he did. That's the traditional age for boys to become soldiers, as you know. Has been for hundreds of years, stretching right back to the earliest days of Rome, when every soldier was a farmer and every farmer was a soldier. But it doesn't happen much today, at least not among the wealthy."

I said nothing, and he continued after only a brief pause. "Your grandfather Jacobus was wealthy, your father's father, that is. He was from Britain, a lawyer. Traveled to Rome to study there, and then remained to practice his craft, at which he was apparently very good—one of the best in the city, I've been told. He could easily have arranged to keep his son at home and out of the army, had he so wished. But he didn't. He let the boy go when he wanted to, and was quite content to do so. Strange relationship between those two, for father and son: they liked each other—loved each other might not even be too strong a way to put it. You don't see that too often among civilized people. Everyone likes to talk about the tightness of family bonds and the obligations of blood relationships and kindred, but it's all lip service, nine times out of ten.

"Anyway, your father had always wanted to be a soldier, ever since he had grown big enough to make a hero out of one of his cousins, Medroc, another migrant Briton. Medroc was a senior officer in the Household Guard, the Emperor's personal bodyguard, and Honorius himself thought very highly of him, trusting him as he trusted few others. From the way your father spoke of him, time and time again, Medroc must have been a sight to behold in his golden parade armor—enameled sky blue insets in cuirass, helmet and greaves, a high horsehair crest on the helmet, dyed sky blue to match the enamel insets, and a military cloak of sky blue cloth, trimmed with gold edges. I would have enjoyed seeing that myself. I've heard of the finery of the Household Guard, but I never saw any of them."

"But you came from Rome, Magister. How could you not have seen them?"

He pursed his lips as he looked at me, one eyebrow rising high on his forehead. "Because they were in Constantinople with the Emperor when I was in Rome, that's how. Rome hasn't really been the Imperial City since the time of Constantine, and that was more than a hundred years ago, as near as spitting. The Roman garrison troops in my day—I mean the permanent troops who never left the city—were famed, and still are, for the ornate richness of their uniforms and armor. They made ordinary troops like us look like beggars, even in our parade uniforms. But the Household Guard were the elite troops of the entire Empire, hand-picked from the best of the best for their size, appearance and prowess, and privileged as no others ever were. Their blue-and-gold uniforms were legendary.

"From the first time your father set eyes on Medroc in his fine plumage, he dreamed of someday becoming one of the Emperor's Guard. The lad's career was clearly laid out, all the way from basic training under Cousin Medroc's watchful eye, to a solid and reward- ing position as an officer in the Household Corps, thanks to his family's influence. It was all cut-and-dried and carefully arranged."

He looked at me, making sure that I was listening closely before continuing. "But there's a lesson there, lad, concerning your father and his cousin that you should keep in mind from this time on: the trouble with things that are too neatly cut-and-dried is that they often break when a strong wind comes up, because they're too dry to bend. Your father had been in the Household Guard for less than a year, still a snotty-nosed trainee recruit, when Medroc got himself killed during a garrison mutiny in the far south of Gaul, near the border with Iberia."

"Iberia? What was he doing *there*? Was he traveling with the Emperor?"

"No, but he was traveling *for* the Emperor, carrying urgent dispatches from Honorius himself to the legate commanding in southern Gaul, and he arrived in a mountain town along his route just in time to get himself and his men safely bedded down for the night and soundly to sleep before the garrison mutinied. The garrison commander, who from all later reports was a complete pig, was assassinated in the darkest hour of the night, along with all his officers, and Medroc awoke shortly after that to find himself being dragged out of bed. He was a witness to their mutiny, and they knew him to be a loyal and trusted officer of the Emperor, because they opened and read the dispatches he was carrying. They killed him right there, probably before he really understood what was happening to him. Of the twenty troopers in his escort, two were lucky enough to escape that night and survived to raise the alarm. So that was the end of Cousin Medroc, and of your father's dreams of an illustrious career in the personal service of the Emperor.

"Medroc's death went unnoticed for a long time, as far as I can tell, lost sight of in the confusion and upheaval of the campaign against the mutineers. It was a hard campaign, too. I remember it because it was my first. I had been in the army for several years by then, but that was the first time I had ever been called upon to fight, and it was the only time I ever had to fight against our own, Roman soldiers just like us. We had no idea what had driven them to mutiny, or if, under the same conditions, we might have been tempted to join them. Fighting them was not a pleasant experience, from that viewpoint alone.

"But besides that, the success of the mutiny from the outset had attracted malcontents and deserters from all over southern Gaul, so that what had started out as a town garrison with an arguably legitimate grievance soon grew to something else entirely, approaching the size of an army . . . a rabble, certainly, but strong in numbers.

Strong enough to defeat the first few units sent out to contain them and put the mutiny down. They won those opening actions easily, because the men sent out against them underestimated almost everything about them. But those early, easy victories were the worst things that could have happened to them. They grew too confident after that. They honestly thought they could win in mutiny, the damn fools—even proclaimed one of their own as Emperor just before we brought them to battle after six weeks of floundering around in mud and rain. That was it. We killed every last one of them, one way or another. Them that survived the fighting died the way mutineers always die, some of them flogged to death, some hanged, and others beheaded. The four ringleaders, soon identified by turncoats desperate to save their own lives, were crucified . . . the only modern army crucifixions I've ever heard of."

Chulderic fell silent after that, and I had the good sense to say nothing and simply wait for him to start talking again.

"At any rate," he began, finally, "by the time the dust settled after all that, the faithful Medroc had been forgotten, long since replaced by some other talented and brilliant young man who doubtless looked just as fine in his parade armor, and Medroc's protégé, young Childebertus, had become just another faceless trainee with no influence and not even seniority to protect him. It didn't take him long to discover that his relationship with Medroc had been resented by more than a few of his fellows, and his life within the Household Guard became very unpleasant very quickly.

"A call went out around that time for volunteers for a new, highly mobile cavalry force to be stationed on the Rhine River, where the difficulty of keeping invaders out had not grown easier in three hundred years. The new force was to be an elite one, and well paid, to compensate for the danger and hardship involved in what they had to do. Your father had always loved horses and was a natural cavalryman. He recognized salvation when he saw it, and he became one of the very first applicants for the new force. Within months of that he was here in Gaul, transferred out of the Emperor's Guard and into the new cavalry division. That's where he met me

and the King, although Ban was only Ban of Benwick at that time."
He broke off and looked at me again, his brow creased in thought.
"Did Ban already tell you all this?"

"Yes, Magister . . . some of it, anyway."

"Then what the blazes did he want *me* to talk to you about if you
already know what I'm supposed to tell you?" This was more like
the Chulderic I knew, snappish and impatient with anything he saw
as being trivial or time wasting, but he said no more after that first
outburst, and I dared to speak up once more.

"About how my parents died, Magister—I asked the King last
night to tell me and he would not, because he had not been there to
see it for himself. But he told me you had witnessed all of it, and he
said you were far more able than he to tell me the truth of what
happened."

"Hmm." There was no sign of impatience in the old man now. He
stuck out his lower lip and gazed into the distance across the lake.
"He was wrong, then. I was nearby, but I was not there. Had I been
there, I would not be here today." He straightened his back and stood
up. "Come, ride with me again while I try to find words for you."

2

Chulderic and I remounted and made our way down the slope,
veering more and more to the left as we descended, so that by the
time we regained level ground we were far from where we had
begun our climb to the summit. Once again we rode in silence,
traversing a landscape of grassland scattered with clumps of scrub
willows, alder and hawthorn while Chulderic searched his mind for
memories he could describe. And then, without sign or warning, he
began again.

"We had barely left the army life behind us when Childebertus
first met your mother. I remember that clearly. It must have been
within the first few weeks of our liberty.

"We were on the road home, I remember, but we were barely out of the German territories, headed south towards Benwick and moving at our own pace, still full of the heady feelings of freedom after so many years of regimentation and routine, and Ban had just finished telling us a story that none of us believed. He told us he had been betrothed, years earlier and at his father's insistence, to an unknown woman. We thought he was gulling us, trying to hood-wink us for his own ends, and when we pressed him for more details, calling him a liar and a lout—which we could do because we were his friends—he admitted that he had been thirteen and she a mere infant at the time. But he swore he had never even seen her, so he could not say if she had one head or two, and we all had a good laugh over his foolishness.

"He could see we were still unconvinced, nevertheless, and so he told us she was the daughter of one of his father's oldest allies, a king called Garth of Ganis, who ruled over a federation of clans among the Salians, the northern Franks, in the rich lands to the south of the Rhine delta. Her name was Vivienne of Ganis, and he swore to us that before leaving home to come on this campaign, he had renewed his pledge to marry her, sight unseen and for the good of his people, when he returned victorious from the wars. Well, he was returning now, he said, and curious to see what kind of burden he had been saddled with to please his father, and so he was going to visit *her* father's place, Ganis, on the way south, since we would be riding close by it, to the eastward.

"Well, we were his friends, so we were not gentle with him when he told us about that. In fact we roasted him for a long time as we rode southward, but when we drew close to where he was to leave us, we decided we should all accompany him to inspect this mysterious intended bride. We proposed it in jest, but instead of being angry, Ban made it plain he was glad that we would be with him when the time came for him to step forward and identify himself to his future wife and her father." Chulderic paused and smiled. "With us around him, it would be obvious that he was being truthful in saying he was on his way home from the wars and had stopped only to pay his respects to his father's old friend in passing, and there would have been no question of his simply dropping by to examine his betrothed. Mind you, had the lady turned out to be less than beautiful, Ban would have been forewarned and able to conduct himself appropriately thereafter, in terms of the speed with which he might rush to take up his solemn marriage duties.

"But as it turned out, there was no need for such caution. King Garth made us welcome and sent for the Lady Vivienne, bidding her come and meet her betrothed. Well," Chulderic turned in his saddle and looked sideways at me, "everyone knows how that turned out." He hawked deeply and spat, and I looked at him in dismay, thinking it a reaction to his memory of the meeting and what it had led to, but his face was serene.

"What we did *not* know," he continued, "because no one had ever thought to tell Ban, was that his lady had a sister—a twin sister, whose name was Elaine."

At the mention of my mother's name, even though I had been expecting it, my skin rose up in gooseflesh and the hairs on the nape of my neck bristled.

"She wasn't there when we arrived, and we saw no sign of her for the whole week of our visit, because she had gone to be with her father's elder sister, who lived some distance away and was ailing. Vivienne was to have accompanied her, but had fallen sick herself, and so had remained at home with her father, which was fortunate for Ban. When he found out that his wife-to-be had a twin sister, however, it seemed only natural for him to ask if the two were identical, but he was told no, they were exact opposites in appearance, and being Ban, he took that to mean that the other twin must be unattractive, as the opposite of the lovely Vivienne. We did, too, in all justice.

"During that week we were entertained like kings, and Ban and Vivienne grew dizzy with love of each other. By the end of the week, Ban had sworn to return and wed her as soon as he could stir his own father to attend the nuptials, and all of us had grown confident that he and she would make a perfect pairing.

"But then, on the day before we were to leave, the other sister, Elaine, returned home, and Childebertus was lost from the moment he set eyes on her. It was absolutely true, what Ban had been told: she was the very opposite of her twin in appearance. Her hair was raven black, instead of Vivienne's spun gold; her skin was dusky olive, instead of lily white; her eyes were dark, deep blue, much like yours, instead of sparkling green. In all things like that the two of them were as different as could be, but the truth was that the Lady Elaine was even more beautiful than her sister, a thing that none of us would have thought possible before we saw her."

"How old was she then, Magister?"

"It seems to me she was seventeen at that time, and had been betrothed almost at the same time as her sister—within a matter of months—but to a much older man than Ban, a close neighbor and trusted friend of her father. This man, whose name was Gundevald, was greatly famed as a warrior, we were told, and had ridden off to join the Imperial Armies two years earlier, leading his own men. He had not been heard from since, but was expected to return soon, since the wars had ended, for a spell at least."

Again Chulderic fell silent for a while. "Within an hour of first setting eyes on the Lady Elaine I found myself thinking it was fortunate that we were to leave the following day, for that young woman, betrothed elsewhere or not, could not turn her eyes away from Childebertus, that night in her father's hall. She claimed all of his attention, too, and a blind man could have seen it would be dangerous to leave the two of them alone together for any length of time."

"Why so, Magister?"

Chulderic jerked up straighter, plainly astonished by the question, but then he remembered who had asked it, and simply waved his free hand, as though dismissing my enquiry. "Because she was betrothed—sworn and dedicated to another. Betrothal is a solemn promise, legally undertaken, to wed someone, Clothar. It can not be discarded lightly. A man who forswears a betrothal insults, defies and challenges his betrothed's entire clan, and by extension of that, any man who knowingly seduces and suborns another man's betrothed commits an act of war against both sides of the marriage contract. The woman is not deemed to be at fault in such things, being a mere woman; the man, the contract breaker, bears the fault, and draws all the wrath upon his own head.

"In this case, the Lady Elaine was already committed to Gundevald, but it was plain for anyone to see that she would have run off that very night with Childebertus had he encouraged her in any way. Fortunately, he did not, and we left the following morning without incident, or so I thought at first.

"In fact, he had made an assignation with the young woman while the rest of us were all asleep, and they had passed several hours alone together. It was the height of stupidity, and it very nearly brought us all to disgrace. What actually transpired between the two of them I know not, but had they been discovered in their tryst, there would have been a butcher's bill to pay, for all of us."

He paused, evidently thinking back, and then sniffed. "I had thought he looked very pleased with himself when we were getting ready to depart that morning, and I wondered why he should be so cheerful when the rest of us were feeling sorry for ourselves, having to be up and on the road so early in the day. The answer was obvious: he had not been to bed at all that night and was still wide-awake and full of vigor when it came time for us to leave. The rest of us, on the other hand, had slept for a few hours—far from sufficient for our needs, after having drunk long and deeply the night before—and so had had to drag ourselves unrested and unhappy from our beds. I overheard heard him talking to Ban, later that day, about Elaine, raving about her beauty and her wit, and although he actually said nothing about it, that was when I knew, in my gut, where he had been the night before. I could hear it in your father's voice that afternoon and see it in the way he carried himself . . . he was cocky, full of himself, walking on air. But it was a fool's risk he took that night, no matter how deeply in love he thought he was and no matter how cleanly he managed his folly. He knew better than to behave as he had. He was a man of seven and twenty at the time, with a duty to consider the welfare of his friends and not set them at hazard."

"Did you confront him with your knowledge, Magister?"

Chulderic jerked his head to one side, hard. "No, I did not. Told myself I had no proof and that no harm had come of whatever he did that night. But I went around for weeks afterwards waiting for something to come of it and expecting to be pursued and challenged. It took me a long time to wipe the incident from my mind. It was the only willfully selfish, inconsiderate and stupid thing I ever knew your father to be guilty of, and I don't think even he realized the risk he had taken or the scope of what he had done."

"And did anything . . . happen?"

"No, nothing at all, as things turned out, and we reached Benwick safely without either Ban or Germanus becoming aware of what Childebertus had done. I was the only one who knew, and I did not let on I knew anything. Life went on, and Germanus rode directly homeward to Auxerre before we reached the bounds of Benwick's lands, and your father and I settled down to live in Benwick with Ban. Be careful here. Mind your eyes."

Our surroundings had changed; the open space through which we had been riding earlier had been swallowed up by encroaching brush, much of it a thorny shrub that rose above the height of a mounted man and was armed with long and vicious spikes that could shred exposed skin or pierce an eyeball. I had become aware of the thorns and the danger they posed just before Chulderic drew my attention to them, and for a short time after that we rode in silence, giving all our attention to the path we were following. At one point, the growth surrounding us was so thick that we had to ride one behind the other, holding our arms up in front of our faces for protection against the wicked thorns, but that was the worst of it, and from then on the growth thinned rapidly until we were riding through glades again.

We came to a stream that was completely concealed from the path we were on by a thick screen of bushes, and we noticed it only because the noise it made in its rocky bed was loud enough to reach our ears. We soon found a way through the barrier of brush that separated us from it, and as we emerged on the other side, Chulderic drew rein and sat staring at the rushing water for a while before pulling his mount's head around to the right and kicking the animal into motion again, allowing it to pick its own way along the bank.

"I know this river," he said, "but I've never seen this part of it. And yet I was close to here last night. I think we're downstream from where I crossed, so we'll probably find the spot . . . That visit to Ganis marked a turning point in all our lives, for nothing was ever the same after it."

The transition from observation to reminiscence was so smooth that I almost failed to recognize it, but Chulderic was already unaware of my presence and heedless of any need for time and logic in what he was thinking and saying.

"Ban was wild with impatience to be wed, now that he had met his bride-to-be, and he spent the entire journey homeward to Benwick making plans to sweep up his father and transport him and his senior advisers back to Ganis as quickly as possible for the wedding. But as soon as we arrived in Benwick it was plain to see that there would be no wedding in Ganis that year.

"Ban the Bald was no longer the lusty, swaggering King of six years earlier—the last time that his son Ban had seen him. He had fallen from a horse more than a year before our return and had aged grotesquely since then. He was so greatly changed, in fact, that Ban himself said later he would not have recognized the old man, had he met him anywhere other than in his own home. I was there when he first saw his father on that occasion, and I saw how badly it affected him. It frightened him, probably more than anything else in his life had until that time, because it showed him that no man, not even his own formidable father, is invincible or immortal.

"The fall had shattered the bone in the King's right thigh, driving the splintered end out through the flesh, and despite the efforts of his Roman-trained surgeons, the wound had festered and would not heal, and so the King had not walked since the day he fell, more than a year earlier. And that inability to walk had brought the old King close to death, because it had robbed him of all bodily strength, since he could no longer fight or ride or even train to keep himself in condition.

"I had never met the King, but I had heard great things about him, and nothing I had heard prepared me for the man I actually saw. He looked to me, an outsider, to be on the very edge of death when we arrived, and in fact he was dead within two months of our return. It was as though he had kept himself alive only to see his son safely returned, and from the moment he saw Ban and assured himself that all was well with him, he simply lay back and allowed death to take him. So what had begun for Ban as a triumphal return home ended in a grief-filled vigil as he waited for his father's life to end.

"We buried the old man at the far end of summer, just as the first tinges of gold began to appear among the leaves of the forest that surrounded the castle, and we installed his son Ban as King of Benwick in his father's stead within a month of that. Then, for a period of months following his assumption of the kingship, throughout the entire winter of that year, Ban struggled mightily to re-establish the harmonious flow of government that had begun to break down during his father's long illness.

"Of course, he had also sent word of his father's condition back to King Garth in Ganis as soon as he had arrived home, so everyone in Ganis knew that the wedding feast would be postponed. In the beginning, spurred by false hopes, the talk was of a brief postponement until such time as King Ban was back in control of himself, but that changed swiftly as his condition worsened steadily, and it was soon known in Ganis that the old King would never return there. By the spring of the following year, however, the old King's death and the changes it entailed had all been absorbed and accommodated, and the marriage of Ban and Vivienne had been firmly arranged for the autumn of that year.

"Your father had much to do with that, encouraging Ban constantly, from the moment of his father's burial and his own accession to the throne of Benwick, to waste no time in returning to Ganis and claiming his bride. The marriage, and the presence of a

Queen in Benwick, Childebertus maintained, would work greatly to the new King's advantage, giving his rule an appearance of permanence." Chulderic paused, appearing to consider what he had just said. "All of which was very true, and excellent counsel," he continued eventually, "but hardly unselfish, since Childebertus knew he could not see Elaine again until Ban returned to Ganis. As Ban's closest friend, he would be the King's witness at the ceremony, as Elaine would be her sister's, and so the two of them would meet again, legitimately, at the wedding of their friends. But his chances of spending time with her, even then, grew daily less as the time for the return of her betrothed, Gundevald, drew ever closer. That time was already long overdue, and your father was almost wild with impatience to return and see Elaine again before his rival could return to claim his bride. Childebertus would be content to settle for that, since he knew it was the very best he could expect.

"And so they met again, in due time, this pair of lovers not-to-be, and still Gundevald had not returned from his campaigning. By that time, however, mere concern over Gundevald's late return was being replaced by grave misgivings."

Chulderic's attention was caught now by something else, something low and dun colored and immobile, out of place on the edge of the stream ahead of us, and he was already spurring his horse towards it. I kicked my own horse forward, following him until he dismounted beside the body of a young buck, less than two years old. It lay half in and half out of the water, its head, complete with immature antlers, almost completely submerged.

"Throw me your rope."

I did as he ordered, scooping the tightly coiled circle of plaited leather from where it hung from a thong by my knee and lobbing it into his outstretched hand. As he worked to unravel it, shaking out the tight-wound coils with both hands, I watched his eyes move constantly, taking note of everything there was to see in the clearing on the bank, from the dead animal itself to the grass around the area where it lay, and the fringe of bushes that screened the clearing, concealing it from view from any distance greater than ten paces.

Finally, apparently satisfied with what he had seen, he stepped ankle-deep into the stream and looped one end of the rope around one of the deer's haunches, tying it securely before throwing the other end to me.

"Here," he growled. "Loop this around your saddle horn and pull this thing up onto the bank, clear of the water."

My horse made short work of the haul, and moments later I had dismounted and stood looking down at the deer with Chulderic.

"Might have been a natural death," he murmured, more to himself than to me.

I shook my head. "I don't know, Magister. It's an awfully young buck."

"Aye, it is. But youth is no great protection against death. There's no sign of any human cause that I can see—not even a wound. But whatever caused it, the beast is newly dead . . . within the day, anyway. I passed by here last night, just before dark, and there was no sign of it then. Look, you can see the marks my horse made, crossing the stream there." Sure enough, the marks were unmistakable, and they passed within half a score of paces of where we had found the carcass. Chulderic was still looking about him. "Well, at least it's clear of the water," he continued. "That's what's important. No point in leaving it to pollute the whole stream. I'll send someone to bury it later, or at least to drag it away from the water, to where it'll do no harm."

"I can do that, Magister," I said, waving the rope I had begun to coil again.

"No, that's no job for you—not today. You have more important matters to attend to today." He moved away, to where his horse had begun cropping contentedly at a drift of lush grass, and raised one foot to the stirrup, but before he remounted he twisted back to face me, speaking over his shoulder as he steadied himself on one leg with both hands braced against his saddle. "You didn't expect to see that today, did you?"

I blinked at him, not knowing what he meant. "To see what, Magister?"

"Death, lad." He grasped and heaved, hauling himself back up into the saddle, where he looked at me again, one eyebrow raised high. "Death in the middle of a fine afternoon."

"Oh. No, I didn't."

"No, and you never will . . . Even in war, when there's danger all around you and the enemy is close and you know someone's going to die at any moment, it's always unexpected when it actually happens." He pulled on his reins, making his horse snort and snuffle as it stamped its feet and sidled around to face me. "What about the deer?"

He had lost me again. "What about it, Magister? It was just a dead deer, lying in a stream."

"Aye, that's right, that's what it was. But how did it die? When? Why?"

This distraction from his narrative was trying my patience. "Forgive me, Magister," I said, "but I cannot think those things are significant. The only thing that matters is that the animal is dead."

He nodded his head sagely, his lips turned sharply downwards in what looked like a pout. "Aye," he murmured, so quietly that I could barely hear him, "that's how it always is, lad. Bear that in mind. The fact of the death always outweighs the reasons for it. I have come to believe that more and more as I grow older . . ."

I was frowning at him, beginning to feel concern over the way his attention was drifting and changing, but almost as though he had noticed my misgivings, he blinked and shook his head slightly, then looked about him, easing himself around in the saddle as he considered where we were.

"Let's go now," he growled eventually. "We'll head over that way, to the north, and then circle back to the south until we hit the trail we came in on. We should be back at home in less than an hour. What was I talking about before we found this carcass?"

I kicked my horse forward and followed him through the screen of saplings and bushes we had penetrated earlier. Then, once we were back on the main pathway, broad enough to accommodate us side by side, I kicked gently until we were even with Chulderic's mount.

"The wedding."

"Aye, well, listen closely and learn. Garth of Ganis was no fool, and no one would ever accuse him of being indecisive. He saw the strong attraction between his daughter Elaine and the young warrior Childebertus—as did everyone else in Ganis—when Ban's party first arrived, and he watched it flower rapidly during the gaiety and excitement of the week preceding the nuptial ceremony. Fortunately, he had no awareness that the pair had met before, on Ban's first visit—that escapade had somehow managed to escape his attention—but he could see at a glance what was happening this time, and he was having none of it. He set some trusted men to watch the pair closely day and night, exhorting them to make sure that the two young people never had a moment alone together. But Garth, being a man, knew it was only a matter of time, as the young people's attraction to each other grew and fed upon itself. He did not distrust his daughter, but he was well aware that she was an impressionable young girl, barely more than a child, and that the buck prancing around her was a seasoned campaigner, a decade older than she, experienced in life and good to look upon. He decided to put an end to their liaison immediately after the wedding, before anything could come of their intensifying attraction.

"On the day of the wedding, Garth watched Elaine, barely paying attention to the bride and her new husband in his concern over his unmarried daughter. He had increasing difficulty in concealing his anger as he saw how eye contact between Elaine and her admirer had given way to touching, their hands constantly hovering close to each other so that their fingers were seldom untwined, even though the clasping was always brief and cautious and, they believed, hidden from the eyes of others.

"That night, the night of the wedding feast, the King made sure his daughter's nurse would have company in her chambers—a collection of visiting children of all ages to keep her awake and thereby ensure that Elaine remained safely where she ought to be, in her own quarters. At the same time, he invited Childebertus to sit among his personal guests at dinner, and took great satisfaction in watching the young man's discomfort as he sought vainly for some way of making his escape. Each time young Childebertus rose to his feet, the King would speak to him directly, drawing him back into the general conversation and making it impossible for him to leave without being ill mannered and obvious.

"The morning after the festivities, Garth rose up early and went straight to speak to Ban as soon as the new husband showed his face. He told his new son-in-law what he had seen going on between his daughter and Childebertus and what he intended to do about it. He then summoned Childebertus to him privately and confronted the unsuspecting warrior with the realities of his situation and the dire punishment he faced if he should bring disgrace, shame or embarrassment to Garth or any of his kinsfolk, and most particularly his daughter Elaine, who was betrothed to another.

"Childebertus listened, and then succumbed to a surge of nobility that he was to regret deeply. He admitted openly and freely that he had fallen deeply in love with the King's beautiful daughter, but swore he had done nothing and never would do anything that might cause Elaine to suffer pain, grief or shame in the eyes of her family or anyone else. He offered to leave Garth's lands at once, and swore by his honor and his love for Elaine never to return. Very noble, passionate and full of self-sacrifice, all of which add up to great foolishness. But the King had been listening closely and he believed every word of your father's protestations. He thanked Childebertus for his tact and understanding, then gratefully and graciously accepted his offer to leave Ganis immediately, granting him the remainder of that day to make his farewells to everyone except Elaine, and promising that he would personally send him on his way the next morning with no hint of shame or scandal attached to his honor. True to his word, as Childebertus was preparing to depart the following day, Garth gifted him with a magnificent horse and all the trapping to go with it, in token of his gratitude and his appreciation as the bride's father.

"Your father thanked the King for his generous gift, then rode away, straight backed and stiff shouldered, filled with rage at himself, he told me later, for his stupidity in offering to leave. He had not even had an opportunity to speak with Elaine, to tell her what had happened. She loved him, he knew, as he loved her, and her father had promised to tell her what he had done, but Childebertus would never forgive himself, he thought, for denying their love to both of them in what he now recognized as a moment of foolish enthusiasm."

"He rode away alone, then? Why didn't you go with him, for company on the road?"

"I would have, had I been there, but I was in Benwick at that time, acting as Ban's deputy during his absence."

"Well . . ." I was almost spluttering, outraged by the injustice of what had been done to my father. "Had he no friends to ride with him? Did King Ban not object to his being sent away alone?"

"Aye, he did. Ban was angry and upset when he first heard that your father would leave the next day. His anger sprang out of his loyalty to your father, for whom he felt responsible, as well as from his own awareness that he himself could not accompany his friend—not now that he had a wife to take back to his own home, with all her belongings and her personal attendants. None of those, he knew, would be ready to leave for another week, at least, and he himself could not leave without them. So he demanded that Childebertus select an escort from among Ban's own men, to ride with him—Ban had brought an unusually large force with him to Ganis, more for display than for real safety, and could easily afford to send a large number of them with his friend to protect him. But your father was still feeling noble then, determined to suffer and endure the agonies of his self-hatred and contempt in seclusion. So yes, he rode off alone."

"What happened then—Magister?" I almost addressed him as an equal, but I caught myself in time to add the respectful acknowledgment of his rank. He did not notice, however, and answered my question without hesitation.

"Ban sent an escort after him, regardless of your father's wishes, but Childebertus must have seen them coming behind him, because he vanished before they could make contact with him and they could find no trace of him from then on. They eventually returned to Ganis, to report their failure to Ban, and he was not happy with them. But there was nothing to be done."

"But that can't be all, Magister! There must be more. How could my father ever have wed my mother, having sworn by his honor never to see her again? Did he forswear himself?"

Chulderic smiled now, amused at my panic. "Easy, boy, calm down. Your father's honor was never in question. King Garth himself absolved him of his promise. I told you the old man was neither foolish nor indecisive. Exactly a month after the wedding, on the very day that Ban and his new wife left King Garth's lands to return to Benwick, Garth received word, in the form of a written report from an imperial legate, that Gundevald of Stone Vale was dead, killed in battle months earlier when his force was surrounded and wiped out by an overwhelming concentration of Ostrogoths whose existence in that part of the world had been unsuspected until that encounter."

I had been listening avidly, because I *knew* Gundevald must have died somehow—otherwise, how could my father and my mother have wed?—and this confirmation of my own judgment pleased me greatly.

"Well, those were the worst tidings King Garth could have received. He knew that Ban, his new son-in-law, was an able man and a valiant fighter and would have made a fine consort to Vivienne, had she ever become Queen of Ganis, but he had always known, too, that such a thing would never be, because it had never been intended. Vivienne would go with Ban to his home in Benwick, hundreds of miles to the south and east, where he already had a people of his own to rule.

"At the time of the pair's betrothal, you see, almost two decades earlier, Garth had been in the prime of his manhood, with a fertile and loving wife who, to that point, had given him three fine, healthy sons and twin daughters. Full of a young man's belief in his own invincibility and flushed with his pride of fatherhood, Garth had foreseen no need then to fret over his own future. The marriage of his daughter to the son of his old friend Ban the Bald had been arranged purely to strengthen the ties between Ganis and his friend and ally, Ban the Bald of Benwick. Since that time, however, Garth had lost his beloved wife, who had died in childbirth along with her infant. He had never remarried, but had kept himself surrounded by women of all ages, using all of them shamelessly to help him look after and care for his children, and most particularly his three sons.

"And then, late in his life and within the space of two years, all three of his sons had been taken from him—one crushed in a fall from a horse, the youngest swept away and lost forever in a flooded river later in the same year, and the eldest and most promising, Dion, devoured by the Spotted Fever. Suddenly Garth was alone, with only one unwed daughter left to succeed him, and his enemies were as aware as he that Garth of Ganis was no longer as mighty as he once had been.

"That knowledge was the reason for Garth's promising his daughter to Gundevald of Stone Vale in the first place. He was very concerned about protecting his kingdom and his people, but he was equally concerned about protecting his unwed daughter. The Salian Franks have very strongly held ideas about women succeeding and taking possession of family holdings. They don't like that at all and they've been trying for years to put a stop to it. They want a dead man's holdings to pass to another male, if not a son, then the nearest male relative. Garth was long-headed when it came to things like that. He could not have foreseen what would happen to his sons, but he was clear thinking enough to ensure that even in the worst imaginable circumstances, his daughter would not end up penniless and disinherited as a helpless woman in a man's world. He saw it as his duty to protect her against the day when he could not be there to see to it himself. Gundevald, like Ban the Bald of Benwick, had been a valued friend of Garth's for years. His lands of Stone Vale bordered Garth's own holding, and although they were neither as fertile nor as extensive as King Garth's Ganis, they were more rugged, easier to defend, and they abutted Ganis on two sides.

"Furthermore, Gundevald was the last of his family, the sole survivor of a long line of successful and enterprising merchants whose ventures, operating mainly out of Massilia, the oldest port of southern Gaul, had covered every part of the Empire for more than two hundred years. By an accident of birth and the attrition of the few remaining heirs of his natural family, Gundevald had become the sole inheritor of a private trading empire so complex and diversified that he could never possibly spend all of his wealth. And his immense wealth enabled him to enjoy a personal power that few men could wield. He counted himself a friend of the Emperor, Honorius, and thanks to the Emperor's blessing, Gundevald commanded his own private army, maintaining it out of his own coffers and placing it at the disposal of Honorius in time of war.

"Garth knew there were some people who thought it less than fortunate that Gundevald was almost twice Elaine's age and so had little youth and less beauty with which to sway or win a young girl's heart, but he knew, too, that Gundevald would make a fine, strong and dutiful husband for his only remaining unwed daughter, and a powerful protector for her lands and her people once Garth was gone. But now Gundevald was dead, and Elaine was almost nineteen, having spent three full years waiting for him to return and marry her.

"Now, as soon as he had received and accepted the word of Gundevald's death, the King also accepted the realities that had changed the world around him. Gundevald's holdings of Stone Vale, which Garth had hoped to use for the defense of Ganis, were now in jeopardy, for Gundevald had left no sons to succeed him and his power and possessions would inevitably pass to whoever among his followers was strong enough to claim and hold them. That, by itself, placed Ganis at hazard, since Garth had no knowledge of who would seize the rule in Stone Vale next, and no way of divining whether that person might be friend or foe to Ganis.

"And so King Garth of Ganis thought long and deeply, then made a swift decision and sent out mounted couriers to overtake Ban's party on the road. Ban's cavalcade, containing all of his wife's prized possessions in a train of enormous wagons, was ponderous and ungainly, and it had set out only that morning, moving very slowly, which meant it would still be well within Ganis lands when Garth's messengers reached it. He sent word that the cavalcade should make camp and await the return of Ban and Vivienne, who were to return immediately to him.

"By the time the pair arrived back at the King's Hall, wondering what was going on, Garth was ready for them and greeted them with a barrage of questions that kept them both reeling, off balance and in absolute ignorance of his motives. This friend of Ban's, he demanded to know, the one he had sent home, the fellow Childebertus, was he trustworthy? He nodded at Ban's angry response, which he had expected, then pressed on: was he a man of means then, this Childebertus . . . did he have wealth?

"Sufficient for his needs and more than he could ever use, he was told. His father, a very wealthy and famous lawyer, had died in Rome several years before and had left all of his possessions to Childebertus, his only son. Those possessions consisted mainly of the monies and portable goods—gemstones and jewels, and gold and silver, both coins and bullion—taken as fees during a lifetime of working on behalf of wealthy clients. In addition to those funds, however, the lawyer Jacobus had also left his son enormous quantities of valuable real estate, most of it rental property generating revenue in the city of Rome and in the new Imperial City of Constantinople, all of it shrewdly purchased throughout the old man's life and now held in trust for Childebertus by his father's closest and most trusted friends and colleagues.

"The King muttered approval when he heard that. He said he would need large resources if he were to protect Ganis and its people in the future.

"*Who* would need large resources? Ban asked, making it plain that he had no idea of what was going on here. Childebertus would, Garth replied, as if that were the most obvious thing in the world. If he was to wed Elaine, he must elect to live here in Ganis, working with Garth at first in governing and strengthening

the domain, then serving as his wife's consort when she became
Queen once Garth was dead. Gundevald was dead—had been for
months. Garth repeated the report he had received and dismissed
the dead man with a wave of his hand. The thing to do now, he
told Ban, was to consolidate his affairs in Ganis before the wars
broke out in Stone Vale.

"Ban asked Garth why he himself was not moving to take
command in Gundevald's stead, but Garth's only response to that
was a quick shake of the head. No point to that, he said. He did not
have the strength at his back nowadays, he said, and couldn't hope
to win a serious struggle against the organized leaders of
Gundevald's army.

"What army? Ban asked. It might be true that they had all been
killed with Gundevald.

"Not all of them, Garth answered. That was impossible.

"Not so, Ban responded, equally forceful. It might seem impossible, but it might just as easily be true. And what if it *was* true?
What if Gundevald's defeat at the hands of the Goths had been so
completely crushing that none of his commanders had survived? No
army can survive, deprived of its command officers; leaderless, the
rank and file were nothing more than a rabble who would dissipate
and vanish within days, hunting for food and sustenance for themselves. Or what if the defeat had been less severe, yet sufficiently so
that those who had survived now had insufficient organized strength
to take and hold Gundevald's place in Stone Vale? Should Garth not
move at least to occupy the territories as a precaution, in self-
defense?

"That stopped the old King short. He had not considered that
possibility. Perhaps he should move in, he growled after a while. All
the more reason, then, to wed Elaine to Childebertus and have the
young man here to work by his side as soon as could be. He wanted
Ban to ride immediately, in haste, to bring back Childebertus as
quickly as possible.

"He might not come at all now, was Ban's response, for
although he knew that Childebertus would crawl over burning coals

to reach Elaine, he nonetheless felt the need to make the old man suffer briefly before giving in to him. Garth had given the poor fellow ample reason to refuse to come again, he pointed out.

"Of course he would come! The King's answer was immediate and confident. He had done nothing to insult Childebertus personally, he said—indeed, he had gone out of his way to show his appreciation and goodwill with the gift horse. Besides, everything was different now. If Childebertus wished to wed his daughter, Garth would look kindly on his suit, provided Childebertus would agree to remain in Ganis and pledge himself and his resources to support the King, standing with Garth and his people against any who might come against them in the aftermath of Gundevald's death.

"Less than an hour after that, Ban was on the road home to Benwick."

"And was my father glad to hear Ban's tidings?"

Chulderic peered sideways at me. "What do you think? He was wild with delight. As soon as he heard what Ban had come to tell him, he sent for me. We were going back to Ganis at once, he told me, as quickly as we could, and we would live there from now on. I would be his Master-at-Arms there, he promised me then, in complete charge of the entire force of men he would be raising immediately to take with him.

"Before we left for Ganis, your father sat down and wrote a letter to Germanus in Auxerre, explaining what was happening and where he was going and why, and telling the legate that we would be extending our northward journey to swing wide of our route and call in at Auxerre in passing. He then asked the noble legate to mediate for him in the matter of the legacy left him by his late father, by contacting the various people involved as custodians of his wealth and requesting that they sell everything that could be sold, as quickly and as prudently as possible, and that they forward the funds in care of Germanus in Auxerre. In the meantime, he hoped Germanus might arrange to advance him some money against future revenues and that he would also agree to use those funds and his military contacts to conscript a force of not less than one hundred men, all cavalry, and more if he could find qualified men in sufficient numbers, and have them ready to accompany us when we left Auxerre to ride on to Ganis.

"Your father had no idea then of how much money was involved in his father's legacy, and I doubt if he ever really came to grips with his own sudden wealth. Germanus told me later that the expenses he incurred on behalf of your grandfather Garth and the fortification of Ganis involved enormous sums, paid for, in the main, by what was realized in the first few years from massive sales of his properties in Rome and Constantinople. Much of that money was shipped directly from Rome to Gaul by sea, then made its way from the coast to Auxerre, and from there to Ganis, in wagon loads disguised as normal military goods being transported under escort. Your father kept the money in his own treasury after that, and used it as he needed it, to purchase arms and men and horses and the like. I remember, though, when I first heard about it—the amounts involved, I mean—the number of wooden chests of gold coin and silver ingots and jewels and the way they were transported clear across Gaul in ordinary wagons, I was flabbergasted. I simply could not visualize the bulk of the treasure."

I sat blinking at that, entranced by the image he had conjured, trying in vain to imagine the size and amount of treasure involved and to see it, in my mind's eye, filling the vast underground chamber of my father's treasury, awash in a sea of gold and brilliant colors as the flickering light of torches reflected from the heaps of gold and jewels.

"What happened to it, Magister, all that money?"

"Clodas took it, along with everything else."

"Clodas. Someday I will kill Clodas of Ganis."

"Aye, mayhap you will. No one will blame you, I know that. He owes you more than one life. Besides, his treasury is yours by right."

I felt myself frowning now. "Clodas of *Ganis*. The King said Clodas wasn't always known by that name. But last night King Ban called you Chulderic of Ganis. Is that correct? Is that truly where you are from?"

The Master-at-Arms barked deep in his throat, and it might have been a laugh, although it might as easily have been a cough. "No, lad. I'm from Ostia, the port of Rome," he growled. "I had never heard of Ganis until Ban mentioned it, and I didn't get that name until I came here with you, ten years ago. Chulderic's a common name in these parts and there were already four Chulderics here when I arrived. Each of them was known by the name of the place he came from, and one of them was already from Ostia, another from Rome. So I became Chulderic of Ganis."

"What did you do in Ostia, Magister?"

He made a formless, grunting sound deep in his chest. "No one has ever asked me that before. What *did* I do in Ostia? I should know, I was there for years . . . I survived, I suppose, and that, considering who I was and where I found myself, was an achievement. I grew up there, fighting for every scrap of food I ate and fighting even harder simply to live when there was nothing to eat . . . I was an orphan and a thief, forced to live by my wits, and they served me well, since I am still here to speak of it. I had no family . . . and no memories of anyone, from my earliest days . . . I lived on the streets, alone, sleeping in doorways most of the time, for as long as I can remember, and the one vision I had that kept me alive throughout that entire time was an image of myself as a soldier. I don't know how or when it began, but I grew up dreaming of being a soldier—not a mere warrior, mark you, but a uniformed Roman soldier, a legionary—because soldiers, to me, were always self-sufficient and dependent upon no man for their food. They were tall and strong and confident, and they had fine weapons and they were clean and wore warm clothing and well-made armor and everyone knew who they were and what they were. I never met a single one, mind you, who showed me any kindness, but somehow, among them all, they saved my life.

"I was fourteen when I first tried to enlist, and they laughed at me because I was a small, undernourished and skinny fourteen. I was so furious that I wept. I tried seven more times after that— seven times in two years—and they turned me away each time.

But then they took me in the next time, on my ninth attempt, with no hesitation. I suppose I had grown old enough by then to look my age."

He glanced across to where I sat watching him, and sniffed. "Now I'm a Master-at-Arms, so who would guess I ever was a thief?"

There was nothing I could say to that, and I only had the vaguest suspicion that there might be a grin hiding underneath his scowl, so I sat mute for a spell, then changed the topic.

"Why did Clodas of Ganis kill my parents, Magister, and how was he able to do so?"

Chulderic stiffened as though I had slapped him, and then his shoulders slumped forward. "Why and how are two different matters, boy. I've been thinking of that, and wondering about it, for ten years now. He killed them because they were there and they had what he wanted. This is a creature born to kill, this Clodas. He is depraved . . . evil. And yet he hides the evil effortlessly, with an almost supernatural ability to dissemble, to appear to be what he is not. Easy for me now to say what I know to be true, that he is without a man's emotions, empty of mercy or compassion, incapable of love or sympathy or sorrow. But this was not the face he showed to us who thought we were his friends. From us, he concealed every inkling of his true nature—from us men, at least, because I seem to recall that most women disliked him and distrusted him instinctively. I suppose that makes men more gullible and foolish than women. It's certainly true that he was able to gull all of us who knew him. Jesu! It makes me sick when I recall how much we trusted him . . . and honored him, for that matter. But then, truth to tell, none of us could even imagine the depths of treachery and depravity that existed within him while he was making us all love and admire him."

The old man stared out across the scene in front of us. "Believe me, lad, he was a piece of work . . . the kind of man to make you doubt every notion you ever had of what is admirable or honorable or worthy of trust.

"How did he do it? Within the six months following your father's arrival, he and King Garth visited every town, every fort and every settlement, no matter how poor or insignificant, in the Ganis federation, and that is how your father first met Clodas, on one of those journeys. In those days, Clodas was not known to anyone as Clodas of Ganis. If anything, he would have been Clodas of Rich Vale, but even that would have been ludicrous. His station was far more humble back then. His father, Dagobert, was the chief magistrate and nominal ruler of the district called Rich Vale, one of the larger fiefs of Ganis which lay far to the southeast of Garth's own lands. But Dagobert was an administrative ruler, more of a public official than a leader in any military sense. He was also some kind of cousin to King Garth, a relative by blood, but I know not how close, although I believe someone once told me that Garth's grandsire had been a brother to Dagobert's grandmother, or perhaps his great-grandmother.

"When Childebertus first met Clodas and his people, there was no slightest sign from any of them that they might all one day disagree. Clodas represented his father that day, for Dagobert had fallen gravely ill and would later die of his illness. Clodas presented himself as a loyal kinsman and ally of King Garth, and welcomed him and your father warmly as honored guests, extending all the hospitality of his father's hall to the King's party. Your grandfather was Clodas's King, and took the welcome as no more than his due, barely aware of anything other than the formality of the occasion. Your father, on the other hand, being the man he was, accepted Clodas's hospitality in the spirit in which he believed it was being offered. It would never have crossed his mind to doubt the truthfulness or the intent of his host. And Clodas took great pains to ingratiate himself with both his visitors.

"Less than a month after returning home to Ganis, they received the word of Dagobert's death, and of Clodas's elevation to his father's rank and holdings, and a month or so after that, they returned to Rich Vale to pay their respects to Clodas, to ratify him as his father's successor, and to commiserate with him over the death of his father. It was at that time that they first began discussing how the garrison at Rich Vale could be strengthened, to their mutual advantage. King Garth, using the combined resources of his regal title and your father's money, with Childebertus's full blessing in the latter, offered to quintuple the strength of Rich Vale's resident forces, which had so far been a mere token presence, providing that Clodas himself would undertake to command his own garrison thereafter, with suitable assistance from Ganis, and to build sufficient housing for his new recruits. Clodas agreed, and it was arranged that a new muster of mercenaries would report to Clodas's command the following spring.

"Well, the new muster arrived, on time and as promised, and from that moment onward the die was cast. Clodas began training his command to serve his own ends. He was his own master, in all respects, and he arranged his affairs accordingly and in complete secrecy. Even the senior officers supplied by Garth suspected nothing, for their tasks were straightforward—to drill and supervise the training of the newly mustered mercenaries until they were battle ready. It was no great feat on Clodas's part to conceal the fact that when his troops were battle ready, they would be ready to attack their own allies.

"May I ask you something, Magister?"

"Of course."

"What did he do to my mother? Before her death, I mean. What did he do to her?"

"What d'you mean? He did nothing *to* her. If he had actually done something, we would have taken care of it then and there, and what transpired would never have happened as it did."

"But he must have done something, Magister. The King told me that he changed from the moment he first set eyes on her. How could anyone have known that? How could King Ban identify the time and place if nothing happened to mark it?"

The skin across Chulderic's cheeks seemed to tighten and he gazed at me fiercely, his eyes narrowing with what I took to be anger. He started to say something but caught his breath and stopped himself, turning his head away abruptly and tilting his chin up as he stared away into the distance. Then he swung back to face me, releasing his breath noisily. "Damnation, boy, I wish you were older. You're too damn young to know about the politics of men and women . . . and that is as it should be."

I had absolutely no idea what he meant, but I schooled my face to remain blank and nodded knowingly.

"It was your mother who first noticed that there was something *wrong* about Clodas. None of us noticed anything, but then, we were only men. Your mother, with her woman's instincts, detested him from the first moment she met him, although she said nothing for a long time afterwards. She sensed something in his attitude that was offensive, and she felt it down deep in her gut. She felt it in the way he looked at her, and in the tone of his voice when he spoke to her. In the months that followed, she heard her husband speak of him often, but she said nothing, merely avoiding the man and hoping that your father's business with him would soon be done.

"But then Clodas confronted her again, appearing unexpectedly one day when she was alone in the household, your father off on a hunting trip and me with him. Nobody knows what was said on that occasion, but there was no doubt in anyone's mind that Clodas had offended the Queen. She called her guards, and she defied him openly in front of them, forbidding him, upon pain of banishment, ever to return to Ganis while her husband was away from home. Then she had him marched out of her gates and sent on his way back to Rich Vale. Everyone who was there heard her clearly. A public rebuke was probably not the cleverest thing she could have done to a proud and self-absorbed man, no matter what the provocation he provided, but she reacted as she saw fit at the time.

"What he said to her that day she would never discuss, not even with your father, but she called Clodas high handed and self-serving and noxiously full of self-love and she told her husband to beware of him and to trust him in nothing.

"That put your father in a vise, right there, because he had already committed himself, publicly, to trusting Clodas in matters of both import and consequence, and to withdraw that trust purely on the unsubstantiated opinion of his newlywed wife would have caused Childebertus much embarrassment. And yet his wife's opinion was of great value in his eyes and in his heart. He knew she would never lie to him and he could not say the same about Clodas. Had your mother told us what really happened between her and Clodas that afternoon, of course, that might have been the end of all of it, then and there, and your parents might still be alive today. But she held her peace, and thereby tied your father's hands, and that led to tragedy.

"I've been thinking about it now for years, wondering why I didn't cut the serpent down myself, simply for causing me to try to imagine what he might have said or done, or even tried to do. But that's a fool's task, because I did nothing. Nor did anyone else. She was stubborn, Elaine of Ganis, and she kept her secret, no doubt for what she thought were excellent reasons.

"Afterwards, both of them behaved in a very civilized manner to each other, knowing that everyone was watching them and waiting for some sign of hostility, and eventually the tension eased and seemed to die away completely. Then, a full year and more after the upheaval, the Lady Elaine announced herself to be with child, and from that moment the priorities of all of Ganis changed visibly. Everyone breathed more easily. Clodas had long since withdrawn into Rich Vale to tend to his own affairs, and your father spent most of his spare time with his wife, anxious to be with her as much as possible while she was carrying you . . . That situation, an appearance of peace, lasted for a whole year, from the end of one summer through the beginning of the next."

3

In the silence that followed, a skylark broke into song and spiraled upwards, its miraculous voice defying comparison with the size of its tiny body, and I listened to it distractedly as I waited for

Chulderic to resume speaking. But the silence extended until I grew concerned that he would say no more, and finally I could wait no longer.

"And then what happened, Magister?"

"Everything, at once." It was as though he had been waiting for me to ask, because his voice betrayed no surprise at my question. "The world fell apart in the space of one afternoon, and the calamity was over almost before anyone realized it had begun."

"But you knew."

"Aye, I did. At least I was among the first to learn of it." I realized afterwards that Chulderic might have construed my comment as an accusation, but his response was instantaneous, a straightforward acknowledgment of truth. "But I was too late even then to stop any of it. As his Master-at-Arms, I should have been there by your father's side, to guard his back and see to his welfare, but no, I was miles away, playing the fool with a woman while my best friend was being murdered—the man who had given me everything I owned and who had entrusted me with his life and his family's safety."

Although I was still only a child of ten, even I could see that this confession was a bitter and heartfelt one, wrung out from a deep well of pain, and I felt sorrow for the powerful Master-at-Arms. I resisted the urge to say anything, however, fearful that I might say exactly the wrong thing and offend him without wishing to.

"I was in love, you see . . . or I thought I was. You were about six weeks old at that time, perhaps eight weeks, and your mother was in fine health again. She had fed you from her own breasts for the first month of your life, but then something happened and her milk dried up—don't ask me what it was; I have no knowledge or understanding of such things. But the upshot of it all was that a wet nurse had to be found—a woman who had lost a child of her own and had milk to feed a starving babe whose own mother could not give him suck.

"They found two, both of them, by sheer coincidence, recent widows. One was called Antonia, a comely little thing, young and well bred of solid Roman stock. Her elderly husband had been a landowner and some kind of local magistrate. The other was called Sabina, a widowed woman from Ganis. Both lived within a day's journey of your grandfather's castle, both had lost their babies in childbirth, and both were in milk. Antonia had a fragile air about her, but Sabina was all woman, beautiful and self-assured and sultry looking. Sabina was also closely connected to some of the senior Salian chieftains—her dead husband, a warrior called Merofled, had been one of Clodas's closest friends—so the matter of the politics had to be considered in the choice.

"In the event, your father went to see Sabina, took one look at her and declared her to be suitable. None of us were surprised at the choice, because the woman was simply too beautiful to ignore . . ." He lapsed into silence, thinking back to what he could remember of that time, then sighed sharply, snapping himself back to the present.

"Anyway, I was with your father that day, as I always was, and he gave me the task of bringing Sabina back to Ganis immediately, to meet your mother. By the time we had ridden the eighteen miles from where Sabina lived to where your mother was, I had already fallen deeply in love with her . . . she was the most beautiful creature I had ever seen, more beautiful than a week-old fawn or a well-trained falcon . . . and to my eyes, at least, ten times lovelier than your mother, who had been until then the loveliest woman I had ever known. When I first met her—Sabina, I mean—she was in mourning for her lost child, but it was plain to see that her grief could not conceal her pleasant nature, and despite her loss she went out of her way to be charming and friendly towards me. She was no longer mourning her husband, however, and she managed to make that clear from the outset. By that time, she told me, Merofled had been dead for many months, and I had the distinct impression she was angry at him, if anything, for leaving her as he had.

"Be that as it may, your mother both liked her and needed her, and so she made Sabina welcome. All of Sabina's love and attention was lavished upon you, and of course that seemed to banish her grief, so that she soon became herself again. That transformation completely overwhelmed me. I became her slave."

I glanced sideways at him. "You said you were playing the fool with her when my father was killed, Magister. Is it always foolish to love someone?"

His eyes narrowed to slits, but instead of snarling at me, he slowly wrinkled his nose as though he could smell something rotting close by. "No . . ." His voice faded away into silence. "No," he grunted again, drawing the word out this time until it was almost a growl. "No, it is not foolish to love someone, but believe me, boy, it is sheer madness of the worst kind to permit love for a woman to come between you and your sworn duty. And it is punishable folly when you allow love for an unknown woman to seduce you from your sworn trust. I was guilty of all of that, and my punishment has been justified."

I blinked at him in surprise. "What punishment, Magister? How were you punished?"

"By being left alive, boy. In all the years that have passed since that time no day has gone by without my remembering my guilt over that afternoon and what I allowed to happen."

"What *did* happen?" I was incapable of masking the frustration in my voice.

"I went riding in the woods, with you and your nurse, instead of doing what I was supposed to do, which was to protect your father. It was a beautiful summer's day after two weeks of rain, and your mother had finally returned to full health. She and your father had spent little time together since your birth and, since the kingdom was at peace and all was tranquil, your father had deemed it an ideal time to spend some time with you and your mother.

"He arranged a small hunting party, a score or so of friends, men and women both, and a small body of servants to look after them. I was in charge of the hand-picked squadron of guards, as always, but on that occasion I was in conflict with your father's own wishes. My first priority was always his security—and his family's, of course—and normally he was content with that. But this occasion, Childebertus told me, speaking as a friend, was for sheer pleasure for himself and your mother and he did not wish it to be spoiled for her by the constant and oppressive presence of a host of guards. I was not happy about that, but there was nothing I could do to change it.

"We left King Garth's castle in the middle of the week, intending to spend three or perhaps four nights by the river in the greenwood, depending upon the weather, and it was soon evident that we would remain for all four nights, because the weather was perfect. We hunted all day the first day out, and killed sufficient meat to keep us amply fed for the entire period. Then, on the second day, we fished in the river, and while we were less successful there, we yet caught enough fine trout to feed us well.

"On the third day, which started out fiercely hot early in the morning, your father and mother decided to remain in camp, close by the river's edge, and they wanted no company, so they sent everyone off to find things to do for the day. Not even I could stay behind, your father said. I argued with him, knowing he was wrong, but he was determined and even more stubborn than I was. Since the day they were wed, he told me, he and your mother had scarcely spent a moment alone together. There were always people around, and he was sick and tired of it, so this one, solitary day, he was prepared to flout all the rules of conduct, to offend anyone who cared to take offense, and to spend some time absolutely alone with his wife. He knew I would refuse to remove his guards entirely, but he insisted that for this one day they should be removed to no less than twice the normal distance they maintained from the encampment.

"And so it was. I posted the guards personally, almost doubling the number of men because the perimeter expanded as they spread outwards from the center of the encampment. Even so, by the time they were all stationed the protective ring around the encampment was a fragile one, at best. And then when I returned to inform your father that I had done as he wished, he ordered me, too, away, insisting that I spend the day with you and your Frankish nurse, Sabina, protecting both of you. He knew I was taken with her. I was unhappy with the laxity he had created among his own people, but I must admit I was lulled by his sense of well-being, and I've told myself a thousand times that no sane person could have anticipated treachery and murderous hatred on the scale of what took place that afternoon.

"But the fact remains that I was more than willing to wander off into the forest with Sabina and you. I carried you in my arms as we went and she walked close beside me—close enough to touch me as she walked and for me to smell the clean, fresh scent of her. She had dismissed the young man—no more than a boy, really—who was always with her, setting him free for the day and promising that she would be almost as safe with me as she always was with him, and he had gone scampering off on his own somewhere.

"Had I known where he was scampering to, I would have cut the legs from under him before he took a step. The whoreson ran straight to Clodas, who was calmly awaiting word, a few mere miles away, that the guards had been relaxed, that I had been removed from the scene, and that he could attack at will. The entire episode had been prearranged, months earlier, and all of us had been manipulated into participating."

"But—" I was unable to absorb what he had just said.

"Aye, but! How could such a thing be possible? How could it be achieved, and who would be sufficiently cynical to arrange it? The answers came quickly enough, once the damage was done—one observation leading to another like swaths of scythe-cut corn in a reaper's windrow.

"Our guards went down quickly, but some of them held out long enough to raise an alarum. I was about a mile away from the encampment when I heard what I thought was a shout and then a blast on a horn, quickly cut short. On another occasion I might have paid it little heed, but I was ill at ease that afternoon. I started running towards the sound, holding my sheathed sword high and free of my running legs as I went and abandoning you and the nurse Sabina on the instant, despite the sounds of her voice crying to me.

"By the time I had covered half a mile I was beginning to flag, for I was used to riding, not running, but by that time, too, I was hearing the sounds of men's raised voices ahead of me where there should have been none. And then I heard hoofbeats coming directly towards me through a dense copse of bushes and I crouched behind the trunk of a tree, hoping that the rider would break cover close enough for me to bring him down. He did, and I was able to grab his reins and unseat him. I was about to stab him but I recognized him as one of my own men, a Panonian mercenary called Fallo, who had been with us for years.

"He had a dagger drawn when I attacked him, and he almost killed me before he recognized me, but we were both falling at the time and instead of sticking me in the chest, his blade glanced off my cross-belt and carved a deep trench underneath my left arm. I bled like a pig and we had to scramble to stop the bleeding, for he had hit a large vein, but while he was tending to me he told me all he had seen.

"Childebertus was dead. That was the main thing Fallo had to tell me. No doubt of it, he said. He had seen the King die with his own eyes. The guards had been overwhelmed in silence, for the most part, struck down by arrows from a distance, but some of the arrows—one of them aimed at Fallo—had missed their marks and the alarm was raised. By then the enemy was already charging into the encampment in force, thundering hard on the heels of the volley of arrows, a solid body of horsemen designed to ride down and obliterate anyone left standing. Fallo and three others that he knew of had fallen back to the encampment, managing to keep ahead of the enemy, and it was as he ran towards the center of the camp that Fallo saw Childebertus at the entrance of his tent, half-naked and clutching a sword and shield.

"Before he could even shout a warning, Fallo saw a horseman dressed entirely in black gallop out from between two tents and bear down on your father, the horse's shoulder striking him and hurling him backwards, to hit and rebound from the side of his own tent then fall over a guy rope and sprawl on his face, his sword jarred from his hand. Clearly stunned by the force of the fall, your father then started to struggle to his knees, but the figure in black was already leaping down from his horse, swinging a heavy one-handed axe over his head. Fallo was still ten paces distant when the rider buried his axe between the kneeling King's shoulders. Your father died then and there, but his killer worked the axe head free and then tried to sever his head, moving around him to the side and starting to take careful aim with his upraised weapon. He didn't even see Fallo coming, and by the time he noticed him he was too late to escape. It was his head, not your father's, that fell from its trunk. And even as he killed the man, Fallo recognized him."

Chulderic stopped abruptly, his jaw set, and reined in his horse, staring through narrowed eyes into some scene that was forever closed to me.

"It frightened him at first, he said, to recognize the whoreson because the fellow was supposed to be already dead, killed a year earlier. The man was Merofled, who had once been Clodas's closest crony and husband of the supposedly widowed Sabina. Fallo had struck off his head with one wild sword blow, and although he knew not how, he sensed nonetheless that this man's identity was important and should be witnessed. But even as he scrambled to pick up the severed head he was attacked by other newcomers and almost died there beside your father. He forgot about Merofled's head then and concentrated instead on saving his own. First two, then five assailants surrounded him, but he managed to cut his way out of the circle and escape, aided by the fact that several of his attackers quit fighting him to join another group who had entered the central tent and captured your mother. Unable to help her—he told me she had been surrounded by more than a dozen men and I believed him— Fallo stole one of their horses, but in fighting to mount it he had to leave behind his sword when it stuck fast in the body of the last man he killed."

Chulderic kicked his horse into motion again. "So, there it was, the entire conundrum in a nutshell, although I could not see it even then. As Fallo spoke the words that bared it all, the connection between Merofled and his 'widowed' wife passed over my head, leaving no impression. I was stunned by everything he had told me . . . stunned, I will admit, into something approaching mindlessness. When I heard Fallo's description of what he had seen, the horror of what he was telling me left me fighting to draw breath, as empty inside as though my guts had been scooped right out. The sudden knowledge of these brutal deaths—your father's and your mother's—hit me as a personal judgment and condemnation. It was a crippling, punishing confirmation of my own worst fears and it was simply too much to absorb at one time.

"It did not occur to me at all then, for example, that your mother might have survived the capture that Fallo had described to me. And it certainly hadn't yet come to me that the attackers were Clodas's men—how, before it actually occurred, could such a monstrosity even have been conceivable? Certainly, when Fallo spoke Merofled's name, my mind tried to form some kind of explanation for his unexpected presence—I remember thinking that the reports of his death must have been in error; he must have been captured and not killed, and thereafter been held hostage to some monstrous threat.

"I had some addled notion in my head, I remember, that the attackers were some kind of Outlanders, some ragtag invading force of barbarian adventurers from the far north, beyond the Rhine. I had half-formed visions in my mind of towheaded, blond-bearded savages carrying enormous axes and heavy shields. But then I remembered that Fallo had only seen one axe, a single-handed one, wielded by Merofled, who was no Outlander. Even then, I realized later, stunned and disoriented as I was, I was beginning, deep in my mind, to sense the presence of evil.

"The deep wound in my arm from Fallo's dagger was not making my problems any less difficult. The bleeding finally stopped, however, thanks to the pressure of the wadded bandage Fallo had strapped around my arm using one of my several belts. He was in better condition than I was, so I rode and he led me back cautiously towards our former encampment. I was fretting at his caution, but it proved worthwhile, for there were large numbers of enemy troops among the woods. Fortunately, they were all leaving, and there was that air of flattened calm about them that affects all of us after the terror of heavy fighting.

"We stopped and concealed ourselves in a dense thicket within a quarter mile of the camp and remained there for almost half an hour, watching as the last of them drifted away into the woods, heading northwards. I had been watching those of them who had approached us, but none had come close enough for me to examine closely, and yet there was something that I felt I should be seeing, something that was plainly there but was eluding me. It was annoying, like the buzzing of an insect in the night, clearly heard but unseen.

"When they were all safely gone, we ventured out and made our way into the camp, where we found your father's headless body, but no sign at all of your mother the Queen. We searched high and low, hoping to find her safely hidden somewhere in the surrounding area, but in the end we found no trace of her and were left wondering what had become of her.

"Whoever these attackers were, they had taken your father's head as a trophy, for his was the only corpse that had been mutilated that way. His and Merofled's, if Fallo was to be believed. But there was no sign of Merofled on the killing field, other than a great outpouring of blood at the spot where Fallo said he had struck off the butcher's head, and the man in whose body Fallo had left his sword had vanished, too. All of the bodies of the enemy fallen had been removed, in fact, the dead as well as the wounded, and only a few slaughtered defenders and two dead horses remained sprawled in the clearing that had housed the camp. Our dead, and the far-flung ring of perimeter guards, had fallen where they stood and fought. I sat light-headed and reeling in my saddle, blinking at the sights that surrounded me, aware that something was wrong but unable to identify what it was. It was Fallo who finally defined it.

" 'They took all their dead,' he pointed out to me. 'Everything. Weapons, gear, trappings from the horses. Everything.' I remember agreeing with him and being aware that I was swaying drunkenly, and my tongue was threatening not to do my bidding, so I articulated my words very precisely. 'Why would they do that, think you?'

"'To hide who they are. They don't want anyone to know who did this.'

"That sobered me slightly, making me concentrate more closely. 'Who are they, then?'

"Fallo looked at me as though I were dull-witted. 'They're Clodas's people,' he said. 'Didn't you recognize them?'

"I remember I scoffed at him, unable or unwilling to really appreciate what he was saying.

"'Then why was Merofled there?' he demanded. 'Clodas's strong right arm. Where has he been hiding for the past year? Those were his men. Did you not see their uniforms? Black tunics and black leather; no insignia. That's Merofled's mercenaries.'

"Suddenly, crushingly, I saw the truth of what he was telling me and everything fell into place. Merofled's 'death' had been no more than a subterfuge to prepare the way for his grieving widow to be introduced into Childebertus's household and into Elaine's trust. No one, of course, could have known in advance that Elaine's milk would dry up; the fact that it had, I quickly realized, was merely a fortunate bonus from the viewpoint of the plotters. They had spent long hours plotting their designs and must have laid careful plans to have Sabina's baby 'die' and then be cared for by someone else for long enough to leave its mother free and piteously qualified to assist Elaine with her still-living child. Sabina's child, then, was yet alive today, as had been her husband, which meant that Sabina was a treacherous, duplicitous whore, set in place to betray the entire household that had welcomed her into their lives, and specifically instructed to lure and seduce me away from the path of my duty, thereby leaving the way free for murderers and rapists to glut themselves in this orgy of slaughter.

"How easy had it been for her to influence the family, given the compassion they had felt for her and the position of total trust they had accorded her? Hers had been the voice goading Childebertus to spend some time alone with his wife and son, and she had used her seductive wiles on me to bring me to acceptance of many things that I would never otherwise have countenanced, all of which had made her foul task easier. And now Childebertus and Elaine were dead and you, their son, were gone, stolen away, if not killed, by the person who had engineered this entire catastrophe.

"Within moments I was riding Fallo's horse hard back to where I had left you and the woman, more than a mile away. Every vestige of weakness and sickness had disappeared from me and I rode like a man possessed by demons, thinking as I went that you were already dead, for I saw nothing strange in the thought of Sabina killing you out of hand—the callousness with which she had arranged the death of your parents made the additional killing of a mere brat insignificant. So convinced was I that she had killed you that I heard myself wailing as I went, aware that it was me making the noise, but that it did not sound like me. I had yelled to Fallo to find another horse and follow me, but I didn't know if he would and in truth he was the least of my concerns.

"My horse broke from the woods into the open meadow where I had left you both and I headed it directly for the place where I had last seen you, hoping, I suppose, to find some traces of your presence there, some spoor that I could follow. And there you were, alive and alone in the grass, tightly wrapped in your swaddling clothes, your face twisted in rage as you howled out your outrage at being left abandoned and unable to move. I almost fell from the saddle, leaping down, and I did fall flat on my face when I bent over to try to pick you up. So for a time I simply lay there beside you, listening to you scream and thinking it the sweetest music I might ever hear."

4

The muffled sounds of our horses' hooves seemed very loud after that, neither of us having anything further to say, but while I found myself intrigued by the thought of Chulderic finding a baby's screams enjoyable, I drew no pleasure from thinking of myself as a screaming infant. And so I rode head down and waited, while counting twice from one to twenty, for him to resume his tale. When he did not, I kneed my mount slightly closer to him.

"What about Sabina, Magister? Where had she gone? Did you ever see her again?"

"Oh yes, and far sooner than she had thought to be seen. She had worn a brilliant yellow scarf that day, when we set out to walk, and I had admired it greatly. Now, when I finally sat up and took you in my arms to try to soothe you, I saw it in the distance—a flash of brilliant yellow in a clump of brambles. It was obvious at first glance that Sabina had lost it without being aware of it, because it hung motionless among the thorns and it blazed like a beacon, showing which way she had gone, so I went to collect it, taking you with me.

"I reached the spot without difficulty, but the ground there, on which the brambles grew, was wet and muddy, almost a swamp, and it was immediately plain to me that Sabina had lost her scarf in falling. There were clear marks where her feet had slipped on the treacherous path and the unmistakable imprint where her body had landed in the mud. She had scrambled to her feet, leaving distinct hand prints where she had pushed herself upright, and had then begun to run, the spaces between her footprints almost twice as far apart as they had been before she had lost her balance.

"Curious about why she should suddenly start to run at that particular point, I followed the track she had taken, walking for about four hundred paces until the path began to drop down the hillside into a little valley, and suddenly there she was, leaning against one of a cluster of three boulders in a depression about fifty paces below me, by the side of the track. Fortunately, you had long since stopped crying, probably lulled by the movement of my carrying you, so I stopped as soon as she came into view, and stood there on tiptoe, looking down at her.

"There was something urgent and anxious about the way she was standing, rising tensely every now and then to peer along the track leading downwards to her right, and I realized that she must be waiting for her husband, Merofled, to come and find her. I was immediately swept by a surge of anger and revulsion, and a strong desire to confront her, and so I began to look for a place to set you down. I knew there was no need to hurry, since Merofled would not be coming, and so I began to retrace my steps, and as I walked and searched I saw Fallo and someone else approaching me on horseback. I moved quickly then, waving them to silence as they drew near. The newcomer was Quentin, another of Germanus's veterans, and I signaled them to dismount and quickly told them what I intended to do.

"Sabina did not hear us approach until I spoke to her, and then she leapt like a frightened deer and tried to run, but Quentin was ready for her and tripped her, bringing her down hard before she could go five paces. He and Fallo then pulled her up again, holding one arm each, and brought her back to face me. To her credit, little though it was, she made no attempt to plead or to placate me; she knew by looking at my face that I knew what she had done. When I told her of Merofled's real death at Fallo's hand, however, every trace of color drained from her face and she would have fallen had the two men flanking her not held her up. I realized then that she had loved her husband and the knowledge that she could truly have a capacity for love and yet be capable of the crime she had committed that day hardened me inside even more than I had been.

"I asked her directly why, having murdered your father and mother, she had left you alive, but then I answered the question myself because the truth had just come to me: she had not killed you, but she had left you to die. Her response to that astonished me, however, because it was emphatic and obviously genuine. Your mother's death, she told me, was a nonsense, talk fit only for a fool. No one sought her death and it had no value to anyone. The most important aspect of all that had taken place this day had been the specific requirement to *protect* Elaine of Ganis. Capturing her alive had been the entire purpose of this venture. Clodas had coveted the woman since he first set eyes on her, she said, and had convinced himself he would make a far better consort for Elaine, Queen of Ganis, than would her wealthy, gullible fool of a husband,

Outlander that he was. The plot that evolved thereafter had centered upon a clean and clear-cut intent: to separate Childebertus from his supporters and kill him swiftly and efficiently, along with his child . . . the sex of the child had been unknown while the plot was taking shape and was of no importance. What was important was that Elaine should be free of encumbrances from her past life when her abductors took her to Clodas, who would protect and console her and see to her safety thereafter. I swear to you, I listened to her talk and wondered whether she was mad and Clodas was mad, or whether it was I who had lost my sanity.

"But then I stopped thinking such thoughts and questioned her more thoroughly, seeking the truth, incredible as it might be to hear.

"Sabina's pregnancy had been fortuitous, occurring at the same time as Elaine's, and it was that coincidence that had precipitated the basic idea behind the entire plot. Clodas and Merofled had conceived the plan and had persuaded Sabina to work with them. Clodas had pointed out to her that the rewards would be great, with Merofled benefiting greatly by the takeover of Childebertus's cavalry, and he had guaranteed her that her own child would be well looked after during the few months when she would be away from him.

"Everything had gone according to plan, she told me, except that at the final moment, when it came time to kill the child, she had not been able to. She had grown too fond of you. And so she had left you in the meadow, alive for the time being and with, she believed, a good chance of being found and rescued. But your mother, she swore, was very definitely not dead.

"By the time she finished talking I was gazing at her open-mouthed, appalled at the depth and scope of her self-delusion. Did she—and Clodas, for that matter—honestly imagine that Elaine of Ganis would ever be grateful for the murder of her husband and their son? They would have to be insane to think such a thing. And what about Elaine's father, King Garth? Was Clodas stupid enough to think that Garth of Ganis would not react to these atrocities with a war of total vengeance?

"I remember her expression grew sullen at the mention of Garth's name and I felt my stomach suddenly grow heavy. Garth was already dealt with, she said, although she had had no part in that aspect of the arrangements and had no knowledge of how his death might have been brought about. She knew only that he was marked to die as part of this day's activities. If Elaine was to be Queen of Ganis—as she would be upon the death of her father— Clodas would be King, by right of conquest as well as by right of being wed to the Queen. And once the old man was dead, Elaine's attitude to Clodas would make no whit of difference to anything. They would be wed, by force if need be, and thereafter she would be his.

"Hearing the indifferent tone of the woman's words, the soulless knell of their disinterest, I turned my back on her and gazed up to the hilltop from where I had first seen her hiding down here, and then I told her what was in my mind. I did not look at her again as I spoke, but I knew she heard every word I uttered.

"I told her that there were laws in Ganis, and in Gaul, to deal with people like her and the atrocious acts that they committed and conspired to cause. I told her that she deserved to be tried and sentenced by the proper regal authorities. And I told her, too, that in the absence of such authorities—an absence caused by her personal actions and intent—she was therefore being tried and duly condemned to death, in accordance with the law, by the next level of power within the State, that power being the military, represented by me as Master-at-Arms of the Kingdom of Ganis. I then turned to face her and nodded to her guards, who had been waiting for my signal.

"Fallo and Quentin forced her to her knees, and then, while Quentin held her arms stretched stiffly at her back, her wrists twisted and locked to prevent her struggling, Fallo undid her long hair and pulled it out in front of her, gripping the tresses firmly in both hands and pulling forward and down, hard, to stretch out her neck. Only then did she begin to believe what I had told her, and her voice grew ever more frantic as she pleaded with me, offering to give me everything a man could desire of a woman . . . everything I had dreamed of before but would never yearn for again."

He paused, biting gently at his upper lip, then turned his eyes on me again, and I could see him taking in my size and, I realized later, my age. "You have no idea of what I mean, boy, but you soon will . . . Aye, soon enough you will." He lapsed into silence again, his gaze sliding away from me to stare, unfocused, at something only he could see.

"My sword was a *spatha,* a long, slender cavalry sword, as you know, intended for stabbing. But I kept it razor sharp and a woman has a very thin neck compared to a man's. She died as her husband had died, her head severed with one blow."

I had been expecting something of the kind, but nevertheless I was left feeling breathless when he spoke the words, perhaps because of the matter-of-fact way in which he delivered them. I could feel my eyes growing round with incredulity and what I can only think of now as consternation.

"You killed her, with your own hands? But you said you loved her! How could you do that, if you loved her?"

"I said I fell in love with her. That is a very different thing from loving her, boy. A boy will love his mother and his grandmother, his aunts and all his sisters, but the feelings that he feels for all of them will be nothing to the feelings he endures when he falls in love with a woman. Falling in love and loving someone are not at all the same. That, too, you will learn someday. But even as you are now, at ten years old, think you I should have spared her?"

That question left me open-mouthed, silenced between the need to scream out "Yes" and the realization that we were discussing the woman responsible for my mother's death. I was unaware of speaking but I must have whispered something of what was going through my mind, because Chulderic answered me.

"No, not responsible, not completely. It was Clodas who was responsible from the outset—his malevolent envy gave birth to the idea—but he could not have achieved what he did without Sabina.

She didn't handle any sharpened weapons that day, but the lethal honey of her coaxing words to both your parents had been more venomous than any poisoned blade could ever have been, and her deliberate seduction of me, undermining my sense of duty and propriety and enabling me to be false to my own code, was malicious and premeditated. And so I killed her without compunction."

I sat silent, absorbing that, then nodded. "That was just. But what about my grandfather, King Garth?"

Chulderic shook his head, as though dismissing my question. "The woman was right. Garth was already dead, that same morning. The previous night, while Merofled was moving into striking range of where we were camped, Clodas himself had arrived at King Garth's door, accompanied by an escort of his mercenaries, telling Garth that he was on his way to visit a cousin who lived in a neighboring territory to the north of Garth's own lands. Garth took him in and made him and his escort welcome without demur or question, secure in the knowledge that Clodas's father, Dagobert, had been one of his oldest and dearest friends. During the night Clodas's people rose up in the darkness and one group killed the old king while he slept, overwhelming his guards easily, since none of them expected any danger. And while they were attending to King Garth, others of their number were busy slaughtering the King's strongest leaders, all of this planned and practiced, with nothing left to chance, so that come morning there was no one left alive who might have rallied the forces of Ganis to withstand the usurper. It was done and over with. Clodas was King of Ganis before the outrage was visited upon your parents later that same day.

"I refused to believe what the woman had told me, hoping against hope that something might have served to warn and therefore save Garth and his people, and so I set out with Fallo, Quentin and some others we had found to ride to warn the King of what had happened, and I had you with me, carefully wrapped and tied into a saddle bag that was strapped across my shoulders. But before we had traveled halfway, the word met us coming from Ganis. The King was dead; Clodas had claimed the throne; his army, far larger than the mercenary force your father had provided the previous spring, had moved into Ganis early that morning in overwhelming numbers; everything was chaos and the King's leaderless army had been disarmed and rendered useless.

"I immediately pulled our little party off the road. We had nowhere to go that might be safe for us, and none of us was of the type that would consider surrendering to Clodas. Besides, we had a nursing infant with us and no way to feed him. Much as I hated having to take the time to do so, I rode apart from the others and sat down alone to concentrate on what we should do next. Your life and safety was my first priority, above and beyond all other considerations. My negligence had made you an orphan, I believed, for I did not know yet that your mother had survived. Now you were the only living remnant of your family's blood, and I knew my immortal salvation depended upon my keeping you alive, to grow to manhood and claim vengeance for your parents' deaths. I had never been more than a nominal Christian until that point, but I became devout thereafter, for a while, believing that I had to expiate my sin of negligence."

"So what did you do, Magister?"

"D'you remember my mentioning Antonia, the other Roman woman who had lost her baby?"

I nodded, wondering what she could have to do with any of this, and he grunted. "Aye, well, I remembered her, too, and I went searching for her, hoping that she might still be in milk, for months had elapsed since I last saw her. She was not difficult to find, for she yet lived in the same house, and she was still producing milk like a brood cow, for she had taken in another baby, younger than you, whose mother had died at the birthing. She remembered me, and when I told her what had transpired with you she volunteered immediately to take you into care. I left you with her and rode off to see what might be done about Clodas and his treachery."

"Did you fight him?"

"Fight him? I could not draw within a mile of him. He was surrounded by his own people, all of them heavily armed and far more vigilant than I had ever seen before in such a large body of men. Their lord and master had just committed a series of heinous sins, including regicide and the mass slaughter of people who had shown him nothing but kindness. It was reasonable to assume that someone would come seeking vengeance and redress sooner or later, and that the avengers might come from any direction, and so the new 'King' had let it be known that he would be openhanded in rewarding any who identified such trouble in advance of its occurrence. Naturally, every man in his army and not a few of Garth's former people were anxious to qualify for such rewards.

"I had to split my group asunder, to take their chances each man for himself, for had anyone seen us together and failed to recognize us as allies, or, God forbid, had seen and recognized us as Childebertus's men, we would all have died instantly.

"I remained in Clodas's camp for more than a week, asking questions, learning little and watching what was going on, and as the days passed I grew more and more discouraged. I discovered that your mother was, in fact, alive but was being kept under constant guard. Clodas, I was told, took pains to visit her twice each day, morning and afternoon, between sessions of governing. That information surprised me, for it had not occurred to me that Clodas might actually seek to *govern* Garth's kingdom, but as I watched the comings and goings of the various identifiable officials thereafter, I found myself admitting, however reluctantly, that Clodas was far more of an organizer and administrator than I would ever have believed before that time.

"By the end of ten days I was forced to accept that I was powerless, as things stood, to do anything to revenge myself on Clodas—I had been entertaining fantasies of sneaking into his quarters and waking him up, making sure he knew who I was and why he was about to die, and then slitting his throat. I was equally incapable of doing anything to help your mother in her captivity, for my face was too well known for me to risk discovery trying to approach the quarters where she was being held.

"That's when I decided to ride south to Benwick and enlist Ban's aid in rescuing your mother. But then, before I could leave, your mother took her own life. They told her you were dead, and presented her with evidence of what they said, and that took all the will to live away from her."

"What kind of evidence?" What, I wondered, could Clodas have said or done to convince my mother of my death while I was yet alive? Such is the innocence of extreme youth.

"The foulest kind," Chulderic replied. "False evidence. She had been grieving deeply for your father, I was told by my informants. I had made a few good contacts during my stay among Clodas's forces and had ample access to information, but none of it was straightforward. My informants, apart from being the enemy, were not close associates of Clodas but simple soldiers, with all the limitations that entails.

"From their conversations I knew that Clodas's prisoner had been prepared to suffer and wait, as long as she believed her son was safe and alive. She believed, too, that Ban of Benwick, her sister's husband, would ride to her rescue. That would take time, she knew, but she was so confident that he would come that she made no secret of it, warning everyone what would happen to them when her brother-in-law came to Ganis.

"Clodas must have heard of this, and connected it with her belief that you had survived his plotting. He did not know you had survived, in fact, but he knew your mother believed you had, and so he told her you had been slain that same afternoon when your father died; that your nurse Sabina had arranged the trap and led them into it.

"Your mother refused to believe that Sabina would be capable of killing you, after having suckled you for months, and of course Clodas could not present Sabina to prove it one way or the other. But three days later, he had one of his creatures present your mother with the dirt-encrusted corpse of an infant that had been butchered and left in a shallow grave for days. It was the same age as you and had your coloring, but otherwise it was not identifiable. Apparently the mere sight of it was sufficient, however, to unhinge your mother's mind, and she hanged herself that same night, with the cord from one of her robes.

"Even Clodas's own were disgusted by that piece of work. No one knew who the child had been or where he came from, and many of them thought it truly was Elaine's own child, but it was common knowledge among some of Clodas's troops that the word had come down to find a suitable child and use it a-purpose.

"That was the night before I heard the tale whispered around a campfire, and the talk was all of Clodas's anger after she was found dead. They said that he was livid with anger, but that no one had dared to ask him why he was so surprised, after what he had done to the hapless woman. Anyway, his fury was ungovernable, and he had all of her guards executed within an hour of hearing the report of her death, even those who had not been on duty that night. He then rode off, still raging, with a small group of his closest cronies and did not return that night. I waited two more days, but he still had not returned and there was no way of knowing when he might even be expected.

"That evening I went back to Antonia and told her everything I had discovered. She listened carefully, asked several questions mainly concerning you, then made arrangements to have another woman take care of feeding the infant she had previously adopted. Then she volunteered to accompany me back to Benwick, nursing you along the way. I felt greatly honored by her commitment to you, an unknown orphan, and accepted her offer immediately.

"Sadly, however, the journey from Ganis to Benwick grew into an odyssey of many months, much of the time spent avoiding wandering bands of brigands and marauders. Antonia barely survived it. She fell ill along the way and died shortly after we arrived safely in Benwick."

I interrupted him with a comment that had just sprung into my mind. "So all the women in your story died."

"What did you say?" Chulderic reined in his horse and sat blinking at me in what I took to be astonishment, but then his eyebrows rose even higher than they had been and he began to nod his head, hesitantly at first and then with more conviction. "Yes," he said. "Yes, by God, you're right. They did, all of them. I've never realized that before. Never even thought of it. They all died."

We rode without speaking after that, each of us with his own thoughts, and soon we were back on the outskirts of the castle lands. With what I have always thought of since then as the resilience of youth, I felt no desire to ask any more questions about my parents' death. I had asked, and I had been told, and I felt satisfied that I now knew the truth, but I felt no grief. How could I? I had never known Childebertus and his beautiful wife. They were mere names to me, people in a tale. I was fully aware, nevertheless, that the tale involved me and that I had an obligation to bring their murderer to justice.

I knew, too, that when I finally brought him to justice, the kingdom of Ganis that Clodas now ruled would become mine, by right of blood and birthright, but I was not yet concerned about that.

One more question remained to be asked of Chulderic, and I broached it as we approached the castle walls. "Magister Chulderic?"

It was the first time either one of us had spoken in almost half an hour, and the Master-at-Arms turned his head towards me and cocked one eyebrow. "Aye?"

"What can you tell me of Germanus?"

"Germanus, is it? Know him well, do you? Most people nowadays call him Bishop Germanus. Those of us who have known him long enough call him General Germanus, or simply the General. No one else that I know calls him plain Germanus. Where did you gain that right?"

"Pardon me." I was duly abashed. "I did not mean to sound disrespectful. It's just that my father says I am to go away with him, to Auxerre, to study. I have never been away from home and I had never heard of Bishop Germanus until last night, so I hoped you might tell me what you know about him."

"Well, lad, I can't. I know you are to go away with him when he comes, and I know you'll miss your home at first. But you won't pine for long and you will never regret meeting General

Germanus. He is probably the finest man I ever met, including your father, but I only say that because your father died before he could achieve the things he wanted to achieve. The General, on the other hand, has had far more time to do what he has done, and he has done it all wondrously.

"Your father and Ban and the General were friends, but it began with your father and General Germanus. You see, they were all patrician . . . you know what that means? It's all a matter of birth and breeding, who you are and where you were born, wealth and manners and education. I was a simple soldier, as I told you earlier, privileged to be included among their number, but I was never completely at ease with them, off duty.

"Germanus, he was five or six years older than me, and rich as an emperor. His family was an ancient and honored clan in northern Gaul, and Germanus was married to a cousin of the Emperor Honorius himself. He had been trained for a military career but he'd felt called to study law and he'd ended up as a successful lawyer in Rome. Honorius changed all that when he ordered him to take up soldiering . . . well, he asked him, really, according to Germanus, but who's going to say no to an Emperor? Anyway, he needed someone to look after his interests back in Germanus's home territories in Gaul, and he thought his friend Germanus was the very man for the job. Germanus's young wife had died, along with her infant, in childbirth, and Germanus was so distraught, his friends were afraid he might lock himself away from the world. Army was the best thing that could have happened to him.

"So just bear in mind he's a bishop, but he's also a warrior, and one of the best, so he'll train your body and your fighting skills as well as he'll train your mind. Here, we're back and I have matters to attend to. Is there anything else you want to ask before I leave you?"

I shook my head, knowing I would never again walk in terror of the Master-at-Arms. I would respect him more than ever after today, but having seen beneath the grim facade he wore habitually, I would never again fear him. "No, Magister," I told him, and thanked him for his patience and forbearance that afternoon.

He nodded courteously and wished me well in Auxerre, after which he turned and rode away, making his way to the castle stables. I watched him until he rounded the edge of the curtain wall fronting the main gates, and I did not set eyes on him again for six more years.

FATHER GERMANUS

1

It has been a matter of astonishment to me throughout my adult life that, having spent no more than half a day in the company of Chulderic, King Ban's Master-at-Arms, I can recall everything he said to me, practically verbatim, and yet when it comes to speaking of my great tutor and mentor Germanus, the renowned Bishop of Auxerre, I often find myself ready to gnash my teeth with fury and frustration because I can remember so little with any clarity. Certainly I can remember incidents, and when I push myself towards recalling those in detail I can sometimes remember the surrounding circumstances quite accurately, but overall I have no sense of any flow of *time* in those recollections, as though my years with the bishop comprised no more than a series of unconnected incidents. I am aware of a series of lacunae in my memory—holes and spaces and missing parts that prevent me from having any solid conviction of wholeness in my relationship with the saintly bishop.

Saintly is not an inappropriate word to use in describing Germanus of Auxerre, for before he ever came into my life, men and women were already speaking in awe of his sanctity, his holiness and goodness. It was public knowledge that early in his first years as Bishop of Auxerre he had cast out demons from a man who had stolen large amounts of money, and in the process of the exorcism had forced the demon to divulge the place where the hoard was concealed—these events had taken place openly and were witnessed by many people, and the results had been indisputable.

Ever since that time, the bishop had been besieged by people seeking cures for illnesses and possession, and he had performed many miracles on behalf of his flock. I was not surprised, then, that within months of his death people had already begun speaking of him as *Saint* Germanus. Whether or not the bishop truly *was* a saint, however, I find myself unqualified to judge, precisely because it was Germanus himself who taught me never to presume to make moral judgments, since those were the sole property of God to make or unmake.

I am content to remember him as my mentor, my teacher and my guide, and latterly my friend. I have never known a time when I did not have cause to be grateful for the example he set me, the lessons he taught me and the principles he instilled in me. The man I grew to become could never have existed or behaved as he did had it not been for the direct influence of Germanus of Auxerre. And that conviction, that certitude that he shaped and molded me to be what I was and what I am today, is the major reason why I find it so galling that I can remember so little of our time together.

Germanus grew to be a constant in my life, the dominating force behind my mental and physical growth for the seven years that followed Chulderic's single day of tuition and enlightenment, and as in the lives of all growing boys, the majority of the mundane events and ordinary, undistinguished times in those seven years have long since been forgotten, leaving only the high points and grand events to be remembered.

As King Ban had told me he would, Germanus arrived at our gates within the month, accompanied by a small retinue, and on the night of his arrival, before dinner, King Ban summoned me to his private quarters to meet my new guardian. As I made my way to the King's chambers, I visualized some kind of wizened cleric, stooped with piety and learning, long-bearded and wearing a high, pointed hat. It was only long months later that I realized I had been visualizing a sorcerer, the image dredged up from some half-forgotten memory of someone else's story told over a fire on a winter's night. The reality was radically different.

The Lady Vivienne emerged from her own chamber to meet me as I entered the long suite of rooms she shared with the King, and she immediately stopped me and took my hands, holding me out at arm's length as she examined my appearance. She turned my hands over and inspected my palms, then turned them back and peered closely at my fingernails, and only when she had satisfied herself that I had bathed that day and was fit to present to an important guest did she nod and ruffle my hair before leading me into the room where King Ban sat talking with Bishop Germanus.

I knew this had to be Germanus the moment I set eyes on him because there was no one else in the room, and that was very unusual. Whenever King Ban entertained guests there were always other people around—advisers and military personnel and other dignitaries—to share the burden of amusing and engaging the visitor and to act as cushions between King and guests on those few occasions when the situation grew strained, difficult or tiresome. No such situation, I knew, could possibly arise with Germanus, an old and much-loved friend.

Ban heard us as soon as the doors swung open and he rose to his feet to greet us. His guest rose at the same time, and my first impressions of him were confusing. He was nowhere near as tall as Ban, nor was he quite as broad across the shoulders, and he was far, far older than the King, yet he struck me immediately as being by far the larger of the two men. It would be years before I encountered the concept of *presence* as it applied to some people, but even although I had no notion of what it was when I first saw Germanus of Auxerre, I was awestruck by my immediate awareness that here was someone larger than life. Rising to his feet beside the King, he seemed to *loom* over Ban, though he was neither as large as Ban was nor as magnificently dressed. He simply radiated appeal, filling the room with it and demanding the attention of anyone and everyone who entered.

He certainly claimed all my attention from the moment I set eyes on him, and I watched in open-mouthed admiration as he strode across the room to greet the Lady Vivienne, his face beaming in a wide-mouthed grin of sheer pleasure. He had no time for me at that moment; all his attention was focused tightly upon his hostess, whom he had not seen, I gathered, since his arrival. As I stared, amazed, he threw his arms about her and hugged her in a very *unbishoply* manner—that word, which sprang newborn into my mind as I watched him, has remained in my vocabulary ever since. Effortlessly, and despite his advanced age, he lifted her clear of the ground and spun her around, kissing her soundly on both cheeks as he told her how happy he was to see her again after so long a time. He then placed her firmly back on her feet and did much the same thing to her as she had done to me mere moments earlier: he held her out at arm's length, her fingertips in his, in order to examine her from head to toe, and then proceeded to heap compliments and blandishments upon every aspect of her appearance, from her gown and veil to her complexion and her hair. The Queen preened with pleasure and her husband the King stood smiling like a man besotted.

But then it was over, suddenly, before I was ready, and he had somehow guided Queen Vivienne into a deep chair and turned the full force of his gaze upon me. I can still recall the sensation of falling that filled me as those eyes met mine; it was akin to the sensation you experience when swinging widely on a hanging rope, far out over water that is deep and still beneath you. Germanus looked at me, and all the gaiety and humor faded from his face to be replaced by an expression I could not decipher. I could almost feel the weight of his scrutiny as his eyes moved up and down and across my body, and in a vain attempt to disguise the effect it was having on me I busied myself in looking back at him, absorbing the details of his appearance.

He was dressed completely in white, which did not surprise me, white being the color of purity and sanctity, according to my step-mother, the Queen. It seemed appropriate to me, in my ten-year-old wisdom, that God's bishop should be dressed in white. The high, pointed hat I had expected was nowhere to be seen, however, and I was observant enough to be able to tell from the condition of the bishop's hair that he had not been wearing a hat at all: it was thick and curly, on the white edge of silvery gray, and he wore it cropped short in the military fashion. He was clean shaven that particular day, although I was to see him bearded as often as not in the years that lay ahead, and his skin was darkened to the color of old bronze by the summer sun. He wore some kind of heavy woolen stole across his shoulders, its ends trailing in front of him and held loosely in place by the bend of his elbows, and beneath that his body was encased from neck to ankles in a long, plain robe of heavy white cloth, belted at the waist with a thick length of white silken rope and otherwise unadorned. Beneath the hem of that long white garment, however, revealed as he spun around holding the Queen, I had seen heavy, black, thick-soled military boots.

"So," he said finally, his eyes fixed now on mine. "You are Clothar, son of Childebertus and Elaine." I waited, not knowing how to respond and not quite daring to glance at my foster parents for guidance. Then slowly Germanus held out his right hand, palm up and fingers extended, and I stepped forward and stretched out my own, palm downward. His long fingers closed around mine, warm and supple, yet callused as though from long, hard work. Still looking deep into my eyes, he smiled and nodded. "I knew your grandfather Jacob, you know, in Constantinople. He was a friend of mine, a very good friend, although he was far more than twice my age. He came from Britain. Jacobus was his Roman name, but everyone called him Jacob. He was a lawyer, and so was I, although he was a famous arbitrator with a lifetime of triumphs behind him by then and I was just starting my career. This was long before I met your father—almost a full decade earlier, as a matter of fact. I was honored that he chose to befriend me, for his own reasons, and I still am." He nodded again, still smiling. "I didn't meet your father until we were both in the army. Your father was a junior officer, and I was his commanding legate, so had I not known Jacob as well as I did, and then discovered almost by accident that your father was his son, the two of us might never have met, let alone become close friends."

He stared at me steadily for a time, then rested an elbow on the back of his left fist and ran the tip of an index finger down the length of his cheek, a gesture with which I was to become familiar over the next decade, knowing it as an indicator that the bishop was thinking deeply, remembering or considering. "I never knew your father when he was your age, but I can see him in you, as you are. Your grandfather Jacob would have been proud to see you standing there, the image of his own son." He was silent then, looking at me still, pouting slightly so that his lower lip protruded against the tip of his finger. It was clear that he was thinking, but still I could not judge from his expression what kind of thoughts were going through his head.

"You are to come with me when I leave here," he said then, "to be a student in my school in Auxerre. Does that cause you concern?" I managed to shake my head, but could not have spoken had my life depended on it. "You are sure about that, are you not?" I nodded. He turned back to my parents, cocking his head. "You didn't tell me he is mute."

Ban laughed aloud, and even Vivienne smiled. "Oh, he's no mute, believe me," Ban said. "He may be awed by you, for the time being, but that will wear off, and when he finds his tongue again you may end up wishing he were mute indeed."

The bishop turned to me again, an expression in his eyes that might have contained a hint of humor. "Will I?" he asked me. "Are you really that loud? I find that hard to credit. Mind you, your father was known to raise his voice from time to time. Come, sit with us. We have things to talk about before we go down to dine, and once there, there will be too many others talking for us to hear ourselves. Sit, and let me tell you what lies in store for you at Auxerre."

I took the chair he indicated, across from him and between the King and Queen, and for a short time everyone spoke in generalities, as people do when they meet after having been years apart, questing to find topics that will neither strain nor test the relationship they had once known together. Finally, Queen Vivienne asked the bishop the question that turned the conversation towards me.

"What will you teach Clothar, up there in Auxerre, that he will not have touched upon here in Benwick?"

Germanus grinned. "Probably little, if not nothing. The concerns and the materials of education are unchanging—reading and writing, logic, debate, philosophy, science, polemic and geography . . . but the focus of everything will be different, if you can understand what that means?"

The Queen smiled. "I understand completely. You are referring to the scope of things."

"Exactly so, my Lady, simply because of the size of the school and the number of pupils. We have wonderful teachers, most of whom I hired myself after lengthy observation." He turned to me. "I wonder . . . I had better make it clear to you from the outset, Clothar, that although you will be in my charge, I will not be your personal teacher. Did you know that, or did you think you would be under my constant attention?"

Still unwilling to trust my tongue, I merely shook my head again, and he grunted, deep in his throat. "Aye," he said. "Well, that is the way of it. I'll be your confessor, and I will keep a close eye on you and on all your activities, serving as your parents' deputy in a double capacity—on behalf of your real parents, who were my friends, and of your foster parents here, who are no less parents and who remain my friends. You and I will meet privately at least once every week to discuss your progress and your life and anything else demanding our attention, but your actual teaching will be at the hands of others, all of them better tutors than I could ever be. I have my pastoral work, as Bishop of Auxerre, and that, I fear, often consumes more time than I have to spend." He sniffed, thrusting out his lower lip again. "Do you know anything about our school?"

I knew a nod would not serve as a response this time and so I coughed to clear my throat. "No, sir."

The bishop nodded and looked at King Ban and from him to the Lady Vivienne. "And what about you two?"

Ban slowly shook his head.

"There is no reason you should, I suppose. Auxerre is a long way from here . . . But I confess I am disappointed that the fame of our school has failed to penetrate this far."

"Enlighten us, then, dear Germanus—" The Queen stopped short. "Oh, forgive me. Should I be calling you by another name, now that you are a bishop?"

Germanus laughed. "Absolutely not! Call me Germanus as you always have. That's who I am and nothing about me has changed simply because I am become a bishop. Titles are for others. Among friends as old as us, names never change."

The Queen bowed her head, acknowledging the courtesy. "Thank you. Now tell us about this school of yours."

The bishop's face grew sober. "It is a school in the tradition of the ancients, where boys are taught the things they need to know in order to be good men, accepting duty and responsibility."

"What kind of boys attend this school of yours? Are they all the sons of wealthy men?"

Germanus smiled at the Queen, but in answering her he spoke to both of them. "No, not at all, although many of them are. Ours is a school for *boys,* my Lady, not necessarily rich boys. The prime entrance requirement to our ranks is intellect. We are looking to train minds and encourage learning for learning's sake. Our world is changing rapidly nowadays, my friends, and many of the old, time-honored ways of doing things are being forgotten and abandoned. And it pains me to say it, but high among those things ranks the education of our children. Education has fallen out of favor, the need for it seemingly eclipsed by the catastrophes and cataclysms shaking the very foundations of the Empire. In a disintegrating world, people are thinking, there is little need for education."

"Think you the world is coming to an end?" This question from King Ban made my eyes snap wide open. The notion of World's End is a Christian one and Ban was no Christian, and yet here he was, asking the bishop for reassurance.

Germanus shook his head. "Are you referring to the return of the Christ in the Final Judgment? I think not. Not yet. The

Scriptures tell us that the Second Coming lies ahead of us, but they also indicate that much requires to be done before it comes upon us. At least, that is what I believe. The Empire may be facing its end and that would not surprise me, but not the world, I think. Mind you, I may be wrong. No man may know the mind of God and it is blasphemous to presume to do so. But it is the possibility that the world might survive that causes me such great concern over the education of our children. And so we believe—we being the elders and bishops of the Church—that we court disaster if we allow our children to run wild. If we fail to teach them how to read and write and use their minds as God intended, then they and our entire world will fall back into Godless savagery. And so we maintain schools."

"To train clerics for the Church." The Queen's voice was gentle, no hint of censure to be found in it, but Germanus caught the inference.

"Of course," he agreed. "But not exclusively. The world needs more than clerics. It needs leaders—educated, Christian leaders."

"And soldiers." This was Ban.

"Aye, indeed, soldiers, too." The bishop's gaze returned to me. "The King tells me you have the makings of a cavalry soldier. We will build on that. Tiberias Cato, one of our brethren, served with me in the army and saved my life on numerous occasions simply because he is a magnificent horseman—the finest natural rider I have ever known. He, too, knew your father, although not, perhaps, your mother. Cato will supervise your training as a horseman and a cavalryman—I know you know the two are not necessarily the same." His pause was barely perceptible. "You do know that, do you not?"

I swallowed. "Yes, sir."

"And do you know the difference?"

"Yes, sir."

"Excellent. What is it?"

"You can be a horseman without being a cavalryman, but you cannot be a cavalryman without being a horseman."

"Absolutely. Good lad. Anyway, Tiberias Cato was a doughty fighter in his time and now he is a marvelously gifted teacher and trainer, but he is more horse than human at times. He will be responsible for your overall development in military things. There will be others working with you, too, in the various disciplines, but Tiberias will be your primary trainer. He will take whatever talents you possess for horsemanship and polish them until they dazzle even you.

"Apart from that—and it is probably sinful of me to prioritize in such a manner, but the soldier in me frequently fights with the bishop—apart from that, you will study all the other subjects that a well-tutored young man should know. You will learn the rudiments of Greek, sufficient for some of your reading, but for the most part you will be taught in Latin. You will have training in logic, debate and polemics, philosophy, mathematics and geometry, geography and the basic elements of imperial law. Also, you will be living among priests and clerics, and so you will behave for the most part as they do, adhering to the Order of Saint Benedict and observing the prayers and ceremonies he has decreed as being proper for a devout man of any age. You will eat well, three times a day, and in return for your food and lodgings, you will be expected to share the tasks of keeping the school clean and its students well fed. That means you will scrub floors, whitewash walls, wash clothes, grow and gather food, prepare it and serve it to your fellows."

He stopped, frowning at me as he watched my reactions to his words, and then his face broke once again into a wide, friendly grin. "But not all of those at once, I promise you. Each of those tasks will fall to you no more than once a month, for one day at a time. We have cooks and gardeners and carpenters and masons who work full time at their various crafts. You, as a student, will be seconded from time to time to assist them, and that means performing the dirty, heavy work most of the time. So you will be required to work and work hard, but the requirements are not brutal and you will have plenty of time to study and to rest between spells of duty."

He sat gazing at me for long moments, and then he said, "Do you have any questions to ask of me?"

"Yes, sir. What . . . what should I call you?"

He barked a short, deep laugh. "Hah! Straight to the point, and a good question. You'll call me what all your fellows call me: Father Germanus. That's the simplest and most effective name we have been able to come up with, and it has taken us some time to arrive at it. I am no longer an active army officer, so General and Legate are invalid, and I have a personal dislike for the term Bishop used as a name. Magister is another term I dislike, because it bears too many overtones of army life, which is notoriously impious and ungodly. Then there is a movement among some of the Church's adherents nowadays, particularly in the east, towards equality in which all members of a clerical community address each other as Brother. We have a number of men in our community whose use of the title Brother is highly appropriate. These are laymen, devout and pious beyond question, who choose to live lives of service to God and to conduct that service in our community, but they have taken no vows and have not been consecrated to the priesthood. They are Brethren in the Christ and I honor them highly. For a time, I even considered adopting Brother as my title, too, but the truth is that to those who attend my school I am both teacher and superior, and I have no desire to be anything as egalitarian as a brother." He paused and smiled again. "As a bishop, I am the pastor and father of my flock, and as mentor and governor to a school full of boys, I am, *ipso facto,* a fatherly figure. So, like everyone else, you will call me Father Germanus. Have I explained that clearly?"

"Yes, Father Germanus."

For the following half hour, the three adults moved on to speak of other things and I spoke not another word, although I missed nothing of what was being said. Soon, however, we were summoned to dinner by the King's Chancellor, formally dressed in honor of the bishop's visit, and I was banished to sit among the lesser family members in the body of the hall. I made sure to seat myself on the side of the table that permitted me an uninterrupted view of the King and Queen and their guest, however, and I barely took my eyes off my new guardian until they rose again to leave.

I spent the next morning preparing to take my leave of my family and friends, and the time passed by in a blink, so that it was suddenly past noon and I was standing outside the main gates of Ban's castle, holding my horse's reins and awaiting the signal to mount. My belongings were all safely packed and stowed in one of the three wagons in our train, and I had made all my farewells to those I loved, including my old nurse Ludda, Allisan the head cook, who had doted on me since my infancy, and Queen Vivienne herself. All three partings had wrung tears from me, and as I stood there waiting for the signal, I was highly aware of the reddened rims around my eyes.

Finally there came a stirring at the gates and the crowd of onlookers parted to permit the King and Queen to emerge with Germanus. There was nothing *bishoply* about his appearance on this occasion, either. He wore a military-style tunic of rich brown-and-white fabric, kilted above his knees, and sturdy, heavy riding boots with spurs. He wore a heavy cloak of plain brown cloth, too, fastened across his chest with a bronze chain and thrown back over his shoulders. He was bare headed and he carried no weapons, but no one setting eyes on him would ever have mistaken him for anything other than a soldier. A trumpeter on the walls above us blew a salute in response to a signal from King Ban, and we swung away, turning our backs on Benwick and riding—I, at least—into a new and unknown world.

2

I adapted to my new life with all the resilience of any ten-year-old boy, accepting everything that came my way, no matter how new or strange, and adjusting immediately to whatever demands or requirements it entailed. Everything that occurred after we left Benwick was new and alien to some extent, and so I quickly learned to catalogue and categorize each event almost as it occurred, assessing, absorbing and accepting the results, for better or for worse, as part of the way things now were, and I threw myself wholeheartedly into every element of the wondrous adventure that my life had become.

All my life, until arriving in Germanus's new school—the Bishop's School, everyone called it—I had regarded King Ban's castle in Benwick as the pinnacle of privileged living. Here in Auxerre, however, I found that the sumptuous luxury of Germanus's family home beggared description. No matter that Germanus himself was now a pauper, having ceded his houses, wealth and all other possessions to the Church; he yet lived in his own former home as bishop and custodian for the Church, and his beloved school, which he considered his life's work and his greatest endeavor for the glory of God, was housed in another of his family's former dwellings, close to his own house and scarcely less luxurious.

I had grown up accustomed to living in strong stone buildings, but now I found myself living in strong, beautiful and graceful buildings, with multicolored walls of fine marble, polished to the luster of expensive glass. For days after my arrival, I walked in awe of the beauty of my new surroundings, but then, being ten, I grew used to them and forgot that they were any different from other houses anywhere, and I lost myself completely in the strange world of living in a school among other students.

Father Germanus had promised me that I would have fine teachers at his school, and I did. Some of them I loved, some I admired, several I endured and a few I tolerated. I only really disliked one out of all of them, however, and the antipathy I felt for him was reciprocated in full measure. His name was Anthony—he insisted that we call him Brother Anthony—and he and I detested each other from our first encounter. He took exception to something in my face or my deportment the first time I went into his classroom and he went out of his way thereafter to make his dislike of me plain to me and to everyone else, and so in response I found it remarkably easy to find a host of elements to dislike and disparage in him. Since he was the teacher and I the newest, most insignificant student in the school, however, he had, and continued to have, the best of our encounters for a long, long time. Even today, looking back across a chasm of years, I find myself hard put to define what it was about that man that offended me, but I have absolutely no doubt that were he and I to meet again today, never having laid eyes upon each other before, we would react to each other exactly as we did then. Some people simply affect one another that way.

Brother Anthony was a tonsured monk, his head shaved bald to show that he was a slave of God, bound to the Church by vows of poverty, obedience and chastity. Such total commitment was a new custom and indicated an entirely new depth of devotion and dedication, Bishop Germanus himself informed me, but one that was gaining great numbers of adherents throughout the eastern portion of the remaining Empire. The people who took such stringent vows, Germanus said, referred to themselves as monastics, and they sought perfection here on Earth by shunning the earthly vices of avarice, pride and lechery and shutting themselves away from the world and its temptations, living in communes known as monasteries. Germanus himself had taken identical vows of poverty, chastity and obedience, but he was at pains to point out that his reasons for so doing were purely personal and pragmatic, to enable him to concentrate solely upon his episcopal responsibilities. He had no interest in monasticism, he maintained; his ordained place of work was squarely in the world of ordinary men, with all its temptations. He was a bishop, with a flock of faithful dependants relying upon him for guidance and example.

Brother Anthony *was* a monastic and had sworn his vows as such, fully intending to immure himself somewhere far from the world and its temptations, where he could concentrate on keeping his sacred commitments, but he was also a brilliant administrator, trained originally as an imperial legionary quartermaster, and so Bishop Germanus himself had prevailed upon Anthony to postpone his departure and remain for a time in Auxerre, tending to Germanus's episcopal accounts and supervising inventories of everything required to keep the bishop's domestic affairs functioning.

Anthony had agreed, and in the brief periods of time left to him between his work and his prayers, he also taught divinity and theology to the students of the episcopal school. He was an able and gifted servant, very pious and devout, the bishop said on many occasions, and whenever I heard him say it, I nodded. Deep within myself, however, I knew that Brother Anthony had somehow managed to deceive Father Germanus and his staff and to keep his true malevolent nature concealed from everyone but me.

There was one unspoken and unwritten law among the fifty-odd students at the Bishop's School: you never complained and you never, ever carried tales. It was a matter of honor among the boys, but as such traditions always do, it carried within it a great potential for abuse. Discipline in the school was harsh, and the rules by which we boys lived were many, strict and inviolable; you broke them at your peril, and when you were caught, as you were more often than not, you took your punishment—always corporal punishment—in silence. You could weep, and depending on the severity of the beating you had undergone people might or might not make allowances for that, but you could not, ever, whine or complain. That was one of the first learned facts of life in the Bishop's School.

Brother Anthony enjoyed beating the younger boys and was despised for it by the entire student body, but he particularly enjoyed beating me, and I have many memories of being unable to walk without limping after one of his "punishments." Of course I, being as stubborn as he was vicious, would never give him the satisfaction of seeing me wince, let alone cry, and so the beatings he delivered grew more savage as time went by and as I grew larger and more able to absorb them. I would often dream of the day when I would be big enough to face him and disarm him and I drew great pleasure from the images I dreamed up of what I would do to him on that occasion.

That day never arrived, however, because long before I grew big enough to challenge my tormentor, I was summoned to an unscheduled meeting with Father Germanus shortly after one of Anthony's "punishments." To this day I have no knowledge of who had reported what was going on, but from that moment my troubles with Brother Anthony were over. Germanus stopped me with an upraised hand as I entered his *cubiculum*—the spacious room from which he conducted all the affairs of his bishopric—and then stalked towards me, an unreadable expression on his face as he raked me from head to foot with his eyes. He took hold of my chin, then tilted my head sideways, right then left, examining my face closely. That done, he reached down quickly and grasped my belt buckle, tugging on it sharply.

"Off," he said. "Undo it and take off your tunic."

Not knowing what he was about, and never suspecting that someone else might have interceded to save me from Anthony, I did as Father Germanus demanded. I loosened my belt and pulled my tunic up and over my shoulders, baring my torso. He frowned, his eyes moving across the bruises on my ribs, and then he grasped me by the upper arm, not ungently, and turned me around. I heard the hiss of his indrawn breath as his gaze encountered the fresh welts on my back, and his fingers tightened on my arm before he turned me back to face him. His face had paled but he said nothing to me. Instead he called to his clerical assistant, Potius, who came in quickly from his station outside the doors of the cubiculum. I was shrugging back into my tunic by then, but the bishop stopped me and waved to Potius to approach and see what had been done to me. Again, a shocked hiss, quickly stifled.

"Take him to the infirmary," Germanus said, and I had never heard such iron control in his voice. "Brother Martin is to look after him in person. Tell Martin to do what must be done and then come here to me. Quickly now." He looked back to me, his face impassive. "Go with Potius. We will speak again later."

I spent four days in the infirmary, lying on my side or on my stomach, anchored in such a way that I was unable to turn onto my back, and on two of those days Germanus himself came to visit me. He said nothing the first time, merely nodding to me and standing in my doorway for a while, contemplating me as I lay immobile, but when he returned the second time he did speak, if only briefly. "Recover quickly," he said from the doorway. "Your time remaining here is none too long and you should enjoy it to the full. Brother Anthony has left us."

Brother Anthony had, indeed. As soon as I was released from my confinement, my friends came rushing to tell me that Brother Anthony had been escorted to his monastic life by Bishop Germanus in person, and would spend the remainder of his life in pious servitude within a monastery selected by the bishop and noted for the severity of its commitment to penance. Therein, Brother Anthony would be cut off forever from the company of boys.

3

We spent our lives training and studying, and only occasionally praying, and none of us would have had it any other way. That is why our time there in the Bishop's School—for my experience was shared by all my friends—passed by so quickly. We were boys, engrossed in doing what boys do, thoroughly captivated by our studies, both military and academic.

A stringently observed aphorism at the school was *mens sana in corpore sano:* a healthy mind exists in a healthy body. The importance of that belief was reflected in the discipline of personal hygiene, both mental and physical, that permeated the lives of the students, driving them remorselessly from cold baths and shivering prayers in the darkness of the predawn, pre-breakfast hours, through days crammed with varying activities, both scholastic and military, until the curfew hour, when we would fall into bed after the communal evening prayers known as vespers, too exhausted even to talk to each other and acutely aware that almost before we had time to close our eyes to sleep, we would be rousted out again for matins, the morning prayers that the entire community shared in the darkest hours before dawn. And yet, for all the hardships and strictures of our life as students there, few of us would ever be as happy in our adult lives as we were then in our innocence.

And yet great things were occurring in the world around us, events that ought to have claimed all our attention and surely would have, had we known they were happening. Entire races of people were on the move at that time, sweeping in mass migrations through vast territories that had once been owned by the Empire and policed by its ubiquitous armies but were now, for the most part, abandoned and unsupervised. And as each race of land-hungry people swept forward—Visigoths and Goths, Vandals and Huns and a hundred other nameless hordes—wheeling from northeast to westward for the most part, they dispossessed other, former occupants, who moved on in their turn and increased the havoc and chaos.

Everything—every stretch of land that had been part of the Empire in the West for a thousand and more years—was in a condition of flux and turmoil in those turbulent days after the fall of Rome, when Alaric and his Visigoths first captured the Eternal City. The Empire, which everyone had thought to be eternal, had collapsed within the space of a few years, and no one, anywhere, was equipped or prepared to deal with the catastrophe. And yet, when the tally was complete and all the initial chaos began to subside, order, or a degree of order greater than anyone could have anticipated, reasserted itself at an astonishing rate.

The reasons for that were not hard to find, for anyone who cared to look for them, for in the decades and even centuries that the old Empire had been tottering, a victim of its own corruption, people had learned to subsist on their own terms, to be more self-sufficient and independent of imperial dictates. And so the crash of collapse, when it came, proved to be less surprising, less demoralizing than it might have been, and even the majority of the peoples who were on the move had benefited from the civilizing influence of Rome for a millennium.

Not surprisingly, since Auxerre was firmly in the center of Gaul, we experienced very little of the upheavals that were happening elsewhere. The Frankish presence in the north and west continued to increase, but that meant nothing to us, since we ourselves were Franks and our migration had been ongoing for more than a hundred years. It was similar with the Burgundians, whose settled borders almost abutted ours in the south. They had practically overrun the entire southwest of Gaul. But although neither of us was amicably disposed towards the other and there were sometimes clashes between our people and theirs, the situation between us never degenerated into outright war. Each of us knew the other and had his measure, and we both knew it was more important to guard ourselves against outside aggression than to fret over what our neighbors might be planning.

Bishop Germanus, of course, was aware of all of this, but he made it his business to ensure that none of us were bothered by such things. We had an education to absorb, he believed, and the form in which we absorbed it would dictate, to a very great extent, the fashion in which we later reacted to such external priorities and distractions. If our grounding in the classical elements of education was sufficiently substantial, he argued, then we would be perfectly well equipped to deal with whatever the world might throw at us, and so we studied logic and philosophy, geometry and polemics and geography—this while the world was changing daily—and we conversed in Greek and Latin and were conversant with the written works of the great Masters: the Greeks Socrates, Aristotle and Plato, Aeschylus, Euripides and Homer, and the Roman works of Caesar, Cicero, Herodotus, Pliny, Ovid and many others. And over and above all of these, we studied the Christ and his teachings.

When I consider that we studied all of these things between predawn morning prayers and noon, and that the second half of each day was given over completely to our military training and discipline, then add the additional consideration that we somehow had to accommodate all of our daily chores and duties within the fabric of those activities, finding and making time between classes to tend to our community responsibilities, I am never surprised that we had no time for talk, or even thoughts, of girls or women.

And then, of course, there was the fighting: the training . . . the horses. I have to admit that that aspect of our education, the physical, militaristic part, was supposed to be a relatively minor element of our growth, recognized and provided for but of significantly less importance than our scholastic and clerical training. That was never the case with me, however, despite the concerted efforts of my other tutors, and to his credit Father Germanus never sought to influence me to conform to their wishes. He had promised Ban and the Lady Vivienne that my training in the military skills would continue and he never deviated from his word.

I had been born and bred among King Ban's horse soldiers and had learned to ride as soon as my legs could spread widely enough to span a pony's back, so I had no inhibitions about thrusting myself, the morning after my arrival in Auxerre, into the world of the school's stables and its small but carefully selected and extremely valuable collection of horses. I walked in through the gates with all the arrogance and innocence of trusting youth only to be stopped short with a barked command before I was three paces over the threshold. I froze, taken aback by the ferocity of the shout and the wild appearance of the man who had uttered it, and my challenger bade me stand right where I was, the tone of his voice defying me to move another step at my peril. He strode towards where I stood gaping at him, glowering at me from beneath bushy white eyebrows that formed a solid bar across his forehead.

He was a small man, *tiny* perhaps being an even more accurate word, because he was not much taller than me and I was only ten. He was carrying a smallish coil of limber, well-used rope—seven, perhaps eight loops in all. I remember that clearly, because when he reached me he slipped his arm through the loops and shrugged the coil upward to hang from his shoulder. Seeing him glare at me, I tried to smile back, but I was intimidated, and my face would not relax, so I simply stared back at him, wide eyed. Finally he hawked loudly and spat off to one side.

"Benwick, right?" His voice was loud and harsh, rough edged as though seldom used. "You're the brat came back with the Gen'ral?"

The General. I realized he was talking about Father Germanus and remembered Germanus saying that a man called Tiberias Cato would be my teacher and that he had served in the army with him. This must evidently be Cato. I nodded, and looked at him more closely.

Although he was small in stature, I saw now that he was built perfectly in proportion and his limbs were clean lined and clearly defined, dense with corded muscle. He was hairy, too, his entire body—or all that I could see of it—apart from his clean-shaven face, coated with a thick pelt of soft blond hair, its color ranging from faded yellow in places to grayish white in others, with one swirling whorl of a cowlick thatch at his crown that showed signs of once having been bright yellowy gold. His forearms and the legs below his knee-length tunic were deeply sun-bronzed, and the hair that coated them was bleached almost white. I was fascinated to see that the hair on the back of his hands grew right down to his knuckles and that the phalanges of his fingers had coarse black hair growing on them, utterly unlike the hair on the rest of his body.

It may have been the thickness and profusion of his body hair that made the bareness of his face so obvious, but irrespective of what caused it to seem so, the man's face, smooth cheeked and deeply tanned and dominated by brilliant, flower blue eyes, glowed with health and a special kind of self-sufficient beauty. His eyebrows, the first thing I had noticed about him, were a thick, unbroken bar of white, and the tangle of hair surmounting his forehead was unkempt and long untrimmed.

"Hmm," he grunted, oblivious to or uncaring of my scrutiny. He lowered his shoulder and allowed the coil of rope to slide off and drop into his waiting hand, and then he threw the coil to me. I caught it with both hands. It was a running noose of the exact kind used by Ban's stable men.

"You know how to use that?"

"Yes," I managed to say.

"Hmm. We'll see. Come."

He led me to a wide, barred wooden gate at the far end of the stable yard and held it open as I went through, after which he closed it carefully behind us and secured it in place with a loop of rope. We were in a long passageway now, with two paddocks on each side, each of them measuring approximately fifty paces in length by the same in width. The first enclosure on my right held eight mares, all of them in foal, and in the one beyond that, I could see others, these accompanied by newborn colts. The paddock on my immediate left held five healthy young geldings, and the fourth space lay empty. I followed the stable master as he led me the length of the passage-way to the gate at the far end and beyond that into a wide, fenced pasture with clumps of trees scattered here and there and a lazy brook meandering among them. I had no idea how big the pasture was, because the trees obscured the boundary fences, but I knew it was enormous and I guessed from the position of the sun that we had to be close to the northern outskirts of the town. There were horses everywhere, and I immediately began to count them, but I lost track as I passed thirty and realized that just enough of them were moving to make my task impossible. The wiry little man looked around him and then glanced at me.

"Bring me one," he said, then walked away. Unsure of myself and even of what he meant, I watched him as he went, and when the trees blocked my view I followed him again, keeping him in sight until he disappeared inside a small, low-roofed building with thick stone walls. He had not glanced back once in my direction, and so I moved closer, stopping only when I drew close enough to identify the building as a small smithy with a forge and a heavy, sturdy-looking bellows. Cato was already bent over the bellows, blasting gales of air into the coals of the forge and filling the smithy with clouds of smoke and ashes. As the scent of the hot ashes reached my nostrils I grasped my coils of rope more firmly and turned back towards the horses.

I knew I was facing some kind of test here, but I had no idea what was being tested, and yet I knew somehow that time was of no great importance in whatever it was. And so I made myself think about what I knew. Cato had told me to bring him one, and the only thing there in numbers greater than one was horses, so he evidently expected me to bring him a horse. Clearly he meant me to select one from the herd, and I was to be judged, in some manner, on the one I chose.

I began to walk among the animals, looking at them, and quickly made a number of discoveries. Scattered among the herd, but numerous enough to be clearly evident, were horses of a breed I had never seen. They were all completely black and larger than any of the other animals in the herd; big, strongly muscled animals with dense, extraordinarily heavy coats of deepest black, long, thick manes and tails and beautiful feathered fetlocks that almost covered their hooves. The other herd animals were of several breeds and sizes, all familiar to me, and their colors ranged from gray to red to chestnut brown. There were mares and fillies, immature colts and a preponderance of geldings, but there were no stallions. And then, mere moments after realizing that, I found the first of the stallions and smiled in admiration. There were six of them, I soon discovered, each one magnificent and each securely confined in its own strong enclosure. The six enclosures were strung along the paddock's perimeter fence like beads, each separated from the others by a distance of at least twenty paces. Two of these six animals were of the beautiful long-haired black breed, and I found myself admiring them even more than I had earlier.

It was evident, however, that I was not expected to select a stallion, so that left me facing a choice between a mare or a gelding— all of the colts were too immature to qualify as horses in this instance, I suspected. I examined all of them again, and all of them were beautiful, but my eyes kept returning to the big black animals.

A short time after that, I reached the door of the small smithy, leading the horse I had chosen. Tiberias Cato, hunched over his forge and peering into the blue-white coals, paid me no heed until I stepped across the threshold and called out to him. He started slightly and straightened up, swinging to face me, his eyes taking in the horse I was holding. He tossed the tongs he had been holding onto a heavy workbench and came towards me, wiping his hands on a rag he had pulled from somewhere.

"Why'd you pick him?" he asked when he reached me.

"He's beautiful," I replied. "I've never seen his like before. What kind is he?"

"Forest horse. Wild stock. But why him in particular? He's not two years old yet."

"He's magnificent, and when he's two, and older, he'll be the best here."

"Will he, by God? D'you say so?" Listening to him say that, I actually believed he had not realized that and was surprised, but I had not yet come to an appreciation of sarcasm or irony. His eyes were already moving beyond me to another mount, and he pointed. "That one. Let's see you mount him."

Not catch him or bring him, but mount him. I turned to look at the bay gelding Cato had indicated and then swung back, tightening my grip on the reins in my hand. "Why can't I mount this one?"

"Because he's not broke yet. Trying to ride him now could get you killed, or it could end up with his being ruined as a good horse. Besides, I showed you the one I want you to mount, and I'm waiting."

Disappointed, but no longer feeling rebellious, I quietly took the rope bridle off the black gelding, then loosened and removed the noose around his neck. I coiled my rope again and went after the bay, which stood placidly watching me and allowed me to come close enough to slip both the noose and the bridle over his head. He was not a tall horse, and his head was too big and heavy to be beautiful or even handsome, but he was stocky and deep chested, strongly muscled. When the bridle was secured, I led him to an old tree stump that was obviously much used as a mounting block and heaved myself up onto his broad back. The bay stood there with his head down, his ears twitching back towards me as though he was listening to my breathing. Apart from that, however, he remained motionless as I made myself comfortable.

Then he exploded into motion, leaping high into the air and spinning in a head-snapping half circle to land stiff-legged, head down, hooves together with his back bowed upwards so that he almost jarred me off, which was his intent. By sheer good fortune, this was a trick with which I was thoroughly familiar, having had to deal for more than a year with a cantankerous horse in King Ban's stables that had mastered the same turning leap and must have been one of this animal's relatives, and so I recognized the preliminary movements under me and adjusted to them practically without thought, relaxing my posture and leaning into his spinning jump, allowing the slackness of my body to absorb the shock of his stiff-legged landing.

He must have been greatly surprised to find himself still burdened after this exertion, because he stood stock-still for long enough to permit me to lock my fingers in the hair of his mane and hammer him in the ribs with my heels, and then he went into action again, bucking, rearing and spinning, determined to rid himself of me. I, for my part, was just as determined that he would not do so, because I had caught a glimpse of Tiberias Cato's face just before this second rampage erupted and it was plain to see that he was even more surprised than the horse was by its failure to reject me. And so the gelding cavorted and reared like a mad creature and I clung on, adapting to his every feint and trick until he stopped again, quivering with fury. I did not relax for a moment, however. I knew he was not yet finished and I stayed poised, ready to adjust to whatever he might do next. Even so, what he did caught me unprepared.

With a mighty surge of powerful muscles he launched himself into a run, his stride lengthening rapidly into a full gallop, and I rode him easily, enjoying the sensation of speed until I saw where he was taking me. We were headed directly towards a huge old solitary elm tree in the center of the paddock, and it was clear that he was either going to run straight into it or brush very closely past it, using it as a tool to scrape me off his back. Incredulous, I watched until there was no doubt of what he was doing: the rough bark of the tree would scrape along the horse's right side, and my right leg would not survive the impact.

A bare two leaps before disaster struck, I anchored my fists more solidly in his mane and swung my right leg backwards across his back, bringing my knees together on his left side, my right hip against his surging side. I allowed my body to swing down, straight-legged, until my feet hit the ground and rebounded, and then I used his speed to swing myself back up to straddle him again. I felt his speed start to flag immediately and he had no more tricks after that, so that I found it easy to turn him around and head him back towards Cato, his speed slackening until we drew to a halt in front of the stable master, whose face remained blank even after I had dismounted.

"They teach you to ride like that in Benwick?" was all he said.

"I've never been anywhere else."

"Hmm. King Ban, does he ride like that?"

I merely nodded, not knowing what else to tell him. I knew, from my riding instructor in Benwick, that even although I was a mere boy, a child, I was one of the best riders in Ban's kingdom and would one day be the best of all, but I did not want to say that to Tiberias Cato, lest he think me a braggart.

"I didn't think you'd last through his first jump."

I was on the point of telling him about the horse with the same trick in Benwick, but then decided to hold my tongue and asked him instead, "Does he do that often?"

The small man nodded. "Every time, even with me. Not many people can stay up there when he does that."

"Did you know he would try to scrape me off?"

He shook his head, frowning. "No. I've never seen him do that before. That's something new. He's a clever whoreson, for a gelding."

I shrugged. "It didn't work, though, so he might not try it again. I mean, it's not as if he's human, is it?"

"No, but there's times when he seems to come damn close. Anyway, take the bridle off him and turn him loose, then get out of here. You're not supposed to be here at this time of day. No student is. Come back the day after tomorrow when your lessons start. What's your name?"

I told him, and he nodded and pursed his lips, and such was my self-conceit that I saw nothing strange in being accepted instantly by Tiberias Cato, Master of the Stables, a unique and formidable being respected and feared by every student in the school. I was, after all, Clothar of Benwick, adopted son of King Ban of Benwick, since birth used to being treated with deference and respect.

It may have taken me as long as a week to realize that Tiberias Cato was no respecter of names or rank and that he cared not a whit what people in the world beyond his paddocks thought of anyone else. In Cato's eyes, there was but one natural ranking in the order of men, and it lay visible in the ease and skill—or in the lack of ease and skill—that they demonstrated in their relationship with horses. Cato himself was more centaur than human being and he rode as though the animal beneath him was an extension of his body. I cannot remember ever seeing him use his hands to control a horse while mounted. All his control—and it was prodigious—was exerted from his hips downward, leaving his hands free at all times to do whatever he required them to do. It was very impressive, even awe-inspiring to watch, and yet in order to watch and appreciate his mastery of what he did, you had to be aware of it, and the astonishing truth was that most people looked at Cato, then through him or past him, without ever seeing how gifted he was. They dismissed him idly as some form of stable groom with the seniority of age and were too blinded by their own inadequacies to be able to discern anything of the magic he worked with horses.

I had no such blinkers hampering my view of the stable master. He fascinated me from the day I first saw him ride a horse, and he quickly became my hero. I made it my concern to find out everything I could about him, but of course there was only one man, apart from Tiberias Cato himself, who could tell me everything that was known about the Master of the Bishop's Stables, and that was the bishop, who knew Cato perhaps better than Cato knew himself, and it would be more than a year before I could be sufficiently comfortable in his august company to come right out and ask him openly about his friend and servant Cato. And so until that time I merely watched and admired this favorite of all my teachers, nursing what little knowledge of his history I had been able to acquire from the stories the older boys told about him, and feeling my admiration for him increase with every new example of his knowledge and understanding of the ways and the lore of horses.

4

The six years that followed my departure from Benwick flew by, as time always does when we enjoy what we are doing, until the day when I found myself, slack mouthed and stunned, contemplating my sixteenth birthday, which was looming in the too-near future. I tend to remember the occasion nowadays as having dropped upon me as a complete surprise, as though I had not even been aware of my increasing age until Father Germanus pointed it out to me in the course of one of our regular weekly meetings. It is a comforting thought, that image of being caught off balance, ill prepared and unready, but that is not really the way it occurred.

I may have been mentally and emotionally unprepared to be sixteen years old, indulging in wishful thinking and foolishly believing that if I paid no attention to the passage of time then it would flow on without changing anything, but the truth is that I had been very much aware of time passing, and of the changes I was undergoing, in common with my friends, as a result of its passing. Bodies that had been slim and soft, hairless and childish, had gradually become hardened and muscular, thicker and heavier, and the downy growth that had been barely visible upon our faces no more than a year earlier had coarsened upon some of us, the darker skinned among us, and hardened into stubble on our chins.

The most noteworthy change of all, however, had been in the stuff of our conversations, the things we talked about. Where once we had discussed and debated little else but physical training and our individual performances in drills and contests, most of us now talked of little else but girls, *women* and the dark and mystical secrets surrounding them and their physical nature. And as a result of our waking preoccupation with such things, our nocturnal lives, once a matter of mere oblivion disturbed very occasionally by nightmares, had changed to encompass exciting and erotically disturbing dreams, barely remembered upon awakening yet no less powerful because of that. Manhood was closing in upon us, we all knew, and although the prospect excited and intimidated us, we continued nonetheless to gull ourselves into believing that we could have and enjoy the satisfactions of physical manhood—the fighting and the womanizing—without ever having to abandon the inno-cence and comradeship of boyhood.

But now all at once, and beyond equivocation, I was to be sixteen, which meant that I would have to leave the Bishop's School and make my way alone in the real world, among real men! The realization of that truth was devastating, because it forced me to accept that this stage in my life, boyhood as I had known it in Auxerre, was close to being over. A boy's sixteenth birthday is his life's greatest watershed, marking the crossing point into manhood and taking him from childhood to adult status, from carefree idyll to the acceptance of a man's responsibilities.

On the day when Germanus reminded me of my age, I had been the acknowledged leader of the senior class, the Spartans, for more than a month, but even that exalted estate had failed to make any significant dent in my lack of awareness. I had been so happy and confident in my own popularity and power among the other students that it seemed natural that things must continue as they were. But my entire world changed in the space of one short, supposedly normal interview, when I found myself having to accept that, with the start of the following year, another boy, a younger boy, would be leader of the Spartans and I would be gone, never to be remem-bered by the boys that followed in my footsteps from year to year. Where I would be by then, I knew not; but I would be a man—if in name only—and probably a serving soldier, my boyhood locked irretrievably behind me.

On a hot spring day in the first half of my sixteenth year, completely without warning, Tiberias Cato announced that the next day would be a day of festivities and freedom from classes for the entire school, in honor of the return of Bishop Germanus from a particularly long episcopal journey. Furthermore, he announced, the occasion would be highlighted by an all-out competition among the senior students, designed to test their prowess and skills and the progress they had managed to achieve so far in this, their final year. The student who emerged victorious from the final stages of the competition would be rewarded with a special prize, something unique and valuable, although Tiberias Cato refused to say what it was.

That part of the announcement caused more excitement among the students than anything else anyone could remember, for although competition in everything was taken for granted at the school, prizes were seldom awarded, and those few that were usually took the form of time off from classes, for one morning or afternoon, in recognition of some stellar achievement. Such rewards were a welcome respite from the normal grind of daily school life, but no one would ever have described them as exciting.

Here, however, was a competition with a valuable prize to be won, and the entire student body was agog with speculation as to what the prize might be.

Everyone competed against everyone else for everything at the Bishop's School as a matter of course, striving to achieve one's best possible performance in everything for the greater glory of God. That Latin phrase, *ad majorem Dei gloriam,* was probably the most commonly heard expression at the Bishop's School. It was Bishop Germanus's own personal watchword, conveying his deeply rooted conviction that if everything a person does on Earth is dedicated to glorifying God, then it becomes impossible for that person to sin and incur damnation. By direct association, the sentiment had become the school's maxim as well, constantly quoted by the teachers and never lost sight of by the student body.

There were twenty-two of us in the senior class that year, a larger number than normal, and according to school tradition we were called the Spartans. The suggestions of discipline, pre-eminence and status implied by that name were not accidental. The soldiers of the ancient Greek kingdom of Sparta were renowned and revered in our male, militaristic society, and the story of their heroic fight at the Pass of Thermopylae was one of our legends. In defending and holding that narrow pass against the enormous invading armies of the Persian Empire for longer than anyone could possibly have expected, three hundred of Sparta's finest soldiers, under the command of their king, Leonidas, had won eternal glory, sacrificing their lives to purchase much-needed time for their countrymen to prepare to defend themselves against the invaders. We therefore, the Spartans of the Bishop's School, were charged with the responsibility of being exemplars to the school, setting the standard of high achievement, scholastic pride and sterling behavior for all the younger students following behind us. Tomorrow, we all knew, one of us would win a memorable prize, and each of us was determined to be that winner.

The truth was, of course, that of the twenty-two Spartans in our current year, only eleven possessed the skills and the prowess that would be required to emerge as victor. The remaining eleven possessed skills and abilities directed more towards generating higher standards of clerical and scholastic excellence. It had become the tradition among the Spartans that each Warrior, as the more physically inclined students were called—they were selected by Tiberias Cato and his staff for their athletic and equestrian prowess—would be assigned one or more Scholars as partners for the year. The unit thus formed would become a team, competing together against the other teams in the class, but also performing together when it came to the supervisory duties and responsibilities incumbent upon the Spartans as senior students. There had been eighteen Spartans in the previous year's class, and of those only six had been real Warriors, and so that class had been split into six teams each of three students. This year, by contrast, we were evenly split into pairs, eleven Warriors and Scholars respectively. My Scholar was Dominic Tara, the smallest and the youngest, but also the most brilliantly gifted student in the class in both mathematics and geography, the areas wherein I was weakest.

Dominic came looking for me soon after Cato's announcement and found me talking with two of my closest friends, Stephan Lorco and Quintus Milo, who, as his name suggested, was the youngest of five brothers, all of whom had attended the Bishop's School. Dominic's face was set in a very peculiar expression and he was moving strangely. I stopped whatever I was saying.

"Dom, what's wrong?" I asked him. "You look as though you've discovered something terrifying."

He said nothing, but looked at me with that peculiar wide-eyed expression and shook his head.

Dom was the only member of the Spartans who was called by his given name. Everyone else in the school, and certainly among the Spartans, was either known simply by his family name—Lorco and Milo were two of those—or by a descriptive nickname. I cannot remember now why Dom should have been different from everyone else in that respect, but I suspect it had to do with his age and his tiny size—he reminded most of us of smaller brothers we had left at home, and we tended to treat him more tolerantly and gently as a result of that.

"Dom?" I repeated, raising my voice to capture his attention, but he shook his head again, disregarding both me and Milo, and spoke to Lorco.

"I'm to summon you to the Chancellor," he said.

The smile vanished instantly from Lorco's face. A summons to the Chancellor was never issued lightly, nor was it treated as anything less than disastrous. Brother Ansel, the Chancellor, was first deputy to Bishop Germanus and was charged with the daily running and discipline of the school whenever the bishop had to go away, which occurred with some regularity. There was little doubt that he was an able administrator, but he was also a man utterly devoid of both humor and mercy. Ansel had become famed for the intolerance and inflexibility of his views and for the ferocity of his punishments. None of us were sure if Germanus was aware of Ansel's other side, and of course, no one rushed to inform him that his deputy was preternaturally cruel and remorseless, and every student in the school behaved with extreme caution whenever the bishop went away.

Lorco's face had drained of all color as he tried to think of what crime he must stand charged.

"No, it's not that," Dom continued, looking quickly from Lorco to Milo and then to me, seeing the effect his words had had on all of us and trying to reassure us with flapping hands. He turned hurriedly back to Lorco. "It's nothing bad . . . at least, I don't think it is . . . He's not *after* you . . . I believe it's your father."

Death. The word, unspoken, clanged loudly in all our minds. The only time anyone ever seemed to speak of parents here was when word arrived that one or another of them had died unexpectedly.

"Wha—" Lorco had to cough to clear his throat. "What about my father?"

"He's here, I think. In the school."

That was even more startling than the summons to the Chancellor. "My father?" The disbelief in Lorco's voice would have been laughable at any other time. "You're mad. My father's more than five hundred miles from here, probably in Hispania, pacifying the Iberians."

Dom merely threw up his hands, palms outward. "I don't know, then. Perhaps I'm wrong. But there's a strange man in with the Chancellor, someone I've never seen before, and he looks like a soldier, and I know your father is a soldier. I went in to do some transcription for Brother Marcus in the vestibule beside the bishop's day room and I heard old Ansel talking to someone, so I peeked through an open door and saw this man. I couldn't hear much of what they were saying, but what I could hear sounded boring. I didn't pay any attention to them at all after that, to tell the truth, until I heard your name being mentioned. And I'm pretty sure I heard the man say something about his son. A little while after that the door opened and old Ansel stuck his head out and sent me to fetch you."

Lorco looked at me, his eyes wide, and I shrugged. "Better get going," I told him. "It's not wise to keep old Ansel waiting, and besides, Dom might be right. If he is, and your father's here, that's good, is it not?"

In truth, I was not sure whether it was good or not. We boys, as the stoic Spartans we were supposed to be, seldom spoke among ourselves about our homes or our parents, and the reason for that was more self-defense than reticence. When you were as completely immersed as we were in a life that offered ample hardship and few comforts, it became foolish to endanger what little equanimity you possessed by dwelling on memories of home and family and the softnesses and luxuries you could find there.

Fortunately, Lorco's face broke into a wide, toothy grin as soon as I asked the question. "Better than good," he said. "It's unbelievable. If my Tata's really here, we'll all have some fun. You'll like him, I promise you."

It turned out to be true. The man with Brother Ansel was Lorco's father, Phillipus Lorco, another former legate who had soldiered under Germanus's command and now held the military title and rank of dux, or duke. As Duke Lorco, he was now the imperial governor of a huge territory in the southwest of Gaul that included the mountainous region separating Gaul from Hispania, but in his time with the legions, even before the advent of Germanus, he had won great acclaim and successes coordinating and conducting hard-fought, relentless campaigns against the Burgundian tribes who had been invading south-central Gaul and spreading havoc there for nigh on a hundred years.

He was now here in Auxerre, it transpired, because he had been urgently summoned by Germanus's military successors to attend a gathering of imperial strategists in the fortress at Treves, Germanus's own former base and still the military headquarters at that time for all of Gaul. The purpose of this extraordinary assembly was to coordinate a campaign against the ever-bellicose

Burgundians, who were once again threatening to break out of the territories they had now occupied for decades, this time to engulf the entire southwest of Gaul. Duke Lorco's contribution to the planning and prosecution of the campaign had been deemed both invaluable and a sine qua non of success.

Faced with a journey of several hundreds of miles north to Treves from his home base in the ancient fortified town of Carcasso in the south, and aware that the most direct route to his destination would take him within a hundred miles of Auxerre, where his eldest son, Stephan, was in school and prospering, the Duke had allowed himself sufficient time in advance of the gathering to visit his old friend and commander Germanus, his primary purpose to arrange to take his son back home with him to Carcasso when the boy's schooling was completed and the Duke's own duties in Treves were concluded.

It turned out that the bishop was not in Auxerre for his arrival but was expected to arrive back in Auxerre the following day. In the meantime, the senior Lorco had three days to spend in Auxerre before striking out for Treves, and Brother Ansel had magnanimously permitted him to renew his acquaintance with his son.

I had the privilege of meeting Duke Lorco that same afternoon, when he came with his son to be introduced to me and Milo as Lorco's closest friends. He was a friendly, affable man with an easy manner and a charming disposition that stirred a fleeting spasm of resentment in me at the thought of how fortunate Lorco was to have a living father. The sensations caused me to flush with guilt and shame at what I judged to be disloyalty to my adoptive parents in Genava, and with those feelings came an abrupt awareness of how much I missed them and how greatly I wanted to see them again. I would give anything to see my stepfather's face again, I thought then, and with the notion, Ban of Benwick stood before me in my mind, gazing at me with that raised eyebrow of his and smiling his slightly crooked grin.

Those feelings passed and left me feeling content as I stood beside Milo, watching Lorco leave the school with his father. They

would dine together privately that evening in the Duke's quarters in
the nearby *mansio,* the local hostelry maintained by the imperial
civil service for the accommodation of couriers and others traveling
on official affairs. Whether Lorco would return to the school that
night at all was something that remained to be seen, although I
hoped that he might not. He was so obviously happy and proud to
see his father and to have had the opportunity to introduce him to
us, his friends, that I felt he deserved to be allowed to spend every
moment that he could in his father's company. The mere occurrence
of such a thing—a student remaining out of the school overnight—
was unusual enough to cause all kinds of talk among the other
students, and for once the boys talked as they never had before
about the places they came from and about their loved ones. More
than a few tears were shed without much effort being made to hide
them, so that there was a subdued atmosphere in the dormitories at
curfew that night that was almost palpable, despite the countering
excitement over the coming day's activities and the promised
competition.

It was mid-afternoon and the celebrations at the school were
already well under way when Bishop Germanus arrived, without
fanfare, at the exercise grounds attached to the school's extensive
stables. All activities ceased, and a respectful silence hung over the
assembled students. I watched my mentor as he dismounted from
the pony he rode that day and walked, alone as always, slowly towards
the raised reviewing stand at the far end of the open-air arena where
most of the afternoon's contests and events were taking place, then
mounted the dais to join the assembled tutors, staff and visitors.

As I watched the bishop on this occasion, however, something
in the way he moved brought the realization home to me, for the
first time ever, that Germanus of Auxerre was an old man. I saw
something different and bothersome in him that day, something
intangible and yet unnervingly suggestive of a lack of healthiness,
although it appeared and disappeared so fleetingly that I was able
to convince myself that I had imagined it. It may have been the way
he walked the few steps from dismounting from the pony to the

start of the stairs rising to the stand. The day had been fine, on the whole, but a heavy shower of rain had fallen half an hour earlier and muddied the ground underfoot, making it treacherous, and just before the bishop reached the first of the steps to the dais he paused, a very brief hesitation, and reached, unsteadily it seemed to me, for the support of the hand rail. It happened, I saw it, and the unwelcome burden of a new anxiety descended upon my head and shoulders.

I was completely unprepared for the revelation and I rejected it even as it occurred to me. I can distinctly remember the anger I felt at myself at that moment for even thinking such a thought—entertaining the very notion of his mortality. But unsought and unexpected as it was, it disconcerted me to the point of causing a strong spasm of anxiety in my breast.

No one else noticed, I am quite sure of that, because Germanus reached the top of the stairs to the dais and strode directly along the front row of seats, his bearing utterly regal and resolute, to where Duke Lorco had risen to greet him. The two men embraced as old friends do and exchanged a few pleasantries before Germanus excused himself and turned to bless the gathering before sending Tiberias Cato the signal to continue with the proceedings his arrival had interrupted. That done, he sat down in the vacant seat by Duke Lorco's side and both men talked animatedly for a while before settling back to watch the competition, which was now approaching the final stages.

I had been doing well in the competition until then and was quietly confident that I was ahead of the field on points. I had been in excellent form in the preliminary events, all of which involved athletic activities on foot: running, jumping and wrestling, and the fighting drills, which included mock combat with clubs, swords and heavy spears, as well as archery and lance throwing.

I had won the running events easily, to no one's surprise. I had grown a handsbreadth during the summer of my third year at the school, which had inspired much jesting and also my nickname, Legs. But Lorco had challenged me seriously on the broad jump, and I had been on the point of giving up, convinced that I could not possibly match his final, inspired leap, when I saw Tiberias Cato watching me, a troubled, meditative look on his face. I knew Cato had no time for anyone who ever quit ahead of being beaten in anything, and I did not want him ever to think such a thing of me, so I rallied and gritted my teeth for one last, all-out attempt. Somehow I managed to fly out and land precisely where Lorco had landed, destroying his mark in the process and making it impossible to discern whether one of us had outdistanced the other. The judges shook their heads and consulted the notations they had made earlier and muttered among themselves for a long time before they called the event a draw.

I had then fought my way more than adequately through the range of fighting drills, too, emerging unbeaten from all but the last category, the lance-throwing event, where my closest rivals were Milo and Gaius Balbus, the boy I liked least of all the Spartans. Balbus was taller than I was, and slightly heavier, the largest student in our class, and although I could beat him easily in most events, including swords and heavy spears, he was the only student who could throw a javelin consistently farther than I could. Fortunately for me, however, he could not throw with anything approaching my accuracy, and that displeased him greatly, since accuracy gained more points than distance. I seldom had difficulty in upsetting him sufficiently to make him lose his temper, and with it his judgment, whenever we competed. He was quick to anger and viciously savage with his tongue when he was angry, which was the reason I found it easy to dislike him, for he had stung me and all of my friends too often with his waspish, sarcastic ill-humor.

On this particular morning, however, Balbus had aligned himself alongside Milo, who was throwing very well, consistently and with impressive accuracy. Balbus had paced himself deliberately and precisely, concentrating fiercely and modeling his performance and his rhythm and tempo on Milo's and ignoring me and my performance completely. It worked well for him, and by the start of the last round of throws—five casts each at the torso of a man-sized target thirty paces distant—he and I had both scored sixteen hits out of a possible twenty-five.

The rules of the competition were simple, but the degree of difficulty escalated hugely with each round of five casts. The initial targets, wooden cut-out figures of men, were set up twenty paces from the throwing line, and the whitewashed scoring area extended from the line of the hips up to the head and included the arms—a relatively easy mark. After each round of five casts, however, new targets were placed two paces farther away from the throwing line and the scoring area was reduced in size, the arms and head being among the first to go, until by the last round the casts were thirty paces long and the scoring area was a wrist-to-elbow-length square on the target's chest.

Going into that last round, Milo was one point ahead of both of us. He had scored eighteen hits, his best score ever and a school record for twenty-five casts. It may have been the lengthy duration of the event—thirty casts of an infantryman's *lancea,* the ancient thonged javelin used so effectively by the Roman armies for hundreds of years, exacts a terrible toll on the throwing muscles— but Milo missed the scoring area of the target with all five of his final casts, although all five hit the wooden target somewhere, and he ended up with eighteen points out of a possible thirty. I hit three out of five to beat Milo's score by one, but Balbus, in a display of unsuspected virtuosity that shook and humbled me, hit solidly with all five casts and emerged with yet another record: twenty-one hits out of thirty casts.

It was purely coincidental that the bishop arrived just shortly before we were to progress to the riding events, most of which were designed to test advanced riding skills and the formal, correct and precise handling of animals in restrictive and difficult situations. Several of the equestrian contests, however—and the most difficult, according to some people—involved grueling tests of both horse and rider in events that measured stamina and endurance, as opposed to precision and obedience. The most brutally demanding of those were point-to-point races over planned routes and fiendishly difficult obstacle courses that had to be negotiated within stringent, close to impossible time constraints.

This was the area in which I felt most confident—far more so even than in the foot-racing events. I did not feel even slightly presumptuous when I told myself that no one among my classmates could come close to me in anything having to do with horses and horsemanship.

At the start of the first race—a point-to-point affair in which each contestant had to ride three miles, collecting three flags along the way and bringing them back to the starting point within the time it took for a sand glass to drain twice—all of us were drenched in a brief but spectacular cloudburst. This was quickly forgotten by everyone but me, because it would cost me the race. I was riding a big bay gelding that I had ridden often before that afternoon, and we were first through the gate leading from the stable yards and along the short, wide lane that led into the open country beyond the town. I gave the bay his head and let him stretch his muscles while I enjoyed the rush of the wind through my hair and the feeling of his enormous body flexing and uncoiling beneath me.

I leaped down from his back at the first pick-up point and snatched up one of the red flags that lay there, and I had remounted and was kicking him forward again when the closest of my rivals, Balbus once again, came thundering down towards us.

The run to the second pick-up point, with the yellow flags, was uneventful despite a couple of obligatory jumps, one of them a downhill leap over a log at the edge of a deep pool of water. I was confident I was outstripping the field easily until I discovered—unpleasantly and most surprisingly—that Balbus was hard on my heels, far closer than he had been at the red flag pick-up. I looked closely at his mount this time as we passed each other—Balbus leaping down to snatch up his flag as I kicked my heels into my mount's ribs. He was riding a huge gray, and it was sweating visibly, but not inordinately so. I crouched lower on the bay's back and drummed my heels against his sides, coaxing him to higher speed on our way to pick up the last, green flag, but I was distracted now, wondering how Balbus could have gained so much ground on me so quickly.

It did not occur to me, then or later, that he might have cheated, for that was simply not a possibility. There were no rules to contravene in this race, other than the rule stating that each rider must pick up all three flags before heading for home and the finish line. There were degrees of difficulty in routing, and each rider had the option of deciding whether or not to deviate from the standard course, which wound through valleys between hills, for it was possible, theoretically, to shorten distances dramatically by riding up and over any hill crest, rather than going around it. But we were all familiar with the dangers that lay in wait there; the slopes were steep and treacherous with loose stones and boulders, and in some places they were simply unscalable. Besides, the normal risks of attempting to go up and over were increased and emphasized by the fact of the race and the consequent need, if the attempt were made, to get up one side and down the other quickly with no failed attempts, no hesitation and no loss of time.

On the last dash for home I decided to leave the flat valley bottom and cut off some distance by riding higher, taking a straighter route along the gently sloping shoulder of the hillside that stretched above me on the right. But just as my mount breasted the last angled line of hillside that lay between me and the finishing line, I suddenly saw Balbus coming down at me from above, on my right. He, too, had chosen to climb, but had gone even higher than I had, gambling that he would be able to cut my lead and beat me on the downhill dash into the last turn. I saw him just in time and kneed my mount to the left, sending him downhill, not steeply but sufficiently to stay ahead of Balbus. My horse, a surefooted animal that I had ridden many times, lost his footing somehow on the slick, rain-wet shale of the hillside and went sprawling, hurling me over his head like a living boulder. Neither my horse nor I was seriously injured, but we were nonetheless effectively out of the race. By the time I had collected myself and clambered back up onto the bay's back after checking him for injuries, five riders had galloped past us and we were unable to catch any of them thereafter.

I arrived back in the stable yards glowering blackly and biting down on my self-disgust, but I could not even have the satisfaction of being angry at Balbus. He had done nothing wrong, apart from inducing me to make an error of judgment and then going on to win the race.

Less than an hour later, my earlier disappointment forgotten, I was in the middle of what we called *the battle,* the most chaotic but also the most enjoyable part of the competition. It was a remnant of the truly ancient gladiatorial contests in which, as the climax of a set of games, there would be a general fight in which it was every man for himself and the last man left standing could win his freedom.

Our version of the event was nowhere near so bloodthirsty, but it was our tradition that the last man standing would be declared the day's victor, which meant that even an underdog who had fared badly in the individual contests of strength and skill had a theoretical chance to emerge victorious over all others. There were almost as many umpires on our battlefield as there were combatants, too, their object being to identify and disqualify participants who were clearly beaten before they could suffer any real physical damage. The combatants all wore heavily padded protective leather helmets and fought in armor built of boiled and hammered layered leather; solid metal was too cumbersome and heavy for most boys. The weapons were standard shields and wooden practice swords of heavy ash or oaken dowel.

The combat began with every contestant mounted on horseback, and the theory was that the man who remained mounted for the longest time ought to emerge as the easy victor. Theory, however, seldom survives for any length of time against reality and human ingenuity. It had quickly become standard activity in our school battles for those who were first unhorsed to join forces on the ground and unseat everyone who remained on horseback. Then, when the last man had been unhorsed, the battle began on foot and in earnest.

The ground-level battlefield was not a pleasant spot for those who took no joy in passages of arms, because the danger of serious injury was very real. There were always students—usually the younger, smaller boys—who would take part gleefully in the early portion of the battle, milling around in the crush until they were unhorsed and then joining forces to bring down their elders and betters. They would then defect soon thereafter, citing self-declared and self-determined wounds during the confusion of the first few moments of the main fighting. The majority of the larger boys, particularly at the outset of each battle, had high hopes of winning the contest by themselves, and laid about them enthusiastically, slashing at everyone who came within reach. Reality asserted itself quickly, however, as arms and wind began to tire after but a few moments of savage, energy-sapping swings that missed their targets but nonetheless took their toll on the swingers.

In the end, the contest invariably boiled down to a struggle between the same eight or ten boys who had been predicted as final-stage fighters long before the event began, and this occasion proved no exception. By the time the initial frenzy began to dissipate and I had an opportunity to take a wary step back and look quickly about me while I snatched a breath of air, I found I was now sharing the arena with five opponents. Even as I counted them, however, one of them, a classmate called Serdec, took a thrust in the gut that dropped him to his knees. His shield fell away, leaving him open to a crushing blow that might have cracked his skull had it not been struck aside by a vigilant umpire.

Serdec was out, leaving five of us, and even then, as I counted, the number shrank to four as another fighter, Balbus this time, was hit savagely between the shoulders and then again on the back of the helmet as he went to his knees, head down. I didn't wait to see him fall forward but swung away, my own shield up in anticipation of being attacked simply because I had stopped moving to look, but there was no one near me and I was in no danger. I was alone in that part of the field and I took immediate advantage of the respite, dropping the tip of my wooden sword to earth to rest my arm muscles as

I looked about me for the best spot from which to defend myself against whoever would eventually come against me.

For hundreds of years the legions of Rome had trained with practice swords that were double the weight of the real swords they would use in battle, and the reasons for that were simple, admirable and perfectly understandable: after having trained for years with heavy practice weapons of oak or ash doweling, a real sword, wielded in battle, felt practically weightless to the soldier using it. For our battle we were similarly encumbered with the brutally heavy practice swords. These often became too heavy even to hold after a period of prolonged use, and so I stood there gratefully, my arms dangling, feeling the deadweight of the weapons I was holding but enjoying the sensation of exhilaration as new strength came flooding back into my tired muscles.

The fighter who had finished off Balbus was a large boy from Germania whose real name had been unpronounceable to anyone when he first came to the school. Because of that, he had quickly been nicknamed Lupus, because someone had said he looked just like a big German wolf, and nowadays no one in the school knew what his real name was. This fellow was now moving quickly towards Lorco, his gait a combination of trotting and sidling as he maneuvered to come in behind Lorco's opponent, another Spartan called Borus. Borus saw him coming, however, and shifted his stance warily, circling away from Lupus and trying to assess whether the newcomer would tackle him or join him in attacking Lorco. Apparently none of them had noticed me, still on my feet and armed, less than thirty paces from them. Borus had done his own calculations, however, and with a wave of the hand he invited Lorco to join him in a combined assault on Ursus, the largest of the three. They closed on him together, from right and left, and he did not last long at all against their combined assault. He lost his wooden sword to a smashing blow from Lorco so that he had only his shield for defense and no offensive weapon at all. The umpires declared him dead immediately, and he slumped and lowered his shield, hanging his head dejectedly as his two erstwhile opponents turned their heads to look at me.

I had taken advantage of the time accorded me to choose my own fighting ground and prepare myself to meet them, and I stood crouched on the only spot in the entire arena that might be described as high ground, a tiny knoll that afforded me a very slight advantage over them in height. I was half convinced that Lorco would take sides with me against Borus if I invited him to join me, but the other half of me argued that even if he did join me, I would then be forced to abandon my position on the little knoll, and then I would have to fight Lorco on equal terms, once we had beaten Borus. I held my ground, facing them both blank-faced and keeping my wrist cocked threateningly, my sword's point up and ready to swing in any direction. They shuffled their feet, hesitating, doubtlcss rcvicwing their own plans should the next few moments bring them both against me. The next move, and the decision that would precipitate it, would be momentous, and at the instant when the die was cast, all three of us knew, the one of us left to fight alone against the other two would be out of the contest, which would then be settled between the pair who remained.

It was one of those moments when everything seems to slow down and stop, as though the entire world were being arrested in its progress. The sun was at my back, a choice I had deliberately made, and I could see both Borus and Lorco squinting against its brightness as they tried to read my expression. But then, unexpectedly, I found myself looking beyond them, to where Duke Phillipus Lorco sat tensely on the high reviewing stand beside Bishop Germanus, gazing intently down at the tableau in the arena almost at his feet and at the picture his son made, crouched and determined, his attention totally focused on the task at hand here in the final stages of the afternoon's competition. And as I saw the Duke, I also became aware for the first time of the cacophony of screams and shouts that surrounded the three of us who were left standing in the arena, only because it faded quickly into silence, in one of those strange and inexplicable occurrences that sometimes happen among the largest crowds. Now there was utter stillness, and into it came the thought, as clearly heard in my mind as though it had been spoken aloud, of how proud my friend Lorco would be to win this contest in the presence of his father, and how equally proud the Duke would be to witness his son's triumph in front of the entire assembly of the Bishop's School.

The thought was unexpected and unwelcome, and I thrust it away almost as soon as it occurred to me. But it would not go away, and then I found myself stepping down from my little knoll and nodding to Lorco. He nodded back and we both turned on Borus, whose face had already begun to sag with disappointment. He knew he could not possibly win against me and Lorco; he could not have won against any pair, by that stage, but Lorco and I were the primary favorites, and to fight us both would be folly.

"Yield." Lorco spoke the word, and for the space of half a heartbeat I thought Borus might do as he was bidden, but then he showed us his true mettle and roared some kind of challenge in his own tongue, swinging his sword high and throwing away his shield at the same time to grip the weapon's hilt with both hands as he sprang hard and to his left, directly at me. He almost caught me unprepared, too, for I had really expected him to yield and had already been planning my opening moves against Lorco.

The tip of his hard-swung weapon whistled by the tip of my chin so closely that I felt the wind of its passing, but I was leaping backwards at the time. I landed awkwardly, unbalanced and unsteady, and most of my attention went perforce to leveling myself, but Borus was still pursuing me, almost on top of me, and a second heavy blow was already on its way towards my head. There was no time to think, but I knew I could not remain on my feet and avoid the descending sword, and so I simply gave way at the knees and rolled away as soon as I hit the ground.

The blow missed. I heard the sound of its passing and the grunt of effort with which Borus stopped the missed swing and tried to reverse it, but then I heard, too, the solid whack of what I knew could only be Lorco's sword against Borus's armor.

Came another grunt and a muttered curse and Borus sprawled on top of me, thrown down by the weight of Lorco's attack so that his cheek came to rest against mine. For the briefest moment I felt the softness of his face and the warmth of his expelled breath in my ear, and I wanted to giggle like a girl. But I was already scrambling away from him, frantically grappling and sliding to where I could regain my feet and defend myself against Lorco, who was now as much my enemy as was Borus.

I was almost successful, too, but as I braced myself solidly on my sword, using it as a staff to push myself up to my feet, Lorco smashed it sideways with his own, knocking it out of my grasp and dropping me straight down again to bang my chin against the ground and drive my teeth into the edge of my tongue. I managed to lurch into an ungainly forward roll and spun around, regaining my feet in time to see Borus's last stand. He had evidently hit Lorco as Lorco smashed my sword away, and now he had his sword above his head, still in a two-handed grip, ready to deliver the final blow. Lorco spun around and swung his sword, back-handedly, up into Borus's groin.

Borus fell like a stone and curled himself into a ball, clutching at his injured parts. Lorco raised his head and slowly pushed himself up onto all fours, looking around for me. I was standing, but barely, spitting blood from my swollen mouth and gasping for air like a winded ox, telling myself disbelievingly that I had never, ever felt so tired. The sword in my hand felt like the heaviest burden I had ever carried, but I knew that I had one more thing to do. I had to finish Lorco before he could stand up again, and he was already rising unsteadily.

I hoisted my weapon and moved forward to claim my victory, and as I did so I saw Duke Lorco again, gazing down wide eyed at his son, and my knees gave way and I found myself kneeling in the dirt, blinking up at my friend Stephan Lorco as he stood above me. I knew I did not have the strength to stand quickly enough and so I swung again, low and wide and as hard as I could, a hacking, horizontal slash at Lorco's knees. His blade sliced down in an opposing blow and stopped my swing almost effortlessly, and I did not see the following stroke that hit my thickly padded leather helm and sent me flying sideways into darkness.

5

"Is he that good a friend?"

The question caught me unprepared, but Tiberias Cato was not the only one who would ask it of me in the time that followed. I had just picked myself up off the ground and begun to limp towards the medical pavilion and I had not even had time yet to realize that I needed to ask myself the same thing: *was* Lorco that good a friend that I would willingly sacrifice my chances of capturing all the triumph of the moment and winning a valuable prize simply to ensure that he might look as good as possible for his visiting father? Or was I deluding myself? Had I, in fact, sacrificed anything? Had I hung back and allowed Lorco to beat me, or would he have beaten me anyway? Apparently I had done something, and done it overtly, for Cato growled his question at me out of the corner of his mouth as he swept by me on his way to present the victor's prize to my friend Lorco, and for a short space of time I was too taken aback to realize the import of his words.

I blinked blearily and swung around to peer after Cato as he strode to where the victor of the day stood spread-legged with exhaustion now that the battle was over. I could hear Lorco panting heavily from where I stood, twenty paces away, and I watched his chest heaving beneath his leather cuirass as he fought to regain his breath, his head dangling and his arms hanging straight from his shoulders. He was swaying on his feet, and he looked as though he might topple forward at any moment to measure his own length on the dirt of the arena, but Tiberias Cato marched right up to him and grasped him by the upper arm, then turned him firmly towards the spot where his father and Bishop Germanus sat watching from the reviewing stand.

I had seen that Cato was carrying a sheathed sword tucked beneath his arm, a long-bladed cavalry spatha, and as I watched him present it to Lorco, I began to appreciate what I had lost and felt the first tug of regret. The spatha was Tiberias Cato's own sword, a superb weapon, probably one of the finest of its kind ever made. It had been bought for him many years earlier by Germanus himself, in Constantinople, shortly after Cato had signed up with the legatus as an Assistant Master of Horse, charged with teaching the garrison's troopers some of the new techniques and skills that he had brought back with him from the lands of the Smoke People, where he was raised. This was a distant eastern land, far beyond the boundaries of the Empire, a place where all people had straight black hair, skin of yellowish brown and strangely slanted eyes. Tiberias Cato's father had traveled there as a merchant, taking his wife and young son with him in his unending search for new and exotic goods to trade, and when he and his wife died there of a fever, their orphaned son was brought up by the local tribesmen and lived among them until he achieved manhood and was able to go in search of his own birthplace and his surviving kinsmen.

That sword had gone everywhere with Tiberias Cato since the day it came into his possession. It had hung either from his waist or from his saddle on every campaign in which he fought for two decades and more. I was astonished to think that he would ever even consider giving it away, even although he had no real use for it nowadays. My astonishment, however, quickly gave way to chagrin that it had not been won by me.

I heard applause from behind me and looked up to where Phillipus Lorco stood by his chair on the reviewing stand, flanked by Bishop Germanus and Brother Ansel and backed by everyone who had assembled to watch the day's events. All of them were applauding noisily, their eyes fixed on Lorco. I sniffed and shrugged off my disappointment, then made my way to the medical stand, where I knew I could at least find some cold water to drink. I had no injuries to speak of, apart from a few bumps and bruises that would soon fade and disappear.

Less than an hour later, having bathed and changed into fresh clothing, I was standing stiffly at attention in front of the work table in Tiberias Cato's quarters, hearing him repeat the question he had growled at me earlier.

"Don't feed me that swill," he barked when I responded as though I didn't know what he meant. "You know damned well what I mean. I asked you if he is that good a friend that you'd willingly give up a prize like that one today simply to make him look good—and don't try to deny what you did, either. I was watching you. You looked up so many times to where his father was sitting that you almost lost count of who was still in the arena. You were swiveling your head from side to side like a thief caught between two angry dogs."

There did not seem to be much I could say in response without lying or blustering, and so I said nothing, fighting against the urge to grow angry and staring directly at the wall behind him, my eyes leveled just above his head. He was partially correct, I told myself. I remembered looking from father to son and perhaps back again, that much was true; but I had not done it as often as he had suggested, and not in the way he seemed to mean. And besides, I was far from sure that I had willingly done anything to give up the fight. The more I thought about that, in fact, the more convinced I became that I had done no such thing. Cato, however, was not interested in any self-justification I might develop.

"Look at me, boy. Damnation, look me in the eye!" I did. "Humph! That's better. Don't ever be afraid to look a man right in the eye while he's tearing a piece off you with his tongue. As a matter of fact, you should teach yourself to be afraid *not* to look him in the eye. Everyone deserves a reprimand once in a while, because God knows everyone makes mistakes. But you show respect for the man who's dressing you down while he's doing it. It's his responsibility to do whatever he has to do to straighten you out and get you to mend your ways. Staring over his head as though he isn't there will just make him angry.

"Now, one more time, from a different viewpoint. Would your friend Lorco have done the same for you? Think hard. If your stepfather, Ban of Benwick, had been up there on the stand, would Lorco have done for you what you did for him today?"

"I don't—"

"*Think,* I said, before you answer."

"But—" He cut me off with a sidewise slash of his hand. I subsided, gritting my teeth, and began to think honestly about his question, since it was plain he would permit me to do nothing else. Would Lorco, in fact, have done the same thing for me, to his own cost?

"And before you answer that one, here's another. D'you think he knows what you did?"

Another question I had failed to consider. But that one was easier. I shook my head, emphatically. "No, Magister. He could not possibly know, because *I* don't even know if I did what you say I did. I thought about it, perhaps—no, I *know* I did—but only in the back of my mind. So, no . . . Lorco doesn't know."

"Well, let me ask you this: if we could restart the battle, would you be tempted to do it again—to give up the fight to make your friend look good? Would you?"

I was able to smile for the first time. "Not if I knew, going into the arena, what the prize was to be."

"Ignore the prize; prizes can change. Would you do it again?"

I thought about the last time I had seen Lorco, as I emerged from the bath house a short time earlier. He had been on his way in, walking towards the main entrance with its multicolored windows of tiny red- and gold-stained glass diamonds mounted between thin strips of lead. He had been talking to his father, his head tilted up towards the Duke's face and his left hand curled around the hilt of his new spatha, which now hung from a belt at his waist. Neither of them had seen me pass, so completely were they focused one upon the other. Now I remembered Lorco's smile as he gazed up at his father and I found myself smiling.

"Yes, Magister," I said. "I would do it again."

"Good!" The Master of Horse almost leaped to his feet. "That was decisive enough, even should it turn out to be a wrong decision."

He paused then, one hand suspended in the air, as though about to bless me—something that he would never dream of doing, being both a layman and a warrior. "But you still have not answered the first question: would Lorco do the same for you?"

I shook my head but spoke with conviction. "I can't say, Magister, one way or the other. I don't know whether he would or not, but I have just realized that, either way, the answer to your question is not important. Whatever I might have done out there, it felt like the right thing to do at the time. I certainly don't feel bad about having done it now. If, as I said, I did it."

Cato shrugged. "Very well, then. You're probably right. He was bound to beat you eventually and today was his time. Lucky thing you're not going to be here for much longer. I doubt you'd enjoy being second best more than once."

"Second best!" That stung me, but Cato had already begun to grin by the time I was able to think of a response, and I immediately swallowed what I had been about to say.

He nodded his head. "Aye, right. Let's forget about it from now on, shall we? The bishop wants to meet with you before dinner. He's tied up now with Brother Ansel and some of the other senior brethren, but he told me to send you in to wait for him when I was done with you. Now get out of here and don't keep him waiting. And let's both hope you'll never have to depend seriously on a friend's willingness to make a sacrifice for *you*. Out!"

I walked very slowly on my way to the bishop's chambers, dawdling unconscionably as I sought to grapple with new and strange ideas. I was beginning to realize, but only slowly and imper-fectly because it ran counter to what I saw then as logic, that Tiberias Cato was not angry at me at all, even while he clearly believed I had lost that day's battle deliberately. But then, even as that thought was occurring to me and challenging my beliefs about the man I thought I knew, I found myself amending it as a new understanding began to build upon itself: Cato would never condone such a thing as a deliberate loss. That is what was so confusing about what I had been thinking. The idea of someone setting out deliberately to lose a fight smacked of cheating; there was a definite connotation of dishonesty within that premise at some level; and that, from all I had come to know and admire about Tiberias Cato, would have been anathema to him, violating every principle of conduct that he possessed.

But then a new thought occurred to me, possibly the first purely philosophical thought I had ever had. The idea of someone deliberately choosing *not to win* was not at all the same thing as that person's making a deliberate choice to lose. As soon as I glimpsed that notion, seemingly solid in its logic, I snatched at it to examine it and devour it whole, but it eluded my grasp like smoke and left me feeling vaguely anxious, somehow mildly threatened, and aware that I had almost mastered a profound and tantalizing abstraction. I wanted to sit down there in a doorway by the edge of the thoroughfare to think the whole sequence of ideas through from front to back and from end to end, but then I noticed that the doorway in which I had paused was the one leading into the bishop's quarters and I was already too late to do anything but make my way inside.

I heard voices from the bishop's day room as I passed along the passageway that ran between Germanus's private quarters and his working, public rooms, and was quietly relieved to know that the meeting of the senior clerics, whatever it concerned, was still in progress and I had not, therefore, kept the bishop waiting. I knocked nonetheless before entering his private rooms and was unsurprised when one of the lay brethren opened the door and, waving me forward with the broom he was clutching, ushered me into the familiar anteroom, where a wood fire burned briskly in an iron basket set in an ornate fireplace in the wall near the entrance. I thanked the man courteously and took the chair he indicated, beside the fireplace, and settled in to wait for the bishop. The lay brother, who had not spoken a word and whose name I did not know, nodded to me and then quietly withdrew into what I knew was the bishop's bedchamber, where he was obviously doing some kind of cleaning chore. A pocket of resin in one of the logs on the fire ignited and spat loudly, making me jump, and I gazed into the burning mass, trying to detect where the explosion had occurred.

I had seen stone fireplaces indoors before—life in King Ban's great stone castle, with its thick walls, tiny windows and perpetually darkened rooms would have been intolerable without huge fireplaces, and logs that were large enough to be considered tree trunks were kept burning in them night and day, to banish the shadows and generate much-needed heat. Until I came to Auxerre, however, I had never seen a smaller version, in a smaller, brighter, better-lit household—and having said that, I must add that until then I had never even imagined the existence of smaller, brighter, better-lit households. I knew of only two kinds of dwellings: the stone huts that ordinary people lived in where I came from, which varied in size but never in design, being either round or square and consisting only of one common room, usually windowless; and the massive fortresses in which the rulers lived. The presence of light indoors, in an unfortified dwelling place, and the feelings of spacious airiness created by that light, had been the single most telling difference I found between life in Auxerre and the Bishop's School and life in the land in which I had grown up with King Ban and Queen Vivienne. Here, in the civilized fastnesses of north-central Gaul, where peace had reigned virtually uninterrupted for hundreds of years, people had learned how to live elegantly, in wondrous houses built with pleasure and entertainment in mind.

Indoor fireplaces were yet uncommon here. I knew of only six others in addition to the one here in the anteroom to Germanus's sleeping chamber. He had worked and soldiered too long under a hot sun, the bishop said, to permit him to be warm away from the sun's direct rays, and so he kept a fire near him at all times, even going to the extreme lengths of building one into his house. I found it amusing but thought-provoking that every one of the other five similar fireplaces I had seen were in the homes of retired soldiers, men who, like Germanus, had spent years and even decades on campaign beneath desert suns.

"Ah, Clothar, you are here. I hope you have not been waiting long?"

I leaped to my feet, not having heard Germanus enter the room, but he was already waving me back into my seat.

"Stay, stay where you are." He crossed the room to the long table beneath the glazed window opposite the fireplace and carefully placed the parchment scrolls he had been carrying so that they would not roll off and tumble to the floor, moving a heavy ink well against one side of the pile to ensure that they would stay. That done, he turned back to gaze at me in silence for some time. I gazed back, but although he was looking at me, I knew he was not really seeing me, for it was clear that his mind was elsewhere. His lower lip was thrust forward, covering the line of his upper one completely, and I knew that this indicated deep thought prior to some momentous announcement, for that expression, known throughout the school as the Bishop's Pout, appeared only in times of extreme deliberation and deep concern, and everyone who knew Germanus recognized it immediately.

"Is something wrong, Father Germanus?" I asked, daring to interrupt his thoughts. He blinked, then seemed to shake himself although he made no visible move.

"No." I could tell from his voice that that was true. "No, there is nothing wrong, nothing at all. It's simply that—" He broke off and frowned slightly. "It seems like an unconscionable time since last we spoke. When was it?"

"Eight weeks ago, Father. The day before you left to go to Britain."

"Aye, right, eight weeks ago . . . Dear Lord, the time is flying nowadays. Eight weeks, gone in a blink, and it seems but yesterday since I was talking to Ludovic about our plans for traveling, and that in itself must have been nigh on half a year ago." He paused, and then asked, "Did you really believe it necessary for your friend Lorco to win this afternoon?"

I gaped at him, caught off balance yet again by the sudden emergence of this question when I had not expected it, but this time, having been through the exercise of discussing the matter with Tiberias Cato, I responded more quickly and more easily.

"Yes, Father. I did."

"Hmm. Why? Do you object to my asking?"

"No, Father, of course not, but Tiberias Cato and you both noticed what happened. Do you think anyone else saw?"

Father Germanus shook his head tersely. "No, I doubt it. Cato and I noticed it because we both know you as well as we do, and we saw . . . shall we say, a certain lack of fire and energy in your attack? Duke Lorco took great pleasure in his son's prowess. You intended that to be the case, did you not?" I nodded. "I thought so. Why?"

I shrugged. "Lorco is my friend, sir, and his father's esteem is important to him. I saw that today, and I first noticed it yesterday, when word came of his father's visit. It was good that he should win and make his father proud."

The bishop smiled a tiny smile and raised his right hand to bless me. "Peace be upon you, then. I shall beseech God in my prayers to furnish you with friends worthy of such loyalty and trust."

I smiled. "Thank you, Father."

"Do not thank me, boy. Friendship is God's gift for fortunate men to share. It is a wonderful phenomenon and it exists according to its own rules and regulations. Its criteria are unique unto itself and it is restrained by none of the usual demands that people place upon other people's behavior."

Once launched upon a favorite topic—and I knew by this time that the bishop loved to talk about the criteria governing friendship—Germanus could be virtually unstoppable. I sat back and listened for a long time as he held forth on all that he believed about friendship, and much of what he told me that afternoon is still as alive in me today, and as fresh and credible, as it was when I first heard it that day.

He talked about the nature of friendship and about its durability; about how it could, and often did, spring out of nowhere, fully formed to take both members of the relationship by surprise, and then he went on to describe how, at other times and in other circumstances, it might grow slowly and almost unnoticeably, unsuspected by either participant. He pointed out to me, too, that friendship is untrammeled and unconstrained in its acceptance in a friend of appearances and personality quirks that would be unacceptable in anyone else; and from there he progressed to a discussion—albeit one sided—of the nature of friendship and its relationship to love.

I listened, fascinated, to everything he had to say, hanging on his every word and feeling no urge to speak or to intrude upon what he was unfolding to me.

Love, he maintained, is an essential part of friendship, although it might be seldom mentioned by the friends themselves, but friendship may not necessarily be a part of love. Physical love—sexual love—and the state of being *in* love he explained as being conditions that completely enfold two individual people, fusing them emotionally and inexorably into a single unit of awareness and rendering them generally oblivious to everything else that is taking place in the world about them. They are a pair, but in the fiery singularity of their love for each other they exist as a single entity that shuts out the rest of the world.

Friendship, on the other hand, while also confined to two people, involved each of the two less exclusively and far less selfishly. Lovers demanded closeness—*propinquity* was the word he used—but friends could remain friends at opposite ends of the world and their friendship was undeterred by years of separation. Each friend in a pair might have many other friends, and those friends might like or dislike any of their friend's other friends, but the initial pair's friendship was a thing unique to the two of them, and though they might choose to extend the privilege of their friendship to others, their own friendship remained strictly and at all times a private matter between the two of them. I blinked, I recall, when he said that, but I managed to follow it without difficulty.

True friendship, he asserted in summing up, was a unique and divinely privileged phenomenon, and in consequence it was a condition that occurred only rarely in the life of any single person.

If a man could name five close, lifetime friends before he died, Germanus said, then that man's life had truly been blessed.

I clearly remember that as I listened to him say that I felt uncomfortable, skeptical and even slightly embarrassed by what I perceived as his naivety, for I was fifteen years old and had a wealth of friends—scores of them, I thought. I was prepared to accept everything else that Germanus had had to say on the subject of friends and friendship, and in fact I had been delighted to hear him endorse some of the ideas that had occurred to me in thinking about my friends, but I really did believe that he was being ingenuous in insisting upon this scarcity of true friendship. Alas, two decades were to pass before I came to appreciate what he had meant.

"Now, I have a task for you, should you be willing to accept it."

I straightened with a jerk, aware that I had been wool-gathering.

"Anything, Father," I said. "Anything, and gladly."

"Hmm. Enthusiasm, without knowing what is involved? Thank you." Smiling at his own observation, he crossed to the armchair on the other side of the fire and sat down, tugging at the voluminous folds of his outer garment and shifting in his seat until he had adjusted everything and could sit in comfort. "I want you to go home," he said, and then, before I could react, he held up his palm to forestall me. "I have just returned from Britain, as you know, and much happened while I was over there—happened here, I mean, in Gaul, not merely in Britain."

I nodded, silently, and waited.

"I was supposed to spend last night in Lutetia, for no other reason originally than the fact that it lies on the direct route here from the coast. But it is also a central point for irregular gatherings of bishops, and one of those was convened while I was in Britain, in response to several urgent matters that arose unexpectedly and could not safely be postponed. It was known that I would be returning shortly from Britain, but couriers were dispatched to find me sooner and to summon me to the gathering in Lutetia as quickly as I could travel. They missed me on their first pass because I had made a detour for reasons of my own, and by the time they found me I was preparing to leave for home, so they only gained a single day on my planned schedule. Thus I arrived in Lutetia one day earlier than I had intended, and spent not one but two nights there, conferring with my pastoral brethren."

His face clouded, and he sat staring for a space of moments into the flames in the fire basket, but then he collected himself again and straightened slightly, looking me in the eye. "You may or may not have heard mutterings of what is going on in the world outside our school, but there is widespread unrest, and troublesome events are shaping up here in Gaul . . . very real threats of another war, which is the last thing any of us needs. These threats are arising from several sources. Most particularly, however, they are emanating from the lands of the Burgundian tribes, to the south and west of where we sit today. The imperial military intelligence people have been warning us for years now that the Burgundians are poised to spill out of their present holdings in an attempt to conquer all of central and southern Gaul, and first and foremost, from my perspective, those are not good tidings for the Church. The Burgundians, as you know, are not Christian and are, in fact, violently opposed to us and to our faith. They seem to delight in killing priests and bishops and in persecuting the faithful wherever they find them, and so we—my brother bishops and our clergy—will be using all the influence at our disposal, marshaling and channeling our combined resources to deflect and disarm the rebels' initiatives however and wherever we can—working in conjunction, of course, with the legions." Again he paused, considering his next words.

"It was forewarnings of a Burgundian revolt that caused the Imperial Administration in Treves to summon Duke Lorco here from his base in Carcasso, but I have received forewarnings, too, from my own sources, concerning another aspect of the same revolt, and that is why I require your assistance—not because you are a doughty fighter and a champion of God's work, although you show all the signs of growing into such strengths, but because you are Ban's nephew and adopted son and Ban is my friend. And so I would have you leave here in four days' time, bearing messages

from me to your kinsman Ban and traveling with your friend
Stephan Lorco and his father the Duke when they leave to return to
their own lands in the south. Their journey home to Carcasso will
take them within sixty miles of where you live, and I have asked the
Duke to provide you with an escort from his group for that short
portion of the journey that will remain to bring you to Genava. He
assures me that he will see you safely delivered home. Will you do
this for me?"

"Of course, Father," I said, attempting to mask my disappointment at being sent home from school before my just time had
elapsed. Even as I voiced my consent, however, I saw that he had
told me nothing other than that he was sending me away. Because
King Ban, my uncle, was his friend, he had said, Germanus wanted
me to leave his school and go home. For what purpose? And if it
were only to bear messages, why would he send me and not a fast-
riding courier? Beginning to grow increasingly confused, I bit down
upon my rising panic and forced myself to try to speak what was in
my mind. "You want me to carry a message to King Ban . . . from
you and in person . . . but what do you wish me to tell him, Father?"

He seemed completely unaware of my discomfiture and merely
smiled, shaking his head very slightly in dismissal of any concerns
I might have. "Nothing that you need lose sleep about. I will put
everything into words on paper in the next few days, because it is of
extreme importance that I say what must be said properly, with no
possibility of being misunderstood. I shall therefore write, and
rewrite, and write yet again. It will be sufficient for you to carry the
missives that I write to your uncle the King, thereby assuring him
that they come directly from me to him, as a friend. That done, and
having spent some pleasant and restful times with your aunt, the
Lady Vivienne, you will hie yourself back here as soon as may be,
for this is merely the first such task I have assigned to you and by
the time you return I will have great need of you—" He broke off,
arching one eyebrow. "You wish to say something."

"I . . . I am to return, then, Magister? I thought you were sending
me away for good."

"I *am* sending you away for good, boy—for good reason and to even better purpose. I am sending you upon a mission for the well-being of God's Church and her faithful servants, which means, in effect, that I am sending you upon God's own work. But I am far from being finished with your education, if that is what you really meant to suggest. I have much in mind for you, and none of it entails sending you back to Genava permanently as a punishment for having reached the age of sixteen." He smiled. "In truth, I see little of Genava in your future, my young friend, at least for several years. That is, at least in part, why I am sending you home on this mission. It will give you an opportunity to take your leave of your family again before moving on to the next level of your endeavors."

As his words washed over me I felt relieved, elated and exalted. I would be called upon to do a man's work here in central Gaul, it seemed. I felt the merest twitching of guilt in acknowledging then that I been dreading my eventual return to Genava, fearing that the life I had known there previously would suffer gravely now by comparison to all that I had known here in Auxerre. Now, however, with the blessing bestowed by these new duties, I could return gratefully to the lakeside to revisit and embrace all my old friends and loved ones before taking off yet again on expanded adventures.

When I left the bishop's quarters that afternoon, I was bubbling inside with excitement, and every philosophical thought that had simmered in my mind earlier had been obliterated by the import of what I could now look forward to doing and being. I had four days left as a schoolboy; four days to wrap up the raiment of my time as a student; and after that, like a chrysalis shedding its outer skin, I would be reborn as an entirely new being: a man and a warrior dedicated to the greater glory of God.

URSUS

1

I do not know where I was on the day my boyhood came to an end, but I remember the occasion very well because the horror of it never left me and still has the power today to stir the hairs on the nape of my neck and make me shudder with dread. I can recall every aspect of the countryside that surrounded me that day, and most particularly I can remember with absolute clarity the last scene I saw before my world was suddenly changed for all time.

I never have known, however, exactly where we were that day. It was our fourth day out of Auxerre, heading south at a leisurely pace. We were riding two abreast, twelve of us and one two-horse wagon. Our party was strung out along a surprisingly hard-packed path that followed the osier-lined left bank of a broad, muddy-brown river that eddied sluggishly, its waters looking thick and viscous beneath a sun that was too bright and too hot for the time of the year, even in southern Gaul. It had been raining heavily to the north and east of us for two entire days; although we ourselves had not seen as much as a storm cloud in the skies around us, there was no mistaking the signs in the river. We had watched the water level rise alarmingly these past two days, swelling and filling up the channel until the banks had entirely vanished and the sullen waters spilled over in several low-lying places to flood the fields on either side. We had managed to remain on slightly higher ground at all times, however, and nothing untoward had happened to us. The river was swollen to the point of threat, but yet the ground around us and ahead of us was firm and almost drought-dry.

Paralleling our path on the left, some distance away but easily discernible, was the wide, dusty swath carved by the small army of Duke Phillipus Lorco as it passed by earlier that morning. We were a hunting party, dispatched the previous afternoon to harvest fresh meat for the troopers, and we had done well that morning, so that now, approaching midday, we were riding to rejoin the main body of our party, avoiding the dusty track stirred up by the earlier troops and staying on the narrow, hard-packed riverside path. The light four-wheeled wagon we had with us was loaded with six large deer carcasses—enough meat to keep everyone in the one-hundred-and-twenty-strong main force smiling and well fed for several days.

Lorco and I were riding together at the very rear of the loose column, close behind the wagon with the butchered deer, and although it was an unpleasant place to be, what with the swarming flies and the thick stink of the fresh, congealing blood that attracted them, it was nonetheless a spot that kept us safely out of sight of our two current nemeses, Harga, the Sergeant-at-Arms, and Dirk, the huntsman, both of whom had been charged by Lorco's father to watch us closely and keep us out of mischief. They were an ill-matched and foul-tempered pair and neither of them even tried to like us or to tolerate us. To them we were nothing more than an imposition, an accursed nuisance to be frowned upon, shouted at and generally held in subjection. And so we naturally set about immediately finding ways of thwarting them and doing as we wished. To that end, we were hiding from them at the rear of the meat wagon as we plotted our escape from their supervision.

Harga and Dirk lent themselves easily, albeit unknowingly, to our mischief. No one with eyes to see would ever describe either one of them as comely, and so we had named them Castor and Pollux, the heavenly twins, thinking ourselves extremely witty. We were now out of their direct line of sight, safe behind the tailgate of the wagon as we enjoyed a laugh at their expense. For their part, the two jailers rode on side by side, unaware of us or of our disdain.

Disturbed by our passage, an enormous flock of crows rose up with a clatter of flapping wings from a recently plowed field to our left and then wheeled away from us, cawing and screaming raucously as only crows know how. Mildly surprised at their number, I watched them go, following the dense cloud of them easily with my eyes until they disappeared into the leafy masses of a trio of huge old conical trees that stood like tapered, towering candles in the distance, close by a distant stretch of river that caught the afternoon sun's light in a silvery dazzle of reflected brightness.

Lorco had fallen behind me by half a length, his horse stomping and cavorting, protesting at the cloud of horse flies that swarmed around us, and as I turned in my saddle to speak to him one of the flies landed on my nose and began crawling down, towards my mouth. I brought up my hand to brush it away as Lorco said, "That's the biggest flock of crows I ev—"

My life changed at that instant, blasted by a sight I should never have seen.

I saw what happened because I was looking directly at Lorco's mouth as his lips formed the words. I heard the sounds that accompanied the event and noted them because they were so strange and jarring. And both sight and sounds were seared indelibly into my memory. And yet I failed utterly to comprehend what I had heard and seen . . . and even now, I find myself wondering which came first, the sight, or the sounds? Such was their speed when they occurred that they were indistinguishable, but in a hundred dreams throughout the year that followed, they broke apart, sounds and sight, and took place again and again, inexorably and appallingly, sometimes sight followed by sound, sometimes the other way around, but always with the power to snap me sharply awake, gasping and filled with terror.

As my fingers brushed at the end of my nose, dislodging the tickling fly, Lorco's entire head appeared to change shape. It was a phenomenon too brief to register, but I saw, or it seemed I saw, his entire head *flex* in less than the blink of an eye, the way a reflection will sometimes undulate in a calm, dark pool when an unseen fish passes beneath. It was as though all the bones of his skull had suddenly been replaced, for a mere flicker of time, by a liquid-filled bladder of some kind. It lurched and instantly reformed itself. And as this odd event occurred I heard alien noises: an abrupt, violent hiss and a ripping, rending, meaty sound that terminated in a solid, crunching *thunk!* as something propelled Lorco towards me with great force, jerking him forward from the waist as his face split asunder in a welter of blood and flying pieces of whiteness that I would later come to recognize as teeth and fragments of shattered bone.

I did nothing, frozen in the instant by disbelief and feeling something within me grasped and crushed in the grip of a massive fist of solid, icy coldness that I could not even begin to recognize. I saw my best friend's suddenly ruined face come thrusting towards me, a spray of blood bursting from his ruptured mouth, filling the space between us with a red, wet mist, and then I saw his eyes, wide and terrified, shrieking at me in eloquent silence, begging me to tell him what had happened. Unable to move, I saw his horse begin to spin and carry him away from me, and as he began to topple sideways to the ground I finally saw the arrow that had killed him. It was a heavy, iron-headed war arrow, triple-bladed and wickedly barbed, and it had struck the back of his neck, severing his spine before passing through the cavity of his mouth to shatter his upper front teeth and emerge through the base of his nose.

Even as Lorco pitched forward, and knowing that he would crash head first to the ground, I still had not begun to comprehend what had happened. Then I heard shouting, and saw movement ahead of me, and looked up towards the rear of our train in time to see the man who had shot Lorco preparing to loose another arrow at me. I remained frozen, but fortunately my horse was already reacting uneasily to the panic it sensed in its companion. It reared sideways, tossing its head and whinnying, and I watched the arrow spring from the killer's bow and leap across the intervening space between us to hiss by me so closely that I felt its passing. And now, as my panicky mount spun me around, I saw that our entire party was surrounded and outnumbered by a swarm of strangers, most of them armed with bows. Even as I looked I saw Harga go down with two arrows in him, one of them deep in his skull behind the right ear, having pierced his leather helmet.

"Fool," I remember thinking, seeing the silvery iron helmet hanging from his saddle. "He should know better than that." I should have, too, for my own helmet hung close by my knee, but I was a mere boy, not a soldier, and so I absolved myself.

Then clarity returned and terror threatened to overwhelm me as I saw that I had mere moments in which to save myself or die. I could see six of my companions, not counting Lorco, already sprawled in the dirt of the path, and I saw several of the enemy take note of me sitting there, high up and empty handed on my fine horse. One of them was almost within reach of me by that time, an outstretched hand grasping for my reins. I snatched them myself, barely in time, and pulled them tight, swinging my horse around hard, striking the man with its shoulder and sending him sprawling.

Someone shouted urgently, a warning to someone else to catch me before I could escape, but I was already spurring my horse hard, roweling him viciously in my need to get away from there. Another form leaped up at me, attempting to seize my bridle, but my horse was already surging forward. I kicked out with a savagery born of desperation and the man fell away as the thick, iron-studded sole of my heavy riding boot connected with his ear. I dug with my spurs again and now I could feel the strength of the horse beneath me as he strove to leap away from the gouging torment of the pain in his sides.

Another man leaped at me and was struck and thrust aside by the plunging horse, and a fourth slipped and fell with a cry beneath its trampling hooves. I heard three sharp, whistling sounds that I recognized as close-shot arrows, but I was almost free of the throng by then, with only two men now between me and the bare fields beyond. The man farthest to my right had a bow, and as I saw him he brought the weapon up and sighted towards me. Acting purely on instinct, I let go my reins, seized a handful of mane in each fist and threw myself down along the horse's left side until I was hidden from the bowman completely. It was a trick I had practiced with this horse many times, for more than a year, and the only means the bowman had of countering it was to ignore me and shoot the horse. Fortunately, he did not. He may have wondered what happened to me, but by the time he stopped gawping I was past both him and his companion and my horse was galloping flat out. I swung myself back up into the saddle and leaned forward as his arrow belatedly flew by me, missing widely. I sighted between the animal's ears towards the dark line of trees that marked the outer edge of the forest wherein I knew I would be safe—safer by far, at any rate, than I could be in the open fields that flanked the river—and raked him with my spurs again.

No one tried to follow me, and an hour later I dismounted by a narrow, fast-flowing stream where I lay on my belly and thrust my face into the water, drinking greedily until I could drink no more. The water was cold enough to hurt, but I made no attempt to get up. Instead, I rolled my head from side to side, soaking my head completely and allowing, encouraging, the chill to keep me numb and thoughtless. When I could stand the cold no longer, I pushed myself up onto my knees and tried to stand but fell instead to all fours in the streambed and vomited up what I had drunk.

I do not remember crawling out of the water, but some time later, it might have been an hour, perhaps even longer, I awoke on my side on the thick grass beneath one of the trees on the stream's bank.

There was a thought, a memory, already in my mind when I regained consciousness that afternoon on the bank of the stream. It was the memory of my own hubris, less than two weeks earlier. When I had learned that Bishop Germanus had great things in mind for me once I had reached sixteen, I had thought of myself as being a man and a warrior dedicated to the greater glory of God. Now the recollection of it made me cringe with shame.

For more than five years I had been among the top students of the Bishop's School and for the last three of those years I had shown myself to be virtually unbeatable in the military training segments of our daily curriculum. I had worked hard and trained constantly, cherishing dreams of being a warrior, until now, today, and my first opportunity to put my training to the test. And I had fled in terror.

A voice in my mind told me to stand up and be a man, but I tucked my hands into my armpits and drew up my knees, hunching myself into a ball and moaning aloud as I allowed myself at last to recall what had occurred. Again and again and yet again I watched poor Lorco's face explode and saw him falling sideways into death, and yet, insanely, I was concerned above all else that he was about to land on his head and injure himself on the hard ground. And then I began to recall the bodies of our companions as I had seen them last: Harga, falling backwards from his saddle, arms spread, an arrow in his skull and another protruding from beneath his left arm; Gorgo, our finest bowman, sprawled face down in the dust of the path, his buttocks thrusting comically into the air because of the way he had fallen; Dirk the huntsman and Alith and Fistus, his runners, and Petrarch the cook, who always liked to see his food being killed, and limping Tamarus, his assistant—all of them recognizable in a single glance, all of them dead within moments of each other, reduced to shapeless huddles of drab, bloodied rags.

And then my mind showed me images of our attackers, more than a score of them, perhaps as many as two score; screaming men, many of them aiming bows, many more running headlong, leaping and charging towards me and whoever else might have survived their first murderous onslaught. They had appeared from nowhere, it seemed, springing fully formed from the earth itself like the demons spawned by the dragon's teeth in the ancient tale that had terrified and thrilled me as a child. As I thought about them at greater length, however, it became obvious that they had been lying waiting for us among the osier willows on the riverbank and in the long grass on the left side of the path we followed.

Harga had committed the primary sin of military command by riding through unknown territory without advance guards, and all of us had paid a fearsome price for his neglect, lulled into false security by the knowledge that we were following close on the heels of our own forces. Once more I saw the ground around our group covered suddenly with leaping, running men, and I heard their screams and felt again the terror that had consumed me. And I saw myself again kicking one man in the head and then spurring my horse into a dead run, running and running and running as far and as fast as the beast would carry me.

I had fled from battle at the first hint of hardship, and the knowledge burned in me like gall. I howled aloud and squirmed and kicked on the hard ground, weeping and wailing like an infant and wriggling and groveling in abject misery, and had I been able to dig like a mole I feel sure I would have buried myself alive, then and there.

Eventually, however, these convulsions of grief and self-loathing died away and gave place to emptiness and a great, welling, leaden-hearted misery. I lay motionless after that for a long time, mentally identifying and exploring the aches and pains I had imposed upon myself in lying there. I had used up all my store of tears and my whole chest felt hollow, like an inflated bladder, weightless and yet filled somehow with tension and unbearable loss.

I must have fallen asleep at some point during all of that, because the next thing I became aware of was a deep, explosive snort and the sound of a hoof stamping close by my head. I jerked awake to see my horse looming above me, and the sight of him filled me with another wave of guilt and shame, for I saw that I had left him fully saddled and bridled. I sat up, groaning with the effort, and pushed myself to my feet, where I stood swaying for a time before I felt strong enough to reach out and take hold of his reins. As soon as he felt the reins in my hand, he snorted again, softly this time, blowing air through his velvet muzzle, and raised his head high, pointing his ears forward and then standing motionless, as though waiting for me to mount. I stroked his neck and muzzle, then slapped him on the neck and told him to wait while I returned to the water to kneel and drink again from the stream, more decorously this time and knowing that I would not be sick again. I dried my mouth with the back of my hand and swung myself up into the saddle, where I sat for a time, simply looking about me and trying to decide what I ought to do. My horse whickered again, his ears twitching as he waited for my signal, and as I bent forward slightly to lay my hand on his neck, my outstretched fingers touched the top of the heavy bronze helmet that hung from the hook on my saddle bow.

I stopped, staring at the helmet and remembering the sight of Harga's hanging from his saddle in the same way. Had he been wearing the thing, the arrow that pierced his skull would probably have been deflected and he might never have had to fling up his arm the way he had, exposing his vulnerable armpit to the second arrow that struck him. I suddenly felt the welcome weight of my own full-body armor: a complete front and back cuirass of hammered bronze, with matching kirtle of armored straps and, strapped to my riding boots, long, heavy leg greaves that came up above my knees. A long-bladed spatha hung by my left side from a sword belt that crossed my chest, and a matching dagger hung in a sheath from my right hip.

I should not have been wearing armor that day at all, as a member of a hunting party, but Harga had been in a vengeful frame of mind that morning and had ordered both of us, Lorco and me, to wear full armor as a punishment for being what he called "insolent smart-arses." He had discovered, the previous afternoon, that the wagon we were using to transport the deer we killed also contained the four chests belonging to Lorco and me containing our clothing and our armor. They had been loaded in Auxerre when we joined the Lorco expedition to ride south with them. Harga had thought it highly amusing to make us undo the bindings and unpack our chests and to display all our goods and possessions to the others in the hunting party. He took a malicious pleasure in trying to humiliate us that way, but we, having spent the previous five years living in communal quarters with close to a hundred other boys, saw nothing belittling in what he made us do, because in fact the complete display of everything brought from home into the Bishop's School was a ritual event, undergone by every new boy who joined the scholastic ranks, and in those instances much, including anything edible, was confiscated by the older boys. Of course, we said nothing about that to Harga.

And so this day we had worn armor in the blazing sun. But we had been on our best behavior for most of the day and even Harga had not objected—in fact he had pretended not to see—when we took off our helmets. A new wave of grief swept over me as I realized belatedly that Lorco, too, might still be alive had he been wearing his helmet. My eyes awash again with sudden tears I would have sworn a moment earlier could not be in me, I gulped and swallowed and bent forward to take the heavy bronze helmet from its hook and slide it over my head. The sudden hollow hush that surrounded me as the leather-lined cask sank over my ears was unexpectedly peaceful, and the restriction of vision caused by the broad, hinged cheek protectors forced me to sit straighter and turn my head when I wanted to look at anything that did not lie directly ahead of me. I unsheathed my spatha and held it up to where I could see the blade, unbloodied, unsullied, unused. I sheathed it again and kicked my horse forward in a walk.

As soon as the animal began to move, my body adjusted to its motion and my thoughts became cogent and cohesive. I glanced up at the sky and saw the sun low in the west, its glare trapped behind all but the edges of a swollen cloud. The attack, I knew, had occurred before noon, so I must have been lying by the stream in the woods for several hours. By this time, I knew, the enemy, whoever they had been, must have collected their booty and moved on long since. But what they might have done with the bodies of my companions was an unknown that I had to address. Bad enough that I had run away from the killing field in the first place, but if I were to return to the Duke as the sole survivor of this debacle, I would have to bring information on the aftermath of the slaughter, verifying and reporting the names of the others dead . . . besides his son.

My jaws began to ache with the strain of gritting my teeth together as I made my way back to the scene by the riverside, following the deeply gouged tracks of my earlier, headlong flight without difficulty and growing increasingly aware that if anyone had chosen to follow me they would have had no trouble finding me and killing me.

I saw the wagon first, standing abandoned near the river, among grass that grew as high as its axles. The horses were gone, as were the butchered deer carcasses; clearly our attackers had had no wish to encumber themselves with a wheeled vehicle. As I approached, I thought at first that I could see a body hunched on the ground beside one of the rear wheels, but on closer inspection it proved to be the broken, boxy shape of one of the chests that had been on the wagon. There were articles of clothing all over the surrounding ground, scattered to the winds as though they had been pulled from their chests and flung straight up into the air, but whether they had been mine or Lorco's I had no idea and less concern. They were garments, clothing, things of less than no value. I moved on.

The first body I found was that of Borg, the cheerful young man who had driven the wagon and had been the friendliest of the group towards me and Lorco. His throat had been slashed open, almost severing his head, and he had been stripped naked. My stomach heaved as I looked down for the first few moments at what remained of him, but then I swallowed hard and tugged on my reins, turning my mount, and my eyes, away in search of others.

I could see most of the others now, their lifeless bodies strewn haphazardly over a surprisingly wide expanse of ground, and I guessed that some of them must have fought hard and long before being cut down so far from the path, irrespective of whether their horses had carried them there alive or dead. There were no dead horses, however, although it did not occur to me to look for any at first. Only when I saw the distance at which some of the bodies lay from the river path did I think to look about me for dead animals, and at that point another element of the enigma of what had happened clicked into place. I remembered waiting for the thump of an arrow hammering into my mount's side as I hid behind its bulk from the aiming bowman, and I recalled being surprised that the killing shot had not come. Now, however, that was no longer so surprising. These men, whoever they had been, had attacked us for our horses and perhaps our weapons, no more than that. They had not been interested in simple plunder.

As soon as I saw the truth of that I tried to recall the attackers. Hazy, confused images came to me at first, of open, screaming mouths and wild, staring eyes; of madly running men brandishing fearsome weapons and intent upon my death; of flashing, naked, dirty limbs, long, bony legs and knobby knees and, in some instances, bare, muddy feet. And then my mind fastened upon an image of one particular man, the man who had flanked the bowman whom I dodged by hiding behind my horse's barrel. He had been facing me, too, crouched and tense, ready to kill should I approach him closely enough, but the fearsome weapon he had clutched in one hand, upraised and ready to strike, had been misshapen and clumsy looking, a club of some kind—a plain, heavy-looking wooden cudgel that looked nowhere near as menacing as the ash wood practice swords I had been using for years at the Bishop's School. This killer had not even had a blade to brandish. From that recollection sprang others, and I rapidly began to revise my opinion of our opponents.

They had been stronger in numbers than we were, but they had not been as well armed, and the impressions I had had of heavily armed and armored men had been born more from frightened panic than from observation. Many of them had been bowmen, true, but I could recall now, looking back less fearfully, that more than half of them had not. The essence of their victory had lain in the success of the trap they laid; in their numbers and the speed and surprise of their onslaught. More than anything else, however, their victory had been our fault, attributable to the slovenly, incompetent leadership of the Sergeant-at-Arms, Harga.

Chilled by that assessment, I sucked in a deep breath and set about my self-imposed task of cataloguing the dead. We had been thirteen, including myself, Lorco and Borg the wagon driver, but I found fifteen corpses scattered about the field, and four of those

were strangers to me. That meant that there was a body missing, and
someone else from our group had survived the attack, unless—
and the idea came to me quickly, surprising me with my own
pessimism—the missing man had tried to escape by the river and had
been killed in the water. I pulled my horse's head around and
turned to look towards the river, and as I did so I thought I saw a
flicker of movement off to my right, among the osier willow that
lined the riverbank.

I froze, afraid to turn my head again and look more closely, but
then, accepting that I had a choice of fleeing yet again or staying
where I was, perhaps to die this time, I acknowledged to myself
with great bitterness that I would never be able to live with the
shame of running away again, and so I gritted my teeth, unsheathed
my spatha and turned to face directly towards the place where I had
seen the movement, seeing the spot slide into clear focus in the gap
between the side flaps of my helmet.

I stared and waited, silently defying whoever was there to step
forth, but no one appeared and nothing moved, and eventually I
began to feel foolish, sitting there on my horse like a living statue
and facing an uninhabited stretch of treed riverbank. I nudged my
heels into my horse's flanks and it began to walk forward slowly, its
ears pricked in the direction we were taking. And then, in a burst of
movement that brought my heart into my mouth, Lorco's horse
lurched out from among the distant willows and came trotting
towards us, whinnying a welcome. The sight of it almost unmanned
me yet again, for I had assumed that the raiders had taken it with all
the others, but seeing it trotting towards me, with Lorco's silver
helmet dangling from its saddle hook, I realized that it must have
run away right at the start of the attack, when Lorco fell from its
back, and not stopped until it entered the river willows, presumably
to find water. It had obviously managed to remain unseen by the
enemy, who must still have been fighting at the time.

The magnificent animal, one of Tiberias Cato's finest blacks
and bred from the same sire and dam as my own mount, came
directly to us and made no move to avoid me as I sheathed my

sword and leaned forward to take hold of its reins. As I straightened up again with the reins safely in my hand I saw something that I had never expected to see again. The magnificent long-bladed spatha that Lorco had won in the school arena weeks earlier, Tiberias Cato's own spatha, hung in its belted, hand-tooled sheath from the hook on the other side of the saddle bow from Lorco's helmet. Slowly, reverently, I reached across and collected it, then removed my own sword and replaced it with Lorco's, hanging mine from the hook on my saddle bow. Then, once again, I unsheathed the sword, and the difference between it and my own was immediately apparent. It settled into my grasp, filling my fist satisfyingly, and in the pleasure of simply holding it and feeling the heft of it, it took several moments for me to remember that I was a coward and undeserving of such a weapon. Grimly then, I sheathed it, and returned to the task of recording the dead.

The corpses were not all completely naked, but all had been stripped of everything of value—weaponry and armor. I had to check each of them, including those not ours, before I could identify the missing man, but eventually it became clear that the man called Ursus, the Bear, was not among the dead. He was a loner, a taciturn, self-sufficient man who asked nothing of anyone and expected to be treated the same way. I had never heard him speak, but even in the short time I had spent in his company, I had learned that he had a reputation as a fearsome fighter. Now he was missing, and I found myself wondering if he, too, had run away as I had.

I had not once descended from my horse since my return to the killing ground, and thus I ended up sitting high in the saddle and gazing down at the carnage on the ground, wondering what I should do next. I had no desire to ride away and simply leave the bodies lying there to rot, but I could see no alternative. There were fifteen dead men lying here—fourteen men and one boy, my best friend— and I had no means of burying them, having nothing to dig with other than a narrow-bladed sword. Nor was there any way to burn them in a pyre. The scrub willows that lined the riverbank were green and wet and no more than an inch thick at any point, and the closest trees of any adequate size were half a mile away and it was growing dark already.

Aching with the knowledge of what I must do, I dismounted beside Lorco, who lay where he had fallen, close by the wagon. He was flat on his back and mercifully his eyes were closed above the ruin of the lower part of his face. I stooped and picked up one of the loose garments that lay by my feet, and draped it very gently over his head, concealing his wounds. That done, I dug into my saddlebag to pull out the small codex that Germanus had given me before I left the school. It contained a transcription of several prayers attributed to the blessed Saint Anthony, and others attributed to Saint Martin, a native of Gaul. I opened it to the beginning of the first prayer, then knelt beside the body of my friend and read the entire selection of the prayers of Saint Martin aloud, dedicating them in the reading to the surrounding dead while focusing on my beloved friend.

By the time I finished reading it was almost too dark to see, and I stood up to leave, knowing I could do no more for Lorco or for any of them, but as I turned to remount my horse, I again saw the garments scattered about my feet and realized that I would be a fool to leave all of them there when I would surely have need of them later. I sorted through the things that I could find, surprised at how much had been left undisturbed in at least one of my chests. I filled my own saddlebags and Lorco's with clean, dry clothing, then improvised a pair of bags from two spare tunics and stuffed those full as well before tying them together and slinging them over Lorco's saddle. Only then, in what was close to full darkness, did I ride away from the killing ground, unwilling to spend a single moment longer than I had to in that place.

I rode though the dark along the riverbank for more than an hour, following the narrow path that traced the black line of willow shrubs along the waterside, and then the moon rose, full and large in a cloudless sky, and I was able to see clearly enough eventually to identify a large stand of trees that would shelter me for the remainder of the night.

I made a dry, dark camp at the base of one huge tree and God blessed me with a sound and dreamless sleep.

2

I awoke with the sun shining directly into my eyes through the screen of leaves that hung over me, and the first thought that came into my mind was a vision of Lorco dead on the ground as I prayed over him. I knew that before I did anything else, I had to find Duke Lorco and tell him about his son, about what had happened to him and about how I had come to survive the attack. It was not an encouraging incentive to leap up and be on my way, but nothing could have induced me to leap up that morning under any circumstances, since I had slept wearing full armor and my awakening body was now busily making me aware of the outrages to which it had been subjected overnight. I struggled to a sitting position and scrubbed at my eyes with the heels of my hands.

Moments later, still barely awake but trudging painfully in the direction of the river to relieve myself and wash the sleep from my eyes, I was astonished to discover that there was no river. The last vestiges of sleepiness vanished instantly as it became clear to me that at some point during my night walk—and it must have been early, probably in the darkness before the moon rose—I had somehow taken a divergent path and wandered inland, away from the river's edge. A fringe of shrubs still edged the path along which I had arrived here the previous night, and I remembered how determinedly I had watched and clung to the bulk of their blackness. But these were hazel shrubs, not osier willow as I had thought, and search as I might, they concealed no broad, placid stream of water.

That discovery led me to think about drinking water and that, in turn, made me think of food and realize that I had none, which meant that I must now think myself not merely as a coward but as a fool, as well. Until the moment we were attacked, it was true, none of us had had any reason to worry about food—we had food in abundance, from fresh-killed venison to dried chopped fruit and nuts and roasted grain. We had ground flour and salt and various dried and smoked meats, too, all of it safely stored on the wagon in boxes and casks. But now I was alone, hungry and thirsty and more than a little apprehensive of what might lie ahead of me.

All the more reason then, I thought, pulling myself together, to find Duke Lorco and his expedition quickly, and thereafter, I swore to myself, I would never go anywhere or venture into any situation without food and at least a full flask of water in my saddlebags.

I had unsaddled my two mounts and brushed them down before going to sleep the night before, and although I had been working in the dark I had tried to be thorough and militarily professional in seeing to their needs, knowing they had been saddled all day long. I was grateful that, thanks to the training hammered into us in the school stables, they had not been without rations, for it was the law according to Tiberias Cato that every horseman carry a bag of grain for his mount and keep it in his saddlebags at all times. So I had brushed the animals down and given them each a handful of grain in their nosebags before hobbling them for the night. Water had not crossed my mind, for they had both drunk deeply merely a few hours earlier, and I had been confident then that the river lay right behind our camp site. Now I examined the animals in the light of day and decided I had not done badly by them, considering the darkness under the trees the night before. I brushed them both down again, briskly, saddled them and then swung myself up onto my own and led the other out into the full morning light.

Open fields stretched away in every direction from the copse where we had sheltered, and it was easy to see from the absence of farm buildings that the land belonged to one of the *latifundiae,* the huge collective farming corporations that provided most of the Empire's annual grain harvest. There were no hills of any description, anywhere, just broad, flat fields with an occasional copse of trees that had been left standing to serve as windbreaks in bad weather. Far to my left, at the very limit of my vision, the fields came to an end, hemmed by dense trees. There was nothing at all on the right. The fields there simply stretched away to the low horizon, and presumably beyond that to infinity.

I turned and rode back and around to where I could see, beyond the copse, the path along which I had traveled the previous night. Sure enough, a single line of hazel shrubs, clearly a demarcation line or border of some kind set up by the landowners, extended from where I stood to the flat horizon, indicating the way I had come, and the direction of the sun on my right told me that I had been traveling from northwest to southeast. The river, I remembered from what Dirk the huntsman had said, had been running mainly southwest at the point where we had been attacked, so I knew it must now be somewhere to my left, westward of where I now sat.

Wasting no more time, and talking aloud to my horses in order to avoid having to think about anything else, I set out to find the river first and then the Duke and his men.

I had ridden about five miles, and the terrain had been changing very gradually for the previous couple of miles; I had been aware of climbing an unseen gradient for some time, a barely discernible slope that only became really evident when it eventually leveled out into a plateau. Near the top my horses had to scramble to crest the steep west bank of a fast-flowing brook that had cut itself a channel in the soft ground in its rush to join the river, flowing down from a rocky outcrop south of me that was the closest thing to a hill I had seen all morning. And suddenly there was the river, straight ahead, beyond the crest of the slope and less than a hundred paces distant.

No osier willows lined the low-lying banks here. The swollen river, broad and silent but sullen and dangerous looking, filled its muddy bed almost completely, its silt-laden waters reaching to within a couple of handspans of the grassy edges of the channel. The river must have been flowing westward for some time, more or less paralleling my own route, to the north of where I was. It must have changed direction, swinging west, within a mile of the killing grounds, and the only reason I found it at all was that it meandered again, southward this time, to cross my path. As soon as I found the riverbank, however, I knew that something was far from well.

I drew rein and peered into the distance, looking for signs of life and confidently expecting to see Phillipus Lorco's horsemen somewhere ahead of me, but there was nothing. Surprised, but not yet uneasy, I turned in my saddle and looked to left and right, but there was nothing to be seen there, either, although I could see that the open grassland ended in dense woodland on my right, about a mile north of where I sat. Nothing stirred there; no flash of sun on metal, no moving column, no pillar of dust. Puzzled now, I turned to look back the way I had come, as though I might have passed them along the way without noticing the dust and the noise or the sight of more than a hundred mounted men, and it was then that I noticed the absence of the track.

Six score of mounted troopers, three fully manned Roman turmae, one composed of light cavalry, one of mounted archers, and the third of heavy-spear-wielding *contus* cavalry, with all of their extra mounts, supply wagons and ancillary personnel, create a significant amount of damage when they pass over a grassy plain, particularly when the troopers are riding in formation, four or five abreast in a single column. It is impossible to conceal the evidence of their passing.

When we were attacked, we had been riding two abreast on the narrow, packed-clay path beside the river precisely because of the mess that had been created and the dust that had been churned up when Lorco's turmae had ridden over the dry fields on our left earlier that morning. We had had no wish to stir up that dust again because all of us knew from long experience how choking and debilitating it would be. We were privileged, we knew, to be apart from the main body of our force on such a hot day, because the unavoidable presence of swirling, choking, all-pervading dust, caking your face and gathering in the folds of your skin and neck, coating your tongue and filling your eyes and nostrils, trickling down your body beneath your armor back and front on runnels of sweat, to dry out and create unbearable itches in unreachable places, was a fact of cavalry life in the late spring, summer and autumn months.

There was no such track to be seen here, no matter where I looked, and so great was my disbelief that I began to ride hither and yonder, searching for it as though it was something I might have mislaid through sheer carelessness. I had good reason to be concerned, for the absence of a track meant, beyond dispute, that Lorco's cavalry had not come this way. They had taken another route, which meant that I was now lost and alone in an unknown and hostile land. I reined in my horse and sat staring up at the cloudless sky while the terror from the day before, reborn at full strength and ravening for release, built up inside me until I found myself incapable of moving. Fortunately, I recognized the peril in that thought even as it occurred to me, and I rebelled against it, hearing a new, angry voice rising inside me and insisting that although I had played the coward by moving too fast the previous day, I would not do the same this day by sitting still.

I jerked my head around hard, breaking my paralysis, and looked to my right, northward, to where the missing troopers now *had* to be, and forced myself to think about what could possibly have gone wrong with them. Duke Lorco, I was convinced, would not have changed direction before we caught up to him, not with his son and me riding with the hunting party. So if they had not changed direction, then they could not have passed this way yet, which plainly meant that something must have detained them. But what? And then the answer came to me, and relief swelled up in me like an enormous bubble.

They would have waited for us to catch up to them in camp the previous evening, and when we did not arrive, they would have assumed the hunting had been poor and we had remained in the field to try again at dusk. After that they would have continued to wait until long after dark before deciding we had opted for another dawn hunt. But Duke Lorco, I estimated, would not have been comfortable with his son's prolonged absence, so he might well have sent couriers to ride back early in the morning—I was convinced, in fact, that he would have done precisely that—to find the hapless and incompetent Harga and to chivvy him into making better time. And then, that done, the Duke would have waited where he was, doubtless fuming, but impotent to change anything before his lost hunting party caught up. He would not have traveled farther without first seeing his son safely back in camp.

Feeling as though someone had lifted the weight of my two horses off my shoulders, I swung them around and set out to the north at a canter, following the river again until it entered the tree line, after which I stayed as close to the riverbank as I could. I had to pick my way in places between the densest clumps of undergrowth, so that the progress I made was less swift than I would have wished. However, now that I had a purpose and a direction I could follow with confidence, I made better speed than I might have otherwise.

As I rode, weaving my way between the trees and through the undergrowth, my mind was racing ahead of me, following the logic of my suppositions about Duke Lorco's behavior. If he had in fact sent out couriers and waited for them to return, then it was likely that by the time I caught up with him he would already have learned of his son's death and of my disappearance. The prospect of not having to be the one to tell him of his son's death was an attractive one, but I could not imagine any meeting between the two of us that would not entail my having to tell him, somehow, of what had happened to Lorco, how he had died and how I had run away, leaving everyone else behind me to be slaughtered. Thus my guilt revived and grew stronger as I rode, and my misery and self-loathing, forgotten for a brief time, returned to drape themselves over my shoulders.

That is how I was feeling when I rounded the bole of an enormous oak tree and found myself face to face with a trio of men on foot, no more than twenty paces ahead of me. The sight of them made my breath catch in my throat, but I have no doubt their surprise was as great as mine, because it was evident in the startled way they leaped backwards, groping for their weapons. For a moment my heart bounded in joy, my first thought being that they were scouts and I had found Duke Lorco and his men, but it took no more than a glance to show me that these were not Roman soldiers, far less cavalry. They were all dressed differently, but in a predominant color of red. Two of them were armored in what looked like legionary plate armor, while the third wore a tunic of bronze-colored ring mail and had dull silver greaves strapped to his legs. This one, the smallest of the three, had been walking with an arrow nocked to his bow string, and as he sprang backwards at the sight of me, he nevertheless sighted hastily and loosed his arrow. It hit me hard and high on the left breast and was deflected by my cuirass, but it caught me off balance, and the force of its impact sent me reeling backwards, toppling me over my horse's rump to land sprawling on my knees and hands.

Fortunately for me, for I was still wearing my heavy helmet, I landed without either breaking my neck or knocking the wind out of myself. My helmet was jarred forward over my eyes in the fall, cutting off my vision, but I managed to push it up and back in time to see, between my horse's legs, the strangers starting towards me, separating widely to come at me from different directions. The bowman with the silver greaves remained in front, weaving slightly as he tried to find an angle from which to shoot me, but the other two were moving quickly now, circling to each side of me.

I had no time even to think of being afraid, although I knew beyond a doubt that if I tried to run away this time I would be dead within moments. Their encircling move, however, forcing me to fight in two directions, was one with which I was more than familiar—I had had the moves and countermoves of that attack and defense drummed into me since I was old enough to swing a practice sword. I looked down at the ground beneath my feet and saw that it was sloping downwards to my right, and then I took two long paces backwards, distancing myself from the two horses ahead of me yet keeping their bulk between me and the bowman in the ring-mail shirt.

Both of the men moving to attack me from right and left carried swords, the one a broad, heavy-bladed thing that looked as though it might be a one-edged blade, the other a long, slender, spatha-like weapon that look well cared for and well used. The man approaching on my left had the heavier, ugly weapon and he was farther away from me than his companion was. He was also slightly above me, beginning to move down towards me. The fellow on my right was below me and closer, just starting to crouch and raise his sword as he came at me in a sidling shuffle.

I took three running steps towards him, which he had not expected. He hesitated, wavering, and I almost beheaded him with my first slash. He barely managed to get his sword up quickly enough to save himself and my blade smashed his aside, by which time I was beside him, pivoting with my whole body and dropping into a crouch as I aimed a hacking slash at the unprotected back of his knees. It was a blow I had been taught by Tiberias Cato himself, years earlier, and when successfully delivered it was crippling. He screamed as my blade severed his hamstrings, and dropped immediately, first to his knees and then forward onto his face, but I knew he was finished as a fighter and did not wait for him to fall.

I spun on one foot and sprang up and back to face the other attacker from my left, but he had seen how I handled his friend and he was more cautious, crouching defensively and waiting for me to come to him. I knew I could beat him—there was no trace of a doubt in my mind about that—but by that time my flesh was crawling in anticipation, waiting for the impact of the arrow I knew must be coming for me at any moment because I was out in the open now, clear of the horses and vulnerable to the bowman, who had all the time he needed to sight on me. Nothing came, and finally I risked looking over to see what he was doing. It was the quickest of glances, no more than a flick of the head, but it showed me what I least expected to see, and I could not resist looking again, even although I knew the risk I was taking by looking away from the sword-wielder on my left.

The bowman was dead, flat on his face on the ground and motionless, with an arrow through his ring-mail tunic and buried almost to the feathers between his shoulder blades. And as I saw that, my opponent attacked. He had seen me look away, then look again, and on the second look he lunged, swinging a mighty over-hand chop that would have cleft me in two had it landed. Of course it did not land, because I had Cato's magnificent spatha with which to deflect it. I swept it aside easily and leaped backwards, only to land awkwardly on a round section of stick that rolled beneath my foot and sent me crashing to my back on a bed of the previous year's oak leaves.

My opponent was above me almost before I had landed. Spread-legged and dark-faced, he rose on his toes to gain the maximum impetus from his ungainly weapon. I tried to whip my sword across in front of me to stab him in the groin, but my blade had slipped beneath a branch or a root when I fell, and as soon as I felt the resistance in my arm I knew I would not be able to dislodge it quickly enough to save myself. Then, for the second time in the space of two mornings, I watched a life snuffed out abruptly by a hard-shot arrow. This one caught my opponent in the hollow of the neck, just above the metal rim of his cuirass, and drove him back-wards, off his feet and into instant death.

I rolled hard to my left, dragging my sword behind me and feeling the moment when it sprang free of whatever had been holding it. As soon as I did, I spun on my left elbow, kicking my legs around, and lunged to my feet quickly if far from gracefully, facing the direction from which the second arrow had come. I told myself that whoever had shot my enemy must be my friend, although I did not dare to trust myself sufficiently to believe it. As soon as I was safely upright, I set my feet squarely and hunched into a fighting crouch, glaring around me to see who and where the marksman was, but he remained unseen. Slightly to the right of where I now stood, the man I had hamstrung lay dead, too, pinned to the ground by yet another arrow. Directly ahead of me now was the massive oak tree that had stood between me and my three erstwhile attackers, and I guessed that the fourth man, whoever he was, must be behind its huge bole. I glared at the tree, willing him to come out and face me.

Moments later, just as I was beginning to feel foolish, a voice spoke from behind my back.

"That tree is *not* going to attack you, boy."

Appalled at how easily I had been duped, I spun as quickly as I could move, raising my sword as I did so and preparing to throw myself to the attack, although I was once again expecting to die, shot down before I could really move forward. But then I stopped in mid-step, astonished. The man facing me was Ursus. He held his arms folded across his chest as he leaned back against the trunk of a tree, his legs crossed at the ankles and his entire weight on his left foot. His bow, still strung, hung from his right shoulder. I was stunned to see him and was incapable of finding a single word of greetings or of gratitude or anything else. I simply stood and gaped at him.

"You handled yourself well, for a youngster. Who taught you to fight like that?"

I had never heard this man speak before, and now I found the sound of him to be more pleasant than I would have expected, based purely upon the things I had heard the others in the hunting party say about him. His voice was deep and sonorous, warm and mellifluous and somehow suggestive of humor. I cleared my throat and tried to answer him coherently.

"Teachers . . . I had many . . . at the Bishop's School, in Auxerre."

"They taught you to *fight*? I thought they were churchmen, priests."

"They are, but the bishop there is Germanus. He used to be an imperial legatus, commander-in-chief of all imperial forces in central and northern Gaul. He was Duke Lorco's first legatus."

"Shit . . . I knew that, but I never made the connection between Germanus the legate and Germanus the bishop."

"You mean the Duke didn't tell you?"

He straightened up from the tree and uncrossed his arms, leaning forward slightly to peer at me, a strange expression on his face. "Are you twitting me?" Before I could react to that, however, he nodded and the expression on his face changed. "I'm a mercenary, lad, a sword for hire. I don't even have a rank that earns me any more than basic pay, whereas Phillipus Lorco is the governor of an entire imperial region. We don't have much in common, Duke Lorco and I. You understand?"

Then he walked straight towards me, and as he passed he waved at me to go with him. I followed him to where my two horses had found some grass growing in a patch between the trees and were busily crunching and cropping at the succulent greenery. Ursus stopped and I almost walked into him.

"Which one do you want?" he asked.

"That one's mine," I said, pointing.

"Good, I'll take the other one, then."

He moved directly to the horse, and I spoke to his back. "You saved my life. Twice."

He paused in the act of stroking the animal's muzzle and turned to look at me. "Aye. You were outnumbered, but you were unlucky, too. If you hadn't stepped on that stick and fallen you would have beaten both those men."

"But I did fall."

"Aye, and you were fortunate that I was there and watching. But don't be too grateful. Next time, you might have to do the same for me, and though you won't find me ungrateful, I might not thank you at the time."

I said something then that I did not know I was going to say, and to this day I don't know why I said it at that particular moment. It may have been relief at finding him to be more pleasant and approachable than people had said he was, or it might simply have been that the guilt that filled me had suddenly become unbearable.

"I ran away."

Ursus looked at me, his face blank, then quirked one eyebrow. "From where, the school?"

"No, from the fight, yesterday. I panicked, lost my nerve and ran for my life."

"So did I. It all happened too quickly and there were too many of them, too suddenly. One moment we were ambling along as though we were the only people in the world, and then, the next, there were men leaping all around us on every side and arrows flying everywhere and dead people falling off their horses, their heads and bodies bristling with arrows. I was riding alone, closest to the riverbank, because my horse was grazing wherever he could find a mouthful of grass, and I saw the two men on my left, the cook and his helper, knocked off their horses, both of them in the same instant, one forward, the other backwards, both stone dead. I've been in this game long enough to know a dead man when I see one, even if he's still falling. I took one look around and saw wild men everywhere, three of the whoresons, at least, for every one of us when we were all alive. Then one fellow jumps up in front of me, coming at me with an axe. I put the spurs to my horse, ran the whoreson down and just kept going, right into the river, where I slid off and got my horse's body between me and the bowmen on the bank who were already shooting at me. I got away, but they killed my horse. One of their arrows hit it in the neck and severed a big vein. Shame. Good thing I can swim, though." He paused, then looked me in the eye. "But I thought I was the only one who got away. How did you manage it?"

I shook my head. "I don't know. I was talking to my friend Lorco when he was killed. An arrow hit him in the back of the head and came out through his face. There were strangers everywhere, screaming and shouting, attacking us on foot, and more than half of the people in our group were dead. I saw bodies lying everywhere. And that's when I panicked and ran away. I didn't stop running until I was deep in the forest."

"Doesn't sound like panic to me. More like good sense. You're still alive. And you stood and fought those people we just killed today. Nothing cowardly there. And you couldn't have done that if you'd been killed yesterday, could you?"

He stared at me, waiting for an answer.

"No," I said, quietly. "I suppose not."

"Don't suppose anything. Accept it and stop fretting. What happened to us yesterday—to me and to you—happened because it was meant to happen. If you and I had been meant to die in that ambush we would have died. But we lived, so we were not meant to die. And if that's the case, then what is the point of whining about not being dead?"

I nodded. "Where is Duke Lorco now?"

"I don't know. I expected him to be somewhere up ahead of me, but I suspect you're telling me now that's not so. Am I right?"

"Yes. That's why I came back in this direction. How could you not have seen him yesterday? You must have swum right by his camp at some point."

"No, not yesterday. After the ambush I hid in a bank of reeds in a pond that once was an eddy in the river. And I mean hid . . . head down and flat on my belly most of the time, holding my breath in case someone might hear me breathing. There were hostiles *everywhere.* The whole countryside was swarming with them, and none of them looked like the people who attacked us earlier in the day. I think they were an entirely different bunch—an army, not just a rabble mob like the crew that hit us. I never got close enough to any of them to hear them speak, but as far as I could tell from what they were wearing, they were Burgundians, and they were well armed and well equipped. The first ones I met were on the other side of the river, and they almost caught me out in the open on the riverbank, but I saw them just in time and managed to make it to the tall reeds around the edge of the pond. And there I stayed for the rest of the day, because there were more of them all around me, on my side of the river. I don't know how they got to be on both sides, because the river's wide, and it's in spate, but there they were.

"All I could do was sit tight and hope to get back into the water as soon as it grew dark enough, and then swim downstream from there. Whoever these people were, Burgundians or not, they had been passing by me all day, all headed south, as far as I could tell, and there were thousands of them. I mean, I couldn't stand up and count them, not without getting myself killed, but I could hear them passing by and they just kept coming and coming.

"Thing was, though, I couldn't tell where they were really going, or where they planned to stop for the night, and that worried me, for if they were going to be sleeping all along the banks of the river, then I wouldn't be able to make as much as a splash, and if I hit a stretch with bad currents, I could give myself away just by trying to stay alive.

"Anyway, late in the afternoon they started to thin out, but as luck would have it, just before dark, as I was getting ready to make my escape, a whole new detachment of them came along and settled in for the night right along the riverbank next to where I was hiding. They set up a guard post so close to me I couldn't even lie back in the reeds and sleep, in case I snored. I was stuck in there until the whoresons left this morning at dawn, and I've been drifting downstream ever since, with my head in the middle of a floating crown of long reeds that I made while I was stuck in the pond, waiting to get away." He paused, then added, "Crown isn't the right word. It was more of a wreath, with long reeds sticking straight up out of it so that no one could see my head in the middle of it. I'm starved. Have you got anything to eat?"

"No." I half turned back to where the three dead men lay behind us. "But they might. We didn't expect to be in need of food yesterday, until we were attacked, but those fellows came here a-purpose, so they probably brought food with them."

"Bright lad," Ursus said, turning smoothly and moving back to check the contents of the scrips that hung about the dead men's waists. Sure enough, we found bread, dried meat and a small pouch of dried nuts mixed with what tasted like chopped dried pears, as well as a full skin of watered wine. We sat down where we were, our backs against the big oak tree, and made short work of all of it, ignoring the dead men and eating and drinking until our empty stomachs were full again. By the time we finished there was not much left to save, other than a heel of bread and an end of the dried meat.

Ursus sighed, finally, and stretched where he sat, grimacing as he did so.

"I don't know," he growled. "We'll live now, for a while, at least long enough to get ourselves killed if we run into any more of those Burgundians. But where's Duke Lorco? That's the question you and I have to answer. We'll have to find him by the shortest route, for our own safety—" He broke off, frowning at the expression on my face. "What's wrong with you?"

I shrugged, trying to make light of what I had been thinking and to dismiss the grim vision that had sprung into my mind. "Nothing, not really. I was just thinking about what you said about the hostiles . . . the Burgundians . . . Thousands of them, you said. Is that true or were you exaggerating?"

Ursus made a face. "No, it was true."

"Far more than Duke Lorco has with him."

"Aye, but Lorco's cavalry are worth ten men afoot, and he's got three turmae."

"True." I nodded, but with no enthusiasm, for the calculation attached to that was not a difficult one. "That's more than a hundred troopers . . . But a single thousand men would match them at ten-to-one odds, and you said there were several thousands of Burgundians. That could make odds of twenty, thirty to one."

"If it came to a fight, aye, it could. But who's to say it would? Lorco's smart enough to keep away from an army of that size."

"What if he has no choice?"

"What do you mean? Of course he'll have a choice. There's always a choice."

I dismissed that, seeing the fallacy behind his bluster. "No, not always. Look at what happened to me with these three. I came around the big tree and there they were, right in front of me, looking at me. I had no choice but to fight. Same thing might easily happen to Duke Lorco."

Ursus pulled his mouth down into a scowl of doubt. "Nah, I don't think so. Lorco would have scouts out. He'd never be stupid enough to ride without scouts."

"Granted, but these Burgundians would have scouts out, too—that's what these three were doing here, scouting. But they ran into us, and now they'll never get the word back that we're here. Couldn't the same thing have happened to Duke Lorco's scouts?"

Now the scowl on Ursus's face had deepened to a glower. "By the Christ, boy, you have a knack for seeing the blackest side of things, haven't you?" He glanced around us, looking at the forest growth that sheltered us. "Well, we can't sit here forever, so let's go and try to find our own before the enemy finds us. I warn you, though, they'll be swarming like bees to the north of us, and if we can't pass through them—which is almost certain to be the way of it—we'll have to ride around them. God alone knows how long that might take. However it turns out, you make sure to stick close behind me, keep your head down, and do whatever I tell you to do *right now,* with no arguments and no questions. If you ever live to be as old as I am, then I'll take orders from you. In the meantime, I'm the *Magister,* understand?"

I nodded, and we prepared to mount up and head northward in search of our friends.

3

We never did discover what befell Duke Lorco and his three turmae. They simply vanished from the ken of men. Ursus and I searched for them for three entire days, and not once in that time did we find as much as a trace of them, although we might have had cause for thanks in that, since the entire countryside was overrun by the force that Ursus had described, and his estimation of their numbers as being in the thousands turned out to be very conservative. We were surprised, too, to see that they had large numbers of horsemen among them, because Ursus had seen no riders among the troops that moved steadily past him on that first afternoon when he had hidden among the pond reeds, and we were forced to assume that they had ridden separately to join the foot soldiers.

We watched these riders closely, after our initial surprise wore off, and although their mounts were healthy and well equipped, it soon became obvious that the riders themselves had had no intensive training in coordination. They were warriors, but not cavalry troopers. That realization, reinforced by our observations of the casual, informal way the riders moved about the countryside, encouraged us to step out of hiding and venture among them as though we had every right to be there doing what we were doing. We moved openly but took care nonetheless to avoid coming too close to any particular group, and we managed to avoid detection, although there were times during those days when we passed within spitting distance of some of the invaders.

Notwithstanding all our caution, however, we were twice involved in skirmishes with small groups whom we met in places where we had no reason for being present, other than trying to slip past the carefully guarded strongpoints that had been built on high elevations overlooking those places where enemies like us might be expected to try to pass by undetected. We were fortunate enough on both occasions to see these people before they saw us. There were three foot soldiers in the first group and two horsemen in the second, and I take no shame in saying that it was Ursus who dispatched four of them, including both horsemen, each of them driven off his horse's back by a single deadly hard shot. I captured the fifth and last of the men by running him down, smashing my horse directly into him and bowling him over, then leaping on him and disarming him before he could regain his breath, after which I held him at the point of my sword until Ursus could tie his arms securely behind his back.

It was in questioning this captive—Ursus, it turned out, could speak a version of his language—that we discovered the enemy were in fact Burgundians from the southwest. A federation of their tribes, our prisoner told us, six in all and numbering close to ten thousand warriors, had left the lands they had settled almost a hundred years earlier and struck east in search of more living space. So far, he said, they had been on the march and victorious on all fronts for half a month. They had encountered no serious opposition and had annexed everything between their home territories and the spot where we had captured him, and it was plain to see from his attitude that even although he, personally, had erred and fallen into our hands, he did not expect to be our prisoner for long. He told us that we would be discovered and killed within the very near future.

Simply by falling into our hands, our prisoner had presented us with a problem, because we could not take him with us when we moved on, and we could not simply set him free. We knew we ought to kill him, but because of the teachings I had absorbed in the Bishop's School, I was incapable of doing that and equally incapable of permitting Ursus to. "Thou shalt not kill" is an unequivocal Commandment. Not that I would have hesitated to kill the man in the heat of battle—or so I told myself, blithely disregarding the fact that I had never yet come close to contemplating killing any man. I knew well that killing in self-defense is permissible at any time, and that in time of war, when the cause is just, killing as the result of armed aggression is justifiable. Killing in cold blood, however, was murder, unacceptable under any conditions, and so we were trapped, becoming, in effect, prisoners to our prisoner.

Fortunately, he absolved us of our quandary by freeing himself in the middle of the night and then foolishly awakening us with the noise he made in escaping. Ursus felled him with a single arrow from a distance of thirty paces, which, at night and against a running target, was a bowshot verging on the miraculous. We scrambled out to where the fellow lay and dragged him back into the cave where we were sheltering. We left him there in the morning, after we had scouted the area and identified a reasonable opportunity to move out of hiding and escape unobserved.

The decision to abandon the northward search for the Duke was made by Ursus, but I made no objection when he suggested it. As we had moved north during the previous two days, the concentration of Burgundians around us had increased dramatically, and it was obvious that to continue moving as we were, haphazardly and without real objectives, was folly. It was already amazing that we had avoided detection for as long as we had. The single alternative open to us, Ursus decided, was to turn back and head southward, to wait for Lorco and his turmae at some spot where the lie of the land itself would dictate that they must pass close by us. That decision made, and its common sense plain and clear to both of us, we turned back with great feelings of relief and headed south to await Duke Lorco and his troops.

For the next two days we traveled steadily, following or paralleling the easiest and most obvious route to the south and finding ourselves being shepherded gradually but unmistakably in the southeasterly direction dictated by the river as it penetrated a wide, forested valley between two ranges of hills. The route we followed was one that had never seen the construction of a Roman road, yet it was wide and obviously well traveled, and by the time we had gone a score of miles along it, it had become obvious that the Burgundian invaders had no interest in it, because we saw little sign of them. The few isolated groups that we did see were making their way hurriedly and single-mindedly to the north, paying no attention to whatever might be going on around them.

By noon the following day, having spent the entire morning watching for Burgundians and seeing none, we finally accepted that we had left them and their invasion route safely behind us. We made a comfortable camp that night, close by the road but sufficiently far away from it among the trees to be confident that we could safely light a fire without risk of its being seen by any late-night travelers, and then we lay awake for several hours in the firelight, talking about our missing companions, wondering where they might be and when we would encounter them again.

We never did. Nor, to the best of our knowledge, did anyone else. I learned later, after my eventual return to Auxerre, that there had been a deal of speculation in their home region during the months that followed their disappearance, but Phillipus Lorco himself had quickly been replaced by a new governor who was faced with his own priorities, and the disappearance of Lorco and his three turmae had quickly faded into acceptance, its urgency diffused by the other events surrounding the Burgundian invasion that summer.

The most widely accepted version of what might have happened was that Lorco and his party had ridden blindly into a trap and been wiped out, but there were those who refused to accept such a notion. Those doubters, claiming personal experience, friendship and long-standing knowledge of Governor Lorco, swore that he would never commit such an elementary error as to ride through unknown and potentially hostile territory without deploying scouts on all sides of his force. Bishop Germanus, having spent years as Lorco's legatus in the field, was a voluble proponent of that belief, but when I heard it, I found myself wondering immediately if there might be some truth to the less acceptable version.

Thinking back to the dilatory conduct and the unconscionable laziness of Lorco's lieutenant, Harga, and that man's failure to take even the simplest of precautions, thus leading us into an entrapment from which Ursus and I should never have escaped, I was forced to wonder about the degree to which Harga's laziness might have been inspired or encouraged by his own superiors' behavior. I felt disloyal to Duke Lorco for thinking such things, but I could not avoid them. I kept them to myself, however, and never expressed my own personal doubts or misgivings to anyone. Lorco was dead and his son had been my closest friend, killed in front of my eyes. I determined that no hint of criticism that might affect the honor of their name would ever pass my lips.

On the afternoon of our third day's journey south we came to a spot where the valley narrowed to the width of a narrow gorge through which the river poured, changing from a broad, placid, meandering stream to a raging torrent within the space of half a mile. Here, Ursus said, was the spot where we would wait for Duke Lorco. He remembered passing through the narrow passage on their way north, and told me that Lorco himself had said that if anything untoward occurred later in their journey and anyone found himself cut off, they should head for this place and wait for the remainder of the group to come back. We searched the narrow riverbank for evidence of the cavalry's passage but we found none and so were able to settle in to wait, confident in the knowledge that the main group was still behind us.

We set up camp, dangerously and precariously, on the steep side of the cliff that formed the left side of the gorge, and we took time to ensure that it was the best site we could find, secure from casual detection from beneath yet affording us an unimpeded view of everything that happened in the gorge itself, on both sides of the river. And there we remained for days, watching and waiting. Several groups of travelers passed by us, going in both directions, some of them strongly armed and alert for interference, others less so. None of them suspected our presence and none of them bore any resemblance to our missing Duke or to any of his people.

After four days our concern had grown too great to ignore. We could not go back, and we could no longer afford to remain where we were. Ursus had shot a deer on the second morning of our stay and we had been eating that ever since, but we had no other provisions. I had found some wild onions and garlic growing along the riverbank, and Ursus had found some succulent mushrooms, so we had been able to augment the taste of the deer meat, if only slightly. But we had no salt and no flour, nor had we anything in the way of dried fruit, roasted grain or nuts. It had become clear to us by then that one of two things, each equally unlikely and unwelcome, had occurred: either Lorco and his party had encountered a strong Burgundian force and been captured or defeated, or they had decided, for reasons unknown to us, to make their way home by an alternative route. Whichever was true, it was clearly futile for us to remain where we were. So once again we headed south.

Ursus had only nine arrows left by that time, and now, accepting that we would not be rejoining Lorco's cavalry and were in fact to be solely reliant on our own resources, those nine missiles took on a greater significance than they had ever held before. They were our sole means of dealing death at anything greater than arm's length, and in consequence we were loath to take aim with them at anything that offered us even the slightest threat of losing another.

Fortunately, Ursus was an excellent fisherman and he also knew how to construct a snare for catching hares and even ground birds like grouse and partridge. He would rummage carefully among a patch of underbrush until he detected the narrow pathways—sometimes more akin to tunnels—along which the small animals and birds made their way, and then he would fashion a noose from an old bow string and anchor it with a solidly driven tent peg before carefully suspending it close to the ground and disguising its outline with cunningly blended grasses. We would then withdraw and leave the noose to do its work, and it seldom failed. We took partridge and grouse and, twice, badgers, neither of which submitted to the noose, far less succumbed to it. Each of them completely destroyed the trap into which it had blundered, and made off with the invaluable bow string, presumably still wrapped about its neck.

We traveled southeastward from the river gorge for six days without incident, avoiding all human contact, proceeding with the utmost caution and moving stealthily at all times, checking lines of sight and being careful never to move into any position from which we might become visible to anyone else.

Within those short days, however, I learned much about woodcraft and the lore of tracking from my companion, who turned out to be far more pleasant company than I had been given to expect. He showed me, expending great patience and tolerance, how to watch for, and detect, the tiny, telltale signs that marked the passage taken by an animal on its way through the undergrowth, emphasizing that once I knew how to see the signs of passing animals I could not fail to see the damage done by humans in their passage. These were signs that I would never have seen had he not been there to point them out, and I knew well that he had spent the better part of his lifetime absorbing the lessons that enabled him to see them—a bent-back twig; a wrongly turned leaf that caught the light when none of its fellows did; a clump of hair caught on the thorns of a wild rose bush; a curled-up leaf that had filled with seepage after being crushed in the center and formed into a cup by a deer's cloven hoof.

We were in a place that had been burned out in a massive fire, probably seven to ten years earlier, Ursus estimated. We had been afoot for some time after breaking camp before dawn and had made good headway until we reached this stretch of forest and were forced to dismount. The brush had quite suddenly become impenetrable, I remember—saplings and bushes that were simply too thickly packed to accord access to a mounted man—and neither of us had spoken for some time, our attention focused intently, for more than a mile, it seemed, upon finding the easiest possible route through a wilderness of springy, immature growth that had not yet begun to assert any order upon itself. We had just fought our way through what we hoped had been the very thickest growth and encountered the first signs that the brush was thinning—everything seemed much lighter and brighter ahead of us—and when I heard water running on my right, I felt a sharp stirring in my bowels that I knew I could not ignore. I muttered to Ursus and handed him my reins, telling him I would catch up to him, and he merely nodded and kept going, paying me no further attention as I made my way towards the sound of the running water to relieve myself in private.

When I had finished and cleansed myself, I made my way back to rejoin Ursus in no particular haste, following the signs of his passage easily beyond the spot where we had parted company. The growth around me was thinning with almost every step I took, and the oppressive feeling I had experienced earlier amid the thickets gave way to one of light-heartedness. There were birds singing everywhere, exulting in the perfection of a magnificent summer morning, and I responded to the music, forgetting for the first time in days to wonder what had happened to Duke Lorco and his party. I stepped around the bole of a respectably sized tree at one point and realized that not only was this the first mature, unburned tree I had seen in a long time but also that I was almost in open ground, standing upon a path of some kind, a game trail that ran straight ahead of me, unrestricted by undergrowth, so that had I so wished I could have spread my arms wide and spun around without hitting a single obstruction.

I started to do precisely that, raising my arms in the air like wings and preparing to spin around, but I froze instead, shocked into immobility by the sight of Ursus's bow and quiver lying on the path less than twenty paces from where I stood.

They lay there, in the open, like dead things, the two most valuable weapons Ursus and I possessed, and even before the first flare of panic had subsided, I was thinking about the reasons for their being there. Clearly they had been left for me to find, a warning of some kind. For some reason unknown to me but evidently imperative, Ursus had decided that I could make better use of the weapons in this instance than he could. That all seemed self-evident at first glance, but I had no understanding at all of what it meant and even less understanding of what had happened to Ursus and the horses. And then I saw how the path, just beyond where the weapons lay, veered sharply to the left and disappeared, concealed beyond the bend by a towering clump of vibrant dark green growth that I recognized as an ancient and impenetrable thicket of bramble briars.

Ursus had gone around the bend in the path with both horses, but before doing so he had stopped and removed the weapons from about his shoulders, laying them there for me. He knew I would be close behind him, but he had no means of knowing how close, and if he were walking into danger beyond that bend in the path that knowledge might be crucial. I snatched up the quiver and slung it over my shoulder, then dropped to one knee and nocked an arrow to the bow string. My intent was to listen, but even as I knelt I heard the sound of metal blades in contact, not ringing as they would in a fight but slithering along each other almost lazily as Ursus raised his voice.

"Come then, you ill-matched set of whoresons. Let's see if four Burgundians—or whatever you call yourselves in the underworld that spawned you—let's see if you can best one Roman Gaul. See, two blades I have, each one of them fit to kill a pair of you before you can puke your fear out. Come to me, then, and taste your deaths."

I edged around the bush in front of me, the bow string taut to my ear as my eyes sought the source of Ursus's voice. He was facing me across a clearing, perhaps a score of paces from me, his back against a tree trunk that was wider than his shoulders. Safe there from attack from behind, he stood on the balls of his feet, leaning slightly forward and rubbing the two long blades of the weapons he held, one against the other. They were his own spatha and mine, the one I had left hanging from Lorco's saddle bow when I took Tiberias Cato's weapon in its place. His eyes were narrowed in concentration but he was smiling, too, the confident smile of a man who knows he is about to take much enjoyment from some imminent activity. He saw me as soon as I appeared around the bush, I know, but he gave no sign of it. His torso weaved slightly from side to side as his eyes moved constantly, watching all four of his attackers simultaneously.

Our two mounts stood close by him on his left side, slightly behind him and beyond the tree, their trailing reins anchoring the animals where Ursus had dropped them on the ground. I knew immediately that he had led the horses there, to place them safely out of his way, and had then darted back to the tree, putting it solidly at his back.

The four men ranged against him, all of whom had their backs to me, had made no move to attack him yet, and looking at their posture, observing the uneasy, anxious way they traded glances back and forth among themselves, I could tell they were bemused, to say the least, by his behavior. He should not have been smiling, not against odds of four to one. I could almost hear their minds working, worrying at the logic here, so much so, in fact, that my mind began framing antic thoughts about what they must be thinking: this fellow had two fine horses, both richly saddled and equipped, which meant that he was not alone. But he *was* alone and carrying two swords, one for each hand, which indicated that his companion, if he had one, must now be somewhere else without a weapon, and that made no sense at all, for no sane man would leave his sword behind him in strange territory. And that raised the possibility that this man had had a friend and lost him to death, burying him and continuing to journey with his possessions. Which meant, in turn, that this fellow—

With a snarl of fury, one of the four gave up his puzzling and launched himself towards Ursus. I let him go, knowing that Ursus had his measure. No sooner had this fellow started moving, however, than his accomplices joined him, all three of them lunging forward to assist the first man. None of them had seen me yet, and so I sighted on the leading runner of the three, a huge, gaunt man with long black hair and stilt-like legs that carried him out in front of the other two. I sucked a deep breath and then released it steadily as I followed his rush, obeying every lesson I had ever learned on sighting and shooting with a bow, and as the first clash of striking blades reached my ears I released and watched my arrow hiss across the space between me and the running target to hit him brutally hard in the neck, just behind the point of his jaw, and hurl him bodily off his feet and head over heels to roll and sprawl in a huddled mass just beyond the kneeling body of his friend, who had already been dispatched without ceremony by Ursus.

The behavior of the remaining two men, after seeing their companion so suddenly and unexpectedly destroyed, might have been laughable under any other circumstances. I saw them hesitate in mid-charge, then break off their attack, spinning away from each other and from the perceived direction of the new threat they had found in me. One of them spun completely around and came running straight for me, covering ground at an enormous rate, while the other ran back the way he had come, pursued by Ursus.

My attention, however, remained focused on the shapeless huddle of drab rags that marked the first man I had ever killed. There was no doubt in my mind that he was dead. I had seen my arrow hit, and it had reminded me exactly of what had happened to my friend Lorco when a similar arrow hit him in approximately the same place. But this death was one that I had inflicted, personally. I had taken this man's life. He was now dead, finished, ended. He would never move or smile or laugh or eat or weep again, because I had killed him.

The fellow running at me now—and I could see him with utter clarity—was wide eyed with terror, plainly expecting me to raise my bow again and shoot him down before he could reach me. But filled as I was with the thought of what I had done to his companion, the thought of rearming my bow had not even occurred to me, and as I watched him come hurtling towards me I saw the white knuckles of the hand that held his upraised sword and accepted, somewhere at the back of my mind, that I was going to die there. Even as he began to straighten up for the death blow and his eyes showed dawning awareness that he was destined not to die before he could reach me, he stubbed his foot hard against something in his path and fell, sprawling forward and crashing heavily against me, grunting in my ear with the pain and with the effort of trying to recover his balance.

He was a big man, far taller than I and easily more than twice my weight, and the impact of our collision sent me flying and smashed the breath from me. Even as I crashed to the ground, however, I knew that the ancient goddess Fortuna had been watching over me. So complete had been his loss of balance that he had had no hope of swinging his sword, even although all his being had been focused upon cleaving me in two, and now we were both on the ground, both in one piece. I refused to yield to the urge to hunch over and hug my middle, which appeared to have been replaced by a ball of solid pain. Instead I bit down hard on my own cheek, focusing upon that pain, and forced my legs to swing up and over my head, rolling violently backwards on tucked shoulders until I could push myself to my knees and see what my opponent was doing.

He, too, had landed badly and winded himself, but where I had fallen on hard ground, he had fallen or bounced sideways into the enormous clump of brambles that had flanked me. His entire face was ripped by the wicked thorns of the bramble briars, as was the palm of the hand he was holding up to his eyes. I could see him gasping for air, too, and hear the great whooping noises that were coming from his open mouth. I scrambled away from him, pushing at the ground in my panic before my common sense began to return to me. He was at as great a disadvantage as I was for the moment and could do me no harm. But that would change if he recovered more quickly than I did. And so I forced myself to sit still and breathe deeply and steadily, willing my body to behave itself and recover its functions before my enemy did.

With a scream of pain and anger that would have frightened me mere days before, the giant facing me dragged himself to his feet, snarling with rage and agony and hacking determinedly with his sword at the briars that surrounded him on all sides. I felt a stirring of awe at his strength and endurance, for I knew how viciously the thousands of long, hooked barbs on those green stems, some of them as thick as a boy's wrist, were ripping at his muscled flesh. Even so, he made headway, gradually clearing a way out of the dragon's nest that held him, and when it became plain to me that he would soon be free, I realized too late that I should have reclaimed my abandoned bow and shot him dead long since. I looked about me then and saw the quiver that had fallen from my shoulder when the big man knocked me down. I counted six arrows in one brief glance, but could see no signs of the bow I had been holding.

And then it really was too late. The big man won free of his prison and reared up to his full height, raising his sword high above his head again and roaring something at me in a language I had never heard before. It was evident that he had no intention of missing his next swing at me.

Strangely enough, I felt not the slightest stirring of fear, though I had every reason to be afraid. I could not see a single patch of skin anywhere on my assailant's body that was not covered in blood. I had never seen anyone so bloodied. He was huge and he was angry and he was covered in severed, trailing lengths of barbed briars and coming to smite me into oblivion for having dared to cross his path and I felt no animosity towards him.

As he lurched towards me, however, I moved easily away from him, circling smoothly to my right, unsurprised by the awareness that I was moving that way in order to take advantage of the fact that he was left handed, and as I moved, the spatha by my side, for so long the property of Tiberias Cato, seemed to spring into my hand by magic. I saw his eyes narrow at the sight of my unsheathed blade, and then he snarled again and raised his right hand to his forehead to wipe the blood from his eyes, and the contempt in his gesture was unmistakable. I hefted my weapon, feeling its balance, and moved again towards his sword arm, inhibiting him and forcing him to step back and away as he sought to raise his blade high for a clean swing at me. I heard Tiberias Cato's voice again in my mind, explaining to us, as he had at least a hundred times each year, that the wooden practice swords we used every day had been used by Roman legionaries for a thousand years, and that they had been designed in the earliest days of Rome to be twice the weight of a real sword, so that a man's muscles, accustomed to dealing with the heavy practice swords, would rejoice in the apparent weightlessness of the real thing.

I reversed direction, moving left and away from him now and freeing him to use the full extent of his long, left-handed swing. I watched carefully, gauging my moment, then leaped away, a long jump that took me well clear of his clumsy, sweeping blade so that it hissed by me a good arm's length from my right knee. I gave him sufficient time to rally and try for me again, and again I leaped nimbly beyond his reach.

By the time we had repeated the same moves a fourth time he was beginning to flag. His blade was heavy, as well as long, and the effort of swinging it and missing was, if anything, more damaging than anything else he might have done. His anger increasing visibly now with every heartbeat, he snarled something unintelligible at me, and I knew he was defying me to stand and fight, or more accurately to stand still and let him kill me. I grinned at him, drawing my lips back to show him all my teeth, and prepared to repeat the dance, even hesitating in preparation for leaping away, but this time he was determined that I would not skip away from him again, and as I began my spring to the left he threw himself after me, withholding his swing until he was sure of me.

Even as he launched himself, however, I had already shifted my balance, and jumped this time to his right, landing behind him as he charged past me and crouching to sweep the end of my blade hard across the unprotected back of his knees. The double-edged tip of the blade missed the hamstrings this time, but sliced deeply into the thick muscles of his left calf.

With a bellow of rage the monstrous man swung around with impossible speed, slashing at my face as he came towards me. I threw my upper body sharply backwards, almost falling over but avoiding the hissing slash of his blade and managing somehow to counter his attack with a blow of my own, blade against blade, my right-handed blow against his left, smashing his blade down and away from me so that his entire body followed the line of his swing and I ended up behind him again. I leaned forward, my weight on the balls of my feet, and closed with him quickly, stabbing hard, but my blade hit solid metal and its tip slid off the back of a cuirass I had not expected, worn beneath his tunic rather than over it.

Again he turned and came at me, but this time I detected a new respect in his approach. He paused, watching me, waiting for me to move, and when I did not, he changed his grip on his sword, holding it differently, more like a sword now than an axe, and began to circle me, moving now to my right, forcing me to move left against my natural inclination. The aversion I felt to moving so unnaturally reminded me of yet another lesson from my mentor Cato for dealing with a left-handed opponent.

I shifted my weight and took two quick steps towards my assailant, leading off with my right foot and then stepping forward and to the left. The sudden move took me right inside his guard and put me in front of him, within smelling length of his unwashed body, my sword arm raised in expectation of his next blow. It was an awkward, ill-formed hack, as I knew it would be, useless from the start because I was all at once too close to him too suddenly. I caught his blade on my own with no effort and turned it aside, and as it fell away past me I dropped my right shoulder, pivoted to the left and thrust my blade into the flesh below his navel, below his cuirass. It was a classic stroke, and I carried it out as I had been taught, twisting my wrist sharply to free the buried blade and jerking it straight back and away before the sundered flesh could clamp around it and before the dying man could drop his hands to grasp it.

He fell to his knees at my feet and gazed up into my eyes, his face twisted into a mask of consternation and terror as he realized what I had done to him. There was nothing worse than a belly wound, I knew. I had never seen one before, let alone dealt one, but I had heard all about what they meant: a slow, lingering, agonizing death.

"Finish him. You can't leave the poor whoreson like that."

I looked away from my assailant's face to where Ursus stood close by, watching us, an arrow in his bow again, and I knew that even if I could do no more, Ursus would put the fellow out of his misery. But that, again, would be an avoidance that I would find difficult to live with. I looked back at my former opponent, who had fallen forward and now hung head down in front of me and moaning quietly, then I stepped to one side, gripped my spatha firmly in both hands and swung hard at his exposed neck, killing him instantly. Then I turned aside and vomited.

I have no idea how long it took me to recover from the sickness that swept over me, but when it was over and I picked myself up off the ground I found that Ursus had confiscated our assailants' provisions and kindled a fire to cook some bannock to go with the cooked meat he had found in one of their packs. The smells were delicious, and I approached the fire slowly, feeling somewhat shamefaced about my latest pusillanimous behavior. Ursus, however, said nothing at all and contented himself with serving me some heated meat on a slab of thin, salty, freshly baked bannock. I accepted it gratefully and devoured it without saying a word. Ursus ate his more slowly, and when he was done he licked the blade of his knife carefully and pointed it at me.

"You did well, lad. First kill's never easy to handle. But it'll never be as difficult or as worrisome again, I promise."

"He wasn't the first." I raised my head and looked Ursus directly in the eye. "The one I shot with your bow was the first."

Ursus twisted his face into the semblance of a half grin. "Nah," he said. "That one didn't count. That was no more than helping a friend in need. If you hadn't taken that one down he would have been on top of me before I could handle his friend, and that might easily have been the end of me. Truth is, lad, your first real kill's always the one whose blood gets on your hands and your clothes— the up-close, frantic one who's trying just as hard to kill you as you are to kill him. He's the one you'll dream about for a while. But you'll get over it, in time. We all do."

He skewered the last piece of meat that lay simmering on the flat iron griddle he had laid on the coals of the fire—he must have found that, too, I realized, in his searching—and dropped it onto the last remaining piece of bannock in his hand, then closed his fist, squeezing the whole thing into a solid cylinder of bread and meat. He held it out to me. "Here, finish this, and then we'll salvage those arrows and drag the bodies out of sight. Can't bury them, but we can't just leave them lying there, either."

A long time later, after it grew dark, he spoke to me again across the dying fire. "Where exactly are you headed? Where are your people from?"

It was the first thing either of us had said for hours and it roused me from my semi-stupor of meditation. I realized that I couldn't answer his question properly, simple though it was. I knew where I was going, but I had no notion of how to get there from where we were.

"Genava," I told him. "It's a lake, far to the southeast, I think, close to the Alps—part of the Frankish kingdom called Benwick. King Ban rules there. He is a Ripuarian Frank and my stepfather, wed to my mother's sister—"

Ursus interrupted me with a scoffing laugh. "A Frank's a Frank, lad, be he from north or south. Leave it at that."

"No, that's not true. The two are very different, no matter that they sound alike. King Ban is a Ripuarian Frank, but I'm not. I'm a Salian Frank, from the north, near the Rhine River. My father's people lived and ruled along the Rhine. Ban rules along the

Rhodanus, which is called the Rhone nowadays. Rhine, Rhone, almost the same, one in the north, one in the south. Are they the same river because of that? I think not."

Ursus raised both eyebrows and pursed his lips, then nodded deeply, maintaining his wide-eyed look. "Prettily put," he said. "A point well made, so I will say no more."

I shrugged. "The fact remains, I know where I'm headed, but I don't know how to set about going there from here. I don't know where we are now."

Ursus laughed, a sharp, deep bark. "Is that all? Well, lad, that's easily taken care of since I know exactly where we are, and I also know the route from here to Benwick and Lake Genava."

I blinked at him, astonished. "You do?"

"Of course I do, and you'd better learn to do the same, and the quicker the better." He paused, gazing at me. "Knowing where you are is a matter of simple self-preservation. Look at me, a professional soldier, a mercenary. If I don't know where I am at any time I could be killed, simply for wandering among the wrong people. And so I pay attention to where I go, always. I'm so used to doing it that I never think about it any more, but I always remember where I've been and I know where I am headed next—even if it's only as far as I can see in a strange country."

"So where are we now?"

"Seven days' south of the gorge on the Liger River, headed southeast, this being the seventh day, and I'd say we've been covering less than a score of miles a day because we've been being cautious, moving slow, keeping our heads down, covering our tracks and taking care to stay out of people's way. Seven more days at the same speed should bring us to Lugdunum. The locals call it *Leeyon,* but whichever way you say it, it's the military administration's headquarters for south-central Gaul." He paused, waiting for my admiration, and when I admitted it he grinned. "What's important about that, though, from your viewpoint, is that if we swing back to the northeast from there and follow the High Road, we can be bathing in Lake Genava in five more days, providing the water's warm enough."

This was momentous news, and I was pleasantly surprised at how close we were to my family home, for had he told me it would take us three times as long I would have accepted that without demur. I felt my face split into a wide grin.

"Well, whether the lake is cold or not, King Ban's bath houses are fine, I promise you. They were built for a Roman governor long ago and they lack nothing that his wealth could provide. Will you come with me, then, to Benwick?"

"Of course, how could I not? I have to see you safely home. We should find word of Duke Lorco in Lugdunum, but even if we are ahead of him and he hasn't arrived yet, we'll leave word there that I've escorted you home and I'll follow him later to Carcasso. Does that sound like good sense? Course it does, so let's get some sleep and be on the road again early tomorrow morning."

4

The twelve days Ursus had estimated for our journey were more than sufficient. We found ourselves approaching Lugdunum at the end of the fifth of the seven days he had allowed us for that portion, and this was mainly because, within three days of setting out on that last lap, we had found ourselves in a heavily traveled area serviced by one of Rome's great spear-straight roads and hence were able to discard all our former caution and proceed openly at more than twice our previous pace.

Lugdunum was a surprise to me. I knew I must have passed through it years earlier on my way north to Auxerre, but I had absolutely no memory of the place, and I found it to be very different, in almost every way that I could think of, from its counterpart city of Treves in the north. Each had a military fortress, and the imperial legions quartered there were the same in both places.

Apart from that similarity, however, everything else was different from one town to the other, beginning most notably with the food but extending to the local people, the farmers and artisans who lived in the surrounding areas. The climate was warmer here, for one thing, since we were now in southern Gaul, but the very appearance of the local folk was completely dissimilar to that of the people who lived in the Treves region. These people here were darker skinned than their northern brethren, and they seemed plumper, somehow, sleeker, more content and more self-satisfied. "Better fed" was the way Ursus expressed it, and in the utterance he made it sound like some kind of cause for shame.

The wine they drank was better, too, I learned, and even though I could not have told from tasting it I could see for myself that the white wine of this region was closer to yellow in appearance, so I was prepared to believe that it might be thicker and more fruity with the kinds of sugar that northern wines lacked notably. It was the local red wine that made this region famous, however, according to what Ursus told me, and I saw no reason to doubt him, although I had no desire to taste any of it. I had tasted my first cup of watered wine at twelve years old. Now, almost four years later, the blend of the two liquids I infrequently drank was barely stronger than that first anemic mixture of one part wine to three parts water. I still found the taste of it unpleasant and preferred the honest tastelessness of chilled, clear water.

We found no trace of Lorco's turmae in Lugdunum. No one had heard of him or from him since he and his party passed through on the way north a month earlier. And so Ursus delivered a formal report to the military authorities, describing all that had happened, to the best of our limited knowledge, and left another written missive with the commander of the garrison for delivery to Duke Lorco when he arrived. That done, Ursus and I ate in the garrison refectory that night and slept soundly for eight hours in one of the barracks rooms before striking out again at dawn along the broad, straight highway that followed the Rhone River to the lake called Genava in the ancient territories of Cisalpine Gaul.

We rode with the river on our right, and at first we had no shortage of companions along the route, teamsters with laden wagons and self-sufficient pedestrians and an occasional string of laden mules led by handlers as taciturn as the creatures they led. But as we traveled farther and farther beyond the protection of the military headquarters, our traveling companions reached their various destinations in hamlets and small towns and villa farms and left us to travel on without them, until eventually we were alone again on the open road.

We no longer had any need to hunt for food, which pleased us both, for once Ursus had established his identity and his membership in Duke Lorco's squadrons, he had been able to draw some of his unpaid stipend from the offices of the military paymaster in Lugdunum. With those funds he had immediately gone looking for a commodious tent of hand-sewn leather panels to replace the one he had lost in the ambush by the river. I was most impressed with the workmanship I could see in the tent's finish, but Ursus waved a hand dismissively, saying it was nowhere near as large or as fine as the one he had lost. Then, having bought the tent, he also bought a horse to carry it, for the thing was much too large to carry on the horse he had inherited from Lorco. I watched closely, but said nothing while he negotiated with the horse trader, but I was satisfied that he had acquitted himself well and had bought a fine, strong animal.

From the horse dealer's premises, we next made our way to the armories, where he replenished his supply of arrows and purchased a bow and another quiver full of arrows for me before taking me on an expedition to purchase rations for the ensuing week, and now our saddlebags were filled with provisions: fresh crusty loaves of heavy, rich brown bread; several kinds of dried and salted meat and fish; four rounds of cheese, two soft and new and two hard and dry; a flask of the garlic-enriched fish oil that had been beloved of Roman soldiers for countless hundreds of years, together with a vial of thick, aromatic black vinegar and even two earthen jars of salty, fat green olives preserved in their own oil. We were men of wealth on this portion of our journey, at least when it came to eating.

On the afternoon of our second day out of Lugdunum it threatened to rain heavily on us and we could see no signs of any rift in
the thick-piled banks of cloud that had swept in upon us from the
north, so we decided we would rather make camp early and sit
warm and dry in our new leather tent than press on for no good
reason and endure the deluge.

We picked a spot in the open, about a hundred paces from the
roadside and close to the river, in the shelter of a huge dead tree that
would provide us with all the firewood we might need. It took us
almost an hour to pitch the tent to Ursus's liking, since this was the
first time we had tried it and every tent ever made has its own quirks
and peculiarities. By the time we had it up and ready to use, my
hands were sore and bruised from struggling with stiff new, abrasive
and unyielding ropes. As soon as that task was done, I went gathering ferns for our bedding, no great hardship compared to pitching
the tent because, as close as we were to the water, ferns grew in lush
profusion among the trees on the riverbank.

By the time I had brought back four enormous double loads of
fresh green bedding, Ursus had built a healthy fire that he felt confident would burn throughout the coming storm, and we settled in to
eat and wait for the storm to break. We ate well that night, and the
storm held off until we had eaten our fill and seen to our horses'
needs for the night. We could hear thunder rolling in the distance
and so knew that the storm was out there, but no rain fell for a long
time and we saw no signs of lightning throughout the time the sun
set and night fell. I fell asleep almost before it grew completely
dark, and Ursus was already snoring by that time, and I slept
soundly through the earliest stages of the breaking storm.

I snapped awake sometime in the middle of the night, my eyes
full of the remembered flare of a burst of brilliant light, and my
breast shocked near to death with the concussion of a single
massive, booming explosion. I sprang upright, leaping from the
softness of my bed to land on my feet, glaring blindly about me and
trying to tell myself that I was not afraid. I had no memory of
drawing the sword that filled my hand and no awareness of where I

was or what was happening. All I knew was I was in pitch darkness
and something terrifying had happened. But then I heard the solid,
steady roar of heavy rain on the leather panels just above my head,
and my memory returned.

I sucked in air, hard, and tried to calm the thumping in my chest,
but it was still pitch black in the tent, and that, combined with the
fury of the storm, was frightening, despite the fact that I now knew
where I was. Another flare of lightning lit the tent, followed after a
moment by a rolling crack of thunder, far different from the one that
had brought me leaping from my sleep. Even as the lightning flared
and flickered out again I thought I saw something moving at the
door of the tent. I opened my mouth to call out to Ursus, and then
heard the sound of a heavy blow and muffled curses.

Without giving myself a moment's pause to listen again and
be sure, lest I lose my nerve, I threw myself towards the front of
the tent just as another lightning flash showed me the flaps
hanging open. I had closed them myself when I went to bed, and
Ursus had already been asleep. I leaped forward and pushed
through the flaps to where I could see movement, a struggle of
some kind, taking place ahead of me. Ursus, I knew, and someone
else. I called his name and moved forward, raising my sword and
trying with my free hand to clear the streaming rainwater from
my eyes as my feet slipped and slid in the muddy grass, and then
I saw more movement looming close beside me, and before I
could begin to turn something, someone, hit me hard across the
head and I went down.

Whatever it was that had struck me, it was not metal, and at first
I thought it had done me no grievous harm. I felt the wetness of long,
sodden grass against my cheek and I rubbed my face in it gratefully
before rolling away. No one was pursuing me, I could see, but that
could change at any moment. I took a deep breath and tried to rise to
my feet, but my head blazed immediately with pain and I barely
managed to struggle to my knees. I made one more effort to stand
and fell instead, to support myself on all fours while the rain
hammered down on me. Appalled at my own weakness, I stared into

the blackness and saw Ursus, his back against a tree again, facing a group of crouching figures. Lightning flared again, and in the darkness that followed it I saw six figures lit in the blackness of my mind. I knew then that Ursus was a dead man, for I was utterly incapable of rising to my feet, let alone of rushing to help him.

"Alive, damn you! I want this whoreson alive!" The voice seemed impossibly familiar to me. Through the pounding of my head I tried to remember where I had heard it before, but the roaring in my ears was growing louder and suddenly I found myself face down in the grass, my mouth open in a puddle of mud. I grunted and spat and tried to roll over, to get my face away from the threat of drowning.

When I opened my eyes again the rain had stopped and I was in great pain and still lying on the grass. I tried then to roll again, but I could not. I couldn't move, and the effort of trying was unendurable, but I gradually became aware of what was causing my immobility: I was on my knees, but face down on the grass, and someone had thrust a stick of some kind across my back, locking it in place with my elbows and then tying my wrists tightly across my belly. The ends of the stick, protruding on each side of me, made it impossible for me to roll to either side. I found that I could turn my head, however, providing I moved it very slowly, and so I worked painfully until I could see what lay on the other side of me. It was Ursus, and he was unconscious, bleeding profusely from what looked like a deep wound on his scalp. He was very close to me and his arms had been tied the same way as mine, allowing me to see that the stick securing his elbows was a spear shaft, which made it likely that mine was, too. But who were the people who had attacked us, and why had their leader wanted to take Ursus, and presumably me, too, alive?

Before I could even start to puzzle over an answer, I heard movement on the other side of me and turned my head slowly and carefully back to see what was there. The soaked logs of our fire, which had not survived the storm after all, lay directly in front of me now, blocking my vision, and the sour stench of wet ash filled my nostrils. But beyond the soaked heap of the ashes in the fire pit, two figures came into view. Looming high above me and ludicrously distorted by the angle of my vision, they moved forward and stood gazing down at Ursus, ignoring me. Both men wore heavy iron helmets with full face flaps that hid their features and both wore heavy military-style cloaks, but neither the helmets nor the cloaks looked Roman, although I could not have said why.

One of the two men hawked and spat on the ground. "This has to be him. He fits the description and he's the only one we found in a day of searching."

"What about the other one?"

"What about him? He's an accomplice and he'll share the other's fate. But I want to get them back as quickly as possible. Looks as though the rain's passed by, so let's get on the road. Call the others and make them ready. Four men to accompany these two. Ropes around their necks and let them walk, or run if they have to. They're lucky I don't hang them. Whoresons." He sneezed, and then cursed loudly, reaching up to pull the helmet from his head with one hand while he wiped his mouth and nostrils with the back of the other, and as a shaft of moonlight lit his face I recognized him.

"Chulderic?" My lips formed the word, but no sound emerged. I stretched my neck and spat to clear my mouth before trying again. This time I tried harder, however, determined that he should hear me, and his name came out as a shout.

"Chulderic, is that you?"

I saw the amazement and consternation that swept his face as he jerked his head around to look down at me, his eyebrows drawing together into a single bar.

"What in—? Who are you, to call me by my name, whoreson?" He was gazing straight into my face but clearly did not know me.

"Chulderic, it's me, Clothar, son of Childebertus, nephew to King Ban."

He stood stunned, peering at me open mouthed, incapable of moving, yet weaving slightly on his feet as though he might pitch forward and fall down.

"*What* did you say?" he asked after what seemed like a long time, and then he took a step and did fall forward, landing on one knee beside the fire and bending forward to grasp my face and turn it to where he could see it more clearly. "Clothar? Is that—? By the white bull of Mithras, it *is* you. How come you here, boy?" He looked up at his companion and barked, "Get him up out of there and cut him free." The man moved swiftly to obey, lifting me gently to my feet and then cutting firmly at the ropes binding my wrists across my belly before removing the spear from across my back.

"I'm on my way home," I said as the ropes fell away from my wrists and before the pain of returning circulation had time to strike. "To King Ban, with messages from Bishop Germanus. My friend here is Ursus, who has been guarding me along the way. Cut him loose, please."

"Urs—?" Chulderic glanced from me to my unconscious companion and then back to me again. "This is a friend of yours? The bowman? Is he a Roman? Can you vouch for him?"

Now I spoke through gritted teeth as I tried to deny the agony in my wrists and ankles, and I had little patience with what I saw as Chulderic's obtuseness. "Of course I can vouch for him, but I don't know what you want. Nor do I know if he's a Roman. All I do know is that he's a good man."

"Ah, so you don't know him that well . . . Has he been with you all day long?"

"Aye, he has, and all day yesterday, too, since we left the garrison at Lugdunum. He has not been out of my sight for nigh on three weeks. Why are you asking me these questions? What do you think he has done?"

"He has nigh murdered King Ban, boy. That is what he's done."

"Balls!" The expletive came naturally to my lips and Chulderic did not even blink at it. "Ursus has been riding by my side since we left Lugdunum yesterday at dawn. I told you that. We have not even stopped to hunt since then. We camped at the twenty-fourth mile marker last night and traveled on today until the storm began to build, late in the afternoon. We made camp, right here, to wait out the storm." I stopped then, realizing what the old man had said about King Ban. "Is the King dead?"

"No. I said he was *nigh* murdered, not killed dead. He lies about five miles from here, in an armed camp. Someone shot him yesterday, from afar—a sneaking, cowardly attack that almost succeeded but fell short."

"You mean the arrow fell short?"

"No, boy, the attempt fell short, of complete success. The arrow struck the King beneath his upraised arm as he stood up in his stirrups to rally his men, and it struck deep and high into his chest, its point deflected upward by the armpit rim of his cuirass. The wound is grievous, but it might not yet be fatal. The next few days will tell, and he is surrounded by physicians and the surgeon Sakander, the best there is. If anyone can save him, Sakander will."

"And you think Ursus did this thing, in my company?"

"We have a description of him, Clothar. He was seen. A tall man, dressed in black and well armored, carrying a bow."

"And riding a high black horse?"

"What? No. We heard no tale of any horse. The killer was afoot."

"Well someone has mistaken Ursus for someone else. He is tall, and he wears black and has good armor and a bow, but he also rides a magnificent horse, the twin to mine. Both are close by here, hobbled in good pasture with a third animal, a packhorse, about a hundred paces along the riverbank there. Did you not check them?"

The old man frowned. "Not in the dark, no. We came up on your tent under cover of the storm because one of our scouts had seen you late in the evening, before the storm broke. But he said nothing of horses." He turned again to his companion and indicated Ursus. "Do as he says, Jonas. Cut him free. We've obviously made an error here. Master Clothar, as you've heard, is King Ban's nephew."

I felt myself frowning so hard that my face was starting to ache. The vision of my uncle as I had last seen him hovered in front of my eyes.

"What is the King doing here, Chulderic, so far from Genava?"

The old man looked at me in surprise, astonished that I should even have to ask such a foolish question. "He is being the King, fighting for his people and their safety. The entire countryside is crawling with two-legged vermin—Alamanni and the accursed Burgundians—all seeking what they call 'room to live.' We've been killing them as quickly as we can, and in the biggest numbers we can find, for nigh on three months now. They must breed like rats, the whoresons, because the more of them we kill, it seems, the more of them spill out of sewers and noisome craters in the earth. And they are outraged, crying to Rome for help against our ravages! Can you believe such shit? They want us to hold up our hands and step aside and let them take over our homes without a word of protest. Oh, it's been going on for a hundred years now, especially with the Alamanni, you know that. But now the whoreson Burgundians are causing us more grief than the damned Alamanni ever have."

He paused, and for a moment I thought he was finished, but he was merely rallying his forces, gathering his strength and nurturing his outrage and disgust.

"And they have imperial backing, it appears, whoreson support-ers at some rarified level of government who maintain that Empire—and tell me, pray, what *Empire* that might be? Tell me that!—Empire, they say, could not survive without their wondrous aid. *Burgundian* aid! They are being given title to lands around Genava—other people's lands—as a reward for what is described as 'faithful and unstinting service in Imperial Wars'! Have you ever heard such rabid filth? What about us, who live here and have fought and died for the whoreson Empire forever, without thought of asking for special privilege or dispensation? Would it ever have occurred to us to ask Rome's blessing upon our actions had we decided we have a right to usurp and dispossess our neighbors? Sweet Jesus crucified!"

I had been waiting for a pause in his tirade and I leaped in before he could begin again. "I need to see King Ban, Chulderic. Will you take us there?"

He nodded, but his eyes still lingered suspiciously on Ursus, who had not moved since being cut free and showed no sign of returning to consciousness. "Aye," he growled, "I will. But we had best see to your friend here. He should have come to his senses ere now."

He was right, and I knelt quickly by Ursus, shaking his shoulder and calling him by name. Fortunately, he heard me on my first attempt and came awake slowly, groaning as he reached up to cradle his head, but then he remembered what had been happening before he fell and he snapped awake, pushing himself up until he was sitting, staring up at Chulderic. I offered him my arm and pulled him up to his feet, and then I made the introductions and told him what had happened.

When I had finished, Ursus stood looking at Chulderic, stooping forward slightly and fingering the swelling behind his ear. "Was it you who hit me?"

Chulderic smiled. "No, sir. That would have been one of our younger men. Strong warriors they are."

"Aye, so it seems, especially when hitting a man from behind his back." He squinted at me. "So now what do we do?"

"We go and visit the King and hope we find him well."

Chulderic cleared his throat, a deep, harrumphing sound that contained all his skepticism. "Little chance of that. If you're the praying kind now, from your bishop's school, pray you then that we find him alive. He was struck down by a freakish chance, but the blow went deep. He might already be dead. Damnation, but I wanted to haul the man who shot him in to his judgment.

"Come then. Let's away."

5

Even from afar there was an air of dejection hanging over the King's camp as dawn broke that day. I became aware of it as soon as we emerged from the surrounding forest and began making our way towards the distant tents. The few guards I could see stood slumped, rather than bristling at attention in the usual way of perimeter sentinels, and the normal bustle of a military camp was subdued, with no one moving at speed anywhere and no upraised voices where normally there would be a babble of sounds and shouts. Even the smoke from the cooking fires seemed to hang listless and inert, settling in flattened layers of varying density above the fires rather than dissipating in the early-morning air. I glanced at Ursus and saw immediately that he, too, had sensed the hopelessness here.

Chulderic and I had talked as we rode about the dispatches I bore for the King from Germanus. I had been carrying them belted about my waist, beneath my armor, and I had already passed them over to the old man, as Ban's senior and most trusted counselor. I knew I could trust him to read and absorb the tidings I bore and, provided the King were fit to hear them, to pass their content on cogently and succinctly enough for the King to understand them and make any decisions that might be necessary. Now Chulderic rode beside me, knee to knee, and his face was wrinkled with concern. I could see his white-knuckled grip on the reins and knew it was only by a great effort of will that he was suppressing his urge to go galloping forward at top speed to be by his King's side. Of course it was much too late for that now and nothing would be served by his making an undignified spectacle of himself in the last few moments of our approach. And so we rode sedately forward and dismounted decorously in front of the King's tent.

As we did so the flaps to the tent were pushed apart and a tall figure emerged, stooping to keep his head clear of the peak of the entranceway. It was my cousin Samson, Ban's second son and my favorite kinsman among his offspring. I was delighted to see him there, because Chulderic had made no mention of his presence with the King's party, but I realized immediately that his attendance upon the King, along with that of his brothers, would be commonplace enough to merit no particular attention. At twenty-three, as I reckoned his age, Samson's natural place as a warrior was by his father's side. Samson ignored me completely in passing, going straight to take Chulderic's reins from the groom who had been holding them. Chulderic gave him no chance to speak.

"How is he?"

Samson shrugged and dipped his head, twisting his mouth in a wry acknowledgment. "Not good. The surgeons say the arrowhead is lodged against his spine, deep beneath his shoulder blade. They can't probe for it, and they can't cut in to it because both the shoulder blade and the collarbone above it are directly in the path of the knife."

"And so they do nothing?"

"Sakander tells me there is nothing they can do without killing him, and I believe him. If they break the collarbone in front to gain access to the arrowhead, they might have to sever it completely, and Sakander says the chances of its knitting again are slight, given my father's age . . . and besides that, he says, even if they could reach the arrowhead, there is still no guarantee that he would be able to remove it—it's a war arrow, remember, heavily barbed—without killing my father."

Chulderic spat an obscenity and then headed towards the tent's entrance, but he stopped and looked again at Samson. "Is he awake?"

"No. He was, until a short time ago, but Sakander fed him a potion and he fell into a deep sleep just before you arrived. Now he should sleep for several hours." Samson looked at me then, and from me to Ursus, a small frown ticking between his brows. "Who are these people?"

Chulderic saw where Samson's eyes were directed and spoke first to that. "That one is Ursus, a mercenary and a bowman. We thought for a time he might have been the one who shot your father."

Samson shook his head again, a short, sharp negative. "No, we found that one. He died before we could question him, but the arrows in his quiver were identical to the one that shot my father, so we know it was him." He glanced next at me, his eyes sweeping me from crown to toe. "And this one?"

"That's your brother. Clothar."

Samson's eyebrows shot up towards his hairline, but then his face broke into a grin of recognition. "By the Christus! Clothar? It *is* you! Welcome, brother." He threw his arms about me, and I recognized the well-remembered scent that always hung about his person, a clean, vigorous smell of light, fresh sweat mixed with something else, a fragrance reminiscent somehow of wild strawberries. He held me at arm's length while he gauged my height and width. "By all the old gods, Chulderic, he has grown up, our little tad, has he not?"

Chulderic grunted, and Samson's expression sobered. "I could wish you had come at a better time, brother, for our father is sorely hurt and like to die." I saw Chulderic stiffen from the corner of my eye, and Samson released me and stepped away, speaking now to the old man, his words blunt. "What, Chulderic? What would you have me say? That the King is but slightly scratched and will be sound tomorrow? Our leader the King has been struck down by a war arrow—an iron-headed arrow with fluted, extended barbs designed to do maximum damage to anything it strikes. I do not like the sound of that, or the reality of it, any more than you do, but it would be folly to deny it or make light of it. He is my father, a man, not a god. We must accept that and plan accordingly."

Chulderic nodded. "Aye, we must, of course. Has word been sent to your mother?"

"Aye, it has, and to Gunthar and the others."

Hearing Samson say those words, I had a sudden image of Gunthar's face, wearing its habitual sneering look of condescension, and I wondered whether time had improved his disposition.

Samson had already moved away to hold back the tent flaps and permit Chulderic and me to enter. He himself remained outside, and I noticed, too, that Ursus made no move to join us, probably aware that he would be denied entry. I caught his eye and nodded slightly to him before I stooped to follow Chulderic into King Ban's tent.

It was dark in there, the strengthening daylight failing yet to penetrate the thick leather panels of the tent, and what light there was came from the flickering flames of a quartet of lamps suspended from poles around the King's bed. The bed itself was heaped surprisingly high with coverings, but then I realized that they were draped over a construction of some kind that covered the King's upper body and had been built to retain warmth while protecting his injuries from the weight of the coverings. A tall, austere-looking man whom I assumed to be the surgeon Sakander sat erect at the head of the bed, close by the King's side, radiating an aura of intent watchfulness. His eyes were already fastened on Chulderic by the time I entered behind the old warrior and he paid me no attention at all. There were other people in the spacious tent, three that I counted among the shadows as my eyes began adjusting to the darkness, but as we approached the King's bed Sakander waved one hand and they all left immediately.

"How is he?" This was Chulderic, growling at Sakander.

"How would you be, given the same affliction?" The surgeon's voice was deep and level in tone, his diction precise and utterly lacking in the pompous affectation assumed by so many of his colleagues. He spoke to Chulderic as to an equal, and I had little doubt that the two of them were friends of long standing. "He is near death and I am powerless to help him. This was a freakish wound, the like of which I've never seen before, but the unlikelihood of it does nothing to lessen its gravity."

"Hmm." Chulderic gazed down to where his friend the King lay sleeping. As though he knew Chulderic would say no more, the surgeon continued speaking.

"Whoever the bowman was, he must have had the strength of a demon, for the arrowhead struck hard and sank deep, dislodging solid bone. It pierced the hollow of the shoulder socket beneath his upraised arm, deflected off the ball of the bone, I suspect, and then again, sideways and inward from the angled plate of his shoulder blade. From there it sliced through flesh and muscle, turning all the time because of the curvature of the arrowhead blades, until it struck his spine, lodging solidly this time, perhaps between two of the vertebrae."

He paused, then cleared his throat before going on. "That is what I suspect, but I have no way of proving or disproving it, short of killing him by cutting into him and mutilating him further, digging for the arrowhead. But we have other arrowheads that illustrate the problem facing us. See for yourself."

He indicated a table opposite him, where lay four war arrows, all identical to each other. "Those came from the same quiver as the one that shot down the King. They are identical in the fletching, as you can see, and in the shaping and weight of the warheads. No reason to suspect that the one in the King's wound should be any different."

I looked carefully at the four arrows, seeing the bright yellow feathers with which they had been fletched, and as I did so Chulderic picked one up, holding it close to his eyes to examine the heavy iron head. I leaned closer to him to share his appraisal. The thing was a work of art, made by a master craftsman and comprising three razor-sharp, wedge-shaped blades of thin tempered metal cunningly welded into a lethal tapering triple-edged point. At the broadest end of each blade the metal had been flared and twisted out of true to form wickedly curving barbs that, once set in a wound, would be impossible to remove without destroying all the flesh surrounding the entry channel. The very sight of the curved barbs made me wince and grind my teeth, imagining the bite of their entry.

"By the balls of Mithras," Chulderic growled, "the man who made these things knows his craft." He wrapped his fingers firmly around the center of the shaft he held, then moved it around behind his back as he bent towards the unconscious form of the King, peering closely at the sleeping face.

"How long will he sleep?"

"Two hours, I hope, perhaps longer. But it could be less. It depends upon how well his mind blocks out the pain."

"That's what you gave him the potion for?"

"Aye. The substance is strong. It induces sleep and stifles pain."

"What is it called, this substance?"

"It has no name of its own. It is one of a range of marvelous powders, all of them white, that are miscible in water and produce wondrously beneficent effects. We call them opiates, and although I know not where they come from, they are supposedly distilled from the essence of white poppy flowers in a distant land to the east, beyond the Empire's bounds."

"The Kingdom," I whispered, remembering something Tiberias Cato had told me about his days as a boy there.

Sakander turned his keen gaze on me immediately. "What did you say?"

He did not call me "boy" but I felt the rebuke nonetheless and I felt myself flushing. "I said, the Kingdom. It is what the Smoke People call the ancient land far to the east, beyond this Empire."

"The Smoke People. And who are they?"

I shrugged, feeling foolish to be talking of such irrelevant and inconsequential things over the unconscious body of the King. "A tribe of nomads, horsemen, thousands of miles from here. A friend of mine, one of my teachers, once lived among them for a while and learned from them about the Kingdom, an ancient place of great wisdom and learning, peopled by men with yellow skin, black eyes and straight black hair."

I was conscious of both men staring at me, and then Chulderic, his voice inflectionless and unreadable, said, "Sakander, this is the King's youngest son, Clothar. He has been away, in the north, attending Bishop Germanus's school in Auxerre since before you came to us. Apparently they have taught him some novel notions." He looked back to the King. "When will we be able to move him?"

Sakander began speaking without removing his eyes from mine. "He should not be moved at all, but since it is clearly both dangerous and foolish for us to remain here, separated from the army, then we may as well move him immediately and hope to achieve the worst of it while he is still in the grasp of the opiate." He turned back to the King then, dismissing me for more important matters. "I have him lying on a board, beneath those covers, for ease of carrying, because I did not know how soon we might want to move him.

Four strong men should be able to bear him easily from here to the largest of the commissary wagons. It is well sprung—as well as any wagon can be—and I have it already stripped of all its contents and layered thick with straw to guard him as well as may from bumps and bruises." The surgeon shook his head. "I don't know whether it is better to move quickly or slowly in such cases, but whichever way we go, Lord Ban will be badly jarred in transit. Fortunately we are but four miles from the main encampment, so if we leave within the hour we can be there before noon."

"Aye, four miles from the army's camp, but we're fifty miles from home."

Sakander nodded, his face expressionless. "True. Will you give orders to break camp?"

"Aye." Chulderic called to Samson, who came in immediately. The old warrior explained what he and Sakander had decided, then instructed the younger man to choose four men to move the King, and then to make the necessary traveling arrangements to rejoin the main body of the army.

Ban of Benwick remained unconscious while he was gently moved, and he slept through the entire four-mile journey to the main camp. Sakander sat beside the King the whole time and his face was somber and unreadable, but I suspected that he was not entirely grateful for the King's lack of awareness. It seemed to me, watching him as he bent forward time after time to wipe the King's face with a moist cloth, that the surgeon might have been happier had he discerned even a hint of discomfort in the King's demeanor. But that was purely a personal conjecture and I had nothing at all on which to base my suspicion, beyond an insistent prompting from somewhere in my own head. It simply seemed to me that the King slept *too* profoundly.

Ban slept that entire day away, and the night as well, opening his eyes only at mid-morning on the following day. I had ridden out of camp by that time, accompanied by Ursus, unable to remain waiting passively for something to happen and even less able to sit quietly by while my father—this title in defiance of the fact that I knew him to be my uncle—fought for his very life. Chulderic told me later that the King was very weak, but free of pain and lucid when he awoke, and that he remained that way for nigh on two hours, during which time Chulderic had been able to pass on to him the gist of the messages I had brought from Germanus. The King had listened and understood, and had made several pronouncements, in addition to which he had had Chulderic summon the cadre of his senior officers, both to witness and thereafter attest to his lucidity, his soundness of mind and his self-possession, and also to bear witness to his issuance of several specific instructions concerning the immediate future of his lands and his people.

Astonishingly, Ban had then, and thus publicly, rescinded his acknowledgment of his firstborn son, Gunthar, as his legal heir and follower, denying him the right to claim the crown of Benwick. His second son, the twenty-three-year-old Samson, Ban had declared in front of everyone assembled, would be his heir henceforth and would assume the crown on Ban's death. It was a momentous announcement and apparently a spontaneous one, in the eyes of those who were present for the occasion, notwithstanding the King's claim that he had been considering it for years, believing he yet had years ahead of him to resolve such matters.

My own belief is that the King's claim, disregarded and generally discounted as it was, was no less than the truth. I knew from comments made by Samson and Brach that Ban had been having serious misgivings for years about Gunthar's fitness to succeed him, but I also accepted that Ban truly had believed there was no shortage of time ahead of him and that he was under no urgency to make such a grave decision. As soon as his circumstances changed, however, Ban the King, who had always been a pragmatist adapting constantly to the real world in which he lived and ruled, made a final and irrevocable decision and announced it bluntly, in the presence of witnesses.

So now my cousin Samson would be king of Benwick. And my cousin Gunthar would not. And wrack, ruin and chaos lay between those two statements.

In the meantime, however, King Ban grew increasingly drowsy and more weakened from day to day, sleeping for longer and longer periods until eventually, four days after his fateful pronouncement, he slipped backwards into a deep slumber from which he was never to awaken.

He asked for me, however, on the day following my arrival while he was yet in fair condition, given the serious nature of his injuries, and when I went into his presence he knew me immediately and made me feel very welcome. He was lying strangely, propped up carefully and off-center on a mountain of soft skins because of the seriousness of his wound, and he still had that curious protective construction about his chest and shoulder. His face was gaunt and haggard, deeply lined and gray with pain, and his voice was whispery, his breathing shallow and careful.

Nevertheless, despite all his discomfort and my own discomfiture, he made it possible for me to gain great pleasure from his company. According me the status of manhood by speaking to me as an equal, he asked me all about my school and my various tutors, all of whom he knew by name thanks to the dutiful correspondence of the bishop's chief scribe and secretary, Ludovic. He asked me, too, about his old friend Germanus, but I had the distinct feeling— why, I could not have explained—that he already knew more about the bishop and his affairs than I could tell him. Then, too, he praised me for my prowess in arms and asked me about the adventures I had shared with Ursus on our way here, eliciting the information from me, almost without my volition, that I had killed my first enemies along the way.

I was aware of Sakander the surgeon sitting at the rear of the tent throughout all this, but the man never stirred and offered no interruption at any time. He merely sat watching, alert to the condition of his charge.

Finally, and in a papery whisper, speaking words that I have never forgotten, King Ban commended me to my duty above all things else and bade me hold myself true to God, Who, he assured me, had great things in store for me and would demand great things of me in return. I must return to Auxerre, he told me, and made me swear that I would permit nothing to deter me from so doing. I swore the oath at his request, but even as I did so it was halfhearted, diluted by a reluctance that was born of a silent, sneaking belief that the King was not altogether strong in mind. In all the years that I had known him I had never heard him talk so fervently about God and God's expectations of real, living people. Truth to tell, I had never heard him speak of God at all, under any circumstances, and had not even believed him to be a Christian. That he should so evidently and avidly be instructing me now concerning my Christian duty and obligations was, I feared, an indication of just how weakened he had become.

He saw my reluctance, and reacted strongly to it, stiffening his voice and speaking with more authority. Unable to move from where he lay, he nevertheless gave me to understand that he wanted to stand up more than anything else, to stand beside me with his hand upon my shoulder as I swore the oath. He bade me be quiet then and to summon the guard outside his tent, and then he sent the man to fetch the bishop who was chaplain to the Christian troopers. We continued talking then of other things until the bishop entered, some time later, and then the King asked him for the pectoral Cross that hung about his neck. He handed the ornate Cross to me and asked the bishop to wait outside the tent. When we were alone again, ignoring the surgeon at the rear of the tent as he seemed to ignore us, Ban repeated what he had said to me about God's expectations for me, and this time, strange as it might seem, I believed him absolutely, so that I swore the oath with passion and conviction, promising solemnly that I would return to Germanus in Auxerre within the year and that I would permit nothing to hinder me or dissuade me.

This time, when I had finished, the King rewarded me with a contented smile and asked me to return the bishop's Cross. I did so, and this time saw Samson waiting patiently outside the tent, gazing off into the distance, his long arms wrapped about his chest. I mentioned this to the King, and he asked me to summon his son.

When Samson came in, the King beckoned to him to bend close, and whispered something into his ear. Samson went away frowning and returned with a powerful, magnificently made bow and a large, heavy quiver filled with arrows, which he stood holding at the foot of the bed. Ban nodded. "Give them to Clothar."

Deeply astonished, I took them from Samson's outstretched hands, then turned to the King. "Lord," I asked him, "what am I to do with these?"

He smiled, and when he spoke his voice reminded me of the rustle of dead leaves stirred by the wind. "Do with them what you will, Clothar. They are yours. They have been the death of me, but they are wondrous fine and should go to someone who will use them well."

I went rigid, realizing only then that these were the weapons that had struck him down—I saw the bright yellow fletching of the arrows and was stunned that I had not recognized them instantly. The large quiver was heavily packed, filled with at least two score of the bright, yellow-feathered war arrows.

"No," the King said sharply, waving his sound hand slightly but sufficiently to stop me and dispel what I was thinking. "No, don't throw them down. They are superb weapons. Learn how to use them, Clothar, and remember when you do that they are merely tools for your direction and use. They had no will to harm me when they brought me down. That came from the man who used them. His was the urge to kill. Treat these with the respect they deserve, as powerful, well-crafted weapons, and they will serve you well, my son.

"Now kiss me and go with God, and I will pass your love and kindness to your father and mother when next we meet. But bear in mind your promise at all times from this day on: within the year, you must return to Auxerre and to Germanus."

His voice was very weak by then, and Samson's face was stretched tight with concern. I looked from one to the other of them, and then to Sakander, who sat gazing at me, his face still empty of expression. The surgeon nodded to me, as though granting me permission, and I stooped and kissed King Ban of Benwick for the last time.

6

Early on the morning of the day of the King's funeral, rubbing the sleep from my eyes, I emerged from my tent to find Samson deep in thought directly ahead of me, staring off into the misty distance and completely unaware of what was going on about him. It was a chilly morning, overcast and damp, and anyone could see it would turn into a nasty, rainy day once the lowering clouds had finished massing overhead and decided to purge themselves of their burden of moisture. I greeted him and asked him what was wrong, and he half turned towards me, surprised to find me there so close to him. I asked him again why he looked so glum, and this time he said, "Beddoc," then turned his head away again.

Beddoc, I knew, was one of his lieutenants, a clan chief who led nigh on a hundred warriors raised from his own holdings not far from Genava. I had met him on several occasions and found him difficult to warm to. He was a naturally dour man—a single glance at his dark, humorless face was all it took to see that—but he was enormous, too, and the sheer sullen bulk of him, draped in drab armor and faded furs, emphasized the air of unfriendliness and inaccessibility that surrounded him.

"What about him?" I asked, when it became plain Samson was going to say no more.

"He's gone. Last night sometime, during the third watch. Left without anyone knowing why or where he was headed."

"He must have told some of his men where he was going."

"No, his men went with him."

"All of them? That's impossible. How could a hundred men break camp and sneak away without being seen? The guards must have seen them."

"They did, but all the guards on that watch last night were his men. He took them with him, too. Left the camp unguarded for the duration of the watch. Sellus, captain of the fourth watch, discovered they were gone when he rolled out to rouse his men."

I did not know how to respond to this because I had never heard of such a thing. A hundred men vanished in the night from a camp site with no one else noticing simply defied credence. I was so amazed by what he had told me that I completely missed the real significance of the event. "Surely someone must have seen something," I protested.

"Aye, we think someone did. A man called Castor, from among my own troops, another called Gilles, one of Chulderic's men, and some young fellow who worked with the commissary people. All three were found dead by their fires, wrapped in their blankets with their throats cut. We think they must have been awakened by the stir, and killed as soon as they were noticed."

My mind tried to process this incomprehensible development. Finally I found my tongue and heard my own question emerge as a bleat. "But why, Samson? To what end?"

My cousin glanced at me and then began to walk, quickly, beckoning me to follow him. "To what end? What about self-interest, will that serve as an end? Beddoc is ostensibly one of my lieutenants, but that is purely nominal and born of political necessity. The truth is that he is one of Gunthar's four closest henchmen. Always has been, since they were boys. I've been watching him ever since my father made his announcement deposing Gunthar as his heir and naming me in his stead, and you may be sure I've been watching very closely. Had Gunthar become king in Benwick, Beddoc would have become perhaps his strongest lieutenant and supporter, secure in one of the king's fortresses as a reward for ongoing loyalty and support. That's what he sees in his own mind, and that's what he seeks to protect now."

"By deserting, you mean? How so?"

"How not? He is scampering to warn my brother Gunthar of what has happened, and the knowledge is making me sick. I should have *known* he would do that. The gods all know I've known him long enough! I should have anticipated his reaction and posted guards discreetly to watch his every move. The King's decree formally making me his heir was public enough to stand as law, but no one at home will know of it yet. As soon as the King was wounded, and never anticipating any of what was to transpire on this matter of the succession, I sent off a messenger to bear the tidings home, but Gunthar knew nothing of the King's decree thereafter. When Beddoc reaches him with his news, my brother will simply announce the King's death and assume the kingship, and once the crown is on his head, validly or otherwise, it will require the strength of Jupiter himself to take it back from him. Gunthar is no weakling and he has no fear. My brother will not be governed by the normal, civil rules that should apply in such a case. 'Honor thy father' has little appeal to one such as Gunthar when the honoring involves abandoning a claim to kingship. He lacks only sufficient strength to back his will. Beddoc has much to gain by warning him and pledging all his men to bolster Gunthar's strength. And understand me clearly, Gunthar will need all the strength he can muster if he is going to try to withstand me and defy the King's wishes."

"What of your other brothers?"

"Theuderic and Brach will stand with me. Gunthar has never done anything to endear himself to either one of them. Nor would he be willing to share any part of what he thinks to gain with either one."

"And the Lady Vivienne?"

"What think you, that Mother would go against her husband's wishes after all these years?"

"No."

"No, indeed. I suspect that my father's decision, long-postponed as it was, sprang from my mother's doubts. The King was always something blind to Gunthar's faults. Mind you, Gunthar leaned backwards close to the falling point to disguise those faults from Father's awareness; it was the rest of us who had to bear the brunt of them. But still, even when he came face to face with the worst of them, our father would always seek and find some reason to explain why this and that were so extreme and why Gunthar might claim provocation in the face of circumstance. It was tedious for the rest of us, but we soon learned to live with it. Mother, however, could always see through Gunthar and was unimpressed by the King's excuses. And as Gunthar grew older, she grew increasingly less pleased with how he was—how he *is*."

"So you are saying your mother influenced your father?"

Samson laughed, a single, booming bark that held no trace of humor. "Influenced him? Aye, completely! In everything he ever did. Of course she influenced him. How could she fail to? Mother is nothing if not direct, and we all know she is the strongest person in our lives. But in this particular instance, concerning Gunthar and his fitness to be king, aye, she has worked for years to change his mind."

"And you believe she was right to do so?"

"I do. Gunthar as king defies imagination. Don't you think she was right?"

"Yet you made no mention of that to Chulderic a few days ago when you discussed this very matter of the King's unwillingness to change his provisions regarding Gunthar."

He nodded. "True. I did not. I knew it and Chulderic knew it, but until the King spoke clearly on the matter of his final choice it would have been disloyal for either one of us to speak of it. Here we are."

We were in front of Chulderic's tent, and it was the center of a beehive of activity, with people running hither and yon, all of them shouting to each other to make themselves heard. I grasped Samson by the elbow, tugging him back before he could duck between the tied-back flaps.

"What? Come inside, we have but little time."

"No, wait, Samson. What will you do now, about Beddoc?"

He frowned. "Follow him, hope to catch him, but he has a long start."

"How long?"

"Perhaps an entire night watch: three hours."

"Is he on foot?"

"He's on a horse, but all his men are afoot, aye."

"And have you already dispatched men to follow him?"

"Aye, as soon as we discovered he had gone. But they'll not catch him, unless he falls sick or dies."

"And when will you leave?"

"Not until we have attended to my father's funeral rites."

"You think that wise? Why not leave now, as quickly as you can, and take the King's body with you? He won't suffer by being kept intact for another day or two and he will feel no pain now on the road. And if you leave now you'll be but hours behind Beddoc, instead of a full day, and Gunthar will have that much less time to decide what he will do."

Samson stared at me intently, his brows furrowed as he reviewed what I had said, and then he gave a terse nod. "You're right. That makes sense. Chulderic?" He shouted over his shoulder, preparing to swing away, but I stopped him yet again.

"Let me go now, with Ursus."

He peered at me. "Go where? What—?"

"To Genava! We have fast horses, Ursus and I, bred for stamina. Beddoc's people are all afoot. We can overtake them by nightfall. How far are we from Genava, forty miles? We can be there by tomorrow, before noon, ten miles and more ahead of Beddoc."

His eyes narrowed as he grasped what I was saying, and then his fingers fastened on my shoulder. He pulled me into the tent with him, shouting again for Chulderic, and within the hour Ursus and I were riding again towards Genava and whatever might await us there.

7

I could never have imagined what lay ahead of me as I followed Ursus out of King Ban's last encampment that day. The weather was foul when we set out and it remained foul for the duration of our journey—indeed, the rain was to persist in varying intensity for three entire weeks—and events and ramifications to those events were to occur within that time that I was simply unequipped to envision, let alone anticipate.

Riding through the driving rain that first morning, I would not have believed, had anyone suggested such a thing, that I might even come close to forgetting or forsaking the last promise I had made to King Ban, to return to Germanus in Auxerre. My faith was still strong in those opening days of what I would come to remember as Gunthar's War, and there was no room yet in my soul for self-doubts or for questioning the values I had been taught throughout my life. My beloved aunt, Vivienne of Ganis, awaited me at the end of my journey, less than forty miles distant, and I could scarcely wait to set my eyes upon her again.

I admit I knew that things had changed greatly in much too short a space of time, and that the welcome of which I had dreamed and for which I had yearned would not—could not—be as I had envisioned it. The Queen who would have welcomed me with love and joy a mere week earlier was now a widow, burdened by a new-born widow's grief, and a tormented mother, too, torn and distracted by the rivalry and conflict so suddenly flung up between her sons. I knew I would be fortunate indeed were the Lady Vivienne even to notice my arrival. All of that was in my mind, as I have said, and in my thinking as a man, but in the hidden recesses of my heart, wherein I was still merely a boy, I dared yet to hope that Vivienne of Ganis would welcome me with radiant smiles and open arms.

We caught up to Beddoc and his band late that afternoon and avoided them easily by leaving the road and sweeping around them, leaving more than sufficient room between us and them to ensure that they would have no suspicion of our presence. They had been marching hard all day, knowing they had a three-hour head start on anyone pursuing them, and to the best of my knowledge, none of them save Beddoc knew that Ursus and I existed, and not even he knew that we had swift horses at our disposal. Beddoc's sole concern was to reach Benwick and align himself with Gunthar before any word could reach the castle from King Ban's party. To that end, he had struck out and away in the middle of the night, knowing that no one he had left behind owned horses that were fast enough to overcome a three-hour lead. His men might be vigilant in watching for pursuers but, human nature being what it is, they would not suspect they might be overhauled as quickly as they had been, and even had they seen us by mischance, they would not have recognized us as representatives of King Ban's men.

Avoiding them was easy. We had known for some time before finding our quarry that we were gaining on them rapidly. The great road that stretched, magnificently straight, all the way from Lugdunum to Genava carried little traffic nowadays, even at the best of times, and this was far from being that. The threats of war and invasion were enough to deter all but the strongest and most desperate travelers, and so we had the rain-swept causeway all to ourselves, and we saw not the slightest sign of military activity anywhere as we progressed.

Solid and arrow-straight, the roadway provided us with significantly greater advantages than it permitted Beddoc and his men. We were heavily cloaked and well protected from the wind and rain, mounted on strong horses that moved swiftly and cared nothing for the driving downpour. Beddoc and his people, on the other hand, were afoot and heavily laden, making heavy going of their forced march, trudging through heavy, unrelenting rain under full military field packs, because when they had crept away from Samson's camp in the dead of night they had not dared to risk the noise of harnessing and stealing baggage wagons for their gear and equipment. They had left their cumbersome leather legionary tents behind, confident that they were but one night's sleep beneath the stars away from home, and so each of them lacked that heavy burden, at least. And so they plodded now through the pouring rain, huddled in misery, footsore, aching and feeling very sorry for themselves, their sodden clothing and ice cold armor chafing painfully wherever they touched skin.

We came closest to them at the point where they had stopped for their last rest of the day. Beddoc's party had been stopping once every hour, as marching legions always had from the earliest days of Rome's soldier-citizenry. Ursus had waved to me to slow down and moved out slowly ahead of me, scanning the roadside, and sure enough, we soon found the spot where Beddoc's men had spilled off the hard top of the road in search of relief from the road's surface and whatever shelter they could find beneath the canopy of the trees on either side. We reined in, and Ursus swung down from his saddle to search for whatever he expected to find. I sat straight in my saddle and dug my thumbs into the small of my back, under the edge of my cuirass, grimacing as I stretched and flexed my spine and stared ahead, over my horse's ears, along the tunnel of the road that stretched ahead of us.

Had the terrain here been as flat as the road was straight, we should have been able to see Beddoc and his party long before this, but the ground in this region undulated gently, in long, rolling ripples that stretched east and west, so that the road ahead rose and fell constantly. You might be able to see as far as half a mile ahead at any time, but then the road would crest and fall away into the next gentle valley and be lost to sight. The sight lines here were impaired, too, by the foliage of the trees that had encroached almost to the edges of the road in some spots, so that their lower boughs appeared from a distance to sweep down completely, to brush the surface of the very stones.

That, I knew, was something new, because I also knew that there had once been a time, extending into the boyhood of King Ban's grandsire, when an entire department of the imperial civil service had existed solely to maintain the roads in central and southern Gaul. Under its supervision the great roads, so long and straight, had been maintained and regularly repaired, and huge swaths of cleared land, fifty paces wide, had been kept free of growth on either side of each one. But after nigh on a hundred years of neglect and untrammeled growth, the protective borders were now choked with growth, and mature trees now towered close beside the roads themselves, close enough, in many cases, for their massive roots to have damaged the edges of the paving, heaving the paved and metalled surface upward and causing cracks and fractures. Those insignificant-seeming invasions of the roadbeds, according to the wisdom of Bishop Germanus, marked the beginnings of a process of disintegration that would inevitably, with the hungry assistance of time and weather, bring about the ruin of most of Rome's wondrous network of roads.

I saw Ursus stoop and pick something up, and then he came back towards me, gazing down at whatever it was he had found, then lobbing it towards me when he was close enough. I caught it and held it up to see it properly. It was the heel of a loaf of bread, just small enough to fill my palm and hard enough that I could clearly see the gnawed marks where someone had tried in vain to bite into it with strong teeth.

"It's still dry," Ursus said, standing now by my knee, "in this weather, save on the very outside. That means we can't be any more than a quarter of an hour behind the man who threw it away. There's an abandoned mansio about five miles ahead. They'll stop there for the night. Or at least, they ought to."

"Why there?"

"No other choice." He reached up with a bent finger and flicked a drop of rain from the end of his nose. The downpour suddenly intensified, the rain falling harder than ever, and I had to bend down towards him and listen closely to hear his voice above the thunder of it on my helmet, even though he was shouting at me. "They've no tents, remember? And it's too damn wet for them to even try to shelter under the trees." He moved even closer to me, leaning against my horse's side, his left hand holding my ankle as he shouted up at me and his face twisted into a rictus that I soon recognized, to my complete astonishment, as a grin. He was absolutely enjoying all of this, the journey, the chase and the deluge.

He removed his hand from my ankle and raised his voice even louder, wiping at his eyes with a forefinger. "The mansio's old and it's been sitting empty for years, long before I was born. It's got no doors or windows but it's still standing, thanks to thick stone walls, and it has a roof, or most of a roof, and fireplaces. They'll be better off there than any other place between Lugdunum and Genava. They might not be completely dry, or completely warm, but they'll be out of the wind and the worst of the rain and they'll have firelight and a bit of heat. They could be far worse off."

"And what about—?" The rain slackened as quickly as it had increased, and I heard myself bellowing. I lowered my voice instantly, glancing about as though to see if anyone else had heard me. "What about us?"

"What about us?" He was standing sideways to me now, his hands on his hips so that his cloak hung tent-like from his extended elbows. "We'll cut away from the road here, ride around and get ahead of them. From then on, every mile we gain on them is worth at least six to us, because they'll be walking to catch up to us and we'll be flying on horseback. Once past them, we'll ride for ten more miles, then stop for the night at a place I know, where we'll be warm and drier than any of those poor fools."

"Ten miles, once we're past them? It will be dark by then, and probably still raining, which means there'll be no moon to light your way. How will you find this place you speak of? Is it on the road? What kind of place is it, anyway?"

"Nitter natter, Master, so many questions." Ursus grinned and swung himself up onto his mount, making nothing of the sodden weight of his cloak. "It's a shepherd's hut, built of stone, solid as bedrock and strongly thatched, and it is never without a supply of fine, dry firewood. And as for your other question, no, it's not on the road. It is four hundred paces off the road, as I remember, and I could find it blindfolded if I had to. But I won't have to. Come, let's go." He looked up at the sky, then kicked his horse into motion, angling it away from the road and towards the forest, shouting back over his shoulder as he went. "I would say we have two hours of daylight left to us, perhaps two and a half. That should be more time than we need to reach our spot without riding through darkness. Once past Beddoc's crew we can really travel quickly, since we won't have to worry about running into them." He kicked his horse again, pushing it to a canter, and I followed close behind him, shouting back at him.

"How do you know this place we're going to, and how do you know it's still there? When were you there last?"

He didn't look back but his voice drifted to me over his shoulder. "I saw it last three years ago. I know where it is because I was born near there. I know it is still there because it was built to endure forever. And I know *that's* true because the shepherd who built it was my grandfather. I helped him chink the walls while I was still a babe in my father's arms. And I know it's warm and dry and stocked with fuel because my brother Doran still uses it today, when his flocks are on that side of his lands." Now he looked back at me, laughing. "Have you any further questions, Master Clothar?"

I closed my mouth, which had gaped open in surprise at what he was telling me, and then laughed back at him, kicking my mount's flanks to bring it level with his, and we rode on through the downpour, out into the forest's edge where we could ride parallel to the road and pass our quarry by without fear of being seen.

It was dark within the confines of the forest, and although I knew the expectation was illogical, I felt it ought to have been drier, but this forest was all deciduous growth, so there was nothing but a thin screen of leaves preventing the driving, incessant rain from falling straight through the canopy to the ground. And so as we rode through the trees we found it worse in places than being out in the open air, facing the rain. Out there, at least, we would be able to tell where the attack was coming from and hunch ourselves against it. Here, in the shadows beneath the trees, depending on what we or our mounts brushed up against or disturbed in passing, we were constantly being caught unprepared by small deluges, and sometimes enormous ones, that crashed down on us from all directions, landing indiscriminately on our heads or on any other part of our bodies that happened to be in the way. I tried hard to empty my mind of anything other than picking my way forward through the undergrowth and remaining alert to the possibility, however unlikely it might be, that Beddoc might have sent out scouts in such weather to check the forest's edge for enemies.

Sooner than I had expected, Ursus held up his arm in a signal to halt, and I reined in close to where he sat staring off to his right, listening intently. I tilted my head to listen, too, only to wonder for possibly the hundredth time at the acuity of my companion's hearing. I could hear nothing but the hammering of rain on my helmet. The noise of it filled my entire world.

"What can you hear?" I asked him.

"Nothing, and that suits me well. We're close to the old mansio, but not too close. I'm going to take a look. You stay here."

He swung down from his saddle and went towards the road, and I could not believe how quickly he faded from my sight, obscured by the mist among the trees and the falling rain, the blackish green color of his heavy woolen cloak seeming to absorb the very air about it and rendering him invisible. I forced myself to sit patiently, waiting for him to return, and in a short time he did, looming up suddenly within paces of me, though I had been watching diligently for the first signs of his coming.

"They're there, settling in for the night about a quarter of a mile up ahead, and a miserable-looking crew they are. They won't all be able to fit beneath the roofed portion of the place, not by a long shot, so there will be a deal of squabbling over who gets to stay where and I imagine the people in charge of them will have a job keeping the peace. I managed to get close enough to hear a few things, but the only important thing was someone giving orders for a squad to come into the forest looking for firewood . . . dry firewood. They won't find any, not in this downpour, but that means they're going to search deep into the woods, trying to find a dry cache, so we had better make a wide loop just to be sure we avoid them. Let's go."

We struck off deep into the woods, and rode in a long semicircle for the better part of half an hour, until we were sure we had left the enemy night camp far behind us, and we came out onto the road again. From that point on, free of the need to worry about being seen, we traveled as quickly as our mounts could carry us. The daylight lasted long after we had expected it to fade, so that it was still not completely dark by the time Ursus reined in and led us off the road, along a narrow but clearly marked pathway that took us, as he had promised, to a dry and sturdy, draft-proof haven that was stocked with an ample supply of cut and split firewood, carefully piled beneath sheltering eaves that had been extended for that purpose. We had a fire going within minutes of arriving and we ate in comfort and then bedded down in the luxury of two narrow, hand-built cots, with our wet clothes hung and stretched out around the inner walls, steaming towards dryness in the heat from the fire.

I was almost asleep when Ursus spoke for the first time in nigh on half an hour, and his words snapped me back to wakefulness.

"Be prepared for anything tomorrow, Clothar, and expect it to be worse than anything you can imagine. You hear me?"

"Aye. But why would you say that?"

"Because that is the only way to go, as a thinking man. Going in expecting the very worst, anything you find that's less than that will appear to be welcome. We are about to be involved in a strug-gle, you and I—perhaps a civil war between brothers—whether we like it or no. The stakes are high enough to justify a war—a king-ship and its power for the winner. I don't believe in auguries but I mislike the way things have fallen out these past few days. This brother of yours, Gunthar, sounds like a bad one to me. He does not strike me as the kind of man who'll be content to sit quietly back and run the risk of being deposed. Granted, he doesn't know yet that King Ban dispossessed him, or that he is dead, but he does know Ban was seriously wounded, and that in itself might have been enough to make him react according to his true nature.

"I hope I'm wrong and everything is well, but we'll find out the truth tomorrow, when we reach Genava. Sleep well, in the mean-time, and hope the rain stops before dawn. At least we'll start out warm and dry in the morning, which is more than can be said for Beddoc's cattle."

BOOK TWO

Brothers and Cousins

GUNTHAR AND THEUDERIC

1

Gunthar's War. I have no idea why I still think of that squalid episode in those terms. It was Gunthar's, certainly; he brought it about and he was the dominant participant, but it was not a war. It never came close to being a war.

Wars have at least an illusion of grandeur and respectability attached to them; there is always the notion involved that, in a just war, some of the participants are motivated by high ideals and honorable intentions and that they fight to defend and protect something of value. Gunthar's War stirred no such thoughts. There was nothing noble or inspiring within its entire duration to stir the minds or imaginations of adventurous boys. The people ranged against Gunthar and his depravity, myself included, fought out of sheer terror and desperation, knowing that to do less, to refuse to fight, was to surrender their lives and their entire world to the dementia of a murderous degenerate. Gunthar's War was a morass of filth and wretchedness from beginning to end. Nothing good came out of it. It was a bloodbath of mindless slaughter and godless atrocities too foul for the ordinary mind to accommodate, and merely being involved in it was a disgusting experience, easily the bleakest and blackest part of my early manhood.

Even so, I came of age in the course of it, and I learned much about the ways of men, because it presented me a study in treachery and an object lesson in how one evil man can spawn corruption and perdition and thrust it on to other, better men. Gunthar's "War" was no more and no less than a vicious internecine squabble. It was born of greed, betrayal, duplicity and the lust for power, and it demeaned and came nigh to destroying everyone caught up in it.

We rode into it, literally, the morning following our night in the shepherd's hut.

I had been dreaming for years of the first view I would have of King Ban's castle after my lengthy absence, and I had seen every detail of the place clearly outlined in my memory, so that even in the pouring rain, which had not abated in the slightest overnight, I found myself almost laughably anxious as Ursus and I approached the brow of the last rise in the road that concealed the castle from our view. And then we were level with the top and I was gazing hungrily at the sight that awaited me, only to find that it was vastly different from what I remembered leaving behind me six years earlier.

An enormous ditch had been dug around the entire castle, and the excavated earth had been used to build a steeply sloping rampart on the far side, in front of the castle walls, which thus became a secondary line of defense rather than the primary one. The work had been done very recently, too. I could see that by the rawness of the logs that had been used to stabilize the slope of the earthen wall. It was a classical Roman fortification of *vallum et fossam:* an unscalable ramped wall of earth and clay excavated from, and used to back, a deep and dangerous protective ditch. The defenders were all but invulnerable, at the top of the sloping wall, where they could overlook and annihilate their attackers, who had to cross the exposed ditch and then fight their way up the steep clay face. In this instance, however, the effect of the fortification was doubly enhanced by the towering height of the castle walls that loomed behind the earthen one, for the stone battlements were more than twice as high again as the new ramparts at their foot, and the defenders up there could shoot down easily and without fear of counterattack into the mass of any attackers who might dare to attempt a crossing.

Ban's castle, I saw at a glance, was now invulnerable behind its new defenses, accessible only by an imposing and weighty drawbridge, which for the time being lay open, bridging the chasm of the ditch. Perhaps the assembled might of Empire would be able to bring Ban's castle down now, but even that was questionable. The fortress beside the lake had its own deep wells, ensuring an ample and permanent supply of fresh water for the garrison, and any successful attack against it must entail a prolonged land siege and a simultaneous naval blockade to prevent reprovisioning of the garrison from the lake side of the defenses. Anyone with any awareness of the logistics involved in such a venture knew too that the Empire no longer had such naval power at its ready disposal.

I was aware of Ursus sitting tall beside me, taking everything in. "All that looks new," he said. "Must be for the Burgundians."

"Alamanni. Chulderic said the Alamanni were on the march."

"Aye, but didn't he say at the same time that the Burgundians were causing him more trouble than the Alamanni ever had? Whichever's right, he's gone to a power of trouble to deter one or both of them. I wouldn't like to be the attacking commander responsible for capturing that place now. Once that bridge goes up, there's no way of getting it down again if the defenders don't want you to."

I had been staring at the bridge as he spoke, having recognized it as a masterpiece of defensive engineering from earlier times, one of the great Roman drawbridges. I had heard of such devices from my tutors at the Bishop's School and had examined ancient drawings and plans for building them, but I had never seen a real one, and now I wondered who had designed and built this one.

Even from where we sat on the hill's crest gazing at it, and even through the drifting curtains of heavy rain, I could see that it was solid and massive, the bridge deck itself roughly thirty paces in length and fashioned of long, straight logs carefully selected for their uniform size and thickness. They had then been hand sawn, lengthwise, and squared so their sides would fit together, after which they had been covered with a layer of thick, heavy planking set crosswise and secured in place with heavy metal spikes. But that was merely the smallest and least important part of the construction. A drawbridge, no matter how soundly built the bridge deck might be, was completely useless if it could not be raised and lowered, and therein lay the challenge of construction. The end of the bridge on our side of the great ditch overlapped the edge of the excavation by several paces and fitted into a deep channel that had been carefully dug to accommodate its thickness and to bring its surface level with the ground. The far end, however, on the castle side, was very different.

The bridge deck there terminated a good ten paces, perhaps even fifteen paces beyond the edge of the ditch in what appeared to be a high, blank wall of stone, so that traffic crossing the ditch had to turn sharply right at that point, immediately veering again to enter the protection of the curtain wall that shielded the approach to the main gates. Halfway between the edge of the ditch and the wall at the end of the bridge deck, however, a huge log, two long paces in diameter, had been carefully sunk across the approach and firmly anchored into the ground above the narrow edge of a long, deep pit, the high, vertical sides of which had been lined with logs to guard against subsidence. The pit had originally been dug as a sawpit for the dressing and shaping of the enormous matched logs that formed the foundation of the bridge deck, but it had been sited in that specific spot to serve another, more enduring purpose: the log across the end of the pit, between it and the ditch, was the fulcrum of the bridge, and the blank wall at the bridge end was merely the front surface of a massive counterweight that made it possible for the drawbridge to be raised and lowered with the help of an intricate system of windlasses and pulley hoists. The counterweight itself comprised several thick sheets of iron, hand riveted and bolted to the thick beams of the bridge deck's end and then surmounted with great squared blocks of solid granite that were secured to the metal plates in turn by welded straps of iron a handspan wide and a thumb's width thick. When the bridge was raised, the counter-weighted end sank into the pit. Twin towers of massive logs flanked the pit right and left and contained the system of giant windlasses and torsion brakes that enabled crews of men to raise and lower the bridge by means of pulleys and enormous chains of iron links.

"You're right," I said belatedly. "Once that bridge is up, there's no way across. The place is impregnable."

"Aye. So what will you do if your brother Gunthar's seized it?"

"He is my cousin, not my brother."

"Cousin, brother, makes no difference to my question. What if he has taken the place?"

"He hasn't." I pointed to where a military standard was visible on the highest peak of the battlements above the main gate. "That's still King Ban's standard."

He squinted at it. "How can you tell? It's a length of soaked, bedraggled fabric beneath a Roman eagle standard on a staff. That's all I can see, through this rain. It could be anyone's."

"No, because it's pale blue and gold. Even wet and dirty, those colors are recognizable. And they're Ban's colors. He was always most particular about visible insignia, and he issued personal colors to each of his four sons with much ceremony as they attained manhood. Gunthar's is pale green with a wide yellow border; Samson's is two broad lateral bars, scarlet and white; Theuderic's is bright yellow with a broad diagonal band of black, from right to left, and Brach's is blue and white vertical stripes. Had Gunthar moved to usurp the kingship, his green-and-yellow banner would be hanging up there now."

"Perhaps he forgot to change it. Could he do that, forget such a thing?"

I glanced at him, wondering if he was being facetious, but then I shrugged. "Gunthar is not the kind of man who forgets details of that kind. Appearances are everything to him, which is part of his particular . . . charm. You'll understand when you meet him. What Gunthar chooses to show you and what you actually see are seldom the same thing." I turned again to look at the rain-drenched blue-and-gold standard on the walls and shook my head, this time more decisively. "No, had Gunthar taken over already, he would want everyone to know it—immediately—and one of the most obvious ways to achieve that would be to hoist *his* standard, *his* colors, above *his* fortress for all to see."

"He sounds like a wonderful fellow," my companion drawled. "But speaking of things that are there for all to see, there's not much to see here at all, is there? Were it not for that cluster of guards above the main gate there, I would have thought this place was deserted."

I looked again, at the walls this time rather than at the bridge. There were some guards above the main gate, as he had said, but there was no one else in sight, and the so-called guards had not yet seen us, although we had been there long enough to examine their new defenses in detail. I felt a kick of sudden misgivings stir in my gut and sat straighter in the saddle, taking up the slack in my reins.

"You're right. They're too few, and negligent. They have not even looked in this direction since we arrived. We had better get down there." I kicked my horse into motion and heard, rather than saw, Ursus's mount fall into line behind me, and all the way from there to the final approach to the bridge I kept my eyes fastened on the men above the main gates.

They finally noticed us when less than sixty paces separated us from the end of the bridge, and then there was a startled flurry of movement, accompanied by a high-pitched challenge. I ignored it completely and kept moving, headed for the bridge deck, and the challenge was repeated. I called to Ursus to follow me and put my horse to the gallop, covering the intervening space in what seemed like a mere instant before I was listening to the thundering of our hooves on the wooden deck. A solitary arrow zipped past me, missing me by several paces before it disappeared in the muddy bottom of the ditch. As soon as we were across the bridge and safe in the shadow of the castle walls, concealed from further fire by the curtain wall in front of us and the overhang of the battlements on our left, I pulled my horse to a halt and we waited for the arrival of the defenders of the castle. Moments later we heard the main gates behind the curtain wall creak open and then came a rush of feet as the "guard" came running to confront us.

They spilled around the edge of the curtain wall and swept back towards us, surrounding us and brandishing swords and spears, all of them shouting at once so that no word of what they were saying could be heard. I sat motionless, my weapons clearly sheathed and untouched, my arms folded across my chest. Ursus, I knew, was doing the same, watching me sidelong and following my lead in everything.

I knew we were in very real danger, particularly since it now appeared that there was no one really in charge here. Any one of these people might decide at any moment to end this situation and make a hero of himself by cutting us down to annul the insult we had offered them by penetrating their defenses so easily. I did not dare to move, for fear of provoking a murderous response. But then came a bellowing roar from another voice behind the curtain wall, and around the corner lurched a man I recognized, albeit with great difficulty and only after scrutinizing him for some time.

It was my old childhood friend Clodio, who, for as long as I could remember, had been in charge of the standing guard at the castle gates. Ever an outwardly bad-tempered, loudmouthed blusterer, Clodio had always been more bark than bite, and he had taken a liking to me when I was a mere toddler staggering about the courtyard with a bare bottom. Throughout my childhood he had treated me with respect and a special consideration due, I now knew, to the fact that he was one of the few who knew the secret of my true parentage. King Ban and he had been boyhood friends and comrades in arms for many years, saving each other's lives on several occasions, and in consequence he had always enjoyed the King's special favor in times of peace, although, for some reason no one had ever defined or even divined, he had steadfastly refused to accept advancement beyond what he himself had decided was his natural station. Clodio, if ever I met one, was a man who had always been content and well pleased with his life, confident in himself and in the friendship, loyalty and high regard of his king. It once amused me to think of the King as being loyal to Clodio, but it was simple truth, and Clodio's loyalty to the King was so much a part of him that no one would ever have seriously thought to question it.

Some gross misfortune had befallen him since I had last seen him, however, for his entire body was twisted upon itself, gnarled and malformed. Whatever injuries he had sustained, they had left him incapable of walking as other men walked. Both legs were misshapen, cruelly skewed, his right hand was clawed, useless, at his breast, and he propelled himself in a lurching, ungainly stagger, dragging his left leg. His mouth was as loud and profane as it had ever been, however, for as he drew near he berated everyone in sight, and his status evidently remained secure enough that they paid heed to him and drew back slightly to allow him to approach us.

He peered up at Ursus, selecting him over me as the elder, bearded man. "Down, whoreson," he snarled. "Off that horse now or you die. Who in—?"

"Shame, Clodio," I said, interrupting his tirade. "Is that the way guests are welcomed to Benwick nowadays?"

He stopped dead, keeping his eyes on Ursus and refusing to look at me, but then he answered me in a snarling voice I had never heard him use before. "Aye, these days, it is." He turned slowly then to glower up at me. "Who are you, that you know my name and speak to me direct? I don't know you."

"Yes you do, Clodio. You've told me many tales and shared your rations with me more than once, when I was small. It's me, Clothar."

"Clothar?" He stiffened and blinked his eyes several times, as though attempting to adjust to some profound revelation. "Clothar? But—How come you here? You should be in the north somewhere, with Germanus."

"I was, but my time there is done now and they sent me home, bearing letters from Germanus to King Ban." I swung down from my horse and walked to where he stood, and no one moved to hinder me. When I reached him he stretched out his left hand and touched my face, peering at me in that strange way common to people who see things poorly at a distance.

"Clothar. It *is* you. You've become a man. I never thought to see that, you've been gone so long."

I smiled at him. "I've been trying to become one, Clodio, learning to be a soldier, among other things. But more important, old friend, what happened to you?"

He glanced down at himself, and I noticed that he looked first at the clawed right hand that was drawn up beside his right breast. "Ah," he said, as if noticing it for the first time. "This." He looked back at me then, gazing straight into my eyes. "Runaway wagon. Five years ago. I jumped off, but one foot was tangled in the reins, so I got dragged. Thrown around, run over by the wheel a few times. It was downhill. Steep grade. Killed two horses."

The expression "Well, at least you're alive" was on the tip of my tongue, but I managed to bite it back because it was very obvious that Clodio was not altogether pleased with that situation. I nodded my head instead. "Forgive me, Clodio, I did not know."

"Forgive? Hah! How could you know? You weren't here, were you?" He suddenly became aware that we were at the center of a ring of curious onlookers and he rounded on them, cursing them for a lazy batch of layabouts and then telling them my name, pretending as always that I was the King's own youngest son and making sure they knew exactly who they had been poised to attack and kill when he arrived. He conveniently forgot, in doing so, that he himself had been prepared to flay the skin from us before I spoke to him, but that was typical of the Clodio I remembered so fondly. The men he was haranguing stared at me in something approaching awe, and I acknowledged them with a courteous nod before Clodio sent them scuttling back to their duties.

We watched them until the last of them had rounded the edge of the curtain wall, and as soon as we were alone, I introduced Clodio to Ursus. The two men nodded to each other cautiously, neither one quite prepared yet to accept the other without suspicion.

"Where is everyone, Clodio, and why is the guard so lax?"

He glowered. "What do you mean?"

I thrust up my hand to cut his protestations short before they could be uttered. "Come, man, look at where we are. We're across the bridge, Clodio, on this side—the wrong side. We came across at the gallop, two of us, unopposed. We might as easily have been half a score. Had we been enemies, we could have cut the ropes and destroyed or damaged the windlasses, making the bridge unraisable before anyone reached us. There were guards up there, above the gate, but they were not even looking out over the battlements. I don't know what they were doing, but they were not keeping watch. We sat on the brow of the hill over there, less than two hundred paces away, for nigh on a quarter hour in broad daylight and no one even glanced in our direction."

"But—"

"No, no buts, my friend. There's no excuse for dereliction of duty. Who is in command here?"

Clodio sniffed, a loud, long, disdainful snort. "I am, I suppose, so I'm the one you'll have to hang or flog, if you think that's called for. Lord Gunthar rode out yesterday to bring home your mother, the Lady Vivienne, from Vervenna. She has a young friend there . . . well, the young wife of an old friend, in truth, Lord Ingomer. He was newly wed a year ago to a young wife, Lady Anne. She was brought to childbed there a sevennight ago. Lady Vivienne went there before that to assist with the birthing, so she has been gone for ten days now, since the day after the King rode out to the west against the Alamanni. Lord Brach accompanied his mother with a score of men."

Lord Ingomer, our closest neighbor, had always been one of Ban's staunchest allies and supporters, and Vervenna was the name he had given to his lands, which bordered on Ban's own. Ingomer's house, a small, heavily fortified castle, was no more than five miles from where we stood. Nevertheless I found myself frowning.

"Why would Gunthar ride out to bring my mother home when she already has an escort? Brach is with her, isn't that what you said?"

"Aye, but yesterday, when the word came that King Ban had been wounded—" Clodio cut himself short, appalled that he might have committed a gaffe. "Did you know that? The King was shot down by an assassin's arrow . . ."

"Aye, we know that, but you say the word arrived only yesterday?"

"Aye, about the middle of the afternoon. I was up on the walls and saw the messenger come over the hill there."

"Sweet Jesu, he took his time in getting here! Four days, to cover a distance we consumed in one?" I was speaking to Ursus, but he frowned and jerked his head in a clear negative, and so I turned back to Clodio, wondering what I had said that Ursus did not like. "Go on, Clodio, what happened when the word arrived?"

"Lord Gunthar grew massy concerned about his mother's health when once she heard the news, and so he rode to pass the tidings on to her himself, for fear she heard them unexpectedly from some other source."

"What other source? There is no other source. Are you saying Gunthar rode off alone?"

"No, he took a strong party with him—his own mounted guards. Three score of them in two thirty-man squadrons."

"And he simply left you alone in charge of the fortress?"

"Nay, not he. Gunthar accords nothing to lesser men than he . . . men below his station, I should say, since he believes all men are lesser than he is. He left the fortress in the charge of your brother Theuderic."

"So where is Theuderic?"

"With the others now, wherever they are—Vervenna or elsewhere by now. I know not. He was away when word of the King arrived, patrolling the eastern boundaries against Alamanni raiding parties, so he knew nothing of it until he returned, about midway through the afternoon. Mind you, he was expected. Gunthar knew he was coming in person to pick up supplies, hoping the King might have returned from his patrol of the west side and would be able to spare him some more men for the eastern patrol."

"So this was after Gunthar had left for Vervenna?"

"Aye. They missed each other by less than an hour."

"What happened then? Come on, tell me, Clodio, don't make me squeeze every word out of you."

"I'm telling you, damnation! I just can't talk as fast as you can think. When Theuderic heard about the King and then found out that Gunthar had gone a-hunting for Queen Vivienne, he was angry—wild angry. Next thing I knew he had reassembled all his men—they were already dismissed and scattered by then, you understand, not expecting to be riding out again that day—plus every other able-bodied soldier in the place, and went thundering off to Vervenna at the head of a mixed force, forty horsemen and the last half century of infantry. As he rode off across the bridge he shouted to me that I was to be in charge until he returned. That was the last I saw of him."

"And you have heard nothing from any of them since? That was yesterday."

"Not a word. And I know well when it was."

I looked about me, seething with frustration. "I cannot believe they left you here with no more than a holding crew. Even so, why is the bridge down? Doesn't that strike you as being unwise?"

Clodio flushed, and his deformed torso writhed in what amounted to a shrug. "Aye, but I didn't know how to raise it."

I blinked at him in astonishment. "You didn't know how to *raise* it? You pull it up and lock it in place, Clodio. It is not difficult to raise a bridge."

"Mayhap not." Clodio was beginning to sound resentful now. "I'm not a fool, Clothar. But that bridge is new and it's Gunthar's pride and joy. He was there, hovering over it like a crow over a dead rat at every stage of its building and he was very jealous about protecting the secrets of its construction and its operation. No one has been allowed to touch it or operate it other than his men since it was built. From what they told us, it has all kinds of new and wondrous bits and parts to it and only people trained to handle it are allowed close to the workings. I've never seen the machinery being used and neither has anyone else who is left here in the castle, so I didn't want to take the risk of breaking or damaging something and earning Gunthar's wrath for my troubles. That's too easy to do at the best of times. And so I decided to leave the whoreson as it was. Besides, I was expecting everyone to return at any moment. They're only supposed to be five miles away."

I bit down hard on the angry response that was filling my mouth and forced myself to count silently from one to ten, aware that from Clodio's viewpoint he had done nothing wrong and reminding myself that we had had no real indication, thus far, that anything was wrong in any way. Finally I sighed.

"Damnation, Clodio, there is no great difficulty in turning a windlass, no matter how newly built it is. All it requires is brute strength, shoulders on a cross-bar and muscled legs to push the thing around. Call back eight of those people you just dismissed and we'll raise the bridge right now. Then we'll go inside and see what remains to be done there."

Almost before I finished speaking, Clodio was waving to the wall-top guards, who were now all watching us very closely, and I heard voices raised up there as someone relayed the orders Clodio had shouted up to them. As soon as he turned back to me, I laid my hand on his shoulder to soften the impact of my next words, should he decide to object to them.

"As of this moment, Clodio, I am relieving you of duty and responsibility for the safety of the fortress."

He grunted and nodded his head, once. "Good. I wish you joy of it. Leave me in peace to do what I must do, that's all I ask. I'll die protecting people in my care if I have to, but I have no love for bidding others die at my orders. Apart from the women and children—and God knows we have more than enough of those—there are less than forty men left in the entire place and none of them are fit to fight. Not a man of them. They're all like me, cripples and old men. All the fighting men are out, most of them with the King and Chulderic and Samson. Another group, almost as big, is on the eastern borders, under Theuderic and Ingomer. Then there's a score more with Brach and the Lady Vivienne, the remaining cavalry squadrons with Gunthar, and the last of the garrison with Theuderic."

"So what does the full garrison strength stand at nowadays?"

Again I recognized Clodio's malformed version of a shrug. "Couldn't tell you," he said. "Not off the top of my head. Not my responsibility to know things like that. But let's see. The King and

Chulderic took nigh on five hundred with them on the western sweep, and Theuderic took almost as many to the east, although his men were joined by Lord Ingomer's people and by another contingent, mainly infantry, raised from among the chiefs of the eastern marches. So Theuderic would have more than a thousand at his beck in the east, for it's a bigger territory with fewer people but more ground to cover than the western borders . . . but of that thousand, say he had between four and five hundred from here in Genava. Then Gunthar had his guards—three score of them here, another three score out with Theuderic but under the command of Chlodomer, Gunthar's right-hand man. The people Theuderic brought back with him are already counted, but then he took away the remaining foot soldiers from the garrison, say forty of those. So what does that give us? Nigh on eleven hundred . . . more than a thousand men, give or take a score or two. That's about the right of it."

I nodded, smiling. "An impressive estimate, my friend, for one whose responsibilities have no connection with such things."

"Aye, right." He inclined his head, acknowledging my praise. "But where does that leave us?"

I glanced at Ursus. "It leaves us with a bridge down that ought to be up. Let's change that, for a start."

Clodio began shouting orders to the men he had ordered down from the battlements above, and while he was instructing them, Ursus turned to me, nodding towards the bridge. "That is excellent," he said, "and all very well. Raise the bridge and keep the wicked ones out. Excellent precaution. But it has flaws. What about Beddoc?"

"What about him?"

"He'll be here soon, probably within the hour." He saw from my expression that I had no notion of what he was suggesting, and so he continued. "You want to keep him outside the gates and away from Gunthar? That's understandable, except that Gunthar is out there as well, on the far side of the bridge."

I stared at him, hearing his words and understanding what he was saying, but completely incapable of responding. He spoke on, ignoring my open-mouthed silence. "So, will you keep Beddoc outside the gates to wait for Gunthar's arrival, or let him inside, knowing that he is Gunthar's man and therefore your enemy?"

"And knowing, too, that once he is inside we have no one here to withstand him or to influence his behavior," I added, finally finding my voice.

"Exactly." Ursus looked at me, one eyebrow raised, and almost, but not quite smiling. "You catch up quickly, no matter how far you lag behind at the outset. I think you've grasped the gist of the problem."

I nodded, slowly. "Aye, but not the solution."

"There may not be one." He turned around in a wide arc, gazing at the layout of the castle's defenses. "Certes, if you raise the bridge no one comes in, but we shut out our friends as well as our enemies. We'll hold Gunthar and his ambitions at bay, safe outside the walls, but Queen Vivienne will be out there with him, as will your two other brothers and the men who ride with them. And then will come the arrival of Samson and Chulderic. An entire carnival, with good and evil ranged on opposing sides, and all on the lands outside your gates. Do you enjoy the thought of that?"

"No, Ursus, I do not—most particularly since these are not my gates. They are the Queen's gates, now, for she is Ban's legal regent until Samson can assume the kingship."

"Think not on that, lad. As long as you control the bridge the gates are yours. All we can do is hope to have the time and opportunity to open them to the Queen and her men."

"Aye, but there are too many unknown factors here and I do not enjoy having that responsibility, Ursus."

"No more do I, but there must be an answer for us somewhere, even though I cannot see it yet . . . Was your uncle Ban a drinking man?"

"What do you mean?"

"Did he drink beer, or wine? Would he keep any of such things available for his use?"

"Aye," I concurred, remembering. "He always had beer to hand."

"Good, then let's raise this whoreson bridge and find some of his beer. In the drinking of fine beer, many weighty problems are easily solved and frequently come to naught."

Half an hour later, secure behind a raised drawbridge, Ursus and I sat with Clodio, holding foaming tankards and discussing our situation. Clodio said nothing, content to leave, at least outwardly, the thinking to Ursus and myself.

For my part, I disliked the taste of the beer but I was willing to think, to make the effort of thinking. Unfortunately, I lacked both the capacity and the experience to be aware of what I should be thinking about at such a time, and so I, too, said nothing.

Ursus sat silently and sipped his beer with grave deliberation, gazing with tranquil, uncreased brow into the middle distance.

"So," I asked him when I could bear his apparent equanimity no longer, "what think you, Ursus?"

He turned to gaze at me and raised his upper lip to bare his teeth, not in a snarl but in the approximation of a smile. "About where we sit?" he asked. "What would you like to know first?"

"Anything," was my immediate response. "Anything you care to share."

It turned out to be the correct answer, for he began speaking immediately and I listened to him closely, finding no need, and no desire, to interrupt the flow of his thoughts.

"We're on a pronged twig, over a fire," he began, "skewered two ways and secured among the flames. We'll be thoroughly cooked, at best. At worst, the skewer we're hoisted on will burn right through and drop us into the fire's heart." He looked at me, one eyebrow cocked, and grinned ruefully. "If we let Beddoc and his crew come inside when they arrive, we might as well surrender to Gunthar right away, no matter what he does or what he might be guilty of, because we have no forces, nothing, no strength with which to withstand Beddoc's strength, and no means of denying him anything he wishes—including access to the drawbridge controls.

"So. What can we do? Nothing, is the correct answer to that question, because there are other things happening out there beyond these walls, on the far side of that bridge, that are beyond our control, although their outcome is crucial to us and to our well-being. The Lady Vivienne is out there, at the mercy of whatever might develop from all this, and as well as Samson you have three cousins—*brothers*—out there, too, Gunthar, Theuderic and Brach." Ursus was unaware that Clodio knew who I really was, and so he kept on talking through his momentary slip, hoping that Clodio might not have noticed it. Clodio, for his part, gave no sign of having heard anything amiss as Ursus continued.

"Among them, they have some two hundred men, but the problems we are facing here all stem from the basic fact that we don't know what's happening among the three of them. They might, for all our fretting, have all joined forces and be on their way back here in perfect amity. We simply have no way of knowing. But if that's so, why are they not already here? It's but five miles, you said, from Ingomer's castle to here." He turned to look directly at me, his narrowed eyes leaving me in no doubt that I was being called upon for a contribution to this discussion, and perhaps for a solution or a decision. "So, Lord Clothar, what are we to do?"

"Get out of here." The words came unbidden to my tongue and were out before I knew I would say them.

Ursus raised his eyebrows high, wrinkling his brows. "Now that is an answer I had not expected. Abandon the castle, you mean?"

"Yes, and no. At this very moment I am not sure what I mean, not exactly. I know it's illogical, but that feels like the right thing to do, here inside me." I tapped my breast.

"You propose to leave the fortress to the enemy?"

"What enemy, Ursus? We don't know yet if there *is* an enemy . . . Isn't that what you have just been saying? We are yet talking about family matters, and to this point no demonstrable treachery has been offered or committed, and no one has been harmed."

"As far as we know."

"Yes, that's the right of it: as far as we know. But there's too much we don't know. You said it yourself, we'll serve no useful purpose penned up in here with no supporting strength while all the other people with a part to play in this are free to move about outside." I glanced again at Clodio, who sat watching and listening, as mute as an old stag. "Clodio, you have not said a word since we came in here. What think you of all this?"

He made a wry face. "Not my place to think about it, is it? I'm only an old soldier."

"Oh, no, don't hand me that 'old soldier' claptrap, my friend. I won't wear it because it never has fitted. You're one of Ban of Benwick's lifelong friends. And besides, if you're qualified to be left in trust of the entire fortress, you're qualified to express an opinion. So speak up and spit out whatever might be in your craw."

He stared at me for several moments, nibbling on the inside of his lip, then nodded his head. "Right. Here's what I think. Ban has four sons: Gunthar, and Samson, Theuderic and Brach. Gunthar is poisonous—a demon in human form. All his brothers know it and fear him for it, because they know there's nothing he would not do on his own behalf.

"That fear is why Theuderic reacted as he did when he heard the word of Ban's being wounded and Gunthar's riding off to find their mother. His first fear was that Gunthar might seize power and might even seize the Queen, his own mother, to make sure that none of his brothers would dare to challenge him. Theuderic's a clever young man and I have a gold piece under the leg of my bed that say's he's right in this."

"But why would Gunthar think to usurp power? He is the King's named heir." I knew that was no longer true, but I wanted to see Clodio's reaction to hearing me say it.

"Aye, that's true, but it's the common word around here that the Queen has no trust or faith in him. She fears his nature. There are some who would even tell you she has been coaxing at the King for years to change his decree and give the name of king to Samson, his second-born."

I was staring hard at Clodio as all this came out, knowing exactly whence he had gained his insight and wondering admiringly at the extent and depth of his evident friendship for and intimacy with the King, and probably with the Queen, too. I was sure that such talk could not be common knowledge, as he claimed. Had it been so, Gunthar would have learned of it long since and, being Gunthar, would have taken steps to guard against it. Or would he? I found myself hesitating there, acknowledging that there was but one man for whom Gunthar had always shown genuine respect and fear. King Ban, his father, had always overawed Gunthar, and now that I thought of it, it seemed inconceivable to me that Gunthar would make any move to fulfill his own ambitions while there was any chance that Ban yet lived and might come home to knock him down and put him firmly in his place. But yesterday the word had come that Ban was gravely injured. How grave the wound might be could be something that was open to interpretation, depending upon the sympathies and loyalties of the reporting messenger.

If that was so, and if the messenger were friend to Gunthar, or if he had an eye to his own enrichment, then the tidings rendered might well have tempted Gunthar to trust his fortunes to the gods of chance.

"The messenger, Clodio, the one who came yesterday from Chulderic. Who was he?"

"His name is Grimwald. Why, is it important?"

"It might be. Is he a friend to Gunthar?"

"No one is a friend to Gunthar. But Grimwald would like to be one of his cronies, there's little doubt of that. He sidles after Gunthar like a lovesick pup after a bitch in heat, sniffing at the great man's arse and falling over his own feet."

I knew then that what I had been supposing was right: the messenger had made his choice and weighted his message, and Gunthar had seen his opportunity to seize the power he lusted to possess.

"Hmm. Tell me, is the old postern gate still in use?"

"What, you mean the old gate in the back wall by the lakeside, above the rocks at the high-water mark? Nah, it's been sealed up these five years now, ever since a boatload of Alamanni almost succeeded in using it to steal into the castle. Ban ordered the door torn out and then he filled the entranceway with mortared stones. No one will ever enter or leave that way again. Why do you ask about that? You look as though you've bitten into something with a nasty taste."

"I have, old friend. What I was thinking was that if we left here now, today, Ursus and I, and some division of the enemy—and I mean Gunthar's forces—were later to take over control of the castle and deny entry to our friends, you might be able to open up the postern gate during the night and let us back in under cover of darkness. But that's not going to be possible, so mayhap we have to stay here, useless as we are in such a case." I looked at Ursus, who sat watching me with pursed lips, his arms folded tightly across his chest.

"He's dead, isn't he? Ban's dead. That's why you're here."

I turned back to Clodio. "Aye, Clodio, he is. It grieves me to have to be the one to tell you of it, but he died two days ago." I described the seriousness of the wound. "Even Sakander the surgeon could do nothing for him."

I told him, then, how Beddoc's men had slipped away in the night to bring the tidings to Gunthar, and how Ursus and I had taken off after them, passing them and leaving them behind by nightfall.

As I spoke, Clodio's eyes did not waver from mine. "But the most important thing in all of this is not known yet," I continued, speaking to him directly and quietly. "Not to anyone here, at least. You were right in what you said about the Queen and how she had been working on King Ban. Before he died, the King assembled all his men and decreed in their presence that he was disinheriting Gunthar and naming Samson to rule in his place. Knowing that, there can be no doubting that Beddoc was on his way to warn Gunthar. Beddoc's people will yet be several hours behind us, but we've already been here for more than an hour, so they can't be that far away. That's why it was so important for me to arrange to use the postern door." I swung back to Ursus. "We have to decide . . . *I* have to decide, I know. We can't simply continue to sit here doing nothing."

"You could come through the caverns." Clodio's voice was so quiet that I barely heard it, and the meaning of his words took some time to penetrate my consciousness, so deeply was I concentrating on what I must do next. I sat up straighter, suddenly alert.

"What did you say?" I asked.

"I said you could come in through the caverns." His voice was still barely audible.

"What caverns?"

"The King's Caverns, below us, in the rock."

I leaned closer to him, watching the tiny half smile on his face blossom into a wide grin as he decided that he had done the right thing in telling me of this.

"Which king's caverns, Clodio? King Ban's?"

"Aye." He was grinning hugely now. "But King Ban the Bald, the old man, your grandfather. And he told his son, our King Ban, that he had been shown the caverns by his father, who had learned of them from his, and so on, back until the days before the fortress was built."

"Wait!" I held up my hand. "I don't understand this. Why have I never heard of this before? I grew up here, and never once in all my boyhood did I hear a whisper about any caverns."

"I know you didn't, nor did anyone else, because no one knows they're there. Only myself and the King ever knew of it, and I only found out by accident. And then Ban swore me to secrecy. You never heard mention of it because you were never meant to, along with everyone else. It's the biggest and best-kept secret in all of Benwick."

"But there must be an entrance somewhere . . ." I was thinking furiously. "If they're right under our feet, as you say, then there must be an entrance nearby, somewhere along the beach, above the high-water mark. But if that's so, then why has it not been found by others, long before now?"

"Because it isn't there." There was no trace of a smile on Clodio's face now. "It's nowhere near the lakeside. There is only one entrance, and it's far from here, inland."

When he told us where it was, I remembered the place, recalling that I once had known it very well indeed, having spent a fair-sized period of my boyhood playing there. But I had covered every bit of space in the caves that were there—I would never have called them caverns—and had found no hidden entrances or exits. One small tunnel I remembered, leading from one chamber to another, but that was all. I said as much to Clodio and he agreed with me. He, too, had played there as a boy, he told me, and had never seen anything unusual. But then one day he had seen the old King and his son emerge from the caves without ever having gone in. He had been playing there all day with half a score of friends and none of them had seen any sign of either the King or his son in all the time they had been there, until both of them had come out.

Everyone had thought it was magic, and they had hidden lest the old King see them and decide they had been spying on his sorcery, but as soon as the two Bans were gone, everyone had descended in a rush upon the caves, searching them from top to bottom in a hunt for some indication of whence the old King and his son had sprung.

A few years later, sheltering from a sudden summer storm with his friend Ban in the same place, Clodio had recalled the event and mentioned to Ban what they had seen that day. No one had ever been able to make more sense of what had occurred that afternoon, he said, and the incident had gradually been forgotten. Now he mentioned it only as a curious memory. Ban showed no reaction. A short time later, however, Ban vanished completely after uttering an unearthly, terrified howl that echoed eerily through the emptiness of the caves.

Clodio scoured the caves and found no trace of his friend, the King's son, and so, badly shaken, he made his way back as fast as he could to the castle, intending to summon help. And there he found Ban, sitting placidly against the wall waiting for him.

For months after that he wondered what had happened, for, of course, Ban offered no explanation. He merely smiled mysteriously, and thereafter he would appear and disappear from time to time, simply to keep the mystery alive. It was not until another three years had passed that Ban had shown Clodio the secret doorway set into a blank rock wall at the back of the cave. By that time, however, they were fully grown and fast friends, having already saved each other's lives in battle, and their trust in each other was absolute. And Clodio had kept the secret until now.

"I know the place, the caves, I mean," I said. "But how will I find the secret entrance?"

"You won't. Even knowing it's there you'll never find it, not if you search for it for a hundred years. You won't find it until I show it to you. King Ban knew nothing of it until his father showed it to him, and Ban the Bald told the same tale of being shown by his father. The secret goes from generation to generation."

An appalling thought hit me then. "So Gunthar knows of it."

"No." Clodio's response was whiplash-quick and sharp. "Never. Empty your mind of that thought. Gunthar has no idea the caverns exist. When he turned twelve and should have learned of it, the King, by sheer good fortune, was involved in quelling a revolt by the Alamanni on our northern borders. When he returned from his campaign, he found his son absent, vanished no one knew where, hunting with his cronies. Even as a twelve-year-old, Gunthar was a law unto himself. Anyway, for whatever reason, Ban never did find a convenient time to show Gunthar the secret. The boy's fourteenth and fifteenth birthdays came and went, and still he had been told nothing, and by the time he had turned sixteen and attained manhood, his father had decided, for reasons of his own, to tell him nothing. It has turned out to be a wise decision. I am glad to have been able to play a small part in it."

"You played a part in it? How so?"

He almost smiled at me, but at the last moment all that transpired was a quirking of one corner of his mouth. "Through friendship, and through shared responsibility. You forget that I, too, knew the secret."

"But—forgive me for being blunt, my friend—why would the King entrust you with the secret and yet deny it to his son?"

"You just said it yourself: trust. Ban trusted me. He could not bring himself to trust Gunthar. And I urged him, quietly, to trust that judgment that bade him remain silent despite the unease he felt over what he saw as a duty to his firstborn. I reminded him that he had sired four sons and that the secret of the castle's strength or weakness need only be passed to one of them to endure."

"I see. So have you told any of the other three?"

"No. You are the only one who knows, and even you know nothing yet."

"But I am not the King's son."

"No more am I. But you will be worthy of the trust, Clothar, and when you—should you—choose to pass the knowledge on, you will divulge it wisely, I have no doubt."

"Does Queen Vivienne know about it?"

"No."

"Hmm." I glanced sidelong at Ursus, wondering how he was perceiving all of this, but he was staring down at the ground between his feet and I had no means of knowing if he was even listening. I looked back to Clodio. "Tell me about the entrance. I find it difficult to imagine any well-used entrance being as completely concealed as you describe."

"I did not ever say it is often used. Ban's tomfoolery aside, it is opened only once every ten years or so. The doorway was built by a master stonemason a hundred years ago and more, but it is a doorway the like of which you have never seen."

"So how will I find it, alone?"

"You won't. You will find me. If you leave now, and should there be treachery so that the castle falls into Gunthar's hands, I will make my way out and through the caverns each day at noon. I will wait in the caves there for an hour, then return here if you have not come to find me. I will do this every day for ten days, and after that I will assume you have been found and killed, and so will stop going. But if you do come that way, bring no more than a score of your best men, and make sure you bring sufficient cloth to bind their eyes, for none of them must see the entrance or the exit on this end. Now you had best leave, before Beddoc and his people reach us. Where will you go, once you are out of here?"

I looked at Ursus and shrugged my shoulders. "Vervenna first, I think. That seems to be the most obvious place to start. But we'll approach it carefully, for only the gods can know what we'll find there. And if there's no one there, that too will tell us something." I stepped quickly towards Clodio and laid one hand upon his shoulder. "Thank you, old friend. I will not forget. Let's hope our expectations are ill founded and we'll have no cause to call for your assistance. But if we're proven right and the madness we fear does break out, we'll be there by the caves one day, waiting for you. Go with God, Clodio."

"I will, young Clothar, but I would far rather have gone with my King. Be careful."

2

We rode into it. Rode unsuspecting into the chaos and destruction that marked the beginning of Gunthar's War and were engulfed by its madness within the space of two heartbeats. One moment we were forging ahead determinedly through the still unceasing downpour, our horses plodding side by side along a broad and muddy woodland path, and the next we had rounded a bend in the path and found ourselves at the top of a steep defile leading down into a tiny vale that was choked with corpses. It was still not yet noon and the noise of the lashing rain was loud enough to drown any noise from the flies that were beginning to swarm here in uncountable numbers.

At first glance, I could not tell what I was looking at, but beyond that first uncomprehending look there was nothing that could disguise the atrocity of what we had found. My first conscious impression was of a score of bodies. The number sprang into my mind as though it had been spoken aloud, and I recall it clearly. *A score of bodies.* No sooner had I acknowledged it, however, than I saw that it was woefully inadequate, for another score and more lay sprawled and half concealed by bushes. And at that moment, as though it had been preordained, the rain stopped falling, for the first time in days, to leave us sitting stunned in a silence that seemed enormous, gazing in stupefaction at the carnage before us.

Ursus, as usual, was first to collect himself. "Well," he said, his voice sounding louder than ever now that he had no need to shout over the noise of the rain, "at least we know now that they have not all joined forces. Whose men were these, do you know?"

"Ban's," I said, still too stupefied by the unexpectedness of what we had found to have thought beyond the fact of it to the implications it entailed. "They're garrison troops, wearing Ban's emblem, see? The blue boar's head." And then, as the import of what we were seeing began to sink home to me, my voice shrank to a mere whisper and I felt my bowels twist themselves into spasms of knotting cramps. "These must be the men Theuderic took with him when he left yesterday."

Ursus nudged his horse forward until he was sitting knee to knee with me. I glanced at him, wondering if he felt as I did, but he was scanning the entire scene ahead of us, his eyes moving ceaselessly over the ranks of slaughtered men.

"Took them on the march," he said. "Must have lain in wait for them, knowing they'd be coming." He tilted his head back slightly, pointing with his chin. "Look at them. Poor whoresons didn't even have time to draw their weapons. Not a strung bow or an unsheathed sword among them. Probably ambushed from over there." He pointed to the hillside facing us on the other side of the narrow valley. "See, on the top of the hill there, those bushes? See how dense they are? You could hide horses in there, and that's exactly what they did. Perfect spot to lie in wait for anyone coming along this path, because once they're on the slope down, there's nowhere else for them to run to . . ." His voice faded away for a moment, then resumed. "Can you see Theuderic here?"

"Theuderic?" The question snapped me out of the trance I had been sinking into, making me look around in expectant horror. It was one thing to see my cousin's men shot down and slaughtered, but quite another to think that Theuderic himself might lie among the dead.

"No, I didn't think so," Ursus continued, speaking quietly as though musing to himself. "There's no dead horses here at all, which suggests that whoever set this trap let all the horsemen pass by first—they would have been ahead of the infantry in any case—and then sat tight and waited for the foot soldiers. And they, knowing that their own cavalry was just ahead of them, would have marched right into death, suspecting nothing. Probably hadn't even sent scouts out ahead of them, although it would have made no difference. Poor catamites walked right into it. Look at those arrows. I haven't seen that many spent arrows since I fought in Asia Minor, against the Berbers there. I've seen hedgehogs with fewer bristles than that. And yet there's hundreds missing. Look, you can see where they've cut the retrievable ones out of the bodies." He indicated the body lying closest to us, and I saw immediately what he meant. The man had taken an arrow in the thigh, which dropped him in his tracks, severing the leg's main blood vessel and causing him to bleed to death very quickly. The ground around him was black with his lifeblood and it had gouted far enough to stain several of the bodies lying ahead of him, as well. The wound that had been added afterwards had not bled at all; its edges were clean and deep, and the hole left by the missing arrowhead was big. I turned my head away before the gagging in my throat could overwhelm me, but Ursus was still looking.

"Look over there! That fellow there was still alive before they came down. They slit his throat when they came back, either to silence him or to make sure he'd tell no one what he had seen." He shook his head in disbelief and blew out his breath explosively through puffed cheeks, looking up again to where the bushes that had concealed the killers stretched across the top of the hillside on the far side of the little valley.

"This is cousin Gunthar's work." I said it quietly, and Ursus looked again at the surrounding scene and expelled another whoosh of breath.

"May God himself be my witness, I would not have believed it if I hadn't seen it for myself, but those whoresons actually came back down here after the slaughter and collected their spent arrows to use them again." He shook his head again, still looking about him as he continued in the same musing tone. "It takes a special kind of attitude to let a man do things like that—especially to people he has known. These were garrison mates . . . That's a close relationship, young Clothar, brothers in arms. But their brothers, like some of your own relatives, were less than loving. Your cousin picks his guardsmen carefully, it would appear, with more than half an eye to temperament . . . I wonder if they are *all* mounted archers. They must be, to account for the numbers of arrows and the rate of fire . . . the short amount of time involved." He waved a pointing finger, indicating the feathered missiles projecting from the bodies. "These are mounted bowmen's arrows, much smaller than the ones you and I have in our quivers. When we come face to face with Gunthar's men I think I would rather have my bow to pull than theirs." He sucked air between his teeth, still looking thoughtful as his eyes moved ceaselessly over the killing ground. "Before we do anything else, though, we ought to take a closer look at what we have here. Come on."

He swung down from his saddle, and I joined him very reluctantly, my gorge rising anew at the stench that had begun to rise now that the rain had stopped. My entire mouth seemed coated with the brassy, almost granular stink-taste of blood. I tried to ignore the feel of the blood-soaked ground beneath my feet, telling myself it was no more than mud, then stood reeling with nausea, clinging to my horse's halter. Ursus, however, paid me no attention. He was already quartering the scene around us with his eyes.

"Go you and look down there, Clothar, among the bushes at the bottom of the slope. See if you can find anyone still alive. And see if you can find any different crests from the boar's head, something that might give us proof of who's responsible for this. I'll search on this side of the slope. If you find anything at all, shout."

A long time passed before I found anything to shout about, and when I did, I almost missed it.

I had lost track of time, walking among the dead for so long that I had grown inured to the horrors I was seeing, and my revulsion and nausea had passed. It was plain to see that Ursus was right. The killers had come down after the slaughter and retrieved as many of their arrows as they could cut out of the corpses, and the number of cut throats showed that many of their victims had still been alive when they came down. Now, all of them were dead, every man and boy, and there had been more than a few very young boys, evidently trainees, among the garrison troops. My guess was that no one had survived this massacre, that even those who had sought to surrender or flee had been shot down without mercy or compunction.

The rain started falling again at some point, and the renewed chill of it reminded me how far removed we were from any kind of warmth or shelter that day, and I had turned in disgust to rejoin Ursus when I glimpsed something from the corner of my eye that seemed out of place. I immediately looked for it again, but this time saw nothing, and I felt impatience flaring up in me. I forced it down, however, and disciplined myself to move slowly and look again, meticulously this time. And then I saw it: a flash of gray and green among the long, yellowed grass at the base of a thorn bush to my right, a long way from where the nearest dead man lay. Whatever it might be, it had not been left there by any of Theuderic's dead foot soldiers.

Ursus came running at my shout, to where I was tugging my prize out of the rank, thorn-filled grass among which it lay. He was leading our two horses as he came and I noticed that in one hand he was carrying an arrow that he had obviously taken out of a dead man. I glanced at it but said nothing, contenting myself with merely raising one eyebrow. He saw my reaction and hefted the ugly thing, its barbs clogged and clotted with gore.

"It's not a memento, and I don't intend to shoot it at anyone. It's evidence of murder and it will be identifiable because it's identical to all the others. Whoever made all these arrows is a master fletcher, and if we find him, we'll find the people for whom he makes his arrows. What have you found?"

"It's a saddle roll. Must have been snagged in the brambles there and pulled off without anyone noticing it. Couldn't have been too well secured in the first place."

I crouched on the narrow path and untied the knots binding the bundle, then rolled it out with a flip of my arms.

Ursus whistled, a long, drawn out sound of approbation. The main binding of the roll was a standard brown woolen blanket, Roman army issue, heavy and densely woven from untreated wool so that it retained its natural water-repellent attributes. It had been thinly layered with beeswax on one side, too, to increase its resistance to rainwater, and then it had been folded and wrapped into a tight cylinder. Within its folds, however, it contained a change of clothing for its owner, including a plain gray, quilted tunic, the left shoulder of which was emblazoned with a sewn-on patch of brightly colored yellow cloth, edged in dark green and cut in the shape of a bull's head.

"Gunthar's bull," I said.

Ursus nodded and held out his hand. "I had a thought it might be. Let me look at it."

I passed the tunic over to him and he peered closely at it, then wadded it up roughly and handed it back to me along with the arrow he had collected. "Good. It's not exactly proof of who did the killing here, but it would convince ninety-nine out of every hundred men I know. Wrap it in the blanket with this and bring it with you.

"Now let's move on and see what lies ahead of us on the remainder of the trail, but brace yourself, lad. You might not like what we find."

I was too enervated by then to show surprise. "Why?" was all I asked him.

"Because there's worse to come, I fear. What would have happened when your cousin Theuderic realized his infantry were slow in catching up?"

"He would have come back to find them."

"Right. And he's not here, is he? My guess is that he made the attempt and rode into the same kind of trap, set elsewhere for him."

"Which means he's dead. Is that what you are saying?"

"He could be, aye." Ursus nodded, sober faced. "Probably is, to tell the truth, for otherwise he would have been here before now, to find out what happened to these people. I think you had better prepare yourself for finding him and his men dead between here and Vervenna."

We rode on, neither of us saying another word, both of us expecting to find another scene of murderous destruction beyond every turn in the road and over the crest of every hill until, about a mile beyond the scene of the massacre, we emerged from the edge of a screen of small trees and saw a wide, smooth, grassy slope stretching up and away from us to the crest of a ridge that stretched all the way across our front. As soon as I saw it I drew rein.

Ursus, seeing my sudden reaction from the corner of his eye, turned towards me. "What," he asked. "What's wrong?"

"I know this place. I remember it."

Ursus sat looking at me patiently, holding his mount tightly reined so that its neck arched tautly and it stamped its forefeet, trying to sidle away from the curbing bit. He said nothing, controlling his restless mount, content to wait for what I had to say, and after a while I continued.

"We used to play here, as young boys. We would run up to the crest there and throw ourselves over the top, then roll downhill on the other side. It's all grassy and soft over there, no trees and not even any stones. The hillside slopes down from the crest on that side for about two hundred paces, perhaps slightly more. It's a gentle slope. At the bottom of it, though, it butts right into another hill and the terrain changes. That whole hillside on the other side is covered with trees . . . hardy old things, stunted and twisted and not very big.

There's a narrow stream cutting through the line where the two hills meet—it's very fast, very powerful, fed by an enormous spring that bubbles up out of the solid rock, higher up the far hillside on the left, close to the top. The channel it has cut over the years is deep but not wide. It levels out only in one narrow spot, where the ford is. That's the only way across the gully, and no more than two horsemen can cross it at a time, side by side. And then to the right of that, the slope falls away dangerously until it drops into a ravine that's choked lower down with moss-covered old trees—ancient old thorn trees and stunted oaks. It's a wonderful place for boys to play, but you wouldn't want to ride a horse down there." I stopped, reluctant to say any more but unwilling to kick my horse into motion again.

"So why did you stop here?" Ursus asked. "If that's all you had to tell me, you could have done it as we rode."

"It's a natural place for an ambush." I had been reluctant to voice my sudden conviction lest somehow, by naming it, I made it come true. "It's a perfect trap. Beyond the ford the slope climbs steeply up to another high crest, but that slope's grassy, too, and soft like this one, so in the heavy rain it'll be a quagmire. There are trees on that hillside, too, on either side, pointing away from you, up towards the crest, and they act like a funnel, pushing people inwards to the center. So you're going uphill more and more steeply, and there's less and less room on either side. And up ahead of you, there's ample cover to screen an attacking force, while behind you, on the far side of the stream at the bottom, there's that beautiful slope for anyone charging at you from the rear to smash whatever troops you have remaining there, waiting to cross two at a time. It's a nasty, nasty place."

I looked Ursus in the eye. "So . . . if your theory holds true and we're to find that Theuderic has been ambushed, this is where we're most likely to find him—on the other side of that crest up there."

He nodded, mute, and then his eyes drifted away from mine and focused on something behind me, in the distance. Before I could begin to turn around to see what he was looking at, he had loosened his reins and nudged his horse forward and past me. I spun my mount around and moved to join him where he sat gazing at a dark scar in the grass less than fifty paces from where we sat.

"It looks as though you might be right," he said quietly.

What he had found was the darkened path worn into the muddy ground by a large number of horses as they emerged from a trail through the woodlands at our back and spilled out onto the soaked grass of the slope ahead. They had been riding in columns of four when they came out of the trees, but then they peeled off, right and left, to fan out and form a single line abreast as they made their way uphill towards the crest of the ridge, and we had no difficulty following them or seeing the moves of individual horsemen. There was a broad and much-trampled quagmire of muddied grass forming a lateral line less than twenty paces from the crest, where the advance had halted and stayed for a time, presumably safe beneath the skyline of the ridge while the leaders rode forward to look beyond and wait for their signal to attack.

Ursus glanced at me again, a wry expression on his face. "Well," he said quietly, "we can't very well ride away without looking, can we?"

"No, we can't, but I wish we hadn't come this way."

He nodded in agreement and dug in his spurs, sending his horse bounding forward, and I followed him, roweling my own horse hard, driving him forward and uphill until I was riding knee to knee with Ursus. As we approached the crest of the ridge the ground beneath us showed all the scars born of the passage of three score of heavy horses digging their hooves in hard to gain purchase in the mud of the slippery, rising ground. Then we were on the crest itself and the scene below us opened up and spread out at our feet.

At first glance there appeared to be nothing unusual in view. The ground sloped gently down in front of us for more than two hundred paces, exactly as I had described to Ursus, and the deep gully that marked the bed of the fast-flowing stream at the bottom was a brown and black gash slanting downwards from left to right, its line obscured from our view by treetops and the natural fall of the land. I looked beyond that, however, knowing that anything there was to see would be lying on the sloping hillside on the far side of the gully. Even so, there was nothing unusual to be seen from the distance at which we sat peering, and so, feeling slightly more hopeful, I kicked my horse again and put him to the downhill slope, hearing Ursus following close behind me.

By the time we were halfway down the slope, we had begun to see what we had feared we might. There were bodies among the long grass down there, but we were still a hundred and more paces away and so the only forms we could recognize were the swollen bellies of horses that had begun to bloat and now rose above the top of the grass. We increased our pace, knowing what we would find, and closed the distance quickly, and as we did so the bodies littering the upper slope ahead of us came into prominence.

It was almost exactly as I had described the probability to Ursus. Deep scars gouged by hooves scrabbling urgently in the rain-soaked ground showed where Theuderic's party had made their crossing and started up towards the top of the distant hill. They had bunched together more and more as they penetrated farther into the funnel formed by the encroaching trees until—and even from the bottom by the ford, looking up the hill, it was plain to see where— at the very steepest part of the climb just short of the summit, they had been confronted by an enemy force. It must have been a heavy concentration of bowmen who had lain concealed until then among the trees. Perhaps a half score of bodies, men and horses, showed how far the advance had gone before that first attack. They had been in the front rank of the advancing party and had taken the brunt of the first volley of arrows. When we arrived there later to look at them we saw how, like their infantry counterparts in the first trap, they lay where they had fallen, without a drawn weapon among them.

It was evident, too, from the deeply scored muddy scars on the steep slope, that the advance had turned immediately to head back down to the bottom of the hill and safety. Save that there had been no safety, for where there had been a pleasantly sloping, empty meadow at their back, Theuderic's force now found themselves confronted by a waiting formation of cavalry that sat safely ensconced on a slight upslope beyond a deep gully with only one narrow ford.

The slaughter that had ensued had been much like the earlier massacre of the foot soldiers, save that this time there were horses among the dead. From the arrows that were stuck in the ground on our side of the ford it was evident that Theuderic had made a stand at the bottom of the hill and deployed his own bowmen against the cavalry facing him, but he had very few of those and their arrows were soon used up. Outnumbered and outmaneuvered on two fronts, Theuderic had then led a charge against the narrow ford, on a two-horse front, in a desperate attempt to win through and establish a foothold on the far bank and thereby give some protection to the troopers following behind him.

We found him quickly, in the mud, pressed against the stream's bank at the bottom of the ford, sitting almost upright with his lower body crushed beneath the weight of two dead horses. The steep-sided streambed on both sides of him was so full of dead men and horses that the water had piled up above the obstruction they formed and found a new path down the hillside. Two broken arrows projected from Theuderic's body, one that had pierced the layered leather of his cuirass and another that had found its way between the rear and front plates of his armor, under his right arm. A third arrow, however, had transfixed his neck just below the Adam's apple and would most certainly have killed him, no matter what harm he might or might not have taken from the other two.

I climbed down from my horse to remove his helmet, for although I believed the dead man was Theuderic, having judged so from the size of him and the richness of his armor and clothing, I had not set eyes on him for six years and so could not trust myself to recognize him properly without seeing the face beneath the closed metal flaps of his helmet's mask. I recognized him quickly, for all that, even before I cut the leather strap beneath his chin and tugged the helmet from his head. Theuderic had always been the most comely of the four brothers, with large, bright, wide-set eyes of dark, sparkling blue and a clean-shaven face that emphasized the squareness of his dimpled chin and the regularity of his strong white teeth. Now those eyes, open in death, were dull and clouded, unutterably vacant, showing none of the laughing, amiable attributes of the cousin I remembered so clearly. He had not been a vain man, my cousin Theuderic, at least as far as I could remember, save in that one matter of keeping his face cleanly shaved at all times, and as I gazed on his dead face now it occurred to me that I could not recall ever having seen him with a trace of stubble marring the perfect smoothness of his face. Kneeling there above his cold, rain-soaked corpse, unable to move him in the slightest way because the mountain of flesh towering beside me was the rump of one dead horse lying on the carcass of another that was lying on his legs, I felt a welling sadness in my chest and then, for the first time since finding Chulderic and the King, a stirring of cold, clear anger. This was fratricide, the curse of Cain; the shameless and inexcusable murder of one brother by another, over the matter of pride and worldly possessions.

The anger grew brighter until I could feel it blazing deep inside me. Unable to kneel still any longer, I rose to my feet and made my way up out of the streambed to my horse, where I tied my cousin's helmet to one of the straps hanging from my saddle. It would constitute proof of his death, should anyone require it later. That thought angered me even more and I walked away, stiff-legged and fighting to put down the flaring rage that now threatened to consume me. I was not accustomed to such anger. In fact, I could not remember ever having felt even remotely as I did then, and that made me walk faster than ever, trying to run away from the sensations bubbling inside me until I slipped suddenly on the treacherously sloping ground and wound up teetering at the top of the precipitous drop into the tree-choked ravine down which the stream cascaded. I regained my balance easily enough, but found myself gazing down to where a horse and its rider had fallen and died while attempting to escape from the trap. The horse had impaled itself on a broken stump some twenty paces below me, and its rider lay close beside it, broken and twisted into an unnatural shape. Not far from where they lay, the earth and moss had been torn up by other hooves.

I shouted for Ursus, and he came to me at once, rubbing his palms against each other briskly, trying to rub off the mud that had caked them. When he reached my side I pointed down.

"Someone got out. Look down there, and over there to the right, beyond the dead horse. It's hard to tell from up here, but it looks as though there could have been three, perhaps four of them got away. You can see where at least one horse went almost straight down here, on this side, see? And another over there on the right. Look at those marks! It doesn't seem possible that anyone could have survived that descent, but there's only one dead horse and rider down there, so someone made the leap."

Mere moments later we were at the bottom of the ravine, having made our way carefully down the precipitous slope by clinging to moss-encrusted trees and lunging with care from one to the next, making sure to lodge our feet behind tree trunks whenever we could, which was most of the time. Now, at the bottom, we made our way quickly towards the marks we had seen from above and were quickly able to establish that a respectable number of mounted men—six at least and perhaps twice as many—had managed to escape the trap. Whether or not they had been pursued was moot, and some of the tracks we found might conceivably have been made by others riding in pursuit of a few escapees, but we were heartened to know that the slaughter in this second entrapment had not been as complete as in the other.

In the exhilaration of knowing some men had escaped, we decided to follow them and try to find them and join up with them if we could, and Ursus turned his back on me, his hands on his hips, to stare back up at the slope we had descended.

"Well," he said, "we should have brought the horses down and picked an easier route. No one was chasing *us,* after all. Now we have to climb back up that whoreson."

Mounted again, we took one last look around the killing ground and then made our way slowly down the swooping slope by a more circuitous route until we could enter the wooded ravine, but we left it again almost immediately to make our way downhill more easily in the open, following the path of the stream and watching for the signs that would indicate where the survivors had left the protection of the deep gully. We did not find any until the hillside had faded gently into a wooded valley where the stream joined a wider brook, but when we found the spot where the horses had finally clambered out of the riverbed to head across the valley bottom towards a denser growth of forest on the far side, the tracks were clean and easy to identify as belonging to fourteen riders, which was a far larger number than either of us had expected. I looked at Ursus immediately, but before I could make any comment he shrugged his shoulders.

"Makes no sense to me, either, so don't even ask me. Some of them must have made their way down the same way we did. Either that or they cut around behind somehow and managed to keep out of the way of the bowmen coming down from above until they found another way to reach the bottom of the slope. It's not important how they did it. What's important is that they escaped and now they're out there, somewhere ahead of us."

It took us until late in the afternoon to track them down, even though we knew they must be close by in one large, wooded area because we had found their tracks, then lost them again on stony ground, but could find no trace of them anywhere beyond that, once the ground softened again and the soil was deep enough to show tracks. We made a complete circuit of the tract of woodland, large as it was, and by the end of it, when we arrived back at the point where we had started, we knew beyond any doubt that our quarry must still be within the tract somewhere, because the only way they could have traveled on without us finding their trail would have been to sprout wings and fly out.

As it transpired, we must have ridden by the entrance to their hiding place three or four times without even suspecting it was there, because it lay in the densest part of the forest, shrouded by ancient clumps of gnarled, moss-covered trees covering the base of a hill that was crowned with a solid mass of thick, seemingly impenetrable brush. Behind that screen of growth, however, and not easily found unless you knew it was there, lay the single narrow, twisting entrance to a small, steep-sided valley—a rift, little more than a wide vertical split in the hillside—that had no exit. The men hiding in there were being very unobtrusive, knowing that they were deep in hostile territory, hostages to treachery, and evidently expecting, for the best of reasons, that they might be the object of a massive hunt.

We found them on what might have been our fifth pass by the entrance to their hiding place, but it is far more accurate to say that they showed themselves to us. They had seen us pass by once before, and not recognizing us but knowing that we had not seen them, they had allowed us to pass unmolested. The next time we returned, however, they took notice of us.

There was a wide, grassy expanse—a natural meadow with isolated copses of beech and chestnut trees—fronting the mass of older, smaller trees that veiled their hiding place from us, and Ursus and I were searching it thoroughly when we returned that time, quartering it slowly with our eyes to the ground, looking for signs that someone—anyone—had passed that way recently. Ursus was on my left, a good hundred paces from me at the farthest reach of my sweep, which took me within a very short distance of the edge of the clearing. At the opposite end of one sweep, however, when I was farthest away from the forest's edge and closest to Ursus, I caught a flicker of movement from the corner of my eye and looked up to see a horseman emerge from the woods on my right and come towards me. He was heavily armored, his face hidden by the closed flaps of a heavy, crested helmet, and he carried a spear and a brightly colored shield, blazoned in yellow and crossed by the black diagonal bar that marked him clearly as one of Theuderic's men.

And then, being almost sixteen, I committed the error of a sixteen-year-old for the first and only time. I whooped in welcome and kicked my horse forward to meet him as I saw two more mounted spearmen come out of the trees at his back. I heard Ursus shout something from behind me, but I assumed it was a shout of welcome like my own and paid it no attention, bent on exchanging greetings with the newcomers.

Only as I began to draw close to the man ahead of me did I begin to suspect that all was not as it should be, because instead of approaching me directly and slowing down, the fellow I was riding to meet angled his horse away, to my right side, and increased his speed, drawing back his spear arm as if to make a cast. I sat up straighter in the saddle, thinking some foolish thought about allowing him to recognize me and with no thought in my mind that, after what they had been through, these people might expect to encounter only enemies in such a place.

Again I heard Ursus shout, his voice closer this time, but by then my own foolishness had begun to dawn on me. I heard the thunder of the oncoming horseman's hooves and saw his arm thrust forward, launching the long spear directly at me, and I leaned hard and far to my left, almost throwing myself out of the saddle and trying to pull my horse bodily out of the line of the weapon's flight. The point of the spear took me in the side, beneath my upraised arm and fortunately on the metal of my cuirass, rather than in the join between the plates. It hit solidly before it glanced off and away, but the force of its impact threw me effortlessly over my horse's rump, so that I saw my own feet fly up in front of my eyes. I had an instantaneous vision of my horse's rear hooves flying up, too, and hitting me in the head as I fell, and I tried desperately to extend the movement of my fall, tucking my head in and kicking my legs back further over my head. I landed awkwardly, with my weight on one knee and elbow, but I felt no flaring pain and I rolled immediately, clutching for my dagger, the only weapon left to me.

My assailant had ridden around behind me and was now driving in for the kill, a long spatha raised above his head as he leaned towards me, concentrating on the angle of the cut that would kill me. The drumming of his horse's hooves was loud and concussive, and I threw myself down, rolling head over heels and managing somehow to avoid the hissing arc of his swing. As he charged past the spot where I had been a moment earlier I was already rising to my feet, pulling the helmet hastily from my head and looking about me for my horse, wondering what chance I had of laying hold of the long spatha that hung in its sheath by my saddle.

Again the visored horseman came at me, and this time, freed from the restricted vision caused by my heavy helmet, I shouted as I threw myself forward and angled my roll so that I passed directly beneath his horse's belly. It was a dangerous thing to do, since I might have been caught by one of the beast's great hooves, but it was less dangerous than risking a deadly thrust from its rider's sword, and my hope was that the beast might be startled enough by my move to rear, and even unseat its rider.

My ruse worked, after a fashion. The rider aborted his blow and the horse snorted in surprise as I passed under its belly, the top of my head brushing the bottom of its barrel. Came a moment of confusion as I scrambled to regain my feet, and then I saw the huge horse standing erect on its hind legs, its front hooves waving in the air and the rider on its back straining forward, his visored face close to his mount's neck and his free hand clutching white-knuckled at the pommel of his saddle as he fought to stay on the animal's back. I caught a glimpse of his two companions, still motionless at the forest's edge, and then there came a whistling hiss and a solid, meaty thump as an arrow smacked into the rearing beast's throat, taking it beneath its upraised chin and toppling the animal over backwards so that its rider had to fling himself free, scrambling to avoid being crushed as the creature fell.

He managed, somehow, to retain his balance and stay on his feet, but a mere moment later he was sent flying as Ursus drove his horse right into him, smashing him with its shoulder. I watched Ursus wrest his mount to a sliding halt and then spring off, dagger in hand, to roll the downed man over onto his stomach, plant one knee in his back, then grasp the crest of the fellow's helmet and pull it back as hard and as far as he could, placing the edge of his blade against the stretched skin of the exposed throat.

"Now, whoreson," he hissed, hefting the dagger again and placing it more firmly where he wanted it. "All you have to hope for is that your friends there place more value on your life than I do." He looked up at the other two riders, who were still coming, but showing signs of hesitancy in the face of such a sudden reversal.

"Stay away," he roared, "unless you want to see your friend here lose his head."

The two riders stopped, glancing at each other for guidance that neither would provide.

Ursus spoke to me then. "Get your bow. No, get mine. It's strung. Don't aim at them but be ready to let fly if they don't listen to me. Try to take one of them down, but if you can't, then aim for the horses and we'll take them on foot. But move slowly now, as you go. Don't panic them into putting up a fight."

As I moved towards his horse he pulled back again on his prisoner's helmet and shouted again to the others.

"We are friends here, not enemies. Can't you see that? Had we not been, this one here would already be dead. As it was, I took his horse instead of him. Look at the boy there. Don't you know him? He's Clothar, youngest son to Ban and brother to Theuderic and Brach. Brother to Gunthar, too, but that's not his fault. He's been up north and just came home, to this. But his fight is not with you. He now wants vengeance for his brother, Theuderic."

One of the two men facing us hefted his spear slowly and threw it down into the ground, where it stood swaying as he reached up and undid the strap securing his helmet. He pulled it off and I recognized him immediately, although I could not recall his name. He was staring at me, narrow eyed, and then he waved one hand in a gesture to his companion to lower his weapon.

"It's true," he said. "I recognize the lad. It's young Clothar, right enough." He looked then at Ursus and nodded. "So be it. Let Charibert go. No more harm between us. Why are you here and whence came you?"

Ursus stood up, freeing the man called Charibert, who rose to his feet without a word or a look at his captor, fingering the skin of his neck and grimacing as he moved his head cautiously from side to side. I had not even had time to collect the bow Ursus had sent me for, and so I left it hanging by his saddle and went instead towards the man who had recognized me, trying to remember his name and recalling it as soon as I reached his side and his eyes turned to meet mine.

"Corbus," I said. "Corbus of Renna. Well met. I'm flattered that you should remember me, for the last time we two met was the day I left here with Germanus, to attend his school, and that was six years ago."

"Aye," Corbus said quietly, smiling. "And you have changed much since then, grown up and put on some meat, but those eyes of yours are unmistakable. That color struck me the first time I ever saw you and I've never forgotten it." He turned to his two companions. "Look at those eyes. Have you ever seen the like? They're violet, my wife said when she saw them first; the color of the flowers. The only other eyes I've seen like them were Theuderic's, but his were bluer. These things are purplish . . . unmistakable." His face hardened then. "But you still have not told me where you came from and why you're here. You know what's been going on?"

I shrugged and glanced at Ursus, who stood watching, saying nothing, his face thunderous.

"Aye," I said. "We have a fair idea. My friend here is called Ursus, and he comes from a place south of here, a town called Carcasso. He was separated from his military unit, which was supposed to be escorting me. He and I have been together ever since." I paused, collecting my thoughts, then spoke again directly to Corbus. "We found the King and Chulderic encamped on our way here, and the King was wounded, as you probably know by now." Corbus nodded. "Aye, well the wound was fatal. King Ban is dead." I paused again, waiting for their reaction, but there was none, and I realized they had been expecting to hear of the King's death. "Before he died, and while we were there, the King issued a decree." I went on and told them about everything that had happened since then, up to the point of our meeting.

"Aye, well you have the right of it," Corbus said. "Gunthar heard the word and made the choice to gamble. He must have been afraid that Ban would do what he did, giving the succession to Samson at the last. God knows what he was thinking, for he has damned himself to a course no man in his right mind could ever choose to follow. Anyway, he set out to find his mother the Queen a bare hour before we arrived back at the castle, and when Lord Theuderic heard of it he set out after him immediately. We thought we had a chance of catching him before he could do anything foolish. But he knew when he left that we were due to arrive at any moment, and he knew, too, that we would be bound to follow him because Theuderic was already deeply suspicious of Gunthar.

"He must have had it plotted in advance because I have never seen a better-marshaled operation or a trap so cunningly set. Gunthar planned his brother's death, very carefully . . . and that, in turn, means inescapably that he has also planned the elimination of his other brothers, Samson and Brach. He'll add your name to those, Clothar, once he knows you are here. All of you will have to die, and quickly, if he is to sit in safety on the King's seat."

The fear that flared up in me at that almost took my breath away. "I have to find my mother. Now, instantly, before it's too late, because he must mean her death, too. He cannot leave her to live."

"Breathe easy, lad. We have the Queen."

"You have—?"

"Aye, she is safe with us, right here, concealed from all the world." He saw the question in my eyes and answered it before I could ask. "We met her on the road, between here and where your brother fell, and purely by accident. The Lord Brach rode with her, accompanied by his original escort. They had concluded their business at Vervenna and were on their way homeward, bringing the Lady of Vervenna and her newborn child with them to await Lord Ingomer's return from patrol. It was an unbelievable stroke of fortune. They turned around and came with us."

"Where are they now, then?"

"Behind us, almost within bowshot, save that there are rock walls between us and them. One of my scouts was born close by here and knows these woods better than his own wife's rump, and so in your mother's hour of need he brought us to the refuge he and his family have used in times of danger for a hundred years and more. His brother still lives nearby and has made us welcome."

"He has made the *Queen* welcome? In her own domain?"

Corbus inclined his head respectfully enough, but his words implied a hint of censure. "The Queen is aware that some of her people have lived here since before this was a kingdom. In their time, they were kings of their own lands."

"I see. How is the Queen?"

"Mourning a new-lost son. Apart from that, she's well."

"And now I have to tell her of her husband."

Corbus nodded, his face solemn. "Aye, you do, and that will not be a pleasant task. But my Lady the Queen already knows her life has changed beyond redemption. She is so deeply steeped in grief that increasing her burden is a mere matter of degree." He sighed. "Still, we should go to her directly. She will be happy to see you, after such a long absence."

"Aye, mayhap . . . until I tell her what she wishes least to hear. Take me to her, if you please."

"I will, as soon as you are ready."

As I turned towards my own horse, I saw the third man extend his arm to the horseless man called Charibert and pull him up to ride double with him. Ursus's horse and mine stood side by side, not far from where we were, and as we walked towards them Ursus finally spat out his last word on the subject of my enthusiastic error.

"It was a stupid thing to do."

I stopped. "I know, Ursus, and I almost died of it. I know that, believe me, I know. I can but promise you that I will never again take the appearance of a stranger at face value."

"Fine, then." He made one last harrumphing sound in his throat and swung himself up into the saddle, and we made our way over to where Corbus and his two companions sat waiting for us. As soon

as we reached them, Ursus nodded to the man Charibert and apologized for killing his horse. Charibert, now mounted behind the third
man, nodded in acknowledgment, his face unreadable, and then
murmured that he would rather be looking at his horse lying dead
than have others looking at him lying dead. They turned their
mounts around and accompanied us, but no sooner had we left the
large meadow and entered the woods from which they had first
appeared than the horses were fetlock deep in standing water.

"I knew it had rained a lot," Ursus said, looking down at it. The
long grass through which we were riding was almost completely
submerged and the lower branches of the trees and shrubbery ahead
of us were barely above water. "But I didn't think it was this bad."

"It's not," Corbus replied. "It's always like this here. It gets
better, too, wait and see."

Sure enough, as we progressed into the woods, the water rapidly
grew deeper until it was knee deep on the animals and the last
vestiges of grass had disappeared beneath the surface. And yet we
were still within the woods. Trees towered all around us, although
we could now see that many of them were dead or dying, and the
dead growth increased as the distance increased, so that the trees
farthest from us were uniformly gray and lifeless, drowned by the
lake in which they stood.

Corbus tugged on his reins and brought his horse to a halt.
"This is as far as we can go in safety." He lifted his hand to his mouth
and blew a low, piercing whistle that was answered instantly from
deeper among the trees, then went on speaking as though we were in
the middle of a common grazing ground. "Something broke, underground, about two lifetimes ago, according to the man you are about
to meet, and what had always been a small, healthy spring became a
raging torrent." He glanced over at Ursus. "You saw the gully carved
by the stream where we were attacked, did you not? That is spring-
fed, too. There's something about the terrain here that causes water
to come up to the surface from beneath the ground with great
force—force that does not abate and is impossible to withstand." He
waved a hand towards the figure who was approaching us, wading

through water that rose almost as high as his crotch. "This is Elmo. He'll tell you about it better than I can."

We sat silent, watching the man called Elmo approach, and eventually he came to a stop just in front of us, still ankle deep in water and clad from head to foot in a single robe of blackish brown wool that was completely drenched. There he stood, staring up at Ursus first, taking in every detail of my friend's appearance before turning his eyes on me and scanning me so carefully that I felt as though there could be no flaw, no blemish on or about my appearance that escaped his scrutiny. Only when he had finished cataloging me did he glance at Corbus, who told him immediately who we were, naming me first as Ban's youngest son. Corbus continued, "They know nothing of you or why you are here, Elmo. I was about to tell them the history of this place when you came, but decided to wait and let you tell them. Will you?"

Elmo's eyes narrowed as he looked at me. "I live hereabouts, and my family has been here more than six full generations. My brother Theo rides with Corbus. My grandsire's grandsire name was Elmo, too, and he lived here before your grandfather, Ban the Bald, was even born, before there was a king of Benwick, and when what is now called Benwick had no name at all. When my ancestor Elmo lived here, though, this place was like that other place at your back, green sward and scattered trees, and we grazed our kine on it— oxen, sheep and goats. It was sheltered, and close to where we lived, yet far enough removed to keep our beasts free from being plundered. It was boggy in places and it could be dangerous, but it was well watered with sweet, clear-running springs, half a score and more of them.

"But then one day, during my ancestor Elmo's sixteenth summer, something happened here—a great shifting, somewhere in the earth, beneath the ground. Elmo was here tending his kine when it occurred and he told people the earth shook and threw him on his back and he could not stand up again while it lasted. And after that the springs all dried up and ran no more. People were afraid, thinking some god had grown angered at them, and they offered sacrifices of all kinds to every god they knew and some even to gods they didn't know but thought might be there, watching.

"Even the Romans heard of it and sent some soldiers—engineers, they called themselves—to look at what had happened. But nothing came of it for nigh on another year. The springs were all dried up, but nothing else had changed, and the ground was still a bog in some places, although different places than before." He paused to scratch his nose, and I found myself wondering, although not yet impatiently, what the import of all this could be. Why were we sitting our mounts knee deep in water listening to a tale from a stranger, when we should be on our way to deliver our tidings to the Queen? Elmo heaved a deep sigh at that point, reclaiming my attention, and turned with lowered head to look at the surrounding water.

"In the spring of the following year, less than a year after the upheavals, my ancestor heard a great cracking noise in the middle of the night and awoke to the terrified screaming of all his cattle and a great hissing, splashing noise of roaring, rushing water. It was the dead of night and there was no moon, so it was black as charcoal here under the trees, and all he could tell was that in the midst of the unseen but frightening chaos around him he felt, and seemed to be, safe against the bole of the tree under which he had been sleeping. He crouched there all night long, waiting for the sun to rise, and when it did he could not believe the sight that awaited him." Elmo paused again and glanced up at us to see if he had all our attention, knowing full well that he had. We all sat rapt, even the three who had heard the story before.

"He found himself sitting on what would turn out to be a spine of stone running most of the way across the meadow. It had not looked anything like that the day before, but something had ruptured in the ground and released a terrifying scourge of solid water that had scoured away all the soil in its path and bared the rocky sides of the spine. There was another outcrop of rock behind the place where he now sat, and it was crowned with dirt and grass, but the face of it was the clean, bright gray of new-split rock and it was out of a fissure there, lower down than my ancestor's perch, that the water was spewing.

"His cattle had all vanished, scattered in terror of what was happening, and so my ancestor's main task that first morning was to escape from the spine of rock on which he had found himself. The great scoured channel swept down to his left and the ground there was collapsing and disappearing even as he watched it, undercut by the ferocious strength of the newborn stream that was causing great lumps and chunks of solid earth and clay to rip free from above and fall into the waters to be churned into mud and swept away.

"The ground on his right-hand side appeared to be sound and solid, however, so my ancestor set out in that direction to remove himself as far as he could from what was happening on his left. But at his first step he sank to his knees and fell forward into what was no more than a sea of thick mud covered with bright, clean growing grass and wild flowers. He almost drowned there, in that mud, but his gods were on his side that day, he swore, and he was able to scramble back to the rocky spine. Once there and safe again, he walked all the way to the farthest end of it, looking for a way to jump off it and on to solid ground, but he could find no place that tempted him to put any trust in what he could not feel solidly under his feet. The gully that yawned on his left was several long paces wide in places by that time, and growing wider and deeper with every moment that passed. At the endmost tip of the spine there was another gap, he said, less than two paces wide and out of the worst of the current on his left, but just far enough away to prevent him from jumping. So he turned around and went all the way back to his starting point, following the twists and turns of the spine as it wound aimlessly back and forth.

"Back at his starting point, he looked again at the rock across from him, from the base of which the water was still hissing and roaring with no lessening of its fury. That rock offered a solid landing place, for he could see the handspan's depth of soil and grass that lined its broken top. But its surface was above the level on which he stood, which meant he would have to jump up and across, and if he fell short, he would fall directly into the roaring deathtrap beneath him and be smashed to a bloody froth.

"He made the jump safely and for the next month and more he watched the gradual destruction of what had been a safe and pleasant grazing spot. And he discovered many things about what was happening. The ground on the right of the spine that had been bog and then became mud simply sank into the earth and disappeared, slowly and steadily, washed and sucked and sifted away by the waters until that side of the spine lay as bare and exposed as the left side.

"But then my ancestor began to grow aware that something other was occurring here. This place is bowl-shaped, it transpired, and he watched and paid close attention as the waters rose and rose until the bowl was full."

"So how long did that take?" It was the first time I had spoken since Elmo arrived, and he looked up at me.

"When my grandsire was the age his grandsire Elmo had been at the start of it all. Our family has paid great attention to the happenings in the place now for nigh on a hundred years, and few things happen here that we are unaware of.

"No one can tell why the waters ceased to rise. They simply stopped one day and rose no farther. A balance of some kind was reached . . . a leveling. The waters are still sweet and fresh, so the torrent is still flowing strongly enough to keep the currents stirring and to avert stagnation, and there is sufficient drainage, obviously, to maintain the level of the waters without loss."

"So how are we to cross it? I presume we are to cross it? I see no boats, but you must have some close by."

"None large enough for horses." The man smiled at me and his entire face was transformed. "We will walk." His smile widened at the look on my face. "The spine, Lord Clothar. The spine I've been talking about is still there, below the surface. We will follow it. That is why I am here—to guide you. You will have to dismount, though, and lead your horses, for the way is narrow in some places. Follow the man ahead of you precisely and feel your way with caution, making sure each foot is firmly set before placing your weight on it. The water on either side of the spine is deep, but we'll be close enough together that, if one of you does fall in, we'll be able to pull you out again. But I am sure I do not have to explain the folly of trying at any time to make your way across the spine without my guidance." He avoided looking at any of us as he said that, but there was no mistaking the tenor of the warning. "Now, Lord Clothar, if you will follow me with your friend Ursus behind you, the others have crossed before and know the procedure."

Having said that, he turned away and waited to hear mc splashing into the water at his back before he moved off into the waters ahead of us. I glanced once at Ursus, and followed my guide, preparing to concentrate completely on where he was leading me and to trust utterly in his own knowledge of the pathway across the open waters.

As I walked close behind my guide, fighting the urge to throw my arms around him and hang on from time to time, I found myself thinking about where we were and what was happening, and my thoughts were whirling as I made my cautious way across the mere. There was water all around us, but we were already more than halfway across and I could see where the trees turned green again up ahead of us, marking the start of dry land again. I stopped and turned to look back the way we had come, and in front of me Elmo stopped moving immediately.

"What is it?" he asked me.

"Nothing, I'm merely looking back. There's absolutely no sign of the route we've followed to get here, and no indication of how we'll progress from here to reach the end of the crossing."

I turned back to find him looking at me and smiling slightly. "Does that surprise you, Lord Clothar? Or do the people in the north leave marks in the water when they pass through it?"

I took the jibe in the spirit in which I thought it was intended and smiled, letting the thought of being insulted glide away from me. "No. Forgive me, Elmo, I was but thinking aloud, about our circumstances. My— the Queen of Benwick lies ahead of us, under your care, and this may be the only spot within her own lands where she is safe. She would not be safe in her own house today, not with her dead husband's firstborn son behaving like a mad dog as he is. But here she is beyond reach of all who might seek to harm her. And you alone hold the key to her safety, because of your knowledge of this pathway through the waters."

"Well, not alone. My brother Theo knows the way across as well as I do. But then Theo is seldom here, whereas I live close by." He looked over my shoulder to the men at my back. "We should keep moving. Our friends back there are at our mercy when we stop thus, for they cannot simply go around us and continue on their own." He began walking again, speaking back over his shoulder. "You were talking about the Queen's safety but you sounded as though you harbor some doubt. In what regard?"

"Accessibility. It's obvious no one can come in here without knowing the way, but is that surmountable? Is there any other way a determined man—or army, for that matter—might penetrate the refuge where you have the Queen?"

Elmo shook his head. "Not without growing wings like a bird, to let him fly . . ." He paused for a few moments and thought about what he had just said, then held up a hand and wiggled it back and forth. "Well, that may not be completely true. If a man is determined enough, he can usually find a way to get what he wants. It is conceivable, I suppose, that die-hard assault could reach us in the valley by coming over the top of the hills, but I really believe it would hardly be possible. These hills are high and rugged, and when God made them, He built them upright out of huge, flat, sometimes knife-edge-thin slabs of stone, then tilted them all sideways and fixed them in place just before they fell over of their own weight. Our little valley lies at the center of that piece of His creation, and the hills all around it slant steeply away from it in all directions, so that anyone approaching from the outside has to struggle constantly to climb unscalable, sharp-edged cliffs that are all tilted towards him and overhang each other in endless ridges, each with its own dangers and threats. I have been there in those hills, Lord Clothar, and it is not a pleasant place to be. I went there of my own free will, as an act of penance, and it is no exaggeration to say that I was truly penitent when I emerged, and that there were times when I genuinely thought I would never emerge at all, but would die in there, in some hidden spot unknown to man."

I was staring at the back of his head, marveling at his fluent ease with words, but his reference to penance took me by surprise.

"Why would you do an act of penance?"

He did not even bother to turn around. "Because I am a sinner. Sinners are required to do penance."

"You sound like a bishop."

"Aye, well I'm not, but I am a priest, and my bishop's name is Erigon. He is my teacher."

"Erigon? My teacher's name is Germanus. He is a bishop, too."

That stopped him dead in his tracks, and he turned slowly to face me, his eyes wide. "Germanus? Of Auxerre?"

"Aye, that's him."

His eyes grew even wider. "You know the blessed Germanus?"

"I know Bishop Germanus of Auxerre." I was careful to keep my voice neutral. I had heard others speak of Germanus as "the Blessed" but I had never known any of the school's staff or residents to speak of him that way, and I had certainly never seen or heard the bishop himself make any reference to such a thing, so the sentiment, as much as the tone of voice in which it was uttered, made me feel slightly ill at ease. "He is my mentor. I meet with him regularly, at least once every week or two. He knew my parents when he was young, before he became a bishop, and he is still a close friend of King Ban and Queen Vivienne. I have attended his school in Auxerre for almost six years now."

"Have you, now? You are a very fortunate young man." Elmo shook his head in apparent wonder and turned again to resume walking. By the time we reached the other shore he had told me everything he knew and admired about Germanus, and listening to him this time I did not feel the slightest discomfort.

Soon we were at the edge of the water with solid ground ahead of us, and I could see people moving among the trees in the distance. Towering rock walls swept up on either side of us here, and gazing up at them, I was awestruck to realize that they had been invisible from the big meadow on the other side of the water, completely concealed by the topography and the cloaking effect of distance and the density of trees on the hillsides. I turned to say something about that to one of the others but as I did so I heard a shout of welcome, and suddenly we were surrounded by the men who now occupied what I had already begun to think of as the secret valley.

BRACH AND SAMSON

1

When we arrived in the tiny encampment within the cleft in the rocks, we made our way directly to find my aunt Vivienne, but there were two guards posted outside the tent she and her women occupied and they waved us away as we approached, their demeanor indicating unmistakably that they took their responsibility for their Queen's peace and safety very seriously. One of the two told us the Queen was asleep and that her physician had ordered that she was not to be disturbed.

I was relieved to be able to accept the decree without demur, because I was deeply reluctant to awaken her with tidings she did not need to hear immediately, and so I sought out my cousin Brach, knowing we needed to discuss the situation now in force.

No one seemed to know where he was, but the place was very small and eventually I found him beyond the camp site, bathing in the water of one of three deep, spring-fed pools in the middle of the small valley. The mere sight of him astonished me. The youngest of Ban's four sons by Vivienne, Brach was the one who had changed most to my eyes in the years that had elapsed since last we saw each other.

When I left for Auxerre as a ten-year-old, Brach had been fifteen and, everyone agreed, a big lad for his age. As I gazed at him now as he strode naked from the water and began to towel himself dry, it was more than plain to see that in the years since then he had not stopped growing. Always thickly padded with muscle and heavily set on long, strong, clean-lined legs, he had expanded enormously until now, at the age of one and twenty, he was gigantic, composed of layer upon layer of corded muscle with nary a trace of fat to be seen on any part of him. His arms and thighs were immense, and his chest was so sculpted, his pectoral and abdominal muscles so distinctly pronounced and perfectly shaped, that it looked as if he wore an officer's dress-uniform cuirass of richly worked leather, ornately carved and tanned to resemble human skin.

I saw him frown when he first noticed me walking towards him. He would have no doubt that I was a friend, since only friends could find their way into this place, but I knew he was trying to place me, wondering who I was and where I had come from. I wondered how long it would take him to know me, or if I would have to tell him who I was. But as I drew within ten paces of him I saw recognition dawn in his eyes and his entire face broke into a great smile of welcome as he threw open his arms and leaped towards me, forgetting the fact that he was completely naked. He hugged me to his bare chest with the strength of a bear and practically crushed my ribs before letting me go. When I stepped back from him, he nodded his head, still smiling, and I realized he had not said a single word, and only then did I remember that that single attribute, his taciturnity, was the thing I had admired most about him when I was a child. I reached out, still grinning, and poked the massive biceps of his left arm with one fingertip.

"You've grown big, Brach. How did you do that?"

His laughter was immense, a deep, booming roll of pleasure, but still he said nothing. Instead, he picked up the towel he had dropped and began to dry himself thoroughly. Then, when he felt comfortable again, he wrapped himself in the folds of the towel and dragged his fingers through the tangles of his long, brown hair.

"I'm happy to see you well, Cousin Clothar," he said. "And big. You grew, too. Why are you here and not in school?"

The last time he and I had spoken, Brach had addressed me as Brother. Now, six years later, everything had changed. I shrugged.

"School is over, Cousin, and Bishop Germanus sent me home with letters for the King."

His face darkened. "You've heard?"

"Aye, more than you."

"What does that mean, more than me?" He glanced about him. "Come, walk with me back to my tent and tell me."

"No." I held up a hand to stop him. "Better I should tell you now, with no one close by to hear. The King is dead, Brach." I saw the sudden pain that flared in his eyes and again I raised my hand to him as though to silence him, although I knew he would not speak. He kept his eyes square on mine then, remaining motionless as I went on to tell him how Ursus and I had been brought to Ban's encampment, and how Ban had made his pronouncement in favor of Samson.

Brach stood in silence until he had absorbed what I had said, then he walked three paces to the nearest tree, where he seated himself on the grass and leaned back against the trunk before wiggling his fingers to indicate that I should keep talking. He listened intently until I finished the story of how we had set off in pursuit of Beddoc and ended up here in this hidden valley, and when I had finally done and had nothing more to say he remained thoughtful. At length, however, he sucked air noisily between his teeth—a trait he shared with at least one of his elder brothers—and swayed effortlessly to his feet.

"Gunthar should have been killed long ere now," he said. "I had thought about doing it myself, several times, but then I told myself he was my brother and my thoughts were unworthy. I was a fool to listen to myself. He's a mad dog and I knew it a long time ago. I was right to think of killing him."

"No, Brach. You could not have killed him and lived with yourself thereafter."

He looked me straight in the eye, and every vestige of warmth had gone from his voice when he replied, "I should have accepted the burden gladly. Now Theuderic is dead at his hands and he was ten times the man Gunthar could ever be, even were he not crazed.

Now he threatens not only me and Samson, he threatens our mother!" He stopped, evidently with an exercise of will. "Now, what of you? What will you do? You can't stay here or he'll kill you, too, if he can. I swear on my mother's eyes, he's a rabid animal. Will you return to Auxerre?"

"No, I'm staying here to fight with you. I've been well trained in warfare these past six years, as both a cavalryman and an officer, so if you will have me, I'll attach myself to your troops and you can judge me for yourself and use me as you see fit. Does that sound fair? And I have Ursus with me, too, who is worth five men—hunter, warrior, fighter, mercenary, and loyal and true as the day is long. Someone in the family has to bring about Gunthar's end, and since it is already too late for that person to be Theuderic, I will make a perfectly acceptable substitute."

"Fine. Accepted. But what do we do now? When will Chulderic and Samson reach home?"

"Today, perhaps tomorrow. But what happens when they arrive depends on Gunthar. I left ahead of them to overtake Beddoc and bring word of the King's death to the castle, to you and Theuderic and your mother at the same time as to Gunthar, but none of us foresaw the possibility of finding the castle all but abandoned. Chulderic and Samson would have made their way homeward, expecting me to have carried out my task and informed everyone of the King's death at the same time, permitting no advantage to Gunthar. By now, however, Gunthar might well have returned to the castle and taken possession of it. If he has, then he has already met Beddoc and knows that the King is dead and that he dispossessed Gunthar before he died. And if that is the case, Gunthar will throw any remaining caution to the winds. He will be prepared to go down to his death fighting.

"Now, if he already holds the castle, then Chulderic and Samson are stuck outside, with nowhere near sufficient men to lay siege to the place. The truth is that there are not enough men in all of Benwick to lay siege to Ban's castle. Our friends then will have no place to go, and there are too many of them to come here. This place is formidable but it couldn't accommodate a hundred people, let alone five hundred. How many are here now, two score?"

"Aye, somewhere in that region. Chulderic and Samson have five hundred between them, and then there are another four hundred in the east, the remains of Theuderic's force."

"How many men can Gunthar muster?"

"Probably about the same as us, according to the last information I received. About a thousand. But that was a month ago, perhaps longer, so the numbers may have changed by now. He had a thousand then only because there were no more available for hire, according to my sources among his people. He may have added others since that time. I simply don't know. However, we have the edge on him in horsemen. The largest part of his force is made up of foot soldiers—infantry and all mercenaries, mainly Alamanni, with a few contingents of Burgundians."

"Alamanni and Burgundians . . . ?" I had been on the point of asking if Gunthar had gone mad, but of course he had. In his need to secure his own kingship, he would care nothing for where his fighting men came from or who they were. He would hire mercenaries from anywhere that he could find them. And that made me think on something else.

"Where is his money springing from? How can he afford to pay mercenaries?"

Brach twisted his face into what might have been a smile, but was utterly lacking in amusement. "Nobody knows. There are rumors. They seem unbelievable, but I'm inclined to think they could be true. Tales of theft on an enormous scale. One tells of a coterie of pederasts who lived together in a villa near Lugdunum about six years ago, just when you were going off to school. All elderly, all wealthy and all depraved . . . what else would you expect of pederasts? Anyway, they could afford to indulge themselves in their degeneracy, bringing in traveling entertainers from all over the empire. One night, they were all killed in their beds, fifteen to twenty of them plus all their servants, and the entire villa was emptied of its treasures. People spoke of tracks a handspan deep, left in bone-dry ground by the wheels of heavily laden wagons.

"Then there was the incident of the talents of gold. Two entire talents of gold bullion, in bars, all stamped with the head of the Emperor Honorius and escorted by an entire cohort of Imperial Household Guards on its way from Carcasso to Massilia, to await shipment to the imperial treasury in Constantinople. Three years ago. They had barely traveled thirty miles, two days into a five-day journey, when they were attacked at night and wiped out . . . all of them . . . and the gold vanished, never to be found again."

"You think *Gunthar* was responsible for those things?"

Brach shrugged his massive shoulders. "Someone arranged those robberies and carried them out successfully, and whoever it was, he had access to enormous resources in men and logistics. Think for a moment about what would be involved not merely in attacking but in overwhelming and annihilating a full cohort of Imperial Household Guards engaged upon the personal affairs of the Emperor . . . and then add the additional difficulties of stealing and transporting two *talents* of solid gold—box upon box upon box of gold bars—and making them simply vanish without trace, permanently.

"But those are only two instances—admittedly the most spectacular two—but over the past five years there have been others, at least half a score of them, similar crimes equally bold and impressive, involving vast sums of money, usually in gold. Gunthar was always the boldest and most brilliant of all of us. And he is an astoundingly gifted strategist. The kinds of operations we are discussing here would be simple for him."

I was stunned, bereft of words by the dimensions of what he had suggested. It was one thing to acknowledge that my own cousin Gunthar, whom I had never liked and had never really known, besides being the firstborn son of King Ban of Benwick was also homicidally insane and a fratricide. It was something altogether different, however, to acknowledge that he might also be a criminal genius of long standing.

"I know how to get inside the castle." I had not known I was going to say it, but suddenly I heard myself speaking the words aloud.

Brach stopped short and looked at me. "What did you say?"

"I said I know how to get inside the castle . . . without anyone being able to prevent us, I mean."

"That's impossible. Even before my father built the drawbridge, there was no way into the castle once the gates were closed."

"No, not true. Far from true, in fact. There is a very simple way into the castle, penetrating all of its defenses, and the knowledge of it has been a secret in your family for generations."

Brach was frowning at me now. "A secret in our family for generations? According to whom? I've never heard of that before. How come you to know of it, when I do not?"

"It was King Ban's secret, to be entrusted only to one of his sons."

"You are no son of his at all, despite what most of the people think. So how come you to know of it?" I was about to answer when he said, "So Gunthar knows of this?"

"No, he does not. Your father never told him. He never was able to bring himself to divulge the secret to Gunthar."

"Well, thank the gods for that. And yet he told it to you?"

"No, to his oldest, closest and most trusted friend, and that friend told me."

"Clodio! The tight-lipped old whoreson."

"Aye, Clodio knows the secret, and it's safe with him. He has held it for forty years and more and holds it safely still. He told me *of* it—that a secret entrance to the castle exists—only because he knew that King Ban would have wanted the castle held safely against Gunthar, but he told me neither where the entrance is nor how it works. He simply offered to lead me in through it, to bring me into the castle secretly should Gunthar take over. That was before we knew of Theuderic's death."

"So, then, what think you, should we take him up on his offer?"

"We have to. There's no other choice. As long as Gunthar holds the castle undisputed, none of our lives will be worth living. We would have to post a permanent guard in front of the castle to bar him exit, and even then there's no guarantee that he would not find some means of coming and going on the lake. We can't surround the entire castle."

Brach held up an imperious hand, cutting me short. "Wait you, Clothar. I am beginning to feel too naked to be discussing such things. Let me put on some clothing before we discuss this further. I'll be thinking of it as I dress, and I'll be back directly. I promise not to waste any time."

We walked together, this time without speaking, until we reached his tent and he ducked inside, leaving me alone to really look about me for the first time since I arrived.

The camp was not large, yet it seemed large because of the number of people crammed into the small space it occupied, and the space seemed even smaller because of the high, steeply slanted walls of rock that hemmed the valley in on three sides. The valley itself was long and narrow, in the shape of a ragged S, and the camp lay in the rear portion of the shape, farthest from the waters of the mere that guarded the entrance.

I looked at the bustle going on all around me and reflected that, had I not known we were in a time of war, the condition of this camp would have left me in no doubt. There was not a woman to be seen, although I knew my aunt and her three ladies were here and every man in the place was involved in something that related in some way to fighting: many were polishing and sharpening their weapons and tending to their armor, scraping and hammering at dents and rust stains; many more were tending to their saddles and riding gear—I had counted almost fifty horses in the front part of the valley and had been surprised that people had gone to so much trouble leading the animals across the causeway under the water when they might have left them safely on the other side. But then I had realized, in the thinking of it, that there could be no safety on the other side, since anyone riding casually by would immediately see horses grazing there and would investigate to find out who and where the owners of the animals might be.

None of the people around me paid me the slightest attention. I was there, and therefore one of them. There was no discussion of that and no question of its being untrue, and so it mattered not that they did not know me . . . they assumed that some other person did and that I had a purpose in being there, all of which was true. In the meantime, they had duties of their own, and they pursued them single-mindedly.

I was thinking about that, and watching two men struggling with some kind of sawhorse, when Brach spoke from behind me.

"So you think we should go back to the castle quickly? Soon, I mean?"

I was disconcerted yet again by the sheer size and bulk of him. Naked and wrapped only in a towel he had been formidable. Fully dressed, he seemed even larger, and I knew that when completely encased in armor fashioned to his own frame, he would seem leviathan. I looked at the breadth of him and was aware that I had to move my head to look from one of his shoulders to the other.

"Sweet Jesus, you're huge!" I could not help myself, and Brach twisted his mouth wryly.

"Aye," he said, wistfully, I thought. "So I have been told. It has advantages attached in time of war, I suppose—the extra strength and superior reach—but it also makes a bigger target out of me, more difficult to miss for the bowmen and the spearmen and the slingers who can stay out of range of a superior reach. Believe me, Cousin, being as large as I am has its drawbacks, even with the ladies. Now, should we go back soon?"

"Aye, we should." I was intrigued by his mention of *the ladies*, but I knew this was no time to discuss it. "And the quicker the better. The odds are acceptable that Gunthar might not have returned yet to take the castle. And even if he has taken the place, he could not yet have had time to gather all his thousand men. Some of them are on patrol in the east, with Lord Ingomer, are they not?"

"Aye, but not many. Two or three score riders, no more. Gunthar's own guards."

"No matter, what's important is that he has not yet had time to marshal all his forces. Once he's in the castle, he can hold it easily and admit them later, as they arrive. But if we move quickly now we can oust him in the middle of the night, from inside the castle itself, where he will least expect us and will not be equipped to handle such a surprise reversal. So I believe we should leave immediately with as many men as can be spared."

"Spared by whom? And what about my mother?"

"She should remain here for the time being with all the other women and the Lady Anne's infant. She is safer here than she could be anywhere else in Benwick, and knowing she is here we'll have no cause to worry about her. We will be able to concentrate on what needs to be done, and to get the task finished. After that, we can send back for her, and she will be safe inside the castle for the duration of this war, if it is a war."

"Oh, it's a war, Cousin. It is war to the death, and our enemy has nothing in common with us, though we are blood kin and siblings." He paused, thinking, then nodded. "So, we should leave immediately, but realistically that means tomorrow at first light. After all, I have a brother lying dead out there and I need to bury him. What then?"

Brach noticed my hesitation, and his brow wrinkled slightly. "You think the timing is too important, that we do not have sufficient time to bury Theuderic and reach Genava as quickly as we should?"

I nodded, grimacing my regret but unable to dissemble. "Aye, I do."

"No matter. We'll do both. I'll find my brother and see to his burial because I cannot stomach the thought of leaving him out there for the crows to pick at. You and Ursus and a few of my men can ride ahead and discover what the situation is. I'll follow you with the rest of my men as soon as we've done what we set out to do."

"That makes sense. A few hours won't make too much of a difference as long as the preliminary moves are set in place, and I can look after those. By the time you arrive I'll have everything arranged."

"What will you have to do?"

I shrugged. "I won't know that until we reach Genava and find out who is there—who's in the castle and who's still outside. If Gunthar is in possession, much will depend on how many of his people are in there with him, but Clodio will tell us that when he comes out to meet us. Once we know that, we will know how many men we need to take into the castle."

"We'll take them all."

"No, Cousin, that's a bad idea. The more men we take with us, the greater the chance we have of being detected. Ideally, we should go in with a score of men—the best men we have. We'll overcome the guard and lower the bridge, let our own people in. Given the surprise of our being inside the gates when it doesn't appear possible, we should be able to achieve great things in little time."

"What if Gunthar's not there? The castle might be in his hands but under the control of one of his men. What then?"

"Nothing changes, except that we lose the chance to capture Gunthar. No matter. We kill or capture those inside and close the gates against the others. Let Gunthar wander about outside in the open where he thought to scatter us."

Brach sucked on his upper lip and nodded thoughtfully. "Makes sense. Now we should visit Mother. She ought to be awake by now. I warn you, though, Cousin, she has taken Theuderic's death very badly. And she has had much to bear, these past few days."

"Aye, and I'm about to add to her burden."

"There's no need for you to do that, Cousin, not if it's that upsetting to you, and I can plainly see it is. I'll be the one to bring her the tidings of my father's death—it's my duty, anyway, as her son. She has to learn of it somehow, but it's not necessary for you to be the one bringing the tidings on your return after so long away."

I stood gaping at him. I had been so caught up in my role of messenger that I had been agonizing over how I would ever find words to tell my aunt my grievous news without endangering her regard for me and making her see me forever after as the bringer of doom and grief. Purely selfish, I admit, and not at all admirable, but

I was fifteen years old and terrified of causing unbearable grief to the woman I loved most in all the world.

Brach, whom few people would ever describe as being an intuitive man, despite his self-possession, seemed to understand the thoughts teeming in my mind, for he reached out with one enormous hand and gripped me by the nape of the neck, squeezing me gently and lending me some of his great strength.

"Hold yourself still, Cousin, and leave the breaking of the news to me. I won't even mention to Mother that you're here, not yet. Mayhap the sight of you tonight, just after sunset, will lift her spirits, even if only for a moment. Sweet Jesu knows she will be in need of comforting, and the sight of you newly arrived might well be joyous enough to distract her from her grief, for a little while at least, and that will be a blessing. So go and find your friend Ursus and get yourselves something to eat at one of the cooking fires. I'll break the news to Mother and comfort her as best I may, and I'll come looking for you later, when she is asleep again."

"Think you she will be able to sleep again today, after she hears what you have to say?"

"She will have no choice. Her physician is very wise and very learned. He gave her a potion today to make her sleep, and when its effects have worn off completely, he will administer another. She will sleep, I promise you, and it is the best thing she could do. I will come looking for you later. Now go—eat something."

2

It took far longer to strike out on to the road than anyone expected. We could not start to leave before sunrise, because our horses each had to be led individually along the spine of the underwater causeway—an impossible task in darkness. As it was, Elmo and his brother Theo were chilled to the bone by the icy water and completely exhausted after leading only half of the horses and riders across, so that they had to rest and recapture some body heat before they could continue. The morning was already more than two hours old by the time the last of our thirty horses and their riders made it safely across, but fortunately it was a pleasant, sunny morning and warm enough for our soaked men to ride on wet, and they dried out gradually in the sunlight without too much discomfort.

We traveled hard and fast from that point on and within the hour had reached the steep hillside path leading up to the place where Gunthar had ambushed Theuderic's force. A quarter of a mile away I reined in and pointed up towards the spot to show Brach where it was, but he was familiar with the place and knew already where the assault had taken place. He merely nodded to me, his face expressionless.

"You should stay down here, on the plain," he said to Ursus, and then to me, "and you, too. The quickest route from here to the castle is to go that way"—he pointed southeast—"around the flank of that hill and keeping to the open fields, avoiding the wooded hillsides. It's about two miles from here, give or take a quarter mile. You'll see a pair of big old poplars as you approach the castle. You can't miss them. You'll turn a corner around the hillside and there they are in front of you in the far distance, standing in an open space with no other trees around them. They're important, because once you pass them, you can be seen from the castle's battlements." He looked at me again, one eyebrow raised. "Of course, you can be seen by anyone from anywhere, if they happen to be looking when you show yourself, so don't be tempted to do anything careless on the way there.

"Half a mile or so beyond where you first see the two big trees, you'll find a shepherd's hut made of stone. Ursus, if you are still of a mind to return home, turn directly to your left there and follow the only path there is in that direction—it's a cow track, no more. It will take you back northeastward for another mile to where you'll see the main road running east and west. Westward will take you back to Lugdunum.

"Now the two of you had better be on your way. Clothar, I've detailed one of my sergeants to ride with you, with five other men to serve as scouts, just in case you should ride into unwelcome company. I'm taking my main party up now to the forge. We'll dig a grave for Theuderic and another, larger one for his men. Not much we can do about the dead horses, I'm afraid, other than leave them to stink until they disappear."

He jerked his head in a terse nod. "So, I'll wish you well, Ursus, and hope to see you again someday on some field more acceptable than this one. Cousin Clothar, I should be in a position to start my men digging and collecting bodies just about the time you'll be arriving in the region of the castle. We can hope that you'll find Chulderic and Samson in possession when you arrive, but be careful how you approach the place. Take no chances." He paused.

"Say Gunthar has the castle. What will Chulderic and Samson have done already if they arrived to find it in Gunthar's hands? Think you they'll sit calmly in the shadow of his walls? They won't attack . . . at least I hope they won't. Samson would not be that hotheaded, would he? No, even if he were, Chulderic would not permit such foolishness. So where are they likely to be?"

I was shaking my head before he finished. "If Chulderic and Samson have not yet come, I'll withdraw to the red-wall caves, where we all played as boys. Clodio will be waiting for me there, to take me in by his secret entrance. You remember the place?"

Brach nodded. "Good, that's a good place to go, far enough from the castle to allow you to breathe in comfort without being watched. If you're not in front of the walls with Chulderic and Samson when I arrive, I'll come and find you at the caves. I should be no more than three hours behind you, four at the most. So, farewell, both of you."

He pulled his horse into a turn and rode away with a loud and piercing whistle that was obviously familiar to his men, for they all put spurs to their mounts at the same time and swung into place behind him, with the exception of the sergeant and five men detailed to ride with me. They broke out of the ranks and rode towards me.

"I'm Clothar, cousin to Lord Brach," I said to the sergeant. "He forgot to tell me your name."

The sergeant dipped his head. "I'm Shonni. I'm to ride with you."

"Aye, I know. Well, then, let's ride, because I want to be at Castle Genava before noon."

A very short time later, it seemed to me, we rode around the shoulder of a hillside and saw, as Brach had predicted, two towering trees in the distance, their upswept branches giving them the slender, delicate-seeming gracefulness that marked them unmistakably as poplars. A few moments later, we came in sight of the shepherd's hut where Ursus's path would finally diverge from mine. We drew rein, he and I, when we reached the tiny building, and I offered him my hand, bidding him farewell. When I tried to release him, however, he clung to my hand, looking at me in a way I had never seen before.

"Perceval," he said.

"What?"

"Perceval. It's my name, my real name. I never use it nowadays." He let go of my hand.

"Why not? It's a fine name."

"I know it is, and it's well known in the country I came from. Too well known. It was my father's name—might still be, for all I know. Dead or alive, my father's condition matters nothing to me. He was a wealthy man, my father Perceval, a landholder and chief of his people. Some even called him King. I never did, though. He and I did not see things from the same viewpoint, ever. Where I saw white, he saw black. Even to our names—I was Perceval and so was he, but he pronounced his Parsifal, to differentiate himself from me, you see. We did not love each other. So much did we not love each other in fact that when I left home I changed my name, not wanting others to know, or even guess, that I might be the Perceval who was my father's son. I killed a bear one day, a big and bad old bear that had turned man-eater and was terrorizing a village where I had stopped for a time. I went hunting for it with my bow and managed to kill it. The villagers were awestruck and gave me the name of Bear-killer. I shortened it to Bear—Ursus—and decided it suited me well. It's what I've called myself ever since, and that's been nigh on a score of years."

I felt myself smiling, slightly bemused. "So why do you tell me this now? Am I supposed to stop thinking of you as Ursus now that you're leaving?"

"No, not at all." He glanced down at himself, checking the few possessions that hung on either side of his saddle, then took a firm grip on his reins, preparing to ride off. On the point of digging in his spurs, however, he looked at me again and pursed his lips, allowing his chin to sink down onto his chest. "You're a good man, Clothar," he said. "Better than many another twice your age that I've met in my travels. I have enjoyed riding with you and I regret having to leave, but we've discussed that. One thing, however, I would like you to recall and understand when I am gone." He paused, and I sat watching him, waiting. "There is no Ursus," he resumed eventually. "Ursus is but a mask behind which my true face, my true identity, lies hidden. I go through life meeting people in the hundreds, perhaps thousands, and of all who have known me as Ursus, I have only made myself known as Perceval to two.

"One of those was a woman, and I was to be wed to her some years ago . . . ten years ago, in truth. She lived in a small town along the southern coast, where people made their living catching fish. I met her when I was stationed for a while in Massilia, which was close by—I was a regular legionary in those days. She was beautiful, and we loved each other from the start, right from the first time we met. But before we could be wed she was violated in a pirate raid one afternoon and it later turned out that she had become pregnant."

He fell silent, and for a time I thought he would say no more, but then he continued, "There was no question of the babe's being mine. She and I had never known each other and she had been virgin. I was hurt by what had been done to her, but I was never angry at her for it. How can you blame the ground for being in the way when the rain falls? So, we decided, we would proceed and be married and we would raise the child whose father could have been any one of five or six men. I went campaigning soon after that, against the same pirates, and you can be sure I was anticipating catching up to them. They had been raiding all along the coast and had finally succeeded in drawing down the wrath of the military governor of Massilia. We were to be wed at the end of the campaign, but winter came late that year and the campaign dragged on, so that by the time I made my way back to Massilia and to her, she had run her term and died giving birth to the pirate's child. Her name was Maria, and to her, I was Perceval."

He sniffed, but it was not a tearful sniff, more a snort of determination. "You are the second one I've told my name to. Remember me as Ursus if you wish—that's all you've ever known me as. But think of me too, from time to time, as your friend Perceval. Farewell."

We embraced once again, awkwardly, mounted as we were, and then he rode away and I watched him until he vanished over a distant rise in the road. Only then, when I was sure he had gone, did I turn myself back towards my own route, where I could see Shonni the sergeant sitting his mount waiting for me halfway between me and the two big trees. I touched my spurs to my mount's flanks, bringing him up into an easy lope that devoured the distance to where Shonni had already kicked his own horse into motion again, and we rode in silence, side by side, our ears and eyes attuned constantly to whatever might come to us from the five scouts who rode ahead of us and on our flanks. I have no idea what Shonni was thinking of as we rode briskly along the road to Genava's shores, but my own thoughts were full of my friend Perceval.

3

We took Castle Genava at the start of things without great difficulty, losing only one man in the process. I had arrived back before the walls alone, leaving my six-man escort concealed among the trees at my back, and I was challenged immediately by a vigilant guard on the walls who was most evidently not one of Clodio's group of aged veterans. I waved up at the fellow without urgency, merely acknowledging his challenge and slowing my mount from a canter to a walk as I did so. On the tall staff above the man's head, where Ban's banner had hung when I was last there, Gunthar's colors now flaunted his defiance to the world. Looking about me as I allowed my horse to approach the walls at a walk, I could see no signs to indicate that Chulderic and Samson had been there, and when I was convinced of that I raked my mount's flanks with my spurs and sent him into a dead run, swerving him tightly around and back towards the safety of the trees. Surprisingly, no one made any attempt to shoot at me as I rode off.

From there I made my way directly to the red-wall caves with my six companions, and this time we were challenged and stopped before we could approach within two hundred paces of the entrance. Chulderic and Samson, it turned out, had elected to set up their camp in the woodlands surrounding the caves while they mulled over what they would do next. Both leaders were surprised but pleased to see me and glad to know, finally, what had happened when I arrived back ahead of Beddoc. They listened in stunned silence as I told them about Theuderic's death at the hands of his brother and about Brach's suspicions that Gunthar had intended to abduct the Queen. There was little discussion of my report, however, for there really was nothing to discuss. What had been done was done and no amount of discussion could undo any of it. I told them that Brach had taken a party of his horsemen to bury his brother's body and that he would be following behind me in a matter of hours.

Then I asked casually if either of them had seen Clodio, and Chulderic told me that he had, the previous day when they had first arrived and were setting up camp. When I asked them where the old man had come from, Chulderic merely shrugged his shoulders before rising to his feet and walking away from the fire.

Samson, however, was more observant and asked me why I was curious about Clodio. He, too, had noticed the old man the previous day, simply because Clodio was as distinctive as he was, but like Chulderic, he had paid no attention to, nor had any interest in, how Clodio had arrived there. I gave him a noncommittal answer, and shortly thereafter I excused myself. I made my way around the camp, drifting aimlessly for the benefit of anyone who might be watching me, until I could wander eventually into the red-wall caves themselves.

It was never quite dark in the caves during daylight—except in the deepest recesses at the rear—because the outer wall of the red sandstone formation that gave them their name was pierced and honeycombed with weirdly shaped and fluted holes that served as windows and provided illumination enough for the purposes of most of the people who used the caves—mainly the local boys, who had come to the caves for generations to escape from adult supervision for a while. I stopped just over the threshold to ensure that no one else was there, and when I was confident that I was alone I moved swiftly across the sandy floor and into the darkness around the corner at the deepest point of the main cave. It was close to noon, I knew, and I was hoping I might be there when Clodio's secret door swung open, but he spoke to me before my eyes had even adjusted to the darkness, and I could have sworn I heard a smile in his voice and that he knew what I had been up to.

We moved back together to where I could see out into the main body of the caves and be sure no one was approaching, but to be absolutely certain that we were alone I signaled him to remain where he was while I stepped out into the light and searched the caves once again, swiftly. Only then did we talk, and I began by rattling off a number of questions, telling him to think about them for the time being and be prepared to answer them when I had finished. I then told him what was in my mind about recapturing the castle, and that I had discussed it with Brach but had said nothing yet to Chulderic or Samson either about my plan or about the existence of the caverns. I assured him that I would tell them, however, as soon as Brach arrived, adding that since we had no time to waste I would have an assault force ready to go into the castle that same night at whatever hour he chose to come and guide us in.

When it was his turn to speak, Clodio was to the point. Beddoc had arrived outside the walls less than an hour after my own departure the previous day, he told me, and Clodio had refused him entry, leaving him and his men to cool their heels outside while Clodio waited to see what else might develop. Some two hours after that, Gunthar had returned at the head of a party numbering in the hundreds. Four hundred was Clodio's best estimate, plus the better part of another hundred brought by Beddoc. This time Clodio had thought it best to lower the bridge and permit Gunthar and his men to enter, because he knew he had planted the seed of a night attack from within in my mind and he knew, too, that it was better and safer to have Gunthar and his men inside, behind the walls, while waiting for Chulderic and Samson to arrive.

Gunthar had by this time met up with Beddoc and learned that his suppositions were correct. He had swept in and occupied the castle as though he intended to use it to full advantage this time, and he had begun his new tenure by doubling the standing guard. Watching him, admittedly from a distance, Clodio had gauged that the usurper was in fine form, bubbling with confidence and deter-mination. No mention had been made of Theuderic by anyone, and Clodio had known nothing of his death until I told him about it, but even in the darkness of the passage wherein we stood I could see the sudden stiffness that came over him as he drew himself erect with a hiss of breath.

In response to my question on the strength of the garrison, he added a hundred to his original estimate. Five score more had shown up shortly after dawn today, he said, from the southward, commanded by a Burgundian warrior whose name was hated and feared by the people of this entire region. This fellow had a reputa-tion as a fearsome and indomitable fighter, but he was also reputed to be an enthusiastic torturer who killed for pleasure. I took note of that, but my sole concern at that time was the vulnerability of the castle's garrison.

Eventually, when Clodio and I were satisfied that each knew the other's mind on the matters at hand, I left him to return to the castle through the caverns while I went outside again to meet with Chulderic and Samson. Clodio would come back to the caves an hour after nightfall, and when he did we would be waiting for him with our assault party. I had thought a score of men would be sufficient for our needs, but Clodio disagreed. He concurred with my judgment that fewer was better, but he knew what we would face once inside the walls, and his estimate was that half a score again— thirty men in all—was the least we would need.

Brach arrived midway through the afternoon, and as soon as the greetings and commiserations over Theuderic's death and burial were done with, I called for attention and asked Chulderic to post guards outside the caves to protect our privacy while we held a command council inside, away from curious ears. Chulderic, clearly astonished at my presumption, glanced wide eyed at Samson and the other senior commanders present, but before he could question my authority, Brach stepped to my side and added his voice to mine, telling the others that there were matters to discuss that they knew nothing about yet, and that I was the one who had access to, and command over, the secrets involved. Still visibly reluctant and even skeptical, Chulderic chewed on his opinion and made quite a show of deciding, with evident reluctance, to say nothing of what he truly thought at the time, but it was clear to me as he issued his orders to post the guards that he would have little patience with anything I might have to say unless it proved to be startlingly original.

Well, it was that, and Chulderic's attitude changed quickly once I began to speak. My first mention of the King's Caverns and the secret entrance to the castle that lay concealed in them brought snorts of derision from my listeners. They had all spent their lifetimes on the shores of Lake Genava and in Ban's castle and none of them had ever heard as much as a hint of a secret entranceway to the castle. Such things were in the realm of sorcery and magic, or were a boy's fantasy. The muffled snorts grew louder as men began to vent their scorn for me and my idiot ideas, but I settled everything by simply raising my hand and stepping forward to face Chulderic, almost nose to nose with him in a fashion that few would dare employ towards the veteran commander, whose lack of patience and shortness of temper were both proverbial. People took note of my stance and paid attention, nudging each other and directing their eyes to the confrontation between us, but it took long moments before the noise began to abate to any degree and even so, it would not have died away completely had Chulderic not asked me what I had to add to what I had already said.

As soon as he spoke, silence fell over the assembly, which numbered eleven men besides myself: Chulderic, Samson, Brach, and eight other senior commanders, all of whom had been promoted to the posts they now held by King Ban himself. I took my eyes off Chulderic's and looked about me, making eye contact with every person there, including Brach, before looking back at the senior commander.

"I have not been in these caves for more than six years, Chulderic," I said. "But today when I arrived I asked you a question . . . a very particular question about someone else. Do you recall?"

Chulderic was frowning now as he glanced at Samson and then back to me. "You asked me about Clodio—about whether or not I'd seen him. And I told you he was here yesterday. What's the import of that?"

"The import is that Clodio is in Castle Genava, behind the walls. Brach, do I lie?"

"No, on my mother's honor." He addressed the others. "Clothar told me when he joined us yesterday that Theuderic had left the castle in the care of Clodio when he rode out after Gunthar, and that Clodio had told Clothar of a secret entrance, through a chain of underground chambers stretching from here into the castle and known as the King's Caverns. Clodio claimed it had been shown to him more than a score of years ago by my father, King Ban."

Before anyone could react, I raised my voice again. "Now ask yourself this, Chulderic: if Clodio is in Gunthar's castle now, how came he here yesterday? You and Samson both saw him. He did not come with your party, because he's too crippled and infirm to ride anywhere, so where did he come from, and where did he vanish to thereafter? Because he's not here. He's not in your camp. I swear to you, he is back in Castle Genava with Gunthar, but he will return here tonight, after dark, to lead us back into the castle in the dead of night with a party of thirty men." Brach was grinning at me and at the effect I had produced, and then I folded my arms and sat on a block of stone, where I waited for the furor to die down.

That night, Clodio selected a score of men from the sixty best Samson and Brach could provide for his consideration, then blindfolded all of them and led them into the castle under the command of two of Samson's captains who had also been blindfolded until they were within the caverns' entrance. I am sure I was not the only person watching the selection process who noticed that Clodio picked only the smallest men from among those recommended. Even the two officers appeared to have been chosen by him precisely because of their small stature.

Before they set out, Clodio told the men that he would lead them through a secret doorway into the first of a chain of caverns that stretched for more than a mile to the King's castle. Once they were through the secret entranceway, their blindfolds would be removed. There were places in the caverns where the passage was both difficult and dangerous, he warned, and none of it was easy, since several of the caverns were enormous and as black as Hades. Clodio would lead them through all the perils, he said, to the deepest level of the castle, far below where they were standing now. It would be damp down there, so far beneath their feet, and dark. No one ever went down there, he said, but even if they did, they would find nothing, for the entrance there was as magically hidden as the one through which their party was about to enter.

The men chosen for the raid wore no armor and carried only the lightest of weaponry—daggers, swords and bows. Their strongest armor would be the surprise and fear they generated by their sudden appearance in the middle of the enemy stronghold. Their task was to move swiftly and silently to silence and dispose of the guards, most of whom would be looking outward, expecting no attack from behind.

I did not join the raiding party, although it had been my hope to go in with my two cousins using the secret approach. Yet Clodio brought us word that Gunthar had a ploy in motion. Even as he spoke, he told us, Gunthar was leading a force of three hundred men, horse and foot, out of the castle under cover of darkness to seek out and destroy Brach and his small party and capture the Lady Vivienne. Brach and I exchanged glances when we heard that. We knew the Queen was safe, and we knew, too, that Gunthar was not going to find and destroy Brach by riding away to search for him on this night of all nights, when Brach was encamped within a mile of Gunthar's gates, under his very nose.

I immediately wondered, nevertheless, if this might be some cunning trap set up to entice our forces out into the open, because Gunthar must suspect that Chulderic and Samson were close by. Perhaps he hoped that by leaving the safety of the walls with three hundred men he might encourage Chulderic to commit to some kind of move against him, at which point he could swing about and return to catch Chulderic's force between his own and the castle. Of course, thinking along such lines tends to resemble searching for the center of an onion . . . layer upon layer of possibility come to light and are then rejected, only to be replaced by another, identical layer.

In any event, I decided that it made more sense for me to use my cavalry training and skills that night than to go trudging through the blackness of the caverns carrying a flickering torch and hoping eventually to grapple hand to hand with some faceless mercenary in the darkness of the castle. Brach suggested to Chulderic that he and Samson and I should all ride with the force designated to storm the castle once the bridge had been lowered. Chulderic agreed, and the three of us transferred ourselves to ride as ordinary troopers with the veteran cavalry commander Sigobert, whose normal rank was second in command to Samson himself. Thus my entry to the castle that night would be, God willing, by way of the hurriedly lowered drawbridge, at the head of a fast-moving column of riders charged with the task of penetrating the curtain wall defenses as quickly and savagely as we could and then making sure that Gunthar's people—three hundred of them were expected to remain in the castle, as opposed to our assault party's thirty—could not rally strongly enough to take back command of the main gates.

It was hot and heavy work and we were outnumbered from the start, but the enemy had been demoralized on several counts, and so we were able to do greater damage than we might have expected to do otherwise. First and foremost, the garrison had been appalled by what must have seemed like the magical apparition of our warriors pouring out of the strongest building in their castle—the central tower with its massive defenses. Few of the defenders actually saw the arrival of our raiders, however. Our men were at their backs and moving stealthily and with determination. Familiar with the layout of the castle and the disposition of the guards, they attacked in silence, using their lethal daggers efficiently, and most of the guards died silently without ever knowing what had happened. Our raiding party slew them efficiently and without compunction because all of their targets were Outlanders—mercenaries whose deaths bore no personal significance for any of our men.

Despite all our caution and efficiency and speed, however, a few men did manage to cry out before they died, and after that the alarm spread quickly, swelling with the clash of steel on steel until the off-guard watch spilled from their beds to see what all the clamor was about. By then, the first wave of attackers had overcome the guards at the main gates behind the curtain wall and flung open the gates, leaving a few men to hold them safe while the rest swept out along the curtain wall passage and around to attack the towers flanking the drawbridge. There they paused while the bowmen among them shot down the soldiers guarding the bridge works—all the defenses had been constructed to guard against attack from the far side, not from inside—and as soon as all the guards were dead they went to work immediately to lower the bridge.

I was waiting with Sigobert and his attack group of horsemen, sixty strong, just behind the first fringe of trees across from the bridge, less than a hundred paces from the edge of the ditch. As the youngest there, I had better night vision than anyone else, and as soon as I saw the top of the bridge begin to move I warned Sigobert, who gave the signal to advance. Our whole group surged forward on a single broad front and was already reshaping itself into something resembling an arrowhead formation as we moved. By the time the bridge end came to rest on the ground we were less than thirty paces distant and advancing at full gallop in a column of horsemen three abreast. The thunder of our hooves on the timbers of the bridge would have awakened the entire garrison at that point, had they not already been fighting for their lives.

We charged across the bridge and wheeled hard to the right, into the passageway behind the curtain wall that led to the main gates, and we were not a moment too soon in getting there. Gunthar had evidently hired some exceptionally skilled people with his levies of mercenaries, and under their leadership the garrison troops had rallied strongly and mounted a concerted attack on the few of our men who had been left holding the gates against our arrival. Our fighters were heavily outnumbered and faring poorly when we reached them, but the sudden arrival of a charge of heavy horsemen was more than our enemies were prepared to stomach and they turned and fled back into the castle, leaving the gates in our possession. Mere moments later, it seemed, we heard the roar as our own infantry followed us through the gateway, under the leadership of Chulderic, and shortly after that the enemy surrendered and the castle was ours. My hand, I discovered, was sore from gripping the hilt of my sword too tightly, but I had not swung a single blow at anyone from start to finish of the fight.

The total cost to us in storming the castle had been one man killed and twenty wounded, and none of the wounded men was expected to die. This would normally have been cause for celebration, but our situation was not one in which to rejoice. Samson, concerned about the Lady Vivienne and her companions, wanted to travel to her immediately to assure the Queen that all was well, that the castle was in our hands and that she and her company would be brought back in safety as soon as it was practicable. What that really meant was that the Queen and her ladies must resign themselves to remaining in the small valley behind its impassable mere for several more days until the tactical situation became less fluid and the dangers of their being abducted along the way had lessened to the point of being acceptable.

But Brach had objected, claiming that duty for himself, and their clash of wills might have escalated had not Clodio announced bluntly that neither one of them should go on that mission unless they were prepared to be stranded outside the walls for a long time, in the event that Gunthar's forces returned to the attack. There were places in the caverns, he told them, that were simply too narrow for anyone as big as Samson to get through, even without armor, and Brach was half again as large as Samson.

Their compromise was to send three of the smaller men to carry news to the Queen. Should Gunthar move against us in the meantime, the messengers were instructed to return to the red-wall caves to await Clodio, who would lead them back through the caverns.

That task attended to, the princely brothers sought a place to sleep, while I, in acknowledgment of my lowly status as both a junior and a newcomer, took over the post of commander of the guard for the remainder of that night.

Within the week that followed we had settled into a routine of boredom that was reinforced by the swift realization that our success in capturing the castle had effectively placed us under siege. Gunthar's forces had begun moving into position outside our wall by dawn on the morning following our attack, and a permanent detachment remained there afterwards, a large body of men whose primary purpose was to prevent us from lowering the drawbridge and leaving the castle. Most of them were bowmen, and by and large they remained out of our sight, safe behind the screen of trees

that began about a hundred paces from the approach to the drawbridge . . . which raised the question of whether or not they were
there, or whether they had merely convinced us that they were there,
while in fact they were elsewhere and we had been tricked into
imprisoning ourselves.

We put that notion to the test twice, sending out mounted parties
to test the enemy's responses, and on each occasion, Gunthar's
bowmen simply moved out of the trees into the open as soon as they
heard the bridge being lowered and then stood there, picking their
targets and launching arrows, as quickly as they could pull and aim,
reveling in their own lethal accuracy and in the knowledge that no
living soul could reach them.

The dilemma that next arose to perplex me was founded in
the fact that I considered myself even then to be a horse-warrior
ahead of everything else. The original attacking party had come
in on foot through the caverns, arriving on the lowest levels of the
central fortifications and making their way up by very dark and
narrow stairways from floor to floor until they were able to
emerge into the courtyard. That, in my mind, precluded any
possibility of even considering the route as an exit for cavalry. An
extraordinary horse may climb up stairs, blindfolded or blinkered
and led by a trusted groom or rider, perhaps, if the conditions are
right and the stairs are shallow enough, but no horse will descend
a steep and narrow stairwell into darkness. I had to wonder, then,
could we not enter the caverns with our horses from the other
side, through the red-wall caves?

I went directly to find Clodio, never doubting that I could enlist
his help.

Later that night, after a long and sometimes impassioned
discussion in which he and I came to know each other far better than
we had before, Clodio took me into the caverns for the first time and
showed me the route to the red-walled caves. I had not seen what he
did to cause the door to open, but when it did, it opened silently,
swinging backwards away from us and up with only the barest
whisper of stone caressing stone as it rose. As soon as we stepped

through into the space beyond, he grasped me by the arm and pulled me to one side, out of the way of the door, and told me to stand absolutely still. I stood motionless in the dark, listening to the silence and hearing the faint sound of the door closing again, and only then did I begin, very gradually, to grow aware that it was nowhere near as silent down there as I had first thought. I could hear water dripping, from many places, and the sounds the drops made as they landed varied from flat, dead-sounding slaps to musical, echoing and rotund plops where the drops were obviously falling into pools of standing water.

There were other sounds, too, that I could hear but not identify, mainly because they were obscured by the noises my companion was making. Listening, I could tell that he was moving about, and it sounded as though he was rearranging his clothing. But then there came a glow, the merest hint of light that spread quickly, and then I saw the shape of Clodio's face as he bent low towards a clay fire box enclosed in a small cage of wood that he must have carried beneath his robe. He was kneeling on the ground close by my right side, and the glow had been revealed when he removed the lid of the box. He began to blow gently on the glowing embers and to feed them with small, teased bunches of fine, dried grass. Within moments a small flame sprang into being and he fed it more fuel. In the growing light I saw a store of twigs and small kindling set against the wall, and beside them an iron brazier and what looked like a small barrel filled with heavy sticks.

Clodio eventually lit the fire in the brazier with a twig from his fire box, and as he waited for the flames to catch and take hold he moved to the barrel, selected a stick and pulled it out, then thrust it under my nose for me to smell it. It stank—a rank, sulphurous stench that made me catch my breath. It was a kind of pitch, he told me, but thinner than the kind the shipwrights used to seal the seams of their vessels. This substance was called naphtha, he said. He thrust the end I had sniffed into the flames of the brazier and the thing exploded with a roar and instantly became a brightly flaming torch, burning hard and fiercely enough to sustain the roar of sound that had accompanied its birth. It was brighter than any other torch I had ever seen, illuminating the entire space within which we stood.

Now I could easily see that this cavern, at least, had a roof, uneven and stained with moisture, arching over my head at about twice my own height. And against the wall, securely fastened into the rock, was a pair of angled brackets clearly designed to hold torches. There was one torch in place, and I looked at it curiously. The top end of it was encased in a cage of rusted wire, inside of which there appeared to be tightly wrapped rags of cloth, stiff and dry and brittle looking. Clodio reached up to it with the torch in his hand and it ignited with another ferocious whoosh of leaping flames.

"The brackets were built possibly hundreds of years ago and probably at the same time as the doors. They're all made of lead, not iron, so they don't rust—it's very wet down here. There's a line of them all along the path to the other side. Most are on the walls, but there are a few in places where there are no walls. Those ones are mounted on poles. Two brackets to a station, post or wall, makes no difference. Look how far apart the holders are. That's so you can be sure that either one will burn without igniting the other. Going across, you light the one that's waiting for you and put a fresh one in the empty holder. See?" He kicked at the ground, where I saw the charred remnants of several old torches, burned right down to the butts.

"Once these things are lit, you can't put them out, so you simply leave them to burn themselves out. But that's why you bring a bucket of ten or twelve fresh ones with you each time you cross. Burn the dry one, leave a wet one. The pitch comes from two places—two pools of the stuff that never dry up. You simply throw in a bucket and bring it out full, then lug it back here and pour it into the barrel there. No trouble finding the pools, even in the dark. You can smell them from half a mile away. Fall into one, though, you'll never come out again. Stuff kills you. King Ban knew someone who fell in, when he was a boy. They pulled him out, but he had already breathed in some of the stuff and he died right there.

"So, those are the rules. The brackets are about sixty paces apart, and there's a fresh barrel of soaking torches every tenth station. There's three ten-station stretches from here to the other end, so it's just slightly under two miles."

"Is it all flat?"

"None of it's flat, lad. You'll see that as soon as we start to move. From here, it's all slightly downhill for about a mile, then it levels out for a very short distance and begins to climb again. Course, it's all irregular, and the path we'll be following isn't very wide in places, and there are some very nasty drops on either side from time to time. But that shouldn't bother you as long as you don't look down into any of them. Just keep your eyes fixed on the ground you can see ahead of you by the light of your torch.

"There's a couple of tiny passages, too—wrigglers, I call them. Those are the places I warned Samson and Brach about. Narrow spots—tight places where you have to squeeze through, and it's best not to think too hard about where you are, but just remember to breathe out and keep moving until you're through and out on the other side. There's seventeen caverns down here. Some of them are tiny, others are enormous. This one here is smaller than some of the rooms in the castle upstairs, but it opens out into another that's ten times as big. Some of them are beautiful, too, even at night. There is daylight down here, in places—holes in the roof, high above your head, and the light falls down from them like beams of solid gold. Then there are places even more strange and filled with wonders that you'll have to see for yourself . . . you wouldn't believe me if I simply told you about them. Now, fill up that bucket over there with twelve of those torches and let's get started." He set out immediately, leaving me to scramble to obey him and then catch up, my hands and arms filled with the means of bringing light to the darkness.

"How do you make the torches?"

Clodio was lowering himself carefully down a sloping rock face and he took the time to regain a solid footing before he answered me.

"I cut handles, good solid ones that offer a fair, firm grip. Willow and hazel sticks are best, I've found, because they grow more or less straight. I cut them to length and then jam the narrower end into the space made for them in the metal cages I have made specially for them. The cages are made from heavy iron wire and the same smith has been making them for me now for fifteen years, so he makes me a batch of them in a single day. Then I stuff the cages with old rags, anything I can scrounge. Old army blankets are best, though, if you roll them tightly enough they burn for hours and hours. Then all that's left to do is leave them to soak in the barrel of naphtha until you're ready to take them out and mount them in the brackets. Given enough time up there without being used, they'll dry out completely and you'd never know they'd ever been wet. But one spark's enough to set them off, even when they're bone dry." He made a choking sound, and it took me a moment to realize that he was laughing to himself.

"What?" I asked.

"Oh, I was just thinking. I make a batch of new torches two times each year, usually around the solstice because that's a good, solid time to remember to do certain things, and each year I might have to change three, perhaps more, of the wire cages." He giggled again. "Old Marcy the smith's been making them for me, as I said, for fifteen years and he still doesn't know what they're for. He's tried following me, asking people about them, he's tried everything to find out, but I never say a word. It's driving him mad. Come on now, we'd best be moving."

It took us nigh on an hour to traverse the caverns, lighting beacons as we went to guide us back, and only in two places did I have difficulty squeezing through the narrow wrigglers he had warned me about. The second time, I came so close to being unable to get through that I found myself on the verge of absolute panic at one point, beginning to believe that I would die there, wedged in an impossibly tiny hole in the center of the earth. When I regained sufficient presence of mind to remember what Clodio had said about breathing out, however, I forced myself to exhale each breath all the way and relax my body, and I was able to win through, but I had to stop and catch my breath then and there, to collect myself and master the fear that still leapt in my chest like a flickering fire.

"If that's the only way through there," I said, struggling to keep my voice level, "then you were right. Brach will never see this place. He's far too big even to fit into the entrance there, let alone crawl through the wrigglers. We would lose him, and Samson, too, because neither of them would ever give in and they'd never back away. Brach would keep trying to squeeze through until it killed him."

"Aye, and it would, without mercy. Almost got you, there, didn't it, until you remembered what I said about breathing out. Are you ready now to move on?"

A short time after that he held up his hand and stopped. "Here we are. This is the end of the road, and I think it's also the place you were asking me about. Low ceiling, close to the outside, easy to supply and big enough to feed and shelter fifty horses. Mind you, it's going to be the end of the secret entrance as a secret."

I nodded. "That is true—but if the secrecy was intended in the beginning as a means of saving the castle and its occupants from disaster and defeat someday in the distant future, then it has already served its purpose, for it can't ever be used and then continue to be a secret, can it? Now we will use it to excellent purpose, and we will maintain at least a semblance of secrecy for as long as we can. If we continue to enjoy good fortune, Gunthar and his people may never find out about it. I'll grant you, that may be wishful thinking, but any period of time we can grasp and maintain in this matter will serve us in good stead. Let me have a look at the place."

We were in the first chamber into which the secret doorway opened from the back of the red-walled caves—and in the light of my flickering torch, held at arm's length above my head, I could see that it was perfect for our needs. Foremost, it was spacious, and the ground was solid stone, dry and almost perfectly flat, save for a few bumps and extrusions that would bother no one—and no horse. The smoke from our two torches was whipped away to some vent high above our heads, and a cool current of air blew gently and steadily around us. I could see where and how we could halter horses in lines of six or eight on both sides of a small central ridge of stone that bisected the floor, and there was plenty of dry, open space in which to pile and store bales of hay and other fodder.

The best feature of all, however, was a spring of pure water that welled from a hole in the stone wall at approximately the height of a tall man and flowed down into a large natural basin before spilling over again to form a narrow stream that ran along the cave wall until it was lost in darkness and distance. Not even in Tiberias Cato's stables in Auxerre had there been such a wonderful source of fresh water.

I told Clodio the place was perfect, and thanked him for his trust, and he grimaced and stepped away from me, towards the wall of the cave. I watched him go, wondering how I had offended him, but he stopped short of the wall beside a spine of rock that thrust up from the floor and beckoned to me. I stepped to his side and looked where he was pointing, but I could see nothing except the rock spine surmounted by a projecting knob of stone. When I turned back to him, my eyebrows raised, he closed his hand over the stone knob, pulling it back towards him. It swung open, hinged in some way, and beneath it was a hollow space. Clodio reached into the space and I saw him twist something to his left. Immediately, a wide section of the solid stone wall at least six paces to the right of where we were standing began to swing silently in towards us and tilt upwards from the base of the wall. It looked wide enough to permit entry to two horses side by side, and, holding my torch high above my head, I stepped forward to look at what was happening and saw the system of levers that were operating the mechanism.

"That is impressive," I said.

Clodio came up beside me, his strange gait appearing sinuous and natural in the flickering torchlight. "Aye, it is, I know, but the opening device is mummery. There's no need for secrecy on this side of the door. Anyone in here already knows why he's here and what's going on. It's only the other side of the wall that needs masking, and *that* works perfectly. Mind you, the door is a long way from the controlling device over there, and if I hadn't shown you that, you'd have thought this thing opened by magic, would you not?" I nodded, and he led me through the door and showed me the corresponding trigger on the other side.

The next day I made the final arrangements for what would become the biggest thorn in Gunthar's side in the time to come, and I began by convening a meeting of my elders and superiors and telling them what I envisioned. They listened closely and, to their credit, made no demur. I did not flatter myself, however, that they had all suddenly become impressed by my bravery and my impressive cavalry skills; to them I was a mere boy, untested and untried, who had taken part in one skirmish without being blooded and before that had been absent in foreign parts for many years, and the truth was that they had nothing at all to lose by humoring me and acceding to my wishes. The horses we currently had inside the castle were useless there, and the cumbersome preparations to raising and lowering the drawbridge ensured that there was no possibility of employing surprise in bringing them out from the castle. The enemy bowmen waiting beyond the walls would have ample time to aim and shoot them down before the animals could even clear the end of the bridge. It was the single biggest flaw in the design of the drawbridge, and there was nothing we could do to change it now, in the middle of hostilities.

Nonetheless, we also had a huge logistical problem that offered us, paradoxically, a means of achieving what we wanted.

We had taken more than two hundred prisoners in our capture of the castle, and now we were faced with the double task of feeding them and guarding them. More than half of the prisoners had willingly thrown in their lot with us when they were captured, switching their allegiance from Gunthar as easily as a horse switches his tail at a fly, in return for their immediate freedom and an ongoing source of comfortable bedding and regular, well-prepared meals that were vastly preferable to what they could expect to receive as prisoners. The hundred or so that remained in our custody, however, were both a nuisance and a massive inconvenience.

I therefore proposed to Chulderic and the others that we set these people free again, but that we do so in a way that would work to our advantage. I explained my thinking and they listened, nodding occasionally in acknowledgment of the common sense involved in what I had to say. When I had finished, all eyes turned to Chulderic, who sat glowering at me from beneath heavy brows. His frown grew even darker as he began firing short, blunt questions at me, and I answered them as tersely and concisely as he phrased them. Finally, when I answered what had been the last of his questions, he surprised me by uttering a single sharp bark of laughter and slapping his hand on the arm of his chair.

"Do it, boy! If it works, it will be the making of you as a man. If it doesn't work, it will provide all of us older men with something to laugh over on a winter's night when we are too old to fight."

4

Just after the evening meal, when the smoke of the cooking fires still hung in the air and the men in both camps, Gunthar's and ours, were feeling well fed and lazy with an uneventful day behind them and their bellies full, the guards on duty herded all our prisoners from the enclosure in the inner defenses where they had been kept since their capture, tied their hands behind their backs and shackled their feet with pieces of rope that were long enough to allow them to walk comfortably but not to run. With longer ropes they tied the prisoners to each other in chains of a score of men each, making five chains in all. With those preparations completed, they then led the roped and hobbled prisoners out through the main gates and along the curtain wall passage and lined them up against the castle wall, facing out towards their former comrades on the far side of the broad ditch.

With a shrill squeak of windlasses and a rattling of chains, the bridge began to descend. That brought the enemy forward through their masking fringe of trees to see what we were about, but when they saw the prisoners all lined up and facing them, they hesitated. There was a period of confusion among their ranks, with people coming and going, and then there was a stirring at their rear as a small party of mounted men emerged from the trees and made their way towards the head of the drawbridge, obviously to discover for themselves what was happening. A trumpet blast from the battlements above us stopped them short, too, just beyond arrow range, as a line of our bowmen, in response to the signal, positioned themselves in the embrasures along the top of the wall above us, showing their weapons plainly. Moments later, at another blast of the trumpet, a trio of riders emerged from behind our curtain wall and rode out under the white banner that symbolized a call to meet to discuss terms.

Chulderic's spokesman, a junior cavalry officer whose name I did not yet know, rode forward to the enemy party and told them bluntly that we were releasing the prisoners because they were eating food that we needed ourselves. He demanded that the enemy commander withdraw his forces as a sign of good faith while the release was carried out, and pointed up to where our bowmen watched vigilantly, the height of their positioning giving them an enormous advantage over their opposite numbers.

As I had anticipated, the enemy commander could scarcely believe what he was hearing, because our message implied plainly that our concerns over our ability to feed ourselves were strong enough to make us release strong, healthy prisoners who would immediately rearm themselves to fight against us again. He complied without further discussion and ordered his men to withdraw. As the enemy fell back, vacating the field in front of the bridge, our soldiers began to shepherd their prisoners across in front of them.

As soon as they crossed the bridge, they spread the prisoners as far apart as the ropes joining them would permit and then held them in place, arranging the five extended rows of men so that they overlapped and formed a wide human screen between the bridge end and the enemy position. Only when they were satisfied with their positioning did the commander of the guard nod his permission and a single drummer began to rap out the cadence of a march that would take the prisoners forward in lockstep, without tripping in their hobbles and falling down. The first few steps were tentative and hesitant, but the rhythm caught quickly and the bound men began to march quite smartly towards their freedom.

At that precise moment, in response to a prearranged signal, the lead riders of a column of horsemen swung around the end of the curtain wall and spurred their mounts hard towards the drawbridge. Sixty riders, gathering speed and impetus with every stride, in a single column three abreast and twenty deep, were across the bridge and veering away to the right before the enemy could react. And when they did react, Gunthar's people were impeded by the strings of helpless, hobbled men spread out between them and the fleeing riders, for flee we did, as hard and as fast as we could, intent only upon riding out of arrow range as quickly as possible and making a clean escape thereafter. We knew they would follow us, but we knew, too, that where we were going they would never find us.

We reached the red-wall caves to find Clodio waiting for us and the secret entrance at the back of the caves already open, and we led our mounts inside, into the darkness of the first cavern. Once there, with the high, blazing fires burning brightly, the horses assumed it was night and settled down immediately, behaving normally as they were secured with the standard horse lines they submitted to every night.

Over the course of the next six days, with the horses safely quartered, we busied ourselves making a temporary home for men and animals in the King's Caverns, widening and digging out the few narrow wrigglers easily now that there was no need for secrecy and we could assign as many men as needed to the task of chipping and digging away the rock walls and widening the gaps in the worst places. There was no observable evidence of time passing down there in the depths of the caverns; it was permanent night, and so we set six consecutive watches of men to work at the mining task, each watch laboring for four hours a day so that the work went on without pause until it was completed. Even so, it took four solid days and nights of hard labor to achieve what we wanted.

That done, and the way open for easy access from one end of the caverns to the other, it was a simple task to bring down bales of straw and hay from the stables in the castle through the open door at the far end and to transport them to the red-wall caves at the other. It was deeply satisfying to know, too, that while we were consolidating our new resources in the caverns, Gunthar's people were turning the countryside upside down in their attempts to discover how sixty men and horses could simply vanish into nowhere.

By the time seven days had elapsed we were confident that the mystery of our escape would have faded from the forefront of the enemy's awareness. From their point of view, our disappearance had been complete and completely mystifying. They could only assume that we had ridden out and away, beyond our own borders, perhaps to gather help or buy the support of mercenaries. In all that time, we made no moves against them from the castle and they had made no attempt to attack us.

As soon as the widening of the wrigglers had been completed, an armed party was dispatched by night, leading a light wagon pulled by a two-horse team, to bring back the Queen, the women in her party and the physician Clement. They returned the following morning, arriving outside the red-walled caves just after sunrise, and the Queen's party was escorted on foot through the caverns and into the safety of the castle without incident. Seven days had passed since Vivienne had learned of King Ban's death.

I had ridden out earlier that morning with two companions, just before dawn, one of four three-man teams dispatched to explore the surrounding countryside and glean any information we could about the activities and disposition of Gunthar's forces within a radius of five miles. Our hunt was to the northeast, covering the ground on both sides of the northeast line, left to the line due north of the caves as far as the edge of Lake Genava, and then right to the line due east of them, so that we covered a full quarter of a circular area, riding

back and forth in steadily increasing arcs as we moved farther out
from our starting point on each sweep and leaving one scout behind
in the cleared area of every third arc in case of any unforeseen
developments at our back. It took us two full days to cover the entire
area, and we knew that our other three teams were doing the same
in the remaining three quadrants, which meant that by the time we
returned to our starting point and assembled all the information that
each of the four search teams had discovered, we would know
everything we needed to know about what was happening within an
area approaching ninety to a hundred square miles around the
castle, and we would be able to draw up comprehensive plans for
dealing with Gunthar's men—their holdings and their disposi-
tions—throughout that area.

Two days after that, I rode out through the red-walled caves for
the first time with Samson and our two cavalry squadrons—sixty
mounted men. We swung far to the south this time, to where team
number three had identified a heavy concentration of enemy forces
they presumed to be Burgundians, billeted in the strongly made and
recently fortified buildings of what had once been a prosperous
farm. I counted upwards of a full hundred men in the place, and we
spent a long time working our way down a hillside at their backs,
through difficult and heavily overgrown terrain, to hit them from
behind, from where they had least expected an attack—especially a
mounted one—to materialize.

We hit hard and fast, giving them no time to rally themselves
against us. Apart from our own mounts, there was not a horse in the
entire place, and so we had no solid opposition. A few hardy souls
formed isolated pockets of resistance, knowing that they were in
desperate straits, but they went down quickly under the weight of
our horseflesh, and we left few of them alive. In what was always
known as "the butcher's accounting," we counted fifty-two enemy
dead, and another thirty-eight wounded, all of whom we gathered
together and left behind us under guard, having first relieved them
of their weapons. A number of others managed to flee the slaughter
nevertheless, and we let them go, content to have them carry the tale

of the attack and its outcome back to whoever might have the responsibility for listening to them. We were happy to have Gunthar know that there was a potent and highly mobile cavalry force out there in his territories, raiding his raiders. However, by the time his exploratory force came seeking us, thirsting for revenge, we had disappeared back into the safety of our secret caverns.

Two days later, while Gunthar's cavalry guards were scouring the southern territories looking for us, we wiped out two similar but smaller posts in the northwest quadrant of our range, attacking both simultaneously with thirty riders. This time, too, we were fortunate enough to find a score of horses stabled in one of the farms, and when we left, having set fire to the buildings and piled the dead in the middle of the farmyard, we took the horses with us, a welcome addition to our own stables.

Those raids marked the formal start of our campaign, and for the next two months we remained neck deep in conflict with what seemed to be an inexhaustible supply of fresh troops spilling out of Gunthar's territories, for territories—his and ours—had been established soon after the beginning of hostilities. Gunthar's forces had possession of a series of four minor but strongly fortified castles that were clustered near to each other in the south and eastern area of what had been Ban's kingdom, and the close linkage of those four strongholds, coupled with the hilly yet densely wooded terrain they occupied, enabled Gunthar to set up a solid and virtually self-sufficient province there that he could hold without great difficulty against any and all comers. There was little arable land within the region he controlled, so he had few convenient sources of supply of freshly grown foodstuffs, but since he and his followers were essentially brigands and Outlanders, they stole what they needed from wherever they could find it.

That brief time removed me forever from the status of boyhood, although because of it, I was never able to undergo the formal rites of passage into manhood. Informal rites there were aplenty to replace them, however, and I never heard anyone complain that my sword was being wielded by someone who lacked a man's credentials. I rode out of the red-walled caves on the morning of that first raid as a complete tyro—a green recruit who had absorbed many of the rudiments of basic training but had yet to distinguish himself in any way in the matter of combat or military conduct or manly prowess. It was true that I had killed more than one man, but none of the people who rode with me that day knew that. In their eyes, I was a mere boy, several years junior to the youngest of them.

Within the week, however, on a raid in which we had divided our force into two squadrons of thirty men each, the group I rode in was trapped by a detachment of Gunthar's mounted guards, who diverted us into a steep-sided valley that had no other way out. They outnumbered us by close on two to one and we had a sore time fighting our way clear, for before we realized what was happening they had herded us into a narrow chute at the extreme end of the valley, where we were so tightly jammed together that we had no room to fight. Caught on the outside of the crush at the rear of our squadron, far from the nearest of our attackers and angry at my own inability to move closer to the fighting, I unslung the bow that hung by my saddle and had been given me by King Ban. I threw the quiver of war arrows across my shoulders, jumped down from my horse and scrambled up the steep hillside that reared above me. It was hard going, for the ground was soft and sandy, and I found it difficult to gain a purchase on the slope with my feet, but eventually I came to a level spot where I could look down at the scene below me. It was chaotic, but I could see everything clearly, and so I began to aim and shoot.

The arrows I was using were the very ones that had killed Ban of Benwick, the arrows given to me by King Ban himself, upon his deathbed. These large, heavy war arrows, with their flared and wickedly barbed heads, could pierce armor from a distance as short as the one from which I was shooting, and the enemy below me were all too close for me to miss. My assault broke the fury of their attack within moments, for it was sustained and deadly, with never a missed target on my part. I drew and aimed and fired as quickly as my hands could move, and I had been well trained in making those movements. I dropped five men with my first five arrows, and by that time even those who had not noticed me before were aware of my presence above them.

The first move by an enemy rider to disengage and ride away caught my eye, and I drove him out of the saddle with a hard shot that skewered his cuirass between his shoulder blades. I heard the noise as he crashed to the ground. Then it became difficult to select a target, because so many men were suddenly in retreat, and naturally, our men were thundering after them, intent now on revenge. As it was impossible to tell friend from foe when they were galloping away from me, I slid quickly back down the hill and salvaged as many of my spent arrows as I could before I remounted my horse and spurred after my companions.

I was feasted that night, the tale of my "counterattack" being the talk around our campfires. We had lost seven men in the encounter, but it might have been far worse and it certainly would have been far more disastrous had I not had my bow and arrows with me. Of all the sixty men riding in Samson's two squadrons, I was the only bowman.

I had good fortune in the next raid, too, managing to quickly spot a weakness in the force that was facing us. It was the kind of occurrence that takes place in the blinking of an eye, when you identify an opportunity, and the decision to exploit it or to let it pass by is instantaneous. In this instance, leading a diversionary thrust across the enemy's front to distract them from advancing directly against our main position, I saw an opening between two sections of the enemy where no space should have been, and I swung aside and charged straight into it. Fortunately, the men directly behind me followed without thought and we were able to act as a wedge, splitting the enemy into two groups that were more easily surrounded and dealt with.

From being the greenest tyro in the group, I had progressed to being known by everyone and acquiring a growing reputation as a man of luck and good judgment, which was extremely flattering but precisely the kind of conceit that Germanus and Tiberias Cato had warned me against more times than I could remember. A short time after that, however, Sigobert, the veteran cavalry commander who had been Samson's second in command for years, was killed in a skirmish with some displaced Burgundian bowmen. His command was taken over by another veteran, Rigunth, but then Rigunth rode into an ambush at the head of a small group three days later and was killed with all his men.

When the word of Rigunth's death arrived, Samson came looking for me and appointed me, temporarily, to the position of squadron commander. I accepted without a blink, having heard only the word *temporary* and fully anticipating that someone would quickly be promoted from the cadre of junior officers to fill the spot. By the time two weeks had passed, however, I was sufficiently perturbed to seek out Samson. I found him sitting at a makeshift table by one of the fires, studying a map that had been drawn by one of our clerks who had a talent for such things, and cleared my throat to announce myself and let him know I wished to speak with him.

He put down the map and the pen he had been holding and looked at me strangely, his mouth twisted sideways in a half smile. I told him briefly what was bothering me and asked him when I could expect to be relieved of my temporary duties, and he leaned backwards, clutching the edge of the table and wiggling his shoulders to loosen them from the strain of having sat still for so long.

"Why are you asking me that?" he responded. "We're in the middle of a war, Cousin. Are you telling me you are not enjoying your command?"

"No, that's not what I'm saying at all, Samson. I'm enjoying it thoroughly, but it has been more than two weeks now and for the past few days I've been worrying that I might be enjoying it too much."

"How so?"

I stared at him, surprised that he could not see my meaning, for to me it was as obvious as the nose on my face. "Because I'm beginning to be afraid that when someone is appointed to fill the post, I'll resent him for taking over."

His expression did not change by as much as a twitch. "Why would you resent someone for obeying instructions and accepting a promotion? That's what soldiers do, is it not?"

"Aye, but—"

"But what? Are you afraid he might do the job better than you?"

"No, how could I be? I don't even know who we are talking about."

"But whoever he may be, he might still do the job better than you can?"

"I doubt it."

Samson raised an eyebrow, perhaps aware that he had dealt a blow to my vanity.

There was a long pause after that, and then my cousin looked down at the map he had discarded to listen to me. When he spoke his voice sounded distant, and carried a distinct chill. "Think about this, Cousin Clothar, and consider your answer well. You are what—sixteen? Sixteen, aye. Now, are you asking me to believe that you can handle this post—the leadership of an entire squadron—better than anyone else I might appoint?"

That put a curb on my tongue. I hesitated, then decided to be truthful, no matter the cost. I ought to be able to speak the truth to my cousin with impunity, and I could see no acceptable reason for pretending that I did not believe in myself.

"Yes, Cousin," I said. "That's what I'm telling you."

He looked up at me, and his face crinkled in a wide grin. "Excellent," he said. "I think so, too. Get on with it, then."

I felt myself gaping at him.

"I said get on with it, Clothar. You are now officially in full command of Beta squadron, so may I return to my map? It really is quite important."

I walked away in a daze, attempting to come to terms with the realization that I was now Commander Clothar in fact as well as in name.

5

Nine days after my assumption of command over my thirty-man squadron, Gunthar launched an all-out campaign to obliterate us, and I began to regret the hubris that had driven me to assume such an enormous responsibility. I lost three men in one afternoon, right at the outset of that campaign, all of them shot out of the saddle by bowmen who had managed to infiltrate our defenses and set themselves up in a blind where there was only one trail that passed by. They knew we would have to use it sooner or later. Their chance came sooner than they had expected, judging from the lack of debris we found afterwards around their hiding place and from the fact that they took their first three targets efficiently. But they died themselves very quickly thereafter, because they had neglected to provide themselves with an escape route.

Three men lost might not seem like many to some observers, but that was one full tenth of my force, and the old Roman word for killing one in ten of one's troops was *decimation*. We had been decimated by a trio of nameless bowmen. We would replace our men when we returned to our base in the castle, but our pool of available replacements was growing no larger and every diminution of that resource was a permanent one.

Gunthar, on the other hand, seemed to suffer from no such constraints. In any encounter between our forces and his, we were more than likely to emerge victorious. No one knew the reasons for that, but there could be no doubt that it was true, because the casualty count at the end of each fight and skirmish was unequivocal. Face to face, hand to hand and nose to nose, the number of casualties demonstrated that we outfought them regularly by a count of at least three casualties for them against every two for us. But there was no parity in the situation. If Gunthar lost a hundred men, he would field two hundred fresh ones in the coming days. Every single man we lost, on the contrary, increased our cumulative weakness, and as each day passed we grew more and more aware of just how weak we were becoming.

We had one turn of good fortune that came when our fortunes seemed at their lowest and we most needed something in the way of a ray of light in the darkness that was hemming us in. Ingomer, lord of the neighboring property of Vervenna, returned from the eastern patrol as soon as he received the word we sent him of Theuderic's death at Gunthar's hands.

Understandably enough, he rode directly to his home at the head of six hundred men to rescue his wife before doing anything else or reporting his presence to anyone, but he found its buildings burned and walls toppled. Distraught, and believing his wife and newborn child dead, he immediately went looking for Gunthar, bent on vengeance. Fortunately, before he could encounter any of Gunthar's mercenaries, he met Samson, who told him his wife and child were safe in Genava. Enormously relieved, Ingomer returned directly to Castle Genava to greet his beautiful young wife and to meet his newborn son, and he and his six hundred men had remained in the castle after that.

Most beneficially for our beleaguered garrison, however, Ingomer rode right up to the drawbridge with his six hundred horsemen, defying Gunthar's watchdogs to challenge them. At the last moment, just as the drawbridge was descending, Ingomer rapped out an order, and two full wings of his riders, a hundred horsemen to a wing, turned their horses smartly and split apart into two groups, then swung into a pincer formation and swept into the woodlands beyond the lea from left and right, routing the hidden enemy there, who, being mainly bowmen, were unable to use their weapons defensively to any great extent among the trees. While the first two wings of cavalry scoured through the woods in opposing arcs and finally spilled back out into the open, Ingomer turned the remainder of his force about and led all four hundred of them slowly and inexorably into the trees, mopping up the last remaining vestiges of resistance among Gunthar's occupying force.

Inside the castle we had never known exactly how many enemy warriors were ranged against us out there, and the wide-ranging estimates that were bandied about were based mainly upon random observations when there was little to observe. Ingomer and his men, however, had left upwards of a hundred of the enemy dead among the trees. Those who remained alive were stripped of their armor, clothing and weapons and set free to make their own way through the surrounding forest to wherever they might wish to go. We had no interest in taking prisoners, and we knew that once disarmed and naked, Gunthar's mercenaries would not find it easy to rearm themselves quickly. Stripped bare, they would be fortunate to make it back through the bogs and forest that lay between them and their nearest support bases, and doubly fortunate to do so without stumbling across any of the local people who lived out there among the trees and had no reason to be hospitable towards any of Gunthar's mercenaries.

That was one of the brighter moments in the campaign, but over and above everything else I can recall about that time is the feeling of hopelessness that grew upon us daily as we suffered continual and irreplaceable losses of men and horses while simultaneously watching Gunthar's numbers swell.

Brach and Chulderic held joint command of the castle and its garrison, although Chulderic was nominally commander in chief of all the forces of Benwick and Brach merely commanded the infantry, a position more or less forced upon him by his immense size. He simply could not find a horse large enough to bear him when he was armed and armored, so any yearnings that he might ever have had to be a cavalryman had long since been abandoned as unrealistic. After Ingomer's rout of the watchdog guards beyond the bridge, we fully expected Gunthar to mount an expedition to replace them, and we quickly brought out our foot soldiers to prepare defensive positions in the woods before new enemy forces could be moved in. The expected attack never occurred, however, and we were left to wonder why Gunthar would simply allow such a strategic position to be abandoned.

We wasted no time while we were wondering such things, however, and we quickly put our newly freed infantry to use against the Burgundian mercenaries, enjoying the fact that, for a brief time, the difference they made was wonderful. At every clash of arms, Gunthar's creatures were sent scampering for their lives and the morale of our troopers swelled for several weeks. But then the same reality that governed our cavalry asserted itself over the infantry, too. Their losses were simply too consistent to be sustainable.

Chulderic had sent out messengers to neighboring kings and governors, requesting assistance, but little was forthcoming. The news of Ban's death was out now and it was believed that the fighting going on in Benwick was among his sons, squabbling for the wealth of the kingdom. Although that was untrue, kings and rulers who had been friends and allies to Ban were reluctant to commit their own resources to what they saw as a family squabble blown out of all proportion. There were too many other real enemies and invading Outlanders abroad in the land to permit anyone who was not directly involved in thc Benwick wars to dilute his own forces.

One afternoon in the second month of the struggle, when things were at their bleakest, we had been pursuing a band of Gunthar's horsemen—Germanic mercenaries who had been celebrated as Roman auxiliary cavalry and magnificent horsemen for hundreds of years—and we had finally brought them to battle. It was an even match, too, all things considered. The Germans were mounted on their heavy, forest-bred horses, and there appeared to be two thirty-man squadrons in their party, which matched our own size. They had been riding far abroad on this occasion, raiding deep inside our holdings and penetrating right to the lakeside about ten miles north of the castle, where they had burned at least one village and hanged large numbers of helpless farmers, simply to encourage their neighbors to offer no help to us. We had received word of their presence two days earlier and had ridden to intercept them and put an end to their depredations, and it had taken us an entire day to find them and cut them off so that they had no choice but to fight us.

We came together head on, in a wild, charging melee that seemed to have developed of its own accord. I had had some thought of splitting my squadron into two groups and spearing into the middle of the enemy formation, but before I could even begin to issue orders I saw them charging right towards us at the full gallop. We had no option other than to fight or run, and so we fought. I led my men directly towards the oncoming enemy, and by the time the two lines met, both sides were advancing at the full gallop.

I was unhorsed on the first pass because my mount went down, smitten in the neck by a hand axe, and I flew right over its head. I should have been killed then and there, for I was winded for a long time, but in the heat of the fighting no one paid me any attention and I was able to collect myself and find a riderless horse. It was a stallion, and it had no wish to be ridden any further that day. Unfortunately, in a battle of wills between him and me, he was destined to lose. As I was trying to catch hold of his bridle, a rider came galloping by on his other side. He knew I was not one of his, but he was galloping hard and could not reach me from where he was, so he slashed at the horse, trying to disable it. His slash was ill timed, however, and poorly aimed because of his speed, so that instead of wounding or crippling the horse, the flat of his blade smacked against the beast's rump, and the animal, already terrified out of its wits, erupted into a run. I went with it, for there was nothing else I could think to do. I twisted my fingers into its mane and ran alongside it in great, bounding strides until I grew confident enough to take my weight on my arms and raise both feet, then drop them back to earth and thrust myself up and back into a vaulting swing that landed me astride the horse's back. Once there, and free of the press for a moment, since we had run far beyond the fighting, I brought him to a stop and gathered up the reins, and as I turned to ride back towards my command, I saw my cousin Samson.

He, too, had evidently managed to swing out of the scrabble of the fight, flanked as always by his two most faithful followers, Jan and Gurrit, a pair of loyal stalwarts who might have been twins, so similar did they appear to be at a casual glance, and who had appointed themselves as Samson's personal bodyguards. I first saw him because his trio of riders were the only people moving in that area and my eye went to them automatically, assessing the potential danger there and recognizing Samson and his escorts immediately.

They were angling back towards the crush of the main fight, riding close together in a tight arrowhead with Samson in the lead and Jan and Gurrit pressing hard on his flanks. It was clear to me in my first, sweeping glance along the line of their attack to their intended target that they were aiming to use the concerted weight of their horses to drive a wedge into the exposed right flank of the enemy formation, but it was equally clear that someone in the enemy ranks had already anticipated what they would do and was moving quickly to counter them, dispatching a group of five riders to interpose themselves between Samson and their own force and give their comrades time to close the weakness in their formation.

I was more than a hundred paces from where the two small groups would meet, but I put my spurs to my new horse and drove him hard towards the convergence point, knowing that I would be too late to take part in the clash of the meeting and feeling the dread of foreknowledge swelling in my chest and threatening to choke me. Three against five was not particularly great odds, but my store of optimism had been sadly depleted during the previous few weeks and I no longer held high expectations of anything other than defeat and disappointment.

Sure enough, while the two groups were yet separated by a gap of twenty paces or more, I saw one of the enemy swinging what appeared to be a slingshot of some kind over his head, and moments later one of Samson's companions, I could not tell which, threw up his arms violently and toppled backwards, the helmet sent flying from his head by the force of the enemy projectile. He had barely hit the ground when the two groups closed with a meaty collision of horseflesh and the clang of hard-swung weapons. Samson's other man, the one on my side of the action, went down, hard, his arms outflung as he fell or was knocked sprawling from his mount. I was fifty paces distant now, galloping flat out, and I saw the blood spraying from the open slash in the falling man's neck, spreading like a red fog as he went down.

Samson's horse was rearing, turning on its hind legs as he hacked at the men surrounding him, making no visible impression on any of them. I howled in protest as I saw one of them, and then a second one, dance their horses clear of the tussle, leaving the uneven fight to their three companions while they distanced themselves slightly and took careful aim with short, heavy, wide-bladed spears. They threw together, and both missiles hit squarely, penetrating my cousin's armor and piercing his back, their blades less than a handsbreadth apart. The two impacts, occurring almost simultaneously, knocked Samson forward at first, threatening to tip him over his horse's ears, but he stopped himself from falling somehow, and then the combined weight of the two dragging spear shafts pulled him backwards and unseated him. He fell in such a way that the butts of the spear shafts hit the ground first, the points driving forward through Samson's chest. For a space of several heartbeats he hung suspended on the upright spears before they fell over backwards.

I was screaming by that point, and almost among the men who had killed him. I saw them turning to face me, their faces registering surprise because until hearing my screams, they had not known I was coming at them. I aimed my horse directly at the two spear throwers, who were sitting side by side and had not yet had any opportunity to arm themselves in any other way. My horse hit the closest man's mount with his shoulder and sent horse and rider flying, and I aimed a short, chopping stab of my spatha at the second man as I passed him, driving the point of my blade cleanly into the soft flesh under his chin. I felt the steel tip lodge against what could only have been his spine, killing him instantly as I swept by and turned in my saddle to allow the momentum of my passage to pull the tip of my sword free.

Another of the remaining three riders tugged frantically at his reins, trying to pull his horse around to face me, but he had reined his horse in so that he could watch Samson as he fell and, in consequence, he had no momentum. He was heavily bearded, but I saw every line on his face above the growth clearly as I killed him, too, driving the point of my spatha through his right eye. I pulled the point free again immediately and swung back-handed at someone who was trying to reach me from behind my right shoulder, and as I did so I saw the unhorsed spearman moving towards me on the ground, carrying the bloodstained spear that he had recovered from Samson's body. Something hit me heavily across the shoulders, once and then again, and I felt my horse collapsing beneath me. I glanced down and saw that the spearman had butchered it, and I threw myself from the saddle before I could be pinned beneath its body. I rolled and came up on my knees beside the body of my cousin, watching the last three of his killers preparing to kill me, too. The spearman on foot had his weapon pointing at me again and the other two were moving apart to come at me from two sides. Then came a sound of charging hoofbeats and a babble of voices shouting my name as a squad of my own troopers charged past me and my three adversaries were cut down.

Shaken by the swiftness of events and my unexpected rescue, I tried to rise to my feet but found that I was incapable of raising either of my knees from the ground. I turned instead to the ruined body of my cousin Samson and bent forward to close his eyes, which, by some strange mischance, appeared to be staring directly into mine, although they were already glazed with that peculiar emptiness that differentiates a dead body from a living one. I remained there, kneeling over him for some time as I tried to find words to pray for his soul. But that was one of the few times in my entire life that I found myself unable to utter a single word of prayer.

The battle had been a complete disaster for us. We had won again, according to the butcher's accounting, but I knew we could never hope to recover from such losses and we were finished as a cohesive fighting force. The enemy had left thirteen dead men on the field and more than half again as many horses—we had no way of knowing how many of the survivors had been wounded or how serious those wounds were. We, however, had lost eight men dead and a full score more bore wounds of one kind or another, although, miraculously, none of those were serious enough to be life-threatening. Unfortunately, the same could not be said for the injured horses. Few horses injured in battle could ever be healed, and although only five of our horses—two of them mine—had been killed outright during the fighting, we had to kill seven more wounded animals. We had not been at full strength at the start of the battle, fielding only half a hundred fighting men instead of our normal three score, but when the activities were all over and the dead all buried—with the sole exception of Samson, whose body we would take with us—we assembled to make our way homeward and we presented a sorry sight, even to ourselves. We numbered thirty-two whole men out of our original strength of sixty.

Weary and discouraged, I gave the signal to proceed, and we headed home with our dead King at our center, laid out on a makeshift bier on the bed of the light two-horse supply wagon that always accompanied us on our expended raids. He lay on his back on a thick bed of fresh-cut reeds, his hands crossed upon his chest beneath the expanse of his war cloak, which, arranged in careful folds, served to conceal his body from profane eyes and the indignities of weather.

My first thoughts at the start of that journey were all to do with my cousin Brach, who had now become King of Benwick with Samson's death. He would be beside himself, I knew, over both the loss of his beloved brother and the unsought, unwished-for accession to the status of kingship. Brach, despite his visual splendor and apparent suitability to play the King's role, was not a man who would ever enjoy the pomp and ceremonies that went with being a monarch. Spectacular as were his exploits in war, he was nonetheless too genuinely humble and too self-effacing ever to be comfortable in such a highly visible capacity as that of King of Benwick. But then, I thought, life seldom asks us for our approval in advance of what it decrees for us. Brach's fate was to be a king. He could not control that, any more than I could control what my destiny might be.

I spent the remainder of the journey, then, deliberating about what I would say to Chulderic when we arrived at the castle, but he was waiting for us when we reached the red-walled caves, and I went into conference with him immediately, drawing him aside to where we could speak without being overheard.

With Samson's death, I told him, we had reached the limits of our cavalry's usefulness as a striking force. We were dangerously, almost fatally, vulnerable in terms of renewable numbers—of both men and horses. We were still able, barely, to continue replacing the troopers who were killed or left unable to ride and fight on, but we had exhausted our supply of able veterans and were now reduced to using untrained riders—foot soldiers and young boys who dreamed of glory in riding out to war but barely knew one end of a horse from the other, with some of them believing that horses had tails purely to indicate that feeding the animal should be performed from the other end. The time had come, I told Chulderic, for us to cut our losses and consolidate the strengths remaining to us by keeping our surviving riders in the castle, acting as defensive garrison troops, and their horses inside the caves where they would be held in reserve pending an emergency.

Chulderic had sat staring at Samson's covered bier on the wagon bed as he listened to me, and now he nodded his head and agreed with my assessment of the situation. We would take Samson in and bury him within the castle walls, he said, and then we would prepare for a siege. But while we were doing that, we would also work to reopen the postern gate, the old, walled-up doorway above the lakeside rocks at the rear of the castle. Thus, he opined, we would have two means of exit should the need for escape ever arise.

Hearing him say those words demonstrated to me, more than anything else could have, just how bad our situation was. At the outset of the war, Chulderic would never have voiced such a possibility. Within the space of a short couple of months, however, his entire outlook on life had changed, and every facet of the changes involved reflected in some way upon the perfidy and evil of the man against whom he was fighting.

Gunthar had never been a lovable person, even as a boy, and my own memories of him from my childhood days were of a sullen, melancholy young man with a foul temper and an unpleasant disposition. He was lavish with incessant insults, utterly uncaring whom he offended. His reputation had grown less and less wholesome and his behavior more and more violent as he aged, too, and most people came to prefer simply to stay out of his way. The most frightening thing about Gunthar, however, was his unpredictability. Of all his many attributes, that one alone was utterly predictable, and it frightened everyone, including his closest allies. And in the very recent past, we had heard persistent rumors that his behavior was growing ever more and more outrageous, erratic and capricious, and that even his closest associates were increasingly apprehensive of being too long around him at any one time, fearful for their own lives. We had dismissed most of what we heard, however, principally because of the way it came to us. Rumors without some kind of solid ratification were seldom reliable.

6

Three days after that conversation with Chulderic, on the day following Samson's interment in one of the castle's interior courtyards, I was summoned to join Brach shortly after dawn. I had been up late, serving as captain of the night watch, and so had been asleep for little more than an hour when I was roughly shaken awake. Annoyed, but knowing that Brach would not disturb my sleep without good cause, I splashed water over my head, my face and the back of my neck and toweled myself into wakefulness before going to join him.

He was waiting for me on top of the main tower supporting the curtain wall across the front of the main gates, and as I strode towards him he stood watching me, one hand cupping his chin while the other supported his elbow. I tried to read his expression as I approached him, but his face betrayed nothing.

"What is it?" I asked.

He jerked his thumb towards the edge of the tower. "Look over there."

I looked down towards the drawbridge, to where a party of three men sat gazing back up at me from horseback. One of the three carried a white banner.

"They want to talk? Who are they?"

Brach sauntered over to stand beside me. "Don't you recognize the one in the middle?"

I stared, trying to place the man's face, but as far as I could tell I had never seen him before. I shook my head, and Brach's mouth quirked wryly.

"That's Tulach, Cousin, Gunthar's senior commander."

"Tulach the Butcher? Are you sure? What would he be doing here, looking to talk to us?" If Brach was correct, the man below was an inhuman creature, whose depravity and debauched behavior had become the stuff of legend within mere months of his arrival here in Benwick.

My cousin sniffed. "I am absolutely sure of who he is, because I have seen him before and spoken to him on several occasions. As to why he is here, I would be prepared to wager that he has come, as Gunthar's official representative, to offer us safe conduct out of here if we will simply consent to leave without further hostilities and surrender the castle and its kingdom to Gunthar."

"And will you accept his offer?"

Brach merely glanced at me sidewise. "Would you?"

"Hmm. Where's Chulderic?"

"I sent for him, but he's not as young as you are. Moves more slowly. He should be here soon."

"So what do you intend to do?"

"Talk to him, I suppose. Listen to what he has to say, then tell him what I wish him to say to my fratricidal brother. Here comes Chulderic now."

The upshot of the ensuing conversation was that I was designated to ride out and talk to Tulach, thereby delivering a tacit message that Chulderic and Brach both considered it beneath their dignity and station to tattle with the enemy. I took two of my own troopers with me, and as the men at the controls lowered the great drawbridge, we rode out towards the enemy delegation. Above us as we went I could hear the tramp of running feet as bowmen hurried to line the walkway along the top of the wall, and as their sergeants shouted orders I could visualize them setting themselves up, nocking their arrows and standing prepared to draw and shoot upon command.

Tulach watched me coming, his face stern and unreadable. I paid no attention at all to the two men he had with him, just as he betrayed no interest in the two men escorting me. He was a bigger man than I had expected, and his face was hard and cruel, with high, flat cheekbones and deep lines graven on each side of his mouth. I was expecting him to state his business without waste of time, and he did, but what he said was the very last thing I would have hoped or expected to hear.

"I want safe conduct," he said, "for me and my men. No more fighting. You allow us to ride out along the main road to Lugdunum without bothering us or pursuing us and we will leave your lands immediately and never come back."

"How many men do you have?" I asked the question for no other purpose than to gain time and cover my own stupefaction.

"Nigh on five hundred, altogether."

"All horsemen?"

"Aye. We have no truck with Gunthar's infantry."

"And how far do you intend to go from here?"

"That's no concern of yours. We can fight our way out, if need be, but I thought we might both prefer—your friends and mine—to sacrifice no more men than we already have."

I nodded my head judiciously, as if I knew exactly what I was doing and talking about, but I was still as completely in the dark as I had been when he first told me what he wanted, and the predominant thought in my mind was that the man obviously thought we were far stronger and had more resources at our disposal than was the case. And if that were true, I thought, I would have to be careful not to disillusion him.

"You have come up with the only viable reason I could imagine for gaining our agreement in this . . . the need to squander no more lives. But how can I be sure that, given my promise, on behalf of my people, that you will not be pursued or harassed, you won't take that as a license to murder and plunder your way from here to Lugdunum? I can hardly take you at your given word, can I? Your reputation for trustworthy honesty and open dealings leaves much to be desired, from where we watch. Your name reeks of atrocity throughout Benwick. Tulach the Butcher, they call you, and you have earned all the hatred that goes with such a name."

His face betrayed no emotion. "Aye, that may be. But now everything has changed and I'll butcher no more. Our days here are done."

"Really, say you so? And what does Gunthar the brother-killer say to that?"

"No single word. Gunthar is dead. He died yesterday, late in the evening, in a fit of rage. His eyes filled up with blood and his face turned black and he staggered and fell dead, clutching his head. I was there at the time."

I was struck speechless, but fortunately Tulach felt the need to say more and kept on talking. "With him gone, our cause is gone and so is our livelihood, so we need to move on and find further employment. Knowing that, I decided to come here and speak with you people. Particularly with Chulderic and Brach, the sole remaining brother."

"Your information is surprisingly up to date. We buried Samson only last night."

Tulach shrugged. "I didn't know that, but I knew he had been killed. Will Chulderic speak with me?"

"No, he will not. Had he wished to speak with you he would have come out here instead of sending me. You have not endeared yourself to anyone here over the past few months."

The big man shrugged. "So be it. Are you authorized to grant acceptance of my suggestion, or do you have to discuss it with the others?"

"They are here. I'll consult with them on this and return soon."
I made to turn my mount around, but he forestalled me, reaching
into the scrip that hung at his waist and tossing me a cloth bag that,
from the way it felt when I caught it, contained a small box of wood.

"Best take them this, then, because they'll no more take my
word than you would."

It was all I could do to resist the temptation to open the bag right
in front of him. Instead, keeping my face rigidly blank, I tucked the
bag into my own scrip. "Wait here," I said, and swung my horse
around, leaving him sitting there.

Brach and Chulderic were waiting for me in the courtyard and
they were as amazed as I had been to hear the tidings of Gunthar's
death, but their wonder and gratitude quickly gave way to suspicion
and fear of entrapment. This was precisely the kind of duplicity we
could expect Gunthar to use to disarm us, Chulderic swore, but while
they were debating I withdrew Tulach's bag and opened the box it
contained. My stomach heaved immediately, but I quickly conquered
my revulsion and held the open box out towards the others.

"I believed him when he told me Gunthar is dead," I told them.
"But here's the proof. Gunthar would never part willingly with his
personal seal, especially when it was yet attached to his finger.
Tulach must have cut the finger off, knowing we would never
believe his unsupported word."

Brach took the box and shook his brother's severed finger with
its heavy, ornate seal out into his palm. He pulled the ring free and
dropped the finger into the dirt at his feet.

"I'm convinced," he said. "The war is over. Let them go home,
so be it they go quickly. We have a land to resurrect here."

I returned to Tulach within the half hour, my features carefully
schooled to give this man no inkling of the reaction his tidings had
caused within the castle walls. Once again, he spoke out as soon as
I came within hearing range.

"Well? Are we to fight?"

"You have a full day to withdraw," I told him, "until this time
tomorrow, at which point we will send cavalry to look for you, but

not to pursue you. If they find you, then they will attack. That is our offer. Accept it or leave it, as you will, but do so now."

He pursed his lips quickly as I spoke, showing quick-flaring anger, but as soon as I had finished speaking, he said, "So be it. My men are ready. We will be far beyond Benwick's borders by this time tomorrow." He nodded to his two escorts, and as he made to swing away I stopped him.

"One more question: where is Gunthar?"

Tulach turned his head slowly and looked back at me, and for a moment I thought he was not going to answer me at all, but then he hawked and spat. "He's in Chabliss," he said, naming the smallest of the four forts clustered in the southeast quadrant of our territories. "He lies where he fell, in front of the fire. I wish you joy of finding him."

He pulled his horse into a rearing turn and sank his spurs into its flanks, and as he and his two fellows disappeared beyond the fringe of trees in the distance I realized for the first time that Gunthar's War was over. It had happened very suddenly and very tamely, with the death of a single man from natural causes, but it had caused as much carnage and grief and misery as any other war during its brief existence.

7

The suddenness of the war's end threw me completely off balance, changing my life instantly from one filled with chaotic urgencies and burgeoning despair, into one in which I had nothing substantial to do, and all the time in the world to dedicate to not doing it. We were aware that there had been Burgundian invasions to the north of our lands, but no evidence of any threat to us in Benwick had materialized, and so we paid no attention to anything outside our own boundaries and were content to wallow in the lethargy that settled suddenly upon those of us who had been most heavily involved in the fighting. The experience could have been a damaging one—I can see that clearly now with the assistance of hindsight—but before I had the opportunity to drift into any set pattern of idle behavior, I recalled a comment that Ursus had made months earlier, during our long journey to the south, on a day when we had been forced to go out of our way and make a wide and difficult detour to avoid a large bear with three cubs.

The sow had settled herself, with her trio of charges, by the side of a mountain river that swept in close at one point—a matter of several paces—to the edge of the narrow path we had been following through difficult, hilly terrain for two days. We saw her fishing in the white water of the rushing stream just as the last stretch of the downhill pathway swooped down from where we were to the riverside where her cubs tussled with each other by the water's edge, still too small and too young to brave the current. It would have been folly to attempt to pass them by unseen, and we had no desire to kill the creatures, so we had muffled our curses and cursed our misfortune and scrambled painfully upwards, leading our horses slowly and with great difficulty, high and hard, scaling the steep hillside with much muttering and grumbling until we reached the summit and were faced with the even greater task of making our way back down again in safety towards the narrow, well-trodden path that was our sole way out of the hills in the direction we were heading.

We had made the ascent in something more than an hour, but it took us three times that long to go back down again, because of our horses and the need to find a route they would accept. In the late afternoon, however, looking down from high above the path we had left that morning, we saw it choked with Burgundian warriors heading directly towards the sow and her cubs, and we knew beyond doubt that, had it not been for the animals, we would have blundered directly into these people and probably died there.

That experience had seduced Ursus into a philosophical frame of mind for the remainder of that day, and he had said something to the effect that God sometimes throws us valuable gifts disguised as uncommon and annoying nuisances. The memory of that occasion, coming when it did, made me look at my sudden idleness as an unexpected gift of time in which to take stock of my life. After ten consecutive days, however, during which I did nothing at all, other than to think deeply about who I was becoming and what I had achieved, I found myself not only unable to arrive at any clear decisions about my life, but not even able to define any new perspectives on which to base decisions. And this despite the fact that I knew there were decisions I must make.

Discouraged by the entire exercise and feeling both foolish and inadequate, I went to Brach and apologized for what I was sure he must see as my laziness and lack of attention to duty in the days that had passed. When I told him I had been thinking, however, instead of being as angry at me as I had expected him to be, Brach laughed and asked me if I knew what I had been *searching* for. When I merely blinked at him and told him I had no idea, he laughed even more and told me to go away somewhere and think further, and at greater length, this time in isolation and free of all distraction. Once I had arrived at some kind of conclusion about what I wanted, I was to come back and tell him.

I took him at his word and did as he suggested, and this time, as he had indicated I might, I came to terms with something that had been troubling me without my being really aware of it. I would be seventeen years old on my next birthday, which meant that Clodas of Ganis had been ruling in my father's stead, unchallenged, for that length of time, and my parents were still unavenged.

King Ban had promised me that, when I was grown, he, or the son who ruled by then in his place, would assist me in traveling to confront Clodas. At that time, the son indicated in the promise had been Gunthar, and I had never been under any illusions about how likely I was to find assistance from that source. But now all that had changed. Brach was King of Benwick and I had proved my loyalty to him, time and again. Now I had little doubt that he would demonstrate his loyalty to me by rewarding me with an escort of warriors to help me to reclaim my own throne in Ganis.

I returned to Brach filled with enthusiasm for the task I had defined for myself. That evening, after the main meal, he dismissed all his attendants so that the two of us could be alone while he listened closely to everything I had to say. When I had finished speaking, however, instead of leaping to his feet and wishing me well as I had anticipated he would, my cousin sat silent, musing and nodding his head. Impatient as I was to gain his blessing for the expedition I was planning, I nonetheless saw that he had more on his mind than I knew about and so I disciplined myself to sit in silence and wait for the cousin who was now my King to arrive at a decision.

Brach did not keep me waiting long. He rose quickly to his feet and began to pace back and forth in front of me, talking more volubly and fluently than I had ever heard him speak in all the time I had known him.

He knew my intentions concerning Clodas of Ganis, he told me, and he remembered and acknowledged his father's promise to assist me in bringing the usurper to justice for the slaughter of my family. That would happen, he told me, and he promised that I would be well supported by warriors from Benwick when the time came for me to march against Clodas. Now, however—and he asked me very graciously to try to see this situation from his viewpoint—was not the time.

Were I to strike out northwards now as was my right, he told me, Benwick would not be able to offer me any assistance in my quest. As King of Benwick, Brach was now constrained by the same concerns that had beset his father, Ban, years earlier, in that he had a domain to govern and a people to serve and sustain and feed, and both kingdom and people were ravaged, weakened and depleted by war. The hostilities were ended, but now the entire kingdom had to be rebuilt and returned to its former condition of wealth and strength. He looked me straight in the eye at that point and told me there was a task for me here in Benwick, and that if I would accept it, he would undertake to equip me, once it was completed, with the men and resources I would need to press my campaign against Clodas in the north.

I found no difficulty in seeing things from his newly acquired viewpoint and agreeing that his suggestions were both sensible and worthwhile. Clodas had spent seventeen years in ignorance of the fact that he would die at my hand, and I saw no great impediment to my plans in permitting him to live a little longer while I attended to other duties. And so I threw myself into rebuilding the affairs and the welfare of our little kingdom—although it seemed anything but little to me at that time—as wholeheartedly as I had committed myself to the war that had ravaged it. Rebuilding, however, meant in this instance exactly what it said, and it involved the physical labor of working side by side with the ordinary people of Benwick, most of them farmers, re-erecting the buildings—and sometimes that meant entire villages—that had been destroyed or damaged during the conflict. It was brutal and difficult work, but greatly satisfying in that the results achieved were plainly visible, and somehow another three months slipped by while I sweated and strained and labored with my hands just as painfully and exhaustingly as any farmer who ever cleared a patch of land by cutting and uprooting trees.

I had seen my aunt Vivienne several times since the deaths of my uncle Ban and her three sons, but not with any kind of regularity, and although she treated me with great kindness, it was plain for me to see that the special relationship I had enjoyed with her during my childhood had been forgotten by her in the bludgeoning she had undergone with the losses in her own immediate family. She had become an old woman, as Brach had warned me, and the trauma of the brief war between her sons had changed her radically and forever, eclipsing the light of her former love of life behind the dark shadow of her bereavement.

It was she, nevertheless, who first reminded me, after Gunthar's War, that I had promised Bishop Germanus I would return to Auxerre. I recall being extremely surprised that she should even know about that, but she showed me a letter from the bishop that had been brought to her some weeks earlier by a traveling priest. In it, knowing nothing at the time of the conflict between the King's sons, Germanus offered his condolences and prayers for the soul of King Ban, but had gone on to mention me and to refer to several tasks that he had in hand for me, awaiting my promised return.

She then told me that she had read all of the correspondence I had brought with me from Auxerre to deliver to Ban. Chulderic had taken possession of it after the King's death and had duly passed it on to Queen Vivienne. She had read it in turn, absorbed it thoroughly, and then passed it on to King Samson. And now King Brach, as his father's sole surviving successor, was in complete agreement with her, and with Chulderic and Germanus, that I should return to Auxerre and to the service of Bishop Germanus as quickly as possible.

I nodded deeply and promised her that I had not forgotten—although in truth I had—and that I would return to the north and to the bishop's service as soon as my current responsibilities to King Brach had been fulfilled. I told no lies in this but I did, however, greatly exaggerate the extent of those few responsibilities I still owed to Brach, because the truth was that I was in no rush to leave Genava and hurry back to Auxerre. I had found love for the first time in my life and was completely enthralled.

The young woman's name was Rosalyn, and she was the most beautiful proof of the existence of God that I had ever seen, because logic dictated beyond dispute that perfection such as hers could not exist had God not shaped it personally with His own hands. She was tall and lithe and lissome and lovely, with a wide, laughing mouth and a neck like a swan's. Our love was pure, for two simple reasons: we never had any opportunity to make it otherwise; and I never found the courage to profess my love to her.

So abjectly did I fail in finding that courage, in fact, that I could barely summon up sufficient nerve to sit in the same room with her and listen to her laughing and talking with her friends. It would have been impossible for me to sit at her feet and talk to her the way I saw other young men doing so effortlessly, making her laugh and singing to her. I could never have found the courage to do that. And yet I know she was aware of me, and she always had a warm and friendly smile for me, and frequently she spoke to me, although only for a short time after we first met. Whenever she did speak to me or ask me a question, I would be overcome with shyness and would stutter and stammer and blush with shame and confusion and frustration. And so, out of kindness I believe, she stopped addressing me directly.

She was a new arrival to Benwick, I learned within moments of having seen her for the first time. Her father was a merchant of some description and traveled widely. I heard that, and I knew it, and yet I failed somehow to understand that she was likely to move on again as quickly as she had arrived. And so she did, after a month-long stay, and I was devastated. One morning she was simply gone, with her entire family, and no one could tell me where they had gone to, or even which branch of the crossroads they might have taken. Inconsolable, I took to riding off alone and spending days on end in the woods, living on birds and small animals that I had shot or snared.

I had been out for three days on one such occasion and had spent an entire morning fishing bare handed for trout basking in deep holes beneath river stones before I caught a truly magnificent specimen, scooping it out of the water and throwing it high onto the bank behind me. As I turned to go and collect my prize, the sun struck me square in the face, dazzling me sufficiently to allow me to see only the shape of a tall man suddenly looming above me, his shoulder blocking part of the sun's orb so that he was thrown into silhouette. Cursing, I scrabbled to one side, clutching for the dagger in my belt, but as I unsheathed it and surged to my feet I was aware of my assailant moving, and then an arm closed around my neck from behind, a strong hand clamped tightly over my wrist, and a familiar voice spoke into my ear.

"Hey, be still! My only thought in coming here was that you might have food enough for both of us."

It was Ursus, and I almost fainted with relief, but instead I kicked backwards, hooking one foot behind his ankle, and pulled him down with me as I fell.

Afterwards, when we had stopped wrestling and laughing in our enjoyment of meeting again, I went in search of the trout I had thrown up onto the bank behind me. I found it twitching in the last stages of expiry, its skin covered with leaves and dry grass, and turned back to brandish it at Ursus, finding him brushing the crushed grass and leaves from his clothing.

"Food enough for both, as you requested. Why don't you start a fire while I clean this, and then you can tell me what brings you here."

It was another half hour before he set aside the bowl from which he had been eating and pulled himself to sit upright, facing the fire.

"What brings me here, you asked. Well, I suppose *you* do. I came to visit you, since I knew you were nearby."

"But you're supposed to be in Carcasso."

"I was, and now I am not. I've had enough of Carcasso."

"Was Duke Lorco there when you got home?"

"No, he wasn't. And not a word's been heard about him. You and I may be the last two living people to have seen him alive. Because he's dead now. Not a doubt of that in my mind. He's dead, long since. Probably since the day he vanished ahead of us."

"He wasn't very good, was he?"

Ursus tilted his head. "What d'you mean, good? As a soldier?" He made a face that managed to be noncommittal. "He wasn't any worse than a number I've served under. He was a fair man, Lorco, reasoned in his judgments and quite likeable for a military commander. But he was sloppy. Lax. And that was reflected in his command. That's the reason we got jumped in our little hunting party. Duke Lorco never worried too much about sending out scouts or outriders, so neither did his people. Mind you, he never really needed to, until the very end when he *did* need to, and by then it was too late to change old habits. It cost him dearly. Us, too."

Ursus snorted and spat. "I made my report to the appropriate authorities when I got back and everybody listened very carefully and made appreciative noises, but I could tell nobody really cared, one way or the other. Lorco had been gone for six months and more by then and his replacement was well settled in and quite happy with his situation.

"Still, appearances had to be preserved, and so they sent me out again, at the head of a search party of a hundred troopers, to retrace our route one more time and make every effort to discover what had happened to the Duke and his party.

"Of course it was futile, but I knew that going in and so I didn't exactly rupture myself searching under every stone. The invading troops, whoever they might have been, were long vanished by the time we got back, and so we were able to travel quickly, but we asked questions at every stage along the way and we learned absolutely nothing. Didn't even find a single soul who remembered seeing them south of the point where we lost them. We found a few who could remember the party heading north, but nobody, anywhere, saw them coming back until we reached the points north of where the Duke and his people vanished. The people up there remembered seeing him coming and going, but that was when we were still with him.

"It took us a month, but by the end of that time we had established that the Duke had vanished and would not be coming home again."

"So what did you do then, once you were sure of that?"

Ursus picked up his bowl again and scooped some wood ash into it, after which he began to scour it with a cloth from his belt. "We moved on, up to Treves and the military headquarters there. Lorco had been expected to return there some time earlier. I had to tell them what had happened and that the Duke would not be coming back. We stayed in Treves for a time, but no more than a few weeks, since we didn't belong to any unit there, and then we headed back south for Carcasso, where we disbanded. None of us felt very uplifted by what we had failed to achieve, I can tell you, but I was the only one of us after that without an employer. With Lorco officially dead, I had no real paymaster and I detested the pipsqueak who had taken over Lorco's position.

"I hired myself out eventually to another commander, since a man has to eat, but I was bored with the life and bored with the work, policing taverns and throwing drunks who might have been me into the cells beneath the civic center. That's no fit work for a soldier."

He grinned his white-toothed, wolfish grin. "So I decided to move on, in search of greener pastures, and here I am. I was mere miles away, heading north again, and decided on the merest whim to veer west and see what you've been up to, so now it's your turn." He leaned back and made himself more comfortable, crossing his ankles and clasping his hands behind his head, his smile still in place. "Speak to me, boy!"

Overjoyed to see him sitting across from me again, for I had honestly believed his friendship gone from my life forever, I told him all about the momentous things that had happened since he and I had parted months earlier. He had heard nothing about Gunthar's War since leaving Benwick, and I found that close to unbelievable at first, although when I thought about it afterwards, in the context of the times in which we were then living, it became less so. From a distance of surprisingly few miles away, the upheaval of Gunthar's War appeared to be little more than a messy family squabble.

That he had heard nothing about our little war, however, also meant that Ursus had heard nothing of the death of my cousin Samson or of the ascension of Brach to the King's chair. I told him about those things first, and then went on to describe as much as I could remember of the conduct of the war, surprising myself more than him by the paucity of detail I was able to recall. Only after that, and having answered all his questions, did I permit myself to move on to talk about my own thoughts and deliberations since the war had ended. Once launched on that topic, however, I went into great detail about all that I had considered and about my decision to avenge the murder of my parents and my grandfather, and to reclaim my father's kingdom from the usurper Clodas.

When I finally ran out of words, Ursus sat silent, staring into the distance. I wanted to speak his name, to ask him what he thought and if he would come with me to help me claim my birthright, but I had sufficient wit to know that he would speak when he was ready and not until then, and that if I spoke to him too soon I might interrupt his train of thought and defeat my own wishes. And so I held myself in peace, with great effort.

"All this thinking you've been doing," he said eventually. "Where does Germanus enter into it?"

I blinked at him. "Germanus?"

"Aye, Germanus. You remember him, don't you? He's a bishop, up in Auxerre, to the north."

I felt my face reddening, not merely at his sarcastic tone but in instant recognition of my own stupidity. But Ursus had not finished.

"Auxerre is far closer to where you wish to be than Benwick is. It's almost within spitting distance of Ganis. It is certainly within attack range. So Germanus will probably be more able to help you gain your ends than Brach is. Brach has promised to lend you men to help you win back your kingdom, and I don't doubt he will, but how many men can he afford to send out now, in view of the losses he has sustained? Germanus has the reputation of a warrior, even though he is a saintly bishop nowadays. His blessing upon your expedition would bring out followers in their hundreds. I would be prepared to wager on that. So, if Germanus blesses you with his support, then he will probably also be willing to make arrangements that would enable Brach to reinforce you by sea, say from Massilia to Lutetia, navigating upriver from the western coast. I'd venture to say that would be a more attractive prospect to Brach than sending his horsemen off on an overland expedition that could weaken his home defenses for months on end. Don't forget, Brach knows how easily Duke Lorco disappeared with all his men."

I nodded, albeit unwillingly, and mulled over his words for a while before looking at him again. "What should I do, then?"

He shrugged. "Decide on nothing until you've met with Germanus. He'll know what you should do and he'll have no difficulty explaining it to you. Leave word with Brach that you'll send word to him with one of Germanus's priests about your future plans. You're almost seventeen, Clothar, not forty-seven, so you should have plenty of time to plan correctly and plan carefully. No need to go charging off to meet your destiny before you catch your breath."

And so it was that I bade farewell to my family and friends easily and in good faith and once again set out to travel north to the ancient town of Auxerre and the Bishop's School that waited there.

BOOK THREE

Holy Men and Sorcerers

BISHOP GERMANUS

1

As we approached the walls of the bishop's town of Auxerre, Ursus remarked on how peaceful it was, but I could hear the ingrained skepticism in his voice even as he said the words. One of the first lessons a mercenary ever learns, he had told me long before, is that outward semblances of peacefulness hold no guarantees of harmony or tranquility. An arrow can strike you just as dead, just as quickly, from an idyllic setting of calm as it can amid the seething anthill of a battlefield.

It was an afternoon in the middle of an autumn that had not yet stopped being summer, and the trees in central Gaul had barely begun to yellow. We were riding slowly, enjoying the heat of the late-afternoon sunshine and feeling no great need to cause ourselves discomfort by hurrying unduly. Ahead of us the western and southern walls of the town that was our destination crested the shoulders of a high hill and met on the summit, their junction fortified by the defensive thrust of a square guard tower. Ursus reined his horse in tightly.

"You know," he said, sounding intensely frustrated, "that tower is about as useless as nipples on a bull." He glared over at me as if expecting me to argue with him. "I mean, if I've ever seen a more stupid, witless place to build a defensive tower, I don't know where it was. Who would ever mount an attack up there, I ask you? No matter what side you attack from, you would have to carry every bit of gear, every ladder, every heavy weapon up there with you, and

435

once you're up there, you'd still be looking up at the tower, inviting them to throw things down at you."

I was grinning at him, knowing he was nowhere close to being as angry as he was pretending to be. "That's true," I said. "But then, if they hadn't built that tower up there, there would be nothing to prevent an enemy from climbing up the hill and scaling those walls, perhaps even while another attack was happening lower down. That would—"

"Shsst!" He held up his palm to silence me. "Listen. What's that?"

I had heard something, too. I cocked my head to the south, listening intently, and heard it again—the distant but unmistakable clack and clatter of wooden training swords. "Someone's fighting, over there."

Ursus had already spurred his mount and I followed him, angling down the slight slope and to his right in order to catch up with him, and together, knee to knee, we rounded the base of the hillside and galloped into a shallow valley. I realized immediately what was going on and waved Ursus down as I reined my horse in gently, slowing him to a canter.

"It's my old teacher," I told Ursus. "Tiberias Cato. That's him, up there on the hillock, supervising sword training. On days like this he often brings his classes out here, away from the school and from the town. I used to love it when he brought us here. It always felt as though we had escaped for the afternoon."

As we drew nearer to where Cato stood on the summit of his tiny knoll, I counted twelve boys gathered around him, all of them now listening intently to what he was saying and ignoring our approach completely, which was purely unnatural. The sight of it made me smile, remembering that even on those few occasions when whatever Cato had to say was boring, you never dared to show that you were less than enthralled by what he was telling you and you never, ever looked away in search of diversion . . . not if you wished your life to continue being bearable.

But then, when we were perhaps a hundred paces distant, Cato himself turned his head to peer at us, then turned back to his class and continued speaking. Moments later, the boys all came to attention and saluted, then in unison began to walk back towards the town gates, traveling in pairs and walking unhurriedly and with dignity as befitted representatives of Bishop Germanus and his associates. Tiberias Cato watched us pull our horses to a halt in front of him.

"Clothar," he said. "You finally return. Be welcome." His eyes moved to Ursus, sweeping him from head to toe. "And you are?"

"Magister," I interposed, "this is my friend Perceval, known as Ursus, which is a shortened form of Ursus the Bear-killer. Ursus, this is the teacher of whom you have heard me speak so often, Magister Tiberias Cato."

Ursus shot me a quizzical look, doubtless because of my use of his real name, then looked down and nodded graciously to Cato. "Master Cato," he murmured, "I feel as though I know you well already, simply from what I have learned of your teachings."

"My thanks to you, Master Perceval, for your courtesy." Cato threw me a sidewise glance, on the point of making some biting comment, I was sure, but he bit it back and invited us to dismount and walk with him. As I slid to the ground, I saw how his eyes flicked to the hilt of the sheathed spatha by my side. I brought myself to attention and unclipped the sword from the ring at my belt, and held it out to him, wordlessly. He took it from me with both hands, the fingers of his right hand fitting around the hilt with the ease of long usage, then drew the blade halfway from its sheath, bringing it up close to his eyes to inspect the edge. Finally he pushed the blade home and looked at me.

"I thought this had been lost long since, with Phillipus Lorco . . . and you, too, for a long time. How came you by it?"

Quickly, I told him of the trap that had been sprung on us, describing how I had seen my friend Lorco die, and went on to relate how I had met Ursus and returned with him to the killing ground, where we had found Lorco's horse with the spatha still hanging from its saddle. "So now it is my pleasure to return it to you, Magister."

His eyes widened and he thrust the weapon back into my hands. "Return nothing. The sword is yours. It should have been so all along, and I intended it to be so from the outset, but your foolery with young Lorco lost it to you for a few days." He tilted his head slightly to one side, appraising me carefully. "You have aged, boy. You have grown up and changed—for the better, I hope. Does the prospect of fighting and warfare still excite you as it used to?"

I saw no benefit in lying to him, and I shook my head gently. "No, Magister," I said quietly. "That admiration and the yearning for such things wither quickly when men begin to die around you. I have no urge in me now to fight or go to war again, nor do I think I ever will have such a need again. But if war comes to me"—I shrugged my shoulders—"why then I'll face it and I'll deal with it. My thanks to you, Magister, on that score, even although they are belated."

He blinked, but never removed his gaze from mine. "What do you mean?"

I smiled. "I have lived through a short but brutal war since last I saw you, Magister Cato, and it was not the Burgundian invasion everyone here was so perturbed about. Our war was fought in Benwick, after the death of my uncle Ban, the King there. I remember you warning us years ago to beware of becoming involved in civil war, where brother fights brother and everyone is hurt. Well, ours was a civil war over a kingship, waged between brothers, and several times during it I escaped with both my life and my hide intact purely through relying on the many lessons I had learned from you. And for that, for those, I thank you now."

"Hmm. You always were an attentive student." He turned his eyes to Ursus. "Did you fight with Clothar in this war, Master Perceval?"

To my great surprise, Ursus flushed crimson. "No, sir," he said, "I did not. I left to return to my base in Carcasso before the war in Benwick really broke out."

"Ursus had no reason to remain in Benwick, Magister." Both men turned to look at me, and I felt myself flushing as deeply as

Ursus had. "He had no reason to be there at all," I added, lamely, "other than to deliver me to my family, a task he took upon himself when Duke Lorco and his party vanished." I looked from one to the other of them and grinned, feeling unaccountably better. "I must have been very young, in those days, to have appeared to be in need of an escort. That was all of seven months ago."

Wasting no words, I then told my teacher the story of the war, and how it had ended suddenly with Gunthar's being struck down by an apoplexy in the course of a fit of rage. "Clement, Queen Vivienne's physician, thinks the apoplexy that killed him was the cause of his madness, rather than the other way around," I added, seeing their uncomprehending expressions. "Clement believed Gunthar's worsening behavior might have been caused from the very beginning by some kind of . . . some kind of alien *thing* growing inside his head." I was fully aware of how stupid that statement had sounded, but Tiberias Cato did not scoff.

"A tumor," he said.

"Aye, that was the word! That's what Clement called it. A tumor. He said it is a hidden, malignant growth that can develop slowly over years, occupying more and more room within a man's head, and then suddenly explode and kill him. And as it grows, he says, it deprives its host—for the man in whom it grows hosts it as surely as an oak tree hosts a mistletoe—of life and strength and sanity. You knew the word, Magister. Have you heard of such a thing before?"

"Aye, Clothar, that I have. I had a friend who died of it, long years ago in the army. It is not a pleasant way to die."

"Did your friend go insane?"

"Not in the way you mean, I think, but by the time he died he was no longer the friend I had known for so long. It altered him beyond recognition, not merely physically, although it did that, too, but mentally—intellectually. The military surgeons were helpless— they knew what it was but they couldn't cut into it without killing him. By the time the final stages hit him, he had been sick for three months, growing worse every day until it eventually killed him." He broke off and spun to look up at me. "Have you spoken to the bishop yet?"

"No, I haven't even seen him yet. We're just on our way in now. We have been traveling for weeks."

Cato frowned. "Then you'd better go directly to his quarters. He'll want to see you without delay."

"Why, Magister?"

"Because he has been waiting for you for more than a month to this point, that's why! And he leaves tomorrow for Italia, on Church business. He is required to be there long before the solstice and he will not return here for at least two months after that, in the early spring. And he has a mission for you to carry out that will not wait until he returns." He waved a hand at me, dismissing me. "Mount. Mount up and ride, you have no time to waste and neither does the bishop. Go directly to his chambers. Hurry! Master Perceval here will walk with me and keep me company on the road back into town and I will see him safely quartered as a guest of the school. Leave your saddlebags and bedding roll with us. Off with you now. We will talk again tomorrow, you and I."

2

Germanus was meeting with several of his senior colleagues when I arrived in his quarters, and the junior cleric who sat on guard before the door to the episcopal chambers was a newcomer whom I did not recognize. He did not know me, either, but I had no trouble seeing that he disapproved of my dusty, road-soiled appearance from the moment he first set eyes on me. He sucked in his prudish little mouth and informed me primly and not quite discourteously that the Lord Bishop was in council and not to be disturbed under any circumstances. I nodded and returned the fellow's disdainful look measure for measure. He was perhaps two years older than me, and every aspect of his appearance befitted the description "cleric."

He was pallid, soft looking and stoop shouldered, his mouth turned down at the edges and his eyes creased with wrinkles from squinting in bad light, trying to decipher manuscripts written by others as insipid as himself.

I turned my back on him as though to leave, but then unhooked the spatha from my side and spun around, dropping the sheathed sword on the table in front of him so that he reared back and raised his hands to fend off a blow.

"I am not threatening you with it, man, I'm offering you an opportunity to save your hide and soothe my ruffled pinions at the same time. Now listen to me carefully. Whether you believe it or not, Bishop Germanus will want to see me. You say he is not to be disturbed. Very well. I am not asking you to disturb him. I merely want you to walk into his chambers, to where he can see you, and to stand there, holding that sword in such a way that he can see it. There is no need for you to speak, no need for you to interrupt him, no need for you to do anything except stand where he can see you and what you are holding. Can you understand that?" He could.

"Now, let us examine the alternative, should you refuse to do as I ask. The bishop, I have been told by Tiberias Cato, has been waiting for me to arrive here for more than a month, although I did not know that. In consequence, I could not expect you to know that, either, so I will not complain about you. But I promise you Bishop Germanus will not be happy to know that you refused to announce me."

The man was instantly on his feet, clutching the sheathed sword in a white-knuckled grip and backing away from me as though I might be rabid and about to leap at him. He released one hand from its death grip and fumbled behind him for the door handle, keeping his eyes on me as he backed through the doorway and closed it, shutting me out.

Within moments the door was flung open again and Germanus himself stood in the opening.

"You came," he said, and stepped towards me, opening his arms to embrace me, and as I returned his embrace, feeling the strength of his old arms hugging me to his bosom, I was struck, despite the vigor of his hug, by the extent to which he had aged since last we met. He was clean shaven and smooth cheeked again, after several years of going bearded, and his mane of hair was snowy white, but still thick and healthy. He held me at arm's length and scanned me with his eyes, his gaze moving slowly, meticulously, over my face and body.

"Older," he said. "And stronger, more vigorous and, aye, wiser, more learned. You are become a warrior, my son, not merely a man." He sighed a great, gusty breath, and smiled. "But then, we expected no less, those of us who know you. Come inside, come in. You and I have much to discuss and little time in which to do it, but your timing could really not be better. My conference with my brethren is almost complete, only a few remaining tasks to delegate for the term of my absence, and then I will be free of my parochial responsibilities until I return from Italia, which means I may have the rare treat of spending an evening at my own pleasure tonight. If you will please me by waiting—in here, I mean, in my chambers, not outside—I shall conclude my affairs and dismiss my brethren, and then you and I will eat and drink a cup of watered wine together. Will you do that for me?"

"Aye, Father," I answered, smiling, "I will, and most particularly if the wine be well and truly watered, for I still mislike its being too strong."

"Then you shall have water. Come inside."

As we entered, the bishop's arm around my shoulders, the officious cleric passed us on his way out, his eyes wide now and his mouth hanging open. Germanus stopped the fellow, then extended his palm for the sword the cleric still clutched. The young priest handed the spatha over, his face paler than before, and Germanus passed it to me without comment. I clipped it into place on the ring in my belt and winked at the cleric, who started in surprise and scuttled away.

We dined together that night, as Germanus wished. The meal was delicious, a simple affair of a roasted hare, served with lightly boiled turnips and some kind of kale, both of them drenched in fresh-churned butter, and fresh-baked unleavened bread that had been liberally salted in the preparation. I eschewed the wine and drank water, but Germanus drank his lightly watered wine with great relish.

Throughout the meal we spoke only of pleasant things, most of them family related. As usual, however, I ended up saying much more than I had intended to, and by the time we finished eating, the good bishop had drained me dry of every last vestige of information I could supply about my lost love, the beautiful Rosalyn. I do not know how I ever came to mention her in the first place, but I do know that I sat down to dine expecting to be asked about such things and determined to say nothing that might lead towards her. I had absolutely no intention of revealing anything about her, or the pain she had caused me. But I had reckoned, of course, without the bishop's gentle, irresistible persuasiveness. It may have been something I said, or equally likely failed to say, that alerted him. I may have hesitated at the wrong point in response to a question. Who can tell? Whatever it was that I did or said, or did not do or say, Germanus was onto the scent like a hound on the trail of a fox, and all my resolve melted like snow in a warm wind. I told him all about Rosalyn and how she had left me, brushing aside the fact that she had had no choice but to leave when her family did. I should have known, however, that I would find little sympathy for my bruised feelings from my Confessor.

I knew that many of the religious brethren had begun decades earlier to distrust and avoid women, increasingly regarding them as vessels of sin; temptations made flesh in order to seduce men away from God. Father Germanus would have none of that, however, and for the simplest and most lucid of reasons: God, he believed and taught, is omnipotent and omniscient and therefore incapable of creating anything less than perfect. He had created woman to be man's helpmeet and companion, equal in most things and unparalleled in one all-important respect: the continuity of mankind itself is the prime responsibility of woman; man's participation in the process is at best incidental and all too frequently accidental.

Without God's gift of woman to share his world, man could not even exist. How then, Germanus asked, could any thinking person allege that women were creatures of evil? The mere suggestion was blasphemous and impious, since it implied that God Himself, the Creator, must be less than perfect. This was a perennial concern for Germanus, inspired by what he perceived to be a collective human weakness—the tendency, amounting almost to a willingness, to demean and offend the Deity by indulging in casual, unthinking blasphemy.

He wanted me to understand the special nature of women, and he was determined that I should treat all women, regardless of birth and position, with courtesy, respect and consideration of their God-given dignity.

He himself had been married for years, he told me, to a wonderful woman who had brought him great happiness simply by sharing his life wholeheartedly, and although she had died while still very young and they had never known the pleasure of parenthood, he yet thought of her, years after her death, as the greatest blessing a bountiful God had bestowed on him. Without the benisons of her friendship and her physical love, he said, he could never have advanced to be the man he had become. She it was, Germanus said, who had awakened in him the confidence and self-assuredness to throw himself completely into any new endeavor he was moved to undertake, and to do so with complete conviction that he could achieve whatever he wished to achieve.

Someday, Germanus assured me, I would find a woman created and designed by God Himself purely to be my helpmeet and my soul mate. I might not meet her soon, he warned, and I might meet others in the meantime whom I liked, admired and even enjoyed, but when I found the one God had made for me, I would know it beyond dispute. As for the others I might meet in the interim, he told me, I should remember that every human being born had a mate somewhere and so I should treat all women with the respect and dignity I would expect to be shown by others to my spouse.

My difficulties with Rosalyn seemed to amuse and intrigue the bishop; he was highly curious about how I could be so bold and daring in combat yet so utterly craven when it came to speaking to a young woman. Looking back on it later, it seemed to me that his interest sprang simply from the fact that I had been vulnerable enough to love, and to love so hopelessly and inadequately.

Much as I appreciated the bishop's amused concern with my amorous misadventures, I was no closer, after our long meal, to knowing what work he had in mind for me, and the mounting frustration of being ignorant about what role I had to play reminded me of a conversation I had had with him more than a year before, when I had approached him after a long period of soul-searching, prayer and meditation.

I had sought him out directly after matins, and he had stopped immediately upon seeing me waiting for him by the side of the path in the predawn dimness. His face had creased in curiosity and concern plainly caused by what he perceived in the very way I was standing, and he had broken away from his brethren to come directly to me.

"Clothar, what ails you?"

"Nothing, Father," I answered. "I merely wished to speak with you, to ask you something."

"It must be important, I can see that from your face." He looked up to where his secretary Ludovic stood waiting for him, and waved the man away gently. "Come," he said to me. "Walk with me and tell me what is troubling you."

In truth, nothing was troubling me at that time. My intent was merely to solicit his blessing upon what I had decided, only the previous night and after months of thinking about it, to do with my life. Bishop Germanus was my hero, and for good reason: his life had been heroic in every respect. He had excelled in every task to which he had set himself and had never known mediocrity or compromise. Living in the school he had created and in the atmosphere that surrounded him, seeing how even the most mundane details of his everyday life inspired and uplifted his companions and his brethren, I had come to admire him so much that I could think of no better way to honor him than by trying to be like him in every respect, voluntarily following in his footsteps and dedicating my life to the glory and service of God by undertaking the triple oath, as he himself had, of poverty, chastity and obedience. And so, with those thoughts in my mind and content to remain silent while I ordered my galloping ideas, I walked beside him through the gathering dawn as he led me back to his day room, where he seated himself across from me, folded his hands in his lap and waited for me to say what I had to say.

I cleared my throat. "I have been thinking, Father, that I would like to join the Church and become a bishop, like you."

My mentor recoiled as though I had tried to slap him, his eyes flaring in incredulity. He recovered himself immediately, and attempted—unsuccessfully—to turn his astonishment into a sneeze, but I felt my face flush with the shame of his disapproval.

"You think me unfit," I said, stricken, feeling my throat swell up to choke my words.

"What?" His face betrayed utter confusion, and even in the pain of his rejection of me I was aware that I had never seen Bishop Germanus so completely at a loss for either words or understanding. And then all at once his face cleared and he was on his feet, gazing down at me. "Unfit?" he said. "What is this about unfit? In all the things I have ever thought about you, Clothar, son of Childebertus, the word *unfit* has never entered my mind. There is nothing—you hear me, lad?—*nothing* for which I would consider you unfit. Look at me."

He reached out and grasped me by the upper arms, holding me tightly, almost painfully, and forcing me to meet his eyes. When I did eventually look at him, I saw his look soften, and he shook his head, making a soft sound that might have been one of regret.

"As God is my witness," he said, "there are few things easier to do in life than to cause pain and grief unwittingly simply by being human." He drew himself erect and heaved a great, deep sigh, expelling it forcefully so that his shoulders slumped again with the release of it.

"Clothar, Clothar, Clothar, what can I tell you? The last thing I ever expected to hear from you was the very thing you just said to me. It had never occurred to me that you might want to join the Church. And you misread my reaction. Misread it completely. Certainly, I was shocked, but it had nothing whatsoever to do with your *fitness* to do or to become whatever you decide to do or to become. It had everything to do, on the other hand, with me and with what I had planned for you, and with what I had decided was to be your role in life, for the next few years, at least."

For the next quarter of an hour, Bishop Germanus led me on a tour of the main residence of the school, where the teachers and lay brethren and others lived and worked. He took me into every room where people were working and praying, and pointed mutely to whatever the people there were doing, bidding me tacitly to pay attention to what I was being shown. I obeyed, but grew more and more confused as we went from room to room in silence until at length we returned to his day room and he crossed to the window, where he stood gazing out into the early-morning bustle of the square enclosure inside the main gates. I stood patiently, waiting for him to speak again.

"Come over here."

I crossed to where he stood and followed his pointing finger to where two of the brethren were manhandling a cart loaded with straw through the main gates.

"They are working for the glory of God," he said, and glanced at me sidewise. "Do you take my point?"

"No, Father . . ."

"Hmm. What do you think I was showing you in that little tour we took?"

I made no attempt to hide my mystification. "I don't know, Father."

"Work, Clothar," he said. "I was showing you work, in the kitchens and the laundry rooms, in the classrooms and the library, and in the stables and the granaries. Work. All of it dedicated to the greater glory of God, and all of it performed by kindly, dedicated souls who are doing their best to fulfill the talents, skills and abilities given to them by that same God." He stopped again, interpreting my continuing confusion correctly.

"The point I must make here, Clothar, will sound uncharitable and perhaps unkind, but it is most certainly valid and accurate. The people performing all those tasks, doing all that work, are, for the most part, incapable of doing anything better or more demanding. To greater or lesser degrees, in the words of Holy Scripture, they are all hewers of wood and drawers of water. Were they capable of doing greater things, performing larger tasks, they would be about them already. But there are some tasks that require men of singular and outstanding abilities"—he looked directly into my eyes—"and there are some men born to achieve and to carry out singular and outstanding tasks."

He turned away from the window and went to his work table, eyeing the pile of documents awaiting his attention and talking over his shoulder to me as I followed him. "I believe, Clothar, that it would be a waste of your time and your God-gifted abilities were you to shut yourself away from the world now and immure yourself as a mere cleric. You might turn out to be a divinely gifted cleric, but not at this stage of your life. Look at me. I am supposed to be a fine bishop, according to my superiors, but as a bishop I am nonetheless very much the man whose life I lived for all those years before I was drawn to the Church." He glanced sideways at me. "Do you know how I came to be a bishop?"

"Not really, Father."

"Hmm. Would you like to hear the tale? It is not long in the telling." I nodded, and he continued. "Well, as you know, I had been in the armies for many years, serving Honorius, who was both my Emperor and my friend, and when the war I had been fighting on his behalf came to an end, he permitted me to return here to Auxerre, which had always been my family's home. Now, as it happened, the bishop in Auxerre when I came home was an elderly and much revered cleric and teacher named Amator. I remembered him well, for he had been my teacher when I was a boy, before I left to study the law in Rome, and he and I had locked horns on several occasions even then, for I was no one's idea of a perfect student." The bishop smiled to himself.

"Anyway, when I came home as the conquering hero of the wars, Bishop Amator was . . . unimpressed . . . that is as good a description as any, I suppose, and shortly afterwards I discovered that he held what I considered at that time to be peculiar ideas about certain things, the foremost among which was hunting. Amator could not accept the idea that animals might be hunted for the sheer pleasure of the hunt. He had come to believe, somehow, that animals had souls just like people; souls of a different order, certainly, but souls nonetheless, and he felt it was a flouting of God's love to hunt them and kill them without pressing need.

"Well, that set the two of us directly upon a collision course, for I had always been a hunter, loving the thrill of the chase and the challenge of the hunt itself. When I came home from the wars, I hunted on my own lands as I always had, relishing the wealth of game that had proliferated since I left, decades earlier. Bishop Amator, may God rest his soul, was incensed, and he condemned me publicly for setting a bad example to my people. And I am sad to report that, in my pride, I ignored him completely and kept on hunting, caring nothing for his disapproval."

Germanus pursed his lips. "But then everything changed, almost overnight. Bishop Amator had a dream in which God appeared to him and told him he was going to die very soon, and that he must quickly prepare *me,* the biggest thorn in his side, to succeed him as Bishop of Auxerre." He looked at me keenly. "Do you ever have dreams, Clothar?"

"Yes, Father, I do."

"And do you remember them clearly, once you wake up?"

Did I? I had to think about that for several moments before shaking my head slowly and with more than a little doubt. "Sometimes I think I do, just after I awaken, but then when I try to remember exactly what I dreamed, it all breaks apart and most of what I can recall makes no sense at all."

The bishop nodded, a half smile tugging at his lips. "That's the way it is with most people. Dreams seldom make sense in the light of day.

"But the dream Bishop Amator had was different. He recalled it in perfect detail when he awoke, and that made him think very seriously about what it meant. He prayed for guidance for days before he finally accepted that the guidance had already been delivered in his dream, and then, having accepted that, he had to act quickly, for he believed that he would die soon but did not know when.

"He said nothing to me, naturally enough, for even although he believed the guidance he had received in his dream was genuine and sprang from God Himself, he knew, too, that I was less than reverent, to say the least. In my younger days I was intolerant and could be highly obnoxious whenever anyone crossed me, and Amator and I were already enemies. Then, too, Amator had to consider that although I had retired from active duty, I was yet a soldier of Rome— a condition that never lapses—and therefore I still owed my complete loyalty, by oath, to the Emperor and the Empire, should they have need of me. That was an extremely important consideration, for it meant that Amator could not simply approach me, even had I been willing, and appoint me to the priesthood as his successor, because there were conflicting vows involved. Before I could be free to take my vows in God's service—as I must, to be a bishop—I would have to be freely released from my existing vows to the Emperor."

"Did Bishop Amator travel then to Rome?"

Germanus loosed a single bark of laughter. "No, he was far cleverer than that. He approached the prefect of Gaul, the Emperor's personal representative and chief magistrate in Gaul, and requested formal permission to absolve the Legate Germanus of his existing vows and responsibilities in order to induct him, as a retired and manumitted soldier, into the ranks of the clergy. The prefect must have been soundly astonished, for he and I had known each other well for many years and I am sure he must have laughed himself to sleep many a night, thinking of me as a humble cleric. In any event, he made no attempt to dissuade the bishop from his designs and gave his approval immediately, and only then was Bishop Amator at liberty to approach me directly."

"And how did he do it? Were you angry that he had done what he had?"

Germanus smiled and shook his head. "No, not at all. He was very careful in how he went about his task of recruiting me. He said nothing until he considered the conditions to be perfect, and he took great care to prearrange their perfection. Then, when I was present among a large gathering of Christians called to celebrate the resurrection of the Lord Jesus, he made his move, announcing to all present that he had had a vision of the Lord, and then went on to tell about his dream and the message it had contained—that I, the Legate Germanus, had been chosen by God himself to succeed him—and that in the light of that revelation the prefect of Gaul had personally absolved me of my vows to the Emperor and the Empire."

Germanus was grinning as he recalled the occasion. "There are times when a surprise is so great that the very word is inadequate. I was stunned by what Amator had told the people, and by what he had done . . . by how far he had taken the matter already, without my knowing anything about it. I was speechless and close to reeling and falling down in my confusion. And yet no one else seemed to be surprised, or outraged or upset. What the bishop had disclosed took everyone by surprise, but the old man was revered by his flock, and he had been bishop in Auxerre for many years, so no one thought to doubt his word. If God were going to communicate in person with anyone in Gaul, Amator would have been the one everyone expected Him to visit, so no one was surprised that it had come to pass.

"Amator told me himself, after everything was settled, that he had been the one most perturbed about the possible effects of his announcement. He considered me to be a hard man, which I suppose I was, and despite his own belief in the divine nature of his message, he expected me to storm off in a fury over his presumptuousness. After all, I had been accustomed to the autonomy of high command and to being answerable to no one but the Emperor himself. How then, he asked himself, would I respond to being manipulated—that was his word—by a mere bishop? He had brought a set of new vestments to the gathering with him, in the hope that I might be induced to take them away with me, and perhaps to think about what would be involved in wearing them, but in truth he had not really expected to succeed in recruiting me immediately or easily."

"But that was not what happened . . ."

"No, it did happen. I left the gathering immediately, as Amator expected, but whereas Amator thought my face was white with fury, it was in truth white with nausea. I was frightened to the point of vomiting. But I did not leave the premises. I merely sought privacy in a nearby building, where I spent several hours thinking and praying for guidance. The guidance materialized, and I returned to Bishop Amator, where I knelt and bowed my head, accepting what I had heard, in the belief and fear that to resist the summons would be to oppose the will of God. I bared my head, then and there, and the bishop shaved my pate to baldness in the tonsure of the Church. And that was that. From being an arrogant, victorious, hunting imperial legate, I had gone to being an impoverished, landless bishop in the space of one afternoon."

I knew I was gaping at him as I sought to absorb that last statement, and he nodded his head, acknowledging my bafflement.

"Mind you," he said, "the transformation was not that sudden. Nothing about me changed noticeably that day, nor for some time afterwards, but profound changes had occurred within me then and there, nonetheless." He paused, then smiled briefly. "I never hunted again, for one thing, and that, in the eyes of many people, was a change large enough to defy belief.

"And I began to pray as I had never prayed before, gaining strength daily as I indulged my newfound belief in God's existence and His goodness. I swore three powerful vows, too, to live from that time on in poverty, chastity and obedience to my superiors within the Church. The latter two oaths caused me little difficulty, since chastity had been a way of life since the death of my wife, years earlier, and obedience to my superiors had been ingrained during my years as a lawyer and then as a soldier. Only the vow of poverty contained any threat of difficulty, since from birth I had been enormously wealthy. But then I considered that I had no family left to whom I could give my wealth—I am literally the last of my line—and I discovered that the mere possession of riches meant less than nothing to me. And so I donated everything I owned to the Church—lands, buildings, chattels, goods and my entire treasury of bullion, jewels, coins and other specie. I rid myself of everything." He glanced at me. "Believe me, Clothar, it was no sacrifice at all. In giving all I had to the Church, I acquired more than I could ever need."

I sat gazing at him as he, in turn, sat gazing into the middle distance. Soon after he had become a bishop, I knew, people had begun to whisper that he had the power of miracles. There was one story of him casting out a devil from a young man that had always seemed truly miraculous to me—if, in fact, it occurred. I wanted to believe that it had, but by the age of sixteen I had long since learned that men were inclined to say more than their prayers before they went to bed at night, and most particularly so when they were passing along hearsay that had impressed them and that they wanted to make even more impressive in their turn. The event in question had been a public exorcism, apparently, witnessed by many people who all swore that Germanus, before he cast the demon out, forced it to disclose the hiding place of a sum of stolen money. True or not, the tale had brought the bishop great fame throughout northern Gaul, and people traveled to Auxerre from all around nowadays, hoping to have the holy bishop cure their afflictions, much to the holy man's discomfiture.

I suddenly realized that he had returned to the present and was watching me watching him, and I sat up straight, clearing my throat in embarrassment. Germanus, however, appeared not to notice.

"So," he said, "Clothar, son of Childebertus, have you understood what I was saying?"

I felt a sudden knot of apprehension in my throat. "I . . . I think so, Father."

"I hope so, my young friend, but I will not test you on it. Instead I will summarize it for you, making it as plain as is possible. Serve God, by every means at your disposal, Clothar, but do it properly, in freedom, while you gather the experience you will need should He call upon you to undertake one of His special tasks. How do I do that? you ask yourself."

He smiled again. "Well, look at me. Consider if I had entered the Church when I was your age. Without the experience of love and marriage and the anguished loss of both, I could never have understood the pain that ordinary people feel on the loss of a spouse or a child. Without my years spent studying the imperial law, I could never have served the Church as assiduously as I have been able to through my understanding of legal issues and the basic workings of fundamental justice. And perhaps most important of all, without the years I spent in military service, exercising and coming to understand the principles of command and command structure, I could never have assumed the position that I hold now as Bishop of Auxerre, responsible for all the people who are in my charge today.

"You have greatness within you, Clothar, and nobility, and God Himself has a design for you to live by. But in order to achieve God's will, I believe you must stay free. Plenty of time to return to the fold later, if your destiny sends you towards the Church. And that is enough of that, I think. Time now to talk of other things."

3

By the time we finished eating it had grown dark outside, and one of the bishop's brethren came in to replenish the fire in the brazier that took up most of the enormous grate. Germanus had always shown a tendency to be cold, even on warm days, and he liked to say it came from having spent far too many years in the warmer countries of the Empire, including Rome itself and Constantinople, to be truly comfortable in the cooler, more temperate climes of his homeland. Now that he was growing older and less resilient, he would add, his body was becoming less and less equipped to deal with chill temperatures and damp, nasty drafts.

When we had finished eating, we made ourselves comfortable in two large upholstered chairs that faced the fire, and Germanus sat staring into the flames for some time without speaking. I of course followed his example, perfectly content to enjoy the unaccustomed warmth of having a fire indoors on a crisp autumn night. The silence was a pleasant one and I felt perfectly at ease, knowing that my mentor would say whatever he wished to say when the time was right. And eventually he did, coming straight to the point without preamble.

"I know I told you before you left for home with Duke Lorco that I had work for you to do, but did I tell you anything of what I meant?"

"No, Father, nothing."

"Hmm." He fell silent again, and I glanced across at him to see whether or not his mouth was pursed in what we students had called the Bishop's Pout, the moue that indicated he was thinking deeply. It was. Presently he stirred again and waved a hand to attract my attention.

"There is fresh, chilled grape juice in the pitcher over there beneath the cloth. Pour some for us, would you?"

When I brought him the cup he nodded in thanks.

"I want to tell you, Clothar, about a friend of mine, a man who lives in Britain. Have you ever heard of the Alleluia Victory?"

Of course I had, I told him. It was legend at the Bishop's School.

Father Germanus, as Bishop of Auxerre, had been sent to Britain to debate the heretical teachings of a British theologian called Pelagius. I had learned about Pelagius from the loathsome Brother Anthony, whose harsh discipline had sent me, and many other boys, to the infirmary. We had learned that the teachings of Pelagius went against the Church in the matter of Divine Grace.

The Church taught that mankind was incapable of achieving salvation without divine intervention on each individual's behalf, in the form of spiritual grace acquired through the sacraments, but Pelagius had proposed the dangerous notion that each individual, made in God's own image, contained within himself a spark of divine consciousness that allowed him to commune directly with God.

Pelagius had argued that the Church's teaching in this matter negated the need for, and the efficacy of, any form of human law. Under the teachings of the Church, when it was reduced to its constituent elements, no man could be condemned for any sin, since he could claim that God had not given him the grace to withstand temptation.

Unfortunately, Pelagius's own teachings, when reduced to their constituent parts, demonstrated that, since each man could speak directly to his God, men therefore had no need of priests or churches. Pelagius had been condemned and his teaching had been declared heresy, but his tenets had appealed strongly to many people, and most particularly so in Britain, where he had amassed a great following after his excommunication and death.

Germanus's role in Britain had been to argue against the heresy in a convocation of British bishops held in the great theater at Verulamium, and on the way there, he and his traveling companions, all of whom were, like himself, Christian clerics unprepared to act as warriors, ran afoul of a band of marauders and would have been killed, had they not been rescued by a contingent of cavalry who happened to be passing through the area at the time on their way to Verulamium. As the horsemen came thundering down to the rescue, the exultant clerics had encouraged them with cries of "Alleluia!" and the tale had grown from one of a simple rescue to a mighty victory over the ungodly.

"Well, the cavalry commander who rescued me that day," Father Germanus said, "was Caius Merlyn Britannicus, from a fortified colony called Camulod, in the west of Britain. He calls himself simply Merlyn of Camulod, and he and I became close friends, even though we had little time to get to know each other. Life works that way, sometimes. Anyway, I saw Merlyn again when I was in Britain several months ago—you may recall that I returned from there just before you left to go home—and he and I resumed our friendship where we had left off. He is a fascinating man, Clothar. Far more so now even than he was when we first met, almost two decades ago. He and I spent much time discussing certain matters of great moment for both him and me, and I made him a promise that I would return within the year to assist him with his plans and to perform a particular service for him." He twisted his face into a grimace. "Alas, the Pope has called upon me to attend a conclave with the senior bishops in Italia, and I am constrained to obey. Unfortunately, that makes it impossible for me to keep my promise to a dear friend, and you can have no idea how deeply that angers and distresses me.

"Merlyn will understand my dilemma when he learns of it, I know, but the thought of merely writing him a letter is offensive to me. That would be too impersonal, and although Merlyn never would think so, I would perceive it as demeaning. And so I decided to ask you if you would be willing to go to Britain and meet with Merlyn on my behalf, to explain why I cannot be there and to carry my suggestions as to what he should do now that I have failed him."

I cleared my throat, and when he looked at me questioningly I asked him if he could tell me about the personal service he was now unable to perform for Merlyn. He nodded.

"I promised him I would officiate at the coronation of his young ward, Arthur. The young man is quite extraordinary. I have never met him in person, but I have been in correspondence with him for a long time, at Merlyn's request, and everything that I have read of his is most impressive. But apart from being scholarly and remarkably self-disciplined in his thinking, he also appears, from all accounts, to be outstandingly responsible in other, equally important areas. If he continues to make the kind of progress he has been achieving in the recent past, then according to Merlyn, and despite his extreme youth—he is a mere two years older than you—he will soon hold overall command of the cavalry forces of Camulod. He is also a devout and dedicated Christian."

There was no hint of condemnation or even accusation in the bishop's voice. "Now, that may cause you and your friends to roll your eyes, I know, but it is of extreme importance to us, within the Church, and I can only ask you to accept my personal assurance on that matter. God's Church in Britain is in great danger at this time, gravely threatened by invading hordes of savage and implacable enemies who are godless and see Christianity as a laughable weakness. The people of Britain, including Merlyn's people of Camulod, refer to the newcomers as Saxon Outlanders, but as such things always are, that name is far too simplistic. It implies that the invaders are of one race and one origin, whereas the truth is nowhere close to that. These so-called Saxons are a mixture of different peoples—Jutes and Anglians, Germanians and Danes, Saxons from the Danube and other, giant, blond-haired people who simply call themselves Northmen. Many of these people—most notably the Anglians—seek only a place to raise their families in peace and free of hunger. Their sole claim to the title of invaders is that they have moved in from beyond the seas, but few of them are fiercely warlike or aggressive. Others among them are, however, and among the most bloodthirsty of those are the real Saxons. Hence the name applied to all of them . . . it is a matter of the basest few earning hatred and fear for all of them.

"It appears, however, that the Saxons have set out to destroy God's Church in Britain, because they recognize it, correctly, as a buttress and a rallying point for the ordinary folk of Britain to come together and withstand the Saxon threat. And so we are receiving reports that within the territories now being held by the invaders, few Christians—bishops, priests or simple faithful—have been left alive.

"The forces of Camulod, properly ranged against the invaders with appropriate backing and the authority of the Church in Britain, could represent the salvation of our Faith. So I have written an episcopal letter to the current bishop of Verulamium, asking him to officiate at the crowning in my stead and to enlist the support of his fellow bishops in the enterprise. That is one of the documents I wish you to take with you when you go."

I nodded my head. "Of course, Father. When would you like me to leave?"

The bishop laughed. "Not tonight, at least," he said, "although I suppose you could, were it necessary. In the hope that you would be willing to do this for me, I have had everything ready for you to take for some time now, since I myself must leave tomorrow, as you know, for Italia. I admit, I was beginning to grow concerned, for both of us, that you might not arrive before I had to leave—but you are here now and nothing is lost. So . . . There is no immediate urgency for you to flee from here but you should not delay unduly, for the autumn gales will soon start stirring up the Narrow Seas between here and Britain, and no sane mariner will embark into the open sea once those begin. If you are tardy and miss the fair weather, you could be stuck on the coast for months on end before you can make a crossing. It happens frequently enough to make the seasoned traveler wary."

"Then I will leave tomorrow."

"Alone?"

There was something in his tone that gave me pause, and I hesitated because I had not even begun to consider what might be involved in this matter. He nodded, his expression grave. "Think about that carefully, Clothar. You may want to find someone to travel with you. I have no doubts of your ability, but you are embarking on a long and potentially harsh journey, filled with unforeseeable dangers, and looking at it purely from the viewpoint of common sense, it would be better not to tackle it alone with no one to watch your back."

"I have a friend who rode here with me. He was with Duke Lorco's party when they came here in the spring and he and I were the only two to survive whatever befell the Duke. He is older than I am, a mercenary and a fine soldier. His name is Perceval and we have become friends. He might be willing to come with me. I'll ask him."

The bishop nodded sagely. "Excellent," he said. "Now let me tell you more of Merlyn and his plans."

For upwards of an hour then, he spoke to me glowingly of his friend Merlyn Britannicus and of Camulod, Merlyn's home, and what it represented. Choosing his words with care, he told me briefly about how two of Merlyn's ancestors, Publius Varrus and Caius Britannicus, had decided to remain in Britain after the departure of the legions and to fend for themselves and their dependants in a self-sufficient colony that they established in their own lands, a colony that had ended up being called Camulod, although the Camulod that they actually built was a stone-walled fortress surrounding an ancient hilltop fort that had existed since before Julius Caesar had landed in Britain four hundred years earlier.

Since its beginnings, the Camulod colony had thrived and expanded, especially after Caius Britannicus became the custodian of hundreds of heavy cavalry mounts abandoned by the armies of the imperial regent Stilicho when they were urgently called home, never to return to Britain. From then on, Camulod had become an equestrian society, and its defenders, who had always been soldiers trained in the Roman tradition, had become heavy cavalry troops, trained in the methods of Alexander of Macedon, whose own cavalry, six hundred years earlier, had conquered the known world and earned their monarch the title of "Great." Camulod's forces were now famed for protecting decency and human dignity within a land where anarchy and chaos had been proliferating now for decades.

Looking me straight in the eye, Germanus told me that Merlyn Britannicus, the third generation of his family to govern in Camulod, was one of the finest men he had ever known, but that he was even more impressive as a visionary. Born of mixed Roman and Cambrian Celtic blood, Merlyn had been taught by Druids for much of his early boyhood, learning the ways of that religion, but he had also been well and thoroughly trained by his Roman guardians in the classical, traditional methods of learning—including reading and writing, which the Druids lacked—and equally exposed to

Christian teachings, so that his education had been far reaching. I found myself unimpressed by that as I listened, but I began to pay much more attention when the bishop moved on to tell me about Merlyn's guardianship of the boy Arthur Pendragon.

This boy was being trained by Merlyn Britannicus not merely to govern Camulod but to govern the entire land of Britain as Riothamus, or High King. Germanus told me that the young man Arthur still had no idea of the destiny Merlyn had in mind for him. The boy believed, rather, that he was merely being raised and trained to be the finest man that he could be.

Any tendency I might have had to scoff at such a high-sounding claim died quickly when I realized that I was in much the same position—not, certainly, in being a king in training, but most definitely in finding myself surrounded at all times by teachers and instructors whom I respected and admired for their integrity, honesty and abilities, and being guided by one towering mentor who was so clearly admirable and incorruptible that the idea of bringing shame or dishonor to him was impossible to think about.

Speaking clearly and explaining his thoughts to me as he went along, Germanus detailed the various things he wanted me to do when I arrived in Merlyn's Camulod. The most obvious of these, and the one requiring least explanation, was the transportation and delivery of a substantial package of letters and documents. Those were for Merlyn's eyes only, and even though the bishop admitted that Merlyn might be one of fewer than a score of non-clerical people in all Britain who still knew how to read—for there had been no schools and no teachers there since the Romans left, four decades earlier—he emphasized the dangers of people perhaps wanting to destroy the missives simply because they could not read and thus felt belittled and insulted. I mulled that point over in silence. It seemed to me that the bishop was exaggerating the danger to the documents.

The second thing he wanted me to deal with was far more in keeping with his wishes as a churchman. In all of Britain, it appeared, there was no permanent ecclesia—no house of God dedicated solely as a place wherein men might worship the Deity. Gaul had many ecclesiae nowadays, and more were proliferating like mushrooms everywhere priests traveled, but they were an innovation that had only come into fashion in recent years. Before the days of Constantine the Great, a hundred years earlier, the Church and its adherents had known much persecution and had met and worshipped in secrecy, but with the conversion of the Emperor himself to Christianity all of that had changed. Now it was not only feasible but desirable for permanent places of worship to be established in populous centers for the greater glory of God. As always, and as in everything, Bishop Germanus thought in terms of God's greater glory.

Germanus wanted Merlyn—and his ward, Arthur—to build a stone church on their own lands, the very first ecclesia in Britain. He had discussed the matter with Merlyn while he was there on the island, but Merlyn had told him that there was no source of suitable stone or rock close to Camulod. He had promised, however, that once his agenda had been fulfilled and he had the leisure to find such a suitable source, he would give serious thought to building a simple edifice of stone that could serve the people of the region as a permanent place of worship. My task was to remind him of that promise.

And then came the most important charge with which I was to be entrusted. Germanus had also asked Merlyn to consider establishing within Britain a new order solemnly dedicated *ad majorem Dei gloriam*—to the greater glory of God. This order need not be religious, nor civil or military. It would be new—something unknown under the sun before now—and its primary purpose would be to glorify God by its very existence. Merlyn, it seemed, had promised to consider that, as well as the ecclesia, and I was to remind him of that promise, too.

"What kind of order did you have in mind, Father?"

Germanus looked at me in silence for a long time, a half smile on his lips, and then he shook his head. "I have no idea, my son." He watched as my consternation and lack of understanding blossomed on my face, and his smile broadened into a grin that was filled with serene confidence. "It is not my place to know such things, Clothar. How could I be equipped to devise such a project? It would be hubris of the worst kind even to think about attempting such a thing. God Himself knows what He requires men to do in His name and to His glory, and when the time comes for something to be done, He will implant the shape and substance of His wish in the mind of someone—perhaps Merlyn, perhaps not—who will then cause it to become reality, and the order will be born. My task, when the idea first occurred to me, was simply to plant the thought in the mind of Merlyn Britannicus, as I am sure I was meant to do. He is facing a life filled with new possibilities, once his new kingdom is established. It may fail abjectly, but it may flourish wonderfully—only God Himself can see into the future and discern what lies ahead. Those of us who are no more than human can only place our trust in His goodwill and wait to be enlightened.

"Now, to other matters. We know what you must do in Britain. Now we must bend our minds to bringing you there safely. You have never been aboard a ship, have you? I thought not. Very well, here are our priorities. We must first deliver you safely to the coast. After that, we must find you a ship that will fit your needs, and we must make sure that you can use it. He turned slightly in his chair to look at me, his eyes moving down the length of me.

"We need to speak of arms and armor now. From what Tiberias Cato tells me, your armor and weapons are well used and serviceable enough, but the overall appearance of your arms and equipment, with the sole exception of Cato's own spatha, now yours, leaves much to be desired in the face of the tasks I shall require of you. That, however, is simply remedied." He called out a name that sounded like Armand, and a tall, strapping young cleric came in immediately from the anteroom, where he had apparently been waiting for the summons.

The bishop thanked him for his patience and asked him to bring in the articles that lay on the bed in his private chambers, and the fellow bowed and left, to return soon thereafter, walking with care and straining beneath the weight of a cumbersome box fashioned of rough wooden planks. It was as wide as my forearm is long, and twice as deep as it was wide. Besides being heavy, the thing was clearly awkward to carry, despite its having been furnished with handles of hempen rope. Armand carried it carefully over to the fireplace and lowered it cautiously to the floor, grunting loudly with relief as he released it and straightened up.

Armand fetched two more boxes, one atop the other, both smaller but apparently no lighter than the first one. The larger of these also had carrying handles attached, but these were of heavy, stitched leather, and the box had been smoothed and stained. It was perhaps two handspans in depth, the same from front to back and at least half again as much across the front. The one that sat on top of that, however, was vastly different. This was a solidly made hinged chest of precious citrus wood with an elaborate brass spring-lock, the key to which hung by a wire from the brass handle on the lid. Ornately carved on all five surfaces and lustrously polished to a sheen that reflected the flickering light from the fire in the brazier, the container was the kind of costly artifact that spoke loudly of enormous wealth and privilege. Citrus wood was so precious, and so much in demand, that there had been rumors circulating for decades that it had been entirely used up and no longer grew anywhere in the world. I had never actually seen citrus wood, and no one I knew had, either, but I recognized the magnificence of what I was looking at immediately and knew it could be nothing other than the fabled wood. I knew, too, that the piece in front of me was probably hundreds of years old, an heirloom of the ancient family of which Germanus was the sole remaining member.

Armand hoisted his burden onto the table, then placed the two smaller containers side by side. That done, he turned and bowed slightly to the bishop and then glided unobtrusively back out to the anteroom.

"Another new face, Father," I murmured, trying not to make my curiosity about the boxes too obvious. "There have been many changes in the months since I went away."

The bishop shrugged. "Aye, I can see where it might seem thus to you, but there have been no more than usual. You simply never noticed it before, because you were always here and for more than five years you absorbed each new face automatically and without thought as it came along. Now you have been gone for more than half a year and are seeing them all at once." He bowed his head and rubbed the palm of his right hand with his left thumb, then looked back at me.

"Tell me about this friend of yours, this Ursus Perceval or whatever his name is. Is he a good man?"

"You mean in the manner of Christian goodness, Father? I believe so. I have never seen anything to indicate otherwise."

"No, that's not what I meant. I meant good in the military sense. Is he trustworthy?"

"Of course, absolutely."

"Are you convinced of that? That you could trust him with your life?"

I smiled. "I already have, Father, several times, and I have never felt the slightest doubt in his reliability, his courage or his strength."

"Hmm. What about money?"

"What about it, Father? I have none and neither has Ursus—he is a mercenary. But we have no need of money."

"There is always a need for money, in some guise or another, believe me. You may drift across the land attending to your own requirements for as long as you wish and you will have no real need for money. But come the moment when you have to undertake a task like those I have set you here, you will need money and a strong supply of it, for you are entering a realm where only money achieves effects. Thus the reason I am asking you about your friend: you will be carrying large sums of money with you and on your person. I merely wish to be assured that this Ursus is able enough to defend you against thieves and trustworthy enough that he will not be tempted to become a thief himself. Tell me all that you know about him."

I did so at length, and when I was finished, Germanus sat staring narrow-eyed at me, absorbing what I had said, and then he nodded and pushed himself out of his chair with both arms.

"Now, come and look at this." He crossed to the large box on the floor, and I followed, eager to know what was to be revealed to me, but I could have guessed at that all night long and never have imagined what he was about to show me. The sides of the box, I could see now that we were close to it, were hinged and secured by a simple metal hasp. Germanus undid the hasp and swung the sides of the box apart, and I gasped.

My first impressions were of rich golden, burnished browns, metal and leather, reinforced by the smell that came crowding into my nostrils, richly scented polish of the kind used to burnish and buff the finest leathers. The box contained an armor tree, a simple frame of crossed pieces of wood designed to store the various pieces of a soldier's gear. I had seen a hundred of them, here and there, but I had never seen one installed in a box, for transportation or, as it turned out to be in this instance, for long-term storage. Furthermore, the armor growing on this particular tree was unlike any I had ever set eyes upon.

Several of my relatives had magnificent armor. King Ban's had been made for him personally, as had my cousin Brach's, and the results were impressive and spectacular, even intimidating. What I was gazing at here, however—and I knew it beyond certainty, for it could be nothing else—was Germanus's own armor, the armor of an imperial Roman legatus, in all its opulent magnificence. Germanus reached out and rubbed the ball of his thumb gently across the deeply ingrained texture of an ancient and much-polished scratch over the left breast of the cuirass.

"Never could get that mark out," he murmured, "but I never really wanted to, not badly enough. It served to keep me aware of my mortality. That was done by a heavy boar spear, thrown by the biggest man I have ever seen. It hit me square and threw me bodily backwards, over my horse's rump. Lucky for me I didn't land on my head and break my neck, but God was with me and the only damage I sustained was this one scratch."

I was astounded, because the cuirass was leather, not metal, and a spear such as he described should have skewered him, cuirass and all. I said so, wondering all the while if he might be exaggerating, as soldiers always seem to do, but he merely smiled and shook his head.

"I cannot speak with any certainty about the harness worn by emperors, because I have never known an emperor who was a true warrior and actually fought and thus wore real armor, as opposed to ceremonial display armor, but I suspect that this suit here may be the finest single suit of armor ever made." Once again he extended a hand and rubbed it gently over the glossy surface of the leather breast plate before plucking the helmet from the wooden ball that supported it atop the tree and holding it up close to his eyes with both hands. "It has been many years since I last wore this," he breathed, "and looking at it now, I could regret never wearing it again were I to permit the self-indulgence." A cloth bag hung from the "neck" of the tree, and he set the helmet atop the box and rummaged in it, extracting a plumed crest made from alternating tufts of pure white and crimson-dyed horsehair. With the ease born of years of practice, he clicked the crest into place on the helmet, transforming it in a moment from a magnificent helm to a thing of startling and imperious beauty.

"Here, try this on. Stand still." I stood motionless, scarcely daring to breathe as he fitted the head covering over my brows. It felt heavy, and solid, but it fitted as though it had been made for me. "Impressive," the bishop murmured. "When one wears such a thing oneself, there is seldom opportunity to admire it. Looking at it now, though, it has a certain splendor, I must admit." He turned back to the tree, leaving the helmet on my head. "But look at the workmanship in this device." He was referring to the cuirass, and I removed the helmet, tucking it beneath my arm before I stooped to look more closely at the cuirass.

It really was superb, an intricate and awe-inspiring creation of boiled, dried, hammered and burnished leather, painstakingly fashioned in the shape of a stylized male torso. The planes of the pectoral musculature were utterly smooth and polished to a mirror-like perfection that reminded me—I smiled at the thought—of my first sight of my cousin Brach emerging from the lake. Elsewhere on the piece, though, there was no expanse of surface larger than a tiny fingernail that was not covered with embossed carvings and workmanship of breathtaking, elegant perfection: rosettes and chevrons and thorny briarwork scrolls chased and embraced each other in apparent abandon yet flawless symmetry across and around the surface of the armor. Germanus stepped back from it, to admire it from farther off.

"Hand it to me, would you?"

Obediently I placed the helmet at my feet, then prepared to lift the cuirass from the wooden frame. I grasped it securely, lifted it— and almost dropped it in my surprise, whipping my head around in consternation to see that Germanus had expected this and was grinning at me again.

"Aye," he said. "Bear in mind I said it's the finest armor ever made. You have almost discovered why. Bring it to the table."

I carried the unbelievably light cuirass, full front and back plates together, to where he was already waiting for me, peering into the second box. As I balanced the cuirass, allowing it to stand on its own upon the table, the bishop held something out to me. It was a flat, rectangular object wrapped in black cloth.

"That's the secret of the armor," he said as I unwrapped the package and then held it up in front of me, staring at it. Whatever the device was, I knew I had never seen one before, and yet it looked familiar. It was made of metal, a grid-like form square in shape and feather light and flexible where I would have expected much more weight and rigidity. And then I realized what it reminded me of. Once, when I was a child, we had had a summer of ferocious heat, and in the course of it my nurse had taken to weaving shades of thumb-wide bulrush fronds to hang in our doorways and window embrasures to keep out the sun while allowing the air to move into the darkened house. The simple square over-and-under weave of the leaves had entranced me, I remembered, because it looked so fragile yet was paradoxically strong. And now I was looking at the same kind of weave, fundamentally simple and straightforward save that instead of rushes, the smith had used slats of metal, extremely thin and a deep, dark blue in color, forming a slender woven plate of steel that I could flex between my hands. Germanus held out his hand for the piece, and I passed it to him. He pressed his cupped hand, containing the blue mesh, hard against the left pectoral panel of the cuirass.

"There is a layer of straps of this woven steel underlying the leather. In fact it lies between two layers, with the edges of the straps overlapping very slightly, and the edges of the leather are sewn together around the outer rims of the cuirass, front and back, very artistically. If you look very closely, you may see where the two layers meet, but it is not easy to find." I bent forward and peered closely, but I could see nothing.

"It is a wonder," I confessed. "I have never heard of such a thing. Where was it made, Father?"

"In Constantinople, where else? The smiths there can do magical things with metal, but the man who made this armor was the finest, most skillful armorer I ever knew. I was able to do him a service when I was in law, and he made this for me specially when I left the profession and joined the armies at the behest of the Emperor. There are arm guards and greaves and an armored kirtle in the box to complete the suit, as you can see, and even the leather dome of the helmet conceals a metal cap. It has served me well, in all my travels and campaigns. I have worn it throughout the Empire." He made a sucking sound through his teeth. "But no more. Never again."

"What will you do with it, Father?"

He tilted his head to one side and looked at me from beneath raised eyebrows. "I shall pass it to my son, my son."

"Your son? I had no . . ." My voice trailed away in embarrassment, but he pretended not to have noticed.

"Of course I cannot give him all of it. The crimson-and-white helm crest is that of a legionary legatus—*the* legatus of Gaul—and the martial cloak and gauntlets that go with it also bear both my personal and my official insignia as legatus of

Gaul. All of those pieces are instantly recognizable to anyone who knows about such matters and so would draw unwelcome attention were someone else to be seen wearing them. But with a plain crest of brown horsehair, the helmet's effect would be much the same, and a plain, functional military cloak of waxed brown wool will go splendidly with all the rest." He glanced sideways at my chest. "You're a big lad, but you still have growth to complete. Nonetheless, the cuirass should fit you well enough even now, over a heavy, quilted tunic, and you'll grow into it soon enough. The helmet's headband is adjustable, so even if your head grows larger, which is unlikely now, the casque will fit you and serve you well."

I was staring at him open mouthed, unable to believe what I had heard, but finally I found my tongue. "You're giving this to me? To me?"

"Aye, but not all of it. As I said, I'll keep the helmet crest, the cloak and the embroidered gauntlets—those are purely decorative in any case, heavy and cumbersome and virtually useless. But the rest is yours to wear from this time on."

He smiled, deciding to take pity on me. "Clothar, Clothar, think about it this way: I have no son of my own and you are the son of one of my dearest friends, and you have given me as much joy and pleasure with your simple honesty and strengths as your father did. I am an old man now, and soon I will die, and when I do, if this armor is still in my possession, venal people will squabble over it and it may end up being worn by someone whose possession of it would make me lie uncomfortably in my grave. Better by far that you should have it, with my blessings. You are going as my envoy into foreign parts, to deal with powerful people and take part in great events. It is fitting that you should be dressed appropriately for the part you may be called upon to play, whatever its nature. So, will you accept this, and my blessings?"

I felt tears standing in my eyes and could only shake my head in acceptance, incapable of speech. Again he affected not to notice.

"Excellent, then come over here, for there is something else I have for you, something that you can use at all times. But it came from far beyond Constantinople."

He went to the table, opened the larger of the two boxes that lay there and lifted out a carefully wrapped bundle, which he laid reverently on the tabletop. He reached into the box again and pulled out what I immediately recognized as a set of supple, well-used and carefully tended black leather saddlebags. He tossed them gently towards me, and as I caught them I noticed that instead of the two normal bags to be thrown across a horse's shoulders, this device had four deep bags, a pair on each side, one superimposed above the other, and a long strap to buckle beneath the horse's chest and hold the assembly secure. I noticed, too, that each bag closed with a strap and buckle.

"Large bags, capacious and useful. I designed them myself, on campaign many years ago. I found that I could never have enough carrying capacity when I was on the move. You'll enjoy those. But this is what I want to show you." He had been working to undo the wrappings around the bundle he had first drawn from the box and now he held up the garment it had contained. It was a surcoat of some kind, a plain rectangle of some strange material, folded halfway so that it hung down front and back in equal lengths. A hemmed, square-cut hole had been provided for the wearer's head to go through, and there were transverse slits, also hemmed and no more than a handsbreadth wide, beneath the shoulders, permitting the shoulder surfaces to project straight out without being pulled downward. Other than that, the sides were open, and it was plain to see that they were intended to be held in place by a belt or girdle and probably a sword belt. It was a plain, dusty-looking shade of the untreated light brown wool called fustian, pale enough to be sandy or earthen.

Germanus tossed it to me, and again I reacted with surprise. This thing, too, was metallic. I held it close and peered at it, then squeezed it in my hands. It contained countless thousands of tiny, almost insubstantial metal rings, all sewn into place in overlapping layers so that the garment itself was flexible and probably more comfortable than anything comparable that one might find in Gaul, although I doubted that there would be anything truly comparable.

"That tunic will deflect a hard-shot arrow fired from close quarters," Germanus said. "I have no idea where it came from or who made it, but it, too, was given to me as a gift many years ago by a visiting king from some far-flung part of the Eastern Empire, and he himself had no idea where it came from. The main thing about it, though, is that it works, and it is light enough and comfortable enough to wear in most situations where you anticipate that there might be danger and yet you do not wish to wear full armor. And it doesn't clink. It rustles a little, but that's all. If you wear it traveling, beneath your new armor, it will fill up the extra room in there. How goes the time?"

"I know not, Father. I have lost track completely."

Germanus called again for Armand, and the large young man reappeared from the anteroom, rubbing the sleep from his eyes. In response to Germanus's question, he informed us that it was the fourth hour of the night. He glanced at the fireplace as he spoke and crossed immediately to blow on the embers, coaxing them until he had a flame going again. When he stood up to leave, the bishop thanked him and gave him permission to retire to bed.

"Time, time, time," he said as soon as the man was gone. "There is never enough of it. Now, to work. We have to get you from here to the coast, as quickly and efficiently as possible. Tomorrow morning, after I have gone, I want you to report to Tiberias and have him select his finest horses for your use. Each of your traveling companions should have two mounts."

"There are only two of us, Father. Ursus and myself."

"Aye, for the time being, but I would like to change that. You will require an assistant, an escort to look after your equipment and your weapons and your horses. I have one for you, if you will consent to take him. His name is Bors and you may remember him. He was in the student intake below yours and he began this year as the informal leader of the Spartans—a brilliant and gifted student, but troubled during these past few months. His parents died in an outbreak of plague late last summer, although we did not hear word of it until after you had left us. But it transpires that it was not only his parents who died. His entire family was wiped out, leaving no one alive. The boy needs something now to rekindle his interest in living. He has been morose and depressed and his studies have suffered for it, but he is still far and away the best and brightest in the school this year. I want you to consider taking him with you. He will benefit by it and so will you, I am convinced. Talk with him tomorrow and watch him for a day or two. If you feel that such an arrangement would work, invite him to go with you. I have spoken to Tiberias Cato and he knows my feelings on the matter, so there will be no difficulties in freeing the lad to accompany you. Similarly, should you feel uncomfortable about this, then Cato will attend to it and no harm will have been done. The boy himself knows nothing of this, so his feelings will not suffer if you reject him.

"So! Horses are looked after. Cato has his instructions. Now, I am assuming that you do not speak the Coastal Tongue, but does your friend, Ursus?"

"I am sorry, Father, I don't know."

"No matter, we will find out tomorrow morning, but it is important that you have someone with you who understands the language. Latin may serve you most of the time, but there are a multitude of tongues spoken in the world of mariners and the Coastal Tongue serves all of them.

"When you reach the seacoast, you will proceed to the town called Gesoriacum, which is the port closest to Britain, and ask there for one of three sea captains, all of whom know me and all of whom I trust. Find one of those three, it does not matter which one, but trust no others. Heed me in this, Clothar, for it is vital to your success. You may have to wait for several days, perhaps several weeks, but one of the three will arrive in the port sooner or later. It is home to all of them. You will give the one you meet a token from me, to prove you are who you claim to be. I have the three tokens, and the names of the three men and which token goes to whom. Put them in your saddlebags."

He now opened the citrus wood chest and withdrew from it a small, slender handmade box of sandalwood that he opened to show three compartments. In each compartment was a small lozenge of leather with a man's name burned into it, and a piece of jewelry. The first, named for Joachim, held a ring with a stone of lapis lazuli; the second, named for Sivio, contained a small silver pendant, looped to accept a chain; while the third, dedicated to Scapius, held a plain silver cross. Germanus read the names aloud, touched each of the tokens and then closed the box carefully and handed it to me.

"Each of those men has an identical piece in his possession, given him by me. By giving him this one, you will have the absolute loyalty he would give to me. On the other hand, however, these men work hard to stay alive, so we cannot rely on their goodwill alone. That would be unjust. So." He reached into the chest again, with both hands this time, and came out with both hands filled. "Here, open this up."

I unrolled a long, supple money belt of soft black leather. It was slightly more than a handsbreadth deep and fastened with triple buckled straps, and the back of it was lined with finely woven wool so that it would not stick to the bare skin against which it would be worn. The main part—the back of the belt, assuming the buckles would be worn in front—was composed of three long lateral leather strips, each of them covering a narrow pocket the depth of the first joint of my thumb, and there were two rectangular areas at the sides, also containing pockets, although these were vertical and only half the width of the others. Germanus was pulling strips of black from a leather wallet.

"These are silver coins, ten to a strip, thirty in all. Tuck them into the three pockets. They'll make a handy addition to your armor should anyone attempt to stab you in the back. These ones here, so much smaller, are of gold—thirty of these as well, in six sets of five. Tuck these carefully into the side pockets, and bear in mind that each of them is worth at least thirty and perhaps fifty of the silver coins. These are emergency funds only. Wear them against your skin at all times, Clothar, and let no one know you have them. You will be moving and living among men who would kill you without blinking for a single one of the silver coins, let alone the gold. For your expenses along the road, in mansios and taverns, use this." He tossed me a small, heavy leather bag of coins. "Those are mostly copper, with only a few small silver pieces. It is the kind of money that will get you whatever you need without stirring anyone's greed." He dug again into the chest and tossed me yet another small leather bag, this one heavy beyond belief. "This you will use to pay for your passage to Britain, across the Narrow Seas. It is gold, but do not be afraid to use it.

"The route from Callis to Dubris is the shortest distance between the two shores, but there has been trouble in the southeast of Britain and the Saxon tribes there, particularly the ones who call themselves Danes, are moving to occupy the entire region and are notoriously unpredictable. Be guided by whoever is your captain, but be prepared to travel westward before you land. Ideally, if you have fair winds and the weather holds, you should round the peninsula called Cornwall and sail up the coastline as far as a place called Glastonbury. Camulod lies close by there. Again, your captain will know of Glastonbury."

I wiggled my fingers.

"What? You have a question?"

"Aye, Father. How many coins should I pay the boatman? I have never handled gold before."

Germanus smiled. "It is the same as lead, Clothar—heavy and cumbersome and valuable only to the extent it is coveted by others. Fall into the sea with bags of it on your belt and you will drown. But it has its uses, too. For a fair-weather crossing, say ten coins. Foul weather, half as much again. For outrageous risk, twenty coins, and for safe conduct all the way to Glastonbury in the west, thirty. That would be generous, but worthwhile.

"Now, what else is there?" He stood looking about him, his hands on his hips, then shook his head. "That's it, I believe. I think we have covered everything. Now, another draft of grape juice, although I fear it will be warm by now."

The fresh juice was warm but nonetheless delicious. As soon as I had drained my cup, however, Germanus rose to his feet again.

"I would like to meet your friend Ursus, if it please you. Will you take me to him?"

"Yes Father, of course, but he might be asleep."

"He *will* be asleep—it is late. But this is a special night." He turned and looked again at the magnificent armor on its tree. "We will leave this here for now, but all my people know it is now yours. You may collect it tomorrow or whenever you wish, but I would suggest you leave it until you have decided about young Bors. If he is to be your assistant, then he should begin with this. And he should learn everything from that point on—the care of your weapons, armor and horses, the care and maintenance of your other clothing, the preparation of your food and the prompt and exact execution of your wishes and commands. This is a learning process for the boy, to lead him into manhood. He has the makings of a splendid soldier, but he lacks this particular type of training, so I charge you to be conscientious in supervising and disciplining him. It will teach him obedience and humility, which is even more important. Now take me to your friend."

We rousted a tousled and sleepy Ursus from his bed, and I introduced him to Germanus. Even under such imperfect and unexpected circumstances Ursus was honored to be meeting a man whose exploits and fame were legendary, and when Germanus invited him to walk with him for a while he accepted with alacrity, merely asking leave to throw some cold water over his head and pull on a warmer tunic. I was not allowed to accompany them, and so I went to my own quarters, where I sat on the bed, leaning back against the wall and going over the astonishing events of this amazing evening.

Perhaps an hour later, Ursus came into my room and shook my shoulder, startling me awake.

"You had better get into bed. You won't sleep comfortably, propped up like that. I enjoyed talking with your friend Germanus . . ." I peered up at him, hoping to hear what had happened between the two men. Ursus nodded. "I've never been to Britain. I'm looking forward to seeing it."

"You're coming with me? I was going to ask you tomorrow."

"Aye, Germanus told me. He questioned me pretty thoroughly. Got me to tell him things about myself I didn't know I knew. Anyway, he ended up by telling me what you're about to do and asked me if I would consider going with you. Of course I had to say I would, because I couldn't live with myself if you went poking about on your own and got yourself killed. The only problem is Tristan. I don't know what to do about him."

"Tristan?"

"My brother. My youngest brother. Believe it or not, I'm fifteen years older than he is." Ursus reached inside his tunic and pulled out a much-folded sheet of very fine parchment. "This was waiting for me when I arrived back in Carcasso. It is a letter from my brother, the first letter I have ever received. Don't ask me how he found me or how the letter reached me, for I have no idea. Someone must have recognized me somewhere, and found out that I was calling myself Ursus, and in some manner the word made its way to Tristan. I have no idea how long ago this was written, or how long it took to reach me, but Tristan was in the legions, stationed in Lutetia, when he wrote it, and he was hoping we might be able to meet again someday. In it he tells me that my father, damn his black heart, died ten years ago, and my brother Simon now rules Montenegra in his place. I liked Simon. He and I were as close as any two in our benighted clan could be. I never knew Tristan at all. He was the smallest tadpole when I left, born to a younger wife after my mother finally died of trying to please and placate the black old boar that I'm named after."

"How old is he now, then?"

Ursus blinked. "I don't know. Yes, I do. I'm thirty-seven now, so Tristan must be twenty-two. He says in his letter he joined the legions on his sixteenth birthday and he's been in for six years, so that would make it right."

"He's five years older than me."

"Aye, that's about what I would have guessed. Anyway, when I left Carcasso, I decided upon a whim to come up this way to ask about the lad, to see if I could find out where he is nowadays. He might be there still, he might have moved on years ago. I don't know. But we have to pass by Lutetia on our way to the coast, so if you wouldn't mind, I would like to stop there and ask about him."

"Absolutely, of course. How long has it been since you saw him?"

"Hmm . . . twelve years, at least, perhaps longer. But he will probably have moved on from Lutetia by now. You know what the army's like."

"Aye, well, we'll see when we get there. Now we'd better sleep. It's late and Germanus leaves at first light. I'm glad you'll be coming with me to Britain."

He left and I lay back to think again about the adventures ahead of me, but I must have fallen asleep instantly, for the next thing I was aware of was the predawn crowing of a rooster.

4

Germanus was in fine fettle as he made his way out of the ancient town that had been the domain of his family for hundreds of years. I was merely one indistinguishable dot in the vast crowd of people who turned out to see him leave and wish him well, and he spent more than an hour moving among the crowd of well-wishers, embracing some and blessing others and thanking all of them for honoring him in this way.

When he spotted me, he came directly to where I stood and grasped me by both shoulders, looking straight into my eyes. "May God be with you, Clothar, my son," he said. "I will be thinking of you and praying for you every day, that your mission to Merlyn Britannicus might bear fruit and bring great blessings to the people and the land of Britain. Go in peace." He kissed me on the forehead and began to turn away, then hesitated and turned back to me, his smile widening. "I wore that armor for many years and during many campaigns, you know, and only ever once did I mar it with a scratch. Try to treat it with the same care, will you? No Saxon axe will cut through it, but a hard-swung axe could make a fearful dent in it, and in you for that matter, so promise me, if you will, that you will stay well away from hard-swung axes."

"I will, Father," I said, trying to smile despite the swelling lump in my throat. "I will. God bless you."

He touched me again, cupping my cheek in his hand. "He already has, Clothar. Walk in His light, my son." And with that he was gone, swallowed up by the crowd.

Later that morning, when the cavalcade was gone and the crowd had dispersed, I went looking for Tiberias Cato and found him, not surprisingly, in the stables among his beloved animals. He waved me to him as soon as I entered the main gates of the horse yards, and when I reached his side he nodded a silent greeting and pointed to a small group of horses in an enclosure close by.

"That one," he said. "The bay. That's the mount I picked out for the boy Bors. As your servant, he'll have no need of a prancing war horse, but that animal will be perfect for him. It's sound and solid, and what it lacks in beauty it makes up for in willingness. The beast has a tractable nature, with enough strength and stamina to do anything he will require of it. It will carry him *and* a full load all day and every day if that's what is required. The other one behind it, the gray gelding, is his packhorse. Same attributes, same stamina, merely less sweet to look upon. Have you decided yet to take him with you?"

"Bors? No, I haven't even met him yet and know nothing about him other than what Bishop Germanus told me last night."

"What more do you need to know, then? If Germanus vouches for him, how can you doubt the lad?"

"I don't. I was merely pointing out that I have not met him yet. I think I may remember his face, but I won't know until I see him."

"Well, that's easily remedied." He shouted to a small boy who was cleaning out a stall behind him, bidding him drop what he was doing and run to the school, where he was to find Brother Michael's class and ask the teacher to send the boy Bors back here to meet with Magister Cato. When the lad had scampered away, he turned back to me.

"I took the liberty of picking mounts for you and your companion Perceval, too. Didn't think you would object to that. Come, I'll show them to you." As he led me back to where he had sequestered four horses for our use, he continued talking about Bors.

"He was always a bright student, right from the outset, and I knew that from the first day I set eyes on him, but everything about him's different now, and none of the changes have improved him. Mind you, there's a part of me that can't really blame the lad, because he's been through more misfortunes than many a grown man goes through in a lifetime. But still, enough is enough.

"It started with the news of his parents' death. That would normally be enough to bring down any man—I mean, it happens to all of us, but none of us are ever ready for it when it occurs and it's always devastating. But then, hard on the heels of the first one, comes a second messenger, this one bearing the tidings that the remainder of his family—his entire clan—had been wiped out by the pestilence, along with three-quarters of the population of the small town they had lived in."

Cato sniffed loudly and braced one of his feet against the bottom rail of the paddock. "That second message is what did the boy in. Until it arrived, he had been grief-stricken but very normal in how he reacted and behaved. After he heard the news about the rest of his family being dead too, however, he changed completely. He grew bitter and resentful, and noisy in his bitterness. He started questioning the very existence of God, demanding to know how anyone could believe in the goodness of any God who could allow such things to happen.

"Of course, that kind of talk was not too well received here, as you can imagine, and several of his teachers began to lean on him, but that only made him worse. He stopped working at his lessons altogether and went from being a bright student and a positive influence among the other boys to being a bitter, cynical recluse who never had a good word to say about anything or anyone."

"So how did the other boys react to that?" I asked, and Cato looked at me with an expression of rueful skepticism that I remembered well.

"Not very well," he said. "Some of them even joined forces to show him the error of his ways. But that was a waste of time, and often painful. Bors is a big lad for his age, and he's always been able to hold his own against lads twice his size. He thrashed a couple of them very badly, and the others soon decided to leave him alone to stew in his misery.

"Germanus is the only one who refused to give up on the boy. I gave him up us unredeemable months ago, but the bishop chewed on my ear for days and weeks until I decided to give the boy another chance. I did, and I kept working with the boy, biting my tongue every day and keeping what I really thought of him to myself. But nothing came of my efforts until a few days ago, and even then there wasn't much to see. But whatever credit there is for that goes to Germanus. I don't know what he did with the boy, or how he penetrated the tortoise shell the lad has built about himself, but in the past couple of days young Bors has become more . . . tractable. Now that's a word I can't remember ever using before to describe a person. It's a word I generally save for horses, obedient, biddable horses, but it fits what's happening with Bors. I wouldn't say the boy's more approachable, because he really isn't, but there's something happening inside that enclosed little world he lives in. Anyway, you'll be able to judge for yourself soon enough. He should be here directly."

By then we had been standing for some time looking at the four magnificent animals in the fenced enclosure he had led me to. All four were bays, of varying degrees of color, and all four were superb. Cato pointed out two in particular, one of them dark enough to be a chestnut, with only a single blaze of white on his forehead, the other with four white fetlocks. "Those two are yours," he said. "There's not much to choose from in the way of differences among the four of them, but those two would be my personal choice were I the one riding off into the unknown on them."

"So be it, then, Magister. They shall be mine."

"Good. They're easy to identify as well, which does no harm. Here comes the boy."

I recognized him immediately, and instantly wondered why I had not been able to recall him by name before. He had been a junior friend and something of a protégé to my own friend Stephan Lorco, following Lorco around for his first two years in the school in a condition resembling hero worship. He had already closed the outer gate behind him and was walking across the main yard of the stables, still several hundred paces from where we stood, and something in his gait, in the way he held himself, immediately caught my attention, making me look more closely to identify what it was that had struck me as being unusual, and before he had halved the distance separating us I knew what it was. He had not seen us yet, standing as we were in the shade of a low hut at the rear of the paddocks, with several lines of fencing between him and us, but there was a lack of diffidence in his walk that was unusual to the point of appearing arrogant.

Summoned from the classroom to meet with the formidable Magister Cato, he should have been filled with trepidation, wondering what he had done to engender such a command. Any other boy in the school would have been recognizably afraid. I would have been, in his place. But this boy showed no such concern. He walked confidently and purposefully, head erect, shoulders back, his pace steady and unhurried.

"He's not afraid," I said.

"No, not that one." Cato's voice was quiet. "A year ago he would have been, but now he doesn't care. Grown up before his time, poor little catamite. There's nothing I could say to him or do to him now that would make him feel worse, or even better, which *is* worse. That's why he needs to go with you, if you'll have him. He's a man now, in his grief, but his body and the rest of him are still in boyhood. Those parts need to grow now, too, but in a man's world, not a boy's school. Bors! Over here."

The boy turned towards the sound of Cato's voice and came straight to where we stood. I saw him recognize me and frown slightly.

"Magister," he said, looking at Cato and ignoring me.

Now that he was beside me I could see how much he had grown and aged in the time since I had last seen him. He was almost as tall as me now and half a head taller than the diminutive Tiberias Cato, and he was solidly made, with wide, strong shoulders, a deep, broad chest and long, clean-lined arms and legs that rippled with well-toned, sharply defined muscles. His face was unblemished and attractive, albeit unsmiling, and his dark eyes held a guarded, reserved look.

It was a measure of my own growth in the months that had passed recently, however, that I saw him as a boy, although the fact that I was looking at him through a man's eyes did not occur to me until much later.

"You sent for me, Magister."

"Aye, I did," Cato growled. "And I thank you for coming." He ignored the slight quirk of the eyebrow that was the boy's only response to his sarcasm. "You know Clothar of Benwick, I am sure. He is visiting us for a short time before leaving on a mission set for him by Bishop Germanus."

Bors looked directly at me for the first time and inclined his head courteously. "Of course, I remember him well," he said, and then to me: "I was there when Stephan Lorco fought you for the Magister's spatha. You should have won."

"I have it here," I said, tilting the hilt forward for him to see. "I was with Stephan when he was killed in an ambush, and I carry the spatha and use it now in remembrance of him."

"Aye, that's right, Lorco is dead, too, isn't he?"

I was left speechless, not so much by the comment as by the tone in which it had been uttered, but Cato had been ready for something of the sort, I think, because his response was immediate.

"Aye, that's right, as you say, he is. But Stephan Lorco was killed in battle, doing what he had been trained to do!"

That was not quite true, for poor Lorco had not even had time to see that we were being attacked, but I kept silent, watching for Bors's response. He said nothing, however, and his only movement was to bite gently at his upper lip, but I clearly saw the pain that filled his eyes. Cato saw it too, I believe, for he spoke again in a gentler voice.

"Anyway, as I said, Clothar is leaving on a mission for Bishop Germanus. It will be dangerous, and Clothar is young to be entrusted with such responsibility, but the bishop chose him above all others for the task because he has great faith in this young man, as do we all. Since leaving here, he has fought in a short but brutal civil war in his own lands in Benwick, and has distinguished himself greatly. And he, too, knows what it is to lose close family, his parents first, and then his guardian and two brothers in this recent war. Bishop Germanus thought it might be good for you to speak with him while he is here. I thought so too, which is why I sent for you. I know not what he might say to you, or even if you wish to speak with him, but here he is, and here you are, and I will leave the two of you alone."

"Wait, Magister, if you would" I said. He had been on the point of turning away but he stopped and looked at me with raised eyebrows. "I would like you to hear what I have to say to Bors." The boy's face was now set in resentment. I am not normally impulsive, but I knew I had to speak now what was in my mind and heart, and what was there was newly born in me, completely unconsidered and spontaneous.

"There is a man in Britain, Bors, two or three years older than I am and therefore less than five years older than you, who will soon be crowned as King of Britannia. His name is Arthur—Arthur Pendragon—and I have been told by the bishop himself that the man commands an army of heavy cavalry the like of which has not been seen since the time of Alexander the Great. Britain is being invaded as I speak, by a tide of different peoples from across the seas to the east of the island. The hordes are drawn to Britain's wealth since the Roman legions left the island two score years ago.

All of them are pagans, and they seem set to destroy God's Church in Britain and to wipe out all signs of Christianity in the path of their conquest. Arthur Pendragon's army is the only force that can gainsay them and hurl them back to where they came from.

"His teacher, a wise and powerful man called Merlyn Britannicus, is a beloved friend to Germanus, and has shaped the new King in much the same fashion as Germanus has trained us, in compassion and decency, but also in military strength, dedicated to the preservation of the laws of God and man and using the full force of his military power to back his convictions. I am to leave for Britain within the days ahead, carrying missives to Merlyn and to the Christian bishops of the land, bidding them rally to Arthur's support and to mobilize the earthly powers of God's Church on behalf of the new king."

I drew a deep breath, not daring to look at Cato, and continued. "I will deliver my dispatches to Merlyn, and to the bishops, in accordance with the wishes of Bishop Germanus, and then I may return home to Gaul. But it is in my mind that I like the notion of this new King and his campaign to save his country from the pagan hordes, and so I may stay there, to ride and fight with him, so be it that I like the man as much after meeting him as I now enjoy the idea of what he represents. I'll take you with me, if the idea pleases you. Will you come?"

The boy's eyes were wide with disbelief. Finally, when he realized that we were both gazing at him, waiting for an answer, he gulped breathlessly, then whispered, "Do you—?" He swallowed, but when he spoke again his voice broke into a squeak on the first utterance—quickly mastered, but nonetheless indicative of his youth. "Do you mean that?"

I glanced at Cato, whose fierce, bushy eyebrows were now riding high on his forehead. "Do I mean that? Mark this, Bors, and mark it clearly. If you do come with me, it will be as my assistant— an extension of your training under my care. I will be the master, you the apprentice. You will not travel as a warrior, or as the equal to myself or my companion Perceval, although in time you may develop into both. For the time being, however, your duties will be onerous and will revolve purely around my needs—my weapons, my armor, my horses, my provisions and any other requirements I might have. In return, I will be your guardian and your trainer and teacher, in trust for the faith placed in me by Bishop Germanus and Magister Cato here. But I warn you, I *will* be your master, until such time as you have proved to me that you have progressed beyond the point of needing to be taught.

"And I warn you, too, incidentally, that you will find few people who will tell you that questioning your master's truthfulness is a beneficial or clever way to set out upon such a relationship. This one time, however, I will ignore the slur. Yes, I mean what I say, and you still have not answered me. Will you come with me to Britain?"

His eyes had filled with tears and for a moment I thought they would spill over, but he blinked them fiercely away and turned apprehensively to Cato, who met his question with an upraised hand. "Don't come to me for guidance. As the man says, he will take you in trust for Bishop Germanus and myself. If you want to go, I have a horse picked out for you."

The young man who walked away from us a short time later still walked with purpose and determination, but there was an air of excitement about him that had not been there when he first arrived.

"That was . . . sudden," Cato said when we were alone again. "Unexpected, but well done, I think. I have the feeling you will not regret your impulsiveness."

5

With Bors dismissed, Cato suggested that I follow him. I never could listen to a suggestion from Cato without hearing an order, and so I rushed to keep up as he walked back towards the camp.

"That spatha was never meant to be the prize, you know," he growled. "I suppose I would have gotten around to giving it to you eventually, but I had something else in mind that afternoon. Then you went and fouled everything up by letting Lorco win."

He led me into a low hut and into the tiny cubicle that served him as both home and workspace. There he pointed towards the farthest corner, where two sheaves of spears were stored.

"Those are what you should have won that day," he said. "Won as a prize, upon the field, they would have been a trophy and would have saved me from the taint of playing favorites by giving them all to you. Now there's no need to fret over any of that. They're yours, a gift. Do you remember how to use them?"

I certainly did. He had brought these strangely strong yet light-weight, delicately shafted spears with him from the land where he had been raised, the land of the Smoke People. Each spear was tipped with a long, tapering, triangular metal head that came to a needle point and could, when well thrown, penetrate even the finest ring mail. The shafts were of the strange sectional and intensely hard wood that Cato called bambu. They were wondrous weapons, their slight weight and utter straightness permitting them to be thrown with great accuracy by anyone who had perfected the tricks of using them. On its most elemental level, the technique required an aptitude for wrapping the shaft quickly in the coils of a thin leather thong. With the thong gripped in the throwing hand, the hurled spear would begin to spin as the thong unwound, adding to its velocity and force. It was a wonderful weapon, and unique.

"They weigh next to nothing, but their length makes them awkward to transport," Cato said. "But that's why I went to such trouble choosing the boy's two horses. You can pack one quiver of these on each side of the packhorse and stow the rest of its load around them. You have two bundles there, with just over a score of spears in each. Might seem like a lot, particularly when you're traveling with them, but it isn't, believe me. The things are irre-placeable, so every one you lose or break takes you one step closer to having none."

Once again I was left fumbling for words by the munificence of such an unexpected gift, and the protests and objections that emerged from my lips sounded inane and self-serving even to me. In response to my witless question about what he would do once he no longer had them in his possession, Tiberias Cato merely smiled and cocked an eyebrow.

"What will I do without them? Much the same as I have done *with* them these past twenty years, which is nothing at all. But I'll have less difficulty in resisting the temptation to use them to rid myself of some of the weaker sisters among our students. I frequently used to imagine myself standing in the middle of the practice ring, picking the slackers right off the backs of their circling mounts. So by taking these out of my reach, you'll be assuring the future safety of the students. They are yours, Clothar, as is the spatha and the legate's armor. Use them as we know you can and will, and we'll make no complaints.

"Now, let's go and find something to eat. Young Bors can pick these up for you later."

6

Five days after that conversation, we rode into Lutetia to inquire after Perceval's brother Tristan, making our way directly to the garrison headquarters, where we were told we would have to speak to the adjutant.

Perceval, I had decided on the day we left Auxerre, while I was still decidedly drunk with power on the assumption of my new role as mission commander, would no longer be known as Ursus. Now that his father had been dead for more than a decade, I argued, he had no longer any convincing need to conceal his given name and could stand tall as who he was by birth, Perceval of Montenegra. We were embarking upon a new life, I pointed out to him—bound for a new land where no one would ever have heard of Montenegra and where he could, if so wished, begin a new existence, free of whatever taint he believed had clung to him thus far.

He had been reluctant even to consider the change at first, let alone accede to it, having been plain Ursus for so long, but he soon relented under my incessant urging and agreed to a trial, a purely temporary assay of the change for a period of three months, stipulating only that he would never claim or acknowledge any association with the name of Montenegra. That, he asserted, would be too much for him to stomach.

In due time the adjutant returned, a pleasant fellow with the Roman name of Quintus Leppo, and assured us that no Tristan of Montenegra was recorded in their annals. Before Perceval could voice his disappointment, however, the adjutant volunteered the information that there was, or there had been, a Tristan of Volterra in their ranks until very recently.

Perceval's head snapped up on hearing that. Volterra, he had once told me, had been a region in his father's holdings of Montenegra. Where might we find this Tristan, he wanted to know immediately, and the adjutant asked him why he wished to know. When Perceval said he was his brother and produced the letter he had received, Leppo broke out in smiles and suddenly became a mine of information. Tristan, it transpired, was a close friend of his and still shared lodgings with him on the principal street of the old settlement of Lutetia. He had served out his mercenary contract and was spending some time in retirement now, debating whether to remain in the north or to seek employment for his skills elsewhere.

Barely an hour after that, we knocked on the door of Tristan's lodgings and found him at home alone. By the end of that night, after he and his brother between them had drunk more beer and mead than I had ever seen in my life, it was decided that he would ride with us to Britain, sharing his brother's fortunes and leaving future wealth or penury to the falling of the dice.

That decision did not displease me. I had formed an immediate liking for my friend's younger brother, who was, I decided upon seeing him for the first time, close enough to me in age to be an equal—three or four years, I thought, flattering myself hugely, was a negligible difference. He was also one of the fairest, fine-looking young men it had ever been my pleasure to encounter. Indeed, the way the young women in the bar in which we drank that evening— the brothers drank, for the most part, while I merely marveled at their capacity for consuming the potions I could not stomach— fawned upon and draped themselves around the blond young man astounded me and made me vaguely envious.

Tristan, in truth, was something to behold. He was fair in the way that few other than the northern people of the snowy lands are fair. His hair was so pale that in certain lights it looked pure white, and his eyes were big and bright, piercingly blue with that hue that only certain flowers can possess. No trace of beard or mustache marred the smooth, gold-bronzed perfection of his face.

He liked me too, from the outset, which is always a sure sign of future friendship, but what moved me most of all was the pure, undiluted and unquestionable love and affection that he evinced for his long-lost brother from the moment of first seeing him and recognizing him there on the threshold of his lodgings. This was a man, I felt, who could ride with me anywhere.

He owned two horses and a full supply of armor and weaponry. He was, he assured me, a mercenary and a professional, prepared to sell his skills and his expertise to anyone who measured up to the criteria he demanded in an employer.

When we arrived in Gesoriacum, four riders and eight horses, we found Joachim, the first of Germanus's three preferred sea captains, in residence, preparing to return to sea in search of one last cargo to trade and money to be earned before the end of the trading year. I gave him Germanus's token of the lapis lazuli ring, and we discussed the price of hiring his boat and crew for our voyage.

We sailed for Britain at high tide on the following day.

I learned about the sickness of the sea on that brief voyage, for the Narrow Seas were rough and unfriendly to mariners, and their harsh lesson was to stay with me throughout my life.

Although I hated Joachim when, after two days of unimaginable agony, he suggested that we avoid the south coast known as the Saxon Shores and veer to the west, around the horn of Cornwall and then north to Glastonbury on the western coast, there came a day when the dawn was bright and golden and I looked out from the prow of the ship to see the high hill he named as Glastonbury Tor looming above the flat shores to the east of where we crept forward through a calm, still sea.

BISHOP ENOS

1

I had never seen such an inhospitable place. Britain, the vaunted land of riches famed by Julius Caesar and the Emperors Claudius, Hadrian and Trajan, was a hole without any redeeming features that I could discern. For the first seven days after our arrival on its coastline, heavy, driving rain fell incessantly and left us chilled to the bone, shivering in our armor and unable to escape the damp, appalling misery of the place. The moist, cold air contaminated every place we found during that time that might conceivably have offered us anything resembling accommodation or comfort and left us sniffling with discomfort and close to despair over the sheer foulness of the climate.

Perceval expressed best what we were all feeling late one soggy afternoon, after we had been vainly trying for the better part of an hour to light a fire using sodden wood. "I hate this damnable place," he said, "and I resent having to live in constant motion, afraid to stand still for more than a few moments lest my armor rust up and lock solid and I be stuck here forever." It was an inept attempt at humor, but we were in sore need of humor by that time.

We had made to land at Dubris originally, that being the easiest access point in the long line of high, white chalk cliffs that formed much of the southernmost coast of the island. An entire stretch of coast there, several miles in length, offered long, shallow beaches and safe havens set into vales and niches along the great white cliffs and had provided the landing place for Caesar's legions on his earliest exploratory expedition to Britain. But even before we had begun to sail in towards the land we had been aware of large numbers of armed warriors lining the cliff tops and watching us with intense, unmoving hostility, evincing absolutely no signs of welcoming activity. Joachim, our ship's captain, held back, eyeing the spectacle warily and looking distinctly unhappy, and when I questioned him on what was happening, he told me that he didn't know. The activity we were seeing here was new, he said, then added that his bones were warning him to stand away. He had sailed into Dubris many times, he said, and had always been welcomed as a trader, no matter who happened to be occupying the port. This approach, he swore, was different. He could feel the danger in the place and would not commit to a closer approach until he could be sure that there were no swift battle boats lying in wait just out of sight along the coast to swoop in on his stern once he had placed his ship and his crew in jeopardy.

The words had barely left his mouth when two swift-moving vessels came into view upwind to the right of us, the spray from their sweeps catching the rays of the midday sun and sending up rainbow showers of drops as the ships drove straight towards us, plainly intent on overhauling us. Fortunately for us, however, they had made their opening move too soon. Without even pausing to consult me, Joachim rapped out orders to his crew and we swung away westward, our ship lying over on her left side with the steepness of the turn. We had the advantage of a fair wind at our back and soon left our pursuers behind.

From then on, the weather began to deteriorate, and so did Joachim's good humor. He had been fretting for hours before that, eyeing the gathering cloud masses to the north and west and anticipating the onset of the winds as he muttered to himself, invoking the ancient gods of the sea to hold back their displeasure and not to send the winter storms too soon. But they were either deaf or angry with him, because all his pleading was in vain. The wind came fitfully at the outset, blowing in short-lived, uneven gusts for the first hour or so, with long gaps of stillness between gusts, but as the

day wore on the gaps grew shorter and the gusts more violent, whipping streamers of stinging spray from the curling tops of the waves
that had suddenly taken on an appearance more coldly hostile than
any we had seen before.

Long before sunset we had lost all sense of sunlight. The wrack
of clouds overhead was low and roiling, the masses of vapor churn-
ing upon themselves as the air grew darker. And then the first rain
squall struck us and abruptly we were all blind, in a world of utter
blackness filled with howling winds, hissing sheets of rain and terrifying, chaotic motion that annihilated all the rules by which we had
been taught to live and move on land. Above and beyond all of those
things, however, were the appalling noises made by the ship itself
under the stresses of the storm, when the threat-filled, menacing
creaks and groans and screams of tortured ropes and planks made it
sound as though the vessel were about to rip itself asunder and
disintegrate under the hammering of wind and water.

All four of us passengers, who had believed ourselves to be ill
until then, immediately plunged to the bottom of an abyss of despair
and abject, inhuman sickness. I know not how the sailors fared
during all that transpired that first night—I have to presume that
they continued doing what they were employed to do, since we
survived the tempest—but we four, embarked upon an adventure,
suffered beyond description. For several days one hammering storm
rolled over us and passed by only to be replaced by another, even
more violent upheaval. None of us could recall having been that
sick, or that helpless, or that frightened at any time in our lives.

I often talked to people about that voyage in the years that
followed, and I was always amazed at the unworldliness and the
indescribably profound ignorance of people who have never been
aboard a ship in foul weather. They simply cannot conceive of the
difference between a storm on land and a storm at sea, and the most
common question I encountered whenever I told the tale was, "Why
didn't you go ashore and get out of it?"

Why indeed? It was a question I might have asked myself, the
day before we set sail upon that voyage. But experience taught

me very quickly that it was a question with no simple, clear-cut answer. In the first place, and most particularly at night, we could not even see the shore, and all we knew was the terrifying truth told to us by our captain and his crew—that we had to hold the ship in safety far away from the land in order to prevent its being hurled against the rocks and crushed like an egg. So great was the power of the breaking waves, we were told, that our bodies would be destroyed by its savagery, pounded into unrecognizable, bloodless meat against the rocks along the shoreline. That was a comforting vision to sustain us in our terror. Then, too, we were prohibited from any simple act of "going ashore" by the size and shape of our vessel. It was a trading craft, broad and deep-keeled, designed to carry large volumes of cargo, which meant that it could not simply be rowed up into the shallows fronting a beach and grounded there.

In order to bring our large ship to land and unload his goods in safety, Joachim required the presence of a pier at which he could moor the vessel, or, failing that—a situation the captain described with no great enthusiasm—he needed to find a straight-edged shoreline or a riverbank along which the water was deep and calm and its surface no more than half the height of a man below the land's. Neither one of these could be achieved with anything resembling safety in stormy conditions, and one or the other of them was necessary for us to unload our eight horses and all the goods we carried with us. We ourselves might leap over the side in relatively calm waters and swim to safety, but we would do so at great cost, since we would have to leave everything, including our armor and weapons, behind us aboard ship and would thus be stranded in a strange land without any means of surviving or even defending ourselves.

Shortly before dawn on the morning of our second day at sea, we felt the wind abating and the motion of the ship became less violent, sufficiently so for me to bestir myself to find the captain and ask him what was happening. He told me we were in the lee of Wight, which left me squinting painfully, wondering if I had lost the proper use of my ears. Wight, he told me then, is an island off the south coast of Britain, and we were now sheltered between it and the mainland, enjoying the respite that its bulk provided from the winds. We would stay there, he told me, in the hope of riding out the remainder of the storm.

Day broke, and even from afar we could see the fury of the waves that pounded the mainland to the north of us. To our left, however, the coast of Wight seemed placid, and I mentioned to Joachim that we might be able to land there. He gazed at me with what seemed like pity, and so long did he take to respond that I began to think he was going to say nothing at all.

"Aye, you could," he said eventually, a half smile quirking at his lips. "No difficulty about that, if you want to. But you might have some trouble after that, once you're ashore."

I frowned. "Why is that? Are the people hostile there?"

"No, they're not. But that's Wight. It is an island. If I land you there, then sail back to Gaul, you might not be able to get off again. There's four of you, remember, and eight horses. I doubt if you'd find a boat on the whole island big enough to carry off all of you at one time, and even although it may not look like a great distance from there to the mainland, this stretch of water is miles wide, so you couldn't swim."

I felt my face flush at my own obvious stupidity, but Joachim laughed. "Hey," he said, sweeping his hand across the horizon in front of us, "you're a landsman, how could you be expected to know about the shortage of ships on Wight? There's no way to tell from here that it's almost deserted, but it's true. Most of the people who once lived there now live ashore, on the mainland. But the only reason I know that is because I've sailed this way before, more times than I can recall. My livelihood depends on knowing things like that when I go to sea. I dare say, were we among your woods in Gaul, you'd be leading me by the hand, because I can't stand being hemmed in. I like to feel empty distances around me . . . nothing but me, my ship and my crew between the water below me and the sky above."

"But you could have dropped us ashore there anyway and made your way directly home, and had anyone asked, you could have said that I requested to be set down there."

He looked at me sideways and smiled more broadly now, although still with an element of ruefulness, as though wondering about my lack of wit. "Think you so? Really?" He shook his head. "I have your gold in my chest, that's true, but there's also the fact that you have come to me from Germanus, and that's worth more to me than gold. If I did anything as stupid as you suggest, I would lose his friendship, and I don't care to do that."

I nodded slowly, acknowledging the wisdom of what he had said. "Then what should we do?"

"Exactly what we are doing. We stay here in reasonable safety, riding at anchor, and we watch for wind shifts while we wait out the storm."

We remained in the shelter of the island for the rest of that day and the night that followed, and by dawn the following day the storm had blown itself out.

We struck out once more to the west, and for the space of several hours we had blue skies and only scattered clouds overhead, although the waves pounding the beaches had scarcely lessened in their fury. Once again, however, by the middle of the afternoon the clouds were blowing in from the northwest in marshaled ranks. Hoping to evade this new storm, we swung in sharply towards the coast, but we could see from a long way out that the coastline here was one of high, unbroken cliffs fronted by ragged lines of rocks against which angry breakers smashed themselves into towers of spuming whiteness. There might have been inlets there where we could shelter, Joachim said, but he was unfamiliar with the coastline here and by the time we approached close enough to search for suitable havens, we would be too late to make our way back out to safety against the incoming storm if we found none. So once again we remained far out at sea, at the mercy of the winds and the waves, and our misery deepened.

The hardened mariners had regained their seagoing constitutions by that time and they ate contentedly despite the motion of the seas, chewing dried meat and hard bread and washing them down with beer or watered wine. The mere sight of them eating and drinking made the four of us landsmen sicker than we had been before.

In due time, we rounded the point of Cornwall, gazing despairingly at the towering cliffs that offered us nothing in the way of moorage, and made our way forlornly back to the northeast, the wind now blowing directly towards us so that our passage became even slower and more difficult than it had been until then. Glastonbury was our destination now, Joachim told us, although if a safe harbor appeared between now and our arrival there, we would take advantage of it.

We clawed our way slowly and with enormous effort up along the coastline, rowing into the teeth of the wind, with all four of us passengers contributing our efforts for the common good until we were barely able to keep ourselves from collapsing into unconsciousness. And as we went, having lost all awareness of day fading into night on several occasions, the storms continued to fall upon us in an apparently endless succession, each new one following closely after the passing of its predecessor. Eventually, however, we entered the estuary of a large river, and the waters quickly began to grow calmer. I had begun to regain control of my bodily functions two days before that and had been improving steadily if slowly, so that I noticed the lessening of the turmoil under our keel immediately and lost no time in asking Joachim for an explanation. He pointed with his thumb towards the distant shoreline that was barely discernible through the curtains of rain on our left.

"We're heading directly eastward now, entering the river channel the local people call the Severn. That shoreline over there, that's Cambria. Never been there but I've heard much about it. Hostile to everyone, the people there, although nobody seems to know why they should be. They have nothing much to be jealous of. Country's mountainous and mostly impenetrable, once you strike inland from the sea. Romans never really made much of an attempt to conquer it, although they say the biggest goldmine in the Empire's in there somewhere . . . some place called Dolaucothi, or something like that."

He pointed again, this time to the closer, low-lying land on our right. "That's your destination, over there. It's mainly flat inland, but boggy and treacherous close to the sea. Glastonbury lies farther down the coast. We passed by it early this morning. Didn't wake you because there was nothing to see and we didn't even approach it—no hope of landing there in weather like this. It's too flat. Too shallow and muddy. And the approaches—there's only a few navigable channels that let you get in there—have probably been destroyed by now, churned up and fouled by these storms. I wasn't prepared to sail into a bog to put that to the test.

"I decided to keep moving up to the estuary here. There's an old river port about thirty miles upstream. Romans called it Glevum. It's deserted now. Or it was last time I came this way, about three years ago. But the wharves were still serviceable then, and if no one's been along to tear them down or burn them up, they should still be usable. Good enough for us to land you on, certainly.

"From there you should be able to make your way easily. There's a main road goes close by there, and once you're on that, you can go anywhere. The road network connects all parts of Britain. At least, I've been told it does. Never was interested enough to go and find out for myself. Roads make me nervous. Too narrow and predictable and too many people use them. Nowhere to escape to, on a road. Give me the sea any day, even in weather like this. A man who knows what he's doing can escape from anyone, any time, at sea, providing he's got a fast ship and an able crew.

"Anyway, if nothing else we're off the open sea and out of the storms, with calm water under our keel from now on. Pass on my felicitations to your friends on surviving the crossing."

He grinned and left me standing watching him as he returned to the business of captaining his vessel, and within a matter of hours we were drifting slowly into the river port at Glevum, gazing at the spectacle of a ruined and uninhabited town as we glided slowly towards an abandoned wharf that was lined with warehouses and appeared to be in perfect condition. For the first time in days, not a breath of wind stirred from any direction, and beneath us the surface of the river would have been mirror calm had it not been for the slashing rain.

The ship's side bumped against the wharf and two seamen leaped ashore with ropes that they quickly secured to massive, oaken bollards. Others rushed to lower the side of the ship, creating a gateway to the deck, while yet more of the crew manned the block-and-tackle cargo hoist and struggled to extract the gangway from its resting place along the center line of the ship and swing it outboard to the wharf. A sudden grunt and a scuffling noise was followed by a panicked curse, and then came a bump and a splash as one of the crew slipped on the rain-slick boards and fell overboard between the wharf and the ship.

All movement stopped instantly as men watched and waited for the screams of the man being crushed between ship and wharf. For long moments nothing happened at all, and then the fallen man splashed to the surface on the other side of the vessel, having dived deep and swum beneath it. With a roar of relief, his shipmates hurried to pull him safely aboard again, and then they all returned to the work of preparing to unload.

Tristan looked at his brother Perceval—I had already stopped thinking of him as Ursus—who stared quietly back at him, his mouth quirked up to one side, then turned to me. "Well," he said quietly, "he didn't die, so let's hope we can accept that as a good omen." He glanced back at Bors and Tristan, who stood watching. "Welcome to Britain, lads. It's wet, and it's dark, and it's none too pleasant, and there's nothing yet to like about it, that I've seen. But at least it looks as though it's solid underfoot. Who's to be first ashore?"

I was, and as soon as my feet landed on the wharf I immediately threw out my arms and lurched forward ludicrously, fighting for balance and trying not to fall headlong as the ship's crew, who had been waiting for me to do just that, roared with laughter and jeers. The others followed me more cautiously, all three of them frowning intently with concentration as they moved, but they had no notion of why I had behaved the way I had and so were equally unprepared and fell about the same way I had, to be greeted with equally loud jeers from the crew.

It took less than an hour for us to unload our animals and provisions, and we all set out for the town, in search of a roof to keep the rain away from us while we lit a fire and cooked the sole remaining joint of venison that we had brought with us from Gaul—a fine haunch that held enough meat to feed all twelve of us in the last meal we would share with our seafaring friends for some time. Sound roofs were few and far between in Glevum, we discovered, although the ruins of the fallen ones offered a wealth of dry firewood, but we found a whole roof eventually, at the extreme end of one of the warehouse blocks lining the wharf next to the one on which we had landed, and all of us moved in gratefully, happy to be out of the incessant rain and within sight of the leaping flames of a real fire.

As we waited for the spitted haunch of salted venison to roast, we salivated over the savory smells of baking bannock and of garlic and onions bubbling in a pot with greens of some kind provided by the ship's cook.

I handed Joachim a small package containing ten more gold coins than we had agreed upon. He looked at it askance.

"What's this? You paid me already."

I shrugged. "I know, but Bishop Germanus told me to spend the funds judiciously, according to my conscience and to what you, in particular, did for us. I believe you did far more than we asked of you and so I think of this, a token of our gratitude, as money well spent. Besides, you still have to win home. And now you and I need to make another tryst. In six months' time, I would like you to return to this same wharf, seeking us. If we are not here, it will be for good and sufficient reason, although I will try to send word to you of why we are not here, and possibly to arrange another meeting at another time. Will you agree to that?"

Joachim tucked the small package into a decorated pouch at his belt. "In six months? Aye, I'll be here, providing I am still alive by then. And I will stay for ten days, should no one be waiting here to meet me. And look you here, come with me." He rose, and I followed him outside. He pointed to the ground where an old, flat, badly rusted piece of iron lay at an angle against the base of the wall. "I saw that as I entered. It's worth nothing and it looks as though it's been lying there for years. If I have to leave with no word from you after the ten days I spoke of, I'll leave you written word of when I will next return, and I'll stuff it under there. That way, if you can't meet me at the appointed time, you can at least leave word of what your plans are. Agreed?" He paused. "You *can* read and write, can't you?"

I smiled. "Aye. I was surprised to find you can, too, that's all."

He smiled back at me. "Aye, well, I had a clever teacher when I was a boy. A crazed man who thought it would be worthwhile for me to know how to read and write when none of my friends could. Afterwards, when I found myself living among people who could do neither, I thought he must have been insane, for nothing is more useless than being the only person able to read and write. But he was right, of course, and it has served me well." He reached out a hand and I shook it gladly. "Go with God, young Clothar of Benwick," he said, "and may He watch over you and those you love. We'll bid each other farewell again later, but this one is between you and me alone."

2

Four days later it was still raining heavily as we headed westward across the first cultivated fields we had seen since landing in Britain. We had been proceeding cautiously, taking all the time we needed and being careful to run no unnecessary risks in this alien land.

We had headed due south from our landing place, following the road that stretched for miles on end with barely a bend or a curve in the length of it, but remembering what Joachim had had to say

about there being no escape on a road, I kept us off the road surface
and safely to one side, concealed among the trees. Only once in four
days had we seen other travelers, and that had been in an area of
gently rolling hills that concealed the people approaching us until
they crested the brow of a rise in the road and passed us swiftly,
riding north, a tight-knit, highly disciplined band of armed men,
perhaps forty strong and moving with determination.

I remembered then what Germanus had told me: that in all of
Britain, only Merlyn Britannicus's Camulod had cavalry.

Knowing the newcomers then to be friendly to our cause, I
spurred my horse out onto the road, ignoring the dismayed cries of
my friends and riding hard after the moving column, shouting at the
top of my voice.

The rearmost riders heard me and turned in their saddles to look
back, then reacted predictably, shouting to their companions and
turning their mounts rapidly to face me. I saw the tight ranks ahead
of me eddy and break apart, then reform swiftly to present a solid
line of men and horses, all awaiting my arrival. Behind me, I knew,
Perceval, Tristan and Bors were spurring to catch up to me, and I
raised my arm and waved them back and away as I slowed my horse
to a walk and slowly approached the faceless men ahead of me. And
faceless they were, because each of them wore a fully closed
helmet, the side flaps pulled together and fastened over their faces,
leaving only a black slash of a hole across their eyes.

I pulled my mount to a stop less than thirty paces from their
front rank and sat there motionless, waiting for someone to come
forward to greet me or challenge me. None of them spoke at all, and
I was conscious of their eyes taking in every detail of my appearance. My fine armor was securely wrapped and slung on Bors's
packhorse, and I knew that I did not appear to be armored at all,
although I was wearing Germanus's supple tunic of ring mail
beneath my heavy, sodden military cloak of waxed wool. On my
head I wore only a knitted woolen cap, soaked through and through,
with a long, brightly colored but bedraggled feather thrust into it.
The ranks facing me stirred and parted, and a man who was

evidently their commander came forward to confront me. He paused briefly, reining his horse in tightly, then kneed it forward again and approached to within a few paces of where I sat waiting, where he stopped and sat staring at me, saying nothing.

I knew this was a test, designed to make me speak first out of fear and uncertainty, and so I sat still, determined not to be the first to break the silence, and finally the stranger spoke, his voice sounding hollow and reverberating as it emerged from the cavern of his helmet.

"Who are you, whence come you, and what is your business here in Camulod?"

So, I thought, *we are within Camulod at last.* I nodded and sat straighter, forcing myself to speak slowly and clearly. "My name is Clothar of Benwick in Gaul, and I come bearing messages and gifts for Merlyn Britannicus of Camulod from his friend Germanus, Bishop of Auxerre, also in Gaul. Behind me are my traveling companions, Perceval and Tristan of Montenegra, and my attendant, Bors. To whom am I speaking?"

"To one who has met Germanus and heard him promise to return here in person." The helmeted head with its high crest tilted slightly to one side. "Tell me, if you will, why I should believe you have come here from Gaul. Did you swim here, horses and all?"

"No, we came by sea, hoping to land at Glastonbury, but we were blown beyond it by the storms." My mind was racing, searching for information that I could present to this man that would assure him of our amity yet reveal nothing of our true business here. I knew he was not really suspicious of us. Our very openness in approaching him from behind must have made it clear to him we had no wish to conceal ourselves. But I knew, too, that I had to say something to justify our presence and to establish our bona fides.

"You have met Germanus. Are you then familiar with the name of Enos?"

"Aye, Enos of Verulamium. Another bishop."

"But a Britannian bishop, is he not?"

"*Britannian*? If by that you mean he is a Briton then aye, he is."

"Well, I bear dispatches in the form of letters from Germanus in Auxerre to Enos in Verulamium, concerning matters which the two of them discussed last year in conjunction with Merlyn Britannicus when last they met—in Verulamium, just before Merlyn had to leave in haste because of the word that Horsa's Danes had sailed for Cornwall."

The man facing me reached up slowly to his chin with one hand and pulled upwards on the end of a short cord that hung there, releasing a metal pin that held the flaps of his helmet together, and as they fell apart he reached higher and pulled the helmet from his head, revealing a strong, evenly featured face, dark haired and dark browed, with a long nose, a wide, square jaw and a mouth that suggested strength of will and good humor. It was the face of a veteran soldier, secure and confident of his own abilities. He flicked a drip of rainwater from the end of his nose with the tip of a fore-finger and inclined his head slightly in a grave and courteous acknowledgment that he accepted what I had said.

"Philip," he said. "Philip Rider, they call me, commander of the Fourth Wing of the cavalry forces of Camulod. Welcome to our lands. Where did you land, the river port?"

"Aye, the place called Glevum. Can you tell me where I might find Merlyn Britannicus?"

"No, Master Clothar, I cannot. I can tell you where you will *not* find him, however, and that is in Camulod. He was there for a few months, but he left some time ago and told no one where he was going. He told some of his closest friends that he will be away for some time—'for as long as it may take' was what he actually said, although no one knows what 'it' is—and he could, or he would, give them no idea of when he might return."

He hesitated, then added, "As to where he went, he could have gone anywhere. Merlyn prefers his own company nowadays, would rather be alone, they say, since his misfortunes in Cambria last year."

"What misfortunes are those?"

The man called Philip frowned. "He almost died in Cambria, was thrown into a fire there and badly burned."

"*Thrown* into a fire? By whom?"

Philip almost smiled. "A mad whoreson called Carthac, big and ugly and evil and as strong as ten good men. They thought he was unkillable, invincible. He thought so, too, until Merlyn killed him. But before he died he threw Merlyn into a fire. Arthur arrived shortly after that, leading us, and we were able to save Merlyn's life. Took him home on a wagon and nursed him back to health. But as soon as he could move freely, he left again, and as I say, no one knows where he went."

"Are your wars over?"

That earned me a quizzical look that told me Philip found it difficult to accept that anyone would have to ask such a thing. "For this year, you mean? Aye, they seem to be. There's peace in Cambria, to the north of here—Carthac was the festering thorn there, and with his death things soon died down. And in Cornwall to the south, the troublemaker was a man called Ironhair. But he seems to have fallen out with his henchman, Horsa, who hanged him for his troubles." A tiny smile flickered at the edges of his mouth. "So there's peace in these parts, at least. But then there is continuing war against the Saxons to the east, although some won't come out and call it that. The Saxons are a permanent curse and the confrontation out there is more of a chronic condition than a state of war. North and south, though, Camulod is at peace for the moment.

"Our leader, Arthur, is on a grand sweep to the north and east, far beyond our lands, showing the banners and the cavalry of Camulod in other parts of the land in the hope of rallying people to stand up together and confront the Outlanders—Saxons and Jutes and Danes and all the other hordes swarming on the eastern side of Britain." He waved a hand to indicate the men behind him. "We are but the advance party of a full cavalry wing of a thousand mounted troopers, coming less than a mile behind us. A strong force, but our mission is peaceable. We ride merely to show our strength, patrolling our territories."

I nodded, thinking rapidly. "I see. And Arthur Pendragon rides to the north and east, you say. Where is he now, exactly, do you know?"

Philip made a wry mouth. "No one will be able to answer that question until Arthur himself returns with the word of it. He has been gone for two months and more. He could be anywhere by now."

"And Merlyn would not be with him?"

Now the man looked puzzled. "Why would Merlyn be with him? Arthur's no longer a student. He's a commander of cavalry in his own right, commander of the First Wing. He looks after his responsibilities and Merlyn looks after his own. Besides, Merlyn could not have known which way Arthur went, other than north, because Arthur left from Cambria, while Merlyn was still abed in Camulod, recovering from his wounds."

"Hmm," I grunted, thinking deeply about what we should do next. "Thank you, Philip Rider. Can you show me the shortest way to Camulod from here? And this damnable rain, does it ever stop?"

Philip flashed a smile. "Why, man, it seldom starts at all. It will blow by within the next day or two, and the weather will turn fine again before winter sets in, you wait and see. And as for the route to Camulod, that's easy. Simply follow this road south from here until you reach a garrisoned town called Ilchester. They're our people there, and they'll point you in the right direction. You should stay here, however, until our thousand pass you by. I'll leave a decurion with you to explain your presence to Commander Rufio, and after that you can proceed. Now, if you will permit me, I have to make up time and distance."

He slipped his helmet back onto his head and saluted me, bringing his clenched fist to his left breast, then turned his horse around and gave the signal to the men in front of him. In a matter of moments they had regrouped, leaving only one of their number with us, and were cantering away from us.

The decurion greeted us with a courteous nod and then sat silently beside us, and within a short time we heard the approaching cavalry squadrons. Their leaders, riding in the vanguard, drew rein on our side of the road as they neared us, and the decurion rode forward to explain our presence. They listened and nodded, then rode on by us with the decurion, nodding courteously but otherwise paying us no attention. When the last of the thousand had passed us by, their remounts, several hundreds in number, followed after them, herded by a large number of boys below fighting age, and we sat watching until the last of the animals had disappeared from view along the road behind the shrouds of falling rain.

Only then did Perceval turn to me with an admiring grunt. "I can't believe that the only thing in this god-forsaken country that I haven't hated on sight is one and a half thousand of the finest horses I've ever seen. Where do they find beasts like that? I can't believe they breed them here in such an unholy climate."

"Believe it," I told him. "They breed them all here now, according to Germanus, but their origins were Empire-wide. Let's be off. It's not far now to Camulod and I would like a roof over my head as soon as it can be arranged. I'll tell you what Germanus told me about their cavalry as we ride."

We kicked our horses into motion, and Perceval and Tristan ranged themselves on either side of me while young Bors rode close behind us, straining to hear.

I raised my voice until I was almost shouting over the noise of the rain. "The story goes that seventy-one years ago, in the year 376, in a place called Adrianopolis in Asia Minor beyond the eastern edges of the Middle Sea, a Roman consular army of forty thousand men, commanded by the Co-emperor Valens, was overrun and wiped out by a mounted force of Ostrogoths. It was a freakish accident and it should never have happened, but it did. The Goths were migrating from one region to another. They even had their women and children with them. But they were all mounted, on small, shaggy ponies, and they crested a mountain ridge to see an entire Roman army below them, marching in extended order along the edge of a lake. They charged immediately and caught the legions before they could form up in battle order, then rolled them up like a carpet. Forty thousand Romans died that afternoon, including Valens and his entire staff, and the word went out that the Romans were vulnerable to attack by massed formations of horsemen." I glanced from side to side and saw that both my friends were listening closely, so I kept talking.

"Theodosius was still Emperor at that time, and Flavius Stilicho, who was half Roman and half Vandal, was his most brilliant legatus. Stilicho had been appointed commander in chief of the Imperial Household Troops—in other words, commander in chief of all Rome's legions and the most powerful soldier in the world—at the age of twenty-two. They say he was the greatest natural military genius since Alexander the Great of Macedon. Anyway, Stilicho launched an immediate-priority program to re-equip and retrain all the legions of Rome in order to counteract this new threat of mounted attack, and within the space of twenty-five years he had increased each legion's cavalry strength from the traditional five percent of light, skirmishing cavalry—mounted archers whose sole duty was to form a mobile defensive screen while the legion was forming its battle lines—to twenty-five percent heavy, disciplined cavalry that operated in the manner of Alexander's heavy cavalry of six hundred years earlier, riding in tightly packed, disciplined formations and carrying heavy spears." I paused, allowing them to absorb what I had said before continuing. "Now that might not sound like much of a feat when you hear someone say it as quickly and plainly as I have just said it, but don't let that mislead you. Think about what was involved in those changes.

"It was an enormous undertaking, according to everything the bishop told me, and he had made a study of all it involved. That Stilicho was able to achieve such a transformation at all was astonishing, Germanus says, for he had first to confront and defeat the opinions and the plotting of the stubborn old-guard traditionalists who didn't want anything to change and who believed that the old ways would always be the best ways. And the fact that most of them resented him for his youth and his brilliance did not make his task any easier. Stilicho never quit, and eventually he won. But that he was able to achieve what he did within twenty-five short years was nothing short of miraculous."

I looked from one to the other of them and they stared back at me, waiting. "I know the bishop likes to talk of miracles and miraculous occurrences. He is a bishop, after all. But it really is astounding. Imagine, for a start, the sheer *scope* of the program that was required worldwide to breed the number of horses needed to equip every legion in the field with that many horses, including remounts and pack animals. Then think about the size of the animals involved. Light, skirmishing cavalry needed only small, light horses, and Rome had always had plenty of those. But for heavy cavalry you need big, heavy horses. Those they did not have, and they needed thousands of them. So where did they find them?

"I'll tell you where they came from. They created them, bred them out of what they had available. Once again, they launched a new, especially designed program all across the Empire. A cross-breeding program, to mate the largest, strongest animals they could find with the finest they had of lesser size, in order to breed larger offspring. By the end of twenty-five years, the results were astounding.

"But then they discovered, too, that the new 'heavy' cavalry, mounted on huge horses, was poorly equipped. They were armored heavily on top, as Roman troops had always been, but now their legs were vulnerable, hanging down among the enemy on foot. So new armor had to be designed to protect the riders' legs, and new techniques for making it. And swords had to be lengthened and strengthened, for even the traditional cavalry spatha was too short to be effective from the back of a large, tall horse. And so a new study of metal crafting and smithing was launched to find new ways of working iron and steel to make longer, stronger weapons. It goes on and on, each problem giving rise to new solutions that led in turn to other problems in a never-ending cycle.

"Eventually, however, after only twenty years, in the period from 396 until 398, when Stilicho was Regent to the infant emperor Honorius, he brought the central corps of his new cavalry forces to train them here in Britain, in secrecy, against seaborne invasions of Picts, Saxons and Hibernian Scots. They were extremely successful." I paused, purely to emphasize the effect of my next words.

"Barely three years after that, however, when Stilicho had to summon the legions home in haste from Britain to defend Italia itself against invasion by Alaric and his Visigoths, they had to leave those cavalry mounts behind, simply because they lacked the means to take the animals with them. A man called Caius Britannicus, grandsire to Merlyn and the founder of the place now called Camulod, had become a friend to Flavius Stilicho during the Regent's campaign here. The Regent named this man legatus emeritus and granted him temporary ownership of all the abandoned Roman cavalry mounts, charging him with keeping them safe and secure pending the return of the legions to Britain. But the legions never returned, and those Roman horses became the foundation of the cavalry of Camulod and triggered the ascendancy of Merlyn's colony."

I fell silent then, and it felt as though I had been talking for a very long time, but neither of my companions made any comment on anything I had said. We proceeded for almost a mile before Tristan broke the silence.

"It has not stopped raining in seven days," he said. "Not once. I forget what the sky looks like without clouds. I can barely remember sunshine. I think we may die here in Britain, drowned in rainwater. Most of all, though, I'm longing for the warmth and dryness of that filthy old warehouse in Glevum. I think God must have forgotten we're here."

I was slightly stunned by the obliqueness of what he had said. And then it occurred to me that he had offered an apt comment on the importance of my impromptu history lesson and its relevance here and now. I nodded, accepting that, and glanced up at the sky.

"Sweet Jesus!" As the others swung to face me I pointed upwards. "Look!"

To the east, a golden beam of sunlight had sprung blazing, clean edged and brilliant from a narrow, bright blue gap in the clouds.

3

From that moment of seeing the first ray of sunshine breaking through the rain clouds, the entire land of Britain seemed to change its mind and welcome us, showing us warmth and beauty and hospitality where before we had known only dankness, gloom and despondency.

The memory of my first sight of the distant fortress of Camulod, sitting high on its wooded hill overlooking the rich and fertile plain beneath, has remained with me forever afterwards. Strangely enough, looking back upon it across the distance of years, I realize now that I did not think of it as a fortress at all when I first saw it. I saw Camulod from afar as a place of great and exciting beauty, rather than as a defensive bastion. I saw that the place had none of the grandeur or magnificence of the great castellated fortresses of Gaul, and in the years to come I would see many finer and stronger buildings and fortifications along the southeast coastline of Britain itself, the so-called Forts of the Saxon Shore, built by the Roman occupying forces hundreds of years earlier and abandoned when the legions left.

What I saw in the distance that first day, for reasons I have never known or sought to understand, was a symbol of hope and, most surprisingly in retrospect, of peace, because it had become obvious by the time we came within sight of Camulod that day that, despite what Philip had told us about being at peace, we were in a land fully prepared for war. There were parties of soldiers moving everywhere we looked, mainly cavalry but with a substantial leavening of infantry, and we were challenged constantly by people demanding to know who we were and what we were about. Fortunately, the fact that we were both well dressed and well mounted worked in our favor, for it quickly became apparent to us that the enemy, whoever they might be, went largely afoot and owned little of the sophisticated weaponry carried by the troopers of Camulod—that word, *troopers,* was a new one to me, but easy enough to understand. Close to the hilltop fort itself, at the bottom of the winding road that swept up to the main gates concealed behind the curtain wall, a vast training ground of hard-packed earth that showed no single blade of grass was filled to apparent capacity with wheeling, constantly moving groups of training troopers.

That close to the castle walls, no one paid us any attention and we mounted all the way to the main gates before we were challenged again, this time by the senior member of a vigilant band of guards who stood before the gates, eyeing everyone who came and went and from time to time questioning anyone who excited their curiosity or caution. I remained mounted and stated our business, saying that I knew Merlyn Britannicus was not available, but asking to meet with someone who could speak on his behalf.

That someone turned out to be a giant of a man, perhaps twice my own age, who strode out from the gates some time later and stood looking down at us without speaking, his arms crossed upon his enormously broad chest as he examined each of us from head to foot. The guards had told us to dismount while we were waiting for this fellow to be summoned, and now that he had come I found myself wishing I had remained on horseback. Even unarmored and wearing only a simple tunic, this man was hugely tall and physically intimidating, even larger and stronger looking than my cousin Brach, the biggest, most muscular and imposing man I had ever known.

He made no effort to speak to us at first, more concerned with assessing any threat that we might represent to him or to his people. His eyes moved over each of us meticulously, missing nothing and even examining the harness and trappings of our horses. Finally, however, he seemed satisfied and nodded very slightly, the set of his shoulders relaxing visibly. He introduced himself, in a voice that was pleasantly deep and surprisingly gentle, as Donuil Mac Athol, adjutant to Merlyn Britannicus. He spoke in Latin, as did we all, but with an intonation I had never heard before. Knowing him to be a local of some description merely from his name—Mac Athol meant son of Athol in the Gallic tongue—I assumed he was a northerner, from the mountains, perhaps a Cambrian. It transpired that I was wrong. He was a Scot, from the island of Hibernia across the western sea, but I would not learn that until later.

I had said nothing to him until then and had no way of knowing whether he had been told who we were or what we wanted with Merlyn, but he addressed me first, ignoring my two older companions.

"You come from Auxerre? From Germanus?" I nodded. "Well, I hope there's no great urgency to your mission. Merlyn is gone, where and for how long no one knows, not even my wife, and that's a wonder, for she knows everything. Tell me your names."

I introduced myself first, and then Perceval, Tristan and Bors. Donuil's eyes moved to each person as I said their names, and when I had finished he nodded again.

"Good, then. Perceval, Tristan and young Bors. Be welcome in Camulod. Come inside now and we'll find someone to look after your things for you, your gear and your horses . . . although I imagine you, young fellow, will want to stay with your beasts and make sure no one touches anything without your say so, am I right?" When Bors nodded, Donuil grinned in response. "Aye, I'd have been disappointed had you said otherwise. So be it. We'll come back and find you in a while. But you three, are you thirsty? We have some fine brewers of beer here in Camulod. Come you and let's see if we can find some of their best."

After dinner that night, on what was merely the first of many long, pleasant evenings by the fire in the quarters belonging to Donuil and his lustrous and beautiful wife, Shelagh, we received our first lessons in the intimate family tale of the development of Camulod and the two families, Britannicus and Varrus, that had brought it into being and shaped it into the self-contained and practically self-sufficient society it had become.

We talked about Bishop Enos, too, and about the mission I had been charged with regarding him. I now believed that I must talk to Enos without delay. No one in Camulod knew how or where to find Merlyn, but my experiences at the Bishop's School had taught me that few organizations were more adept and well qualified at communicating among themselves and finding people than was the Church itself. Bishop Enos had work to do, both with and for Merlyn, on behalf of his friend and colleague Germanus of Auxerre, and I, too, had information to communicate to Merlyn. It seemed to me there was a far better chance of reaching him through Verulamium and the ecclesiastical contacts of Bishop Enos than there was of finding him through the offices of anyone in Camulod.

Donuil listened to all this, impatiently I thought, and would have demurred had not his wife forestalled him, agreeing with my viewpoint. After that—and it was plain that the giant Donuil had not the slightest desire to challenge Shelagh's judgment—the only objection he could think to raise was that Enos might not be in Verulamium when we arrived there.

"I prefer the odds on that gamble," I told him. "Even if Enos isn't there when we arrive, chances are he won't be far away. Verulamium's not merely his home, it's the center of his activities. As the bishop there, it's unlikely he would stay away too long. His duties and responsibilities depend too much upon his being there most of the time. Over in Gaul Germanus seems to be forever traveling, but he is seldom absent from his bishopric in Auxerre for more than a few weeks at a time, even although he has an entire staff at his disposal because his territory is a lot bigger and broader than is Enos's."

By the end of that visit we had agreed that my friends and I should continue our journey without delay, heading north and west, following the route Merlyn himself had taken with his party at various times on the way to, and back from, Verulamium. Donuil would provide us with all the instructions we would need to find the town itself, and he generously offered us an escort of Camulodian troopers. We declined that, at first, believing, rightly or wrongly, that we would be less conspicuous traveling as a small group, but Donuil and Shelagh were both adamantly opposed to our going unescorted. We had no notions of the dangers we might have to face, they told us, reiterating their warnings until we threw up our hands and complied with their wishes.

I asked them then about the assistance we had been assured we would find provided by Cuthric and Cayena, influential Anglian leaders that Germanus had told me about. Husband and wife, they were Christians of long standing and had established themselves and their people widely in the lands surrounding and to the south and west of Enos's seat of Verulamium. Cuthric was what Germanus termed both a sage and a mage—a wise man and a devout Christian by nature and education, but also a man learned in the mysteries and esoterica of his people's ancient beliefs and rituals. Cuthric was accorded great respect and honor by his people, and his wife, Cayena, was the perfect consort to his presence. Even Merlyn and his party, Germanus had told me, had accepted the couple's beneficent influence on the Anglian community, and the fact that Merlyn and the forces of Camulod would recognize such people as a community rather than a nest of invading Outlanders went a long way towards explaining the kind of people these newcomers must be.

Donuil and Shelagh, however, could offer us no realistic hope of finding support among the Anglians, simply because they had no evidence to suggest that the Anglians were even out there any more. No word had been heard from Cuthric and Cayena since Germanus had returned to Gaul, and that entire eastern half of Britain had been sinking into a quagmire of escalating warfare and invasions. Beyond the boundaries of Camulod itself, which was not large, they told us, the entire land was in the grip of anarchy, a condition that they swore we could not begin to understand, having lived our whole lives under the benign influence—no matter how weak or tawdry that might now be—of the Pax Romana.

They were correct; we were to discover that very quickly and be forever grateful that they had made us heed their judgment, for had we ridden out of Camulod as we had first intended, four of us with eight horses, secure in the hubris of knowing our own prowess as fighters and warriors, we would not have survived the first five days of travel. Until we experienced the lawless condition of the country for ourselves, assessing it with our own eyes against the standards we had been taught to apply to life in all its aspects, we could not possibly have anticipated the immense and frightening differences that now existed between life at its worst in Roman Gaul and what passed as "normal" life in Britain. And all of those differences that we were to discover in such a short time—the utter lawlessness, the disregard for human life and dignity, and the rampant hostility, violence and brutality that we found everywhere—had all sprung into existence in the mere two score of years that had elapsed since the legions left, taking with them the power of the state to sustain and enforce justice.

4

We were less than ten miles beyond the outer boundaries of Merlyn's colony, guarded as it was by vigilant horse troopers and infantry manning an outer ring of defenses day and night, when we saw the first evidence of the lawlessness that would be all around us from then on: a sullen, heavy column of black smoke twisting upon itself and rising straight up into the afternoon sky. We veered off the road to investigate at my insistence, for the Camulodian troopers who escorted us would have ridden on by, too inured to what they would find even to bother looking for a cause, and soon we came to a clearing that had contained a squalid, rudimentary farm.

The burning buildings were already falling in upon themselves, their walls made of bare sapling trunks, rather than clay and wattle, and their roofs unthatched, mere racks of crossed poles layered with filthy straw that burned greasily. The farmer still spun slowly at the end of a rope and had been disemboweled after hanging. The naked, broken body of his wife lay under his dangling feet, partially covered by his trailing intestines. Two dead children lay nearby, one of them killed by an axe or sword stroke that had split the tiny skull asunder, and the other had been thrown into the inferno of the burning hut, leaving only a thin pair of legs and feet protruding into the farmyard.

I swung down from my saddle, expecting to do I know not what, but as the visual impressions swarmed upon me in quick succession, each of them worse than what had gone before, I was unable to contain the violent retching that swept over me. I staggered to one side, clutching for something to hold on to and finding nothing as I fell to my knees and vomited.

I was not alone, I saw as I straightened up. Young Bors had offered his sacrifice along with mine, and Tristan, although he had apparently retained his morning meal, sat stone-faced and ashen, staring into the trees and obviously unwilling to look at the carnage around us. Perceval was the only one of our four who appeared unmoved, although I knew him well enough by now to be able to see that he was deeply angry. Beside him, the young tribune whom Donuil had assigned to head our escort sat gazing at me, his expression unreadable. I spat to clear my mouth of the sour taste of vomit, and Perceval wordlessly tossed me the water bottle that he always kept hanging on his saddle. I rinsed my mouth thoroughly before crossing to the young tribune.

"Who would have done this, Cyrus?"

The young man shrugged, his mouth twisting downwards. "Anyone," he said. "Bandits, thieves, envious neighbors, perhaps even Saxon raiders."

"Envious neighbors? How can you find humor in a thing like this? And Saxons, this close to Camulod? Are you sure?"

He shook his head. "I see no humor here and I am sure of nothing, Lord Clothar, although I doubt this would be the work of Saxons. It's too small a thing—despite its immensity for those who died here. If there were Saxons in this region, there would have to be large numbers of them and we would soon find out." He was looking about him as he spoke, his eyes on the ground. "There were no large numbers here, no swarming footprints that I can see. This was probably done by a small group of bandits. There could have been nothing here worth stealing, save for a few skinny animals." He waved towards an empty sty and a trampled pile of filthy straw. "A pig, perhaps a cow."

"And they killed for that? A pig and a cow?"

Cyrus looked at me strangely. "That could be a rich haul for starving men, Lord Clothar. Well worth killing for, nowadays."

"Sweet Jesus! What kind of a place is this Britain?"

Cyrus sniffed loudly, managing to sound disdainful and condescending at once, and his choice of honorific when he named me again conveyed something of the depths of his contempt for me as an Outlander who knew nothing yet disparaged everything.

"It is a place without leadership, Master Clothar. A land without law, where the only right to life that a man has is the one he holds in his hand to defend himself and to enable him to take what he needs in order to keep himself and his family alive. There is no state-run *civitas* in Britain now, no government granaries, no public relief in time of famine. No food at all, other than what a man may hunt or grow for himself. That ensures a harsh, cruel existence for those who cannot fight or claw their way to the top of the ruck of despair. This is only the first sight you have had of it, but you will see more, believe me. Of course, things are different in Camulod. Camulod has law. But Camulod is not yet large enough for its laws to cover all men. And by that I mean our army is not large enough. You cannot uphold or support the rule of law unless you have the means to enforce that rule. Someday we will expand from Camulod and govern more widely, but not yet. We are close to the time, but it is not yet right."

I found myself looking now with dawning respect at this young officer, seeing beyond his outward condescension to the mettle of the man underneath. I had been in his company only since dawn that day, and other than a casual nod of greeting when we were introduced to each other I had paid him little heed. I had noticed that he kept to himself, content to ride alone at the head of his men, followed by his two decurions, and that he seemed completely comfortable with himself and with his relationship to the thirty men in his charge. This young man Cyrus, I had thought, was a typical young squadron commander of Camulod, where thirty-man squadrons, each with two decurions and a squadron commander, were the norm according to Donuil, and the word *turma,* normally used in Gaul to denote a sixty-man squadron, was unknown.

It appeared that I had been in error yet again and that there was more to young Cyrus than first met the eye. Either that, or the typical young squadron commanders being trained in Camulod were several orders of magnitude ahead of their counterparts in Roman Gaul, for over there no incentive was offered to young officers to develop either philosophical opinions or moral platforms, both of which this young man appeared to value. Cyrus the tribune might have been three or perhaps four years older than I was, but I accepted after having listened to him for mere moments that he might be twice my age in terms of self-possession and analytical prowess. I decided to say nothing about either his tone of voice or his offhand treatment of me. I could see plainly that, in his eyes, I had laid solid claim to deserving both.

I noted the way he stared back at me clear eyed, his face devoid of expression, and then I looked again at the hanging farmer and the ruins of his little family.

"This happens often, then." I did not intend it to be a question, and Cyrus made no response. I glanced back at him. "The people who did this can't be far away. They haven't had time to travel far, encumbered by cattle."

He shook his head gently. "No, they have not. They must be close by. Would you like us to hunt them?"

Now it was my turn to quirk my brow. "You don't want to. Why not?"

"Because if we hunt them we will find them and then we will have to hang them and they will die in utter misery and great pain, and what will we have achieved, for all that pain and misery?"

"Justice, for these people!"

Cyrus glanced towards the hanged farmer. "I think not, Master Clothar. Vengeance, perhaps. Revenge. But justice? By whose criteria? Justice in your eyes, perhaps. But who are you, in the absence of any and all laws, to judge what might have happened to reduce the people who did this to such a condition? Or do you believe they might have been born as monstrous as they were today when they did this? Something made these people behave like this, and many of those might be things the like of which you could never imagine: starvation, suffering, deprivation, cruelty at the hands of stronger folk. But even if they are simply monsters, I would say no to hunting them. There are too many thousands like them between us and Verulamium, and our task is to find Bishop Enos, not to right the wrongs of a godless world."

I nodded, a single, abrupt dip of my head. "You are right, Tribune. Inarguably. And I am an ignorant Outlander with too many questions and no appropriate answers. Ride with me, if you will, and educate me further."

I pulled myself up into my saddle and wheeled away without another glance at the charnel house in the small clearing to ride with Cyrus at the head of our column as we trotted back towards the high roadway that cut across the horizon in a perfectly level slash of blackness.

We talked together at great length thereafter, Cyrus and I, and I learned much from him about the rule of law in Camulod, as devised and laid down by Merlyn Britannicus and his forebears: his father, Picus Britannicus, his grandsire Caius Britannicus and his great-uncle Publius Varrus.

Cyrus, it transpired, was a student of law, not merely the laws of Camulod but those of Rome itself. His grandsire's father had been a lawyer in the days before Camulod was founded and had later worked with Caius Britannicus to establish the colony, which at that time had no name, and to draft the first of what would become Camulod's own laws in later years. Since then, Cyrus told me with pride, his family had been involved in governing the colony, as members of the Council of Camulod and custodians of the justiciary of the colony. It was their right and privilege to guard and maintain the written annals and records of the Camulodian law and its tribunals, and they had steadfastly upheld that responsibility since it was entrusted to them by Caius Britannicus himself, the founder of Camulod.

Cyrus himself was now fully prepared to assume the burden of his family responsibility whenever it should be passed on to him. For the time being, however, he served the colony, as all its men did, in a military capacity.

At one point while he and I were talking I noticed a trio of horsemen watching us from high above, on the side of a hill, and when I mentioned it to Cyrus he merely glanced up at them, then returned his gaze to the road ahead.

"They're bandits. They won't bother us because we're too strong for them. And we won't bother them, because they're too far away and we would have to work too hard to come in reach of them, with no guarantee that we ever would. The fellow in the red cloak is notorious in these parts. They call him the Ghost, because he seems to have the ability to be in more than one place at the same time. He's instantly recognizable by the red cloak, of course, but it doesn't seem to have occurred yet to people that he might own more than one and that he might perhaps issue them to certain friends of his for specific purposes. It's always the cloak that's seen; seldom the man's face."

"How many men does he have?"

"Altogether about a hundred, perhaps a score or so more, plus all their women and camp followers. That's a lot of mouths to feed, for a bandit chief, so he has to keep traveling and raiding."

I was looking up to where the so-called Ghost sat on his horse, watching us. He seemed utterly unperturbed by our presence.

"If he has a hundred and more men, why do you say we're too strong for him?"

Cyrus chuckled. "Because we're cavalry. He might have twenty horsemen, at most, and none of them are trained in anything except staying on a horse's back. The rest of his men are all leg-mounted. We would crush them like a rotten nut, in one charge."

"He doesn't seem worried about being caught."

"Nor need he be. He knows he is not at risk, not today. One of these days, though, we'll catch him and his marauding will be ended."

"What will you do to him then? Hang him?"

"We might, although we have yet to hang anyone merely for being in disagreement with us. If he were to do something truly heinous, something that cried out for dire punishment, we might hang him and put an end to it. One of the men with whom we were at war in Cambria was such a creature—Carthac. He was a real devil, utterly incapable of mercy or compassion, and he received none from us when his time came. Merlyn killed him without compunction. There is simply no other way to deal with, or to control, someone like him.

"Simple banditry, though, as carried out by the Ghost up there, really boils down to feeding and providing for his people, and although admittedly he does it wantonly and at the dire expense of others, we have heard no reports of gross atrocities being laid at his feet. For that, and all his other crimes, we would probably simply disarm him and turn him loose afoot and weaponless, with a warning of what he can look forward to should we ever encounter him again at the same game."

Cyrus turned in his saddle then and gave the arm signal for our column to increase speed to a trot, and for a while after that there was no opportunity to talk further.

The network of magnificent roads that stretched all over Britain was, in my opinion, the single greatest marvel in the entire land, particularly so since it had existed for hundreds of years and was now barely used. That lack of use allowed an observer such as me to appreciate the complexity of all the work and planning that had gone into the construction of the network in the first place, but it was disconcerting to see such roads so deserted, because the traffic on the main roads of Gaul was so often dense and frantic. I had discussed the matter of road use at length with Donuil and Shelagh the night before we left for Verulamium, and what they had told me was fresh in my mind.

Donuil had said that the roads had fallen into disuse simply because they provided a focus for all the disruptive forces that existed to prey upon travelers. Bandits and thieves knew well that if they positioned themselves properly along a road they would, sooner or later, be easily able to intercept and rob any travelers who came along and were unequipped to fight strongly in their own defense. We, being who we were, were safe from any such threat, but few other people could afford to travel in the company of guardians strong enough to discourage attack, and so the roads had lain largely unused since the departure of the legions who had built, used and maintained them.

The roads represented the pragmatism of Rome's military genius. Knowing the shortest distance between two points to be a straight line, the ancient Romans had made it their first priority, from the earliest days of their military expansion, to construct roads for the convenience and the provisioning of their ubiquitous armies. The Roman legions, moving at the forced march pace along these magnificently straight causeways, could cover greater distances in less time than any other armies in history.

But mobility and ease of transportation were merely the most obvious aspects of the genius underlying Rome's road-building program. Another aspect, equally important, solved the ages-old problem of how to keep soldiers disciplined and usefully occupied during those times when they were not involved in war or preparing for war. In the ancient days of Republican Rome, the answer to that problem had been twofold: at the end of each day, after marching all day and eating on the move, the soldiers of each individual unit had been required to build an entire camp, fortified and defended on all four sides by a ditch and a defensive wall, to a specific plan that remained unchanged for hundreds of years. Only after the camp had been built and occupied were they permitted to relax and enjoy their only hot meal of the day. Then, the following morning before they resumed their march, they had to break down the camp they had built so painstakingly the night before. Thus the moving units of the armies were kept occupied, and effectively tired, with little time for dreaming up mischief and mayhem.

Their stationary counterparts, soldiers on garrison duty or those not currently marching over long distances, had their time filled for them by their superiors, too, all day, every day. They were kept hard at work building new roads or expanding and maintaining existing roads and buildings.

Over time, of course, what was temporary became permanent, and many of the overnight marching camps became permanent outposts, positioned at strategic road junctions or along particular stretches of road that had been identified as being in need of close supervision. And over the course of years and decades of the same efforts to keep soldiers busy and hard at work, the palisaded earthen ramparts of the original camps gave way to permanent walls of quarried, hand-dressed stone.

Meanwhile, outside the walls of these selfsame camps, the stalls and lean-to shelters of the tradesmen and merchants whose livelihood depended upon supplying the garrisons with all their needs were gradually replaced by solid, substantial buildings containing shops and manufactories for all kinds of commodities. And as these premises grew larger and required more and more support, they attracted workers and gave rise to towns.

Looking at those wondrous, unused roads in Britain, so different from the great, bustling highways of Gaul, I remembered clearly my own awestruck fascination when I first learned, at the Bishop's School, about the Roman roads and how they had transformed Rome's world. Because once the Empire had been pacified and the Pax Romana established, what remained was an open, universally accessible network of beautiful, publicly maintained roads connecting thriving towns everywhere, and that reality combined with the ease and swiftness of transportation and communication gave rise to commerce, so that eventually the hurrying bodies of troops for whom the roads had been originally built were supplanted by the caravans and wagon trains of trading merchants who bought and sold goods from all parts of the Empire and beyond its boundaries. And as the merchants prospered, so, too, did their society.

But then had come the beginnings of the dissolution of the Empire and the ending of the Pax Romana, and what had since happened here in Britain was a microcosm of what was happening to a greater or lesser degree in the rest of the Roman world. The roads were no longer safe because they could not be protected, and so almost overnight they had been transformed from avenues of opportunity and growth into long, inimical, tree-shrouded lanes filled with the threats of imminent violence and the constant fear of invasion and enslavement. Cyrus's words about Camulod's army not being big enough gained more and more relevance as I thought about what he had meant, and although the notion seemed strange to me at first, I soon began to accept that much of the rule of law might be restored here by the simple expedient of having bands of armed men patrolling the roads to safeguard travelers and discourage thieves and bandits.

5

It took us nearly two weeks to travel from Camulod to Verulamium. That was several days longer than it ought to have taken us, yet the journey across the belly of Britain was largely uneventful, and in fact highly enjoyable once we had reached the truly uninhabited uplands, and when we finally reached Verulamium we found Bishop Enos in residence.

Verulamium was a shell of a place that could barely lay title to the name of town any longer, and the bishop's residence was a plain, unimpressive building, long and low and purely functional, with no single element of beauty to distinguish it. But it was built of stone and it boasted a solid and enduring roof made of tiles imported many years earlier from Gaul.

The town had once been a thriving regional center, and the evidence of that was plain to be seen everywhere and most particularly in the surviving public buildings of the old administrative center, many of which were imposing and spacious. With the departure of the legions, however, and the subsequent eruption of anarchy over the ensuing decade when people lost all fear of being punished for anything they chose to do, Verulamium became, like most of the other towns in Britain, too dangerous a place in which to live, because it attracted plunderers and looters the way a carcass attracts flies. And so most of it had been abandoned, left to the mercy of the elements.

One thing had saved the place from being completely abandoned to neglect and decay, however, and that single thing was the reason for the continuing presence of Bishop Enos and the long line of bishops who had lived and worshipped there before his time. Verulamium had been the home of Britain's first Christian martyr, a saint called Alban. Alban had been executed by the Roman authorities two hundred years earlier, in the third century of the new, Christian calendar, for saving the life of a proscribed Christian priest during one of the periodic persecutions of the sect in the days before the Emperor Constantine had emancipated them and their religion by taking up the Cross himself. When arrested and challenged for his so-called crime—providing aid and sustenance to an enemy of the state—Alban had steadfastly refused to recant his newfound belief in the one true God and had been decapitated for his faith.

After that, the town had quickly become widely revered as the home of the blessed Saint Alban, and a shrine had been erected there in his honor, in response to the occurrence of several miraculous and unexplainable wonders. Even to the present time, according to Bishop Enos, miracles continued to occur as the result of the saint's blessed presence, and the shrine continued to attract more and more visitors with every year that passed. The town of Verulamium might be as dead as its Roman past, Enos remarked to me, but Saint Alban's shrine would never know oblivion, and in recent years people had stopped talking of the town as Verulamium, referring to it nowadays simply as Saint Alban's Shrine.

There was a gathering of some kind going on when we arrived there, and the unexpected appearance of a large band of disciplined horsemen caused no small amount of consternation among the participants. Bishop Enos himself, who was a much older man than

I had expected him to be, was the first to recognize the armor and trappings of our Camulodian troopers and he quickly brought his flock to order, explaining to them who we were and promising that no one had any reason to be afraid of us.

Listening to the bishop as he called for the attention of the panic-stricken assembly, and carefully observing the unfolding activities in the meadow outside the town walls where the gathering was being conducted, I was impressed to see—and there was no possibility of it being other than it appeared—that the mere mention of the name of Camulod had an immediate calming effect on the crowd. As soon as they heard Bishop Enos mention the name, people began repeating it and they turned to stare inquisitively at the mounted representatives of the distant colony where, rumor had it, the rule of law was still in force and men and women could live in freedom from threat and fear.

Sitting as I was, however, slightly apart from the main body of the troopers, I saw something else. There was one small band of men among the crowd whose behavior was greatly different from that of the people surrounding them. When we first swept into sight of the gathering, the assembly had scattered in panic, reassembling only very slowly after they had seen for themselves that we were not poised to murder them. But one band of men had refused to scatter and had indeed closed in upon themselves, grouping tightly around one man and what appeared to be his family: a woman and two children. The man at the center of this group stood taller than all the others, dominating all of them by at least half a head, and he was carefully coiffed, his hair and beard meticulously trimmed. His eyes were moving even as I noted him, cataloguing our contingent of troopers and flitting from Cyrus to his decurions and finally to me and my small group. I heard Perceval's voice.

"The tall fellow over there, Clothar, surrounded by the body-guard. He looks like a chief of some kind—a leader, certainly, what-ever rank these people give their headmen. Wonder who he is."

"I noticed him, too. He could be a king, judging from his bearing, but he might just as easily be some kind of champion or chieftain, as you say. We will find out about him later, from Bishop Enos. Cyrus, put your men at ease and take me to meet the bishop, if you will."

Enos, however, was not to be idly diverted from his responsibilities. Our arrival had interrupted a prayer gathering in celebration of the anniversary of the martyrdom of Saint Alban, and the bishop invited us to step down and join with him and his congregation in the final prayers of the ceremony. Only when it was over and he had blessed the participants and sent them on their way did he approach me and acknowledge that he had heard me say earlier that I had messages and missives for him from Germanus. He was most hospitable, graciously accepting the leather pouch of writings that I had for him and betraying not the slightest indication that he might be impatient to sit down somewhere and start reading them. Instead, he went out of his way to arrange accommodations for all of us, quartering the troopers in the central hall of the town's basilica, the administrative hub of the former Roman military government. Germanus, he told us, had cleaned out this and many similar large rooms years earlier, setting his followers to sweeping away the detritus of decades of neglect and turning the refurbished premises over for use by the hundreds of pilgrims who had flocked to Verulamium to attend the great debate he staged here between the orthodox adherents of the Church in Rome and the misguided bishops of Britain who had chosen to follow the teachings of the apostate Pelagius.

Bishop Enos, aware of the ongoing needs of the legions of pilgrims who visited the shrine of Saint Alban each year, and anticipating that the steady increase in their numbers might lead to the town's having need again of spacious accommodations in the future, had seen the wisdom of maintaining the public rooms in good condition for use as dormitories. The main hall was perfect for our uses, featuring two great stone fireplaces, one at each end of the long room. Wooden cots were already in place at one end, strung with rope netting, and an ample supply of straw-filled palliasses set up on end on some of them, to allow the air to circulate between them and keep them dry, while at the other end of the hall someone had arranged rows of tables and benches. A large courtyard at the rear of the building, paved with cobbles and covered with straw, was easily capable of accommodating all our horses, and the yard itself lay but a few moments' walk from the grazing meadows beyond the town walls.

Only when he was absolutely satisfied that our needs had all been attended to did the bishop leave us to our own devices while he retired to read the material that I had brought with me from Gaul.

6

Enos sent for me the following morning and began our meeting by asking me how much I knew concerning the information I had brought to him. I told him truthfully that Bishop Germanus had discussed the matter with me at some length, that he had selected me to come to Britain to convey his hope that Enos would stand as substitute for Germanus in the solemn ceremonies that would surround the coronation of Arthur Pendragon as the Riothamus, the High King of Britain. Bishop Germanus, I said, had hoped that Bishop Enos would not merely consent to deputize for him but would use his powers of persuasion to exhort his fellow bishops within the congregation of Britain to lend their support and their ecclesiastical backing to Merlyn's undertaking in recognition of the benefits and advantages that the Church itself would gain from enlisting the support of Camulod's formidable military strength.

Enos sat silent while I said all this, nodding his head only occasionally as I approached the end of what I had to say, and when I was finished he sat frowning into the distance for a spell before nodding his head once more, this time emphatically, and rising to his feet.

"Every word of what you have said makes perfect sense," he said, "although of course it demonstrates only that you are a gifted listener, since the sentiments you express are Germanus's. But I have decided to do precisely as he wishes in these matters, and to that end I will do all in my power to enlist the support of all the bishops in Britain for the task ahead." He hesitated briefly.

"I know Merlyn Britannicus well, and I have always admired and respected him. His entire family have been friends of mine for many, many years. And because of that, I pay no attention to the outrageous statements that silly, presumptuous and ignorant people love to make about him—this nonsense of sorcery and magic. Merlyn Britannicus is no sorcerer. The very idea is ridiculous. He is a man of his word and devoted to the study and pursuit of truth, albeit his personal idea of truth might differ greatly from that of many another. I have met Arthur, too, Merlyn's ward. A sweet child, when he was a child, but now grown, it seems, into a formidable young man. He will do well in anything to which he turns his mind."

The bishop paused, staring into the distance and nodding in contemplation. "He was impressive, young Arthur, even as a boy. He showed evidence of piety and knew the meaning of respect, and he had a brain capable of great subtlety, corresponding even with Germanus himself." He straightened abruptly, almost as if shaking himself awake. "Of course, he is a warrior now, and I have no measure by which to judge him in that. Merlyn says he is the best, however, and I see no reason to start doubting his word now on such a matter."

"So, pardon me, Bishop Enos, but will you attempt to contact Merlyn now?"

"Of course. Immediately. Merlyn must learn of this at once, by the fastest possible means. I shall send out priests tomorrow at first light, to Cambria and Cornwall in the west—for he could be in either place or between there and here by now—bearing word for him to meet me here."

I was gaping at him, wondering how he could sound so confident. "Pardon me," I said again. "But how many priests will you send out?"

The bishop frowned, but I saw that he was merely counting in his head and not annoyed by my question. "A score," he said. "I believe I can spare that many."

"And you believe that will suffice? Twenty men?"

"No, twenty *priests,* and each of them will spend this night and the remainder of today transcribing copies of a letter I have already written. Each man will carry ten copies, and one of those two hundred copies will eventually make its way to Merlyn."

"Eventually? How long will it take?"

The bishop looked at me as though I were an obtuse schoolboy. "As long as is necessary. The first portion will be longest. It will take a week and more for our first score of men to make their way across the country. After that, once they are arrived in Cambria and Cornwall, the search will progress more and more quickly as they meet and mingle with others like themselves. The word will quickly spread among God's servants. And those who know will share their knowledge, including the knowledge of the letter I have sent to him. He will be found, and as soon as he is, a copy of the letter will be taken to him."

He broke off and looked at me quizzically. "Now there is something worth considering. As soon as Merlyn reads what I have written he will come running right here, to Verulamium, but in the event that he cannot do that, he will at least send a letter here to me by the fastest possible means. Allied to that, it occurs to me that you are probably thinking of returning now to Camulod. Am I correct?" He waited for my nod and then returned it with one of his own. "I thought so. Might I suggest that would be unwise? Merlyn's opinions and decisions will come directly here to me, either in the person of Merlyn himself or in a letter. In either case, you will want to be present when that occurs, to take part in what comes out of it. You won't be able to do that if you're in Camulod, so I would suggest you remain here for the next few months. Once you know what has been decided, you can then return to Camulod and deliver the word of what will happen, while we—myself and my fellow bishops—may follow at a more dignified and stately pace, permitting Camulod to make adequate arrangements for housing all of us. What think you of that?"

I could find no grounds for disagreeing with the old man's logic, but since he was talking of months of waiting, I began to feel uncomfortable with the prospect of keeping Cyrus and his thirty troopers here with me, and consequently absent from their duties in time of war, for such an extended period. I spoke with Perceval and Tristan about what I was thinking and they agreed with me, so I sent for Cyrus and thanked him for his company on our outward journey, then released him to return to Camulod with his men. I was sure the young tribune was relieved to be able to return to duty, but he was still conscientious enough to demur, out of professional concern, wondering how my companions and I would make our way back to Camulod when the time came.

I set his mind at ease on that by pointing out that we would take the same route that we had followed to come here, the straight route to the west, by road from Verulamium to Alchester and south from there to Aquae Sulis and to Camulod. The territories through which the road passed were probably the last remaining ones in Britain that were completely free of threats from the Saxon invaders, since all of their conquests still lay to the east of Verulamium.

Cyrus agreed, and within two days he had reprovisioned his squadron and set off homeward at their head, hoping to reach Camulod in safety before the winter really set in, although it was already December.

7

We settled down to pass the winter peacefully in Verulamium.

It snowed heavily towards the middle of the month, and that snowfall turned out to be merely the first of many as the temperature plummeted to depths that everyone swore were unprecedented. The snowstorms were accompanied by strong winds that whipped the snow into strange and wondrous drifts that served to isolate the countryside, so that travel became impossible and supplies of food and fuel were used up in those places where people were stranded. We were bored beyond belief, although our boredom was alleviated by the need to seek out new supplies of fuel and food.

Neither I nor my three companions had experienced a winter to compare to this before. It snowed only infrequently in central Gaul, even in the deepest winter, and when snow did occasionally fall, it seldom remained on the ground for longer than a day or two. It never fell and froze and remained for weeks and months as it had this year in Britain. Consequently none of us had ever hunted in the snow before, and we discovered it to be an entirely different kind of science, calling for skills that we had never learned. Fortunately, however, we found excellent teachers among the group surrounding Symmachus, the tall, distinguished-looking man we had noticed when we first rode into Verulamium.

Symmachus was a Roman name, but the man who bore it, although he carried it proudly enough, was a Briton through and through. He claimed direct descent from the ancient Cornovii, the warrior people of northern Cambria whose indomitable strength and refusal to succumb to the Roman invaders in the time of the Emperor Claudius had necessitated the building of the giant legionary fortress of Deva that had housed the ten-thousand-strong complement of the Twentieth Legion, the Valeria Victrix, for upwards of three hundred years. Sometime in the course of that three hundred years, Symmachus maintained, a Roman officer had managed to bypass the disapproving frowns and scowling menace of the Cornovii elders and wed himself to one of their daughters, adding his bloodlines and his Roman name to the annals of the clan. The Valeria Victrix was gone now, with all the other legions, Symmachus told us on the first night we spent in his company, but their enormous fortress was still there in Deva—it *was* Deva, he declared—and so were the Cornovii, although they had fallen out of the habit of calling themselves by any special name and simply called themselves the People of the Hills in their own dialect and Cambrians in the common Coastal Tongue. Symmachus was their king, and he and his people, number-ing in the region of five thousand men, women and children, now made their home in the ancient fortress, which they called Chester.

He was a strange man, Symmachus, and for reasons of his own he never liked me and never acknowledged me as the leader of my small group. Instead, he addressed himself to Perceval, as the eldest of our group, at all times, thereby steadfastly refusing me the legitimacy of place that would have been accorded by his addressing me in person. Tristan in particular was highly offended by Symmachus's attitude towards me, but I went out of my way to make light of the situation because I knew what it was about me that the king resented most of all.

Symmachus was accompanied by his wife and two daughters. The wife, a lady called Demea, was still young and exceptionally beautiful, a radiant, laughing creature with bright yellow hair and wondrous green eyes. All the men in the town were at least half in love with her, and the recognition of that truth afforded the king much amusement and enjoyment. After all, he was a strong and well set up man in the prime of life, and his young wife was most obviously besotted with him. And indeed, as we had quickly discovered, his wife's love for Symmachus was the reason he was here in Verulamium, so many miles from home. They had been married now for eight years and were without children of their own, the two daughters being the progeny of Symmachus's first marriage.

The Lady Demea, a devout Christian, had heard about the miracles attributed to Saint Alban, all of them centered around his shrine in Verulamium, and had prevailed upon her doting husband to bring her here, where she could beg the saint in person to intercede for her in Heaven and bless her with a pregnancy. That Demea was fully confident her prayers would be answered was evident to anyone with eyes to see, and the manner in which she and her husband conducted themselves made it plain that they were giving Heaven every opportunity to bless their endeavors. Thus, it was evidently not his beautiful young wife who was the cause of Symmachus's distemper.

It was his daughters, I believed—or one of them, the elder of the two—who cost him sleepless nights and justified, in his mind at least, his continuing disapproval of me. The daughter's name was Cynthia—again a Roman name, or perhaps even Hellenic—but she was obviously not, by her very coloring, the daughter of Demea. Cynthia's real mother, a black-haired, blue-eyed woman from the far northern lands beyond Hadrian's great wall, had died years earlier, giving birth to her second daughter when Cynthia was only four years old. Cynthia was now almost sixteen, breathtakingly lovely and desirable and making no slightest attempt to conceal her attraction to me.

It made no difference to Symmachus that I went to great pains to distance myself from his daughter and avoid her company. He saw nothing of that. In truth, while I acknowledged Cynthia's great physical and facial beauty, I experienced no attraction to her beyond the first few days of knowing her, and she herself had given me the reason to feel the way I did.

Young Bors had fallen in love with her from the moment he set eyes on her, and he was utterly incapable of hiding his infatuation. I know how true that is because I was there when he saw her for the first time and I almost laughed aloud at the spectacular transformation that came over him: his eyes went wide and then almost glazed over and his mouth fell agape and it seemed to me that he forgot how to move. He simply stood there, gazing at her slack jawed and open mouthed, incapable of speech or movement.

Of course, Cynthia saw it immediately. Unfortunately, however, her recognition of his stunned submission to her beauty brought out her worst attributes. Where I took pains immediately to dissemble and conceal my delight in my young servant's reaction to her beauty, Cynthia proceeded from the first to exploit it ruthlessly, treating Bors shamefully and using him imperiously and cruelly, keeping him dancing attendance on her and accepting his every adoring look as no more than her due while she deliberately spurned him, belittling him and insulting him.

Her behavior, uncalled for and excessive as it was, upset me deeply because it impressed me as being quite natural and unfeigned. I found it repellent that she should be so quick to cause my young associate pain, for no reason other than his natural attraction to her beauty. Bors was my servant, and although I strove to keep our relationship as one of master to apprentice, I had found him to be a willing worker and a conscientious student, as well as a naturally friendly and enthusiastic soul—his truculence and sullen behavior had vanished within hours of our setting foot upon the road to Britain. He had done absolutely nothing to earn Cynthia's displeasure, but she poured wrath and disdain about his head in equal and unstinting measure, treating him far less kindly than most people treat animals, and I soon found myself harboring a deep feeling of dislike for her that I was never able to disguise completely.

Cynthia, of course, believing entirely in her own allure and fascination, was never able to bring herself to believe that I could be genuinely immune to her attractions, so that the more I attempted to avoid her and discourage her, the more determined she became to enslave me with her charms and to bend me to her will. Unfortunately, thanks to my education and my many talks with Bishop Germanus concerning women and the rules governing a decent man's behavior towards them, I was never quite able to bring myself to tell her how deeply she had taught me to dislike her, or how her treatment of Bors repulsed me. That would have been too cruel, by my own assessment at that time, although it occurred to me not long afterwards that had she been male and my own age I would have thrashed her soundly for her hectoring cruelty and ordered her to stay well clear of me until she had learned how to control the baseness of her nature.

This, then, was the reason for the tension between the two of us all the time, and that was what her father reacted to with such hostility. His reading of the situation was wrong, of course, but I could hardly come right out and add insult to his imagined injuries by telling him that I found his firstborn daughter ill natured, morally unattractive and generally unpleasant and that I would far rather spend time with her quieter, far less aggressive and offensive twelve-year-old sister, whom she called the Brat.

And so Symmachus distrusted me because he felt I lusted for his daughter, and I resigned myself to being spoken to through Perceval at every turn.

Symmachus was a warrior, however, and he had heard tales of Camulod, and he wanted to know if it was feasible that Merlyn Britannicus and Camulod might consider an alliance with himself and his people in Deva. His question caused a long, uncomfortable silence because none of us was qualified to answer it with anything resembling authority, although I felt that the distance between the two locations alone—almost two hundred miles—would render impossible the kind of arrangement that the king was thinking of. I said as much, and although he seemed to accept the logic of my explanation after examining it for a short time, I could tell that Symmachus was not too happy with me for having stated the obvious and created difficulties for whatever it was he had been considering. Once again, however, I kept silent, venturing no more opinions and showing no more signs of curiosity.

Symmachus and his party had been on the point of leaving for home when the weather broke in mid-December, effectively stranding them in Verulamium for several more months, and so it was that we came to know him to the extent that we did. Although I found him less than comfortable to be around, I had no such difficulties with his companions, who were in fact his family's bodyguard. I came to know several of them very well, and my friends and I spent many pleasant hours with them among the woods, learning to hunt as they did in deep snow. They, in their turn, were fascinated with the spears given to me by Tiberias Cato. The Cambrians had never seen their like, but were unimpressed by the information that no one else had, either. They were quite convinced that somewhere along the edges of one of their northern mountain lakes they would soon find reeds long enough and strong enough to dry and shape into light, strong, durable spear shafts like mine. I made no effort to convince them otherwise, for they simply would not have believed that people had already scoured the reaches of the Empire looking for such things.

They were particularly fascinated by the technique I used to throw the weapons, and by the accuracy I managed to achieve, although they pretended to be overly concerned about the amount of time I spent practicing. They were correct in that. I did spend inordinately large amounts of time practicing that winter, but there was little else to do most of the time. When the weather was too cold and the snow too deep to do much outside, I converted the largest hall in the basilica into a practice arena, piling all the cots and tables and benches up against one long wall and throwing my spears from one end of the vast hall to the other. The distance was slightly less than forty paces, which was ample room for practicing throwing with accuracy, and I had ranged a series of tables and benches of differing heights across one end of the room so that I could make my way from one side to the other, jumping or stepping from one level to another and throwing from any of them as I went. At the far end, I had mounted a series of five boards to serve as targets, each of them painted with pitch in approximately the size and shape of a man. My watchers were amazed that I could announce my targets from any throwing height, specifying the area I would hit—head, chest, thigh and the like—and then hit accurately from thirty to forty paces distant eight times out of any ten. That, to them, was magical. To me, it was the result of incessant hours of brutal, unrelenting work.

As time passed the weather eventually grew more pleasant, and as the worst of the snow began to melt and disappear, I was able to move outside to practice on horseback. Everyone else did the same, of course, happy to be able to ride out again after having spent such a long time immured by the heavy snow. The others rode abroad, however. I was more than content to ride by myself most of the time, exercising constantly in the courtyard that Enos had originally allocated to the cavalry mounts from Camulod. It was not a large space, but it was suitable for my needs, offering me sufficient room to wheel and weave and to accustom myself again to the rhythm and disciplines of casting a spear with accuracy from the back of a moving horse. Again, watching me at work, my new companions from Cambria, who rode small, sturdy mountain ponies and were not at all familiar with large horses, merely shook their heads and looked at each other in rueful recognition of my interminable folly. All of them, at some time over the winter, had taken their turn at trying to throw my spears, and some had tried much harder than others. None of them, however, had had the slightest success in mastering even the basic elements of the throw.

The only person I ever knew who showed a natural skill with my throwing spears from the very outset was, astonishingly, Cynthia's younger sister. The child would often come to watch me as I practiced, and so unobtrusive was she that I quickly grew accustomed to her presence and eventually lost all awareness of it. She never spoke to me and never interrupted me in any way, but simply sat watching me out of wide, bright blue eyes beneath the thick, black fringe of hair that framed her forehead. Her cheekbones were magnificent, high and slanted, and combined with her long, slender neck they gave her a swan-like, regal look. I had only ever seen her smile on two occasions, neither of them inspired by me, and in consequence I always thought of her as a solemn, humorless child who took little pleasure in anything, although I was quite aware that there was precious little in her twelve-year-old life to give her pleasure. There were few children of her own age in Verulamium but even so she was forbidden to mingle with them. She spent her entire life surrounded by her elders, and her sole sources of enjoyment were the things they deemed enjoyable.

One morning towards the end of that long winter, when I had chosen to work indoors, Bishop Enos summoned me while I was in the middle of my practicing, and when I returned from speaking to him I found the tall, almost painfully thin child standing alone in the hall, hefting one of my spears speculatively in her right hand and eyeing the target closest to her, which I estimated at a glance to be somewhere in the region of twenty paces from where she stood. I had stopped short in the doorway and she was unaware of my presence, and I remained silent, waiting to see what she would do next.

Then I realized she already held the weapon in the throwing grip, the thong wrapped around her fist. She whipped up her arm, glided forward effortlessly and fluidly onto the ball of her left foot and executed what appeared to me to be a perfect cast. The weapon hurtled out of her grasp, the tip of its tail spinning only slightly out of true, and shot towards the target, where it passed so close to the edge of the board that its whirling tail clipped the wood. Knocked off its true flight then, the spear clattered to the ground and slid across the floor to come to rest against the great fireplace. I muttered an involuntary exclamation of amazement.

At the sound, the girl spun to face me, her hands flying up to her mouth and her eyes flaring wide in panic. And then, before I could do anything to stop her or reassure her, she fled, throwing the great doors open and dashing out into the courtyard. I ran after her, calling to her to wait, but she paid me no attention and only ran the harder until she vanished from view around the corner of one of the outer buildings.

Annoyed and more than slightly exasperated, I returned to the long hall and picked up the spear. I was interested in my memory of how the child had thrown the thing. Admittedly the weapon was extremely light, and the probability was high that only by a fluke had she managed to combine the angle of her throw with the speed and pressure necessary to whip the spear forward with anything resembling accuracy, but nonetheless it had been an astonishing performance. None of the grown men who had attempted to throw these weapons over the previous months had even come close to doing what the Brat had done at first attempt.

In the ten days that followed I never once set eyes on her again. No doubt afraid that I must be enraged at her, she took the greatest of pains to stay well beyond the reach of my displeasure. Early in that period, I had thought of asking her father where I might find her, but, remembering that Symmachus had shown almost as much apparently ingrained disapproval of the child as he had of me, I thought better of it and sought out his wife, Demea, instead.

Demea greeted me courteously when I approached her that evening before dinner, making my way through the throng of her admirers and waiting patiently until she found the time to turn to me. The child, being a child, was not among the diners. She ate all her meals in the kitchens with the junior servants and the children of the serving staff, which was the custom. Children seldom ate with the adults at the main meal of the day, and most particularly so when the evening gathering was large and could become unruly and boisterous. Gaining a seat at the household table was one of the distinguishing rites of passage from childhood to adult status for people of both sexes.

Demea turned to me eventually with a gracious smile and asked after my health, plainly wondering what could have brought me to seek her out on this occasion, since in the normal way of things I would have contented myself to acknowledge her from a distance with a courteous nod of greeting and a pleasant smile. I cleared my throat uncertainly, suddenly uncomfortable and almost embarrassed by the remembrance of what this woman's husband believed to be my motivation concerning his elder daughter. Demea cocked her head slightly, waiting for me to speak, a vaguely uncertain smile hovering about her lips. I cleared my throat again, then begged her pardon for imposing upon her in this way and asked her what her younger daughter's name was.

The lady's face almost froze in puzzlement, mixed with the slightest hint of consternation, and it was plain to see that she had expected me to say something about her other daughter, Cynthia. Fortunately, that realization alone permitted me to overcome my own uncertainty and speak more easily. Managing to smile without a hint of strain, I told her that I had encountered the child a few days earlier and had realized only after she left to go on her way that I had forgotten her name, if I had ever known it at all.

Her eyes were wide and troubled. "Is it important that you should remember the name of a child so young, Master Clothar?"

I grinned at her then, suddenly enjoying this situation. "No, Lady Demea, I doubt that anyone could think such a thing important. I merely found it unfortunate because, after I had seen the child and passed her by, I suddenly remembered being ten years old myself, and I recalled clearly how convinced I had been of my own importance in this world. It was a short-lived feeling, because almost as soon as it had occurred to me, I was crushed to discover that a close friend of my father's, whom I had known most of my life, had absolutely no idea of who I was or what my name was."

Demea sat blinking at me, a tiny, vertical frown between her brows, and I found myself growing aware that, beautiful as she might be, Symmachus's young wife was not a creature of great intellect.

"I was greatly hurt by that," I told her, saving her the pain of wondering what I had meant. "So hurt, in fact, that I promised myself I would never hurt any child that cruelly when I became a man. And until now, I never have . . . although I fear I may have caused your daughter to suffer exactly as I did myself, and that has made me bold enough to come and ask for your assistance."

The lady's face blossomed suddenly into a wide smile as understanding dawned upon her.

"Her name is Maia. She was born in the month of May, and although she is not my own daughter, her father and I first met in the month of May."

I bowed deeply, thanking the lady for the information, then excused myself and made my way to my own table, planning how I would seek out young Maia the following day and settle our imagined differences. I wanted to see how she would handle a spear on a second attempt.

8

The next day, the weather changed again for the better, and I decided to ride out hunting with Perceval and Tristan. Young Bors would carry our tents and hunting paraphernalia in the body of a light high-wheeled, single-axle cart drawn by two horses. There was still a deal of snow on the ground in many places, and the combined strength of the animals together with the high, narrow wheels of the cart would allow us to take the vehicle almost anywhere we wished to go.

Unfortunately, it enabled us to take the cart to where we had no wish to go. Tristan shot a large hind in a dark, barely accessible spot at the base of a cliff late that afternoon, and after we had gutted and cleaned the carcass we experienced some difficulty in getting the meat to where we could transport it easily.

Perceval took the measure of the cliff above us. It was perhaps as high as the height of five tall men standing on one another's shoulders, and he estimated—accurately, as it turned out—that we could save ourselves a great deal of grief by pulling the wagon to the edge of the cliff up there and lowering ropes by which we could haul up the meat.

Everything proceeded smoothly until we were raising the last hindquarter of meat, when something startled one of the horses. The beast shied and its harness mate reacted in equal panic, leaping away from its companion as far as it could and causing the wheels of the cart to shift slightly. It was enough to cause Perceval to over-balance. He fell out of the cart and over the edge of the cliff, where he crashed solidly to the ground as all of us watched in horror, too stunned to move.

He was alive and conscious, we knew, as we made our way down to him, because we could hear him cursing savagely, using language that one seldom heard coming from his lips. But his left leg was twisted violently up behind him so that it lay beneath his back.

Fortunately, Tristan's days of service as a mercenary had exposed him to the harsh realities of military life, and now it appeared that he had learned how to deal with such things in the field. As soon as he reached his brother he knelt behind Perceval, ostensibly to support his back but in reality to conceal his hand as he unclipped his large dagger from his belt and grasped it by the sheathed blade before bringing the heavy metal handle down solidly across the back of his brother's neck, knocking him unconscious on the instant.

He wasted no time after that. Perceval's body slumped to the ground as Tristan shifted rapidly around towards his brother's legs. He grasped him about the waist, then squatted there above him, gulping in great breaths of air.

"Right," he grunted. "I'm going to lift him as high as I can. You two take hold of his leg and pull it around to where it should lie naturally. Then pull it straight. Quickly now, and be careful but don't be timid. Haul back on that leg with all your strength and straighten it until the ends of the bone are back together, or as close as you can get them. If you don't do it properly the first time, he won't thank you later for attempting to be gentle! I don't know how long he'll stay unconscious, but he'll never be able to stand the pain of trying to straighten that leg out if he's awake, so on the count of three, I'll lift and you pull. Ready? Now, one, two, *three!*"

Tristan thrust upwards with all the strength of his thighs and legs and managed to hoist his larger brother clear of the ground while Bors and I, not daring to look at each other or reflect upon what we were doing, seized the broken leg and pulled it around into its normal position, or as close to it as we could manage. The break appeared to be high on the thigh, and Perceval's breeches were doused with thick, fresh blood. The ends of his splintered bones grated audibly as I pulled on the leg, which was amazingly heavy, and my stomach lurched as nausea swept over me. Remembering what Tristan had told us to do, however, I gritted my teeth, fought down my revulsion and threw all of my weight backwards, pulling with all my strength until I felt the leg I was gripping flex and almost seem to stretch.

"Do you have it?" Tristan's voice was close to breaking with the strain of holding up his brother's body, and as soon as he heard my affirmative shout he allowed Perceval to drop heavily. He spun around to look at what I had managed to achieve.

"Good," he hissed. "That looks excellent. Bors! Quick as you can, break me two long boards from the tailgate of the cart—I need them to splint his leg. Be quick, and bring rope, too, the thinnest rope we have, to tie the boards in place. Move, now!"

As Bors scuttled away to do his bidding, Tristan was already turning back to me, looking at my legs. "Yours are longer than mine. That's good, because I need to be doing other things. Sit here, and take his leg between your own. Lodge your left foot securely in his crotch, making sure his balls are on the outside of it." I wriggled myself into position. "Right, now wrap your right elbow around his foot—the left one—and lock it in place with your other hand. Get as strong a grip as possible. Good, that's good. Now here's what we're going to do. When I give you the word you're going to lean back, pulling against his leg as hard as you can and bracing yourself with that straight left leg of yours. You understand? What we're trying to do is stretch his leg . . . farther than it ought to be stretched." He scrambled away as he was speaking and took up a kneeling position ahead of me and on my right, facing his brother's broken leg. "What's happened is that the bone is splintered, like a tree struck by lightning, and the ends are too jagged to come together again on their own."

He pulled out his dagger and slit his brother's woolen breeches lengthwise, peeling back the cut cloth to expose the flesh beneath it. The skin there, where it was not slick with blood, was white and pallid, and the flesh bulged out in an ugly swelling just below the point where jagged ends of bone protruded through the shredded flesh of the awful wound, which oozed blood sluggishly. Tristan kept talking to me, his eyes moving ceaselessly over the damages beneath his hands, and in a vain effort to keep my mind from dwelling on what I was looking at, I fought to concentrate upon the swirling, drifting snowflakes that filled the air around us, falling in utter silence, those of them that landed on Perceval's bared leg changing from white to crimson in an instant. Tristan was oblivious to the weather and the cold.

"Well at least he hasn't severed any major bleeders. So, young Clothar, you are going to use every iota of your strength to pull that leg straight out until it's so long that the jagged bone ends pull apart from each other. Once you've done that, I'll guide the ends of the bones back into where they should be, and then we'll splint every-thing up and it'll be in the hands of God." He bellowed up to Bors, whom we could hear banging on the cart above our heads. "There's an axe in the toolbox by the driver's bench. Use it." He turned back to me. "Right, Perceval might be coming back to life at any moment, so let's get this over and done with, if we can. Are you ready?" I nodded that I was. "Good. Do it, then. Pull, and don't stop until I tell you to stop. Go!"

I threw myself backwards, my eyes screwed tightly shut against all distractions as I concentrated upon keeping my body at full stretch, pulling at Perceval's leg, which felt heavy and lifeless. Once, twice, I felt as though something shifted and then I felt a lateral movement and heard Tristan grunt.

"Right," he said. "That's it. You can stop pulling now. I can't do any more. That's as close as I can bring it to being where it was before."

I relaxed and immediately felt myself on the verge of total collapse, exhausted by the effort I had been sustaining. Above our heads, Bors was now chopping hard, but even as I grew aware of that the noises stopped, and moments later we heard the sounds of him scrambling down to join us again. He brought four long, narrow boards with him, and a long coil of thin hempen rope.

"I brought some water, too."

"Good lad," Tristan said. "Do you have any clean cloth? I'll need one piece to wash his wound and another to use as a bandage."

"I've got cloth," I said, remembering that I was wearing an extra tunic of plain white cloth beneath my quilted one, for additional warmth. I quickly stripped it off and shrugged back into my outer clothes before the cold could even penetrate. Tristan ripped it into two pieces, one much larger than the other, and used the smaller piece to wash away the blood that was now crusting on his brother's thigh. He used a corner of the larger piece to dry the skin, after which he folded the remainder into a pad that he placed directly over the wound, binding it in place with strips of the wet cloth. I had noticed that the bleeding had lessened perceptibly since Tristan's ministrations ended, and apparently that was a good thing, because Tristan mentioned it, too, in an approving murmur.

He then splinted the leg, cutting the rope into lengths before calling on Bors and me to hold the boards in place along the limb while he tied them into place. He worked swiftly and with great confidence, and I was much impressed with his self-possession and the competence with which he had managed the entire affair, from the first moment of his looking at his brother, assessing the situation and what had to be done.

"Where did you learn to do all that?" I asked when the last ties were in place and he sighed and slouched back against the bole of a tree.

"Hmm. I didn't learn. I saw it done once, though, after an action against the Burgundians, not far south of Lutetia. One of our senior centurions, an old sweat called Lucius, fell into a ravine, from horseback. The situation was quite similar to this one, in fact, except that Lucius had an arrow in him, too. That's what caused him to fall in the first place. Anyway, an old friend of his, who had been a medic decades earlier, before becoming a centurion, knew what to do. I was in the situation you were in today, so I wasn't nearly as sure about what I needed *me* to do. But I remembered the old medic talking about how we needed to stretch the leg and bring the broken bone ends back together."

"You've never done that before, ever?"

Tristan heard the wonder in my voice and frowned slightly. "No, and I'd feel a lot better about it if my beloved brother there would just wake up, or grunt, or puke or something." He stooped forward and placed the flat of his hand against Perceval's brow. "Well, he's still breathing, at any rate, so I suppose there's nothing more for us to do but wait." He glanced up at the cliff above us and shook his head in rueful wonder. "I have absolutely no idea how we're ever going to get him out of here."

"I have, sir."

Both of us turned to look at Bors. He shrugged and held up both hands in a curiously helpless gesture.

"I found a set of pulley blocks in the toolbox with the axe." He looked from one to the other of us, but when neither of us showed any reaction he continued. "There's no poles, but we have an axe and we're surrounded by trees, and we've lots and lots of rope."

"So?" Tristan was clearly not understanding what Bors was telling him, and neither was I. "What are you talking about, Bors?"

He blinked at us both in astonishment, and then he grew suddenly confident. "We can build a hoist, like the ones the sailors used to load the feed for our horses when we left Gaul. It only needs four stout poles, a few ropes and a set of pulleys, and we have all of those. Once it's assembled, we need simply strap Master Perceval to a board and hoist him up directly to the cart, straight up the face of the cliff."

I remembered seeing the device he was describing, swinging heavy sacks from the wharf and delivering them safely to the ship's deck, but I had paid it no great amount of attention and now my memory of its workings was clouded, to say the least.

"Straight up the face of the cliff. Can you build such a device, Bors?"

He looked at me wide eyed. "Aye, sir, I can."

"Where did you learn to do such a thing?"

His face went blank with astonishment. "Nowhere, Master Clothar. I simply watched what the mariners did, and paid attention to the way the device worked. It was very simple. And then I remembered having seen a similar thing, but much larger, on my father's farm when I was a boy. One of the workers there, a foreman, taught me about pulleys and tackle and the way they work. He showed me how a single man can lift many times his own weight simply by using ropes threaded through pulleys."

"And so you now believe you can build such a device and use it to haul Perceval to safety up there on the cliff top?"

"Aye, sir, I do."

"And the first step towards doing it is what? Cutting down four trees?"

"Four, aye, Master."

I looked at him one last time, setting my chin and pursing my lips before I spoke. "You are absolutely sure you can do this?"

I saw the determination in his eyes. "Aye, Master, I'm sure."

"Well, then, let's go and select our trees."

Twenty-four hours after that—having found our trees and felled them, then dragged them close to the top of the cliff, cut them to size and harnessed them together to form a tripod and a hoisting arm—Tristan and I had learned how to thread a rope through a set of pulley blocks and how to set up a simple gin pole hoist.

Perceval had regained consciousness about the time we set off to hunt for suitable trees, and he had been suffering unimaginable pain ever since, so that lines newly stamped into his face appeared to have been etched there years earlier. We fed him rich, blood-thickened venison broth spiced with wild garlic and onions that grew in profusion close by where we were camped at the cliff base, but he had little appetite, too badly in need of rest to care about eating and in too much pain to be capable of resting. By the time we had erected the hoist, however, he had lapsed into unconsciousness, and although that would make our task of raising him easier, it also worried us deeply. We strapped him securely to a stretcher made of wrist-thick sapling stems and raised him quickly, straight up the cliff as Bors had promised. Once we had him safely there, we trans-ferred him to the bed of the cart, which we had loaded with dried bracken from the sheltered bottom of the cliff to cushion him as much as possible.

By that time, however, it was growing dark, and after a hurried discussion, weighing the pros and contras of attempting to travel through unknown woodland in the dark of night, we decided we had no other choice but to remain where we were for another night and set off for Verulamium early in the morning. So we lit a cooking fire and set about cooking more of Tristan's venison, which we ate with the last of the bread we had brought with us.

We retired early that night, looking to be astir and ready to move off before dawn broke, but I for one could find no rest, fret-ting over the health of our helpless friend. Bishop Enos had some wonderful healers and physicians among his priests, I knew, and I would not be satisfied until Perceval was safely delivered into their hands.

9

We arrived back in Verulamium before noon the next day, having been absent for five days, and we were traveling very slowly, painfully aware of the agonized sounds coming from the rear of the cart at every bump in the surface of the ground. Once within the town, however, it was the work of mere moments to deliver Perceval to the building that Bishop Enos had dedicated to permanent use as a hospital. There, a tall and gaunt old priest called Marcus, who had once served as a military surgeon with the legions in Africa before the invasion of the Vandals in 429, took Perceval off our hands and promised he would have the finest care anyone could have. Father Marcus stripped off the splints Tristan had applied and examined the work that we had done to repair the leg, and was lavish with his praise for Tristan. We were grateful to be able to leave our friend and brother in his care.

I made my way directly to Bishop Enos's quarters to inform him of what had happened to Perceval, only to find that the Lady Demea was there, deep in conversation with the bishop. I slipped away without either of them having seen me and went outside, where I found young Maia sitting on a concrete water conduit, her long shadow stretched out before her, her slender feet bare in the gutter by the side of the road. She was completely unaware of my presence as I walked up behind her.

"Maia," I said, "I'm not angry at you, so there's no need to run away from me."

She jumped to her feet as I spoke and spun around to face me, her face flushing hotly, and after a few moments when she was plainly searching for words, she said, "I'm not afraid and I'm not running anywhere."

"Good, I am glad to hear that, because I need to talk with you. I would like you to come by the basilica tomorrow when I am practicing with my spears and show me how you threw that one. I am not at all upset about that, I promise you. In fact the opposite is true. So will you do that? Will you come tomorrow?"

"I can't. I won't be here."

"What do you mean? You won't come to the basilica?"

She shrugged, her face regaining its normal color. "No, I mean I won't be here in Verulamium tomorrow. We are leaving for home in the morning, returning to Chester."

"You are? That's very sudden, isn't it? Why?"

She shrugged her shoulders, the movement emphasizing how thin and insubstantial she appeared to be, and yet I knew she was as strong and lithe as a whip, despite the impression she conveyed of being like a young deer or a newborn foal, all eyes and long, unsteady legs. "Because the King and Queen's prayers have been answered," she replied. She spoke without inflection, and nothing in her demeanor indicated that she might hold any opinion of any kind on what she was reporting, but there was something impossibly subtle about her words that made me look at her more closely, wondering if there was really cynicism in her speech. She paid me no attention, however, and was already continuing. "Saint Alban has interceded in Heaven on their behalf and Queen Demea is now with child and so we must go home now. That is why I am here. I'm waiting for the Queen. She is talking with Bishop Enos."

I continued to stare at her for the space of a few more heartbeats, then told myself not to be so silly. The child was only twelve, after all. That was a marriageable age, certainly, but only for rare unions between young girls and very old men whose mortality was questionable. It was no indicator of either womanhood or intellect. "I see," I said, nodding slowly. "Has she been there long, with the bishop?"

"No, not long. Why?"

"Oh, no reason. I'm sorry you are leaving so soon. I shall miss you."

"*I'm* not. I can't wait to go home."

"I don't suppose you would care to show me how you threw that spear right now, would you?"

She cocked her head and looked at me strangely, her elfin face with its enormous piercing blue eyes unreadable. "Now? But you have no spears."

"True, but they're nearby. I can have them here in moments. What say you, would you like to try for that target again?"

Her eyes sparkled, and as she straightened her back I noticed again how tall she was, unusually tall for a girl her age, and thin as a sapling tree. She smiled, very slightly, white teeth gleaming briefly behind wide red lips. "I don't know if there's enough time."

"Of course there is. There's always time for what we love to do. Stay here until you see me cross the street over there, then follow me into the basilica. It won't take long for you to show me how you throw."

I had been right the first time I saw her. She threw naturally and without thought, uncoiling into the cast reflexively and following through perfectly simply because she had that kind of grace in her normal range of motion. She threw three spears, and two of them hit their targets. I was full of praise and I could see she was delighted with her own prowess. But she never lost sight of the fact that she ought to be sitting outside the bishop's house, waiting for the Lady Demea, and so I thanked her for her demonstration and allowed her to go on her way. She flashed me a dazzling smile and darted away like a deer towards the door, where she hesitated and looked back at me, lingering.

"What? Say it."

"Where did you learn to throw spears like that?"

I shrugged and grinned at her. "Like what?" I was being facetious, but she took me seriously.

"Like magic, the way you do, with the cord wrapped around the shaft. I've never seen that here."

"No, you wouldn't, not in Britain. I learned to do it in Gaul, across the sea."

"I've never seen anyone who throws better than you. I have never seen spears like those, either."

"That's because there are none. These spears have no equal."

"I shall call you Hastatus," she said then, sounding very grown up and sure of herself. "It means a spearman. Do you mind having a new name?"

"No," I said, smiling again. "Not at all. Not if it is bestowed by someone as skilled and gracious as you are, Lady Maia."

A flicker of something that might have been annoyance crossed her face, and I thought I had offended her with my levity, but then she nodded. "So be it, then. You shall be my Hastatus. And I'm glad you don't like Cynthia. I don't either, but most people simply can't see beyond her face." She flicked a hand in farewell and was gone.

10

In the morning we turned out to bid farewell to Symmachus and his party, and I was surprisingly reluctant to see them go. Cynthia, I noticed, had apparently changed her mind about me, for she did not address a single word to me, and she left for home without deigning to glance in my direction. Maia the Brat sat beside her, and although she did not smile upon me either, she at least rewarded me with a tiny, private flip of the hand as her carriage pulled away.

Tristan nudged me as the wagons left and nodded towards Bors, who stood forlorn, gazing hopelessly after his disappearing love.

"Look at him, poor fellow. I remember how that feels, to watch your first love ride away forever. But he'll get over it quickly. We all do." He looked back at the retreating wagons. "That's quite the young lady. I don't think I have ever seen anything quite like her."

I managed to find a smile to mask my disagreement. "Cynthia? She's unique, I'll grant you, but I think I may not die of grief if I never see her again."

He grunted, a single, muffled bark of amusement and agreement. "I believe you there, but I wasn't talking about the beautiful Cynthia. It was her sister I meant."

"Who, Maia the Brat?" I laughed aloud. "She is a delight, I'll not begrudge her that. And she's quick, and clever, and has a mind of her own. But she's just a child, for all that, a little girl."

"A little girl . . . Aye, right. You come back and tell me that in three or four years, if we ever run into her again. I guarantee she'll be the loveliest creature you'll ever have seen. She'll bewitch you, just as her sister bewitched Bors."

I laughed again. "Not me, Tristan. I'm unbewitchable."

"She doesn't think so now, not that one, believe me. She likes you very much, and not in the way you obviously expect of a twelve-year-old."

"Maia? Come on, man, I've barely spoken to the child, and when I did we talked of throwing spears."

He shrugged elaborately and held up his hands. "Fine, forget I mentioned it, but I know more about that young woman than you do."

I looked at him in surprise. "You do? How can you?"

He grinned at me and danced away, his arms raised defensively as though he expected me to pummel him with my fists. "I ask questions, and I listen to the answers, and so I learn much more than those who never ask and far, far more than those who ask but never listen." Knowing he was baiting me, I refused to rise to his goad, but he kept going anyway. "The young woman has a mind of her own . . . but she has secrets, too. And she would rather be a boy, at this stage in her life, so she trains with weapons when she is at home in Chester, where all her people love her. And her name is not Maia, although she wouldn't tell you that."

Suddenly I found that I had lost patience with his bantering. "Don't play the fool, Tristan, of course it is. I had the name directly from her mother."

He sobered instantly, looking at me eye to eye, the smile on his face fading as swiftly as the humor left his tone. "Stepmother, Clothar. Demea is her stepmother. The child was born on the first day of May—hence the name, Maia. And Demea and Symmachus met and fell in love in the month of May when the child was three, and they were wed the following May. But only after that did Symmachus start calling the child Maia, to please his new wife and to ingratiate her to the child. Little Maia's name had been the same as her real mother's prior to that, and the Lady Demea preferred not to be reminded of that name or to have her husband reminded of it. The child's real name is Gwinnifer. Mind you, she seldom uses it, save among friends."

Gwinnifer. I had never heard the name before but it resonated, somehow, in my breast. I swung around on my heel to look after the cavalcade, but they had long since passed out of view, and the road lay empty.

MERLYN

1

"Tell me about the dream you had . . . when Germanus spoke to you."

I sat gaping at my questioner, wondering how he could have known of such a thing, and he smiled and waved a hand towards a table to his right, where papers and parchments were strewn in apparent chaos.

"Enos sent me a letter telling me about it and alerting me that you were on your way here. He had no way of knowing which of you would find me first—you, personally, or one of his priests—but he sent the letter anyway, anticipating that one of his people might reach me and warn me of your coming. So, when was this dream?"

I shrugged and leaned back into my chair. "I cannot say, with any certainty, Master Merlyn. It was at the end of the winter. Most of the snow had vanished, and Bishop Enos had finally been able to go out into the countryside, about his work. The earliest bloom of flowers had come and gone again . . . it was the end of March, perhaps early in April."

I was sitting comfortably, in a folding, curule-style armchair that had a leather seat and back, and the man across from me, in an identical chair, almost smiled, the right side of his mouth twitching upwards. "Do you mean to say that you had lost track of time?"

"Completely. It sounds ludicrous, I know, but it is true, nonetheless. We were very bored in Verulamium and it was a long, harsh

557

winter. We would have left much sooner than we did, purely for the sake of moving, had it not been for Perceval's injury. We were held down by that, waiting for his leg to heal."

"It did heal, though, and remarkably well."

"Aye, considering the damage he did to it. He walks now with only the slightest limp, and that will soon be gone. He grows stronger every day. But it was fortunate that his brother Tristan was there with us and knew what needed to be done."

"Aye, it was indeed. Now tell me about this dream of yours, if you will."

I shrugged again. "It was a dream, what more can I say? I dreamt it."

"But it had a salutary effect upon you, did it not? Greater than any dream you had ever known. You told Enos that it was the most realistic dream you had ever had, and that it had forced you to change your plans. It sent you off to look for me, did it not?"

"Aye, all of that is true."

"And why was that? What made it so different? You will forgive my insistence, I hope, but the matter is important to me."

I sucked in a deep breath and sat straighter, stifling my impatience with this man whom I had met less than an hour earlier, after pursuing him three times across the width of Britain.

We had arrived back at the gates of Camulod without giving anyone warning of our arrival, but our presence had been noticed even before we reached the outer perimeter of the territories ruled by the colony, and as we approached the *castellum,* it was to discover that we were expected. Merlyn Britannicus, I was told then, had convened a gathering of Camulod's senior strategists earlier that day and would be unable to join us until the meeting was completed with its agenda satisfied. Fortunately, the guard commander told me the assembly had been in session since shortly after dawn, and no one expected them to take more than another hour to conclude their business. In the meantime, we were taken to the bath house, where we cleansed ourselves of the accumulated dirt of ten days on the road, and then to the refectory, where we stuffed ourselves on freshly prepared food far richer than any rations we could ever carry in our packs.

Sure enough, soon after we left the cookhouse with our bellies full, a soldier came looking for me. Merlyn had emerged from his conference and invited me to join him in his private quarters. I went with the messenger immediately, my mind swarming with thoughts of finally meeting with the man I had come so far to see.

I had heard many things about Merlyn Britannicus in my travels across Britain and some of them were simply incredible, defying both logic and belief but titillating and terrifying the very folk who whispered of them. Merlyn Britannicus was a sorcerer, these people said, perhaps the blackest sorcerer ever to live in Britain. Even his clothing proclaimed the fact that he was a practitioner of the black arts, a familiar of the gods of darkness. He dressed in loose, long-flowing robes of deepest black, and no man or woman was permitted to look upon his face. But then, the person speaking always added, who would want to? This was Merlyn Britannicus, of Camulod, a man whose death at the hands of his archenemy hundreds had witnessed. And then, after his death, they had continued to watch in horror as the head was struck from his corpse with his own sword.

Carthac, the monster who had killed him, carried Merlyn's head back to his camp, swinging it by its long, golden hair as he went. The camp was enclosed and virtually unassailable, high in the mountains and miles from the scene of the fight where the rest of Merlyn's corpse had been left lying. Carthac had shown Merlyn's severed head to his whole army, swinging it high around his own head before casting it into a bonfire, where it exploded in a fireball the likes of which no one had ever seen, filling the air with billowing, choking smoke and whirling sparks. And from that cloud of smoke, to the consternation and awestricken terror of everyone who saw it, Merlyn Britannicus had leaped into view, miraculously reborn, to kill and strike the head off Carthac in his turn and send all his followers screaming out into the open air, where they found Pendragon bowmen waiting to shoot them down from the mountain slopes above their camp.

From that day forth, these storytellers said, Merlyn had walked in silence, shrouded in robes of deepest black, and all men shunned him.

That was the people's version, the tale told in hushed voices throughout the land on dark nights when the wind howled in the distant emptiness beyond the firelight.

The version I had learned from Merlyn's friends was very different. The man Carthac had beheaded was actually Ambrose Ambrosianus, Merlyn's half brother, close enough to Merlyn in appearance to be virtually identical. The two brothers had worked hard to turn that close resemblance into a tactical weapon, cultivating it in such a way that they wore identical clothes and armor and were never seen together. Because they were frequently seen fighting on the same days, but at great distances from each other, the story spread that Merlyn the Sorcerer could win simultaneous victories and be seen triumphant on the same morning or afternoon on two battlefields twenty or thirty miles apart.

On the day when Merlyn was "reborn," he had penetrated Carthac's camp disguised as a sick messenger, and he was sitting by the fire pit, nursing a pouch full of some mysterious fire powder. It had been his intention to use the fire powder to create a diversion that would allow him an opportunity to kill Carthac, taking him by surprise in his own camp, by his own fireside, where he least expected any threat. Unaware that Carthac had even met Ambrose, let alone captured him, Merlyn was therefore taken completely by surprise himself by what transpired, and he had barely begun to assimilate what he was seeing when Carthac threw Ambrose's head into the fire. Then, intent upon recovering his brother's head before it could take further harm, Merlyn had dashed into the flames, forgetting that he was carrying the bag of his magical fire powder. The powder spilled into the open fire with a terrifying explosion of flames and smoke, and from that cloud Merlyn had emerged in front of Carthac, stunning everyone and stabbing the enemy leader to the heart before he could react.

Carthac, however, was not to be easily killed. Panicked perhaps by the miraculous reincarnation of a man he had just beheaded, and ignoring the wound in his chest, he scooped Merlyn up and threw him bodily back into the heart of the bonfire from which he had sprung. Merlyn landed flat among the coals and sustained grave injuries, but fortunately—although he himself would come to question that good fortune in the long, exhausting months of rehabilitation that stretched ahead of him—the explosion of fire powder had blown the blaze apart and scattered the fierce-burning branches and bright embers that would otherwise have consumed him completely. As it was, he emerged only slightly disfigured and incapacitated, although his burnt legs ensured that he would never ride a horse again with any ease and would forever afterwards walk with a pronounced limp. His left arm and hand, too, were badly damaged, his fingers reduced to little more than claws, and his face, particularly the left side of his mouth, bore scars of what could have been a far more hideous burn. Whenever Merlyn smiled, his mouth was pulled awry on that one side, twisted downward artificially to expose his lower teeth. But then, whenever Merlyn Britannicus smiled, everyone who noticed—and there were very few of those— was invariably glad, because his natural self shone through. The eyes of the people who made up the rest of the world never penetrated the darkness beyond the long, black outer robes he wore, or the hood that overshadowed his face and kept even his eyes concealed from unwanted scrutiny.

This was the man who sat across from me now, the hood of his outer robe pushed back to expose the yellow hair—now showing broad streaks of silver gray—that swept back from a wide, high forehead and keen, deep-set and piercing eyes beneath straight, golden brows.

It was hard not to stare at him, because this man had become a legend and much of the legend had to do with his unseen face, so I was signally aware of the honor he was doing me by allowing me to look upon his face. It was a strong face, but strangely coarse looking, almost as though the skin had undergone some kind of abrasion that had almost broken it. I was dissatisfied with that explanation even as it occurred to me, but I could find no better way to describe it.

The first, ridiculous idea that sprang into my mind upon seeing him was that here was some kind of lion man. I had seen two caged lions, in a traveling entertainment that had visited the Bishop's School in my second year there, and they had impressed me greatly with their quiet dignity, their strength and their coloring. Stretched out in the dusty afternoon sunlight on the floor of his cage, and surrounded by chattering, gesticulating boys, the old male, dusky, dusty and stoic, had crouched motionless, ignoring everyone and everything, his eyes closed in disdain as he contemplated some other reality far removed from where he lay.

Something about Merlyn Britannicus had immediately reminded me of that old lion—perhaps the coloring, I thought at first, but then it struck me that it was the man's face that had prompted the memory. Merlyn Britannicus's face was *leonine,* and that had to do with the curiously roughened quality of his features. His nose was broad and spatulate, beginning between his brows, where it appeared to have thickened and grown flatter, and that general impression of additional and *recent* thickening persisted all the way down to his mouth, where even his upper lip showed signs of thickening, rather than swelling.

All of these thoughts and impressions flashed through my mind in the space of a moment, but I turned my eyes away quickly when I became aware that my host was watching me watching *him*. What I did not know, and would not learn for many more years, was that this leonine appearance, caused by a thickening and coarsening of the facial skin, is a primary mark of mid-stage leprosy.

I was thinking hard about what I hoped to gain from this meeting, but it was plain to me, even as I prepared to ask my own questions of him, that he would tell me little or nothing of what I wanted to know until he had heard all he wanted to hear from me. He sat watching me gravely from the opposite side of the fireplace in his personal quarters behind the Great Hall of Camulod, and the fire in the iron basket had died down to embers, wisps of smoke wafting up between us. There was not much light in the room, though the sun was shining brightly outside, and he sat between me and the only window, effectively placing himself in silhouette. Merlyn Britannicus of Camulod, soldier and warrior, philosopher and leader and, most recently by all accounts, sorcerer and warlock, sat waiting patiently for me to tell him all about something that mattered greatly to him but which barely signified with me at all. I had absolutely no interest in visiting the subject he was most curious about, because I had been living with the outcome of it for months past. I did recognize, however, that I had no option but to get on with it.

"Very well, Master Merlyn," I said, successfully stifling a sigh. "Let me start from the beginning.

"We set out to find you last year and it was already late autumn by the time we left Auxerre. Bishop Germanus had set out for Italia before that, to meet with the Pope and the other bishops, but before he left he gave me lengthy and explicit instructions about coming here and finding you, and he made it very clear to me that there was an urgency governing my mission to bring you his word."

From that point I went on to tell him about our entire voyage: our landing at Glevum, our arrival in Camulod, and finding Bishop Enos in Verulamium.

"Bishop Enos had his men out looking for you," I said in conclusion, "but it took a long, long time to locate you, since you apparently had no slightest wish to be found."

Now Merlyn shrugged. "Why should I? The wars were ended and our home was safe again for the first time in years. I had been deeply involved in much of what had happened and had lost too many close friends and loved ones during the conflict without ever having time to grieve over any of their deaths. I felt then that it was time for me to withdraw, as far away as possible from everything, and be by myself for a while.

"Besides, in addition to my mourning, I had other matters to think about and decisions of some import to conclude, none of which would have been made easier by having other people around me. Had I expected or anticipated your arrival I would, of course, have returned earlier than I did, but Germanus had assured me that he would be coming in person this year and I took him absolutely at his word, never imagining that he might have superior orders that would preclude his coming here."

I nodded, accepting the truth of that. "Well, it seems it was our fate to remain in Verulamium to endure what everyone has assured me was the longest, harshest and most brutal winter anyone can remember."

"That is true. I have never witnessed anything comparable to it. We had one like it many years ago, when I was young, and it killed many of the oldest and least healthful of our people here in Camulod, including my great-aunt Luceiia Britannicus. But even that winter, brutal as it was, was shorter and less savage than this one just past. Coming from Gaul, it must have been an unpleasant surprise for you."

I nodded. "My young assistant, Bors, had never seen snow before. He comes from Iberia, to the southeast of Gaul on the shores of the Middle Sea, where he was born and bred to an unvarying climate of high heat and desert sunshine. He was thrilled by the first snow here, the newness of it, but that wore off quickly and left only the fact of a winter such as he had never imagined. The first two months of snow and ice and chill almost killed him. He wore more clothing during that time than any other·three men in our group, and it required great effort at any time of day to prize him away from the fireside to do his daily tasks. He may never overcome his distaste for Britain's climate now."

Merlyn smiled. "Some of our own people feel the same way, and they were born here. A single trip to Africa, or to any of the warmer climes to the southward, can spoil a person forever afterwards in their expectations of Britain. And after the winter had passed, you had to wait for your friend to heal?"

"We did, and were frustrated by the knowledge of time wasted. And then one night, in the blackest hours of the middle watch, Bishop Germanus came and sat on the edge of my cot. I knew he was there and I could see him clearly despite the darkness. I even felt his weight pulling my cot to one side as he sat down, and yet I could see myself as well, asleep on my cot and completely unaware of him. He reached down and shook me by the shoulder, but I was deeply asleep and merely sought to turn away from his grasp. He shook me again, and then a third time, whispering my name urgently, as though he wished not to be overheard by anyone else. It seemed to me I was standing apart, by the top of the bed, looking down at both of them—Germanus growing impatient with my unconsciousness and me, refusing to awaken. I remember wondering how the sleeping figure that was me could possibly be so unaware of what was going on, and then it came to me that I had been astir before dawn the previous day and had worked in the stables with Bors, almost without stopping, from then until I fell into bed late that night.

"Eventually, however, Germanus took my left hand and dug the point of his thumbnail into the very base of mine. That woke me up, quickly. I came up out of darkness snarling, aware of the pain in my hand and preparing to defend myself, only to find Germanus's hand flat against my chest, pushing me down as he called my name again, bidding me wake up. Then, when he was satisfied I was awake and aware of him, but before I could even think to question him about his being there, he spoke to me.

" 'Clothar,' he said, 'listen to me. Listen closely, for I have but little time. You must find Merlyn Britannicus, quickly. That is the only reason now for you to be in Britain. Find Merlyn. Give him the information that you carry from me. Go, now, and do as I bid you.' And then he placed his outstretched hand over my eyes and sent me back to sleep, and the part of me that stood as witness watched him rise and walk out of the tent. And even although he had carried no light, the tent darkened into blackness as he passed out through the flaps. In the blackness that remained then I grew dizzy and fell into I know not what. But I awoke the next morning with every detail of the dream brilliantly clear in my mind and went searching for Bishop Enos immediately."

The man across from me, whom I still could not regard as the Merlyn Britannicus I had envisioned, nodded his head slowly, sucking his upper lip down into his mouth to where he could grasp and nibble it between his teeth. "Hmm," he mused, "that is what Enos told me in his letter, although he lacked the details you have just supplied. Tell me." He fixed me with a sharp gaze. "Do you believe the visitation really happened? You have already said that it was no more than a dream, and yet you acted upon it. You left Verulamium and came west. What do you really believe?"

I answered cautiously but firmly, choosing my words with great care. "I believed it at the time. I believed it was, as you say, a visitation, a vision of some kind. I had no understanding of what I had seen, or dreamed, or imagined, or of how it came to pass, and all the logic of my training told me that such things are quite impossible. And yet our faith teaches us to believe in miracles, and I have no difficulty in believing in those things when they involve holy and devout people in extraordinary circumstances." I stopped and searched for words to express what I wanted to say next. "There are many stories told in Gaul of miracles performed by Germanus. Were you aware of that?"

"No," he said. "I did not know that, but it hardly surprises me. Is it true?"

I shrugged. "It's true that there are stories told of it. Whether or not there is truth in the stories is beyond me. But people over there speak of him as being saintly, and I truly believe he is. He himself, however, will have nothing to do with such tales. He has sworn to me in person that there is no substance to any of those reports. He says that people merely perceive what they wish to perceive and will bend truth and facts to suit their own requirements. I asked him once, when he was in full flight over this, if he was denying the existence of miracles, and of course he was not. He corrected me immediately and with great passion on that. But what he was denying—and he was adamant on this—was his *personal* ability to perform miracles or to contribute to anything that might ever be described in any way as being miraculous.

"I continued to believe, throughout the months that followed my dream, that contrary to logic and to all the laws of probability and possibility, Bishop Germanus came into my tent that night and spoke to me. I believed it happened. And I believed he had come there to tell me I had to come here, seeking you. And thus, I suppose I believed I had experienced a miracle. It was a wonderful sensation, although almost frightening, for as long as it lasted."

"And do you no longer believe it was a miracle?" Merlyn was looking at me now through narrowed eyes, and I shrugged dismissively in response.

"How can I, now that I know the truth? Miracles are *miraculous,* Master Merlyn. They are supernatural occurrences originated and performed by God Himself, often through human intermediaries. They are ungovernable and inexplicable under the laws or the expectations of mankind—Bishop Germanus's own words. That says to me, by extension, that they must therefore be incapable of error. If that visitation had been truly miraculous—had Germanus somehow found, or been divinely granted, the ability to travel mentally and incorporeally to Britain for the sole purpose of visiting me in my sleep—then how could he not have known that the coronation ceremony, which was his primary concern, would take place in Verulamium and not in Camulod?

"My dream of Germanus sent me off across Britain seeking you *after* you had already made extensive preparations to have everything take place in Verulamium, for all the best and most logical and obvious of reasons. Your letter to Enos, outlining your wishes in what was to take place within his jurisdiction, as well as describing all the arrangements that you had already set in motion long before then, must have arrived in Verulamium within mere days of my departure. In other words, your letter had been written and sent off to Enos, and all your arrangements had been decided upon and their organization delegated to those responsible for them, long before I had my miraculous dream. *Ergo et igitur,* as my old teacher Cato would have said, there can be no talk of miracles in this, because a Germanus possessed of miraculous powers would have *known* what you proposed to do, and would have been aware of everything you had arranged. He would not have dispatched me on such a worthless chase as the one I have been pursuing ever since then."

Merlyn had been sitting with an elbow on the arm of his chair, supporting his chin on his hand as he gazed at me and listened to my rant. Now he sat up straighter, releasing a deep, pent-up breath. "Is that really what you think Germanus did? Do you honestly believe he would send you off on a worthless chase?"

"No, Master Merlyn, not at all. What I believe *now* is that I had a vivid dream that night, and because the details of it remained with me the next morning—which is unusual in itself— I chose to allow myself to become obsessed with what I had dreamt. All the foolishness that has followed since then has been my own fault, attributable to my own overheated imagination and to nothing else."

He sat looking at me, unblinking, for a count of ten heartbeats, then grunted deep in his chest. "Hmm. So you believe that everything you have done since leaving Verulamium has been futile, a waste of time."

It was more a statement than a question, but I felt myself rearing back in surprise. "How could it be otherwise? Our pursuit of you, sir, achieved nothing but disappointment and ever-increasing frustration. Acting on the single trustworthy report we had received about where you might be found—a report from a wandering priest who had not known we were seeking you—I traveled directly from Verulamium to Caerdyff, in Cambria. I arrived there to find that you had departed more than a month earlier, to travel west along the coast to the Pendragon stronghold at Carmarthen. I followed you then to Carmarthen, by road, only to find that you had long since left there, too, again by sea, accompanied this time by the Pendragon clan chiefs and their warriors, to sail across the river estuary to Glevum, on your way home to Camulod. But that departure, I discovered, had occurred even before our original arrival in *Caerdyff,* and so our entire journey to Carmarthen had been futile and we were already more than a month—almost two months, in fact—behind you.

"Even then, however, I would have followed you directly, but your departure with the Pendragon levies had stripped the entire coastline of large vessels, and we wasted four more days trying in vain to find a ship capable of carrying us and our horses. And so we had to make our way back by land, along the entire length of the south Cambrian coast and up the river until we could find a way to cross to Glevum, losing more time and distance with every day that passed. By the time we finally arrived at Glevum, with several more days yet ahead of us before we would reach Camulod, we had lost twelve more days in addition to the time that had elapsed between your leaving Carmarthen and our reaching there.

"I had estimated by then that we were at least two months behind you, and as it transpired, I was correct. We were two and a half months late. And I have since found out—because everyone we met along the road is bursting with the tidings and talking about the wondrous and magical events that ensued—that in the course of those two months you returned to Camulod and then traveled immediately onward to Verulamium with the Pendragon clans in the wake of Arthur's armies, which had marched there earlier. And once there, you crowned Arthur Pendragon as Riothamus, High King of Britain, with God Himself apparently blessing the event and bestowing upon the new King a miraculous new sword.

"You then sent the new King off to fight a great battle, at the head of the largest army ever assembled in Britain since the Romans first arrived with Julius Caesar. He won the battle, of course, and it was a great victory, which people think will be but the first of many, and flushed with the fruits of success, all of you have now returned home to Camulod, where I am finally permitted to find you and meet you to present my respects and admit my shame at having been so far removed from everything of importance that has happened in this land since I first set foot in it nigh on a year ago."

The anger that had been smoldering inside me was now threatening to spill over, and I was aware that I needed to bite down on my ill humor. Evidently the man across from me felt the same way, because he raised one hand quickly, palm outward, stemming my flow of words with a peremptory gesture born of years of command. I could feel my heart pounding in my chest. Merlyn met me eye to eye.

"Germanus is dead."

I blinked hard, I remember, because I felt I had been staring for too long and my eyes had begun to tingle strangely, and then I shook my head, slightly confused, and cleared my throat. "What . . . ? Forgive me, what did you say?"

"Germanus is dead. He died in Italia, after his meeting with the Pope and his fellow bishops. The word was brought to us a month ago, in a letter sent to Bishop Enos by Ludovic, Germanus's secretary. You know the man?" I could only nod, the import of what Merlyn was telling me beginning to penetrate my awareness. "Aye, I thought you might. He has been with Germanus for more than thirty years."

"Forty," I whispered. "Ludovic has been with the bishop for forty-three years. He is the bishop's secretary, but they are close friends, too. They started out as students of law together, Germanus told me. He became a successful advocate, but Ludovic quickly found that he preferred building cases to disputing them in open court, and so the two men became associates and remained together ever afterwards."

"I knew they were close, but I would never have suspected such a long friendship. Forty-three years is more than half a lifetime. Anyway, Ludovic knew how important our affairs here in Britain were to Germanus, and so he took the time to write a long letter to Bishop Enos, describing the bishop's final days and the circumstances surrounding his death, and he described in detail several of the conversations he himself had had with Germanus concerning our activities here and the coronation we were planning. As you know, Germanus firmly believed that the salvation of the Church in Britain will depend upon the emergence of Camulod as a military force under Arthur, and neither Bishop Enos nor I can see any reason to doubt the accuracy of his expectations."

Merlyn stopped talking and sat watching me closely while I struggled to absorb all that I had just learned. Finally he leaned slightly towards me, his gaze still fixed on mine, and asked, "How do you feel?"

Even in my daze I recognized the futility of the question. I remembered having asked it myself of other people in pain, in just the same hapless way because there are times when you have to ask, and those are the only words that come anywhere close to framing the concern you are trying to express. I gulped and nodded my head, waving one hand in a small gesture to indicate that I was well and needed no help. It was a lie, of course, and we both knew that, but it served as an acknowledgment that my mind was still functioning. Merlyn accepted it and resumed speaking, still leaning towards me with the same narrow-eyed gaze.

"I want you now to think again about your dream, Clothar, in the light of what I have just told you. From all the information I have been able to gather—from Ludovic's letter and from the eyewitness account of the priest who brought the letter to us— Germanus must have died very close to the time when you dreamed of his presence in your tent. I mean *very* close, Clothar . . . perhaps that selfsame night, and at the very hour you saw him, for he died in the deepest part of the night. His death occurred on the last night in March. Your dream, you said, occurred at the end of March or the beginning of April. I would like you to think more closely about that now, because it is of great import. I have asked Enos if he can remember when it was, but he was not in Verulamium at the time and did not return until several days later. He recalls only that you were excited by the dream and impatient to be on your way, and that you had waited for his return purely out of courtesy."

I frowned, thinking about that. "I remembered the dream itself, no more. The particular night of its occurrence was unimportant."

"Well, do you believe now that it might have been important after all?"

I felt myself frowning harder, knowing what he was now suggesting, but I was far from convinced that this theory of his might have merit. "How so?"

"How so? *How so?* Because, my young friend, if your dream occurred the night Germanus died, then he might really have been there in your tent, and for a purpose."

I sat gazing at this man about whom I had heard so much and who now appeared to be disappointingly normal and quite incapable of performing any of the heroic exploits I had heard attributed to him. "That is nonsense," I said eventually. "What possible purpose could he have for doing such a thing?"

"How is it nonsense?"

"I have already explained all of that, Master Merlyn, and even although it makes me sound ill mannered to say so, I thought I had made myself perfectly clear. If *any* of what happened that night had been real—if Germanus really had come to me in a dream—he would have known that everything was changing and that he was sending me off on a useless journey."

Merlyn sat for a moment as though weighing what I had said, and then he nodded abruptly. "True," he said. "From your viewpoint and as you perceive it, absolutely true. But look at it for a moment, if you will, from my viewpoint. What if I were to suggest that your journey was not merely *useful* but necessary, and utterly unrelated to anything you have envisioned? I have been thinking about that for some time now, but most particularly since you arrived here today, and I now believe that is the truth."

I had no idea what he meant, and seeing my incomprehension, he said, "These," and bent down to the floor at his feet and picked up the fat leather wallet I had given him on my arrival, an hour earlier, the wallet that contained all the documents Germanus had sent me to bring to his attention. He had accepted it graciously when I presented it and had then asked for my indulgence while he scanned its contents. His examination had been cursory, for the most part, and he had set several documents aside with barely a glance, quite irrespective of the imposing bulk of some of them.

One document, however—it appeared to be an epistle several pages long—had claimed his full attention, bringing him to his feet with muttered excuses as he walked away to read it in a muted whisper in the afternoon light of the window embrasure. That document now rested securely in the folds of his long outer garment, but he had stuffed all the other papers back into the wallet that he now brandished in front of me.

"The information contained in this wallet is the true essence of your task here in Britain, Master Clothar. I suggest to you now that it is the *sole* reason for your being here today, far more important in Germanus's eyes than the matter of Arthur's coronation. I invited Germanus to participate in that event because I knew his presence would add *dignitas* and authority to what we did, but he and I both knew, back then, that the event would take place whether he was present or not. So . . ." He paused, continuing to look me directly in the eye, then began again.

"Ask yourself this. Why did Germanus send *you* here, to me? He could just as easily have sent you directly to Enos at Verulamium. The letter you brought to him explained everything to Enos, did it not? Anything that he asked you after reading it was born of curiosity and not of a burning need to know important details, is that not so? Am I correct?"

I nodded, unsure of where he was going with this, and he returned my nod with greater emphasis. "Aye, so here is what I believe." He raised the leather wallet and turned it back and forth in front of my eyes. "I never gamble for pleasure, but I would be prepared to wager a substantial amount that if either Arthur Pendragon or my affairs in Camulod and Britain are even mentioned in any of these documents, it will be but briefly and in passing, to illustrate some point or other that Germanus wants to bring to my attention. For Germanus *did* want—and still wants—all of my attention to be focused upon what is here in this package. I have no doubt of that, and you should have none, either."

"The letter that you read so carefully, then, was from Germanus." I spoke it as a statement, not a question, but Merlyn answered it.

"It was. From his hands, to my eyes. When he compiled these documents, and sent you off to bring them here to me, he could have had no knowledge of how events would develop—no one could have known that, at that time, including me. And so what happens? Think about this. Here in the west, in Cornwall and Cambria, in the aftermath of our victory over implacable enemies whose sole intent was our destruction and the obliteration of everything we stand for here in Camulod, great passions were stirred up and momentous events began to unfold that could easily encompass all of Britain and change life throughout this land. And then I received word from Bishop Enos that Germanus was unable to come as he had promised, but that he had exhorted Enos to stand in his place and to organize the events surrounding Arthur's coronation so that they would demonstrate credible, solid evidence that the new Riothamus would have the blessings and support of God's Church in Britain to assert and reinforce his authority." He held up his left hand, and a young man whom I had not previously noticed but who had evidently been awaiting such a signal came rushing forward. Merlyn stayed him with an upraised finger and looked at me.

"Are you thirsty, Master Clothar? I am. I have been talking without rest for almost six hours today. We have mead and beer, and even wine from Gaul. I am going to have some mead, myself. What would you like?"

I thanked him and asked for mead, too, and the youth vanished as quickly as he had appeared. Merlyn settled back farther into his chair.

"As soon as I had read the letter Enos sent to me, and read the copy he had attached of Germanus's letter to him, it became clear to me that they were both right and that it was of vital import to our cause to hold the Riothamus coronation in Verulamium. It had not occurred to me until then, but once aware of it, I could not deny the rightness of it. Physically, the great theater there has a grandeur not to be found anywhere else in Britain today, and it can house seven thousand people—seated—at any time.

"Emotionally, too, the place recalls the glory days of Empire when, despite all the moaning and weeping that some people indulge in today, this land knew naught but peace and prosperity. And then there was the additional consideration that the theater has already served as a point of focus for the Church and the affairs of

God, when it was used as the venue for the great debate hosted by Germanus himself two decades ago. And then, last in recollection but by no means last in order of importance, the place is neutral, politically speaking. If, as Germanus had suggested, Enos was to use his bishops and their influence to bring the regional kings and the clan chiefs of Britain to attend the events we were planning, they would probably find it easier to attract them all to Verulamium than to Camulod, first because Verulamium is more central—Camulod lying far to the west—but second, and more important, because Camulod itself stirs envy, and perhaps disquiet, in the hearts of the very men we wanted to attract."

The young man returned with our drinks, and Merlyn waited until he had served both of us and left again before continuing. "And so the decision was made, by me and me alone, to move the events we were planning to Verulamium in accordance with the wishes expressed by Germanus and Enos. You had already been here in Britain for several months by that time, and before you left Gaul, Germanus could not possibly have foreseen my decision or how a change in my thinking might affect his plans for you. And so you were in Verulamium—in the wrong place and at the wrong time."

He held up a hand quickly, smiling as he did so in order to deprive his next words of any sting or implied rebuke. "Allow me to finish my thought, if you will, before you object. Here is the meat of what I am saying: none of us, as it transpired, could have any real control over developments, once the entire affair of Arthur's crowning had begun to gain momentum. Had you been in Verulamium when I arrived, you would have been lost in the midst of a turmoil, because Arthur's armies had already been there for several days by then, and bishops and kings and chiefs and their various adherents and followers were assembling daily from all over Britain, all of them seething like ground oats boiling in a pot, and clamoring for my time and attention. The town was full to overflowing and surrounded by armed camps—Arthur's multiple encampments being the largest of all, although several of those belonging to some of the lesser kings were almost equally impressive, given that they lacked the horse lines and cavalry capacity Arthur commanded."

He leaned forward and looked me directly in the eye. "And so had you been there when I arrived, Master Clothar, and had I found the time to meet with you, our meeting would, of necessity, have been a very brief one, with no hope of discussing anything at length or in detail. You would have presented me with your documents from Germanus and I would have accepted them gratefully and set them aside to read later, with the best intentions in the world of doing so. But the matters you were bringing to my attention would have had nothing to do with the tumultuous happenings under way at that time, and thus, by definition, they would have been irrelevant in the context of Arthur's coronation. I would have had no other choice than to set them aside in favor of more urgent priorities. Do you take my point?"

I nodded, albeit grudgingly, and wondering what his true meaning might be here. "Yes, I do."

"Excellent, because my point is that Germanus's appearance in your tent that night *was* miraculous, and the sole reason for its occurrence was his need to *remove* you, to send you away from Verulamium before the storm broke and the chaos began to eddy and swirl about the town. Thus, your travels across Britain were quite the opposite of useless or futile. They were intentionally designed to keep you safely away from me until my work with all those other factors was complete and I could give my full attention to these writings you have brought for me. I believe that, Master Clothar. And I believe, too, that Germanus came to you the night he died and that his visit was a miracle tailored, perhaps for the only time in his exemplary life, to his own requirements and his personal priorities. He wanted you to keep this wallet and its contents away from me until now, when I can deal with whatever they contain and might require of me."

I sat gaping at him, unable to speak either to agree or disagree with anything he had said, and all he did was smile, watching the varying expressions as they crossed my face. Finally I coughed to clear my throat, and found my voice.

"That would make these documents extremely important."

"Extremely so, I agree. Germanus never was a waster of people's time."

"But what could be in them? What do they—?" I stopped short, abashed by the awareness that the answer to those questions was not for me to demand. The documents were for Merlyn's eyes only.

He did not react to my impertinence, however, but merely held the wallet now in both hands and raised it up in front of him, gazing at it. "I have glanced very briefly at some of them, Master Clothar, as you are aware, but I must confess I am eager to learn more. So, if you will pardon me, I will go now and make a start upon the task of reading them, for I think it might take me several hours to read through everything and absorb the meaning of it." He stood up and started to bid me farewell with a nod of his head, but I stayed him with my own upraised hand.

He eyed me courteously, one brow slightly raised as he waited to hear whatever it was that I had to add, but although my lips were parted, nothing emerged from my mouth, for I answered each point in my own mind even before I could begin to articulate it, until eventually I felt my cheeks reddening with embarrassment.

"Forgive me, Lord Merlyn," I said then. "I have half a hundred questions in my head, all of them demanding answers, but there are several that I find particularly distracting and frustrating."

"And to those you would prefer more immediate and satisfying answers. I can understand that, knowing how long you have been in pursuit of me." He eased himself back into his chair. "Tell me about these other considerations, then, and let me see what I can do to set you at your ease."

I remained silent, nonplussed, searching for the correct response to his invitation and failing to find it. What *was* I concerned about? And then suddenly, two things crystallized in my mind and I knew where I must go in this. I cleared my throat again.

"I would like to speak to you, if I may, about your ward, Arthur, the new King. For two years now I have been looking forward to meeting him, anticipating the event of his coronation as Riothamus and savoring the opportunity to offer him my services and my support in his endeavors as High King. I have even persuaded my friends Perceval and Tristan to join me. So I was deeply angered to discover that, through no fault of my own, not only had I missed his crowning in Verulamium but I had also managed to be absent for the first important battle he fought as King—his first strike against the invading Danes led by Horsa, and in all probability a battle that could define the course of his reign.

"I know it was an important battle—how could I not know? It is the talk of the land. Everyone has been talking of little else since it took place. Believe me, Master Merlyn, we have heard about it from many people, but none of those from whom we heard of it was actually present at the event—not one of them. None of them saw the fight, none of them knew the truth of what occurred, and the information they passed on to us when the tidings were fresh and new was already polluted by ignorance and the boastful claims of empty-headed loudmouths." I drew a deep breath, forcing down the anger that was always so close to welling up in me nowadays and compelling myself to remain calm, at least in my speaking.

"We heard reports of everything that went on ahead of us as we crossed from Cambria to here, Master Merlyn, and we could trust none of it to be free of distortion or bias. On the purely personal level, all I really know to be true is that great events have been unfolding far from my ken and that, despite a deep belief that Bishop Germanus sent me here precisely to be involved in these events and to stand with Arthur the King and his people, I have somehow managed to miss all of them—to the point of utter and unhappy ignorance."

As I spoke, intensely aware of my own frustration yet unable to control a burgeoning sense of unwonted anger, Merlyn had turned his head towards the fire basket, and when I had finished, he sat silent for a while longer, his lips pouted in thought.

"It is easy to see why you are angry," he said at length. "On the matter of the King's coronation, there is little I can do to ease your disappointment. I know there are stories circulating concerning what went on at the high altar, and I know, too, that they seem incredible and undeserving of belief. But I can offer you a few hard facts that are indisputable, despite their appearance of being fantastical. Mere moments after the King's corona had been set upon his brow at the high altar by Bishop Enos, and after swearing a mighty regal oath to use his armed might to defend God's Church against all pagan and godless aggression, Arthur Pendragon drew a magnificent long-bladed sword from the altar itself—from the altar stone—in full view of thousands of people. I have seen the sword, and held it in my hands, and there has never been a weapon of such beauty and splendor ever seen before, in this land or any other. That is the truth, Master Clothar. These events occurred. I was there and saw them take place with my own eyes. And as the new King held this wondrous sword aloft for all to see, a beam of purest sunlight shone through a gap in the clouds above and outlined him in golden glory in an unmistakable demonstration of God's own approval of his crowning and his sacred oath.

"Those events you missed, and their like will never occur again, and I regret deeply that, after all the troubles you have gone through, you were unable to witness them. I can assure you, however, that you may trust my version of what occurred that day, and you may also be assured that Arthur will be happy to accept your sword, your service and your loyalty when the two of you eventually stand face to face. Lose no sleep over that one, Master Clothar. Arthur Pendragon has a mighty task ahead of him and he will require, and be grateful for, all the assistance, loyalty and support he can find.

"As to the other matter, the King's first battle, I can provide you with accurate information on what happened there. I have in my possession not only the reports of the battle but the plan of battle from the King himself, drawn by his own hand, and I will gladly share those with you at another time—perhaps even tomorrow, if Arthur does not return in the interim."

This was the first indication I had received since my arrival that the King was not even in Camulod, and I asked Merlyn where he had gone.

"He is on circuit patrol. Traveling around the perimeter of the colony, checking each guard outpost and patrol garrison, then striking outward to visit our outlying garrisons in surrounding towns and communities."

"The King does that in person?"

"Aye, and happily, of his own choosing. It enables him to meet and speak with his men as men, and he enjoys that."

"Commander to trooper, you mean, rather than king to subject."

"No, man to man, rather than superior to minion. It is important to him."

"Important to his men, too, I'll wager." I was remembering Chulderic's story of how King Ban and my father had met Germanus. "How long might he be gone?"

Merlyn shrugged. "Who can say? It all depends upon who and what he encounters on his patrol, but we generally allocate ten days for each sweep—that's what we call our routine patrols—then add sufficient discretionary time for them to extend that by two days. After that, if we have not received word from them, we send out rescue squadrons."

"Have you ever had a patrol that failed to return?"

"Aye, several, but very few overall, in a sixty-year period."

"So you are not concerned about the King's absence?"

"Concerned?" Merlyn laughed. "No, not at all. He is not *absent*, Master Clothar, he is on a sweep, of his own lands, and he has only been gone for ten days. We expect him to return at any moment— he could be entering the gateway as we speak—but even if he fails to appear today, he yet has two days before we will begin to grow concerned. And even then, we would need evidence of some kind to arouse our suspicions to the point of sending out a rescue mission. This is not some junior subaltern or local kinglet, Master Clothar. Arthur Pendragon is Riothamus of Britain and a battle commander of supreme abilities. He will not be bullied, nor will he be easily dissuaded from completing whatever tasks he sets himself before returning home to Camulod."

I nodded. "Yes, I understand what you are saying. I look forward to meeting him."

"Good. You will, and very soon, I promise you. And now, if there is nothing else—"

"There is one more thing, if you will permit me?"

He hunched his shoulders expressively, his face indicating surprise but with a willingness to listen, and I felt myself flushing scarlet as the words that had been in my head began to drain rapidly downwards, avoiding my lips. Merlyn sat waiting.

"Well," I continued, floundering. "I know not if I can find the proper words . . . but I think it is important that I try to say what I wish to say, if only to clear the air and allow myself to think logically." I took a breath and thrust straight ahead. "May I ask you, Master Merlyn, whether Bishop Germanus mentioned me by name in the letter I brought to you?"

Merlyn slowly raised his hand and scratched delicately and deliberately at his chin with the nail of his little finger. "Yes, he did. But why would you ask me that? The content of that letter is my concern alone."

"It is, sir, I know. But I must ask you to be patient with me and extend me your forbearance, if you will, no matter how ill mannered or clumsy I may appear to be in this . . . I have been asking myself for some time now why Bishop Germanus chose to involve *me* in these affairs when he could very easily have sent one of his own priests to deliver letters for him. He had no shortage of young priests at his disposal and they cross the seas on God's business all the time, so why would he pick *me* and send me off to a foreign land with no idea of what I must do once I have carried out my task for him? He had a purpose in mind for me, of that I am sure, but he told me nothing of what it might be. And now you tell me he is dead and that confounds me, for I know not what to do now, or where I should go. My mentor is dead. My task, as far as I know, is completed. And I have no clear indication, mental or otherwise, of what I should do next. I feel . . . abandoned, I suppose . . . cut off from all certainty.

"I have an unfinished task in Gaul, where the man who slew my parents and my grandfather yet rules in a kingdom that is rightfully mine, but although I intend to return there someday and claim his head in vengeance, I feel no burning urge to rush off and do it now. Part of me wishes to believe that my place is here, at this time, and yet I have no sense of . . . place—no sense of what awaits me or of what I should be doing next. I will meet the King soon, and that particular question may be resolved, but still I know nothing of what Germanus planned for me, if he planned anything. And so I must ask you more, and beg your understanding and indulgence. Did the bishop speak of me specifically? And if so, pray, what did he say?"

Merlyn grimaced, sucking breath between his teeth, then shook his head and blew out a great breath. "Damnation, Master Clothar," he said, "you come upon me with this request at the worst time, because while I can answer you truthfully, I cannot tell you what you want to know.

"I have told you that he named you in his letter to me. But he has also enjoined me to be careful in what I say, to you or about you, until I have read everything that he has sent me. Don't ask me why, boy, because I simply do not know why, and I will not until I have had time to read all this."

"He told you to tell me nothing of what he has to say of me?"

"He told me to say nothing until I have learned everything there is to learn about you."

"But what is there to learn that you do not already know?" I bit down on my anger yet again. "No, Master Merlyn. That makes no sense at all, because it makes too much of me, and for no adequate reason. Bishop Germanus was my mentor, but he was mentor to many others, too, all of them more worthy of his time and attention than I was. His interest in me, from the outset, was an obligation. He had been a close friend of my parents and my foster parents, too, and he had stood as godfather for me at my baptism, after the death of my parents and long before he became a bishop. So when I grew old enough, he took me into his school as a pupil. My father was a king, and he served in the legions with Germanus. But he is a dead king, almost seventeen years in his grave. He was murdered soon after I was born, and his lands usurped by his murderer, and in order to protect me and guard my identity after my father's death, I was raised in secrecy by my uncle Ban, King of Benwick, in southern Gaul. That is my life, in its entirety. There is no more to learn."

Merlyn shrugged. "Apparently that is not so. Perhaps you yourself do not know all that there is to know."

"About *myself*? That is iniquitous," I said, my anger spilling over. "Am I now to believe that I am unworthy to know some truth about myself—some arcane secret that no one thinks me capable of handling? Germanus himself told me nothing of what the letters contained regarding me before he sent me off to spend a year and more wandering through this land carrying his wallet. And now, having done so in all obedience and to the best of my ability, I feel slighted and insulted . . . deemed unworthy of trust, even with knowledge of myself." Raising my voice to Merlyn Britannicus this way, this man I did not know but had every reason to treat with the utmost respect, appalled me, outraging every tenet of behavior with which I had been raised and leaving me with a sinking feeling of imminent remorse. But I had no way of stopping now. "Master Merlyn," I continued, the bit between my teeth, "I know I have never done anything to earn, or to deserve, such treatment, and that makes me deeply angry, because I am utterly at a loss to understand why it happened, and that ignorance, that not knowing, is the most perplexing and infuriating thing about this whole situation."

Merlyn rose fluidly to his feet, betraying no sign of any of the damage he had sustained from being burned in Carthac's fire. "Very well, so be it," he said, enunciating his words precisely and slowly. "This much I will promise you. I will tell you what-ever is said about you in these documents, so be it I judge the information to be harmless to you. The only proviso I will add to that, having said it, is that I will pass along nothing that Germanus might ask me specifically, for whatever reason, to conceal from you. I say that because I cannot imagine him doing such a thing and then blithely sending you off to deliver the material to me in person. That kind of information only applies in situations that involve heinous crimes and shameful secrets, and Germanus himself clearly respected and admired you when he chose you for this task. He would never dream of using you so cruelly, so I believe you may set your mind at rest on that concern. Will that suffice?"

I nodded, mollified by his straightforwardness. "Thank you, Lord Merlyn, it will."

"Good. But now I really must take leave of you. I have much to do, as you know, and there are other matters claiming my attention before I can be free to apply myself to our affairs." He waved a thumb towards the door at his back. "I will have young Mark escort you back to the quarters assigned to you and your three friends, and you and I will talk at more length tomorrow, once I have mastered what you brought to me." We exchanged nods of farewell, and he pulled his hood firmly forward to conceal his face again, then swept out, limping only very slightly.

Left alone in the room, I glanced down at the cup I held in my hands and was surprised to find it empty. I had no recollection of drinking its contents. I was still angry, too, although in the face of Merlyn's courtesy and consideration I could not quite tell myself why that should be so. And then the answer came to me. Despite all his charm and courtesy, Merlyn had nonetheless committed himself only to telling me what he considered harmless to me. Any request from Germanus that specific information be kept from me, for whatever reason, would be sacrosanct in Merlyn's eyes.

The anger boiling inside me grew stronger and I stormed out of the room, headed for the bright afternoon sunlight and spoiling for a fight with someone—anyone at all.

2

It was probably fortunate that I encountered no one in my distempered journey from Merlyn's quarters to my own, for my anger continued to build, demanding an outlet. It was probably equally providential, when I think of it, that when I arrived back at the accommodations assigned to us, neither Perceval nor Tristan were there and I could not even find young Bors. My only options were therefore to remain alone or to go in search of them. I had paid little attention to the weather as I stalked from Merlyn's place, but now that I had time to look about me I had to admit, albeit grumpily and with reluctance, that this was a perfect day on which to be walking and breathing deeply, savoring the scents of the world. It was one of those long, warm late-summer afternoons that are so universally seductive and alluring, beguiling normally responsible people into deserting their appointed tasks and wasting their time instead on self-indulgent frivolity. At that moment, on that afternoon, having found no one on whom I could vent my anger, I was perfectly open to, and in exactly the right frame of mind for, temptations of that kind. I was in no mood to do anything constructive. Besides, I thought, if I went walking I might find someone I could provoke into a fight.

Bors had leaned my two quivers of throwing spears upright, as he always did, against the wall in one of the back corners of our quarters, and the long, needle-pointed metal heads gleamed dully in the afternoon light that filtered into the room. I stood in the doorway, looking at them and thinking that it had been far too long since I last practiced, and shortly after that I found myself striding towards the stables, a small bundle of four spears tied with thongs and dangling behind my right shoulder.

I paid no visible heed to any of them, but I was aware of people noticing the spears as I passed by, for the weapons were extremely unusual and most of the people crowding the open spaces and narrow walkways I traversed were soldiers and warriors, conditioned to examine other people's weaponry. No one made any comment on my spears, however, and I saddled up my horse and made my way out of the gates.

Below me at the foot of Camulod's hill, as was normal at this time of the year, the enormous drilling ground was almost completely obscured by the clouds of dust stirred up by the ceaseless circling and maneuvering of the riders training there. I avoided the place, purely because there were too many people down there, and steered my horse well clear of the swirling dust clouds, angling it towards the woods that lined the outer edge of the approach road to the fortress. Once in the green-hued shade among the trees, I began to ride around the base of Camulod's hill, following a route I recalled from my first visit. About a mile back there, I knew, behind the hilltop fort, there was a gently sloping meadow, bisected by a wide, deep brook that was bridged by a trio of well-matched logs supporting a deck of heavy planking, and slightly downstream from the bridge was a hole that was full of fine trout and deep enough to swim in. My intention was to go directly to the meadow, spend some time there practicing my throwing, both from horseback and afoot, and then perhaps to spear a fat trout and cook and eat it immediately. To that end, I had gone first to the cookhouse, where I procured a loaf of fresh bread and a twist of salt before heading for the stables.

Alas, the entire countryside was swarming with men—Arthur Pendragon's victorious armies, freshly returned from their victory over Horsa's Danes—and there was no avoiding them. I hoped at first to simply ride beyond them into something at least approaching solitude, but it was not to be. There were too many people around to permit anything close to privacy.

As I penetrated deeper and deeper into the woodlands and drew farther and farther away from the fortress on the hilltop, I found myself becoming increasingly resentful of the persistent presence of others around me. Most of them were men, but no army in history has ever failed to attract its share of women. There were enough camp followers scattered throughout the teeming throngs to keep everyone at a high pitch of excitement, for one reason and another. Fully three times I made my way towards spots that appeared to be deserted, only to find them occupied by lovers in varying stages of undress and coupling.

Other activities were going on, too. In one spot, some enterprising soul had set up a game in which men threw horseshoes at a pair of iron spikes hammered into the ground some twenty paces apart from each other. The object of the game appeared to be to land each horseshoe as close as possible to the spike. I was unsurprised to see that, as usual among armies of any kind, large amounts of money were changing hands among the onlookers. Intrigued in spite of my foul humor, I watched the play for nigh on half an hour and saw only one man achieve the highest points by dropping his horseshoe cleanly over the spike, to the uproarious delight of those who had bet on him.

In another spot, a clearing in the woods, I came upon a number of men throwing knives and axes at a range of targets and from varying distances, and several of these fellows followed me with hostile, watchful eyes as I rode through. There was no gambling taking place there that I could see, and it seemed to me that everyone involved was taking the entire exercise very seriously. I looked directly at one of the participants in passing, a tall, dark-haired fellow who looked as though he would be happy to fight any casual foe that life might throw at him, but he ignored my truculence, following me with an unblinking gaze as sullen as my own.

As soon as I realized he would not fight me merely for looking at him, I looked away and kept moving, for I knew exactly who and what he represented: that brotherhood of veterans in every army who have survived everything they encountered and have learned to trust and rely upon their own close comrades and no one else. I had shared that comradeship of veterans myself, during Gunthar's War, and I knew from experience how powerful a bond it forms. But somehow, and I now saw that my expectations had been foolish, I had not expected to find its like in Britain.

Now that I had become aware of this phenomenon among Pendragon's armies, however, I found myself watching for similar instances as I rode on, and I found no lack of them. But what surprised me most, as I paid closer attention to the men I passed, was that I began to fancy I could gauge a man's war experience merely from the way he reacted to my presence. The more I saw, the more I became convinced that I was right and that the true veterans, the hardened core of this army that was all around me, were a highly distinctive group, easily identifiable despite the countless human differences between each man and his neighbors.

Engrossed in this new and intriguing train of thought, I eventually lost all awareness of where I was and what I was about. I rode by one group of veteran spearmen, all of them wearing what came nigh to being a uniform of drab green tunics with bright yellow blazons at their left shoulders, and I put my theory to the test by approaching very close to them, almost to within touching distance.

The silence that fell over them at my approach was profound. I counted a score and a half of them before one of them finally looked up and saw that I was bearing directly down on them. He frowned and cleared his throat but no words emerged from his mouth. The expression on his face, however, made words unnecessary, and heads began to turn towards me more and more quickly, until thirty pairs of eyes were glaring at me in outrage, their owners shocked into silence by the suddenness and effrontery of my approach.

I had identified the group leaders some time earlier, and now I nodded gravely in acknowledgment and greeting to the one I deemed to be the senior of three. Showing no sign of curiosity and making no eye contact with anyone lest it spark a challenge, I rode steadily through their midst, and they moved grudgingly but wordlessly to grant me passage.

When I had passed safely beyond them I made no attempt to look back, for I could feel the burn of their collective gaze in the center of my back. I did, however, permit myself to smile then, knowing that it was only my appearance that had saved me from being dragged off my horse and thrashed for my presumption. The fact that I was in this place at all, riding among them, meant that I must be an ally of some stripe, but that would have mattered not a whit had any of those men decided that I needed to be taught a lesson in good manners and decorum.

There was sufficient foreignness about my appearance, however, to have given them pause; not only was I mounted but I was superbly mounted, on a magnificent and richly caparisoned horse, and although I wore none of my wondrous armor, the clothing I wore, I knew, spoke loudly of wealth and privilege—loudly enough to suggest unmistakably that I might be someone with a great deal of power, whom it were better not to offend or accost.

I rode then for a short time through a lightly wooded area where I encountered no one. It was the first time I had been free of the sight and sounds of people since leaving the fort, and for some time I was not even aware of the change. But eventually I relaxed so that I nearly slouched in the saddle, allowing my horse to pick his way forward at his own speed. When he carried me to the edge of a pleasant and fast-flowing brook, I considered dismounting and simply lying on the grassy bank for a while, listening to the sounds of the swift-moving stream, but as I reined in, preparing to swing my leg over his back and slide to the ground, I heard the sudden, familiar rhythmic clacking of heavy, hard-swung wooden dowels spring up nearby. Someone was practicing sword play, and the rapid, stuttering tempo of the blows told me that the people involved were experts. Instead of dismounting, I pulled my horse around and walked him towards the sounds.

I saw seven of them as I emerged from the trees surrounding the meadow where they were and recognized the place as my original destination. I had reached it almost by accident, but I saw at a glance that my memory of it had been accurate. There lay the bridge of logs covered with crosswise planking, and on the far side of the stream the gently sloping sward was dotted with copses and clumps of low trees, mainly hawthorn and elder. I saw now that the seven men were all young, strong and vigorous warriors whose clothing, like my own, declared them to be well-born and privileged in all they did. Two of them were fighting skillfully with training swords of heavy wooden dowel similar to those I had used since my earliest days at the Bishop's School. These swords, however, were longer and heavier than those we had used in Gaul, although neither of the two opponents seemed the slightest bit inconvenienced by the extra length and weight.

They were well matched, the fighting pair. Both were of medium height, wide shouldered and heavily muscled, their bare forearms taut with the tension and strain of controlling their whirling weapons. They circled each other as they fought, leaning forward on the balls of their feet and grinning ferally, their friendship as apparent in their faces as was the iron determination in each of them to win this bout. The man facing me as I emerged from the trees was the first one to see me, and as soon as he did he took a backwards leap and grounded his weapon, shouting something I failed to understand. Every eye in the place turned towards me as I brought my mount to a halt, watching the group carefully albeit avoiding eye contact with any of them.

There were nine of them, I could see now. Two had been lounging on the bank of the stream, my view of them obscured by a low-lying clump of heather, but now they had raised themselves on their elbows to look over at me. Something white flashed from a dark place on the far side of the stream, and as I squinted in that direction my eyes adjusted to the light and the distance and I made out the shapes of several horses—nine of them, I presumed— hobbled in the shade of a clump of hawthorns. All of them were saddled, indicating that their owners were on their way to some other destination and had merely stopped here to rest for a time.

I nudged my horse gently with my spurs and rode forward slowly, angling him towards the bridge. But I knew I would not pass unchallenged this time, for none of these people's clothes were shabbier than mine. No one man among them made any overtly threatening move or betrayed any kind of hostility towards me, but suddenly they were all moving, perhaps in response to some signal unseen by me, and so fluid was their movement that I quickly found myself facing an entire line of them, seven men shoulder to shoulder across the front of the bridge. I kept moving, guiding my mount with my knees until a mere ten paces separated me from the line of warriors. I took note that three of them were smiling but I drew little pleasure from it, since the likeliest reason for their smiles was anticipation of the pleasure they were about to take in thrashing me. Of the four who were not smiling, two were frowning and the other two had blank faces from which wary eyes watched me intently. It was one of the latter two who spoke to me first, his tone of voice as expressionless as his face.

"Come now, fellow, how offensive need you be? Who are you and where have you come from?"

I merely shrugged my shoulders, answering him calmly but ignoring the matter of my name. "I had no thought of being offensive. I am merely passing through."

"Well, pass through at some other place, you inconsiderate lout. Can you not see that you are disturbing our leisure, trespassing upon our goodwill?"

I felt all apprehension suddenly leave me. I had been spoiling for a fight since the moment I left Merlyn's quarters, but I had no intention of getting myself killed and thus had been looking for a safe fight, an outlet for my frustration. I knew now that I had found what I was seeking. None of these people facing me bore me genuine ill will. Had it been otherwise they would not have spoken at all, outnumbering me as heavily as they did. They would simply have acted, and I would be dead or unconscious. But now I knew that what I was facing here was the same kind of unit pride that I had been watching among the common soldiers. These young men were all officers, all leaders, sharing and enjoying one another's strength and companionship in a place of safety. My presence among them, as an unexpected newcomer of their own stature, afforded them an opportunity for sport, at no cost, and I was sure they would not consider swarming me. The combat shaping up here would be single combat, one against one.

I glanced over to a patch of close-cropped turf on the riverbank. Heavy spears had been arranged in two pyramids there, and helmets, cuirasses, greaves and a number of swords and axes had

been neatly propped against them when their owners had stripped
down to their tunics to rest and enjoy the sun. Now I looked back to
my challenger, with one eyebrow raised in wry amusement that I
hoped would provoke him.

"Goodwill, say you? You lay claim to goodwill, behaving this
way, accosting and bullying passing strangers? You and I obviously
come from different places, with different definitions of goodwill."

"Aye, we do, and I can hear the country clodhopper in your
voice. Where, in God's name, did you learn to speak Latin like that?"

Again I shrugged, refusing to rise to his bait. "In a place far
removed from here, a place where anyone as surly and ungracious
as you appear to be would be tied and left outside on a cold night to
feed the wolves."

He blinked, but he rallied quickly enough. "You are in Camulod
now, fellow. We mislike foul-tongued Outlanders here. You should
be praying to whatever gods you own to help you out of here in one
whole piece."

"I have a God—the one, true God, as much yours as mine—and
I had been thanking Him for leading me to this fair Camulod, until
this place and this meeting. Now, having found that you are here,
too, I find that the awareness of your presence kills my appetite for
the place."

I saw his face flush at that and knew that I had penetrated his
defenses, and when he spoke again his voice was heavy with truculence. "Ride away, little man. I've told you once already and will
not do so again. Ride back to where you came from, or find another
path across the stream, it matters naught to me. But you will not
cross here, and if you move to try it, we'll have you down off that
pretty horse before you can put spurs to him. I asked you who you
are and you have not yet answered me."

I sat straight on my horse, staring down at him and nibbling at
my upper lip, and he and all his companions stood gazing up at me
in silence, awaiting my response. The fellow who had spoken was,
I guessed, close to me in age, perhaps a year or two my senior but
no more than that. He was tall, too, but no taller than I was, and he

lacked my breadth of shoulders. Had I been offered my pick of them to fight, he was the one I would have chosen instinctively, perhaps because he was so fair of face that I suspected he might take care to avoid disfigurement in any fight that was less than deadly serious—yet I had no doubt at all that he would be formidable when the die was cast and real fighting broke out.

I could almost feel the tension in the air as everyone waited to see how I would respond to this last insult, but I merely bowed my head very slightly and answered again in tones of mild civility. "Nor will I answer you, asked thus. My name is my own and I have no intention of divulging it to a nameless brigand on the road simply because he has a posy of pretty blossoms as sweet as he is to back him up in his prancing and posturing." I watched their uniform reaction of amazed disbelief as my words registered in their minds and I continued before any of them could find his voice.

"As to where I have come from, you know that already, or you should, had you a brain with which to think and take note." I pointed backwards over my shoulder, then pointed towards the far side of the stream. "I came from there, I'm going there, and you are in my way. Now stand aside and let me pass."

My challenger smiled now and his face was transformed into radiance, but he shook his head slowly from side to side. "No," he said, "I feel no overwhelming need to move aside—no *urgency*. I fear you may have to bludgeon your way past me—unless, of course, you would prefer to lead your horse across, farther downstream."

"*Bludgeon* my way? Against all seven of you?"

"Why not? These are our lands and you do not belong in them. Do you mislike the odds?"

"That depends upon how you intend to fight me, *fellow*—to the death, with you afoot and me mounted, then so be it. I'll kill all seven of you, using these." I reached back and touched the bundle of spears that hung behind my shoulder.

My tormentor laughed. "You have only four of them, and there are *nine* of us, not seven."

I had forgotten the other two men, and that made me angry at myself, but before I could respond a voice spoke from my right, where the two from the riverbank had approached me unseen and, even worse, unsuspected.

"That's enough, Bedwyr. Let the man go on his way."

The man called Bedwyr swung his head to face the newcomer. "But, Magister, we can't let him ride by without a toll of some kind."

"Of course you can. Besides, I think he might have the advantage between the two of you."

Bedwyr's expression changed from protest to outrage. "What advantage, Magister, other than the horse? If he fights me on foot, face to face, I'll crush him."

I turned to look at the man they called Magister, the title by which I addressed Tiberias Cato and my other teachers and which meant, in my understanding, a person who was teacher and patron combined. To my utter astonishment, he appeared to be no older than the man Bedwyr, but he was huge, and he wore no signs of rank or any other rating other than his physical presence, which stamped him unmistakably as a leader. He was taller than I by a good handsbreadth, I estimated, and he was wide shouldered, broad of back and massive through the chest. His hair was dark brown, shot through with wide bands of a lighter golden color, and his eyes were unlike any I had ever seen, the irises golden yellow, flecked with black. He was close by my side, looking up at me as curiously. He nodded to me, his expression grave, but I saw a hint of something in his eyes just before he spoke again, something that might have been humor. He spoke again to the man Bedwyr, although his eyes never left mine.

"But if he fights you afoot, Beddo, then win or lose, he will tell us nothing about these strange-looking weapons he carries, and while that might sit well with you, it would please me not at all. Those spears look to me to be more than they appear to be at first glance. I suspect they might be an entirely new weapon. Am I correct, stranger? Is this a new weapon?"

I shook my head. "No, it is a very old weapon, but there are none like it in Britain—or in Gaul, for that matter."

His eyebrows rose in polite disbelief. "Do you tell me so? Then where do they come from?"

"From far away . . . far from here. They were made in a land a full year's journey eastward from the Empire's eastern border."

His eyebrows had come down, and they stayed down at this additional piece of information, but his eyes narrowed as he studied me, assessing whether or not I was bluffing him. "A year's journey beyond the *eastern* borders? That seems unbelievable."

I shrugged. "Believe it or not, as you will, it is the truth. The man who brought them back from there is my old teacher. His name is Tiberias Cato."

The big man was looking now at the spears. "What kind of wood are those shafts made from?"

"A kind that does not grow within the Empire. It is called bambu and is very light and very hard. We know nothing like it."

When it became clear to him that I was going to say nothing more, he nodded. "I see. You have nothing more to say on the topic. So be it then. But I fear, in light of that, that you will have to fight and best our Bedwyr here before you can proceed."

I looked over to where the man Bedwyr stood glaring at me and shook my head slowly. "No, I think not. There will be no fight between your bully Beddo and me."

"Why not?" There was genuine surprise in the Magister's voice.

"Why should I?" I rejoined, turning back to him. "What have I to gain by fighting him? Bruises do not seem like worthwhile gains to me, nor does the prospect of providing entertainment for the rest of your crew—particularly when I have the option of refusing both choices."

Bedwyr spoke up then. "If you win you can go on across the bridge."

I looked at him sidelong. "The water in the brook is barely fetlock deep for the most part and I can make my way across anywhere, without fighting, as you pointed out."

"Are you afraid to fight, then?"

"No, sir, I am not afraid to fight. I simply choose not to fight you, and I do not do so out of fear." I turned back to the Magister. "I will fight *you*, however, upon the clear understanding that when I win I will be allowed to go on my way without further trouble."

There was a chorus of gasps at that, and sounds of growing outrage, but the Magister laughed aloud and quelled them all by the simple expedient of raising his hand. Then, when the noise had died down, he spoke to me again, his hand still upraised, enjoining silence from his men. He was smiling at me openly now.

"Let me feed you back your own medicine. Why should I fight you and run the risk of injury when I can order any of my men to do it for me?"

"Because you are their leader—their Magister—and I am challenging you directly. Besides, if they attack me, singly or in any other way, you will never learn anything more about my wonderful spears."

His grin grew wider. "What is to stop us from simply depriving you of them now? It would be no great feat, with eight of my men against you alone. I would not even have to be involved."

"Very true, and there is nothing to stop you doing it, if that is what you wish. But even when you have them in your hands you will know nothing of them, or of what they were designed for, or of how to use them. I have only four of them, and you could never duplicate them."

"Never? That sounds like bluster to me. What do you mean, we could *never* duplicate them? Wait! Of course, the shafts . . . *bamboo,* you said?" He fell silent for a few moments, then resumed. "You said that if we attacked you we would learn nothing of the spears. That implies, then, that if I myself agree to fight you we might learn something of them. Am I correct?"

"You are. That is what I meant."

"Dismount, then, but I hope you have strong bones and a hard head." He turned to his men. "Who has the training swords? Bring them forward."

There were mutterings and mumbles among the others, but they quickly stilled as I leaped down from my horse and hung my thin bundle of spears from a hook on my saddle before moving to face their leader, who stood waiting for me with a long, heavy practice sword in each hand, extending them towards me hilt first. He was even larger, seen from this level, than I had thought at first, fully half a head taller than me, broader in the shoulders and longer of arm and leg. An intimidating adversary.

"These are our standard training swords," he said quietly. "They are made from ash wood, so they have resilience, as well as strength and weight. Choose whichever one pleases you more."

I took one in each hand, hefting them and feeling for balance and weight. "They are heavier than I am used to, and much longer."

"Aye, they are half again as long in the blade as a spatha. Do you normally use a spatha?"

"I do."

"We don't, in Camulod. Our swords are longer—stronger, too. Hence the heavier weight, based on the principle that a training weapon should be twice the weight of a real one. Will this be too much for you?"

I looked him straight in the eye and managed a smile for him, then crouched into the fighting stance and began the circling dance of the blade fighter half a step before he did the same. Before we had made half a revolution, the others had surrounded us, silent but watchful, plainly expecting to see their leader teach me a lesson in short order. I felt the difference in the practice sword immediately and straightened slightly, realizing that the increased length and weight of the weapon would call for a different technique in handling the thing. It felt cumbersome and ungainly in my grasp, but I noticed, too, that the hilt was twice as long as the hilt on my spatha, and that told me that the swords these people wielded could be gripped with both hands and swung ferociously.

My opponent immediately taught me something else about these weapons, because he held his in both hands, one on the hilt in the normal grip, and the other cradling the heavy end so that he held the weapon horizontally as he moved opposite me, assessing my capabilities. I could have told him I had none with such an alien weapon, but I knew he would reach that conclusion unaided within a very short time. Until that time, however, I would watch and hope to learn how to survive this encounter without disgracing myself. I began by holding my weapon the way he was holding his.

Decades have passed since that day, but I can still recall it clearly, and the clearest recollection I have is the easy half smile on my adversary's face, the supreme confidence expressed in his every move and the crouching grace with which he faced me. I knew that my weapon was going to hinder me, but I found myself taking encouragement from the way it nestled in my hands. And when he opened his attack by springing at me, changing his grip swiftly to hold the hilt in both hands and bring a mighty overhead blow down on me, I was ready for him. I could have jumped backwards or to either side to avoid the blow, because I saw it coming from the outset, but I chose to step into him instead, raising my weapon high in both hands to meet and absorb his blow before it could develop full momentum.

From the moment his sword hit mine, I lost all awareness of any newness or strangeness in my weapon and I fought as Tiberias Cato had taught me to fight, using all his tricks. Inside the big man's guard as I was, I turned and rammed my elbow into the soft, vulnerable spot beneath the join of his ribs. He grunted heavily and staggered backwards, and as he went reeling I spun again and slashed hard at his left knee. He managed to block the blow with a down-thrust blade and then exploded into a cat-like leap that won him enough distance to leave him safe for a few moments. And then the fight began in earnest.

The exhilaration of combat and the thirst for victory combined to increase my focus and my concentration, so that all my normal fighting techniques were enhanced and I adjusted quickly and easily to my new sword, manipulating it at times as though it were a spear with a solid, heavy shaft.

We fought long and hard, neither of us able to gain a lasting advantage over the other. When he attacked me, hacking and slashing ferociously, I would back away, fending off his blows and concentrating wholly on absorbing and avoiding his ferocity until the moment when I felt the vigor of his charge begin to wane. Then it became my turn to pursue him. Back and forth we went, time after time, the entire meadow echoing with the hard, dry clattering of blade against blade. We lost awareness, right at the outset, of the people watching us. We had no time for others. Our entire attention was focused upon each other because we both knew, within moments of our first clash, that we were equally matched and that this fight would go to the first man fortunate enough to land a solid blow. And each of us intended to be that man. But on and on it went, advance and retreat, neither of us able to land that solid blow and both of us growing more and more fatigued with every passing moment.

There came a time, and I had known it must come soon, when I began to feel, and to believe, that I was incapable of lifting my weapon above my head one more time. But he attacked again, hewing wickedly at my flanks, and one of his blows, a lateral slash, knocked aside my guardian blade and hit me at mid-thigh.

It was not a killing blow, for my own weapon had countered it and absorbed most of its strength, but had we been using real weapons it would have cut me deeply and been the end of me. As it was, I felt the crushing impact and my mind transported me instantly to Gaul where, three years earlier, I had been kicked in the same place, and with much the same force, by a horse. Then, as on this occasion, there was no pain, and I knew this time I would feel none until later. For the time being, however, my entire leg was numb. I could move on it without falling only if I did so with great care.

Knowing he had hit me hard, my opponent held back instead of rushing in to finish me, and in doing so he gave the initiative back to me. I took full advantage of it, using a two-handed grip to unleash a rain of blows, pushing him inexorably backwards with a fierce but unsustainable attack. I knew I was using the last of my reserves of strength but I had gone beyond caring. I knew that I would be finished the moment my attack began to falter, but I was determined to go down fighting. And then, in jumping backwards to avoid a crippling slash, my opponent caught his heel on something and fell heavily, landing hard on his backside and losing his blade.

It was my victory. All I had to do was step forward and place the end of my weapon against his chest. Instead—and to this day I do not know why I did it, but I am glad I did—I grounded my weapon, and then stepped forward, offering him my hand to pull himself up.

Only when he was standing facing me again, his right hand still holding mine and his other gripping my shoulder, did I realize that he was breathing every bit as laboriously as I was. He finally sucked in one great, deep breath and held it for long moments before expelling it again, and when he spoke his voice was close to normal.

"That was well fought, stranger, and it was a task I would not care to undertake again today or any other day. You are . . ." He paused, searching for a word. "Formidable. Yes, that describes you. Formidable. Now that you have thrashed me, will you permit me to ask who are you and whence you come, and who taught you to fight like that?" He released my hand and waved away one of his men, who was trying to attract his attention, and I knew that he genuinely wanted to hear my answers.

"My name is Clothar," I said, looking him in the eye and seeing the black flecks in the tawny gold of his irises. "I am a Frank, from southern Gaul. A Salian Frank reared among Ripuarians in the south. I was sent here more than a year ago by my patron and mentor, Bishop Germanus of Auxerre, to carry letters and documents to Merlyn Britannicus of Camulod. As for the fighting, I went for six years as a student to the Bishop's School in Auxerre, and the stable master, Tiberias Cato, was a former cavalryman. It was he who, as a much younger man, brought those spears back from the other Empire in the distant east. He, too, it was who taught me how to fight. And now I am here in Camulod awaiting the return of Arthur the Riothamus."

"Arthur? Why do you wait for him? Do you bear letters for him, too? And have you been carrying them about with you for a year and more?"

I smiled. "No, no letters for him. But for years I have been hearing about Arthur Pendragon from Bishop Germanus, who heard of him through Merlyn. And now that my mission for the bishop is complete and the bishop himself is dead, I intend to offer my sword and my services to Arthur, if he will have me."

"Oh, he will have you. Never fear on that."

Something in the way he spoke the words prompted me to ask, "How can you be so sure?"

He grinned again. "Because I know. I can speak for the Riothamus. What did you say your name was?"

"Clothar."

"Aye, Clothar. It is . . . different. I've never heard that name before."

"It is common enough where I come from, and it is purely Frankish. Am I permitted to ask your name?"

He grinned, showing white, even teeth. "If I tell you my name will you show me the secret of your spears?"

I knew he was baiting me, gulling me in some manner, but I could not see how and I shook my head, smiling still but now uncertain of what was happening here. "I have already said I would. I said so before we fought."

"That's true, you did." He drew himself up straight, and his smile was open and forthright. "Come, then, return to Camulod with us. I am Arthur Pendragon, and men call me Riothamus, the High King of Britain, but that is only a title. I have yet to earn the right to it, and fill in the truth behind it, and I fear I have a long way to go before I can admit to the name without feeling inadequate. But my given name is Arthur, and I am the chief of Pendragon, and so be it you were serious about joining with us, I think we two could become friends. What say you, Clothar the Frank?"

My jaw had fallen open as he spoke, and I knew that I was gaping like a simpleton, but now I dropped to one knee in front of him, meaning to kiss his hand as I would a bishop's, but he caught me by the arm and pulled me back to my feet. "No, no, none of that. I have done nothing yet to earn that kind of treatment, and you have newly knocked me on my arse. Folly, then, to follow that by kissing my hand." His smile widened. "When the time comes to swear loyalty to me, I will let you know. For the time being, if you feel a need to be ceremonious, you can call me Magister, as the others do. Now, what about those spears you have? Will you show me how they are different to ours?"

I had to breathe deeply and calm my racing, exultant heart. I could hear a blackbird piping somewhere among the woods to my right and a thrush singing its heart out behind us and I felt all at once that anything would be possible in this new land to which I had brought my friends with the thought of serving this impressive man. And when I felt able to speak again without quavering, I bowed my head, partly in acknowledgment, partly in respectful awe.

"Aye, Magister," I said, addressing my King thus for the very first time, "I will."